Magnetic Island: a novel

Magnetic Island

a novel

HARRY CUMMINS

Connor Court Publishing

Published in 2019 by Connor Court Publishing

Connor Court Publishing Pty Ltd.
PO Box 7257
Redland Bay QLD 4165
sales@connorcourt.com
www.connorcourt.com

Phone 0497 900 685

ISBN: 9781925826296

Cover design Maria Giordano

Printed in Australia

Front Cover Photo: Jetty at Picnic Bay Magnetic Island, 1937-1938, State Library of Queensland

This is a work of fiction.
Names, characters, businesses, places, events, locales, and incidents are either the products of the author's imagination or used in a fictitious manner. Any resemblance to actual persons, living or dead, or actual events is purely coincidental. Furthermore, certain long-standing institutions and public offices are mentioned, but the characters involved are wholly the author's imagination.

Connor Court Publishing Fiction

Chapters

Part One

GULLIVER'S TRAVELS

When the plane landed, Tray initially found his new surroundings very depressing. "A crowded Lilliput" was the expression he used. After the fresh and glassy green and blue of the Southern Hemisphere, the monolithic brown and grey to which Europe is reduced each Winter can be very off-putting, like Sickert's paintings of Camden and Dieppe after the radioactive colour of an Emil Nolde. And everything seemed so tiny after Australia, especially the houses. Someone had been trying to pack in as many as possible, even into the smallest snippets of land. Every London home looked as tiny and absurd as a chocolate. And they were identical. They were more like the bricks that made up the Mondrian-mosaic of a Hershey Bar than the individually shaped berries and phalluses you find in a box of chocs. Britain was brown and relentlessly occupied. There was no non-human place where nature lived on its own. In Australia, even in the rare cities, man's excrement plays second fiddle to the natural world. It's overwhelmed, as in central Sydney, by green mountains, blue bays, and an oceanic sky straight out of a book on the dinosaurs. But in Britain, brown towers filled every empty space, covering even the countryside: domes of chickenpox for midgets, parasites. Even the air was brown, and resembled recycled water.

I was appalled that Tray was so down. He had come to London at my invitation. I am a gallery owner, eponymous maestro of "EMPORIO PATRICK MYNTS". (As well as selling contemporary art, I am a specialist in the Late Roman, Islamic and Byzantine periods. And their artefacts). I had promised Tray that I would launch his international career from here. What could he do in Australia? It is totally isolated and so would he have been had he stayed there. Australia is the Garden of Eden: it's too complete to be part of the world. It's so complete, so much a world in itself that most of its people never think of leaving, never imagine that there's a world beyond their own to be conquered. In a sense, they're right. They find, like Adam and Eve, that everywhere else is inferior. The world surrounding their atoll isn't the Pacific, it's the grey Atlantic. To leave Australia is to enter the Underworld, not the open air. It is not to go out of something, but to go into something. Artists are of course sometimes expelled from Australia. Overboard, they never find themselves in the mouthwash-blue of their native seas, they find themselves like Jonah in the belly of a big fish. Its caviar comprises dishwater suds that humanity has used and re-used about a thousand times. But isn't it better that way? How can Australians discover their country, and that it's perfect, unless they leave it? Didn't Marcel say that "the only true paradises are those we have lost"? So "how can they speak of Australia, who only Australia know?". The rest of the world is so used up compared with Australia – it's the only virgin left on Earth. I suppose we should be grateful that, like the Golden Palace in mediaeval Baghdad, it's populated exclusively by eunuchs: intellectual ones. Eunuchs who only know the market rate for what they don't have: ie balls, the ability to generate new life. Artificial life. What is civilization, after all, but artificial life? But wouldn't real life be better? Australians pine for artistic Europe and the US, not realising that art is the search for a perfection they already enjoy, that there is no need to live in a brown hive like London or New York when you already shit in royal jelly; that it is better to be art than it is to make art. And it's certainly better to have their art – the naked statues of Sydney and a pure, melting sky like the sky at the start of the world – than it is to have artists. Who would prefer a handful of bees to a handful of honey? The Australians are eunuchs who know the value of what they don't have, but don't know the value of what they do have: Australia.

They're like the eunuchs in the Golden Palace in mediaeval Baghdad who once guarded Buran, the little ten-year old daughter of Hasan, Prime Minister to the Caliph Mamun. Buran had been promised to Mamun, but the law forbade him to marry her until she turned 18, which would be in 806 AD. Until that time, Mamun had to ensure her virginity, and the eunuchs guarded it in the Golden Palace, the bullseye of the concentric ripples of the stewpond. They jerked around her like goldfish, or drones around a queen in the ribcage of a hive. Neither the eunuchs nor the little girl were permitted to visit even one of the circular suburbs beyond the palace wall. You wouldn't have thought that would matter: what could be nicer than the palace? But the eunuchs put no value on the palace because most of them had known nothing else. They had grown up there as the sons of slave-girls; they had been castrated there in childhood. They certainly had no eyes for Buran, who was as beautiful as Australia. All they cared about were the brown mud-brick slums they could see from the palace walls. The slums crawled, like shit with flies, with the Caliph's Turkish soldiers. Had it not been for the Caliph's cruelty, the eunuchs said, the Turks might have sodomised them. They pushed around Buran's legs like cats on heat, clutching at her like bees with their thighs . . .

Still, you have to admit that when eunuch-Australians do leave the hive, they invariably succeed in our fallen, flyblown world. Having grown up without any knowledge of the world beyond their own – which split the atom and discovered Stalinism and the wheel a good few years ago (it is in fact a little bored with these discoveries) – Australia's émigré painters and thinkers and film-makers triumph everywhere. They have the confidence that comes from imagining that they are thinking things and hence doing things for the first time. It doesn't matter that what they do is old hat, indeed old crap. It's the solipsistic zest with which the Germaine Greers and the Peter Weirs declaim banality that enchants. Contrary to what the founders of America once said, no truth is self-evident – or automatically self-evident. First, somebody has to discover and draw attention to the axiomatic qualities of the truth. Discover it, not create it, because the truth has always been there. It is not the discover-ies, but the discover-ers, that are new. It used to be the case that the truth only got discovered once. Once was enough. It was the expat Australian who proved that it could be "discovered" more than once; who proved, in fact, that it is not truth, but discovery, by which we mean publicity, which is as eternal and original as sin. Tray was my discovery, but, not being Australian, I hoped that mine was a discovery that would not be repeated.

11

NOUKI KEEPS MICE

Nouki keeps mice. She told him – Tray – that she was in the habit of secreting the animals about her person. Once, she had done her hair in a bun and the mouse trapped inside the funnel of the bun "sprang a leak" and she couldn't get it out. She ran around screaming, tearing off her clothes, trying to melt the cone with a pail of water. This had happened during a wedding – her sister's second marriage. Nouki ran squawking down the aisle shedding her finery like a chook chased by a Cockie with a panga. "Just can't understand it", said Nouki. "They can go for ages without getting pongy. And then you clean out their cage one day and they're *terribly* pongy". Nouki was thinking of her own existence, but Kurwen knew how worried Tray was, and she tried to distract him. She announced that her mother had also had to go to London for an extended stay. It was in 1976, during that year's "British heatwave", which she had found "about as hot as a Black Duck's cuntie". Tray turned towards Kurwen and tried to smile. The flesh of her perfect-featured baby, Earl, was a transparent grey, like that of a scallop: Earl's lips were purplish. The baby was clinging serenely to a pamphlet he had pounced on at the local clinic: *"Sexuality – Finding Our Balance".* Tray peered out of the car window. He watched hundreds of bright little stars swarming like white tadpoles on the black back window of a car that was passing them – each a reflection of the pitiless sun. Men in shorts with wide, floppy fluorescent orange hats were mending the traffic lights. The tall gum trees, the glaring heat and the absence of pavements were already making him feel homesick, and he hadn't even left Australia yet . . . How strange to think of the period immediately prior to a disaster. "Why on earth did I go and agree to it?" he kept asking himself: "Sydney is *so beautiful".*

Sydney is a virgin, a eunuch. Its buildings are clean, like cubes of feta cheese and tomato. They remind you of London, but a perfect, imaginary London, like the one you see in children's books; ideal buildings in an unfixed, timeless world. Despite the heat, there is a cool, fresh wind that smells of eucalyptus. Man is absent from this city of four million people in a way that has no parallel anywhere else. It's like a city at the bottom of the sea. Nature dominates it as it does the ancient ruined cities of Asia Minor. Every day brings a bright, windy afternoon, and from Martin Place, Sydney's Trafalgar Square, you can see, through hilly streets, the vast eunuch Bridge and the glittering harbour, like the ocean at the South Pole. A sort of monstrous innocence haunts the middle of town. Nature is Number One, even there. The big Australian sky, for instance, makes human beings and their world insignificant. You look up: what you see is the sky at the start of the world, fresh and glassy and wet. The sky is clean and transparent, duck-egg blue in colour. Tray tried to enjoy it because today he was flying to London. The sky would be small there and the sun weak. They would be trivial things there and he would no longer notice them. People didn't notice their physical environment in Europe, they only noticed each other. People only noticed human things in Europe, things inside themselves, things inside other people. Cold, grey weather connives at the victory of the mind, just as mental illness does. Living in Europe isn't like living, it's like reading.

They drove along the North Shore, the skyscrapers of Circular Quay rising and falling, seemingly only feet away, beyond waves of wooded urban hills. They passed the most distinctively native of all the Sydney suburbs – low, elaborate art nouveau pasteboard shops, little battery-hen houses with sculpted verandah grilles. On either side of the road the silvery olive-green of wattle and gum, enlivened here and there by great puffs of purple jacaranda. The harbour was everywhere too – deep turquoise – ultramarine – cochineal – speckled with sails - hemmed in by thin, fantastic peninsulas and hills; raw, unfinished looking, as the hills of England must have looked in prehistoric times. The taxi crossed the Harbour Bridge. He would never see the blue of that harbour in the Northern Hemisphere. It was a bizarre tropical blue like toilet detergent. They drove down the Cahill Expressway towards Wooloomoolloo. The park – The Domain – was the unreal green of soft-drink. So fresh, so unreal, like a paddock in the Amazon basin, just set down there amid the skyscrapers. The canopies of its gum trees – the spiky, vaginal calligraphy reminded him of parsley. He would have to make a note of that. He was a painter. Because he was a realistic one, he always tried to describe his ideas, even to himself, in terms of something else, something that other people could understand. An abstract painter can afford to express himself transparently, in prose, because he doesn't want to make the unintelligible self intelligible. Tray, on the other hand, was concerned with dialogue, with getting his thoughts, his own version of things, across. As a bleak realist, he had to use fresh metaphors, adapt to poetry, the only language everyone can understand.

Kurwen and Nouki, two of his young models, were sharing the taxi, at least to the City Centre. They were going shopping. The girls were sitting next to him (they were all in the back), Kurwen, in profile, a sunburnt Vermeer, Nouki an oily brown all over, with fiercely blonde hair, like a plastic doll. The two girls were discussing now an impending holiday in Bali (Australia's Benidorm). Then Nouki leant out of the window and cried ecstatically, at a passer-by: "Kenny, I'm going to your *hayume*!" . . . They drove past the little park in Boomerang Street. Everywhere they saw the most beautiful people. The Australian torso is exquisite. Lines of muscles are arranged in columns, like the flakes in fried fish. The Irish-Australians are the fillets that haven't been cooked yet, the pink ones beneath a covering of flour. Cubed Turkish Delight in icing sugar with warty, iris-free nipples. In the less atavistic Aussies, the powdered fillet has been fried by the sun. These muscles have a syphilitic golden richness, like the bumpy scum on a Lobster Mornay.

He said goodbye to the girls. He asked the taxi driver to stop for a while at the Art Gallery of New South Wales, which is up from the Docks overlooking "Harry's Cafe de Wheels". One of Tray's worst paintings, of the legendary activist Gopi Panicker, was hanging there. He had found Panicker a Bush turkey: straight-backed, imperious of mien and dignified in her movements, but sensitive and very easily flustered. Like a turkey, she had the bulging jet eyes of a prawn and wattles at her neck like dead flowers. Her face, like a cockerel's, was the carmine red of Athlete's Foot. Tray's painting of her formed part of an exhibition of portraits which had been submitted to the Art Gallery of NSW for the Archibald Prize. He was visiting the Gallery to buy presents for his friends in London from the famous shop. It certainly wasn't to reaquaint himself with Ms Panicker's features. His abortion – which looked a bit like an abortion. All bolognese red, with a tangle of cobwebs and an opal-grey skull (a dead, nesting mother bird whose egg could still be seen in her skeleton), it had been undertaken by both artist and sitter out of naked ambition. The ambition of Tray Beautous, who was unappreciated in avant-garde circles, was of the conventional variety. Panicker's was of the descending, or condescending sort. The Lady Ottoline Morrel of Coogee was publicly producing a motherless joey from her pouch. Also, she had felt she needed a definitive public statement of her "new image", and Beautous' diptych, an open sandwich at so seminal a smorgasbord, would do nicely.

The development of Panicker's image had reflected the changes in "the Movement". In the beginning, in the late Sixties, she had, like the rest, equated a prudish form of heterosexuality and its attendant pornography with liberation. She had posed for photographers with budgerigar eggs – which she had later boiled and eaten on an Arnott's cracker – in a nest of her own pubic hair. These, she explained, were "my own balls, mate" and she was committing public *Hari Kiri* with these photos in order, like the Pelican, to feed her "daughters" – soon to be hatched from said balls – with sustaining blood. Beautous had been born in the city of Townsville in North Queensland, Australia's north-eastern province. When Gopi related the "daughters of the revolution" anecdote, he asked her why she had felt impelled to eat such things. She replied with the New Left mantra about it being impossible to make an omelette without breaking eggs. Tray recalled at this point a story about the founding of Townsville. This had occurred in 1863. Apparently, when the first settlers arrived, the entrepreneur who had lured them to a remote swamp with tales of milk and honey said that he had nothing to feed them on but turtle eggs. Later, it turned out that they had in fact been eating crocodile eggs, which were the only local source of food. It struck Beautous at the time that creators of new societies spent far too much time breaking eggs – not to mention stuffing their faces with *Oeufs Arnold Bennett* – and far too little in hatching out their fancy little crocodiles. Gopi, for instance – "feminist daughters" notwithstanding – was never to have any children at all. This didn't stop her, when the Feminists decided, after several convulsions, that motherhood was actually good, from setting herself up as an expert on breast feeding and Chlamydia. First though, came the *de rigeur* interlude as a sophisticated lesbian. And now, like everyone else in the movement, she wanted to look venerable, motherly and elegant, like a kangaroo. Tray however had painted her as an Emu. He had defined a fat grey torso which made one think of a cattle tick, and a long, fibrous neck. He had given Panicker a butch homosexual's small, muscular Emu head and a poofy one's big black Emu eyes. She hadn't looked unsympathetic but she hadn't looked attractive either and this had incensed her. Her public persona – and no-one was more ruthlessly publicity hungry – suggested that she lived a purely dialectic life devoted to female autonomy. This was the truth. But we can choose our political identity precisely because ideas, however much we like them, lie outside our own minds and souls. Our minds and souls are not subject to our outward-looking intellect, and are therefore immune to its beliefs. This was why Gopi Panicker – cerebral, political, *recherché* , anti-man – was as besotted by blokes as a little playground flirt, and, more unfortunately still, couldn't believe that any man could behold her without abandon. That was why she had hated Tray's painting, which wasn't even technically good (not that she could have judged that). "Have you ever had the AIDS Test?" she asked him, not believing that any man could find her other than intriguing, or hornier at least than the smirking Stymphalian creature Tray had described. Tray said that he hadn't: "I'm waiting until I've sucked as many cocks as you have!" . . . They then discussed literature, by which Gopi always meant the Feminist Canon and nothing else. (This was the result of a perceptive view of art which saw every novel, play or poem as a political tract in

17

'

favour of patriarchy or the ruling class: so why not just dispense with these metaphors and concentrate on the "real thing" – polemic?) Had Tray read the "seminal" **Female Eunuch**, she wanted to know? "I would have thought that was right up your street." Tray agreed. He was fascinated by eunuchs; he was in fact thinking of writing a book about Byzantine eunuchs – "a huge and unexplored subject". He said he wasn't very interested in female eunuchs, though: "or female non-eunuchs, for that matter."

Anyway, the Art Gallery of New South Wales was bright and marvellously airy. It was one of those old buildings whose modern interior makes it appear bigger inside than its exterior would seem to permit. What made it the loveliest gallery in the world were the views of the Harbour. The whole back wall of this big three-storey mansion had been torn off and replaced with a plate of glass. On every floor, you looked past the canvases at a huge blue tank that seemed to fill the whole room. Sedate sailing boats moved across it, as in some impudent fantasy. The effect was even stranger from far away, when the boats on the Harbour – or rather, right inside the gallery – appeared themselves to be paintings. Tray, who was buying some Wattle-printed nick-nacks for his English friends in the Giftshop (he didn't go near the Archibald), wished that he could have achieved the same effect with the forest of porn he had painted on the walls of Beverley Brownbill's sauna. Those images of naked people, even though they were depicted in settings out of doors, had seemed to intensify the interior qualities of the room, rather than to suggest a paradoxical infinity of outwardness, as the harbour did. Something about the gallery – perhaps all those sails on the rich, almost reddish blue – reminded Tray that Bev had always loved to wear white. This was probably to show off how rich she was: white obviously necessitates a larger wardrobe. When Tray had first met her, her celebrated embonpoint was not what it had been. Her body like that of a rat or a cat was slightly hunched and pear-shaped, yet, like a rat or cat's physique, it was still sleek and very flexible. Beverley had the reddened Drambuie eyes of a rat or a cat, the drizzly nose and exquisite mouth and teeth of one of those creatures. Above all, she had their kindly, inquisitive look of slightly malicious self-interest, a look that expresses all that organic, animal knowledge of human nature which – far more than Stanley Baldwin's "power without responsibility" – is the defining glory of rats, cats and whores of all sexes.

Tray had met Beverley, his first real patron, at a family Coroboree at Noosa Heads, in the South of Queensland. She was a gold-digger – a "Golden Retriever," as they are called in Australia – who had married his great uncle, the grazier Piers Brownbill. (Some members of Tray's family were well off, but it could only have been an outsider like Bev who took the interest in art to support him). Naively anglophile parents had named Piers after Piers Gaveston. Like the infamous catamite, he had been "the most beautiful boy in the world": in other respects, they were not much alike – in fact, they were not much alike in that respect either. Tray had never meant to attend the Noosa party. He often quoted Madame Verdurin: *"Families are such a bore, one longs to get away from them."* Unfortunately, circumstances had compelled him to stay with relatives in Brisbane, which is close to Noosa. Though they were boycotting the event themselves (because of one of those obscure feuds that gorge on families like tapeworms), they insisted that Tray go: a nice – and typical – distinction. Imprisoned in one of the last stifling "Queenslanders" (unique old Queensland houses) on Kangaroo Point (he had descended on his aunt and uncle simply to sell paintings to the Singaporean millionaires said to inhabit the new apartment blocks that littered the surrounding paddocks), he reluctantly gave his consent. It was doubly annoying, because, the prosperity of Brisbane, which was all that had lured him south, had proved as illusory as the febrile health which Tolstoy describes as clinging to Moscow, when, in **War and Peace**, Napoleon glimpses it, oasis-like, after the battle of Borodino:

> **"Moscow was empty. There were still people in the city ... but it was empty. It was empty in the sense that a dying, queenless hive is empty. In a queenless hive no life is left, though to a superficial glance it seems as much alive as other hives."**

There were certainly plenty of queens in Brisbane, but of the Taiwanese and Singaporean Croesi for whom the frail little Queenslanders had been crushed like ants' nests, for whom the giant condos had been raised, there wasn't a sign. The empty apartment blocks soared above tiny, wooden cottages on stilts as in some fantasy by Salvador Dali. The endless, empty balconies made one think of gnawed cobs – of combs drained of honey.

Seb and Aunty Mary weren't bad people, but they were hardly congenial. Mercifully, they were childless, but barrenness had made Mary a fanatical dog-breeder, a placebo which brought all the horror of family life into sharp relief. Tray found it strange how perverse childless women could be, and how little separated the tracts of the Feminists from the photographs that Mary plumped defiantly down of her dogs in fancy dress. On the morning of Piers' "do", as Tray sat in agonies, picking at Mary's obsessionally elaborate breakfast, Uncle Seb plied him with questions about crossword puzzles and then, head held up, with open arms and open, upraised palms, like Rodin's *"John the Baptist"*, he began, under the cover of a diffident heartiness, to probe. Did the various members of Tray's (immediate) family get on? The French: a peculiar lot, were they not? And did he have a "girl"? (A seemingly throwaway line, but Seb was fixing him with a frightened, desperate stare). Klima, another, more remote relative rang. The relief was profound. She it was who was going to drive Tray north from Brisbane up to Noosa. He was elated at having "sorted things out" and he posted the postcard he had distractedly written to his Father in Mourilyan.

Klima arrived. She was much older than Tray had imagined her. Small, slight, scrawny, over made up. No trace of the moist fat peach remained, only its wrinkly stone. So many Australian women were like that. In photographs taken of them in the 1950s and 60s you saw them in elaborate clothes that made them like women in the rest of the world. These had now been abandoned for pink or white tee-shirts and shorts. What had happened to those wonderful old clothes? The women of Australia had let their outside go and the inside had gone as well. When Tray ran into women he had known before, they looked like seeds of their former selves. Even the young were invariably shrivelled brown mannekins, like the tiny corpses to which firestorms reduced the people of Dresden. It was amazing how one sort of human density, akin to that of the hive, could be converted so quickly to quite another sort of density, akin to that of the bee. Everything was so speeded up in Australia. It wasn't that complexity and profundity didn't exist. It was just that, under the pitiless richness of the sun – which, like the Nile, gave birth to and drowned everything – profundity and complexity were incubated quickly and then cremated, as Pompeii and Sodom had been. Nobody was given the time to notice them. In this respect, the humans in Australia resembled the great civilizations of the Muslim world. Like the palaces in *The Arabian Nights*, these civilizations had risen and vanished with the frequency of waves. Tray often feared that Sydney – salty, squishy Sydney – so staggering and so perfect, a city of garish fairground buildings and palm trees waving on the cornflower-blue night sky – would simply vanish one day like Baghdad – the Abbasid Baghdad where *The Arabian Nights* were set and composed – a city which had been bigger, more civilized, and more beautiful than Rome, Constantinople and Venice combined, and of which not a brick survives. What Australia needed, Tray thought, were not the athletes for which its politicians were always calling – beautiful though these might be (the athletes, not the politicians) – but artists who could freeze Australia's beauty as it gouted, like spunk, into oblivion. Only artists could put a slice of protean Oz on show for all of time, just as Spain's Christian Crusaders had, in capturing Granada and Córdoba, preserved them. Had these wonderful cities remained in the hands of the Muslims, their creators would have destroyed them, just as they destroyed Alexandria, Quarayan and Samarra, and are now in the process of destroying Beirut and Amman. Muslims, like Bower Birds, may, in an unknowing way, embody or create the beautiful, but, like Australians (or Bower Birds) all they are conscious of is the wish to destroy.

Klima escorted Tray to her sportscar. She had closely cropped designer grey hair, which made her look like an old poof. Her fingers, like those of an unwrapped mummy, were caked in huge, geometric gold rings. Tray engaged her in conversation about the doomed magazine she had set up. Klima made it all seem very jolly. That self-deception, acknowledged as such, which soothes for a while. She would always refuse to deal with advertising people, she said. She had been warned. Her boyfriend had called them "piranhas". Then it was "barracudas". **BRISBANE NIGHT**, which sounded more like a poem by Kevin Hart than a listings freebie, a cash-in on "Expo", was for her boyfriend. He was the "Editor". Klima, having slept with half of Bjelke-Petersen's cabinet, had thought that the Queensland Government would lave her in advertising revenues, just as they had oiled her naked bottom with oysters, "Four X" and ghee, but she had failed to grease the palm, or any of the other members, of the Poujade of the Great Barrier Reef himself, so it was no deal. **"NIGHT"** was withering on the vine.

Now they were tearing up the incongruous pine-fringed freeway that Tray remembered seeing on the train from Townsville. They stopped at "The Giant Pineapple" at Maroochydore. It was fifty foot high; its pitted cement glistened with orange emulsion. Klima could joke about this but earlier, at Gin Gin, when they had passed a painted concrete dinosaur and Tray had hailed another Australian Phidias (the reptile was bigger than the Athena in the Parthenon), she had said: "With tongue very firmly in cheek, of course?!"

Acres of grenadillas, sausagefruit and mangoes surrounded "The Giant Pineapple", and there were tours of the estate for the public. The brutal green of the crops made the recently cleared red earth look very naked. It was fresh and gashed and did not resemble the soil of a farm at all. Klima ravenously unwrapped Tray's gift. "Do you want to remove this?" she asked, flashing her **Clockwork Orange** eyes. He duly removed the price tag, remembering, not amused, the words of Proust: *"A book in which there are theories is like an object which still has its price tag on it"*.

They boarded a sugar train that was touring the estate. "I hope you're taking all this in," Klima observed drily: the guide's commentary was being drowned by the shrieks of the youngest passengers; all Tray could make out was: *"And what kid, even a grown up one, could resist a ride in a real-life sugar train?!"* "The usual screaming hype over nothing" Klima snarled, but she didn't mean it, she was just angry because of the children. She was one of those "difficult" people who, rude and tactless themselves, you have to tiptoe around – the least little thing could offend her. You couldn't be an anus with Klima, you had to be a vagina: you had to expand and contract unnaturally to accommodate her perverted sensitivity. You soon became aware of your unnatural and guarded responses: they felt odd. They gave one a feeling of power as well as of resentment, for her interlocutors were forced to be aware of the situation while she, lost in selfish tyranny, was blind. It was like dealing with a mongol or a lunatic, and, as with so many powerful people (who all share, to some extent, the self-destructive blindness of eye-gouging Byzantine emperors), you wondered how, given her tactlessness and the horror of her company, she could ever have got so far. The children – most were babies – continued to bray, much to Klima's distress. Tray was fascinated by the pink vulnerability of their bodies in this intense heat – for they looked very foreign in this glassy Queensland heat – children of the Varangian Guard, aliens, conquistadors. He loved to catch their suddenly interested-looking faces in the middle of a vacant tantrum. He asked to take Klima's photograph. Thrilled, amazed, she pretended to demur.

They drove on to a ginger farm, which was attached to a factory and shop, in Yandina. There was ginger this, ginger that, all extolled in commentaries whose tone couldn't have been more depraved if the bottles of chutney had come from the Tomb of Tutankhamen. This excitement about the one unimportant thing struck Klima, who had lived in "LA", as "very Australian", and, in fact, a guide to the various stages of ginger production hailed "OUR AUSSIE" techniques in a series of superlatives. Klima ostentatiously admired a jar of honeyed ginger, and the then poverty-stricken Tray had duly been obliged to buy it for her. There were pictures of women working on a production line and Klima said: "Those people must be mentally retarded. I would kill myself if I had to do that. Are they being *tested?*" Such a bohemian attitude was alright for those, like Klima, who would never have to work, but Tray – who was at that time forced to live as precariously as Klima, in her cool, corn-fed stupor demanded – felt envy for the cosiness, security and routine that the women enjoyed.

He grew increasingly agitated as they approached Noosa. Despair would not be too strong a word. There were mountains and reflecting pools. The mountains were big, wierd things shaped like dog turds. The mountains in a fairy tale. Southern Queensland looked as if it belonged in a film of **The Lost World**. The billowing paddocks – like the sea you see from a ship – were a brilliant irridescent green. There was an utterly pure sky. There were large, boiling white clouds brimming with sunshine; palm trees; sheets of blue-ish sugar cane. Then came the town on its smoky beaches. The beaches looked like mottled pancakes. The sand dunes drifted on a cut-glass Arctic blue (it was so different from the milky grey sea off Townsville!) There were tea-coloured creeks and jade-coloured canals running into forests fabulous with rare koalas. These canals, like its rich, lubricious *canaille*, made Noosa a "Canopus" to Brisbane's "Alexandria". The teak and stucco villas were uniformly squat because the citizens, decadent old money, had wished to preserve the resort from the pokies and Japanese golfers that went with the Atlantic Citys on "the Gold Coast" *south* of Brisbane. They had kept out what Klima mysteriously called "the Australian people" – always a wise precaution – and there wasn't a tall or geometric building to be seen. "Look," Klima shouted over the car's engine, "look over there: *'Capricornia'*!" Piers and Beverley's house was amazing. It was a ziggurat formed by three white cylinders. Each cylinder rose on top of the other like a wedding cake, and each was smaller than the one underneath it. A green dome crowned the topmost tier, and the two bottom tiers had balustrades running around the edges of their flat, circular roofs so that the windows and French windows in the cylindrical storeys above overlooked balconies where you could lounge on red pouffes. From a plane, the house would have appeared a dartboard made up of four concentric circles – four because the whole house was surrounded by a circular moat: the swimming pool! Its harsh, disinfectant blue clashed very oddly with the platypus colours of the nearby creeks. In fact, "Capricornia" looked utterly terrifying in sleepy, provincial Noosa, like one of those exotic Sikh temples you see peeping out of the bland canefields south of Cairns, or the Bahai Saint Peter's that blazes over the dumb grey Bush north of Sydney. Piers had built the house from scratch after his second marriage. He had invested millions of dollars at the insistence and according to the specifications of his new wife, or rather of Gaybum Fortnightly, the firm of Melbourne architects she retained. Beverley – who had been upstaged at parties umpteen times by builders' wives and the like wearing her "unique" Versace dress – a not infrequent hazard for the brand-name-starved Queensland rich – had demanded a house like nobody else's. And so André Fortnightly (who wore a dowager's choker beneath his plaid shirts, causing his friends – in deference to his pierced nipples – to talk of "pearls before swine") would assure her that the design he proposed had never been attempted since the first Abbasid Caliph, Al-Mansur, had built the "Round City" of Baghdad in 762 AD! This city would also have looked, from the air, like concentric rings. As at Noosa, the outer circle would have been a moat, and the "bullseye" would have been the "Golden Palace" of the Caliph himself, which was crowned by a huge green dome.

André's plan was highly original, but he probably picked the Arabian simile out of the air to flatter his client. *"The Second Mrs Brownbill"*, as the snobbish old bags thereabouts dubbed Bev, had the zeal for culture of a true philistine. She informed her Noosa neighbours that "Capricornia" was called after "the great Australian novel" of that name. Some found it hard to see how her Xanadu expressed the ideals of Xavier Herbert's famous *Bildungsroman*, a rather austere *tour de force* set in the Northern Territory. Her neighbours believed that **The Australian Ugliness**, after the tome by Robin Boyd, would have provided a better soubriquet, or, given the odd shape of the building, **The Magic Pudding**, by Norman Lindsay or **Caddie** (as in "tea caddy") by Catherine Elliott-Mackay. The cruel made sport

25

with the subtitle of **Caddie,** ie: *"The Autobiography of a Sydney Barmaid"***,** but someone said that Bev wasn't a barmaid at all, but an Ansett hostie from Windora whom Piers had met flying around Australia visiting his estates. Unfortunately, Bev – who had taken up with a man twice her age while his first, elderly wife lay skewered with cancer – was widely despised, and the retired burghers of Noosa – and their wives – could give her the titles of plenty more "great Australian novels" for her home. Some, with heavy irony, called it **Man-Shy**, after the book by Frank Dalby Davison, others (with less irony), **Her Privates We**, **Naked Under Capricorn**, **Power Without Glory**, **My Brilliant Career**, **The Little Bush Maid**, or **Careful – He Might Hear You** (for she was not thought to be very uxorious); then there was **For The Term of His Natural Life** (ditto); **Landtakers**; and, with reference to Piers himself, **Here's Luck** and (rather less optimistically), **Wake in Fright**.

It is unusual for a Queensland grazier to live in a resort all the year round, but Beverley had made Noosa Piers' permanent home. As a newly enriched woman, the idea of always being on holiday appealed to her peurile sense of the sybaritic. "It's a whole new world," as André Fortnightly had said, seemingly referring to *la vita Capricornia* (he was actually referring to the villa's concentric, cosmological design, which made him beg his patrons to name it **The Solid Mandala**, after a book by Patrick White). Bev certainly had no wish to live in Piers' existing house, an ancient bungalow like a public lavatory, whose tin roof blazed like a windscreen under the Darling Downs, baking the perfume of possum piss within and making the leather on the armchairs sweat like the nut-brown skin of an old queen with AIDS.

Piers and Bev really enjoyed themselves at "Capricornia", which may have been the reason why their elderly neighbours hated them. The bare boobs and torsos of the locals had reached the beaches of Ithaka-Noosa after a long, perilous journey and were now just useless, bubbly brown seaweed. How could Piers and Bev, who were still relatively spry, get away with being Lotos Eaters, while they, the "natives", had only been allowed to taste

Bundy-Rum-and-Cokes as broken, long-denied Odysseuses? They bitched to each other about it like old Nazis who had "had" to waste a lifetime (as dentists) gassing people and picking things out of their teeth, or performing evil and useless human experiments (as doctors), or (as judges and lawyers) herding the innocent behind the chicken wire; above all, they resented the fact that their new neighbours' enjoyment of a tropical hideaway was never shattered – as theirs so frequently was – by the lawsuits of surviving victims and the public "witch-hunts" of the authorities.

Klima and Tray were now driving into the lawns that surrounded "Capricornia". They were flat and vilely green and unnatural-looking, as lawns tend to be in the tropics, where the proper grass for lawns doesn't grow. An awful substitute, which is the colour of paint and resembles a mosaic of tiny lettuce plants, is coaxed into life with cubits of liquid. It is so difficult to create lawns in Queensland that, where they do exist, they make themselves rather violently felt: they don't melt into the landscape, as a lawn should. The lawns of "Capricornia" drew attention to themselves by their wierd flatness and their scaffolding of sprinkler plumes. Tray was reminded of the tiaras of spray on a Hockney swimming pool. There exists a horrible moment, which is only a moment, when you arrive at the home of a dreaded host. Crossing the border into their much feared world passes quickly, like the pain that takes you into death. It is as big and as bad an introduction as it should be, but it is so quick that, mercifully, you have no time to absorb it. Suddenly you enjoy a new existence where you can feel no pain, no matter how heightened or strange it all is, because you left your old personality, which would have registered the difference, in the old world, and now, all at once, you have the new personality of the new world, which feels nothing. The Cerberus at the gate of this world, which was also its Virgil, was a cattledog called "Benjy", which rushed out to meet the guests. Curiously (like Virgil), he was a representative of the old as well as the new. Apart from Cynthia Brownbill, who was allowed to drift gibbering around "Capricornia" like the first Mrs Rochester because she had Cancer and would shortly

27

die, Benjy was the only reminder of the life Piers had shared with his first family on the homestead at Goondiwindi. Bev was in denial about her husband's first incarnation, and had caused the destruction of nearly everything in Piers' world that was pre-Bev, and pre-her illegitimate daughter Kay (the child of an old flame and now Piers' sole – and legitimate heir; his children by Cynthia had been disinherited). Bev was Nurbanu, the widow of the Turkish Emperor Selim II, who, in 1574, had denied her husband's death and strangled every last one of her son Murad's fifteen half-brothers, scions of more senior wives and concubines, while Selim lay in an icebox with the yoghurt. Until, that is, Murad alone could reach Istanbul and seize the throne. (Nurbanu took pity on only one of her stepsons: guessing the tastes of the strange little moth, she was "merciful" to him, and locked him in a windowless dungeon with two naked black women). Or perhaps Bev was just typical of any second wife, who invariably inflicts pointless carnage and exerts a greater tyranny than the first, legitimate spouse because, like all usurpers, she assumes a hostile environment. Bev certainly got one when she married Piers. Aldour Brownbill – an unmarried thirtysomething – stood behind his new mother at the altar and screamed *"SLUT, SLUT, SLUT!"* so that Queensland snickered. (The nuptials of Piers, one of the state's oligarchs, had been televised live by Brisbane 4TO). Then Aldour ruined the group wedding portraits by posing for them with an erect penis standing out of open flies. The flamboyant photographer connived in this outrage, which had given Tray the idea of printing huge blowups of newspaper photographs of society weddings. The artist had then painted turgid graffiti phalluses on respectable trousers and gasping hilarious female lips. He had exhibited the resulting wall-sized canvases at the Perc Tucker Gallery in Townsville. The newspaper text occupied the lower half of the pictures, as it had done on the page, and the lifeless black letters were painted in warmly by hand as a laconic comment on the images above:

"While the bride and bridegroom were signing the register, the choir came down to the top of the aisle and sang most beautifully 'Song of the

Old Bullock Driver', *which was very moving, and much enjoyed by all the guests. After the ceremony, everyone drove a few miles to the reception and wedding luncheon at Colonel Kevin Coca-Cola's beautiful home* 'Darkies Creek'. *Our dear kind host is such a perfectionist that the car parking had been arranged quite sensibly and comfortably in a section of the farm opposite the abattoir*".

Tray and Klima found "Capricornia" moist and red beneath its sugary crust, like a pavlova. From the kitchen they could see, through a tunnel of mahogany, a misty green arbour of desolate gums and a rutted hill cleared for building. The darkness tinkled here and there with reflections and the glint of pointless, horribly stuffed glass cabinets. It suddenly struck Tray that Sydney and Melbourne, which have mild, Mediterranean summers, are like cities in the high Roman Empire: their people live out of doors. Sydneysiders are rippling statues and their home is a landscape. In tropical Queensland, which is blue and paradisal to look at, it is actually too hot to spend much time outside. Queenslanders spend life indoors, in the latticed darkness of a louvred verandah, or the vacuum-sealed coffee-scented cold of an air-conditioned flat. When you cross the Queensland border at Coolangatta, you exchange the athletes and agorae of Sydney and classical Athens for the dark, shut-in world of a Byzantium that repudiated the nudity and openness of antiquity. In "Capricornia", as in Queensland as a whole, heat and light could only be viewed from darkness, coolness, as Monet so often described them. The light at the end of the tunnel was a particular, pastoral image that did not, however, offer the oasis that the specificity of its counterpart, in England, would have done. Those few gums offered no repose because they were the start of a Bush that would repeat itself forever. And the darkness wasn't comforting either. The Tandoori Chicken-coloured wood and Bel Air interiors of "Capricornia" were not the luxury they would have appeared in Europe, but something painful because the infinite Bush, just outside the door, would never ruin their undefended perfection. This was Art divorced from, unthreatened by, its threatening environment, and, therefore, painful and meaningless. What is unthreatened by its environment is also isolated from it, and what is isolated from its environment is unreal. These gorgeous suites, made poignant for Tray by the cleanness of Kay's untidily strewn toys, were as frighteningly unreal as the ones he saw on breakfast television.

"Now Tray," said Bev, "your father says your sistah is a lovely girrule, and has a lovely little bayeebee. And he was a bit sorry she hasn't gotten married yet. Has she gotten married yet?" Bev looked too perfect, too "normal" to give birth. Her flabby, vinyl features were those of a sunburnt transvestite. Her teeth – yellow, succulent, and numerous – reminded Tray of buttered corn. She wore a blazing white smock: it could have been a man's oversized shirt. She had left its tails hanging down outside her skirt; a very ugly gold belt made it puff out on top to hide, perhaps, dugs no longer gelid. She fingered her necklace – an old gold watch-chain – with purposefulness that betrayed her concealed power, and the interest she took in her new guest. Tray tried to avoid her eyes, which were shrewdly hidden behind dark glasses. His own, he feared, must betray all the boredom, fear and disgust he always felt in such company. Piers gave him a tour of Beverley's paintings. Being perfect, in an anal, Laura Ashley way, meant being an "artist" as well as a "mother", and Bev had brought forth endless dulcet visions of Abos and Humpies in the approved *École de Kaymart* style. Piers admonished Tray for drinking beer. "There is a time when you will appreciate the finer things of life!" Tray was only drinking beer out of politeness, because he knew they wanted to keep the wine to themselves. "Just taste that," Piers advised him, "and see what you think." Tray sipped the lees of a half-finished Chardonnay Piers had asked a hotel Dining Room to send up to his suite about a week before: Tray pronounced it ambrosial. Piers had never been to Britain, so one could only admire his English accent. His prune-like brown head and toothbrush moustache made him look like one of Mussolini's generals. He had a big, boyish face like a paedophile.

A brief discussion of Tray's situation ensued. He was astonished to hear them offer him a commission. It reminded him of what Proust had written in his novel about the incorrigibly dreadful Monsieur and Madame Verdurin, who suddenly, and in a way that seemingly belies their entire existence, come to the financial rescue of Saniette, a friendless protegé of theirs whom they have done nothing but mock and torment for years. *"I was sorry I had not known of it earlier,"* says Proust's Narrator. *"For one thing, the knowledge would have brought me more rapidly to the idea that we ought never to bear a grudge against people, ought never to judge them by some memory of an unkind action, for we do not know all the good, that, at other moments, their hearts may have sincerely desired and realised."*

Bev had asked Tray if he could decorate her Sauna-cum-Dunny: with a "myural" of all world races living together in perfect harm - on - y. At this point she burst facetiously into song, with a line from the famous Coca-Cola ad:

> **"I'd like to teach the world to sing,**
> **In perfect har - mon - y!"**

"Well," she winked, "I *am* a Labor supporter," picking her nose to emphasise her splendid iconoclasm.

Tray took this as an explanation for her (well-known) love for mankind. He was surprised to learn that *he* in fact had put the match to her molten philanthropy. "Darling," (her accent, unlike her husband's, was pure Aussie, if sweetened with many a Dunny spray), "I know you're not very successful. Your draw-rings aren't very successful, are they? Have you looked at mine? I guess it's cos people can't stand it – not you, *personally*, darling – but you must admit that those muscly Surfies are creepy – they're for poofs. No wonder you need our munny! But if all you can do is Surfies, that's just what you'll have to do. But if it's *our hayume*, Troi, it's gonna be *all man-coined* in the nyewd." (She winked again). "Me and Piers – he used to be Country Party! – you know what we believe in, Trayoy? Fair-dos is what we believe in. Yers. Equal doos. I don't *cayare* what people say, I'm sticking to my guns. We'll just have to be like poofs and put our Nuddies where our mouths are – not on *that* wall, darling, I don't want your stuff where people can see it but in the Dunny and the Sawnie where Piers can look at your Surfies and mebbe have a wank. . . ." (She laughed again). "Darling," [now she was addressing her husband], "it's such a pity about poor Trooyy" (Tray). "*We've* got plenty of shrapnel, haven't we darling? *We* can help him out!" Tray wondered how on earth this offer could be squared with Piers' less than Neronian liberality, but he had reckoned without Virtue, or the desire to *appear* virtuous, which is the most seductive vice in the world, more powerful than avarice and certainly less unnerving than actually getting off your backside and helping folk physically. "But of *course*, old boy" Piers chortled, "When you're rich enough to own *two houses*, you can *afford* to be generous!" So it was a deal. Tray was to paint his Nuddies in Bev's Saunie.

Just then, Cynthia drifted by in her Forties finery like the embalmed corpse of Eva Perón. She offered Tray a plate of Twisties. Bev was very much an adherent of the "waste not, want not" school. She didn't want her husband's ex-wife, and she wasn't prepared to waste her either. The neighbours would glimpse Cynthia, who was old and sick and in the first throes of Alzheimer's, and who had never had to lift a finger in her life, compulsively raking up leaves under the orange tree, her knickers round her knees, or trying to wash her soiled bedclothes in the swimming pool before Beverley found them and slapped her and shook her like a doll. Or they would see her vacantly swabbing the drive, like the servant she now was. Fortunately, and to Bev's evident satisfaction, she evinced a touching gratitude. "And she was climbing those rocks," Cynthia gushed, spraying Kay, Bev's daughter, Tomcat-style, with débutante saccharine, "as if she were a *little rabbit* ...!" Tray, feeling sorry for her, expressed admiration for the cheap handbag that she mysteriously and rather grandly bore as she attended to her servile cares. He asked her if she had owned it long, (it certainly looked old). He immediately realised this was a mistake, for she launched into a long, convoluted story about how it had replaced a bag that had been sitting on a desk in the hall when a "lubra" came to the door and asked her to guess how many jellybeans there were in a bottle – it was a raffle for ***Planet of the Boongs*** – an "alternative" musical about "Captain

32

a novel

James Crook" which the denizens of the Palm Island Reserve were putting on at the Civic Cen-tah that Christmas. Then Cyn had turned round and the handbag was missing and the police had eventually brought it back, empty, but she had refused to accept it. "I couldn't bear to touch it once the darkies had had it." She seemed to think that she, not Bev, was the chatelaine of "Capricornia". "Yes," she murmured humbly, as if she had a plethora of such mansions from which to choose, "this is a nice, comfortable home; you can just live in it; you can't compare it to the stately homes of England". . . Cynthia was one of those Englishwomen who are peculiar to plebeian immigrant colonies – the sort you would never find in England. She was like a souvenir miniature of Bundaberg Rum which nobody in Bundaberg – or anywhere else – would dream of using. An artefact with the right clothes and voice – like a national doll – but too right. She scratched nervously at her clitoris. She had lidded yet staring eyes, a white, papery face, cherry-pink lipstick. Her bone structure suggested a Death's Head and the impression was heightened by her popcorn-like teeth.

Two of Bev's exhausted relatives were led into the salon by Piers. They were already somewhat the worse for drink: they didn't look the type that his "beer only" policy would have troubled. The lady, with a bullfrog breast and gaping eyes, looked like a Brahmin bull. Things were livening up, and more and more such strangers appeared. Though the party was meant to be a celebration for and of his family, Cynthia, Piers and Klima were the only people Tray could recognise; the majority seemed to be siblings of Bev. *"Capricornia"*, whose tapering upper storeys made it resemble an old-fashioned, cylindrical beehive, began to remind Tray again of the "dead hive" to which Tolstoy had compared Napoleon's Moscow in *War and Peace*.

> *"The bee-keeper opens the upper compartment and examines the top storey of the hive. Instead of serried rows of insects sealing up every gap in the comb and keeping the hive warm, he sees the skilful, complex edifice of combs, but even here the virginal purity of old is gone. All is neglected and befouled. Black robber-bees prowl swiftly*

and stealthily about the combs in search of plunder; while the short-bodied, dried up home-bees, looking withered and old, languidly creep about, doing nothing to hinder the robbers, having lost all desire and all sense of life. "

"Having lost all desire and all sense of life" was a description that certainly fitted Cyn, but the robber Queen, Bev's mum, Peg, was "withered and old", too. She was an Irish Materfamilias; the sort of woman who is deeper than her children, more tragic. She had accepted her fate: she looked like a Chou-En-Lai. She had just left hospital. She held her arms straight and stiff and frail by her trembling side, and raised a stiff, skeletal hand to her mouth, shaking, as she smoked. She bestowed upon Tray a horrible, penetrating look. "Call me Peggy, please" she commanded, when he addressed her as "Mrs Murphy"; but he got a feeling – not a nice feeling – that she liked him. She must have known she was dying. She was surrounded by her offspring. They all had incredibly Irish faces. Dermot, Bev's brother, was tubby, powdery and red, with white hair. His children's fierce snub noses and high cheekbones looked solid, like green berries. Then there was Bev's sister, Shirelle, who inexplicably wore slippers and what looked like a shapeless blue nightie; a fag was constantly trembling in her fingers. She hugged a black poodle called "Tonie" with a pink bow in its hair. "You're not wild about animals, are you?" she informed Tray . . . There was another brother, "Babe", a simple, wiry ocker, who lived with his mum. The sight of Babe climbing into the back seat of the taxi that was taking Peggy home – she, decrepit, frail and yet imperious in front; he, lithe and muscular, clambering into the back like a dog, bound to what was weaker than him as if by magic – was troubling.

Notwithstanding the havoc she had wrought in and on her family, Klima was fond of Bev. An heiress to whom everything had come easily, but who liked to think herself a shrewd, frightful businesswoman, Klima claimed to admire the way that Bev, like some crow raiding a nest, had destroyed Klima's cousins. She admired even more her own "courage" in admitting to such a sympathy. "You can't make an omelette," she would insist – like some member of the Khmer Rouge about to execute her own mother – "without breaking eggs." Piers' children – Klima's rellies – were lazy parasites, she said. They were not like Klima. Klima had her "work" and her "relationship". Sperm being, for a woman, thicker than blood, "K" and "B" were hardly likely to clash, as Bev had no designs on Klima's "man". (The word made it sound as if she were the hostage of some hairy-chested Bluebeard rather than the employer of a seedy remittance queen: "relationship", with all its Swinging-Sixties and yet pre-Feminist connotations, has the same glutinous, deceitful ring). The fact that Klima's "man" was, in financial terms, a shrivelled appendix and not a life-giving pharynx made it extremely unlikely, in fact, that Bev would ever pursue him; he wasn't even attractive (people used to joke that Klima couldn't even *buy* a decent bloke). Alas, like many powerful women, the illusions Klima entertained about her own attractiveness meant that she was seldom alive to the real appearance of her lovers. Just as a scab of smallpox pus put up the nose of a child is sufficient to stop it ever getting smallpox, a powerful woman who has looked into the mirror with pleasure – as they all do – is hardly likely to be defeated by the pug-ugliness of her "man", even – indeed especially – if she has bought him. So Klima and Bev got along. Like most unpleasant people, they were not even consciously unpleasant. Both suffered mildly from mental illness. Malevolence was its result, not its cause. Each was therefore ignorant of her own nastiness, just as a crocodile would be. Each thought of herself as a kindly, gracious person. Because of their blind malice, though, both were extremely dangerous, especially to each other. But somehow, like the flame and the paraffin in a lamp, they had failed to combine and explode. They were "mates". And yet Klima could not resist offering the cruelty, in the presence of one more fortunate, which leads the mother crocodile, in the billabongs of Townsville, to bite the heads off some at least of her darling children. At Bev's Wedding Luncheon, and despite being well disposed to her, Klima had been driven into a rage because Bev had been speaking to some idiot at her table – probably the Prime Minister of Australia – whom Klima had no interest in, but whose position in

35

society made Bev's proximity an affront. On that occasion, Bev's rellies had been as thin on the ground as they were numerous now. They had multiplied like bacteria in every new wound that Bev had inflicted on her husband's family. Then, all Klima had needed to do to wreck the bride's happiness was to tell her about the "fascinating" interview she had just had with Bev's brother Sean, a motorcycle policeman who had regaled "youse" ("K's" assembled siblings) with tales of the bags of limbs he had collected from the site of a suicide on the Murgon railway. But now that Bev's relatives were, in more ways than one, so common at "Capricornia", and their *esprit de corps* so much the State Religion, there would have been no point in mentioning them. In order to hurt one of her best friends (as was only natural), to pay her back for her success, Klima now had to refer to her own, ie to Piers' family, not to Bev's. The Brownbills were the exotic liabilities now. "How is Aldour?" she called out. Bev was carrying a small roast crocodile stuffed with prawns back to the fridge: it had awed everyone, as intended, like something out of the **Satyricon** – its jaws were fastened on a rugby ball made of a paupau dipped in chocolate – but now there was a danger that someone might eat it (it did, after all, constitute the buffet), and why should they? Croc was Bev's favourite. "Wasn't Aldour invited, Bev?" Klima asked. Bev's face tightened, as if she had already enjoyed the radical surgery Piers had promised her for her birthday. "Is Aldour married yet, Bev? . . . Oh, I had forgotten – he doesn't really *enjoy* weddings, does he?"

Aldour Brownbill had lived the Life of Riley – until he had ruined Bev's wedding. Theoretically an "Interior Decorator", the only interior he had ever decorated was that of his own Indooroopilly *"à terre"*, and he didn't even live there very often, spending most of his time in a suite at the Conrad, which is probably Australia's, and certainly Brisbane's finest hotel. There, he enjoyed interminable solitary lunches and dinners in the restaurant, steeping himself in *Bouillabaisse Barrimundi* and Yalumba champagne. Then he would piss away the allowance he drew from his father at the Casino in the old Treasury building next door (for, like most of the Australian rich, Piers was as generous where he and his family were concerned as he was mean to other people). Hours not consecrated to the pokies were lavished on the Performing Arts Centre just over the river, where Aldour would cry into his vase of Lambrusco over Barry Bogiatsis' "ravishing" versions of the latest Sydney operas. His favourite by far was Okelle de Bahn's **The Eye of the Beholder**, which was about the Eighth Century Emperor Constantine VI of Byzantium, a subject no doubt dear to "de Bahn" (real name Papagos), the mercurial daughter of a Warumbul souvlaki vendor. Pius Anadu, an aboriginal who had been castrated (accidentally) during a tribal circumcision, *was* the "I" of the **Beholder**. In Brisbane, he sang the Emperor in a (childish) falsetto to emphasise the 30-year old's unnatural dependence on his mother, and nemesis, the dowager Empress Irene. (Using the specious excuse of his depravity, Irene, seventeen years into Constantine's reign, had had him deposed, and blinded so roughly – in the same palace room where she had borne him – that he died, giving her the solitary power she had always craved, and earning her a scorching rebuke from Pope Leo III, who declared – much to the delight of the Brisbane opera crowd – that no human being stained with menstrual, much less filial blood, could ever ascend a throne. Leo went on to crown Charlemagne in Rome to displace Irene as ruler of the Christian world, thus splitting Western Catholic Europe from Eastern Orthodox Europe for good).

Pius, who had the only *castrato* voice on earth, also sang, inevitably, the part of the eunuch Stavrakios *("Stauraccio"* to the Spring Hill *cognoscenti*), the then (800 AD) Prime Minister of Byzantium, who had risen from the dirt to where he could put rellies in whatever public job he hadn't flogged to the highest bidder – so what could **THE SYDNEY MORNING HERALD** mean when it talked of the opera's "startling relevance to contemporary Australia"? (Stavrakios, Irene's nominee and her creature, had finally been banished by Constantine in a rare spasm of *amour propre*, thus anticipating the career of his mistress, whose reign as "Emperor" – for she always denied she was a woman – soon collapsed in yet another palace coup, whereupon she was banished – perhaps without regret – to the island of Lesbos).

Unlike most Australian critics, who had hailed the opera as a "masterpiece" – because Anadu, as the victim of *"racial, sexual and gender-specific abuse"*, had hit the jackpot as far as the anally passive Left were concerned – Aldour knew something about music. He could see that de Bahn's score was abysmal, and had largely been plundered from the contemporary French composer Edgar Varèse. Why then did he find the opera exciting? Although he had seen the first, 1981 version in that crumbling pavlova the Sydney Opera House, Aldour greatly preferred Bogiatsis' Brisbane ***Beholder***, which was in the best (ie worst) traditions of Australian *Époque Mauve*, to the modern (set in Rose Bay in 1968) *mise-en-scène* Gabriel Bristly had offered Sydney in 1981. Patrick White was – appropriately as a Philhellene – the Obscene Mum in Bristly's '81 production, and Robert Helpmann, as Stavrakios, was an Oscar Wilde-like Gay Martyr for campaigning – in those benighted days! – for the creation of the Australia Council over the sensible objections of Constantine VI (Sir Sidney Nolan: his blindness explaining a mystery that had long perplexed the Australian art world). Perhaps it was the Freudian echoes in de Bahn that had appealed to Aldour. ***Eye of the Beholder*** was virtually ***Oedipus Rex*** in reverse: it even shared the royal Greek setting. Perhaps Irene reminded him of his own natural mother, who had turned on him like a dog when his attitude to Bev had begun to threaten the cast-off's position at Noosa. The fascination the opera exerted on him may even have been because he saw a presentiment of his fate in its plot. He was anything but stupid, and, soon after Bev had got Piers to cut his son out of "their" will, she secured the withdrawal of Aldour's allowance. The burning wrath of the Sun Queen melted the costly plumage of the opera queen as quickly as the dawn had plucked Cinderella's: it sent him tumbling, Ikaros-like, from his penthouse in the 'Pilly to a stifling basement near the Brisbane River. There, he was forced to share three darkened rooms and a Dirt Dunny with with two young aboriginal girls, both addicts, who worked as ten dollar whores in the

Transport Centre on Roma Street. Aldour himself secured an unremunerative niche in the China Department of *DAVID JONES*, where, for once, his dubious taste was appreciated. It was hardly surprising, given all this, that Aldour had been conspicuous by his absence at Bev's party. But he did come to learn – ironically enough through Klima – of the "myural" with which Tray was to decorate Bev's Saunie. This was a circular, windowless room directly under the dome of "Capricornia", the bullseye of its concentric design. At Bev's suggestion, Tray covered its never-ending, rotating wall with a painting called *"The Human Race"*. This featured representatives of every "oppressed minority" that the Australian Labor Party had ever favoured: Abos, Gays, Muslims, the Mafia, the Irish – even, grotesquely, the Disabled. They were painted running in the nude and in profile, like the never-ending runners etched on the side of a Greek vase. The Disabled – even the paraplegics – had, like the rest, been miraculously "empowered". Those without limbs sailed through the air like Stymphalian Birds shitting – as such birds must – on their blasphemous oppressors. Everyone was in the nude to prove that, as Bev mockingly intoned, "we are all the same". It was good, she said, that the walls of the sauna ended at the point where they began. That meant that, true to Party theory (heavy irony here), no runner could end up ahead of any other. Just as there should be no losers in life (no oppressed), Labor had forbidden the existence of winners. *"The Human Race"* was to be fair, as the real human race so manifestly was not.

Aldour found all this a challenge (as indeed did Tray). The sauna at "Capricornia", he "joked", should be dubbed "the Gas Chamber" as it featured "all the world's most crapulous bludgers". It was "the best place for 'em!" He tastelessly suggested that the artist should embellish his fresco so that it indicated the likely – and characteristic – reaction of each group to imminent asphyxiation, like "the gypsies in Hitler's Europe" who had "rooted like dingoes" as the crystals in Auschwitz had "singed their Kelly Neds". (He related his own visions of the various types of sectarian activity at this point: they are too hateful for repetition). Despite knowing the origin of the name of Bev's home, Aldour had long been in the habit of calling the house, after the book by Balzac, ***Splendeurs et Misères des Courtisanes***. Upon learning that Bev had, in addition, named each of the villa's rooms after the chapters in Xavier Herbert's novel, he set about rechristening them with chapter headings from ***Splendeurs***. Bev and Piers' bedroom became *"À combien l'Amour revient aux Vieillards"* ("What love costs old bastards"), and the room that rejoiced in the heroes of *"The Human Race"* became *"Où mènent les Mauvais Chemins"* ("Where the bad roads lead") . . .

. . .

. . . Recoiling from all these unpleasant memories, which the ghost of the lovely grey harbour had inspired, Tray turned away from the Art Gallery's haunted catacombs to its Giftshop. After he had bought a number of coffee mugs decorated with Brett Roger calligraphy, and a collection of hideous Ken Done prints, which looked as if they had been painted by a schizophrenic, he fled the Gallery of New South Wales and stumbled back to his taxi. Hours would pass before his plane to London, but he liked to arrive at airports as early as possible. At Kingsford-Smith, he luxuriated over the vast variety of coffees on sale in the restaurant: "Flat Whites," "Short Blacks," Capuccinos that looked like Pavlovas. He would never enjoy so sophisticated and differentiated a range of goodies in England. He would never again witness the encyclopaedic epicureanism of an intellectually poor society. It was amazing how every single Australian town and village, however small and bland, could offer the guilty glutton extreme unction. Each Urunga or Taree might strike the foreigner as being identical, artificial, and identically artificial, wherever it might glisten on the vast continent, but though the town itself might resemble some airport dinner set down in the Bush, the random epicure could choose there from a *Trompe d'Oeil*. In a roadside caff, under the brightly painted twenty-foot-high statue of a prawn or a toad that the Civic Fathers would have erected to put the place "on the map", "Violet Crumbles" (a form of chocolate) would tumble like turds over a ziggurat of "Lamingtons" and, diving into the fridge, the connoisseur might well find an ice called a "Golden Gaytime" beside the croc burger and the dead kangaroo. What a contrast to England! As the tourist speeds down its autobahns, towns and villages drift past in the milky air like gallstones . . . Each is old and unique, as a gallstone is, and, like a gallstone, each is the residue of a unique past. But just try finding something to eat! All you'll get is the local variation on Kentucky Fried Chicken or a rissole glowing with streptococci. Why is it then that the plastic hamlets that litter the Outback offer smorgasbords of the finest, most bizarre fare? Why is it that each Greyhound Stop in Gympie or Bundaberg resembles a sideboard banquet in the France of the pre-Escoffier era, such as Flaubert describes in **L'Éducation Sentimentale**, and where, on the one table:

> *"there was a sturgeon's head drenched in Champagne, a York Ham cooked in Tokay, thrushes* au gratin, *roast quail, a* vol-au-vent Béchamel, *a* sauté *of red-legged partridges and, flanking all this, stringed potatoes mixed with truffles."*

Tray, Europe-bound, would never taste real prawns again: prawns as big as bats, and sweet, metallic and crunchy, smelling of babies. The English variety would be tiny, white, limp and tasteless: cold McDonald's chips. And the milkshakes would be *à la McDonald's* too: tubs of sexless sludge, like children's buckets brimming with sandcastle. Why couldn't they make a proper milkshake in England? Bubbly and icy, its texture should be that of satinny milk; its resinous heart is restless chocolate death. And where, in England, could he breakfast, like some pervert, on the "Little Red Riding Hood" of a lobster? He had purchased one for a pittance that very morning from a Fish and Chip shop in Curl Curl. He had washed down its tough white abdomen – which had tasted as bitter and opulent as vodka or *Pouilly Fumée les Logères* – with a glass of Coke.

There was, most unusually for an airport restaurant (though not an Australian one), a glass oven for barbequeing chooks at Kingsford Smith. It gave the Gateway to the Continent the feel of a Bowen Milk Bar. Golden torsos revolved in the misty case. Rugby League players were soaping themselves in a shower. Golden and puffy case: the hollow brass bull of King

41

Phaleris of Agrigento, the bull where he would roast his enemies, but which would ingeniously convert their screams into nice airport music. Because there was a TV in the restaurant too, another interesting innovation. An advert came on for "Big Rooster", a Brisbane-based Fast Food chain, which was trying to associate Queensland, in the mind of the Australian people, with Kentucky. "Big Rooster" had a patriotic jingle which now blared out, converting the sufferings of the napalmed chooks into melody. It reminded Tray of how Kierkegaard, using Phaleris' bull as his metaphor, had said that when a poet cries out in verse from his misery, all the public can hear is a dainty song:

> **"Yes, it's our big chicken, for our big state,**
> **Barbequed or fried, it sure tastes great;**
> **If Queensland makes you feel great, mate,**
> **Then you'd rather have Big Rooster!"**

The next advert on the television was part of a Government drive against citizens who dumped unwanted pets in the Bush, where they promptly consumed the priceless marsupials: *"It's a reprehensible act. It really shows your lack of intentional fortitude. If you're* really *brave, have it put down!"* A brief newscast followed. The Caucasus and the Middle East were uncoiled, as was the fascinating disclosure that *"Missie, a three-legged terrier, has been lost in the Bush between Kiama and Mittagong"* (this may have been a botched execution, a tribute to the Government's wise propaganda). Then there was a current affairs show, which was being beamed in live from a school hall in Barraba. It was a programme about the impact "on the community" of crime and punishment. Two high school girls had been suspended for shoplifting. No graduation or leaving certificates for them! The mothers, who only looked a little older, were being interviewed. *"My baby, my baby, they've done this to our babies,"* said one, adding, in an aside to the audience, *"they've done this to your baby, too."* *"But what can Derry Blair and her daughter DO?"* the interviewer pined. *"I can dent the red tape. I'm gonna go right to the top. I'm going for it four bore. My daughter wants to be a veterinary nurse. Now she's gonna be a shopgirl. No way."* Tray agreed. It didn't seem a very appropriate vocation. Another unfortunate was introduced. Nathan Golding, *"a good, gentle boy,"* was in prison for armed robbery. *"He's a bit of a handful,"* his mother admitted, *"the authorities are trying to sedate him with teargas."* The interviewer refused to be detained by these futilities.

"Mrs Golding, they've called your son a freak of nature." "He has taken steroids, which is unfortunate." "Nathan is very big. How can he be controlled?" "Through kindness. Through the right psychiatric treatment. Through skills that might enhance him as a human being." . . . Suddenly, Tray's plane was announced and he shuffled to the Departure Lounge, where everyone was delayed because a drunken Mancunian (*never* board a plane from Australia to Britain whose ultimate destination is not London) kept going up to a machine-gun wielding policeman, daring the officer to shoot him and unfortunately being denied his request. There was a delay of about two hours before they could board the aircraft.

. . .

He was just tucking into his chicken in coconut milk (he was flying on an oriental airline) when London was announced below. The cubes of glazed breast looked like little tree frogs. They suddenly, unpleasantly, reconstituted themselves as "Our Big Chicken" as Tray remembered the "Big Rooster" song. It was like the passage in Benjamin Britten's ***Saint Nicholas*** when the saint sits down to eat and the minced bits of the murdered boys – which his cannibal hosts are serving him – leap out of the pot and sing:

> **"Well, it's our big chicken, for our big state,**
> **Barbequed or fried, it sure tastes great;**
> **If Queensland makes you feel great, mate,**
> **Then you'd rather have Big Rooster!"**

Lines of Australians, not having taken ample opportunities to go to the bathroom before, were crowding the aisles by the cubicles, clutching sponge bags. Their open flies and awful clothes put him horribly in mind of students just in time for brekkie in a Hall of Residence. (Tray had trained under the great Nuggety Bouquainiste, painter of Mrs Whitlam, at

Townsville's James Cook University). Beside him, two nouveau-riche Sydneysiders (though they couldn't have been that *"riches"*, as it was only Economy) were making life hell for the inscrutable oriental slaves. The gent, with a red, spherical head and a long nose, objected loudly to his victims' plover-with-a-broken-wing-like fatalism. "Come on Flossy!" he suggested (he had christened her "Flossy", though her name, according to the badge, was "Wati"), "come on Flossy – make my day!" He wanted her to lean her udders over him, as the She-Wolf had over Romulus and Remus. "Come on Floss, let's have a bit of elbow grease on this porthole here!" . . . "She's in a buffet situation," he remarked to his paramour, a middle-aged former secretary-type who looked like an overfed dolphin. "No eye contact – she's just pissed." "You shut your mouth," his girlfriend said, "you've had too many beers." "Poor Flossy," said the man, deep in thought. His girlfriend wasn't listening. "You remember you said this morning you'd packed condoms . . . ?" "Yairs . . ." "And I said I was worried because we hadn't used condoms for ages . . ." "Yeah," he said, "I picked up a few tips! . . . Look at that boy!"

He was alluding to Miki, Wati's colleague, a Chinese Antinoös with a huge mouth and eyelashes who was fluttering around a pair of drunken Kiwis (everyone seemed pissed on this flight) like a goldfish.

"Look at that boy," the man snorted again, "it's bloody hard, that!" Miki was bearing yet more trays of cane rum and cashews towards New Zealand tormentors. His face, like the Mona Lisa's, was a picture of melancholy, understanding and contempt. "He looks like an Australian, that bloke," the philosopher averred. Tray, scrutinising Miki, could not help feeling that the designation was a little inapt.

His attention strayed to the video screen, which, funnily enough, still showed a map of Australia. A little black plane like a fly was crawling over Toowoomba. Apparently, though circling Heathrow, they had only travelled about fifty kilometers from Sydney. Then a newscast came on, the national TV news in Wati's country. The passengers had seen it about a hundred times before. At one point, over the Bay of Bengal, it had simply been repeated, over and over again, for two hours. There were endless shots of old buildings being torn down and wondering glimpses of a hideous aseptic skyscraper. This was the country's new, silicone-induced erection. The idea was that such things had never been built before. As if the people weren't replacing their own originality with something you could find everywhere, and were already sick of. The national capital looked like Cairns. It had big, prehistoric grey trees with large, simple leaves. They looked like first attempts at a real tree. There was a modern mosque bigger than St Paul's, silver apartment buildings that shone like a stapler – it was all rather depressing. The rough first draft of a real society. Even the national language, preposterously adopted, on board the plane, to nappy containers and overhead lockers – a language that had been designed for a swamp tribe – looked like the undressed building blocks, the primitive first stirrings, of a real language. The new-rich peasant country on the screen resembled a giant airport with endless malls, dark green tropical plants, brand names and (an exotic, tourist touch) public hangings and whippings, for it was made very clear that Islam ruled beneath the Christmas Tree squalor. There was, in fact, no connection between this new society and the Western values of which it sought to boast. The pictures made Tray reflect on the writers and politicians, back home, who insisted that Australia was an Asian country. If only it were true! The fact that Australia's "intellectuals" were in charge of Asianisation, though, meant that what Australia got was the worst of both worlds: a guilt-ridden subservience to Asian racists born from the same pathetic Eurocentric insularity that made the prophets of Asia behave as if they weren't in Asia at all. It was only the poor, travelled or "stupid" Australians, thought Tray, who seemed to realise the finite luckiness and the infinite fragility of their country. It was only Australians decried as parochial who were uneasily aware of the proximity of Asia amid the myopic European safeness of Melbourne or Sydney, with their "Ladybird Book" suburbs and their all-white children in English straw boaters and uniforms. The indefinable danger that he felt

Australia, like any beautiful innocent, was in, added to the invincibility of its calm. It strengthened that calm. What psychiatrists call "denial", creating as it does a parallel universe, is always as potently sedative as it is hallucinogenic. Australia's custodians and most of its citizens, were, like the protagonists of a fairytale, impervious to unease, so convinced were they that nothing lay beyond their Ruritanian idyll. They really did think that their unreal society constituted a reality in the horrible Asian world in which, in fact, they lived.

"Not only that", the first Kiwi was explaining to his colleague, "I don't the cunt's hardly even got a job." "Well," his friend replied, "that's nothing major, is it?" They appeared to be businessmen. Each had the sharp, androgynously perfect face and the broad rich body of the middle-class white Pacific male. One was a Minotaur with the head of Alexander the Great. Miki's orgiastic quietism had failed to impress them, and when they caught sight of the exquisite Wati, they said that her appetite for hospitality was greater. They speculated loudly on her tenderness, her rapacity. One of the Kiwis leaned forward and told his compatriot to ask her over: "Just walk up and talk to a sheila!" "What," his friend demanded, "a boong?" This remark released a whole cache of romantic memories in Alexander the Great, who hadn't married a "boong", but who had, he assured his friend, ended up with the next best thing. "My first missus was the only one in my life who gave me a blow job – and that's when we were separated. Gave me a blow job! Never did it when we were married or living together. All I did was open my legs – and I haven't seen her since!"

The newsreader on the video screen was blowing repeated kisses with downcast eyes like a chanting Buddhist monk. A picture of Wati's capital formed a backdrop behind him. Unusually for so forward-looking a place, the symbol of the city, the giant postcard behind him, was an old domed building of the British colonial period. It was quite ugly, but Tray could quite imagine why the provincial inhabitants had preserved it. The grand buildings of Paris and London are harmonious and alive because, Tray felt, they are the random products of a long and living national history. They are like the flowers on the Sydney jacaranda, which grow straight out of the tree. In Wati's capital, as in Sydney and La Paz, there was no native greatness, no history, and so greatness had to be imagined and imposed, as suburban England is imagined and imposed in the khaki wastes of Turra-Murra. In consequence, the building on the screen – like the *Capitolio* in Bogotá or the Treasury in Brisbane – was as grandiose as it was insignificant. It was too simple as well as too elaborate. It had no internal harmony because it had no internal anything. It had just been set down on nothingness because it was "magnificent", and had been saved from nothingness for the same reason. It made some of the Australians on the flight think of the despicable old Queen Victoria Building in Sydney, which people who had never been there said was "just like London." What it was "just like" was Moscow or Dundee. It certainly looked awful in Sydney: it should have been blown up. The hideous Victorian pineapple patch behind the newsreader was puny, grainy and ruinous. Especially as it was set off by autistic slabs which orientals had erected behind it. Dwarfed by a wall of blank skyscrapers, the colonial version of Angkor Wat looked like a row of little elaborately marked toads on a piece of white canvas – all its littleness and ugliness were magnified. One couldn't help feeling that modern architecture far better suited the climate and mentality of this half-made country, as indeed it better suited Australia. Old-fashioned buildings were simply dwarfed by the heat, by the momentous peurility of tropical landscapes that seemed more in proportion to dinosaurs than humans. With no human history worthy of the name, it was natural for Michelangelo – or his native equivalents – to leave things as a shoebox block of Carrara marble. Why fashion something in man's image, when man has made no impact here, left no human associations?

The lights above the video screens began to flash. It was hoped that the passengers would patronise the airline again – "especially those of the Islamic faith" (which fortunately did not include Tray). The "Fasten Seatbelts" sign went on and the descent into London began.

RUE OF THE REEF GAUCHE

The year before his arrival in the UK, I had seen Tray's work at an exhibition called *"New Australian Painters"* in Canberra. I had been enchanted. That was why I had invested in his ticket to London. I had even promised to put him up until he could find a studio here. As eponymous maestro of *EMPORIO PATRICK MYNTS*, I had been invited to Canberra by the Australian (Federal) Government with the representatives of about thirty other European and American galleries. There were also journalists, critics and arts functionaries, and direct bulk art buyers from South Korea and Japan. It was supposedly a junket connected with the Bicentennary of Australia's colonisation. Given that all the other visitors were far more senior than I, I suspect that the fact that I am related to the Prime Minister of Australia played a part in my own participation. *"I'm Dreaming of Coming"*, as the Painting and Litfest was deathlessly styled, was meant to "celebrate our cultural coming" and simultaneously to offer a sort of slave market *des Arts* to stimulate a vice for Australiana in jaded metropolitan chicken-hawks. A bit of a contradiction in terms, in other words. Because, if Australia was so self-confident, so anti-colonial, why was it important to influence foreigners from old (and new) imperial powers? *"What,"* as Whitman once memorably wrote, *"have I* [ie Australia] *in common with them? And what with the destruction of them?"* In any case, the bored old queens at the exhibition weren't even slightly interested in *"our Meanjin Dreaming"* (the Coming was another matter). They had availed themselves of the Department of Foreign Affairs' hospitality simply to get away from the Northern Winter, or, on the beaches of Sydney, to bow down to those delicious idols who represent, as I have pointed out, the most authentic aspect of Australian civilization. The esteemed foreign guests were fat and scaly, like freshly baked loaves. They all looked as if they were wearing masks. Their stunned eyes, slow movements and (for Australia) elaborate coûture made them resemble the dressed-up goanna lizards I'd seen on Australian postcards. I laughed out loud at the image; it put me in mind of the wolf dressed up as granny in *Little Red Riding Hood*: an apt simile, considering their proclivities.

Australia House had sent me an airline ticket on the same flight as Edward Semper-Adonis, a Press Officer at the Tate Gallery. I knew him slightly. (We obviously weren't VIP's – we hadn't been entrusted to QANTAS, Australia's national carrier, which is twice as expensive as other airlines). Semper-Adonis rang to ask if we could synchronise our travel arrangements. This was not a cause for joy, but unfortunately I could think of no reasonable excuse at the time. He descended on my suburban Surrey home the day before departure. It was October and he looked like an old man in the olive-oil light. He could hardly have been more than 40. His skin was the colour and texture of a macaroon – young and old, alive and dead, female and male. He was very boring and self-important like all nonentities. He had the Frankenstein forehead and bulging fledgling eyes of a dwarf (perhaps I'm being harsh). He dressed rather nicely.

On the morning we left, Tia, my housekeeper, took our photographs. At 8.20 she said we should all sit down and watch television. She did so with an avidity. She said she had learned from the Aussie soaps that, in Australia, everyone says *pin*jamas rather than *py*jamas. Just then she said: "Isn't that your car?" She was already crying in the hall. We packed and off we drove, with a tearful Tia waving, still waving in the doorway. The chauffeur drove us through the dear country of my favourite memories and associations: the copse by the Golf Course by Marney's Pond; the turn-off for Chestnut Avenue; Esher; Oxshott Woods; Oxshott; the Great Roundabout near Leatherhead from which you exit for Sussex. Just after we'd cleared Oxshott we saw, on our left, a lovely mock-Tudor villa in a yellowing garden – naked brick, leaded windows, black beams. I thought with envy of its probably retired occupant, the life of fear, of struggle, over, the perfect retreat her (or his) reward.

We were in Gatwick just after 9, had a cup of tea, and taxied off the runway at about noon. Initially, I felt fine. My obsessions/compulsions seemed to melt away with a suddenly enhanced sense of diffidence and will. I made an attempt to start a novel – **The Twyborn Affair** – and dozed off, dreaming of Scotland and the avenue of oaks that leads off the Perth-Coupar Angus road to Kinrossie, where there is a Pictish or Scottish (ie *Irish*) Cross. I kept thinking: *surely* it can't be this easy, this pleasant – something is bound to go wrong. I almost felt the need to pre-empt the neurotic disaster I feared was inevitable. Eventually, alas, I submitted to neurotic compulsion and upset myself. It teaches me, at least, not to do so in the future. In the meantime, I listened closely to the snatches of conversation which were drifting out of the kitchen to which our seats were directly adjacent. The stewards/stewardesses (American – it was Continental Airlines) were talking among themselves. "Sounds like a bullshit story to me." "She is a tramp, she is. Really short curly hair. Always dressed to kill." "Two amazon women," the effeminate steward rejoindered. The stewardess agreed. "She is, she's got to be a Lesbian. She's a sick girl. Have you seen her little girlfriend?" The stewardess went on to discuss her sister's divorce in a disingenuously censorious way. "She got to keep a 2.5 carat ring. It's disgusting. *He's* disgusting. He's a great guy, he's got a great personality, but he's overweight, he's a slob ..."

Edward was remonstrating with me, asking me, over lunch, not to eat a custard-filled chocolate éclair when what seemed like the jet from a very powerful hose struck me on the side of the head, soaking me, and drenching my new business suit. One of the stewardesses had been opening a bottle of champagne – it had prematurely exploded at the wrong angle. Anyway, I got a free glass of champers for my trouble and they promised to give me a dry-cleaning slip for presentation in New York (which I couldn't have used anyway), but they never did.

We flew north-west over Ireland, Iceland and Greenland, then south-west into the middle of Canada. Then we veered south-east to glide over the St Lawrence Seaway, Albany, West

Point and the Hudson into Newark, New Jersey, which from the air looked ghastly – decayed, polluted. It was as brown and roofless as Ostia – a city in ruins.

We were subjected throughout the flight to rather horrible American films – one set in New York, at night, in Winter. My earphones were broken – no impediment to the student of the modern American cinema. How alien and crushing (I reflected) those vast buildings always seem, what a horror they are. And then one has to consider the fact that the average American lives under a reign of terror – imposed by his fellow citizens – that makes the *Yezhovschina* pale by comparison. This air of violence – of threat – even invaded Newark airport where we were greeted by a portrait of President Reagan, who looked like a dyspeptic mongol. You can see why Europe-bound Australians vastly prefer to cross Asia – with its clinical dictatorships and its clean, secure, calm-inducing airports – than to risk the States. Newark International was an absolute shambles – like Calcutta. God knows how we got our flight to Honolulu. I certainly couldn't have done it on my own. At one point I asked a security guard – an Irish immigrant – for directions. I would guess by his accent that he was a Northern Irish Catholic. He was most helpful. I felt most sorry for him. Imagine leaving Ireland, with its poverty, yes, but beauty and certainty, for this, this ugly chaos . . .

There were a lot of New Yorkers on the flight from Newark to Honolulu. The faces of the New York ladies were, frankly, ape-like, and seem to have anticipated the American physiognomy as a whole. As did their dress sense – everything of a falseness, newness – ageing, death, denied, and so accentuated. Nylon pink hair like a doll's hair for ladies of 70 – synthetic peppermint-green coats, rouged and powdered faces. The impression one of cheapness, of hopeless dissimulation, imminent decay. Like the clothes and wigs they put on dogs – that's what they resembled. The old man in front of me looked like something out of a turn-of-the-century Viennese magazine – an elephant man – yellow flesh, with a grotesque nose and (for someone so small and old and frail) vast yellow fingers, like parsnips. He would curl them over the top of the back of his chair, so I had a good chance to study them. He was wearing big incongruous modern rings.

The plane we boarded at Newark was rather more comfortable, with larger seats and working headphones (I watched a little of *A Streetcar Named Desire*), but problems arose because they had to move a wildly overdressed young man to make way for a girl who was claustrophobic and had to sit by a window. "I have a fear of claustrophobics!" the young man shrieked. He talked to a teenage boy about "Franz Liszt's Symphony Number Two – killer stuff really." The second in-flight movie was another depressing landscape picture: a weatherboard American town in the mountains, but even the olde-worlde shops and *"Bohemia Antiques"* had neon lettering and a vicious, sterile air. In Europe, old redecorated buildings retain a miasma, an odour of their previous incarnation; in the States, where the attempt at restoration is so whole-hearted, the past, like the past of its human beings, is completely exorcised and disinfected. Replaced by something frightening – of marzipan. The movie starred Steve Martin – a simulacrum (of humanity, humour, heterosexuality) if ever there was one – the archetypal American homonculus. The whole production made me shiver . . .

The only "taxi" available at Honolulu Airport was a block-long white limousine. I didn't want to get in, suspecting foul play, but the driver, a native Hawaiian, assured us that his limo service was off the road for the night and that he would only charge us cab-fare. (In fact, he charged us less than for the standard run into town). It was very hot inside the car, a three-year-old Lincoln Fleetwood – "the best car in Hawaii" according to our impartial coachman. There was no air-conditioning – broken. It was about 2 o'clock in the morning, and as we glided along a freeway past thin, burning sky-scrapers I found myself intrigued by the illuminated cabinet that formed the centrepiece of our darkened cabin. There were two crystal goblets and an ancient box of chocolates on the red felt floor of its glass tank. It was filled with yellow light – a vision of hearse-like desolation in the heat of that night.

At the Hotel Waikiki in Honolulu City I found myself on the Eighteenth Floor. I was getting off to sleep when an argument broke out next door between two middle-aged American women who had just returned to their room. Their voices – thin, clipped, almost Canadian vowels – were very alike – but they weren't sisters. *"I've known you for 27 years now – a stranger all these years!"* "You're too forthright, too abrupt. I accept you for what you are, why don't you just let me be me?" *"I'm not capable – take* **that** *for your choice of words!"* "I almost lost my job two and a half months ago – my mind stretched!" There was a "look what I've done to myself" mentality at work here. It was sterile-seductive, like a children's argument. When you know how pointless, how nihilistic it is, but you go on. It's comforting, the abyss. *"I wanted to have a good time!"* one of them began to wail.

Next morning, when I returned to the hotel to change (it was a roasting 90 degrees), I heard the ladies chuckling together, the TV blaring. The blue and scalding paradise outside, the reason (I had supposed) for their visit, clearly held few attractions.

Watching American TV, you get the impression that America is a totalitarian society; there seems to be an unspoken consensus – about the justice of virulent, marginalising free enterprise – that no-one will admit to. (Not of course that there is anything wrong with virulent, marginalising free enterprise, but one feels that it should at least declare itself, as virulent marginalising socialism has the grace to do in Communist societies). And yet the ferocious commercialism is calming, assuaging. Freedom, peace, can be bought, and for very little. We breakfasted at a beachside café on beautiful pancakes, bacon, eggs, maple syrup, iced water and as much coffee as we could drink for about a pound, a fawning androgyne fluttering at our elbow. You can see why the Australian resorts will never take off – the bracing obsequiousness of the American people – which they divorce from all sense of self – is beyond most human beings.

Honolulu, we found, was a Rio de Janeiro-like city with wide boulevards and tall, thin white skyscrapers. As in Rio, the surrounding mountains and the forest that covered them were a gruesome viridian and had a youthful, Cretaceous air. They seemed strange – as did the bright sunshine – we had only recently been among the freezing mists and the venerable yellow oaks of Oxshott, Surrey. We seemed to have exchanged the real for the unreal, and a rooted society, rich in layers, rings (like the transverse slice of a Deodar) for something brutal, simple, fantastic. In Australia, I felt, the phantasmagoria would be brought to its logical conclusion. The clouds seemed very close to us, very loose – as they appear in tropical countries. They brushed the woods like gunsmoke. Huge shadows preceded them. The pink Moorish hotel for which Honolulu is famous was very close to our own. It was delightful. The sand was white, the sea glassy and hot, purple and turquoise, like the sea around Sicily. Honolulu was a city, like many American cities, which envisaged human relationships only if they were of a commercial nature – it was impossible to find an official, ie a non-capitalist building. The one Post Office serving this vast conurbation, which I happened on quite by chance, was clearly a cause of shame and comprised a single desk in the back of a Bijoutière's. I shuddered for those unable to be consumers: the poor, the homeless, the mentally ill, the unemployed. In this unreal society only the consumers were real, only the consumers could be citizens – indeed the two concepts were interchangeable. There was something depressing, overwhelming, about the fact that every second shop (and there were nothing but shops – gift shops mostly) was an eating house. It put me in mind of a wealthy collector of my acquaintance, the heir to a retail fortune, who buys himself treats every day he hasn't earned. He is trying to buy himself peace, but peace has to be earned, it has to be looked forward to, an oasis in a desert, and in a desert of oasises, like Hawaii, it suddenly struck me how awful his life must be. All these restaurants, with their aggressively endearing names, were offering a sort of kindness, of comfort, which they didn't feel, and yet, really, they (or their British equivalents) were my self-indulgent client's only friends.

We dined in "Perry's Smorgy" – as much lobster as you could eat for $10.95 – and wrote letters in a lovely seaside bar. On our return to the hotel, I related the history of Communism

55

to Edward Semper-Adonis. For some reason he had asked me about it – maybe the depravity of the prevailing *mis-en-scène* had produced the same effect on him as it had on me – a certain *Nostalgie de la Boue* for Pol Pot and the Khmer Rouge.

Later that evening I wrote a few letters in a depressingly fulsome bar in Honolulu airport. We were the only customers. I felt sorry indeed for the waitress, to whom we spoke. She earned some pittance and she worked very long hours – not an unusual state of affairs in a nation that people style the Elysium of mankind. She put a brave face on it like other Americans we had met. Blond hair with black roots; bronze, almost green skin. A denim jacket. She was about 30, by which time an ordinary American woman is as strong and worldly as platinum. Over-ripe, over-strong, like a gone-to-seed rhubarb plant. She had a child – or children. No husband. She had missed the boat. Yet, in contrast to foreigners in similar positions, such Americans have dignity, they work hard, show an interest. The culture inoculates them, keeps them working, hoping, gives them a belief in a success they will never have. The American poor are like people who are inoculated with the smallpox virus and so find themselves immune to its progress. Their smallpox – in scabs of pus from the seriously ill – keeps them stuck in this world, though it seems no different from the smallpox of their wealthy benefactors, which propels its bearers to Heaven. The waitress had hard eyes – a delicate face with high cheekbones. She had so little – intellectually, spiritually – to equip her for her workload, her parodic sexual status, her lack of standing in a horrible society. That's what always amazes you about Americans – how they manage to accomplish so much with so little. How they can attain computer wizardry, create amazing cinema, make complex issues sound simple, child-like – yet they cannot write properly, they cannot speak.

We said our goodbyes to the barmaid and boarded the Sydney plane at around midnight. I woke at about 5 in the morning; there was a red glow on the black horizon of the Pacific, turquoise above it, and then, glowing on the deep, stilly blue, the Southern Cross. An hour or two later I was awaiting our descent into Sydney. We could see nothing. Then we dived into the blanket of cloud that was covering the city and came out over a landscape of diarrhoea-coloured scrub with brown rivers and hundreds of blue swimming pools, like broken tesserae on a recently unearthed mosaic. We flew over the Paramatta River – the Opera House and Harbour Bridge to our left – and landed at Kingsford-Smith at around 7 AM Sydney time. The airport was more chaotic, if less menacing, than that at Newark, and was overrun by Japanese tourists: even the trolleys were sponsored by SANYO.

The people whom Australia's officialdom had arranged to greet us were rather late in picking us up. Mesdames Doreen Reuter and Queenie Hoare were *Grandes Dames* from Sydney's Eastern Suburbs. (In Australia, we were to learn, the norm is always the opposite of what prevails elsewhere – in Paris, London, Berlin etc it is the west of the city that is rich; in Sydney only the eastern suburbs are exclusive). Mrs Hoare had what I would discover was the archetypal Australian face. Exposure to the sun had made her skin as gnarled and shiny as a braided loaf. Her glazed snout and her goat-like golden eyes made me think of a Salt-Water Crocodile. Mrs Reuter had soft, feathery black hair and soft, reddish-pink skin. She had the wet-eyed, drowned-kitten look of an alcoholic. Neither lady was a civil servant. They were volunteers who regarded their contribution to the Australian Government's cultural programmes as a form of charity, like making Lamingtons for refugees. The same wealth, the same isolation from real issues makes every Australian a dilettante, I find. Because they have no real problems, everything Australians do, despite its seeming resemblance to human activity elsewhere, is as authentic as the fevered humanism of Diana, Princess of Wales. Every human act was as "real" in this land of milk and honey as the self-conscious "profundity" in a Patrick White novel.

We were picked up in a sort of minibus. Mesdames Reuter and Hoare occupied the seats immediately behind the driver. The airport in Sydney is on Botany Bay. The clouds finally parted as we were driving away from it and though the sun wasn't completely out, I was struck by its fierce glare. The smoky light was much more intense than that of an English – or even a Hawaiian – summer. External concrete things were suddenly far more present. It was like being woken up from the dead. After the rest of the world, the land was oddly fresh – the sandbanks, sheets of shiny creek, birds soaring up, tumbling over salty clouds, the lettuce-green marsh grass, eucalypts like naked adolescents – everything physical, natural, suddenly seemed to be pushed right in front of one's face. Notwithstanding its assumed familiarity, you noticed it, and only it, for the first time. The magnetic inner world, which we had borne into Australia from the Northern Hemisphere as a pregnant woman carries a kicking child, slackened and died in our crania like a balloon wilting in its *papier-mâché* mould. "What's the name of that park?" I asked Mrs Reuter. "Centennial", she replied – of Patrick White fame! – and here I was staring at it! Hard to describe it – to describe Sydney – or at least the central part of Sydney, which we were now entering. Very comforting, English, down-at-heel, intimate, after Honolulu. On a human scale. The older architecture was the dowdy paste-board epic of Worthing or some other English seaside town that had seen better days – the facades looked like stage props. Curiously provincial, impermanent architecture for a major city. The "skyscrapers" were equally slip-shod and frumpish. They seemed ashamed of their would-be hyperbole. They looked as out of place in Sydney as those that grace the Elephant and Castle. The real thrill came when we began to cross the bridge that links one side of the harbour on which Sydney is built with the other. (The Pacific has taken two bites out of the coast of eastern New South Wales; Sydney Harbour is the second; it lies due north of Botany Bay, the first excision). The approach to the Opera House, which seemed up close to be made of yellowing china, was magnificent. It was now a bright, windy day. I was shocked by the glorious gelatinous blues and greens of grass and sea, the red and white villas that rose and fell on woods that plunged across the confectionery-blue harbour like volcanic islands, the vast transparent sky. We were in Byzantium in its heyday. The puniness, the parody, of the central business district – human, internal, risible – had given way to something open, vast, unbelievable – once again we felt we'd been woken up from the dead. Flocks of white sails flecked the deep ultramarine basin like floes of ice.

We reached the other side of the Harbour: what is called in Sydney "the North Shore". The wide hilly streets, like those in Hampstead to the east of the Finchley Road, were set off by the sea that emerged everywhere on the green horizon and by a pale, gold, ice-clear sky. Bougainvillea, rather than ivy, struggled with stained glass, stucco and ginger-coloured brick, but there were English flowers in the gardens . . . St John's Wood on the *Côte d'Azur*. It is this quality of the unreal, of an unreal, oriental abundance and perfection, like the paradise of the Koran, this mixture of the English and the sumptuously tropical, that gives Sydney its peculiar flavour.

Mrs Hoare and Mrs Reuter were discussing racing tips with the driver, a brawny "Ocker". Their talcum-powdered voices were a mummified version of his – like a pharaoh's perfumed organs. Their accents sounded strange in contention with his. Everyone was supposed to be the same in this egalitarian society, and in a sense they were. The ladies' accent was a museum piece, a coprolite; his a reeking poo. They discussed their families. Mrs Hoare, the less plummy, leaned foward and alluded to "Dean and his boyfriend, Terry" . . . "She was just about to open the dogfood ..." said Mrs Reuter. I didn't hear the *dénouément*.

The whole international party was put up at "The Reef Gauche", an hotel which overlooks Chinaman's Beach on the Middle Harbour. The setting was predictably histrionic. Clouds of jacaranda, like the purple smoke from a firework, drifted through a gorge full of beautiful European and Australian trees. There was a meadow beneath the gorge filled with English grass that was the fantastical green of dye. Soft, inviting alien grass – an important distinction in Australia where the native grass is coarse and sharp and matted with a thorn called "Bindi-Eye". Between the meadow and a dark blue bay, which glittered in a clear light such as you never get in Europe or the States, the beach was as white as cocaine. The breeze smelt as fresh as it felt: in Sydney, even on hot days – even in the centre of the city, among skyscrapers – there is always a strong eucalyptus-scented breeze, cleaning everything, making things new. Or rather, bearing witness to the fact that things have never been old – to the fact that, in Australia, nature remains untouched, untrampled in the heart of even man's domain. It was a cold breeze, heady and sweet. It clashed deliciously with the hot, clear sunshine.

The Reef Gauche, we found, wasn't up to much. You could see the British ideas behind the building, as you could see the British inspiration of every building in Sydney. That, as I said, is what gives the city its tantalizing unreality. Australians, after long hermetic isolation, have forgotten the British pattern of their material culture; they do not realise that the frivolous-looking intestines of their cities appear as if they might also have graced the esplanade at Bognor Regis. Only foreign visitors can identify the provenance of these things. But foreigners are also perplexed by their untroubled existence in a perfect, innocent world, such as the British originals – in Britain – only now enjoy in the illustrations in a children's textbook. The Reef Gauche looked like a Bingo Hall in Carshalton, half ox-blood brick, half rough, white-painted stucco. What made it different from its British parent was that, inside (and perhaps because of the climate) it was naked, a shell, with no cartilage, no inner layering, like a public toilet or a bus shelter. It had obviously originally been an apartment block, but it was an unreal, an ideal apartment block. It was borne up – its incompleteness obviated, completed – by its beneficent environment, as a weak-kneed summerhouse is, or one of those bosky pergolas on the terrace of a Sorrento restaurant, whose three dimensions are sunshine, drunkenness and the timeless consciousness attendant on a holiday. Only visitors from less external places would ever look at the grey, friable limbs of a summerhouse and wonder what will happen to it when Winter comes. But, in Australia, Winter never comes. It is the nation, perhaps the only one, *"that but lives where motley is worn."*

The entrance to The Reef Gauche was like the foyer of a cinema: it was set between two pylons sprinkled with harsh square windows. Two androgynes – one a pink android, the other a tanned Englishwoman like one of those naked gold-painted mannikins – awaited us at the desk. In our rooms, which were fairly large, each of us found a basket of Australian fruit whose golden cupolas and frightening spikes reminded you of a table-piece by Cellini. There was also a great deal of promotional material.

None of us could make head nor tail of the literature that had been produced in conjunction with *"Our Dreaming"* (or *"How Green Was My Coming"*, as some of our dissenters had already begun to call it. The *"New Australian Painters"* exhibition in Canberra formed only one part of the event; other parts, like the literature and film festivals, were to be held in Sydney). I had been a long time in Australia before I could decipher the language used, not only in these brochures, but in all Australia's cultural publicity. Everything was written, like Longfellow's **Hiawatha**, in an English whose jejune grandiloquence was meant to suggest the speech of an aboriginal people – in this case *the* Aboriginal people. This was because, as with **Hiawatha**, the destruction of the natives had given the authors – from the new European ruling class – a bad conscience. Why the pseudo-infantilism produced by over-using the English present participle ("the Dreaming", "the Coming", "the Quickening") should evoke the speech of a people whose language had no such grammatical forms – a people who no longer spoke Aboriginal anyway – was never explained. We exiles from the real world, who had real worries, couldn't help being touched by the quaintness of it all. By the spectacle of a gorged colonial people who had so little to worry about that they had to manufacture "guilt" and "race". Who had to prove that they, too, had "real" problems, that they too had been *soignés* enough to commit "genocide". But there was something troubling about their imaginary masochism. One felt, at one level, that it was as destructive, and as self-destructive, as they said it was. Australians were subverting themselves in unacknowledged, pathological ways that had nothing to do with the street theatre versions. It was like the damage inflicted by the selfless charity of a paedophile. Because we were foreigners, we could see beyond the purely Australian world that, for our hosts, formed the absolute limit of the universe. This universe, dulled by European comfort and ruled by second-rate, second-hand European ideas – as cut off from its immediate geographical environment as a beehive – seemed so safe to its inhabitants that they felt they had to invent the problems which life had withheld. The problems were there, but, strangely, the more intelligent Australians, though truffle pigs of pain in all its forms, didn't notice them. That was because the threats they ignored actually existed: they owed nothing to Australia's borrowed, Barbie-Doll world of self-flattering guilt. The *real* issues, as my mother's cousin might have called them, lay outside, not inside, the beehive. China, with its two billion people and the world's largest army and economy, was just off the coast of the vast, rich, empty island. The one hundred and fifty million Indonesians, who had no land, an army of millions and a history of conquering their neighbours, were even closer. Meanwhile, our hosts invented their wickedness and found themselves very angry about it. They reminded me of the Incas of Peru, who thought that the world came to an end at the boundary of their empire. The Incas used to mummify their ancestors and to provide them with necessities. Though very efficient farmers, famine was always threatening them because of the amount of grain that had to be set aside to "feed" the increasingly numerous but not very industrious mummies. It was a bit like the relationship between the modern Australians and the Aborigines! Eventually, one group of Incas said that it was foolish to divert resources in this way while the living went hungry: they proposed that no more food be wasted. The religious Incas resisted, and a civil war broke out on what was obviously a very important topic. So important that nobody had any time to fight the Spanish. For, confounding the principles of Inca geography, the Spanish suddenly appeared in the empire at this point (1532) and, despite not officially existing, rapidly destroyed it. The same thing was to happen to the just as laterally-minded Aborigines when the European ancestors of our hosts, defying all logic (since "Dreamtime" Australia formed the whole universe, and nothing existed beyond it) appeared in Sydney in the 1780s.

Fortunately, all that imperialist nonsense had been forgotten. Indeed, it appeared from our brochures that our hosts had forgotten even their own language, and had adopted the "speech" of the Aborigines no less than their somewhat restricted world-view. As I have said, I was the first of our party to "crack" this mysterious code. In 1799, Jean-François Champollion, a philologist attached to Napoleon's army in Egypt was able, for the first time, to decipher Ancient Egyptian, when he found an inscription in that language which had been repeated, word for word, in Greek. The inscription dated from the Ptolemaic period and so was not real Ancient Egyptian at all. By the time of the Ptolemies (circa 200 BC), the language denoted by the hieroglyphs had not been spoken in Egypt for centuries. It had been dead, in fact, since the country's conquest by foreigners, first the Persians, then the Greeks. The text Champollion found etched on the Rosetta Stone was, like "Aboriginal", a phoney language specially created to flatter the nostalgia of modern usurpers. Luckily I, like Champollion, had found a text written in a current language (English) as well as under the influence of the "Dreamtime" (though Lithium initially seemed the more likely culprit). I used the former, a poem entitled *"The Queen Mother Rides Through Townsville, 1968"* to decode the latter:

> *"Wite/ Motha/ Fucka - Whitey;*
> *Wite/ Motha/ Fucka - Prossie;*
> *Wite/ Motha/ Fucka - Pig"*

(the same title, but as you would allegedly hear it beneath a cairn of stubbies in Redfern). "One of Australia's greatest women poets", Black Gin Boree ("formerly Harmony Trickle"), had framed this lyric, both in "meh slave tark" (English), and in "meh tark dat di Holokost meh tek frahm" ("Aboriginal" – though this sounded suspiciously like English too – albeit a strangely facetious English that echoed for some reason the patois of the Carribbean). The "English" version of "The Queen Mother" was Augustan, even Shakespearean, in its prosody:

"Yes, evil Brisbane! three years have elapsed
Of dreary banishment, since I became
In thee a sojourner; nor can I choose
But sometimes think on thee; and tho thou art
A fertile source of unavailing woe,
Still, thou dost awaken interest.

But now the touchy bitch who mocked the boongs
Turns the corner from
One decade to the next,
The haunting vices that she left behind
Rise like a dong.

Early morning howling wind through windows
Ghostly shreadded [sic] *wheat of pain,*
Small & getting smaller,
I, fuzz-headed, young & daft,
Bleary-eyed, proud, angry, BLACK,
Stared crudely, still and hard
As a dildo:
Her hat, her hat, O! like a cake universe!
How rediculous [sic]*!*
(Again and again the Queen tells us
Of the cake we must eat!)
We witness total neglect!
We are bombarded
By sick feasting! And festivals!
Her landrover cavalcade because up here
We are slightly rough,
This is not quite grouse
Country but we are surely slaves, alas.
My arrow was not aimed at you,
Lady of another time, O no!
But at the Sun,
The big egg we hardly saw,
For were we not about to pull down France
& lay Chicago low? O yes!

Those were itchy times,
Each shattered moment that you poured through Townsville,
We did not care
For you, pale, piss-eyed, rigid facèd one!
We watched the ugly thump of monarchy
Parade its ghastly airs!
Uncaring she rides past, oh wicked mother!"

As I studied the position of this poem, provocatively placed opposite a photo of the Queen in our *"Welcome to Australia!"* booklet, I immediately discerned the hand of my mother's cousin, the Prime Minister. I knew as well as anyone that Sir Dewy Popkiss had fought fearlessly for an Australian Republic – with himself as Life President, naturally. He was an extraordinarily magnanimous man. Just to show his lack of vindictiveness, and to "heal our Aussie hurting", he had sought a knighthood – a sop to the "pa-the-tic" monarchists. It was a very unfair burden for a man who, "unlike the sort who'd suck a horse's dick if it had been in Prince Edward's mouth," had devoted his life to the *issues*. The Americas Cup was one example of his concentration. Antique Australian commodes (on which he was the world expert) was another campaign. He had transformed Kirribilli Lodge, the Prime Minister's home when in Sydney, into a shrine to "The Australian Commode". (The handout for the Paris Exhibition *"My Brilliant Commode"* – which Nicole Kidman had opened – had been penned by Sir Dewy, as had **Hiroshima Mon Commode** [sic], an account of his battles with Apartheid and nuclear fission, a memoir which proved, like Ruskin's **Praeterita**, that moral perfection always follows a profound love of the Yartz).

HATERS OF THE BEAUTIFUL

A day or two later and my colleagues and I were waiting in the luxury bus that would take us to Canberra and *"The New Australian Painters"* exhibition. Everyone still felt shattered after lunch at Kirribilli. We had been forced to sit on Poo-Chairs that our host had bought in a job lot from the Old People's Home into which he'd turned the Queen's Sydney residence. We had had to eat turtle soup from Mrs Whitlam's chamberpot. The more discerning, knowing how profound my kinsman could be, had interpreted this as a reference to Buñuel's **The Discreet Charm of the Bourgeoisie**, but most of the others, to whom I had unwisely boasted of my relationship, now examined me with suspicion. The Exhibitions Director of the Museum of Modern Art in New York, who was sitting in the seat next to mine, was dousing us both in *"Southern Belle"*, his Eau de Cologne, which was as fragile as Agent Orange. He had the big brutal lips and senseless eyes of a Coral Trout. "You know," he said, "yoh motha's cuzzin is a *verreh strayange mayahn*." He placed his hand consolingly on my knee. "And when *ah* say someone's strange, he's *reeyahlly* strange."

We drew out of The Reef Gauche at around 3. After crossing the Harbour, we drove through a southern suburb called Annandale. Interminable facades out of a Spaghetti Western. Flat roofs projecting over the pavement in an endless colonnade. The streets were festooned with white, red and green streamers for an Italian festival. All the shops on one block seemed Italian, all those on the next Greek, all those on the next Chinese, and so on. It seemed rather a ghetto-riven city, with an American rather than English vision of the cosmopolitan. Then we drove past the newer Shopping Centres. They were low, brick emporia. They boasted vast, leering fluorescent bubble graphics. Everywhere one saw invitations to *recherché* orgies: Cambodian, Mexican, or Turkish food, exotic vegetables and drugs – rare wine, tons of seafood and meat, and over it all, the perky dayglo signs, like graffitti. Instead of satisfying, the arcane abundance gave one a feeling of ashes in the mouth, of desolation. Here was a client society, a consumer society that didn't know what

66

it was missing of the finer things of life. A society like Argentina that made nothing (all the car places were Mitsubishi) and produced only food. Behind me, the lady from the Burrell Collection in Glasgow was chatting to one of the Australian officials who were accompanying us. "They see something, and they feeyule, they feeyule," said the Scot ("they feel, they feel"). The Australian, meanwhile, was alluding to the Glaswegian's admiration for *"Dog Dunny"*, "our Aussie" Silvio Pufulette's "sandpit sculpture": "I've never seen anyone liked playing in the dirt like you do – it's like having your own private chook!"

The outer suburbs of Sydney were on a dizzying, gargantuan scale. They bore no relation to the human, European proportions of the inner city. Australians, expanding in space as in time, had discovered themselves, become Australian, out here, and only within the last 30 years. This is where they had left the "Old World" behind, realised that its restrictions no longer applied. Realised that they might in fact just as easily have discarded them at the beginning. That there was no need for the first Sydney to have clung in baby's fingers to the harbour rocks like Mycenean Troy. It could, right from the start, have have been what the Emperor Constantine's Byzantium was, or the Caliph Motassim's Samarra, or the Tenochtitlan of Montezuma: a purpose-built "Paree" with Assyrian-sized palaces and squares. But that honour was to fall to Melbourne – and to Canberra – which didn't have nearly as good a location. The millions of houses we saw in outer Sydney reminded me of the interminable bungalows of Slough or South Central LA. But these were bungalows that had been built for men and women twenty feet high. Every little suburban cul-de-sac – and there must have been thousands of them – was longer and wider than The Mall. The streets were lined with giant gums. It was like driving through the Amazon – and this was the deepest suburbia! The flanks of defoliated hills sprouted enormous stucco ranches in pink and white like Hindu temples. Everywhere the churned up dirt was littered with white branches and Karnak-sized chateaux that evoked the stupendous, unadorned brick monuments of the late Roman Empire. There was no centre, no focus to it all.

It was frightening to think of the endlessness of such enormity, of the extent of virgin Bush that must have been razed to make way for it. But when we finally cleared Sydney, "the Bush" seemed antedeluvian, infinite, unaffectable. It was more frightening than the city. The driver, somewhat impudently given the seniority of his guests, turned the radio on. Someone droned on about a terrible Irish atrocity that might have taken place on Neptune, so impermeable and prehistoric did our environment appear. The newsreader, in any case, gave far more weight to "the *bashing* of young fine defaulter Jamie Partridge". I must have listened to this bulletin twenty times and this curious expression *"bashing"* was always used. On one occasion it was referred to as *"the Jamie Partridge Bashing"* . . . The scenery – of tall olive gums, sometimes walls of grey rock – never varied. Though once, as we were gliding through another endless, nameless forest, I saw a little boy neatly dressed in blue sitting on a bank of raw dirt. He appeared to be watching the traffic. This intensely suburban person sitting there, pointlessly, in the middle of nowhere, gave the wilderness a new aspect. It reminded one that it had been touched, possessed. There wasn't an inch of the seeming desolation that hadn't been possessed. I remember too a girl in a short red dress, a uniform, kneeling on the top of a tanker. I remember her big, stained mits and her shiny calves like suppositories. She was a pretty girl . . . In the middle of the deadest, densest, greyest forest a sign emerged: "ORANGES, ORANGES, AND MORE ORANGES!" For some reason, it made us all laugh (we had seen a truly awful production of Prokofiev's **Love of Three Oranges** in Sydney Opera House the night before). Then, in Goulburn, the giant statue of a ram hove into view. It was made of cement and of an Ozymandian vastness. More than one of my colleagues remarked that it was the best piece of art we'd seen in Australia. "I wish they'd taken us to that instead of the crap they showed us in Woollahra," the editor of **THE LONDON MAGAZINE** observed. With this one exception, the Australian country towns we passed were all alike. Their wide streets, emptiness, and sterile, grassy modernity were extremely depressing. To see them after seeing towns in England was to feel that they

68

harboured even less of the human spirit than they appeared to. Petrol-station-like settlements, but with forty-thousand-year-old aboriginal names, they not only lacked historical associations, they seemed to repel them. Their modernity was not the modernity of the United States: it was *real* modernity. There was nothing behind it. Modern America is old Europe in its decadence, and American modernity is even richer and gamier than what, in Europe, is old, just as Byzantium was richer and more succulent than classical Rome. Rome in its senility – Byzantium – added something new to Rome: it was the mould on the *Mortadella*, a deliciously corrupt Cognac to Rome's earthy Bordeaux. It was the diseased liver of the sacred goose in Juno's temple – the goose whose night honking warned Rome that the barbarians had come. Europe, like Rome, is the goose, but America, like Byzantium, is the golden egg it has dropped. History has well and truly cooked Europe's goose, and London makes a lovely Christmas lunch, but how could a connoisseur prefer it to New York, the golden egg in its rotten guts? Who could prefer roast goose to *Foie Gras*? Like Byzantium, the United States has managed to combine Christianity with a truly Roman paganism, piety with horrible violence, grotesquely fat eunuchs with lecherous, power-hungry women, puritanism with intrigue, sadism and decay. Like Byzantium, it is the last bolt-hole of civilization, and the biggest force for barbarism on earth. Everyone alive today was born, as the Byzantines were, in the death throes of a world-civilization. The United States, the ghost of Europe, is the Byzantium that arose on Rome's death. Australia is the Roman Britain of those times: an aboriginal island abandoned by the imperial power before it was properly civilized, or even touched, left defenceless before a new, more cruel invader. Australia is an abused baby girl: the United States a magnificent old courtesan. That was why Australia's modern towns and cities were not like New York. They were not like Las Vegas or LA. They were totally new and inhuman, like unpacked syringes, and the juxtaposition of their moribund freshness with the virginity of the ancient Bush, whose human associations, if they exist, are lost on the white man, makes Australia, for me, particularly impenetrable.

After about two hours, we stopped in Narooma next to a park. A withered gentleman in an incongruously virile baseball cap, his wife, and a thin, frail young man were in the process of sitting down in front of a bank of flowers. When they had settled, another man, with a handbag, took their photograph. I remember thinking: how strange. This desolate nothing of a town and its plastic sponge of park are an historic oasis to them, the Tuileries or the Villa Borghese. When the group rose, I noticed that the man in the baseball cap was carrying a white stick. Just then, our driver had cause to open the pressurised doors and there was a surging roar of cicadas like the shaking of a thousand tambourines. We felt besieged.

The Australian official insisted on our stopping again, at "The Big Peanut" in Tathra, for refreshments. Here, we were confronted by an orchard of pink and yellow ices on sticks, the varieties of which we had never seen before. The *"Golden Gaytime"* looked intriguing, but I demurred when someone offered me his *"Heart"* instead. The iced lollies were beautiful, and uniquely Australian. Australians only produced authentic and original art when it wasn't their intention. When "art" was on their mind, their work was derivative, and curiously indifferent to its place of origin. (I thought of the Australian cinema, which so often turned a blind eye to the country's Martian landscapes, and the fondant-coloured opera sets that were its inner cities, and tried, instead, to recreate the pathetic English social dramas of the Sixties in those few parts of Sydney and Melbourne which resembled the Manhattan of the Fifties). I dug into the valve of my *"Heart"* like an aborigine biting a crocodile egg. Liquid ice cream in a shell of opaque sorbet. There was a curious tension in its transitory nature and the (potentially) eternal nature of its attractiveness. This contradiction, the desire to bridge which gives us art, reminded me of a passage by the Byzantine historian Niketas Choniates, when he describes the final illness of the Byzantine Emperor Manuel Komnenos in 1180 AD:

"He [Manuel] *reflected on human frailty at the end of life, and the wretchedness of the body cast around us like an oyster shell* [the sorbet] *and united with the soul* [the cream]."

Like the first European botanists in Australia, who were confronted by numberless plants unknown to man, I tried to isolate and itemise the thicket of "aboriginal" lollies that could be seen in the tall, upright fridge. Its door was completely made of glass. The frosted coffin was also full of wet, fern-smothered roses. (These have to be imported into sub-tropical Australia, where it is too warm for them to grow. They are sold singly from fridges in confectioners' shops. They are outrageously expensive). Perhaps because of the strong sunlight, or because the glass door had been left open a long time while our party made its purchases, the lollies inside were visibly melting. Skewered on spatulae and surrounded by leafy bouquets, they and the roses put one in mind of the gaudy, bloated bodies of the fathers of the Byzantine city of Prusa, who were impaled (according to Niketas Choniates) for having rebelled against the Emperor Andronikos Komnenos (Manuel's brother) in 1184:

"He allowed none of the impaled to be buried. Baked by the sun, they swayed in the wind like scarecrows suspended in a garden".

Across the table from me, a group of Australians were sitting with dead eyes and toffee-apple skin, like roast sucking pigs. I heard a girl ask a stranger: "How did you break your arm?" "What a chat-up line!" I thought. I think the civil servant who had brought us to *"The Big Peanut"* was in league with the owner of *"Ye Olde Crafte Shoppe"* nearby. (The incongruity of this title struck me, not for the first time, with horrible force). Its owner ran into the café wearing massive shades and incredibly brief pink shorts, aflame with his attractions. We were so amused by the innocent violence of his manner that some of us went over to inspect his stock. It was the usual dross, but I was very impressed by a black Australian swan – floppy neck, wings – that had been carved from a single flat tyre.

As we approached Canberra, all the green – or what green there was – went out of the landscape. The leaves became a purplish brown, the grass yellow. We entered a vast, flat

71

featureless plain encircled by smooth, meaty hills. The plain was so featureless, so open and naked to the mountains and the distance and the sun! I wondered if the Aborigines had ever had a sense of place. Perhaps not. Everywhere seems to have been the same to them. Place, particularity, withdrawal are peculiar to the European: the desire to scrape out a hole, to hide. Hence the extraordinary nostalgic compounds one found bestowed on non-Aboriginal Australian towns and villages: "Salisbury Downs," "Strathvale". I found these old names – with their promise of England, and the provincial nullity through which they failed to fulfill that promise – painful to look at. But Australia's cemeteries, creations of the white man, resembled, not the anal caves of its European consciousness, but the aboriginal openness of its landscape. They were brand-new, naked, vulnerable, and they were always positioned right by the main road, unprotected, unvandalised. There were never any fences. The graveyard in Bega, which we were now gliding past, was just a terribly exposed lime-green slope. Its gravestones looked absurdly fresh and artificial, like shells. This is how the ancient author Pausanias describes Greece's monuments as looking in the Guidebook he wrote after visiting the country in 155 AD. When one reads his notes on the statues and temples he saw, still intact, in cities and the countryside, one is always struck by how flimsy and accessible the things are, and with what timeless safety his complacent descriptions invest them. Yet they were protected by none of the practical defences of old things today, nor by the divinity we give them, which radiates a force field that will save them forever. Pausanias describes art and architecture he knew to be of great value as if it were garden furniture. It is fragile and elaborate in his descriptions, but also unremarkable, ubiquitous, touchable. His Greece is like a recreation of the ancient world by Poussin or Hollywood, where columns and porticoes litter a workaday countryside like used cars. There is no concession in Pausanias to the danger to come, when, in the 250's and 260's, Gothic invaders would sweep through Greece and knock down its undefended monuments like bottles. Pausanius inhabited, in his ignorant confidence of eternal safety, the unreal, gravity-less paradise of the modern Australian. As I studied the fresh, open cemetries of Australia on the bus to Canberra, I felt the anxiety that its complacency frequently induced. One wondered how long it would be before the Indonesians or the Chinese punctured this perfect, pre-historical world like a balloon. How long would it be before someone brought it down to earth, into the real world, just by entering it, just by opening the door and introducing gravity, history? History, in Australia, always means a bomb in the pressurised perfection of a plane's interior . . . Just before we entered the capital we passed through Bredbo and I saw a single folorn hat on the railway line.

Canberra reminded me strongly of Ankara: we drove along the same endless straight roads lined with shoeboxes all about six stories high. Like Ankara, it was an ersatz capital built from scratch on an ancient site (in this case an aboriginal one). Like Ankara, it was surrounded by mountains and occupied a circular bowl of valley strewn with isolated modern temples (*à la* Washington) and an artificial lake. Its *raison d'être* being polemical rather than human, it was the only Australian town of any size not to be built on the beautiful coast. Instead, it occupied a site deep within the interior which was surrounded by sheepfarms: hence the Cenotaph to the Unknown Shoulder (of lamb) in Goulburn. This meant that, as in the Baghdad of the eunuchs, everything crawled with flies (sheepflies). Canberra was like one of the great monastery complexes deep within Byzantine Asia Minor. Its dependent, artificial population of politicians, students and officials had been driven into exile from Sydney (the only inhabitable city in Australia) by foaming ambition. In Canberra, as in Dante's Hell, the corrupt and the ambitious were alternately roasted and frozen by the extreme continental climate. They reminded me of those Byzantine monks, men of position and erudition, who, to save rather than to lose their souls, had once made the opposite journey, from the fleshpots of Constantinople (the imperial capital and, physically, the *Doppelgänger* of Sydney) to Cappadocia, deep in Asia Minor, where, in their caves and cells, they would scarify their bodies in extremes of heat and cold.

It was getting dark now, and, even in the pressurised bus, I could taste the odour of a thousand sickly barbeques. These funeral pyres of animals, like something out Homer, make every Australian city smell like Auschwitz. Smoky basilicae were now being ignited by kleig lights, so that, with its neon craters and geysers, the city looked even more like a concentration camp than normal. Incredibly, the town had been built in a series of expanding, concentric rings, with the Parliament Building and the Prime Minister's Residence in the central circle. This heightened its resemblance to Dante's Hell, which – like mediaeval Baghdad – he describes as being composed of circles within circles, with the criminals and the punishments that fit them deepening in ugliness as one proceeds from the outer circle to the centre. One couldn't help feeling that the pilgrimage of the Sydney exiles through Canberra, who generally start their careers in the suburban universities, and then march inwards towards the ministries, the Parliament Building and the Viceregal *loggia*, was a similar *Hegira*.

Bush fires circled us on the mountains, adding a hint of baked eucalypt and Koala *au gratin* to the already torpid air. The rotating bushfires reminded me of the coffee beans they set light to in Rome and float in Aniseed to give it extra flavour. I remembered the flickering beans that circle one's glass of *Sambuca* like *Fiaccole* in the Trevi Fountain. And so another image came to me as I contemplated the city and its venal anchorites: a description of the monasteries of Palermo by Giuseppe Tomasi di Lampedusa. (Palermo, like Canberra, was built – in 990 AD – on the dartboard model of contemporary Baghdad. By Sicily's Arab invaders. Like Canberra, it was intended as the brand new capital of a conquered island). The year is now 1860, and just like us, Prince Fabrizio, hero of Lampedusa's 1958 novel **Il Gattopardo**, is travelling by coach into the middle of town. Republican insurgents, fighting, as Sir Dewy's army did, to liberate their island from a corrupt Bourbon court, have already begun a seige:

" 'Look excellency,'and he pointed to the mountain heights around the Conca d'Oro. On their slopes and peaks glimmered dozens of flickering lights, bonfires lit every night by the rebel bands, silent threats to the city of palaces and convents. They looked like lights that burn in sick-rooms during the final nights . . . The road was now beginning to slope gently downhill and Palermo could be seen very close, plunged in total darkness, its low shuttered houses weighed down by the huge edifices of convents and monasteries. There were dozens of these, all vast, often grouped in twos or threes, for women and for men, for rich and poor, nobles and plebeians, for Jesuits, Benedictines, Franciscans, Capuchins, Carmelites, Liguorians, Augustinians . . . Here and there squat domes rose higher, in flaccid curves like breasts emptied of milk; but it was the religious houses which gave the city its grimness and its character, its sedateness and also the sense of death which not even the vibrant Sicilian light could ever manage to disperse. And at that hour, at night, they were despots of the scene. It was against them really that the bonfires were lit on the hills, stoked by men who were themselves very like those living in the monasteries below, as fanatical, as self-absorbed, as avid for power, or rather for the idleness which was, for them, the purpose of power ".

The monk-clogged squirrel drays of Canberra were its universities and ministries. Now, at night, they blazed with empty, exposed halls and offices, like open fridges. They appeared equally dead, though, during working hours, when the atrociously fierce Australian light pounced on their unnatural qualities and their black, dusty fragility. Then they were broken televisions discarded in the Bush. Each Uni and Government Department was a symbol of Canberra and the completely unreal society its insularity made possible. Canberra itself symbolised Australia's hermetic defiance of the world as it really was. It was therefore unsurprising that the definitive history of Australia – **Terror Australis** – the only introduction most of us had had to the country we were visiting – had been written by an academic at a Canberra university. Each of us had read it – or glanced at it, rather – in Europe, Asia or the States (it was in fact the only Australian book everyone abroad knew, rather like **Mehmed My Hawk** in the case of Turkey), and Brooklana Fagan's dirge had tasted instantly (unlike say, the average Australian film) of its country of origin. This was not only

75

because of the naive way Mrs Fagan had dilated on the "genocide" of the Aborigines, which she compared to the gassing of the Jews ("Well, I'd like to see you get a *coon* in a shower," was Sir Dewy's comment on this, a curious observation given his party's support for "the Black Struggle", but he had turned against the author by then). No! The distinctively Australian note in the book was not its banality, but the innocent quality of that banality. There was a shamelessness about its sententious peurility that reminded one of Patrick White's novels and, like a drop of iodine in Townsville tap-water, it turned all bad to good. Like a kangaroo, ***"Terror"*** was strong and fascinating as well as ludicrous, because, like the kangaroo, it was, after all, *real* as well as absurd. And it *could* be real because it had arisen in a vacuum, in a world without predators. In Europe or America intellectuals (real intellectuals) would have pounced on the first "kangaroo" and torn it to pieces. It was obvious from reading Fagan (and other Australians) that she had picked up concepts like "terror" and "alienation" from foreign books without realising that, in the world beyond Australia, these words were connected to real suffering as well as to the purely literary glamour which had attracted her. The author could relate to terror theoretically, of course, but as neither she, nor the Aborigines, nor Australia itself knew what real suffering was – real "terror" and "genocide" as experienced in the societies which had framed these concepts – she did not see what inappropriate metaphors they made for the Australian condition. Inappropriate, but not implausible. For, like the foxes and Cane Toads which had also been imported into Australia from Europe and America, these big, bad words may have been out of place in the Antipodes, but they were not *visibly* jarring. After all, the Australian public knew neither the non-Australian world from which the monsters came, nor the old Australia that had been ignorant of English foxes and Alabaman toads. And that was why invaders like this term "terror" flourished, gulping down the delicate native fauna which was exclusive to Australia, and which might, one would have thought, have provided an apter range of metaphor for the local literati: why rely on international bombast when you can access a unique, if diminutive poetry? Like the foxes and cane toads, "terror" and "genocide" and other pompous similes destroyed everything Australian that was worthwhile, for, though they had no right to be on the continent, they had no predators there either. Nobody was erudite – or travelled – enough to point out how absurd they were. It was therefore natural that when Brooklana Fagan, once the doyenne of Labor intellectuals, finally denounced my mother's cousin, it was in rather a hyperbolic way.

It was hard to forget Brooklana, having once set eyes on her. We never met, but she was often on British TV, the Australian intellectual's native habitat. She had the cherubic face of a seal, spoilt by an arrogant, self-satisfied expression that reminded one of a ferocious seabird sitting on its eggs. Brooklana was the wife of Knut Fagan, Sir Dewy's predecessor as Labor Prime Minister. Knut's appearance was also distinctive. He had the wrinkled, papery face of an Ourang-Outang, its balding pate with a wisp of orange hair, an Ourang-Outang's tragic, effeminate, painted-looking eyes. Knut had been baptised by his Trade Unionist father after some hero of Scandinavian Social Democracy – sometimes his Christian name was deliberately mispelled, alas! He had been treacherously ousted by Dewy in a secret, brutal party coup. Much to his wife's disgust, he had done little to defend himself. According to her colleagues in the History Department of the Australian National University, she had punished the coward in the way another famous historian, Anna Komnena, had punished *her* spouse Nikephoros Byrennios when he missed the chance to seize the Byzantine throne from Anna's hated brother John (father of the Emperors Manuel and Andronikos) in 1118.

Niketas Choniates again:

> *"It is said that the Kaisarissa Anna, disgusted with her husband's frivolous behaviour and distraught in her anger, and being a shrew by nature, felt justified in strongly contracting her vagina when Byrennios's penis was deep inside her, thus causing him great pain."*

How could anyone worthy of Sir Dewy's designation as "truly, a red-blooded Aussie" have objected to such a reprisal? *Au contraire!* But what but distaste could one expect of Knut "who, if he could hold up as many waves as he could shirts would not have found himself in the position he now does, comrades!"

Brookee (as she was affectionately known) revenged herself on Popkiss by circulating a biography which compared Dew to the worst tyrants who had ever lived: she who – when Dewy was a faithful member of her husband's cabinet – had drawn analogies between the Minister for Sport (a more important portfolio in Australia than Foreign Affairs, which in fact it embraced) and the greatest saviours and sages of mankind! ("He's Trotsky to Lenin, and Lenin is in my Kunt", she had once incorrectly announced).

When Mrs Fagan was in her Seventies, fertility technology became available which would enable her, she was told, to bear the children she had always craved, and had never (for some reason) been blessed with. After her husband the Prime Minister had supplied her doctors with a penn'orth of his jism (some said that, beforehand, he had been obliged to consult the *"Men of League"* Christmas Calendar), Lady Arkana Muckadilla, the famous Aussie international media magnate, made all the necessary arrangements for Brookee's *accouchement.* (La Muckadilla was patron of the Australian Labor movement at the time. She was also patron of the Australian capitalist movement: indeed, like the goddess Parvati in Hindu mythology, her determination to control the universe as a whole compelled her to assume every conceivable incarnation, demonic and divine). It soon became evident that, as a result of the perverse therapies, Brooklana was carrying an incredible *eight* babies, and would have to abort seven if the last was to survive. (In the **Mahabharata**, Vishnu allows the demon Kamsa to destroy seven of the foetuses in the goddess Devaki's womb so that the eighth, Krishna, can be born). But "Lady Muck" (as she was known) said that Brooklana should fight to keep *all* of the Prime Minister's children. She romantically appealed to her conscience as a Roman Catholic: a not entirely transparent move, dialectically, after having

78

convinced her of the wisdom of IVF. And, in fact, the only reason she wanted Brookee to go on carrying the infants was so that the pregnancy – rather like Peter Brook's film version of the **Mahabharata** itself – could provide a lurid and interminable treat for the audience of her Australian newspapers and TV channels. Soon, the massive Vicereine was popping up like a dead and swollen toad between the wheels of the Japanese Utes on the adverts that punctuated Muckadilla's TV shows at seven minute intervals. "The doctors think they can tell us what to do," the first lady smugly observed off-camera, in a promo for an "exclusive" on her Fallopiana in one of Mucky's tabloids, "but only *we* know what is best for *our family*!" When "our family" ended up in the bidet, as expected, after a night on the local vodka and two bottles of "Mildara Chestnut Teal", the Muckadilla **STAR** reported breathlessly on how Mrs Fagan had wrapped each tiny body in a series of teatowels depicting the attractions of the Sunshine Coast. Then she had solemnly named each one. "Nelson" (as in Mandela), "Bobby" (as in Sands) and "Germaine" (as in Greer) had all migrated to the top of the Fagans' Aga in jars of balsamic vinegar from "The Eureka Delicatessen", but, after his namesake's coup d'état, little "Dewy" (as in Popkiss) was seen floating down the Molonglo River, Canberra's *Cloaca Maxima*, like the Tiber-borne corpse of the obscene Roman boy-emperor Elagabalus after the revolt of his nemesis, Severus Alexander.

There was a certain poignancy here, as Mrs Fagan's erstwhile admiration for Popkiss had not been confined to public statements. In a book called **For The Perm of his Natural Wife** – a "frank" account of her marriage – Brooklana had licked the (then) Minister of Footie's arse like an Echidna vacuuming an anthill. There might have been displacement in this, a refocusing of the womanly feelings her husband was unable to satisfy. (The wife of a *former* Prime Minister had once found Knut in her bedroom, dressed up like Joan Sutherland playing Lady Macbeth and wearing a chamberpot – the very one we had so admired at Kirribilli – as a diadem: "*I* am Mrs Gough Whitlam" Knut had informed the intruder – who also rejoiced in that name – "*who* are *you*?"). In *"Dewy My Hawke"*, one of the chapters in

Perm, Brookee had used a line of Whitman to characterise the bond between Knut and the other caryatid of Australian socialism as *"the dear love of comrades"*. In deference to Popkiss' then portfolio, she had enigmatically added, again quoting Whitman: *"An athlete is enamoured of me – and I of him!"* Like most old Australian men, Popkiss resembled a turtle: long years in the sun had left his mouth and eyes lipless holes. As in a turtle, it had turned the flesh on his face into the same hard, inhuman leather as composed his long, wrinkly neck (for there is no dichotomy in an Australian – as there is, for instance, in a European – between the soft, complex face and the hard, simple body). Even though Dewy wasn't everyone's cup of cocoa, ***Perm*** had compared him to Antinoös, at 19 the most beautiful man in the world, the *amour fou* and intellectual inspiration of Hadrian (aka Knut), the most artistic, erudite and philanthropic of all the Roman Emperors. (Curiously, like Hadrian, Knut was given to describing his own Empress as *"morosa et aspera"* – hardly surprising, given the circumstances; he was also fond of Hadrian's observation that *"to be a wife is a duty, not a pleasure"*). During a state visit to Egypt in 130 AD, when he and Hadrian were drifting down the Nile in a gorgeous barge like Antony and Cleopatra, Antinoös leapt into the water and drowned himself. He wanted to divert, in advance, what he saw as imminent retribution by unseen forces: he wanted to draw the revenge of the supernatural world away from its just object, the Emperor. The embryonic "Dewy Fagan", slipping from his womb with the cloves and the cocktail onions, floating, defunct, past the pyramid of the Parliament Building and the Telstra Tower on Black Mountain, was also a human sacrifice. He too had been offered up (or rather, flushed down) to propitiate the anger of Heaven and save the political life of his patron. He failed: Knut fell, and the revolution in Heaven didn't end with his removal.

Dewy, now that he was Premier, was in the habit of commandeering *"Poofter"*, the brand new, state-of- the-art yacht with which the Australian team were trying to lift the next Americas Cup. (Mindful of the unseen powers, as active in the modern Pacific as they were in the ancient Mediterrannean, the Federal Government had wanted to call the ship *"Lifter"*

– which was half-way to "shirtlifter" – hence "poofter"). Dewy could be seen enthroned on *"Poofter"* every morning on Lake Burley-Griffin, the artificial sea in Canberra's heart (though it was the well-oiled Myrmidons of the Brisbane Broncos rugby team – Dewy's personal bodyguard – who actually did the work: their glinting torsos were glimpsed bobbing in the sun). Now, in **Tie Me Chien Andalou Down, Sport** (the tendentious "biography" of Popkiss she released on her husband's dismissal), Brooklana compared Dewy, not to Antinoös in his barge on the Nile, but to Nero, the Nero of that horrible chapter in Suetonius where we see him cruising the artificial lake in the grounds of "the Golden House", the grotesque palace he built in the middle of Rome, which Brook had the insolence to link not only with "Yarralumla", the chaste official residence of Australia's leaders on Lake Burley-Griffin, but to the "Golden Palace" of the orgiastic Caliphs, the complex that formed the pupil in the giant iris of Abbasid Baghdad. She wrote about how Nero (according to Suetonius) would set up brothels on the banks of his lake, staffed with the most respectable of the senators' wives, whom he would service on striking land (this analogy was regarded as tastelessly near the knuckle in modern Canberra). And she would recall how, in Ninth Century Baghdad, the tyrannical Caliph Amin, having seized the throne of the Abbasid Empire from his saintly brother Mamun in 810 AD (just as the evil Andronikos succeeded his just sibling Manuel in Byzantium, and Popkiss displaced Fagan), would cruise the Tigris in front of the Golden Palace in a variety of pleasure-craft, one shaped like an eagle, one like a water-snake. How foolish she had been, Brook wrote, to think that "Dewy, My Hawke" was the former animal, when really, he was *"an Anaconda in a Yabbie Pool . . ."*

All this represented such an abrupt reversal in Brookee's attitude that the Fourth Estate, Mucky's eunuch seraglio and Dewy's faithful ally (it was in fact Lady Muck who had decided that Fagan, "that Turd-Burglar", was too vulnerable to serve as her prophet further), had a field day with their former First Lady's "sense of honour". (Their own, of course, was immensely tenacious). In articles about the coup such as *"Knight of the Long Knives"*, they wondered aloud whether Brooklana was as similar to Anna Komnena as she was to another Byzantine historian, Prokopios of Caesarea. They reminded their readers that Prokopios spent the whole of his professional life (530 - 565 AD) shovelling molasses at the then Byzantine Emperor Justinian and his wife Theodora: until they were safely dead. Then "Prokee", their bosom pal, with an adroitness that would have put even Mucky's concubines to shame, "revealed" (in his best-selling ***Secret History***) that the pious Justinian, in Prokopios' former books Christ's greatest friend on earth, was in fact a demon whose head would fly off as he mulled over affairs of state in the long watches of the night. (The same thing would happen to Sir Dewy's teeth and the contents of his nose during particularly interminable cabinet meetings). The Empress Theodora, meanwhile, whom Prokopios had previously cast as the Balkans' answer to Hilary Clinton, was now a life-long murderess, auto-abortionist and whore, who had performed her first blow job for cash at the age of six, and who was fond of lying naked in the Hippodrome in front of thousands as geese pecked millet off her pudendum. As she lay spreadeagled, each of her rabid openings – Prokopios says that she regretted there were *"so few"* – would lunge out and gulp down male members of the audience and then spit them out, unsatisfied, like a goanna in a paddock full of cane toads.

Despite all this, Popkiss would probably have put up with Brooklana's vituperation had she not taken to invading the chamber *à la* Théroigne de Méricourt, interrupting his Cicero-like thrusts at the "stunned mullets" and "dog-vomits" of Her Majesty's Opposition (he was inordinately proud of these) with Philippics of her own. Les Majesty, the new Foreign Minister, who had conspired with Popkiss to oust her husband, called Mrs Fagan a "mad cow" and ordered the staff to remove her, but she only shrieked louder that Les was Patrikios, the Byzantine ambassador to the court of Al-Mansur, the Caliph who had built the round city of Baghdad in 762 AD. (During an audience at the Golden Palace in 765, while Al-Mansur was in the process of asking the envoy what he admired about the new city, a cow, which a butcher was trying to slaughter in the first of the circular markets that surrounded the Throne Room in a series of rings, broke free and cantered, lowing, into the Caliph's presence. Answering Al-Mansur, the Byzantine drily observed that Baghdad would have impressed him had its concentric design not meant that *"your enemy"* [ie the common people] *"is with you in the palace."* The mortified Caliph thereupon ordered the whole non-official population of Baghdad to be expelled from the Round City to "Al-Kharkh", a new suburb well to the south of the Tigris). Brookee screamed that she was now that cow being led away to slaughter, the doomed Rosa Luxemburg-cum-Cassandra of the common people of the land: the plebs who, like the non-elite of Baghdad, had been expelled (shortly after the foundation of Canberra in 1913) from the enchanted "Round City" girding the Golden Palace at Yarralumla to the grim 'burbs south of Lake Burley-Griffin.

La Fagan, however, was not the only one who could play at being Spartacus. In a speech to the Annual Conference of the Wharfies' Union, the new Prime Minister (whose family had owned a supermarket chain) declared that he, as an "ordinary, yes and a *decent* bloke" was far better suited to lead "the Labor Movement" than the shirt-lifting husband of an haute-bourgeoise fellow traveller like Ms Fagan. He didn't, of course, use that term, dismissing her instead as one of the "pot-throwers of Pymble". (This was Dewy-speak for the radically chic and was a blatant rip-off of Paul Keating and his "basket weavers of Balmain" line). The next day found Popkiss haranguing the "pot throwers" of Parliament over their "sentimental" and "pa-the-tic" adhesion to the idea of independence for East Timor. He praised Indonesia, which he had just agreed to supply with arms, as a paragon of anti-imperialism on a par with "our sacred mother, Ireland". Indonesia had been ruled by Holland, and he dwelt with lachrymose relish on the sufferings of the satay-nibblers at the hands of those wicked Dutchmen (well-known enemies of Human Rights), for it was a paradox of the Australian Left – no doubt traceable to its peasant-Irish roots – that the denizens of all its "holy lands" (not just Palestine!) had to be victims *as well as* victors, parasites *and* parricides.

Brookee had entered the Chamber undetected. Having been permanently excluded after the recent shenanigans, she had been forced to disguise herself as an Aborigine – her face was smeared with Vegemite. There was what Cynthia Brownbill would have called a "Blacks' Camp" nestling on the lawns outside the Lower House at the time, composed of white masochists and *soi-disant* Aboriginals campaigning for "native land rights". Brooklana knew that Popkiss had informed the stewards, that "as regards our coloured brethren" – here even the Rednecks in the long white socks could discern an ironical tone – "let the gins in first: the bucks'll be on their best if they can smell a bit of cunt. And for Christ's sake keep the Phenol for cleaning the dunnies out of sight: those bastards'll sink anything that's more than 2% proof." Dewy knew an international photo opportunity when he saw one and that black faces in the syndicated image of a white politician are like seeds of caviar on a slice of boiled egg: they increase the value of the host by about 900 per cent. What a cosmopolitan! The insouciance of the man, his diffident, easy-going humanity! Or, as Dewy more tersely put it: "one drop of possum shit on the pavlova and move over Nelson Mandela!"

Dewy was just getting into his stride as Brooklana took aim – "the long years of Indanoysia's agony – Timor independence movement backed by CIA [as Dewy himself was] – *Mum always told me – Dewy, you're gunna go far, mate . . .*" "Free Nelson Mandela!" someone screamed. Brook, her twisted features streaked with brown like the face of Bobby Sands during the "Dirty Protest," leapt to her feet in the Public Gallery. She hurled a jar of vinegar containing "poor wee Nelson" at the usurper. It exploded with a crack, knocking off his toupée and drenching both the Cabinet and a Versace lounge suit in blood, stinking shivers of glass, and a skein of consommé and squishy white limbs like a chicken casserole . . . *"Chroist Al-moighty!"* . . . The Prime Minister thought he had been blown up. As the faces in the amphitheatre whirled around him like birds he thought he was in Hell, the Frisbee-shaped

Hell of Dante that the old Jesuits in St Ignatius' College had taught him about. There they were (the blotchy astonished heads of the Honourable Members jumped between the whizzing circles of their pews like dice on a roulette wheel): circle on circle of black and orange killers, crooks and pervs. He was staring into a pizza on a fucking record player, and strewth, didn't that mean that he was dead? . . . "How's that for pot-throwing you fat, dishonest cunt?!"

Brookee was really in very good form. She was dragged away by a scrum of gorgeous Amazons from Securicor before she could deliver the rest of her speech, but later, in an interview with *THE MELBOURNE AGE* (the only broadsheet not yet in Mucky's paw) she explained the significance of her protest. She reminded the interviewer (a cub reporter who hadn't even reached Grade 7) of how Hypatia, the last of the pagan Greek philosophers and (unusually for the times) a woman, had been hacked to death by a Christian mob in Alexandria in 415 AD. (This old professor, the leader of Alexandria's town council and the final, dying ember of the Periclean civilization that had somehow managed to survive for a thousand years, was dragged from her chariot and cut to pieces by a rabble armed with sharpened bits of broken pot. It has been suggested that Cyril, the then Christian Patriarch of Alexandria, set monks from the Nitrian Desert on Hypatia because he was jealous of the intellectual esteem in which she was held throughout the Roman world, especially by her lover Orestes, the local Governor. Cyril, some say, also wanted to see Hypatia dead and Orestes undermined because he was determined to appropriate their prerogatives in Egypt: bishops were, with the recent triumph of Christianity, increasingly seizing the powers of imperial viceroys and independent town councils at this time). Duane, Brookee's Boswell, chewed a spliff with a beatific expression as "the greatest historian in Australian history" explained that she, the last Aussie with any claim to a classical European education (she nearly said the *first* Aussie as well – a strange boast for a nationalist and a republican) was the new Hypatia; that Knut recalled Orestes; Dewy, Cyril, and that she had shattered a "pot" over the Prime Minister's head in order to supply his entourage, the *castrati* chorus of Canberra's useless monasteries (its bureaucrats and politicians) with the shards with which to pare her buxom (*ha!*) limbs!

Dewy, in fact, far from taking reprisals, was desperate to prevent more attacks, and moved swiftly to buy off his tormentor. Reminded of the residual monarchism of their constituents, the Labor majority in Parliament was persuaded to announce that Knut Fagan would one day replace Elizabeth II as "Queen of Australia". This would occur on the happy day when the Windsors were finally expelled, like the Bourbons from Sicily, by the red-clad Samurai of Dewy Garibaldi. It was acknowledged that the Esky-hugging serfs might not even then be prepared to accept Dewy's idea of a "queenless commonwealth" . . . Perish the thought! Knut – now reconciled by Dewy's concession with the Prime Minister – had linked this, the favoured régime of the Aussie Left, to the type of polity which Plato – a Proto-Popkiss, in Knut's version – describes in his book **The Republic**. In 369 BC, Plato had imposed the régime advocated in **The Republic** on Sicily while he was working as tutor and mentor to the island's pretty young tyrant, Dionysios II . . . Fagan flattered himself that he was the image of Dionysios, though James the First of England – with his ugliness, cowardice, and weakness for well-hung ephebes chosen by his wife – would have looked a more convincing role model.

The solution to Australia's "pa-the-tic" monarchism, as Parliament agreed, was for Knut to assume the throne as "Dionysianna" upon Elizabeth's removal. The coronation would be a special "Aboriginal" ceremony, and the House voted credits for the operation which Knut was demanding in return for accepting what he ungratefully dubbed (echoing Frederick of Prussia, who had refused the German throne in 1848 because that offer also came from republicans) *"a crown from the gutter"* . . . Several Senators pointed out that the surgery Knut was insisting on would render him more like the eunuch Stavrakios than the Empress Irene, but Fagan, quoting the speech that Elizabeth the First had made on hearing of the Armada, insisted that, *"though I have the body of a weak and feeble woman,"* (he was jumping the gun a bit here, too – in more ways than one), *"I have the heart and stomach of a king, and a king of Ireland, too!"* (Elizabeth had actually said "king of England", but that was too much for a "Reb" and a nationalist like Fagan).

Popkiss, meanwhile, got on the right side of Brooklana by appointing her head of The Australia Council, "the Federal Government's arts funding and advisory body." In that capacity, she set the ball rolling for the *"Dreaming of Coming"* festival, in which I was now taking part, and in which so many unsightly queens were to flourish with such a signal lack of enthusiasm.

Her first act however was to organise a glittering opera benefit for the oppressed Greeks of Cyprus, whose northern provinces were being occupied by the Turkish army, "just as Northern Ireland is being occupied by the Brits" – and as northern Australia soon would be (as anyone but an Australian could see) by "Indernoyszia". In arranging the bash (which was held at Sydney Opera House), Brook, now back in the bosom of the Faithful, was keeping an eye on the Labor Party's standing in Australia's Greek community, proportionately the largest in the world outside the Peloponnese . . . However, the whole thing – the meddling in issues which were real (Cyprus, Northern Ireland) by the citizens of a country which was emphatically *not* real – was symptomatic of Australia's defining malaise. It showed precocious children at sanctimonious play in a lifeless, protected environment which was not, however, as safe as it appeared . . . "Physician, heal thyself!" But the rulers of Australia weren't physicians, they were ignorant, indifferent kids playing Doctors and Nurses. While the Crèche was burning down!

The Australian intelligentsia (the very word, the idea it carried that "intellectuals" had to be separate and self-conscious, showed the provinciality of those described and that, therefore, there never would be an Australian intelligentsia) didn't understand this as well as the stupid common people. The peons in thongs had become highly alarmed at the left-wing play-acting of their rulers, which had the very real consequence of subjecting them, not only to operas they would never see about problems which didn't exist, but to genocidal levels of immigration from their rich, empty continent's hostile and pullulating neighbours. Canberra had initiated an open door policy so that Australia – a tiny European democracy in an ocean of despotisms and million-strong armies – would have the multicultural cachet of other western countries. These were thousands of miles away, and the scraps the local Caucasians threw black and yellow immigrants were tossed there because whites were confident – perhaps wrongly – of their own security and of the invincibility of the homeland's European core. In Britain and France there was no intention, or "possibility", of surrendering power to foreigners. Why should there be? Would the ancestors of the Asians and Africans in Brixton or Saint-Denis have surrendered power to the British or the French – had it not been forced from them at the point of a gun? Relations between people, even the most benign, are ultimately about power, and all talk of human equality and solidarity is ultimately a lie. The people in Australia who were poor and victimised understood perfectly well what Australia's elite (given the second-rate nature of its vaunted erudition) never could: that kindness, humanity, liberalism (call it what you will) depends on *power*, which is to say, cruelty. There can never be humanity or liberalism for anyone unless there is inhumanity and illiberalism for someone else. All the philosophy in the world is mute before the fact that people, whatever they say (and their humanitarian eloquence is usually proportionate to their Darwinian violence) fight constantly to be among the advantaged group rather than the disadvantaged. Once a country has been taken by force – as Australia had been by the ancestors of both the *Nomenklatura* and the tattooed men in thongs – there can only ever be humanity and kindness for the descendants of the conquerors: unless they wish to give their acquisition up to a new conqueror or to the people from whom they took it in the first place. But what human being would ever do that? The naive policies Australia's deeply provincial rulers had adopted towards the Asians and the Aborigines implied that they were about to hand the continent over to either or to both, but, in fact, they were no more prepared to do that than were the sunburned Celts who had voted them in. And why on earth should they? . . . Because, perhaps, those were the signals they had unwisely sent out. Okelle de Bahn, for instance, who had been commissioned by Brook to write the opera for the Cypriot evening, had set *The Rise and Fall of the City of Abalone* (having plagiarised Edgar Varèse, she was now ripping off Brecht and Weill) in an "Aboriginal City" (there were none: the Abos were nomads who had raised temporary bark shelters) which was being beseiged by "Westerners": ie the first European settlers in Australia, a fleetful of British convicts and their jailers who had conquered the environs of Sydney (aka "Abalone", or, as Dew termed it, "Abo-loony!") in 1788. She had conflated this totally imaginary event (for there was no "conquest": the immuno-deficient natives keeled over and died from the Europeans' germs before the crims had even set eyes on them) with the seige of Constantinople, the capital of Byzantium, and, physically, the double of Sydney, by soldiers from Western Europe during the Fourth Crusade. This had happened in 1204. This metaphor was chosen to please the Greeks of Australia, and indeed of Cyprus, whose island – in 1204 part of the Byzantine Empire – had also been conquered by these Crusaders.

You see, in 1185, the people of Constantinople had risen up and murdered the brutal Byzantine Emperor Andronikos: he was publicly despatched with a spear thrust to the anus in the very Hippodrome where the Empress Theodora had swallowed phalanxes of phalluses centuries before. The Emperor Isaakios II, of the Angelos family, was raised to the purple in Andronikos' place. But in 1195, his brother Alexios III deposed and blinded him, as Niketas Choniates records:

> *"At first, Isaakios could hear only unintelligible sounds, but soon he observed a huge throng running towards the imperial pavilion and heard his brother being acclaimed Emperor. Shortly afterwards, messengers told him of the shameless* coup d'état *and he came to a halt, whereupon he made the*

sign of the Cross over himself and cried out 'Be merciful to me, O Christ, my Emperor!' *and invoked God many times to save him from this hour."*

Isaakios's son, the self-styled "Alexios IV", escaped, and fled to Palermo, where his sister was Queen of Sicily. His sister took him to see the Pope in Rome. Alexios IV begged Innocent III to give him the means to unseat his uncle and to win back his father's throne. In return, Alexios assured the Pope, he would, once in power, bring the Byzantine Empire back into the political and religious embrace of the Roman Catholic Church, which it had rejected during the Empress Irene's tiff with Pope Leo. Innocent was naturally delighted with Alexios' offer. He instructed the Venetian fleet which was carrying the Fourth Crusade to Palestine to make a detour to Constantinople, before whose walls the vengeful young Alexios appeared with an army of French and German Crusaders in Spring 1204.

Constantinople in the Thirteenth Century was like the tomb of Tutankhamen. It was an Aladdin's Cave of undisturbed ancient art and architecture: the only classical city to have survived unscathed into the high Middle Ages, the only one which had never been plundered or changed by barbarians. Paris, London, Antioch, Alexandria, Athens – all the other great cities of the Roman Empire – even Rome itself – had by 1204 long been reduced to tiny squatters' camps within fields of ruins: these cities resembled in fact the "Blacks' Camp" that now fluttered between the unfinished or already ruinous stumps of Dewy's Ceaucescu-like Canberra. But when, in 1204, the French crusader and historian Geoffrey de Villehardouin looked out from Alexios' camp at Constantinople, it was at the untouched colonnades and stadia of the Rome of one thousand years before that he gazed. This is what he wrote in his memoirs:

"You may imagine how they all stared, all those who had never before seen Constantinople. For when they saw those high ramparts and the strong towers with which it was completely encircled, and the splendid palaces and soaring churches – so many that but for the evidence of their own eyes they would never have believed it – and the length and the

breadth of that city which of all others is sovereign, they never thought that there could be so rich and powerful a place on earth. "

The Crusaders' sense of having seen a ghost anticipated that of Governor Phillips and his convicts as they studied the perfect, Pleistocene Australia that had, by 1788 – when it was destroyed – survived unchanged for ninety thousand years. Indeed, their feelings weren't very different from our own as we smiled at a doomed, innocent land which, like its meaningless obsession with republicanism and the Noble Savage, had, in defiance of its environment, somehow plunged, vaccuum-sealed, into the Eighties.

Anyway, Alexios IV, having won back the crown from Alexios III, now found himself reviled as a Quisling by his own people, who had no intention of re-embracing the Catholic Church or emptying their pockets for his Crusader mercenaries. The citizens of Constantinople revolted and overthrew him, replacing him as Emperor with a nobleman called Moutzophlos Dukas. Dukas promptly had Alexios IV throttled. In response, the Crusaders, instead of making their way on to Palestine to fight the Muslims, turned their seige engines on the greatest Christian city on earth. They decided they would sack Constantinople and steal its ancient treasures, divide the Byzantine Empire among themselves – ie destroy Christendom's only bulwark against the Islamic Empire based in Baghdad – and place a Roman Catholic on Mourtzophlos' throne.

After the seige began, the Byzantines, crazed with fear, turned their superstitious rage on the city's statues. These sculptures were the cream of the plastic art of the ancient world and had been collected from all over the Meditterranean basin by the Emperor Constantine. He had placed them all in Constantinople when he had re-founded it as the new capital of the Roman Empire in 324 AD. In the Forum of Constantine, he had raised, next to the huge column which bore his own image, Phidias' famous statue of the goddess Athena, which dated from 440 BC and which had formerly been the sole inhabitant of the Parthenon in Athens. Now, in 1204, the rabble of Constantinople smashed the statue, insisting that, with its outstretched arms, it was welcoming Alexios' men into their homes. It must have been, for the invaders soon fought their way into the city. Its incredible past was burned alive. In one day the Crusaders destroyed everything which luck alone had managed to preserve for over a thousand years. According to Choniates, elegant colonnades dating from the Fourth and Fifth centuries went up *"like so much brushwood"*; the churches and palaces *"and everything within was consumed like candlewicks"*. *"These barbarians,"* he writes,

> *"haters of the beautiful, did not allow the statues standing in the Hippodrome and other marvellous works of art to escape destruction, but all were melted down and minted into coins. Thus great things were exchanged for small ones, and works fashioned at huge expense were converted into worthless pennies . . . They broke open the sepulchres of the Emperors which were located within the Heroön erected next to the great church of the Holy Apostles and plundered them all in the night, taking with utter lawlessness whatever gold ornament, or round pearl, or radiant, precious, and incorruptible gems were still preserved within. Finding that the corpse of the Emperor Justinian* [died 565] *had not decomposed through the long centuries* [it was now 1204]*, they looked upon the spectacle as a miracle, but this in no way prevented them from keeping their hands off the tomb's valuables."*

Like mediaeval Constantinople, or Aboriginal (and indeed European) Australia, Justinian's body was the incorruptible past, miraculously conveyed into the present and miraculously destroyed there. It was hardly any wonder then that in Okelle de Bahn's opera, for which Black Gin Boree (who else?) had written a libretto, Justinian represented both Wandjina Namaaraalee – in Aboriginal myth the spirit who had created Australia millions of years before – and Bennelong, the Abo Chieftain who had betrayed it to the Europeans in 1788. Bennelong, according to the Aussie historian Robert Hughes,

> *"was an Iora tribesman, the first black to learn English, drink rum, wear clothes and eat the invaders' strange food. He was rewarded for his curiosity with the friendship of Governor Philip - and a small brick hut, about 12 feet square, in which he lived on the end of what is now Bennelong Point . . . The Iora ate immense quantities of shellfish, mainly oysters* [though also Abalone!] *which were gathered by women. Bennelong*

Point, where the Sydney Opera House now stands, was first named Limeburners' Point by the colonists because it was mantled in a deposit of mollusc shells, built up over thousands of years of uninterrupted gorging. Gathered again – this time by white convict women – and burned in a kiln, these shells provided the lime for Sydney's first mortar [as the ancient marble statues of Constantinople, when consigned to the flames in 1204, provided lime for the crusaders who had to rebuild the city]. "

In the ***Parastaseis Syntomoi Chronikai***, a guidebook to Constantinople written in about 700 AD, the author makes it clear that the Christian Byzantines loathed the wonderful statues Constantine had bequeathed them. As a Christian people whose artists had lost the ability to represent the human body, they thought that figures as life-like as those created by Phidias must be haunted by spirits. They regarded the Athena Parthenos – which the twentieth century would have committed murder to see – as Niketas Choniates did the dying body of the Emperor Manuel Komnenos: as an oyster, a lifeless shell in which something dangerously alive lingered. One could have described modern Australia – with its lovely European heart and yet terribly artificial (indeed unrelated) culture – as just such a paradox, or indeed anathematised Sydney Opera House in the same vein: it rises from a heap of shells and looks like a wreath of opened "whitèd sepulchres".

On the opening night of Ms de Bahn's ***City of Abalone***, Pius Anadu (again, who else?) leapt naked from the tomb of Justinian, which had been re-erected in the middle of the Opera House's Concert Hall. The severed head of an Emu and two of its massive eggs (painfully affixed by golden wire) bobbed in the cavity where his penis should have been. They were meant to suggest the exaggerated stage phallus of the *"Commedia dell'Arte"*. (Tray Beautous, who was also to design ***The Love of Three Oranges*** for Sydney, would present Prokofiev's piece, too, in *"Commedia dell'Arte"* costume: a shrewd touch as ***Oranges,*** though a Twentieth Century composition, was based on a *"Commedia dell'Arte"* play by Gotti from the Eighteenth Century). Okelle, as we have seen, had lifted the scenario for ***Abalone*** (which was set in the 1790s) from events surrounding the siege of Constantinople in 1204, and Pius sang the aria delivered by the body of Justinian. He was, in other words, something both living and dead (like a freshly shucked oyster), and in that sense representative both of the "present" (Bennelong) and the eternal Australian past (Wandjina Namaaraalee). He was seen being prised from a giant oyster (his sepulchre) by a scrum of burly Crusaders played by the Brisbane Broncos rugby team (Dewy's Varangians: being a charity benefit, **Abalone** featured the *Jeunesse Dorée* – and indeed the *Vieillesse délabrée* – of the Labor Party as well as seasoned professionals). The gaping oyster tomb was meant to recall the building in which the piece was being staged and hence *"emblemised,"* as Okelle was keen to point out, a *"ployy within a ployy"* ['a play within a play']. Beautous, meanwhile, told journalists that the inspiration for this scene had been "Aphrodite emerging naked from the scallop-shell in Boticelli's *"The Birth of Venus"*. The hacks duly reported that Anadu had looked like a gay strippogram jumping out of a giant pavlova. They also noted, with the usual false dismay, a scene where the "Crusaders" (who doubled as Governor Phillip's 1788 Marines) assaulted the genitals of Justinian-Namaaraalee, stripping his shell-like coffin (as had the tomb-robbers of 1204) of "round pearls": Emu eggs, in other words! After severing Justinian's penis (it was this act, interestingly, which, in Black Gin's libretto, put the zombie out of his misery), a Marine shook the severed Emu-head in the faces of the audience. (The Emperor Commodus had once treated spectators in the Colisseum in Rome to just such an exhibition, using the head of an ostrich he had killed there while pretending to be a gladiator. He was dressed as a woman at the time – he wanted people to think he was an Amazon).

But these tidbits were bland and tasteless compared to the main report that the Fourth Estate filed that evening. This concerned Brooklana Fagan. Brookee, one of the opera's "celebrity stars", was playing (in Amazonian drag) "Pemulwuy", an aboriginal "resistance leader" of the 1790's who was meant to recall, in de Bahn's extended Byzantine metaphor, "that Thirteenth Century Mandela" the Emperor Mourtzophlos. When the Crusaders captured Constantinople, Mourtzophlos had fled to the Balkan city of Larissa. His wife's father, the Emperor Alexios III, had been living in exile there since being driven out by Alexios IV. Mourtzophlos not unnaturally expected to be welcomed by his Father-in-Law. Instead, Alexios III had him blinded and sold him back to the Crusaders for a hundred pieces of gold. Like Constantine VI, Mourtzophlos was betrayed and mutilated by the very loved one who should have loved him most. Once Alexios had handed him over, the Crusaders took Mourtzophlos to the top of the towering column in Constantinople on which the statue of Constantine the First had stood since 324 AD. Then they pushed him off.

In his one concession to abstract art, Tray Beautous had made Constantine's column, in the opera, a giant version of an Emu's vertical neck. The Emperor's statue was an Emu's Auschwitz-inmate head. Brookee stood on the beak and sang **De La Plus Haute Tour,** an aria by another famous Aussie composer, Brian Howard. (For, just as the company of the opera had not been confined to professionals, not all of the music in the piece was Ms Okelle de Bahn's). It had been arranged beforehand that, emulating Mourtzophlos, Brook would then do a "Charity Bungee Jump" from the bird's cranium. (The beneficiaries would be "Cyprus" and "the Crack Babies of La Perouse"). Just at that moment – under Dewy's orders – one of the Brisbane Broncos playing a Soldier of the Cross surreptitiously sliced the elastic bungee-cord, sending Brookee slamming into the marble orchestra stalls at Dewy's feet (the Prime Minister was the evening's guest of honour). Red brain fragments and slivers of skull peppered the quail eggs that popped in perfumed fingers, and Brookee's fragmenting false teeth removed a cataract from the eye of the Italian Ambassador, who had thought he would never see again.

Knut, who was sharing the Royal Enclosure with Popkiss at the time (what the Byzantines would have called the _"Kathisima"_) was mortified. Might his truculent wife's demise not lead Dew to peform an abortion on his own future? Who else was there to keep Dewy to his word about the Australian throne? Knut leant forward to whisper encouragement.

He also found the composure to mumble, in his desolation, a passage from a biography of Nero by the Roman historian Suetonius. Suetonius' words would, he felt sure, exorcise the Prime Minister of any of the guilt he might, irrationally, feel:

> **"In the** 'Daedalus and Icarus' **ballet** [Knut reminded Dewy], **the actor who played Icarus, while attempting his first flight, fell beside Nero's couch and spattered him with blood".**

To which he added, in homage to his wife, a line from a poem by the great Russian Revolutionary Maxim Gorky: *"He who is born to crawl will never fly!"* (Rather an ambiguous compliment in the circumstances). Sir Dewy, after glutinous condolences, assured Knut that there were no plans to deny Australia "its own dear queen". He urged his predecessor to put "the tragic accident" behind him and to throw himself into a new commission from Parliament, that of "Big Mr Bi-Guy", ie Lord of Misrule for the celebrations attendant on the Bi-Centennial of Governor Phillip's landfall. These were just about to commence. Knut, in his capacity as "Minister for the Bi", even addressed the Chamber on his plans for the commemoration. He spoke at length of his "belovèd" wife. Who, he demanded, could now remember her? (There were some present who would never forget her). Her death, he insisted, was not the death inflicted on "Mourtzophlos in the Constantinople of May 1204". Its only precedent was the destruction, by the mob, of Athena, goddess of Wisdom and Virtue, in that city the month before. Like the Marxist film director Pier Paulo Pasolini, or "Sebastian", in Tennessee Williams' play **Suddenly Last Summer,** she had been turned on and destroyed by the very "sub-proletarians" she had tried to help. (Dewy and Les Majesty exchanged nervous glances at this point).

Knut, of course, was only speaking figuratively. The rest of his speech, though quite as fanciful, was intended to have utterly literal consequences. As his contribution to the "Bi", Knut promised Australia – his originality was dazzling – "a fresh start!" The capital – he told the Chamber in his capacity as "queen" – would be moved two thousand kilometres north from Canberra to Townsville, his own place of birth on the Barrier Reef in isolated, tropical

North Queensland. This gesture would conclusively turn Australia's back on "imperialism", he said, since all the original British settlements, like Sydney and Melbourne, were in the "Deep South" of the country. The move, Knut explained, would recreate Australia as the Asian and Aboriginal state it always had been – or should have been. Townsville was the closest large city to Asia, twice as big as Darwin (which was technically closer): indeed it had been hailed, in the Dark Age before the birth of the Australian Labor Party (which had been founded in Townsville – another reason for promoting the place), as "the biggest purely *white* city in the tropical world." Actually, far from being white, Townsville had always had more Aboriginal inhabitants than any other Australian community. Didn't this, Knut asked, make it doubly blessed? A "town of towns," as its name implied? That wasn't all. Byzantine history, on which Knut had stumbled while discussing his wife's operatic demise, provided Australia (he assured the MP's) with a perfect analogy and rationale for switching capitals. In 663 AD, the Emperor Konstans II moved the court and government of Byzantium from Constantinople, which sat in the dead centre of the Empire, to Syracuse, the pre-Arabic capital of Sicily, which lay on its far western edges. Drawing himself up like a kangaroo on the podium, Knut suddenly produced *The Golden Honeycomb*, a famous book Anthony Cronin had once written about Sicily. In a sneering voice which seemed to defy the Chamber to contradict him and which made him sound like John Pilger, he declaimed aloud from one of Cronin's descriptions of Syracuse. The Queensland representatives had to agree that the passage uncannily seemed to evoke Townsville and its offshore suburb, Magnetic Island:

> *"A wide, sheltered harbour, an island detached from the mainland by the narrowest strip of sea, and on that island a fresh water spring: such was the site of the second Greek settlement in Sicily, a colony founded by Corinthians, destined to be one of the world's great cities."*

Like Australia's "caring, sharing Government," Knut observed, Konstans II had wanted to move the bowels and brains of the state closer to where its past and future lay . . . And like Labor, he might have added, the Emperor was completely deluded. Greece, North Africa and Italy (the western provinces of Byzantium, whose hinge was Sicily) had been the scene of the Graeco-Roman world's greatest achievements, but, by the Seventh Century, they were, like Twentieth Century sub-Saharan Africa after independence, barbaric, vandalised and economically worthless, and so strategically exposed that Italy would soon fall to the Lombards, Greece to the Slavs and North Africa to the Arabs. How could Konstans have been so foolish? (And how, given the proximity of Townsville to Jakarta – it had been flattened during the war by Japanese planes from Timor – could Knut?) Subsequent Emperors would realise that only Anatolia in the east was rich and defensible enough to sustain Byzantium, and that therefore only Constantinople, its capital, could be the seat of Empire. Remarkably though, even in the Seventh Century, the Dark Ages and their lower expectations had overtaken man physically, but not conceptually. It had been a thousand years since Plato had worked in Syracuse as the tutor to Dionysios II, but Konstans II believed, as did everyone alive in 663 AD, that he inhabited the same continuous, continuing classical world as Plato had. (Konstans' vicious and perverted nature was not dissimilar to that of the philosopher's famous charge, notwithstanding his insane, typically Byzantine piety).

Konstans and his entourage spent years touring the rotting cities of Greece and Italy as they made their leisurely way between Constantinople and the new capital, Syracuse. Horse badges belonging to his barbarian mercenaries have recently been dug up in Corinth, and the base of a statue to the Emperor has been discovered there: the last statue ever to be erected in "Ancient Greece". In Athens, large holes have been found in the floor of the Stoa of Attalos, where Konstans' men sank wooden pillars with which to keep up the ceiling of the collapsing building, one of the few in the shattered village still in good enough repair to house the Imperial Court. To Konstans and his people, the ancient world was still alive. We, however, from the vantage point of modernity, can see that, by the time that they absorbed it, it was utterly extinct. But don't we, as we survey our decaying world, make the same mistake as they did? Is the civilization that surrounds the modern Westerner really a living forest with its roots in Christianity and the Renaissance, as, for instance, the Nineteenth Century undoubtedly was? Or is it more like the Byzantine Empire or the embalmed body of the Emperor Justinian? Something linked to a life-giving past which is, however, as putrid within as it appears outwardly blooming?

Rome was Konstans' last stop before Syracuse. It was still, despite having been sacked innumerable times by Goths, Vandals and even the Byzantines themselves (who had contended with various barbarian peoples for its possession) physically the city Nero would have recognised. It was Konstans the Second who gave it the aspect it has today. He ordered its hundreds of metal and marble statues to be taken down and transferred to his fleet, some to beautify Syracuse, his new capital (itself a ruin), some to be melted down to make weapons with which to fight the Arabs. These tribesmen, fired by their new religion, had just conquered Syria, Palestine and Alexandria and were already raiding every other part of the Empire. The bronze roof tiles on all of Rome's public buildings shared the fate of the statues, as did the metal clamps that pinned the massive walls and columns together. The city simply fell apart, like a set of teeth stripped of its fillings and even its gums. Konstans, in fact, resembled the people of modern Australia. They too never marvel at how inferior their own works are to those bequeathed by the ancestral culture. They too destroy a priceless legacy as casually as they might shoot an endangered animal. Thinking that what they have inherited from the British is, like imperial Rome, as universal, inexhaustible and neutral as oxygen, they vandalise and deride it even as they rely on it and use it up. They forget that the British past, like the Australian future, is fragile, unique, and might be very easily destroyed.

As Konstans' ships approached Sicily, groaning (as had Constantine's three hundred years before) with the accumulated art of the ancient world, an Arab fleet pounced on them, and carried their fabulous cargo off to Alexandria. This was now the city of Mohammed rather than of Hypatia or even Cyril. Konstans, however, managed to evade the Arabs. As promised, he set up his government in Syracuse. A few years later, however, a chamberlain called Andrew, one of the beautiful creatures with whom he was in the habit of sharing long steam baths (miraculously the technology had survived from Roman times), grew homesick for Constantinople. He was desperate to provoke the court's return. One day in 668 AD, as they shared a tub, he brained the Emperor with the metal bucket with which he was supposed to be dousing him. The new Emperor, Constantine IV (Konstans' son), immediately ordered that the capital be transferred back to Constantinople.

Knut, of course, never mentioned any of this in his speech before Parliament. He left Canberra the same day and, embarking on *"Poofter"* at Tathra, made his way by sea to Townsville. He put in at Brisbane, which is about half-way to North Queensland, and he collected the Broncos. Their naked, knotted bodies tumbled into his teak hold like ears of maize, just as Konstans had once harvested Rome's statues.

Aldour Brownbill was watching *"Poofter"* depart from the vast pink cliffs of the Brisbane River, which are so awe-inspiring that the stupendous river below can remind you of the Amazon. The local paper, **THE COURIER-MAIL,** had reported Knut as saying that, just as the soldier bees follow their queen to a new hive, so too the Broncos' brown and hairy bodies must now accompany Australia's new queen to Townsville, Australia's "Golden Honeycomb". "When in Rome," he had added, "do as the Romans do:" and where but in "our Aussie Rome" should its Praetorian Guard reside?

Aldour – jealous perhaps – wrote a complaint to the **MAIL** about a eulogy which Knut, in justifying the change of capitals, had delivered in Konstans' honour at the University of Queensland's Saint Lucia Campus in western Brisbane. (A somewhat eccentric gesture: "the voice of Queenie" was interested chiefly in letters about Abo child-molesters and cases of Gas Gangrene among sugar-cane farmers). Anyway, Aldour wrote to point out that Konstans II had been named after the Emperor Konstans the First, the son of the

Constantine who had, in 324 AD, rebuilt and renamed Byzantium. According to Edward Gibbon, in **The Decline and Fall of the Roman Empire** (which Aldour gleefully quoted), the *first* Konstans was addicted to interfering with the tall blond German warriors who fell regularly into Roman hands after barbarian wars. He was even deposed by one of them while he was *"pursuing in the adjacent forest his favourite amusement of hunting, or perhaps some pleasures of a more private and criminal nature."* Like "Sebastian" in Tennessee Williams' **Suddenly Last Summer**, Konstans I was *"famished for blonds."* Why, Aldour demanded – evoking visions of Knut falling on the Broncos' fluted torsos *"like a fat Gin munching Big Rooster buttered corn"* – should "big Mr Bi-Guy" declare his allegiance to the *second* Konstans? The *first* was clearly his mentor. But events were to prove Knut's analogy inspired and Aldour's false.

When he arrived in Townsville, Knut installed his entourage in the Breakwater Casino. Then he made arrangements for a giant concrete statue of his late wife to be erected on Magnetic Island. It was to be painted, like any elephantine wayside prawn or toad, in the most garish of colours. Knut insisted that this would not only be in the tradition of Australian monumental art (Australians being the first acknowledged experts in this field since the ancient Egyptians), it would also recall Phidias' Athena and, indeed, the Parthenon itself, both of which had once rejoiced in a David Hockneyesque riot of catatonically violent colour. We forget, he opined, that all the great monuments of antiquity were caked, during their heyday, in bright and horrible paint. Today each, with its bare ivory stone, resembles the Taj Mahal, but *then* they were psychedelic wedding cakes like India's modern Hindu temples. Their elegance was cancelled out by elaboration and repetition, the greatness of their art was made to look easy and cheap: perhaps the greatest compliment one can pay the artists of antiquity, for nothing is more simple, as the West's lazy modern painters have discovered, than to suggest that art is difficult. How much harder it is to make profundity look banal than it is to pass the banal off as something complex, as they do! All great art begins its life as very bad art. The difference is that, in the past, it only *appeared* to be bad;

nowadays it really *is* bad, but everybody conspires (myself included!) to hail it as something else. Today, "great art" begins and ends its life as shit but, this time round, nobody comes to their senses, as they did to acknowledge the genius of Phidias when the pink and blue icing finally fell off, and the scales fluttered from people's eyes.

That's why I think I would have liked the two-hundred-foot-high statue of Brooklana Fagan (made to resemble Phidias' Athena) which Knut arranged to erect on Magnetic Island. I would have liked it for the same reason that – I believe – I and the other *aficianados* on the *"Dreaming of Coming"* tour enjoyed Australia's giant painted animals. Like Phidias' Athena and the works of Michelangelo (which were purely religious objects, indeed religious instruments; "sculpture" was the last thing on their creators' mind), these monsters had not been created as "art". The citizens of Mutarnee and Alloomba would no more have regarded them in that way than the pious contemporaries of Michelangelo's *"Moses"* or the Athena Parthenos would have regarded what were, for them, avatars, as footnotes in the history of culture. Because they had not been *created* as art, we could hope that Australia's cement *colossi* would one day be *recognised* as art, a hope we could never entertain for the posterity of the currently fêted works of Damien Hirst or Antony Gormley, or of the painters we ourselves tried to push. It was impossible for even the most cynical of us to think that our luck would hold, or that generations to come would remain in hock to the blind Post-Modernism of the Twentieth Century, which insists on finding "art" in every historical era most inimical to the concept, even its own . . . Unhappily, we were never to admire the statue of Brooklana-Athena. Knut was found dead in Townsville shortly after it went up. With Fagan out of the way, Popkiss demolished the giantess, and abolished what was to have been Australia's native monarchy. The capital, too, was transferred back to Canberra long before we even set foot in Australia.

In Townsville in 1985, however, everything appeared to be going Knut's way. He arranged for his cement Athena to contain a magnetically-charged iron core so that, like a Siren, it would pull all the neighbouring tankers and cargo boats towards itself. There were plenty of these in the vicinity, as Townsville was the port from which the mineral wealth of Australia was exported to Japan. And it wouldn't be the first time "Maggie" (as the Townsvilleans dubbed their exotic 'burb) had disturbed the tropic calm. James Cook – the Englishman who claimed Australia for Britain – had given the island its name after magnetic ores in its black, burnt-looking cliffs sent all the compasses on his ship haywire as he sailed up the Barrier Reef in 1770. In a sense, the atoll stood for Australia itself (which may have been the reason behind Knut's positioning of the statue), for it was "Captain James Crook" – as the Aborigines (and Knut!) now hailed him – who had first suggested how "magnetic" the continent would prove to European settlers. It was this advice which had led the Government in London to send Phillip's convicts to Sydney eighteen years later, the Bicentennial of which Knut was now celebrating.

The original plans for the Bi had seen a fleet of large sailing vessels from all over the world – "the Tall Ships" – entering Sydney Harbour on the same date, in 1988, as Phillip's boats had arrived there in 1788. That, however, left the initiative with the foreign owners and masters of the Tall Ships. It would put, according to Fagan, "Western Colonialists" in the same driving seat as they had unjustly occupied two hundred years before. (It was an article of faith with Knut, and indeed with other members of the Australian Labor Party, that the British founders of Australia had nothing to do with *them*, and that the native-born Australians who were the Brits' descendants were somehow also their victims – the targets, rather than the beneficiaries, of "British imperialism"). Reminding the party of a famous phrase of Lenin's, Knut warned that this unjust *"correlation of forces"* would "pander to imperialism". Knut's plan however – to pull foreign freighters towards Australia whether they wanted to go there or not – would give Australians the upper hand. According to Tray Beautous, who designed the Magnetic Island colossus, its implementation would make Australia resemble, not an ordinary human being, but an *artist*, the only person on earth who

103

can choose his own king – his own court, even! Australia under Knut would no longer be Uranus in a galaxy where the Sun – Europe and the States – was Louis Quatorze. An artist (Tray announced to the *"Bully"* – **THE TOWNSVILLE BULLETIN**) can create his own "stars" from the models whom he, and he alone, can rescue from the obscurity of the crowd. And these happy individuals (like the magnetised trawlers off Townsville) are humanity's only *real* stars (Tray preposterously insisted), as they alone are chosen by an artist, the only human being qualified to judge human value. *("Such,"* as Anna Komnena once wrote of Pope Gregory VII, *"was his arrogance!"*) Those luminaries (Tray continued) who have *not* been chosen by artists – the Mandelas and Monroes (the Europes and Americas) who offer *themselves* up as magnets – are deceived in the estimate they put on their own fascination. They are not artists. Like their admirers, they are not infrequently "insects". Therefore, Tray declared, the unilateral decisions they make in their own favour are irrelevant, however successful each might turn out to be . . .

That, anyway, was the idea behind the monstrosity that now loomed over twenty miles of the Barrier Reef. Its dress was the off-white, sour-milk blue of the muddy sea surrounding Townsville itself. Its bronze breastplate and helmet was the tinned salmon orange of the blazing rock from which Townsville – a city completely bereft of green – emerged as miraculously as Athena had from the head of Zeus. Its face and arms were, for political reasons, the "aboriginal", almost Dravidian purple of Magnetic Island when it is glimpsed from its metropolis, a visual effect produced by a covering of dense, low scrub, so that the island ends up looking every evening like a bunch of cloudy grapes on a blue dish. On one fiery Thursday, the 26th of September 1985 arrived. It broke over Townsville like an egg. Transparent heat rolled over the city like the last clear flat tongue of a wave on a beach. Because it was the white part of the egg (the sun was the other part), the air started to cook, to whiten. It was bubbling and viscous, salty and milky: a cataract. The candied houses were standing on stilts like circus clowns. Almost every street was made of wood and very flimsy looking. A beach with papery colonial huts was nothing but a playground sandpit strewn with crisp packets. The Government offices and the shops were the only buildings not to have stilts, to dare to squat directly on the earth and its tapestry of snakes, spiders, giant poisonous toads and floods. The concrete in which they alone rejoiced was deceptive: it had been hollowed out by omnivorous termites. (Australian termites can eat anything – even cement!) These public buildings, like down-at-heel villas in Sussex or Miami, were painted in very bright colours. As the Townsvilleans started to throng around them, each structure looked from far away like a boiled sweet that a child had spat out on the ground and which ants were now crawling over. From the Nelly Bay Resort on Magnetic Island (appropriately enough), Knut was scrutinising the city with interest. He had been woken by the cicadas, which had started screaming like a chain-saw at first light. (Nobody has ever described how noisy insects and animals make even urban Australia both day and night. Lyndon B. Johnson, who, like General Macarthur, was based in Townsville during the war against Japan, observed that the city would *"fit twice into Brooklyn Cemetery and still be twice as dead."* He still had a point. But firework displays of shrieking parakeets, fruit bats that screamed incessantly when they weren't hanging dead from telephone lines like swatches of blackened bananas, and attic-dwelling possums that howled and thumped through the night like poltergiests made the lazy, stupefied town noisier than Manhattan). Knut had hardly slept a wink, but he wasn't complaining: he was relaxing with his buxom Broncos. By the pool, the swellings and curves on the bough of a eucalypt had been painted to look like the tits and bum of a girl in a polka-dot bikini. (Anthropomorphic tree decoration was Townsville's speciality). As had happened when works of art were inaugurated in Greco-Roman antiquity, Brooklana's statue was to be unveiled the next day amid athletic contests – rugby tournaments and swimming fests. This would delight the sports-mad Australian public as much as it tickled the antiquarian in Knut.

In the afternoon, the Broncos won a game against "the Townsville Tree Frogs", played at the National Fitness Camp at Picnic Bay at the southern tip of Magnetic Island. Knut went into the shower afterwards and rewarded his team with a bottle of Seaview Champagne, and a "cooked chook" from "Big Rooster". (In ancient Greece, a cockerel was the gift an older man gave his young male lovers). The chook, like a fat yellow oyster in the silver shell of the "Big Rooster" thermos-bag, was an artist's model: an ordinary bloke unconscious of his appetising nature. The silver vacuum bag represented consciousness; it was the self-conscious pervert, the artist who knew the bloke's true worth, and made a model, a meal of him. Shucked him and sucked him from the horny lip. It was as if a pearl had enclosed an oyster, not the other way around. As if the quotidian flesh of the oyster was in fact more valuable than its spermy gall-stone. Knut's erect penis was the Philosopher's Stone that turned the chook's everyday body into gold. Through the misty glass the buttery orange Broncos were swelling up like pumpkin scones. Feather-boa-constricted big roosters struggled between each leg. They were singing. This is what they sang:

"Yes, it's our big chicken, for our big State,
Barbequed or fried, it sure tastes great;
If Queensland makes you feel great mate,
Then you'd rather have Big Rooster!"

Two hours later, the bloodied body of Knut Fagan was removed from the shower-room of the Tobruk Baths by members of the Queensland police. Highly biddable public servants, they announced that "Big Mr Bi-Guy" had slipped on a piece of soap and cracked his skull. Others, however, whispered that a Bronco, acting on Dewy's orders, had lobotomised "his own dear queen" with the silver bucket in which the Seaview was being cooled. The golden bottle was left at the scene of the crime: the perspiring globe of an oyster and its silver shell.

• • •

Our bus was drawing out of Manuka Circus and turning into the road that ran through Telopea Park, right in the middle of Canberra. The sky was a glassy black. I loved the huge, watery golden stars, and a moon twice as big as the sun, the colour and size of a grapefruit. Nothing prepares you for the titanic nights of the Southern Hemisphere, their skies like El Greco's paintings of the sky in Heaven. Two Australian cultural officials, thick-set young ladies, were fiddling with their personal stereos in the seat in front of me. They were tough cookies alright. "I've got George Michael on one of 'em," the first observed. "Got that song *'Wild Horses'* on?" the other asked. Suddenly there was a thud, a brassy ripple. The bus slowed down. Someone waiting in the Bush (parks in urban Australia tend to be just enclosed Bush) had thrown a brick through the windscreen. It had narrowly missed the driver's head. The first four rows of seats had been showered with glass; not shards, just thousands of little cubes. The cookies rushed to investigate. They returned abashed. "*'Get to the back of the bus!'* God I miss my schooldays." "There sure are some sickos about," the other observed. "Someone must have thrown it," mused an American, who was clearly in the running for the Nobel Prize . . . I fell into fitful sleep.

THE COOK, THE THIEF, HIS WIFE AND HER LOVER

The next thing I knew, "the Australian National Gallery, Canberra!" was being announced. We all alighted and plunged into its billowing halls. We were going to attend a nocturnal Gala there for the *"New Australian Painters"* exhibition, but I made sure I had time to check out the Gallery's permanent collection as well. There was a somewhat unearthly atmosphere, because a daylight venue had been put to nocturnal use. It was like visiting a school on a parent-teacher evening. At European or American gallery openings, I always feel completely at home, but among these suburban Australians – who really did look like the parents and teachers of my youth – I was as disorientated as when, as a kid, I used to stray from the bedroom into one of my parents' parties. The brackish beery mystery of deep voices and bright artificial light: a light that was so new! It really seemed I had never seen it before. A light which completely recreated familiar things. Not that there was anything beery about this glittering *soirée*, which was as sophisticated as only Australians can make a sophisticated gathering.

The first of the Gallery's famous pictures to catch my eye was Arthur Streeton's *"Spirit of the Drought"*: a naked, pink pubescent pulling a wedge of raiment above her breasts, and, beneath her feet, the skeleton of a cow. It was extraordinary, but not as odd as the milieu I found myself in. The building was filled with funny little old Australian ladies. Who were they? Politicians? They had the self-sufficient "all-dressed-up-and-nowhere-to-go" look of widows or drag queens. "Vivid imagination," said one, scrutinising a canvas. " *'Young and Beautiful'* – to me it would be an old sheila like . . ." " *'Land of the Black Roosters' "*, another intoned, theatrically, "well, yairs, you *can* see a chook there!"

The French Impressionist and Post-Impressionist paintings were very small – all Australia could afford, obviously – but there was a fantastic little Cézanne, *"An Afternoon in Naples"*. Two naked women on a bed, seen from the back. A negro servant, also seen from behind, was lifting a curtain on the women with one hand, and holding a blue tea-set aloft with the other. But for an orange bum-wrap and a yellow turban, the negress was naked too, with shiny blue-grey flesh like Magnetic Island. I paid my respects to a pair of classics, *"Burke at Cooper's Creek"* and Drysdale's *"The Drover's Wife"*, a reproduction of which I have at home. It was difficult to enjoy them because there was a semi-circle of leather chairs nearby and a group of stupefied Australians was watching, of all things, a noisy film for tourists which gave a history of the (extremely recent) building we were standing in. Wherever these tautological films are offered, Australians gather like flies. *"Millions of people visit Canberra each year,"* the film announced, *"interested, questioning people eager to visit the Theaterette we have built on the Gallery landing!"*

There was a "Retrospective" of Fred Williams' work. He's my favourite Australian artist and the exhibition was simply wonderful. He's a great portrait painter too: gets in just enough manginess, obesity, but doesn't make his sitters look ugly in an ideal, "political" way. So realistic: the most realistic portraits I've ever seen. I admired his gum-trees in a landscape, swimming in haloes like bugs under a microscope: the same amoebic shapes you get in Miró and the Paris-period Kandinsky.

The aboriginal artist Albert Namatjira had a room all to himself. He painted Outback lakes and mountains in the Nineteen-Sixties like a lady watercolourist of the Nineteenth Century: a very prissy European sensibility, but not as phoney as the modern tourist-political interpretations of "tribal" art that graced the same gallery. These Milky Ways of dots on a brown background were drifts of ant eggs in a broken nest: propaganda for "the Black Struggle." They were allegedly the work of aboriginal activists. But being products of a self-conscious awareness of the tribal genre which no real tribesman would ever have – working as he does within a tradition, and blind as an insider must be to that tradition – they were purely decorative, and made me think of wrapping paper. They had an imposed, external spirit. They completely lacked the bizarrely non-human quality of real aboriginal art: cave-paintings, for instance, whose embryonic snakes and 'roos recall streptococci or algebra.

I was drawn to a canvas by the window. Somebody calling himself "Tray Beautous" had done it – the name was a new one. He had given the painting a rather unassuming title: *"The Old Folks Home"*. It was a long, rectangular piece, divided into four sections, all the same size. The first was a painting of a termite hill, the sort that is common in North Queensland: I later learned Beautous came from there – like Fagan, he was a native of Townsville. It's difficult to describe what these termite nests look like if you've never seen one. Imagine a very tall, thin sandcastle. They have the brown, sandy look and the fantastic wierdness of the towers on that cathedral in Barcelona by Gaudí.

The first picture showed one of these nests in the spear-like state in which they crowd the Bush around Townsville; it's like a cemetery, there are so many of them. Beautous's termite hill was a penis, not so much erect as solidly mummified. This (I later learned from the artist) was because it was meant to represent European Australia. That was why, in the next quarter of the canvas, we got a cross-section of the nest, this time seen from above. It was a circle full of rippling, ever-contracting circles. Circular chambers. White things – pearls or termites – wriggled in the narrowing bands. The white race were souls in the concentric, cloacal hell of Dante. They were tapeworm in the severed tree-trunk of a turd, parasites, potential bloodsuckers. Aboriginal Australia on the other hand (or was Tray just mocking the po-faced official culture?) was sick with life. The last two quarters of the painting featured a giant Tolga melon like a green Zeppelin. This was phallic symbolism at its freshest. The cross-section of aboriginal society was longitudinal rather than (as had been the case with the termites) vertical. The black seeds within – the Abos – were enclosed in a cartouche like beetles in an Egyptian hieroglyph. They looked like the tiny Africans you see laid out in rows in those Eighteenth Century prints that give an imaginary X-Ray overview of elliptical slave ships. Whether shackled or not (and of course they currently claimed they were), at least the darkies didn't (according to Beautous) share in the death of Western civilization. They were tadpoles wriggling in a womb: their very blackness shivered. Seeds are the shape of things to come. The Abos were in their bloody element – life. The sugar-melon. Its lovely horrific red. The *Dolce Vita* you want a lot and soon get sick of. The sweet juice that trickles down your legs like liquid rubber.

A brutal-looking queen with a face like a wombat pushed a tray of "drinkies" at the small of my back. Instead of champers (there was only Seaview, of course), I chose a fiery cup of tomato *pressé*. There was a crystal ashtray nearby filled up with caviar (an amusing local touch), and I scooped up some black seeds and sprinkled them on my drink. Another androgynous-looking truck driver came up and asked me if I wanted to meet the Prime Minister. I said that I did.

I was led into one of the side-galleries that opened off the main exhibition like a chapel sprouting from the nave of a church. A line of Brisbane Broncos stood guard at its entrance, dividing Australia's First Couple from the prying eyes of the Hoipolloi. The Broncos slouched around naked to the waist wearing faded tracksuit bottoms. Because of their glistening muscles, they looked like bowls of profiteroles in gooey syrup. Dewy and Bon were devouring a television. An absurd attentiveness was written on their faces. They were sitting on Poo-Chairs: antiques which followed them to every official event. They didn't (of course!) need them. They just wished to show their erudition. The back rests of the commodes were covered, like an Australian armchair, in comfy bobble shawls with fierce synthetic colours. I noticed how old they both were, and how small and simple decades of sun had made their big confusing bodies. They had put away, not the "childish things" the great Apostle says to leave go when we reach maturity, but – like all Australians who hit the heart of darkness – maturity itself. It was senility, a second childhood. In common with all the other senior citizens Down Under, the Vice-Regal pair sported brutal, revealing clothes like the shapeless things people who are operated on wear. I found it oddly horrifying, remembering as I did the Sixties' statesman in a *lamé* three-piece between Whitlam and Harold Holt, as overdressed as a middle-aged queen, and his wife, looking like a sea-horse in a figure-hugging plate-mail shift by Mary Quant. She had given the fabulously available Mrs Holt more than a run for her money! But now it was "the Age of Innocence". Dewy was a man in a mental home in ill-fitting pyjamas. He had pealed off his complexity. Was rejecting life, which is double-breasted like a female dog. All Australians reject it, and sooner rather than later. Return, alive, to the womb. But, as Nicodemus asked Christ, when the Lord told him he had to be "born again", how can anyone do that? Like the Byzantine Emperor Manuel Komnenos when he sensed he was going to die, each Australian over forty is an oyster who shucks away the shell. The historian Niketas Choniates once explained the sartorial implications. He said that, on the last day of his life, the Emperor, deducing that the end was nigh, took off his stiff and golden robe and asked for the gown of a monk. The only one that could be found was filthy, so small that it barely reached his cock. Tray once told me that in Townsville, as a child, he had sat in a Yellow Cassia tree and torn the golden chrysalis off a pupating caterpillar. The mummy he discovered was the one the Crusaders found in the tomb of Justinian: it was half intestine, half ribcage, as white and muscular and pungent and skeletal as a nude old man. It was a monk: both foetus and corpse, half in one world, half in the next. Dewy, like the Emperor Manuel, had assumed an anchoritic austerity. Like most Aussie blokes, he had been blessed in his prime with the Irish "eagle" look. He had been broad-chested, with massive eye-brows, deep-set, dead yet staring eyes, a steeply angular face, jutting shoulders, and a covering of super-fine body-hair like feathers. At that time, he was in his political prime too. One might justly have said of Dew then, as the Sixteenth Century theologian Erasmus once said of the animal he most resembled:

> *"The eagle is the image of the king, neither beautiful, nor musical, nor fit for food: but carnivorous, rapacious, a brigand, a destroyer, solitary, hated by all, a pest."*

Now, sitting in a cavernous sarong that looked like a broken egg, he more resembled a feeble glutinous nestling than a bird of prey. I thought immediately of Saint Gregory the Great, who gazed on the ruins of a once-great Rome in 593 AD and cried:

> *"The eagle has grown bald all over its body; growing old, it has lost all its feathers, even those on its wings!"*

It was incredible to think that this maleficent braised *poussin* could dominate a vast continent. Complaining of his one-man rule, a brave minority of journos did indeed ask, as did Saint Gregory when he surveyed Rome, and with as little effect:

> *"Where is the Senate; where is the people? . . . The Senate is gone, the people perish; pain and fear grow daily for those who are left!"*

Like his enemy Joh Bjelke-Petersen, the Nationalist Premier of Queensland, who had seized office during my first visit twenty years before and was still in power, Dew just kept on surviving. Mysteriously, maliciously, and without external supports. Politically as well as physically, the odalisque on the Pooer put me in mind of Joseph Conrad's sketch of the ancient revolutionary "Karl Yundt" in *The Secret Agent:*

> *"The knob of his stick and his leg shook together with passion, whilst the trunk, draped in the wings of the havelock, preserved his historic attitude of defiance. He seemed to sniff the tainted air of social cruelty, to strain his ear for its atrocious sounds. There was an extraordinary force of suggestion in his posturing . . . The famous terrorist had never in his life raised personally as much as his little finger against the social edifice. He was no man of action; he was not even an orator of torrential eloquence, sweeping the masses along in the rushing noise and foam of a great enthusiasm. With a more subtle intention, he took the part of an insolent and venomous evoker of sinister impulses which lurk in the blind envy and exasperated vanity of ignorance, in the suffering and misery of poverty, in all the hopeful and noble illusions of righteous anger, pity and revolt. The shadow of his evil gift clung to him yet like the smell of a deadly drug in an old vial of poison, emptied now, useless, ready to be thrown away upon the rubbish-heap of things that had served their time."*

But still he clung on. How could he fail to, when it had taken him such an effort to get to where he was? Ordinary people, when they contemplate leaders like George W. Bush or Dewy Popkiss, think that there must be more to them than meets the eye. How could there not be, considering the position they occupy? Despite all the evidence to the contrary, the masses always attribute remarkable gifts to their leaders. They are inclined to think that they are, of necessity, secretly brilliant, whatever venality and indeed stupidity none makes any attempt to hide. They forget what Conrad called "the exasperated vanity" of the ignorant, and how psycopathically cunning and hence successful – like a cretinous serial killer – a moron with a one-track mind – deluded as to his fitness for office by vanity – can be. Alexander Protopopov, for instance, was Tsarist Russia's last Prime Minister. The last because, in fact, he *was* the Prime Minister; because the Tsar had been mad enough – egged on by Rasputin (whose creature A.P. was) – to make him a Minister at all. Everyone else pointed out that syphilis had rendered the man terminally and mentally ill, that he practiced necrophilia (the one thing he had in common with Popkiss, going by Bon's appearance), and that he never took a decision without interrogating the icon on his desk, to which he gabbled incessantly. In January 1917, courtiers who feared for the Tsar's survival cornered the statesman – a former book-keeper – and begged him to resign. They warned him that, otherwise, a revolution was inevitable. "How can I give up being *Prime Minister*?" Protopopov asked, "I never even thought I'd be a *book-keeper*!" . . .

So much for Dewy Popkiss. But dare we put our trust in the aptitude of even benign politicians? Even they rarely pursue or attain office for the broadly selfless and intellectual reasons we ascribe. We think that they are evangelists for a particular religion – "Socialism" or "Neo-conservatism" – mere cyphers and foot soldiers who subordinate their personalities to uphold an idea. That's what it looks like from the outside. But what human being, even the most virtuous, has ever thought of anyone but himself, has ever been able to go beyond the experience of his own personal world, his own personal needs? Even a "saint" can't do

114

that. Indeed, the decision to put others' interests before one's own is proof of an ability to stand apart from and judge oneself that is, in ontological terms, profoundly egotistical. As are the motives for doing so. These might be fear of God's punishment, hope of God's reward, or – as is most common among friends of mankind everywhere (white anti-Apartheid activists, for instance, who wanted black majority rule in chi-chi South Africa, but didn't care if Kenyans and Zambians never got it) – the desire to be thought saintly by other people. And what is wrong with that? Even Our Lord requires us (or so it seems) to sacrifice our own interests for purely mercenary reasons. For He will reward us if we do. He doesn't seem to demand that we *conquer* the consciousness of our own interests. He seems rather to appeal to this consciousness. Remember the parable He told about the steward who was about to be sacked, who cancelled what his master's debtors owed the better to butter up potential patrons when he was on Skid Row? Didn't Christ say, after telling that parable, that, as Man is evil, he should also be shrewd, and make friends with God by means of "unrighteous mammon" – ie by giving it to the poor – so that God will take him in, just as the debtors later received the steward? Doesn't this show a tolerance for the essentially self-centred nature of man? Why then should we expect selflessness or competence of even intelligent politicians? God doesn't seem to expect it of *us*? Not even the best or wisest are the "socialists" or "conservatives" – ie the bees or termites – they claim to be. They are solitary fantasists, like artists, and like artists they use a collective ideology ("Cubism," "Abstraction") as an excuse for self-expression. But they lack the knowledge of their hypocrisy. This is what makes them different – and loathsome. Artists, on the other hand, are self-aware. I can think of a hundred politicians who had more learning and ideological commitment than Dewy Popkiss, but it may as well not have existed, as they certainly never used it in office. There, like Dewy, they were the servants neither of ideas nor of "the people," but of those supreme works of art, their egos.

My presence made Dewy and Bon grunt and very briefly glance my way, as if I had just returned from the gallery toilet after an absence of two minutes, rather than from Europe and a hiatus of over twenty years. (Dew had hosted the Kirribilli luncheon – flying from Sydney to Canberra a few hours later – but we had never found a chance to meet over the *"Yabbies Yarrawonga"* and the *"Larves Wichities farcies en Croûte"*). The rellies seemed unprepared for the coïtal extremes of the salutation I had prepared – or any salutation at all, for that matter – and I began to feel uneasy, not knowing what to do. They just sat there, transfixed by the television. They made no attempt to stand up, nor did they ask me to occupy the nearby banquette. "Are you watching the programme on the gallery?" I asked, despairing of a less sardonic introduction. "No," Dewy said. He spoke without irony, as if I had made the most obvious mistake in the world. "It's **Days of our Lives**: we never miss it." This was a soap opera – not even one of the famous Australian ones. Dewy and Bon built the "days of their lives" on its foundations. Cabinet meetings were cut short in its honour, cannibal orgies of fellatio on visiting Asian Hitlers suspended, and when there was a reception beyond the "hayume", the TV escorted them. The shot which opened the programme, and which was repeated after commercial breaks, showed sand dripping from the upper vase of an hourglass into the bottom receptacle. Meanwhile, some great queen announced off-camera, in a ripe Midwestern voice*: "Like the sands of the ocean are the days of our lives!"* . . . *"Melissa, you're not just a* doctor, *you're* a woma*n*," one of the cast observed. It was quite engrossing: the actors were completely absorbed in their ludicrous mission. The cheap, same-room intimacy suggested that Australian soap, **Neighbours**, but the protagonists weren't at all like gawky lads and lassies in an Australian soapie. Aspiring as they did to the American ideal of beauty, they were beefy and androgynous like over-the-hill porno stars. The cheap, unstable film made their faces red and grotesque and their clothes an acidic blue or yellow: they looked like paintings of whores by Emil Nolde . . . I nearly jumped out of my skin: another air-hostess type had started shrieking now. "'Pressure' *me?*! *Of* course *you're pressuring me: you're wearing her damned wedding ring, aren't you?!"* One of the more buxom heroines said she was going to visit her father, who had just suffered a coronary. *"I won't excite him, I promise,"* she somewhat mysteriously swore.

It was strange to look from the soap to Dewy and Bon – both sinister and rather elaborate people – and to find them glued to the screen with a dreamy smile like a pair of infants. One sensed in faces from which the intellect had been withdrawn the love and the miracle of marriage. It's a feeling one often gets observing elderly couples watching television; it would be good to paint their portraits then – you could get the truth. Bon was wearing a cheap smock with a green Paisley motif. It was as grubby as it was crude – I wondered if she had given birth in it. She was smoking a roll-up – mean bitch. And yet she wore earrings in the shape of the Australian continent which seemed to have been cut from huge opals. Her feet and legs were completely bare as if she were reclining in her own sitting room – her "lounge" as she would no doubt have called it. She had eyes like a furtive, protective mother dog, and her dirty dress and foxy face, set against the unnaturalness of her laquered perm, created the oddest impression. I had sometimes found Bon a real pain. She prided herself on coming from "the Australian aristocracy" – or what passes for one – in Australia. Her boast always put me in mind of a response the Greek poet Constantine Cavafy made when someone asked him if he were from "the Greek aristocracy". "Aristocracy!? In Greece?!" he cried, "... to be an aristocrat in Greece is to have cornered the market in guano in the Morea in 1843!" Bonnie had cornered the market in quite another type of excrement. She could flirt and growl with pleasure like the mongrel cur she was. Then a completely innocuous remark would make her puff up with a wounded snarl like a Pig Dog that had swallowed a Cane Toad. As the interlocutor struggled to extricate himself she would cut his flounderings short with ironical wondering contempt. "Let's just drop it, shall we?" she would say, as from the depths of a much put-upon magnanimity which deserved a full revenge but was prepared to forgive out of sheer weariness and the realisation that her underlings knew no better.

Australian women "of good family" are generally like cattle dogs: they are friendly and nasty, faithful and lecherous. Above all, what you see is what you get: they're animals, they don't dissemble. That wasn't Bon. There was nothing fresh or naive about her career in barbarity. She thought she was the greatest thing since the invention of the wheel and she insisted everyone bow down to her stuck-up neurotic rudeness as to the appurtenance of genius. She let it be known that she was "sensitive" (she was about as sensitive as a dose of oral clap). In that respect she was rather like Tray Beautous' relly Klima, but Klima was popular because her naive ghastliness made her (unintentionally) striking and funny. Bon's rudeness just got on people's nerves: the narcissism it revealed sat so ill with her evident mediocrity. Strangers were nevertheless careful to propitiate her: a rumour had confirmed her as the power behind the throne. There was certainly no truth in that, but the local culture lent itself to the surmise. Like all societies ruled by a degenerate machismo, Australia is a land of rough-bitch Femelles and gangling eunuch men, their muscles as big and soft as an egg. A beehive with drones and queens and a certain dearth of workers. It's strange that modern societies like Australia and the States all have male foundation myths and yet tend to be matriarchal, while ancient ones like Greece and Rome – which prided themselves on being founded by women – were (that favourite Feminist word – God knows why) "phallocentric". Men in Australia look strong and solid: so did the cocoons Tray would pick off the Yellow Cassia Tree. Like chrysalises, they are golden and voluptuous: the torso-hugging breastplate of a Roman Emperor. And they crumble like chrysalises in their girlfriends' ugly lizard mouths. Australian males seldom make much of an impression on foreigners, for instance (our own party was something of an exception!) Despite the magnificent density, no guest is left holding more of the somnolent giant than his ectoplasm. What more evidence can you find for a slug than its papery spunk? Though the mind is supposed to suppress the bad memories of one's past and to preserve the good ones, it is only Australia's monster women you remember after a visit (Australia presenting the visitor, in this repect as in so many others, with an exact inversion of normal healthy experience).

Bonnie's family came from Mareeba on the Atherton Tableland, an important dairy farming district. Her father had extracted clarified butter from Malanda milk and made a fortune by exporting it to India and the Indian communities in the Pacific, where it is a staple of Hindu religious practices as well as of cuisine. (India was once as full of milk – and indeed of water and forests – as it was empty of people. The **Rg Veda**, composed around 2,000 BC, portrays a sub-continent that looks very like New Zealand. Now it is dry and smelly like the dick of an old kelpie). The only milk-producing state near India is Australia: Bon's Dad saw the opportunity and he took it. China has no cows, and Europe – as they say of France in Poland – "is too far away" (though not far enough for most Australians, who would rather see it in the Andromeda Galaxy, to which the Republic's experiments with nuclear fission on Muraroa Atoll are in danger of blowing the Great South Land). Bon's family, abject Donegal peasants, had become so rich that she could afford to marry a mere solicitor (as Dew then was).

I had been quite young at the time of my first meeting with Dew, and so, at the start of this second visit Down Under, I was a bit unclear as to the details of his early career. I had asked the colleague sitting next to me on the Sydney-Canberra bus to help me out. Cloke Wainberg, now Exhibitions Director of the Museum of Modern Art in New York, had once been a minor civil servant in the American State Department. In 1966, he had formed part of the suite which accompanied President Johnson when he had visited Australia to drum up support for the Vietnam War. (Brooklana Fagan had been on her way to the Aboriginal camp at La Perouse on the day of the President's visit to Sydney. A group of young activists had invited her to "listen to the spirits singing". Unfortunately, the only spirits she ended up hearing the unearthly cries of were the methylated variety: she was bearing a gift of ten bottles of the *Château-Neuf du Pape* of the Outback down Castlereagh Street just as the

119

Presidential cavalcade turned the corner. She just had time to bung a hankie in the mouth of one of the ten and light it as the last but one Cadillac hurtled by. She missed of course and "the napalm that is splashed on Vietnam like Bundy rum on a Chrissie pud" – interview with **THE SYDNEY MORNING HERALD**, 2 September 1966 – ignited a hot pie cart – soon to be a *very* hot pie cart – that Okelle de Bahn's immigrant father was pushing down King Street. Tray, meanwhile, had been among the infants – the only citizens enticeable into a chorus of approval – who had welcomed the President when he had made the nostalgic trip to his wartime headquarters in Townsville). Dewy had been introduced to Cloke in '66 as a "rising star" ("he could *rise*, baby, but he was *no star*"), and I asked Cloke what sort of pracititioner Dew had been before he took up politics. What sort of law did he specialise in, for example? ". . . *Spesh*-a-lahze eyahn?!" The eminent biographer of Picasso, who was dismembering a barbequed chook with the dexterity of an abortionist ("Ingham Chicken – *Love* 'Em" as the radio jingle kept saying), nearly choked on his tongue. (I was always fascinated by it: it was long and pink and would sway this way and that, slowly, like the tail of an angry cat). "*Spesh*-a-lahze eyahn?!" . . . *Dawg* bite cases, baby; anythang he could *git*!" I inferred from this that, from Bon's point of view, my mother's cousin could hardly have been a "catch". They had met on a tennis court near the exclusive convent to which Bon had been sent in Sydney's Rose Bay. At the beginning of Dew's political career, she had moved with him to Canberra, and, being Irish, they soon found themselves with as many children as a pair of Cane Toads.

Bon was genuinely devout, and even dragged her husband to a priest – of all people – for advice on how to stem the Kennedy-like volcano in her ovaries. (Tray once told me that in Townsville you could see piles of ten or twenty mating toads sitting on each other and dribbling with bluish syrup "like waffles at Cole's"). It was a hot day in Woden (the extraordinary names of these Canberra suburbs!), and all the doors and even the walls of the modern church had been opened to catch the wind (it was a fibreglass affair and such things are possible in Australia). Behind the altar, there was a deep blue screen with golden stars, like the Australian night. The priest had a booming voice. It was rather at odds with his appearance: his face was oily and pitted, like an orange; his eyes were fascinated. He spoke through clenched teeth, which suggested stifled passion. He introduced the couple to his "dear friend", "the Sexual Healer" – a lay specialist whom the parish had hired to assist "the people of God" in matters relating to copulation (well, that figures!) The avatar of coitus-interruptus was corpulent, like Father Twomey himself. He had bushy untidy hair, bushy black flyaway eyebrows and Vegemite-pot eyes. He looked like a possum and spoke with a poofy English accent – the first one that Bon, that pillar of the Australian aristocracy, had ever heard. (One finds these ambiguous English sophisticates in the oddest places on the Australian continent and one always wonders how they got there). "Bonnie comes from Mareeba," the priest announced, reverting at once to first name terms in the nauseating manner of clergymen. "Would you mind if I recorded this interview?" the "Sex Machine" whispered, motioning towards an oddly stained white tape-recorder that was bigger than a dansette. His round black eyes, extravagant eyebrows and sticky, bloated whiteness reminded Bon of a moth. "I am sure there are *so many* young couples who could benefit from your unhappiness." "Not as many as there are fucken enemies of *mine* who could!" Dew exploded. (No doubt he had in mind the sad case of Senator _____, father of five and a pillar of the RSL, who had poured out his troubles to a sympathetic young companion in the back room of the *Café La Mama* on Sydney's Myahgah Street, only to find his Foucault-like utterances on the complex nature of human sexuality brutally simplified in the next issue of Arkana Muckadilla's *STAR:*

> " 'LES GIRLS' *BOY SHOCKER!*
> *MINISTER FOR COMPO IN POOFTERS' BAR!*
> *WIFE DOESN'T UNDERSTAND ME - HE SAYS!*
> *MALE MALLEE ROOT TELLS ALL!"*)

The Intercrural Mage seemed to lose all interest in the couple's problems after that. He told Dewy that his "bigotry and rigidity" were "a great disappointment to the poor". (Dew and Bon never understood this statement, which "probably had something to do with Vatican 2"). All he could recommend to them was that they pursue "natural" methods of contraception from now on. "What about *un*-natural methods?" the priest suggested, with a horrible wolf-like laugh. This indiscretion appeared to unnerve his Diaghilev-resembling friend, who – appropriately enough – suddenly made himself red and stiffly erect.

Though she was never to say so, her husband's reticence had proved an equal disappointment to Bon. She was quite a little trooper in her way and had a deep need – when the demon of sulky bitchery was not upon her (and even when it was) – to "perform", to "confess", to "let it all hang out". In the days when she still took pains over her appearance, she loved nothing better than to dress up like the glittering Katherine Hepburn of **Dragon Seed** and belt out *"I Am What I Am"* with Knut Fagan (who was always similarly attired) in the *entracte* between the end of the Labor Party Conference and the moment when the leaves of tape and Acapulco Gold would flutter down like cockroaches.

On entering the Labor Party Bon had taken a vow of (intellectual) poverty (the only sort of poverty, mercifully, that ever afflicted the socialist faithful). She had entered the Monastery of Mediocrity: the one type which does *not* impose a rule of silence. Like a bad experience on LSD, a monastery cuts its inmates off from reality and makes each believe that his or her little cell is the universe and that everything that happens within is of fantastic significance. Bon was convinced that Earth and Heaven waited with baited breath to learn of the latest convolutions in her marriage and that, just as she did, "Significant Others" would sift through the history of her uterus and vagina much as augurs in the Roman Empire used to prod the giblets of a chook to discover the future of mankind – and for much the same reasons. But why condemn her for that? Gopi Panicker and Germaine Greer had made an entire career out of such "revelations", which could hardly have been a

a novel

revelation to anyone who had ever attended a housewives' coffee morning (though perhaps
Gopi and Germaine were infrequent habituées of those). Bon obviously thought, as the
Australian Tourist Board did (we had seen their giant advertisements on hoardings along
the Sydney highways) that *"Familiarity Breeds Content!"* (An odd pun for a nation to use about
itself, one might have thought – content obviously being for Australians what contempt is
for people in other parts of the world: the bread of life!) The fact is, though, that familiarity,
like heroin, breeds, not content, but a restless desire for a deeper, more perceptive
experience. Bon forgot that, when it comes to the sexual truth (or any type of truth), the
more a human being is told, the less he feels he knows, and he is obliged to pursue his
quarry to ever darker corners where, however, it still remains elusive. Such great institutions
as marriage and pornography are based on this paradox, which forms their *raison d'être* and
indeed their *modus operandi*. It comes down to the often-quoted banality that no human being
can ever really know another, and the deeper their intimacy, the less just, the more incredible
their distance, total possession of another human mind, or even one's own, being an
attribute of God rather than of man. Furthermore, Bon revealed to others, or wanted to
reveal to others, what she had formulated to herself. And there was one item on her menu
of what she coarsely termed her "coming attractions" that she was not prepared to divulge,
perhaps because she could never come to terms with it herself. Which was hardly surprising,
for if we were able to recognise, and hence analyse and neutralise distorting events, they
would not have the effect on us they do. And, conversely, it stands to reason that the
psychological traumas and problems we say we have overcome – holding their little corpses
up with pride as Italian hunters hoist murdered song birds – are precisely those which have
never done us any harm. If they had, we wouldn't have been able to locate them in the first
place. Another cliché, "Knowing Thyself" – the goal of the Greek and his philosophers – is
impossible for even the acutest intellectuals (and Bon was not one of those), self recognition
having the same effect on its subject as an X-Ray has on a tumour, in that it brings the kiss

of death as well as of life to its discovery. However, to add a further twist, Dew knew all about the incident in question, though he also found it impossible to confront. This double deception created an obstacle in Dew and Bon's marriage – which was a genuinely happy one. It was like a pearl in the flab of an oyster. Two people can look into a pearl's murky crystal ball and see different things. One sees a cloudy jellyfish with long white legs, the other a bowl of Chinese soup streaked with vermicelli like a cataracted eye. Neither could tell – especially the other – what the incident contained, or might lead to; only that it was hard and that it was there. They acknowledged it as an oyster must acknowledge a pearl – dumbly, without comprehension.

What had happened was that Bon had "bunked off" one night with Princey Dinners, a starry-eyed young Law student who worked as a Labor party volunteer in Dewy's office (this was while Popkiss was still just an MP). Bon's motives were far from clear as she was fairly pissed at the time: she had run into Princey at a party. At the end of the evening she asked the young philanthropist to take her to his bed, which he was unable to do, for, like many a Revolutionary, he lived with his mother. Instead, as he was sexually very repressed and did indeed crave an outlet (another characteristic he shared with many revolutionaries), he prevailed on Bon – the wife of an MP! – (or perhaps it was she who prevailed on him) to escort him to Telopea Park, the *Forum Romanum* of the Australian people, which was at that late hour wreathed in darkness. And there, clutching his thin, muscular waist – such a different waist from Dewy's! – she had administered an expert blow-job. They were naked (had they contemplated a more extensive exchange?) and were in full public view – though fortunately for them night had turned what was usually a playground into a monastery (the fall of the Empire had had the same effect on the *Forum Romanum*). Its openness and crowdedness had become inwardness and solitude. Night had made the park, as it had made the encounter, and as it perhaps makes all sex, a mental rather than a physical experience. (Tray told me he was aware of the same dichotomy when he passed from New South Wales into Queensland, or from Australia into England, or from the contemplation of Rome to that of Byzantium. Because, you see – if I may digress for a moment – for an Australian, living in England is like dreaming. He finds this true even when he experiences England's externals: its nature, for instance, its sky, its buildings. In his own intrusively natural environment it is the human – and his paltry works – who is the intruder, but in England, whether because of the climate, or the light, or the pitilessly human nature of everything – even of nature itself – the external world bows down to the observer and becomes a part of him – as Bon had bowed down to and become part of Princey – and an interior and intellectual part at that. This is the biggest difference between the two countries. Sydney, for instance, sitting insignificant and isolated on an overwhelming natural scene, strikes observers as a piece of rubbish would look to a jogger on a beach. The beach's pure and violent externality brings the runner's physicality and that of the rubbish to an unbearable pitch. London on the other hand – even in its physical externals – exists for Londoners and visitors purely in the mind's eye, in a crystal ball).

The lovers were like that, inside the mind as a painting – however physical – is. Dewy and Bon were a canvas by Francis Bacon: the same eyeless open head, like the baby monster in *Alien*, and a shapely male torso like a skinned yellow calf in a butcher's shop. And then there was what Walt Whitman (in his poem *"The Sleepers"*) called *"the hunger that crosses the bridge between."* Bon was gasping on a white inhaler like an asthmatic. Eating Princey's dinner reminded her of when she had first tasted Caviar: then, as now, she wondered what all the fuss was about. Brown and tasteless and sticky, it had been like sucking her husband's toes when she had been trying to cure his Athlete's Foot. Where was her Catholicism, though, when the epic southern night found her with another man's penis in her mouth? Where was consideration for her husband, or her children? In Proust's novel, the Narrator, noting the paradoxical viciousness and snobbery of declared humanitarians (socialists for instance), turns for enlightenment to the philosopher Leibnitz, who once wrote that *"it is a long way*

125

from the intellect to the heart." Fortunately, the road that leads in the opposite direction is a fairly short one. In matters of the heart (ie of the spinal cord and the urethra), people do exactly what they want, and make their moral code – if indeed they are one of the infintessimal minority that has one – fit in. Even for the most devout Christian the idea of sacrificing sexual pleasure for a religious principal – ie what the Bible insists on – is revolting, incredible, like tearing out your own eyes or arms (though that is precisely what Christ once said we should do). There is an awareness among the religious that people once *did* think it reasonable to make such sacrifices but today, whatever other sacrifices are required of a Christian (these sacrifices he is, in fact, quite willing to make), sex must not – cannot – be one of them. It's not even a matter of the religious rejecting Christ's words – they cannot even be considered in today's climate, and they *are* not. There is a pre-existent taboo on even the contemplation of sexual restraint. Not that it's a taboo – it's completely uncontroversial: it has never been challenged and it never will be.

The party from which the lovers exited that night had been hosted by Bon for Dewy's staff, so Dew soon discovered everything. Because he was unable to confront his wife, the incident assumed the hideous, limitless power of anything that remains unreal. When he tried to contemplate the incident it was like trying to contemplate the universe. He thought that if only he could come to terms with its reality, he could exorcise its force. "Familiarity breeds content!" But the more he thought of it, the more literary it became, like nature in England. The very process of ratiocination rendered it abstract. He felt comfortable with intolerable images when he thought deeply about them precisely because they were, in fact, far from real. He needed to somehow seize that tiny grain of truth, of fact, if he was ever to dislodge it. He had to learn how to come up on the incident unawares, so that he could swallow and excrete it as it was, undissolved by the gastric juices of the mind . . . He found, however, that such set pieces were always unsuccessful, just as the "cure" is when you are ill and dream that you are better. Then the sickness shoots through your sleep like a sword.

It was only when the image descended unawares – and fleetingly – that Dew saw things as they really were. Then he experienced – briefly – its vastness and physicality. It was a loathsome gallstone. The pain rocked through him as the pain of life does in a cancer person grey with morphine. Maybe that was why he had always been so cruel. He didn't look cruel. Except when he was haranguing the Chamber or a crowd, when politicians always assume a factitious personality, his manner was mild and robotic, like a pervert's.

Days of our Lives came to an end and there was a news broadcast – much to my surprise – about the final, unexpected fall – after more than twenty years – of Joh Bjelke-Petersen. His overthrow, like that of most politicians, had not been the work of "the people" – much less his enemies – but thanks to an intrigue by his closest friends, the career of a democratic leader being no different, at its conclusion, from that of any dictator. Human society differs from other societies on earth – a termite hill, for instance – in that, despite appearances, its organising principle is always individual rather than communal – there is never any true co-operation. The members of a political party – especially an Australian one dedicated (as Australian society is) to utter conformity – are like the inmates of a prison or a monastery: they give a convincing appearance of unanimity, but each is cruelly different, and each makes his own way to Heaven or to Hell. Those two places are the only real human societies where people are at one. "Why do they laugh like that?" Dew asked, clearly rattled, as scenes were relayed descriptive of Brisbane's unwholesome joy at Petersen's downfall. Few in the city – or anywhere else in Queensland – had voted for Bjelke-Petersen. He was a venal nonentity who had simply taken over and adapted to his own ends a gerrymandered electoral system that had been created to perpetuate the state's former Labor Government. One of the Brisbane Brutuses started to speak to the camera and Sir Dewy's eunuch mask broke. It was like when a demonic nestling struggles out of an egg. The Prime Minister of Australia barked out the word "Rats!" over and over again, like a peahen. It was extraordinary, but it didn't discompose his entourage at all. They were clearly used to such gems of exegesis. It was all the more bizarre in that Petersen had been a mortal enemy of Sir Dew, his regime – the corrupt right-wing government of a major province – a terrible thorn in the flesh of the corrupt left-wing national administration in Canberra. Joh had even described Dew, with the strange apt poetry of the moronic, as "an evil insulting animal"! It was an animal which, like the body of Justinian, now crawled out of its whitèd sepulchre in Joh's defence. To the extent that he had political anger at all, Dew's was focused on members of his own party, the only ones who could do him harm as an individual, rather than as the adherent of a particular, political faith. He was fairly indifferent to the enemies of "the Movement". The Australian Labor Party resembles every left-wing party in that, like the Church, it regards the perfidy of its opponents in the way it regards its own virtuous lovingkindness, ie as something pre-existent, a given. This enables certain socialists, like certain Christians, to be as nice to enemies as they are loathsome to humanity and each other. When he saw Joh disintegrate like Ikaros in a clear blue sky – and that there had been no warning, that he was at the height of his powers – Dew saw in the sweaty figurine his own transparent ghost. It was a wax image of the Prime Minister of Australia, not that of Queensland, that the gloating Brisbanites were sticking needles in, burning like Joannie of Arc. He saw the waxwork of himself from "CANBERRAWORLD" in Dimboola melting in the gutter like an iced lolly. Squashed by kiddies on the pavement like a queen termite. That was all that he, invincible, was.

Bonnie hadn't been told of the birth of my niece, Agnes, nor about my cousin Helen's new daughter, Tassie. "I'm a witch, I'm a witch!" she cried: she had suspected these things. She was a small woman but she looked like a big one because her head was big. (It sure was!) The encephalitic dwarf Truman Capote in his debauched final years. I kept on thinking of Tarkovsky's sci-fi film *Solaris*, and the shot of the gigantic baby floating in the golden ocean of the planet "Solaris" like Tray's statue of Brook. In the movie, the baby is the projection of a mental image that a Kosmonaut cherishes of his dead son, just as Joh was the embodiment of Dew's worst nightmare. The resemblance Bon bore a baby was heightened by the way she walked (for the two Olympians had now stirred from their crapper thrones and were making their way to the door). She walked like a crow – another big-headed ungainly creature. She had a crow's bandyleggèd rolling gait ("back problems, darl' "), and she kept looking fiercely for something this way and that, as a crow does. She invited me to dinner and to stay with them that night at the Viceregal Mansion.

I was taken aback by her hospitality given the diffidence I had earlier detected. I should have known better. Everyone in Australia is kind – even the nasty people – but, unlike the English, they don't think they have to put their amiability into words. (The English, on the other hand, think that they don't have to put their *hostility* into words. And they don't. They always have beautiful words for you whether they like you or hate you. An Englishman's words are completely free-standing and form their own reality, like words in the philosophy of Wittgenstein: they are never related to anything. In the same way, reality in Australia is never connected by its inhabitants to any *word*. In this respect, both nations are *sui generis*. Most of the world's nations are poems, metaphors. They are a mixture of body and soul. Each shares in a particular reality – then you have the words that the citizens have created to denote that reality. You have the local plants and animals, and you also have the steam, the smell of the natives cooking them. The Anglo-Saxon world is different. Britain is all words and nothing else: a big head without a body. Its former colony however recalls Prokopios' description of the Emperor Justinian: it's a kangaroo, a big lovely body bereft of a head: a pure, Platonic fact still waiting for its echo, its image).

Bon warned me, as we walked down the gallery stairs, that two friends might be sharing our "tea". The lady – Rhoda – was, she intimated, "rough as bags". She had been married three times – obviously a very shocking thing for a Catholic adulteress like Bon. Her last husband, "Tommo", had succumbed to the ubiquitous cancer. (This disease has reached pandemic proportions in Oz. Some think it comes from the radioactivity in Malanda milk, which is drunk all over the continent and is said to be contaminated by the French nuclear tests in the Pacific, which are conducted right opposite Bon's native Tableland. That is where the dairy cows are raised). "I couldn't 'ave done what she done," Bonnie confessed, in deference to Rhoda, "sittin' in 'is chair pooin' isself, cleanin' 'im up!" I wondered, remembering their own "Pooers", whether this was a daring deconstructionist joke.

I told a civil servant from the *"Dreaming"* tour that I would not be returning to the hotel with the other arts functionaries. I had found this young man, whose name was Russell, rather forward and naive. His face reminded me of a mudskipper. It was lipless. There was a big gap between his two front teeth and between the iris and the rim of his eye. He was drowsily effeminate, with protruding ears. "Are youse going with *them*?!" he asked, as if describing a pair of shoplifters. "Yes, Russell". "To their *hayume*?! . . ." He found it inconceivable that anyone could prefer the Prime Minister's Residence to the Koala Kontinental Metro Motor Inn – and, as I was to discover, his amazement was well founded. The Broncos were climbing into one of what looked like two red English mail vans. They were parked in front of us on Edward Terrace which was leaden, even at that late hour, with the heartrending smell of Lantana. Bon apologised for what would be the defection, from her "meat tea" (I adored this phrase) of their daughter Kommode (sometimes known as "Komodo" as in "dragon" by colleagues at the Australia Council, where she had replaced Brooklana Fagan). Kommode's hubby wouldn't be there either. They were obliged to attend a funeral in Benalla. It was the daughter of a "mate" . . . Leukaemia – a hopeful breakthrough . . . treatment in New Zealand . . . then death. "Death with a capital *Doy*," Bon observed. "The worst kind," I explained. A conversational pattern had been established. Constant anecdotes of mortality and suffering. I was limp with exhaustion.

Bon amazed me by rattling on, like Joh Bjelke-Petersen, about "Bung-it-ons" (the word sounded like an expensive luggage maker): people who "bunged it on". "Bludging" for sympathy. Or was it benefits? Dewy, who was otherwise completely silent, cackled rudely.

Perhaps he was thinking of Brook and the "Bungee-dathon" (as it was styled) at which she had met her Kismet. Now that we were outside the gallery – in which he had been the centre of attention – his tropical gown suddenly appeared heavy and bombastic, like the stole of a priest when he shakes one's hand in the sunlight outside church. Bon veered back to decay, miracle cures (her mother, improbably, from Alzheimer's Disease), brushes with the Reaper, hideous accidents, operations. Notwithstanding the "tea" she was allegedly going to provide us with, she had grabbed a mangy glutinous chicken from the exhibition buffet and was gnawing at it like a puppy. She told us she had been for a brain scan ("find anything?" Dew inquired), and (again improbably) that she felt nauseated and giddy. It was a contagious feeling. Now she was describing a neurological operation on a torn hand. The doctor had told her that he couldn't save her finger. "Positive thinking, doc," she had demurred, "I *need* that little finger!" (She was separating an oily pink cartilage from the chicken bone as she told me this). In the hospital, she had found herself, by chance, next to an injured journalist she had been "keeping an eye on". "Run over by aboriginals. Lost her spleen. Of course, her leg was smashed to bits . . . 'What you doin' in here, Bon?' . . . 'Keepin an eye on *you*, darl.' "

She continued with her self-flattering *extempore* speeches as we clambered into the back of the second of the mail vans. It was strange, and it brought to mind a beggarwoman I had once met in London, in the Euston Road. A high toned sort she was. Like the Sexual Healer, she had the puke-making voice of the school tart at Eton. How she had ended up as a panhandler, I don't know. It was as mysterious as the Healer's pilgrimage to Australia. She wore ageless black bohemian clothes – chic jumble sale stuff. She clung tragically to her left-wing dignity, her life in the 60s, when she had enjoyed status. When she had been in the in-crowd – like everybody else. As I fumbled for my change, she noticed a badge I was wearing – "LESBIANS IGNITE!" – which I had bought at a left-wing bookshop. "That sort of badge is only meant for women!" she exploded, before going into an inappropriate self-vaunting rant about her Left-Wing past. It had been a glittering interlude, as she made clear. It was exactly like the speech delivered by the Oona Chaplin journalist character in Robert Altman's film **Nashville**. "I knew some contenders!" the old has-been, or rather the never-was, proclaimed. All she knew was how to feel better than other people. In that sense a middle-class childhood had been a perfect preparation for a life of Left-Wing mendicancy (is there any other sort of Left-Wing life?) Without that unjustified pride, she would have gone mad. I felt at the time that I had found in this woman an explanation for the behaviour of an entire generation. Hers was a curious monologue, and I sadistically enjoyed it. It veered this way and that – it was grovelling in parts – but then she would be contemptuous of her benefactor, standing on her status as a cultivated person who, being "of the Left", was *better* than him, a woman whose affiliation had endowed her with a ringside seat in the theatre of History. To hear her speak, you would have thought she was one of the lice-ridden Bolshevik leaders who had used to sit in the Imperial Box in the Mariinsky Theatre after the fall of the Tsar. But she also wanted my cash and didn't want to alienate me, so her rage and self-praise were oddly qualified. I noticed the same madness in Bon, like a poor relation who has had too much to drink and – almost – forgets her place. It puzzled me. Why should the wife of the Prime Minister of the Australian Commonwealth – whose status was obviously greater than my own – betray so transparent an inferiority complex? I don't know. All I know is that I have never met an Australian, however nationalist or left-wing (in fact they're the worst), who doesn't behave in this way when an Englishman is around.

The Mail Vans – as I had thought them – were in fact very old trucks from the 1950's, with long, windowless metal cabins at the back. We were now sitting in one of these. Inside, a light sticking out of the ceiling like the bulb in the sleeping compartment of a train poured brownish ghee over a reproduction of the nudes that Tray Beautous had knocked off in the Brownbills' circular Dunny in "Capricornia". A photographic lithograph of Tray's painting of the superbly challenged ones covered all four of the truck walls, and initially made an unfortunate impression (later on I thought it marvellous). Hairy abs, like braided bread covered in poppy seeds, sloshed around me in a crayfish *bisque*. I thought myself in the back of that butcher's van in Peter Greenaway's film ***The Cook, the Thief, His Wife and Her Lover***, the one in which the adulterous lovers are imprisoned, and in which a row of pigs' heads and calves' torsos have been left, unrefrigerated, to rot. Flies cover the oily stinking pink like the black hairs on a plucked and well hung mallard. Lovely fannies and tummies are hairy too.

The "Moveable Feast" in which we now started to lurch and jolt was in fact a very old "Shit-Cart". Sir Dewy, following his unerring nose for coprophile memorabilia, had bought both vehicles as antiques from Karratha Shire Council in Western Australia, where they had only recently been decommissioned. (Tray Beautous told me later that "Dunny Can Vans" – as Australians hail them – were still *au courant* in the Townsville of the 1960s, when he was growing up). The cubicle container in the back of these trucks, where I was making my second appraisal of Beautous' work that night, had customarily been filled to the brim with sloshing human shit (it still was!). Manned by aborigines – poor darlings – who hung off the side of them like little black Bengalis clinging to an overcrowded Calcutta tram, they were always painted bright red to warn people of their approach – not that they needed to be warned. Like "ambulances" in Philip Larkin's poem of that name, they had *"threaded the loud noon"* of Australia's cities until about 1975, when the last suburbs had been converted to piped sewerage. Citizens affected not to see when the big red shit-cart bobbed along against the atomic white of the tin roof and the ever present gums, sterile, feminine and calligraphic, like trees after Hiroshima. They might have been Gestapo trucks in Hitler's Germany pulling up at innocent Jewish bungalows for all the notice people took as the bizarre galleons docked. They would explode like pregnant Red-Back spiders. Little black spiders scurried this way and that, emptying cesspits and backyard dunnies into the back of the cart, often with no more than what looked like a dustbin.

Inside, the van was like the carriage of Catherine the Great, the Eighteenth Century Empress of Russia, who would zip around in a wooden box as big as a house that sped over the snow on skids. The Empress Cath and her lover would always tuck themselves up in bed throughout each journey, keeping their tootsies warm by resting them on heated stones. It was oven-like in the Shit-Cart and Dewy and Bon, perhaps to express their feelings about the dead historian, now cooled their unclad feet on the aboriginal skulls that Brooklana Fagan had made a great hoo-hah about retrieving from England, those of an Eighteenth Century aboriginal chieftain and his wife. The bones of the hallowed pair had been taken to the UK in triumph after the chief's anti-British revolt had been quashed by the Eighteenth Century colonial authorities. Pemulwuy had, of course, been the leader whom Brookee, alluding to Mourtzophlos, had parodied in Okelle de Bahn's *City of Abalone*. "Bukky Gawina" was his spouse. The dunny can van, red like the porphyry sarcophagus of a Byzantine Emperor, was an obviously fitting receptacle for their dust.

We were moving very slowly and swaying, like a wooden Queensland house being moved from one group of stilts to another on the back of a truck – another familiar *aperçu* from Beautous' Townsville childhood – though a better analogy might have involved the scarlet-painted state barge of the Byzantine Emperor. Feeling queasier than ever, I asked Bon how Cynthia Brownbill was. Part of the reason for my coming to Australia was to see Cyn one last time. My Mum and Dew were Cynthia's (much) younger distant cousins (Cyn was sixteen years older than the Prime Minister), and Dew had been immensely impressed with Tray's painting *"The Human Race"* when he and Bon had been summoned up to Noosa some years previously to collect the old dear and take her back with them to Canberra. Her condition had deteriorated. Now that Bev realised that Cyn was no longer conscious of the cruelty she delighted in inflicting on her, she saw no point in further tolerating the old girl's presence. ("Strewth," she complained to Bon, after she had discovered her faithful retainer's limitations as a scullery maid, "the old cunt even did a number two in the Waring blender!").

Piers, who had the backbone of a *Mange Tout*, had reacted with predictable vigour to the prospect of his ex-wife's dismissal into the loving hands of her kinsman, the extent of whose philanthropy was perfectly well known, at least to his family. "Well, old boy, I'm sure you could take better care of her than we can!"

Dewy, who always had one eye on his "BO" (for "Box Office": the surprising extent to which the voters regarded him as altruistic – significantly he often translated it as meaning "Boongs Okay?"), decided to make the best of a bad job. He went north with Bon and the Broncos in a blaze of secrecy, taking about as much care to hide his grief as Diana, Princess of Wales. When the Press asked him if installing the imbecile *Chez lui* wouldn't represent a burden, he replied, elegantly, that he was as pleased to get back this "bonza old girrule" as the Greeks would be if "the Brits" were to return their "lost marbles". Cyn, who really had lost her marbles, was sitting next to Dew at the Press Conference at the time, panting like a happy dog. Her foamy tongue was hanging out like a piece of under-fried bacon. The forest of mikes in front of her resembled a mangled bike. Her head moved slowly from one of its jutting limbs to the next, like a Praying Mantis gnawing at her husband. She had a Praying Mantis's vacant frogspawn eyes, its ominous rigidity. She stank of poo. While Dewy rubbed his scented temples and fiercely closed his eyes in what he thought was a "philosophical" manner she took a sharp swig from his gigantic bottle of *"La Plus Belle Lavende"*. Suddenly, she cried out . . . Nobody could tell what she was trying to say. Old people are like that, strangers in our barbarous world, just as beautiful life-like statues, remnants of a very recent, but lost, civilization were strangers in the suddenly awful world of the early Middle Ages. Even though the existence of many of these statues, like the life-times of the elderly today, spanned the new age and the old, and so were a bridge to a better past, the Byzantines – to talk only of the *most civilized* of the mediaeval peoples – regarded them with horror, as though the Classical World in which so many of the oldest early Byzantines had been born had never existed. Or if it had, as if the mental universe they had absorbed as children had been extinguished in their minds as utterly as by the lobotomist's knife . . . *"Stocheion"*, the word for "statue" in mediaeval Greek, also means "ghost". The verisimilitude of classical plastic art was beyond (they imagined) what a human could create, and so, as we have seen, the Byzantines believed that three-dimensional portraits were the outward excretions – the chrysalises if you like – of evil spirits who did not so much inhabit the idols as inspire them. The statues were the opposite of man, whose eternal spirit inhabited a transient home, and they weren't "Galateas" either, into which life had been breathed by a conqueror artist. This accounts for the fury with which the mediaeval Christian attacked his ancient art. By reducing "eternal" marble to lime or dust he was miraculously bringing its "eternal" spirit to an end too. He could crush the metaphysical with the physical. But many an image remained to walk the earth, and the ghosts inside them would often cry out in a voice as mysterious to the new age as the voice of the elderly – unhinged or not – is to us today . . . But this is to speak tautologically. If the new and "iron" age had still understood the language of the Age of Gold, it would never have destroyed both it and its denizens in the first place. Similarly, if modern man still held the "torch handed down by his fathers", he would forbear to treat the last generation to be touched by Judaeo-Christian civilization – the old – with such cruelty.

In 391 AD, twenty-five years before a pious mob tore Hypatia – like Bev and old, defenceless woman – to pieces, we read of Christians in Alexandria becoming enraged by the mysterious voices emanating from the statue of Serapis, a vast wooden idol in the main temple of the city. A mob of them attacked it. Serapis' worshippers had warned that if his effigy were even touched, the universe would return to its primaeval chaos, but when a soldier lashed at the cheek with an axe, all that happened was that a head toppled to the ground and a horde of rats spurted from a cavity, like Abos from an Aussie shit-cart. Then the looters discovered a cubbyhole in Serapis' chest – just like the belly of the Trojan Horse in which we were now riding. They realised that this was where the "god" would hide while he was hollering his oracles through a silver tube. The temple was razed to its foundations and Theophilos, the Patriarch of Alexandria, built a church to St John on its ruined podium. It was in this church that Cyril, Theophilos' nephew (and his successor as bishop) inspired the mob – perhaps the very same one – to race out of the precinct of the former *S erapeion* and pounce on Hypatia, last of the Greek philosophers. They dragged her from her carriage and hacked her into slimy *goujons*, burning her carcass in the town's main square, the very fate they had visited on Serapis. There are many other examples of unfamiliarity (with what had been one's own culture) breeding anything but "content".

Cassiodorus, for instance, writes, in 526 AD, that when gold thieves in early mediaeval Rome set about dismantling the city's ancient gilded statues with their iron (age) hammers, the idols would "cry out" under the blows, like Cyn when Bev would strike her. The Night Watchmen – the *"Vigiles"*- though ignorant of their language, would none the less rush over to save them. (Cyn, unfortunately, had no such helpers at Noosa, though there were always plenty of witnesses). The Western Roman Empire had only just been destroyed by German barbarians (the Eastern survived as Byzantium). Theodoric, one of the German leaders, had mounted the throne of Italy, though, as he was completely illiterate, he ruled through his Chancellor, Cassiodorus, an educated Roman Quisling. Cursed, like Bev, with a naive nostalgia for culture that would have been repugnant to any real highbrow (prejudices which are both very common, by the way, in modern Australia), Theodoric did everything in his power to preserve the material remains of the ancient past. Such a project would never have occurred to the erudite Romans of the time, whose families had actually *created* these masterpieces. Saint Gregory, for instance, a contemporary Pope and the greatest intellectual of his age, was the last surviving member of the *Anicii*, Rome's oldest and most exalted family. He gave away all the family's money, turned their palace on the Coelian into a monastery, and, in his writings, declared himself indifferent to, sometimes even exultant over, the ruin of the "pagan" city around him. An intellectual moves with the times, which

137

is to say, with the ideas. It is only the philistine, cut off from contemporary intellectual currents (which by the Sixth Century had condemned all "pagan" survivals) who can afford to take the purely aesthetic view. (Just as we can, looking at these events from the Twentieth Century and imagining that temples, say, appeared as harmless to Gregory – for whom the old religion was a recent and active force – as they look to us, we who – to paraphrase Guiseppe di Lampedusa on modern Italian Catholicism – *"are too unbelieving even to be* anti-*Christian"*). I believe that subjectivity, being real, spontaneous and unchanging, bequeathes a clearer view of the created environment than the "objective" approach that everyone favours. "Objectivity," in any age, owes more to the reigning ideology than to detachment. One need only consider our own epoch, and Political Correctness, its presiding genius – the god which is, according to the wise, the only deity that has ever existed (for won't the heavens fall if we so much as breathe on its throne?) – the great hollow sawdust gateau in which so many unclean and indistinguishable mammals have found a home – to realise that. When censorship forces an intellectual to put an orthodox fable from above where an honest response should be, the art and analysis of his era will contain nothing that reflects the world around him. In an era such as ours, it is time to look, for a real witness, to the remarks, such as they are, of the "ordinary" people . . . Anyway, it was the bloodstained tribesman Theodoric, not Gregory, "last of the Romans," who hired the *Vigiles* that guarded the statues of the saint's family. And that was not the only measure he took to prevent the people of Rome from vandalising their own city. (Does this phenomenon not bear perfect witness to how a community can become estranged, in a time like the Sixth Century – or our own – from the past, which is to say, from itself? Would the people of London, for instance, pull down half of Kensington? Well nowadays, of course, they almost certainly would).

"Petrick *[Patrick]*, Nana Brownbill doesn't actually *live* with us anymore. Y'see, she's tairbly SICK!" "Nana" was La Popkiss' revolting shorthand for Cynthia, though, needless to say, the old pest was certainly neither her nor Dewy's grandmother. I thought Bon looked shifty, or shiftier than usual, as she unburdened herself of this, though it was actually impossible to tell, as her face, like that of the Husky it resembled, had a permanent air of both naivety and criminality. However, I definitely detected unease, and I tried to help her out by changing the subject. I reproached myself but I was fairly indifferent to Cyn's misfortunes (as even the most devoted loved one can be: it is a grave crisis indeed involving the extended family member that penetrates the Brazil nut-like carapace of his non-nuclear sibling). So I stared pointedly out of one of the tiny porthole windows in the truck's flank and gushed over a particularly hideous Spanish-mission-style villa. It flew by like a galah, lit up by arc lights concealed in its swimming pool. It burned with pink stucco like a prawn cocktail. "That's a lovely house, isn't it?" I said. "The man in there hung isself," Bon observed. He had been unable to endure the cancer that had struck him – in the midst of all his wealth. "It started in 'is stomach but it came out 'is neck. Ate half his face away. The smell was awful. They had a daughter and my mate Kahra had to help her lift 'im up to the bedroom when 'e got stuck in the dunny down the first floor." The daughter was "a Catholic girl. Couldn't stand anyone touchin' 'er body. Wouldn't go to the doctor. They found her in the house. Died of a strangulated hernia. Unmarried. Taught music at the convent. Didn't turn up a couple a days. They broke the door down. Lyin' on the kitchen floor like a possum. Dead a waik. Smelled like a boongs' picnic!"

"Bon, why isn't Cynthia living with you?" I asked, suddenly forgetting myself in the midst of this carnage. I immediately regretted it. Bon looked like an injured bird when someone approaches it and it realises that it cannot fly away. Her eyes betrayed the same terror. One universe – as in the bird's case the world of morality, humanity – had invaded another which had no understanding of it. Which usually found itself protected from it by an impenetrable if transparent screen. It was clear that Bon inhabited, like a queen termite, a world that was biologically amoral and sycophantic, where nobody had ever dreamed of approaching her in a manner that implied criticism. Like an injured magpie, all Bon's experience could prepare her for was the idea that all creatures are maleficent and that, by framing the question, I had meant to do her harm. But even had she been able to read my intentions correctly, I would still have been at fault. It isn't wise to dislocate the feelings of "difficult" people. Mounting a challenge they cannot deal with in polite, rational terms simply renders the pull of the conventions – to which they have a great but feeble attachment – invalid. It drives them back into the mad champagne air of their native forest – where anything can happen. Like Moray Eels or nesting crows, such individuals are only safe when they are not at home. Bon's now livid, hateful face showed a wonderful fluency and confidence I had never seen before.

"Petrick, I *tiled* yew that Nana Brownbill was SICK. Howdja expect us to look afta herr in our *hayume*?! We've got the fuckin' President of Indernoysza stayin' fer toy and some old sheila wanders in moanin' like Joannie Sutherland with a boil the size of a rock melon on her twat. We *troy* to make polite conversation; then – how would you be – she blinks like a cockie and shits all over the axminister! Without so much as a by your leave. It's not a matter of ex-kyuze *moy* your excellency: djamoind? Just stands there – squittin' like a heifer!" "I'm terribly sorry," I averred, "I really didn't mean to . . ." "The old dear kept on shittin' er guts out. She troyed to wash her sheets and undies so *oy* wouldn't foind 'em. In *moy* tropical aquarium! The rainbow carp thought the *'Exxon Valdeez'* had hit the fuckin' Barrinjoey Lighthouse! Her insoids was rotten, soy, *rotten*!" . . . I couldn't help thinking at this pass of Arius – like Cyril a Fifth Century patriarch of Alexandria. Arius created one of the most damaging heresies in the early Byzantine world. *The Chronicle of Theophanes Confessor*, which was composed in 814, records that, in 335 AD, an attack of diarrhoea brought Arius to a public latrine in Constantinople – he was in the capital trying to get the Byzantine Emperor to embrace his heresy. Here, instead of liquid ordure, he ended up expelling his stomach, intestines, life itself:

"Swifter than a word, divine justice overtook Arius, cutting him off from this life and the life to come in a place suited to the filth that flowed from his tongue!"

"And your uncle's no help," said Bon. "Who had to get her into *The Lovely Aujourdh'ui Veterans Memorial Nursing Home*? Moy! *Hoy* won't even go and visit the old bastard."

In connecting Bon with her forbidden self I had thrown her, like a tidbit, into a raucous owl's nest of resentments. In the sunny conscious world, each resentment had its own cause, effect – and nature – like birds on the branches of a tree. Deep inside the hollow bough, at source, where the indistinguishable cannibal nestlings lived, all the resentments were interchangeable, and if reference were made to one bone of contention, the response it elicited was likely to refer to to quite another. History is full of the phenomenon. For instance, Eugénie, Empress of France, was told in 1870 that her husband, the Emperor Napoleon III, had been defeated by the Prussians at a battle in far-off Sedan. Consequently, the French had, in shame and rage, risen up and destroyed their corrupt régime. They were now rampaging through the Paris streets below, baying for her blood. The Empress was, like Byzantine Theodora, a seething *Femelle* beneath her airs. She made no comment on her husband's political or military acumen. Instead she startled the pampered queens, her *poupées*, who had only ever seen *Madame* piss-elegant and full of shit, by spurting a geyser of detestable obscenities and criticising the penis *royale*'s Odysseus-like hegiras in foreign cunt. Her response when the courtiers urged her to flee (the mob were already dismantling the palace railings) was equally beside the point:

"I feared nothing [she later wrote] **except falling into the hands of viragos, who would defile my last hours with something shameful or grotesque. I imagined them lifting my skirts, I heard ferocious laughter . . . "**

Dewy said nothing as Bonnie ranted on. He just smiled with the absorbed, self-important look a teenage boy has when his mother is discussing his problems on TV. Mum, inveigled into a documentary or chat-show, has the foolish candour that comes from believing that "fame" has bestowed permanent protection, permanent invincibility, that this experience is the epiphany for the audience, for mankind, that it is for her and her son, an epiphany which which will justify, cancel, the shame, the family consequences. Their crucifying folly is in fact totally irrelevant to those watching, less important than the potatoes on a TV dinner. They've ruined their lives for nothing. How strange people are, unable to see that once we cross the line that separates our world from that of other people, we cease to be significant! To others, we are so many battery chooks, but we fuss around our little nests as if they formed the Universe, with each of us sitting at the centre like God in a mediaeval painting of heaven.

Dewy began, for the first time, to look at me with interest. He had the mocking *castrato* eyes of the Buddha. "I wouldn't go back after I saw her with the doll," he said. This upset Bon even more. The cabin was swinging now, the truck was getting up speed, and the naked figure paintings around us were moving. They jolted against each other in uncertain light. Muscular columns swayed like punchbags. They were clusters of bananas in a cyclone on a Townsville plantation. Hairy yellow muscles, drooping, drizzling willies, welts and tits were the upside-down ears of maize that formed the banana stalagtites. Each swatch was a statue of the Diana of Ephesus with her many breasts, the beaded swarm that surrounds a straying Queen Bee. My mind drifting, I felt I was witnessing, on the walls of our truck **Les Papillons de la Nuit**, the last ballet that Nijinsky ever composed (the great dancer became insane, though, before he could perform it). According to the **Memoirs** of his wife Romola," **Les Papillons**" -

> "*was to be a picture of sex life, with the scene laid in a* Maison Tolérée. *The chief character was to be the owner, once a beautiful* Cocotte, *now agèd and paralysed as a result of her debauchery; but, though her body was a wreck, her spirit was to be indomitable in the traffic of love. She would deal with all the wares of love, selling boys to girls, youth to age, woman to woman, man to man!*"

What a different type of artist – a film-maker – once called **The Spirit of the Beehive** lived in *"The Human Race"*. Cynthia was that spirit, condemned to a living death like the pariahs in Beautous' painting. It was easy to pick her out. She was the agèd Madam (a role she had played to perfection at "Capricornia"), a shambling mummy (Aldour's), her breasts and bandages the sticky flaps on a column of kebab meat.

"You know what he's talkin' about, dontcha Patrick?" Bon seemed terribly agitated now, terribly upset. (I admired her for it). "In that Hayume they giv'em dolls – big ones like Cabbage Patch Dolls. The old dears don't know whether they're spittin' or shittin' – they got about as much sense as a chook in a Chinese dinner. They giv'em dolls to focus their attention, see, giv'em somethin' to love, to talk to. It remembers them how to spoik. Reminds 'em that they're yewman!" "But surely, *human* visitors would better ensure that?" I tactlessly observed. "But that's just the point, soy? *Oy* have to go and visit her. He would no more go near her than put his piece-and-vegemite on a poofter's hankie! . . . Got a right shock he did once. Went over there and found her talkin' away to a doll. Mesmerised she was – like some old bastard tryin' to teach a Mynah how to say 'fuck'! Gave her a wide berth after that. It was enough to put a Croc off a Coons' Ceilidh – as they say on the Murumbidgee. He told me so hisself." I thought of Tsarist Russia's last Prime Minister, Protopopov, gabbling away to the icon on his desk, and the edicts of the Iconoclastic Emperors of Byzantium (who ruled the Empire between 717 and 843 AD), who justified their proscription of images by reminding their subjects of how benighted Christians had lugged along life-sized cut-outs of saints to church to interrogate as God-parents and witnesses at weddings. I remembered, too, the talking statues of the early Middle Ages (of which Cynthia was one), and the strange way in which Protopotov's employer, Tsar Nicholas II, had once been warned of the murder of his uncle, the Grand Duke Serge, Governor of Moscow. The Cassandra in question was one of the "Holy Fools" who attended on his wife, Alexandra. The Empress was extremely pious – a nurse in the First World War – and had a weakness for the company of what Walt Whitman (in his poem *"The Sleepers"*) calls:

"the gashed bodies on battlefields, the insane in their strong-doored rooms, the sacred idiots!"

One of these, Mitya Kolyaba, was a retarded peasant of nearly eighty, who was said to have the gift of direct communication with God. He was an epileptic and during a seizure was *"completely overcome by religious hysteria"*. The Seer was made even more formidable by the fact that he was a cripple and had two stumps in place of arms, which he waved wildly in the air during his ecstasies to a timpano of *"painful gasps"* and *"a terrifying howling and spitting"*. As a lackey once noted: *"One had to have extremely strong nerves to endure the presence of this imbecile."* Shortly before the Seventeenth of February 1905, when Revolutionaries threw a bomb at the Grand Duke Serge's carriage in Red Square, reducing him to the same bite-sized fragments that had dignified Hypatia's carriage after the Christians (also millennarian rebels) had done their stuff in the main square of Alexandria, the Tsar ran into Mitya on an offical visit to Saratov. The Seer was standing on a riverbank with a crowd of other peasants carrying a huge ugly doll which he struck violently as he screamed the word "Serge! Serge!" . . . It was whispered that Cynthia had shrieked "Brooklana!" at *her* doll on the day that Dewy had gone to *"The Lovely Aujourd'hui"*, a day which fell exactly a week before Mrs Fagan's fatal accident, for which the Prime Minister, mysteriously, was as mystically prepared as his informant.

Bon was going on now about how the staff at *"The Lovely Aujourd'hui"* had stolen Cyn's wedding and engagement rings. "How could anyone do that to a defenceless person?" It was extremely galling as a brief crisis of conscience had prevented her from taking them herself, which is just what Cyn "would have wanted".

The truck, which had inexplicably spurted forward, began, as abruptly, to brake: I almost found myself in Bon's lap, which is quite funny when you think about it.

Q AND A

When we got out we were right in the middle of the city and yet the atmosphere, outside, was exquisitely suburban; it reminds me of descriptions Tray Beautous later gave of tropical nights in North Queensland. Quiet, peripheral and holy, the extreme and strange land was suddenly safe, European, old, as if there had never been catatonic Bush there only twenty or eighty years before. A child like Beautous who had been born into this recent and artificial world, knowing only it, growing up with it, would have looked at his natal suburb and seen something as redolent and immemorial as Rome. Everywhere on Earth has always been old because mankind has always been young. Whatever new environment a child enters, whether by birth or other means, and whatever it intrinsically is, it is always like a painting by Paul Klee: venerable and beautiful, rich with unknowable, because (or so the child thinks) *ancient* associations. Whatever new environment an adult enters, on the other hand, is like a painting by de Chirico: it is always old, too, but in a different way, because the new in it can be neutralised, explained away by the adult's past, and by his awareness of mankind's past. The past which an adult confronts is a past that is known, defined and (being the past) rejected. The past that impregnates the adult world is also a limited past, as big or as small as the knowledge and experience of the individual. The illimitable, unknowable past that opens up to us in childhood, in which we take so much pleasure, of which we are far more aware, then, than the "limitless future" (consciousness of which is a retrospective adult gloss), soon closes up and is lost to us. And yet I would say that this is the real past, full as it is of human and divine power, based as it is on a correct estimation (albeit an imaginative one) of man's potential.

The crickets whirred and Dewy and Bon, accompanied by a shoal of dark Broncos, made for a steepish bank and a cosy horizon of lit brick like the comforting illuminated entrance of a hospital. The sky was fresh, transparent like stained glass, dark, but lit from behind. The moon was as big and new as a golden carp. It was pale pink and veined with pithy halva like a peeled orange. Clear stars with long thin arms shivered like Daddy Long-Legs. We entered the Viceregal Mansion through what appeared to be its garage (the shit-cart, though, had not been parked there). Bricks had been left out of its walls in a regular, crossword pattern, creating a colander effect. Bon showed me the electric saws and other fiendish machines with which she and Dew, forsaking the assistance of minions, had executed home improvements and periodically ripped themselves up. "Now you won't mention Cyn again, will you?" she said compulsively, as if her fanaticism were my own, "we can go and visit her tomorrow, after church".

The inside of Australia's ***Domus Augustana*** resembled that of many posh Aussie homes: the walls were of raw unplastered brick and the floors of polished, uncarpeted wood. These interiors – like those of a gymnasium – epitomise Australia in that they seem unfinished. The idea for them originates in a European idea of luxury and completeness but they don't go the whole way. They don't need to go the whole way. In the prehistoric social and climatic conditions of Australia a house, even a luxurious one, even, in this case, the most important house, is finished once it is only half finished. You are aware that you are in an easier, less exacting climate – in every sense of that word. The lunatic heat and the babyishness born of an untamed nature mean that you expect less of the human spirit. (Australian books, for instance, all look like coffee-table books; they have huge print like that in books for people who are going blind). Australians, unless they had been, as I had, in a more complex society, were apt to see this sort of morgue-like cretinism as the ultimate in finish and refinement, as if there were no haunted, layered cosy interiors anywhere in the world. There was a massive difference, for example, between the authentically Australian bowels of the Prime Minister's residence and the "Surrey-meets-Palm Springs" style of "Capricornia", whose presiding genius could as easily have been Fergie, Duchess of York, as Beverly Brownbill, avid reader of the European editions of ***HOMES AND GARDENS***. It was a chasm that separated the grim, airy Versailles of Louis XIV from the more intimate, homely Versailles of Louis XV. The subdivided rooms of Louis Quinze, like those at "Capricornia", had been turned into something juicy and pungent, like the cloaca of a roast chicken. The only concessions to arterial plaque in this, though, the *Palatium Sacrum* of the Australian people, were sheepskin rugs and pieces of outdated modern furniture – 1970s-style leather chairs and sofas, their pillowy black flesh like that of the cave-men they dig out of peat. Here and there one saw the stuffed corpse of a favourite Bronco whose neck, I presume, had been broken on some rugger field, his glass eyes staring from the taut laquered face of an old fag-hag. These were used as mannikins for the gorgeous dresses by Rykiel and Courrèges that Bon no longer wore, and which now, like the Eighteenth Century clothes you see in museums, had lost their inner bloom, their life, making you wonder how they could ever have rejoiced in the tropical flesh, the inner architecture, they display in photographs and paintings. Like classical statues, classical *Coûture* draws its life, not from its physical components, but from a tutelary ghost. Once that has fled, a suite of clothes reminds you of a dead seagull. It has no inner life. It is oppressively dirty.

Bonnie and Dew's pictures, some rather good, were all by Australian masters. There was a vast painting of World War II aeroplanes in one of the rooms. All different types of planes, rendered colourfully and exactly against a flat unvarying sky. They were butterflies in a case, immobile and yet caught in an attitude of movement, like those peacock-coloured weevil-things that Kandinsky used to swat wriggling in cobalt blue. I later found that these canvases had been plundered from public collections. So one wondered at the taste of the Australian public - and of the imperial couple. Several, which dated (like the aircraft) from the 1940s, were repressed, "justifiable" studies of the male body. One by Donald Friend of *"Soldiers Guarding Jeeps on a Raft"* was quite outrageous. You find the same thing in Arthur Dobell's war work, but nothing quite as prurient. I made a comment and was assured by Bon that this material had all been assembled by Knut Fagan. It clearly displeased her. Why then did the Popkisses retain it?

147

We were led into a room that really did look like a gymnasium and perhaps was one. It had very high walls, once again of livid unplastered brick, and high windows, like a Roman basilica. Just as in the *Basilica Nova* at Rome, whose apse had once held a giant statue of the Emperor Constantine (you can still see its ten foot high head on the *Campidoglio*), a gigantic nude statue of Dewy sat enthroned in front of the furthest wall: very generously proportioned it was, too! It had been cast in cement (you could see by its rough, unpleasing surface) and was painted in an androgynous pink that made one think of false-teeth. I noticed a fissure in its neck. The head had originally been Knut's but Dewy had replaced it with his own profile. Brooklana had compared this, at the time, to the way Caligula had swapped the head of a statue of Jupiter with his own head in Rome's main temple. But partisans of Dewy (there were a few – a very few –*"intelligents"*) said it was, on the contrary, like Vespasian's beheading of the huge statue of himself which Nero, a perverse predecessor, had erected near the Colisseum in 65 AD. The good Vespasian had crowned the newly headless torso with the bonce of the benevolent Sun God . . . And why not? Was not Sir Dew "the Sunburnt Country's" *Roi Soleil?* Another change Dew had made was that he had seated the Colossus on a dunny rather than on Knut's curule chair.

As in the *Aula Regia* (Audience Hall) of the Imperial Palace in Rome in the late Third Century, the longer walls of this chamber were lined with nude male statues. They were erect three-dimensional casts which Knut had had made of particularly charming Broncos while each was still in his prime. Knut's rationale had been imparted by Tray Beautous, whose whole artistic project was the rescue for posterity of what was finite, beautiful, unique to the age . . . Sir Vidia Naipaul has written that *"the world we inhabit . . . is always new"*. Each generation is offered beautiful things that have never been seen before, and will never be seen again. Unless we record them – preferably while they are at their peak – the one-off voyage that their uniqueness has made through our era will be in vain. Knut had got the best of his Broncos to walk, naked, into a wall of wet concrete, and then to back themselves into another such wall. When these walls dried he caused them to be joined together so that the reliefs on each, united, would form holograms of each model into which wet clay was poured. The process was the same as in Pompeii, where the flesh of transient lava-clad corpses has rotted to leave shapes which, when filled with plaster, have served as midwives to eternity and a metaphor for the artist himself.

Once Knut had created his statues, the sandwiches of cement were divided back into rectangular slices and used as walls for a Dunny – a memorial to his family - which Knut had set up on The Strand in Townsville at the same time as the statue of Brook was being built on Magnetic Island. It was a monument modelled – in both form and concept – on the *Ara Pacis Augustae* ("Altar of Augustan Peace") in Rome, the memorial which the Senate put up to the Emperor Augustus's family on the Via Flaminia in 9 BC. (One can view the remains of this altar to this day. Its design *does* make it resemble a public convenience). The official title of the Knut Fagan shit-house was the *"Ara Pacis Faganoi"* (an apt legend), but it was also known, demotically, as *"The Boulder where a Bum Cunt Pees"*. The Roman *Ara* was a marble box whose walls displayed a relief of Augustus' family in procession. Townsville's was a cement box whose walls were indented with impressions of aroused sportsmen, the moulds for the statues that now graced Dew's mansion . . .

But to return to the *Aula Regia* . . . In Knut Fagan's day, light in what was, in effect, the Vice-Regal Banqueting Hall had been provided by jets of lighted gas that had blow-torched from each of the naked statues' phalluses. Dewy's mutilation of these one drunken night (*"filthoy disgusting poofter!"* – though he kept and caressed the severed heads) had signalled the start of his anti-Knut revolt. (In Plato's Greece, as Brook was keen to point out, the "fascist" plotter Alkibiades' decision to smash the erections on the statues of Hermes in Athens had been this "proto-Pinochet's" declaration of war on the city's democratic government). Dewy had not, however, used Knut's destruction as an excuse to demolish the *"Ara Pacis Faganoi"*

– the fate he had visited on the monster on Magnetic Island. "To do so would be a *croym agensst yew manitee*," he gurgled – thinking of shit, as usual.

"Well, wodgya think of moy doyning room, Petrick?" Bon was digging me in the ribs. She was already much happier. She felt no more enthusiasm for the prevailing décor than I did, but her question was a breathless expression of lightened feelings. Now that she had extruded me, like a kidney stone, from her inner world, she could be nice again, or what passed for nice *chez* Popkiss. She could reverse into the industrial forms of politeness (now I really am making her sound like a denizen of Versailles, but you know what I mean). Her feelings were no longer engaged, she could relax. She probably found, as I did, that the conversation attendant on intimacy is as unpleasant as that attached to enmity: it forces one to dig a new channel for one's feelings in full view of others, like Odysseus in Hades when he had to dig a trench and fill it with his own blood for the souls of the dead to drink. Otherwise they wouldn't speak to him, couldn't speak to him, any more than a friend or enemy or family member will if we hesitate to a perform a similar sacrifice. With ordinary exchanges, such as Bon and I were now enjoying, one's spirit, the world we always carry within us, the real world, our heaven or hell, remains mute, unseen. The blood stays inside your own body, following the same immutable channels in veins and arteries as the stale pleasantries you swap. You can have a nice revery while dictating quite unrelated words to a dear sweet friend. You can "keep your feelings to yourself", the only place where they give you any pleasure.

I told Bon that the room was beautiful, but what I actually felt was that it was far too brightly lit. Down both of its longer sides I saw tables covered in white rice-paper, like tables at a children's party. There were cheap folding chairs for each diner. In the middle of the room, a group of guests were standing chatting to each other with that absurd look of fanatical intimate absorption, oblivious to surroundings, that characterises people with drinks in their hands. There was the usual sound of a gull colony, pierced, as in a gull colony, by sudden hilarious cawings. During the Knut Fagan régime, flickering flames and shadows would have made the statues in the room look real, or appropriate at least. They would have called up the torch-lit shades of the cella of an ancient temple – the *Serapeion* perhaps. Flowering surfaces and flushed stone faces emerging from darkness would have appeared the natural excrescences of the room, as coral appears to snorklers. The harsh electric light that now bore down on everything made the partygoers visibly black and solid: they looked like basket-ball players. It turned the statuary into something fragile and dirty and totally divorced from its environment, as if it were installation art in a gallery, the sort that so rapidly appears decrepit.

Les Majesty, Australia's Foreign Minister, was the first person to whom I was introduced. Broncos (new ones?) were breezing through the crowd offering the guests nibbles and drinks. Each was wearing a beehive-shaped tiara made of a rugby ball taped with three tinsel crowns. "Good Catholic boys!" whispered Bon; the first time she had ever made a joke. The Broncos were naked but for jockstraps: these resembled *"Commedia dell'Arte"* masks, with bulbous eyes and a long curling nose intended to suggest the head and proboscis of a butterfly. The Broncos also wore yellow muslin wings which protruded from the nape of their backs. They were attached to a sort of corset. The Broncos' "uniform" was another hangover from Knut Fagan, who had put the male stewards on QANTAS in it. In official Australia, as in *Ancien Régime* France, the staff in every official institution – Australia's Versailles, Australia's *"La Muette"*, Australia's Fontainebleau – wore a livery unique to their own place of work. Indeed, just as Madame du Barry, the prostitute who became Louis XV's *"Maîtresse déclarée"*, insolently appropriated the dress peculiar to Versailles flunkeys for her own staff at Louveciennes, a chateau some distance from Versailles that her royal lover had made her a present of, Beverley Brownbill had pulled family strings and was allowed to put her cooks and gardeners at "Capricornia" in an official QANTAS livery. And why not?

At "Capricornia", to paraphrase Horace Walpole's eye-witness account of the home life of a Du Barry -

> *"This street-walker . . . received the homage of mankind . . . The Papal Nuncio, and every ambassador but he of Spain . . . waited on her, and brought gold, frankincense and myrrh."*

The costumes of what were now Dew and Bonnie's staff had been delineated by Knut with a characteristic prudence and taste. *"Psyche"*, the word for butterfly in what Knut called "Gin Creek" (ancient Greek), can also mean "soul", and the QANTAS livery was meant to suggest a soul launched from its earthly cocoon into the sunburnt air of Paradise. The papal helmet was supposed to evoke "a fragment of chrysalis".

Butterfly metaphors for the human life-cycle were familiar to Knut from his excursions into ancient literature and art. Greek vases and intaglii often depict butterflies hovering over erect penises and their jetting sperm, which the Greeks thought was the evaporated essence, the cordial, of the soul. Knut, however, denied looking in that direction. He said he had got the idea from verses in the *"Purgatorio"* section of Dante's **Divina Commedia**:

> *"O proud Christians, wretched and exhausted,*
> *Who, sick in mind, and not seeing aright,*
> *Go confidently in the wrong direction;*
>
> *Do you not realise that we are grubs,*
> *Born to turn into the angelic butterfly*
> *Which flies towards justice without protection?"*

A more depraved misuse of Christian simile would be difficult to imagine, but to misuse Christianity is very much in the tradition of a certain shitstabber aesthetic. Knut, in his physical appearance, had always remained defiantly in the pre-butterfly stage. He was one of those shirtlifters who look like they should be lying in an open coffin: puffy flesh – overdressed – too-perfect clothes dominating rather than serving the body. One of those degraded truck-stop queens who, as if blind to the coarseness of their lives, are forever tinkling like a Christmas Tree about "art". "Culture" is their life-blood: the deodorant that runs in their veins . . . *Homme-Femmes* are different from others in that they can get terribly worked up about "culture", which everybody else just pretends to like. Everyone says that thought and art are the most important things in life, but they are only really important to those whom life never touches . . . Knut was one of those pansies, moreover, who seemed indifferent to the fact that the art of the past that he worshipped, forsaking all other gods, the art he would presumably have wished to preserve man's ability to create, was often the product of, would usually have been impossible without, the Christianity that his grim life defied. The poems and operas and paintings he loved were usually expressions of a faith that condemned everything about him, just as he condemned everything about it. (What sort of culture, one wonders, could such fastidious fistfuckers possibly have created themselves?) But aren't bluestocking fisters the perfect spokesmen for a world which has, like the world of late Antiquity, lost touch with its animating spirit? Knut reminded me of those snobbish Byzantine bishops like Photius and Sidonius Apollinaris who were always wittering on about their mauscripts of Homer and Virgil, monuments which nobody either understood or cared about anymore, and whose pagan aura should have been anathema. We live in the same kind of world as they did. Only the shell, the appearance of a civilization remains to us, and, like the people of the Fifth and Sixth Centuries AD – or the Australians, who use and abuse their British inheritance like "rebellious" kids running through a trust-fund, their pique a threat only to themselves – our world is living on borrowed time, on auto-pilot, on a moral and intellectual system it no longer accepts. No doubt it can drift on for a few decades more, as a glider does, the real motors of its civilization long since dead. But the next crisis to hit us will see our sleepwalking civilization, or its ghost, disintegrate instantaneously, in less than a second, as happened to classical civilization in the Mediterranean world when the Muslims invaded in the Seventh Century. It will leave the historians of our era, like the historians of theirs, to scratch their heads and wonder how a culture trailing millennia of "vitality" could suddenly disappear.

The Broncos' chest hair dripped in the fierce light. Rather a young one filled my paper cup with "Orlando Carrington Blush", a pink Australian champagne. He crossed the hall with quick geisha steps, his upper body uninvolved. He had the muscular cicada chest, lined locust belly and black dead eyes of a prawn. He smelled like one. I was talking at the time to Mr Majesty, who, though Dewy's partner in crime, was as different from the Prime Minister as could be. He was in his early dotage, very tall, red- and hatchet-faced, full of energy. He seemed impatient and irascible, as if he had something to do, as if one were a contemptible item obstructing him. Yet, for all that (and in complete contrast to the torpid, judicious Dew), his electric storms were curiously unfocused, as if all the projects about which he raged, and into which, briefly, he threw everything, were a displacement. He complained to me about the "White Leghorns" (old ladies driving home, slowly, from bowls) who had held up his chauffeured limousine. They needed to be "kicked like a footie" he suggested. His wife, "Jaw", was short, with yellowing white hair and spectacles. She had the acorn head of an Amazonian Indian. Her skin was yellow, like polenta. She was sweet and gentle. I am afraid to say I thoroughly disliked her. One sensed in her, as in so many sweet, gentle people, a selfishness, a moral inertia. I always think "sweetness" is a function of cowardice. This old sweetie would have been quite capable of indifferently watching a stranger's intense suffering. You could see that she lived, mentally and morally, only within her family, whose limits, for her, formed the furthest shores of mankind, the furthest limits of the place where one had to be human. She resembled Australia's myopic liberals for whom the coastline of Australia formed the *ne plus ultra* of the moral universe. While I was talking to her, I sadistically raised the most contentious subject I could think of, that of Sir Dewy's favourite fallen Broncos, those who had been *"farcies en haute coûture"*. They reminded me, I said, of the enemies of King Ferrante, a medieval King of Naples. This ornament of

154

the Aragonese dynasty would arrange for the "plotters" he had just had throttled to be embalmed and erected along the corridors of his palace, each got up in his (or her) everyday clothes. Every moment of the day he had his victims triumphantly and tantalisingly at his fingertips. He could address pointed mocking questions to each one, much as Cynthia did with "Brooklana", her doll. Naturally, conversing with Jaw, I hastened to distinguish Dew's mummies, which were those of darlings, from Ferrante's, who were brutalised dissidents, adding with equal sincerity that it would of course have been impossible for the Broncos to have flounced around, while alive, in Balenciaga, as their funerary attire seemed to indicate. "They shall not grow old" I intoned, "as we who are left grow old!" Needless to say, these apothegms went completely over the head of Australia's Madame de Sevigné. Nonetheless, my patent hostility roused her for the first time in years to a form of assertion. It was moving to watch the feeble laboured way she tried, like an octopus, to void a defensive poison. She was not one of those elegant old female fungi – hard and glossily *glans penis*-like without, rotten and powdery within – that, stepped on, expire in a sharp sticky fart. It was hard for her to make any response at all as her life as a sharp-toothed bitch was long behind her, she thought, and the social and intellectual part of her brain, the non-family part, which in the uneducated is connected solely with malice, had long since lapsed, not so much with avoidance as disuse, into an organ preserved but dead, something equally and ineffectually both saccharine and foul, like a holy relic. Jaw Majesty had to stop the whirring bin of candy floss into which she had been wont to stick her tongue every time she opened her mouth, and, like the vicious old puss she really was, lick her own stinking arse instead, which she could hardly even now locate. All she could pick up on in my remarks was their reference to "royalty", wherepon she made what she thought were nasty, ie "sympathetic" comments about the current state of the nuptials of the then heir to the British throne. (She believed in the Australian way that every human being in the United Kingdom is a sort of next-door neighbour of the Queen and would be suitably abashed at remarks to her discredit). "He laid down his wife for his country," she observed of the husband of the Prince's alleged strumpet, who was said to be *complaisant*. "Speaking of which," said Les, as Dew bore down on me, "your uncle wants you to meet someone."

Dewy was still wearing his ridiculous *peignoir*, which made him look like Chaliapin in Mussorgsky's **Boris Godunov**. "Pehhhtrick" he said, stressing and resting on the middle vowels of each word, which made each sound suspiciously ironic but might have been a regional solecism, "you've never met *Night*cliffe and *Jing*ili [his son and daughter in law], *hev yew?*" . . . He led me through what was quite a throng. Drinkies and dinner were in honour of Labor's *"Aboriginal and Islander Support Group"* – "the black sheep" as Dewy called them - but various other odds and sods had been invited as well. Aborigines beamed their charming radiant smile at me, like a flock of Rosellas. The Torres Strait Islanders were less affable. They towered immobile over the group like the statues on Easter Island – I was staggered by their immobility and the way that, like dolls, their listless bodies appeared to repudiate any relationship with their cheap, violent clothes. Their huge misshapen heads, which bulged in all directions, reminded me of loaves of *Focaccia*. Their eyes, like those of an idol, were red and full of contempt. Their peaty flesh had the fantastic black blackness of Christmas puddings or twigs from a stagnant pool. Like the tribes who in fact erected the stones on Easter Island, these Islanders were Melanesians. They had no links whatsoever with the Aborigines – who are probably proto-Dravidians, from India. The Torres Straiters had emigrated to Australia from their home in the Timor Sea in the 1890s, about a hundred years after the Europeans and at least a hundred thousand after the descent of the Aborigines. Nevertheless, to the *évolués* of Australia, the skin colour of the Islanders – it is indeed delicious – entitles them to the same aureole of martyrdom and the same prior rights to Australia as the white ruling class has assigned to Aborigines. There were a good few such avenging European angels at our party: they fluttered around the Islanders like

Cabbage White butterflies magnetised by the aubergine flesh of a horse turd. Alexander Protopotov's contemporary, the Russian poet Osip Mandelstam, once wrote:

> **"I will not return my hired dust to the earth**
> **Like a floury white butterfly! "**

- but he didn't live in the era of the self-abhorring white orgiast. These "writers" and officials - who were fawning and trembling like a Daddy Long Legs - reminded me of the *"Khlysty"* and *"Skopsty"* that the Empress Alexandra had used to patronise, Russian sectarians who saw salvation in self-flagellation and castration. (It is interesting to note that when they had completely dug out, with razors, their "will to power" – "the organ of increase", as Shakespeare terms it – the *"Skopsty"* were known as "little white doves" or "little white lambs;" they had received what was called "the Great Imperial Seal"). These "liberals" (a curious word given their taste for censorship) also reminded me of Elagabalus, the obscene boy Emperor who ruled Rome between 218 and 222 AD. Elagabalus, a degraded Syrian priest from Homs, worshipped the sun in the form of its local cult object, an erect-penis-resembling boulder. A piece of bitumen-black rock, such as Magnetic Island is made of. (So we should not be surprised that would-be white suicides see what Mandelstam calls *"the black sun"* rise in the Abo's arsehole. Though it is, of course, in the *white* man's arsehole that they would prefer to see the "black son" rise!) This black stone, a meteorite, sat in the temple in Emesa (modern day "Homs") where Elagabalus worked as an acolyte. He was an extremely pretty creature and served as a mascot and boy-whore to the Roman legion based in Syria. The soldiers raised him to the purple during a coup in 218 AD in the belief that he was the illegitimate son of Caracalla, a former Roman emperor. In fact he was no more related to Caracalla than the Islanders were to the Aborigines. On assuming power, Elagabalus had the black prick of his god conveyed from Syria to Rome in a chariot drawn by six milk-white horses. He installed it in a temple right in the middle of the Imperial Palace on the Palatine Hill, just as the *"Penitenti"* had installed Torres Straiters here in the *Palatium Sacrum* of Australia. He then proceeded to transfer Rome's oldest and most autochthonous religious objects – the *"Palladium "*, the *"Ancilia"*, the sacred hearth of the Vestal Virgins – from their real homes to the shrine of the new-found *Lapis Niger*. He imagined that this would raise a carbonised termite nest – the charcoal corpse of a stalagtite of napalmed donner - to the level of the Empire's Crown Jewels. (Here, too, in the Holy of Holies, the *"Khlysty"* had promiscuously dared to mingle Australia's ancient natives with these pseudo-authentic blow-ins, the Islanders). And that wasn't the end of Elagabalus' innovations. He opened the baths of the Imperial Palace to the public so he could share his ablutions with the Roman plebs and so discover which of his subjects had the largest penises. Pre-empting the acuity that Australia's ruling class would show in awarding native title, he made the size of the *Membrum Virile* his sole criterion when selecting contenders for high office. As in Australia, the artificial reservation of plum jobs to patricians and the *literati* was reversed and careers were (like the sacred person of Augustus) "thrown open to the talents". P. Valerius Comazon, a dancer, became Prefect of the City; Gordius, a charioteer, was made Consul; while Zoticus, first a grocer, later Prime Minister, was driven from the palace in disgrace when it was discovered that his *"Ami de la Maison"*, inflamed, was only eight inches long ...

As I pushed through crowds towards my family (who had been unable to come to me as Bon's back was playing up, rooting her and the kids to a chair they had found for her on the far side of the hall), I saw the Anglican bishop of Wodonga excitedly *à deux* with a strapping and cretinous-looking Islander. I was suddenly terrified by his queeny face – a mask of passion: he looked like some bloodthirsty Aztec goddess, and who can blame him as it didn't appear as if the monster on whom he had set his sights (he was no doubt considering him for some evangelical position) laboured under Zoticus' impediment. The room was full of people who disseminated "Orthodoxy" (it means, in Greek, "correct belief"): artists, "intellectuals", people who worked in academe and the media. Their horrible weak faces, so different from the average Australian face – like faces by the Belgian painter James Ensor – all mixed together in the one place – made me wonder, as such gatherings always do, why "educated" people wish to seek each other out. How can they bear each other? *"Water, water, everywhere, and not a drop to drink!"* Or eat, for they too are predators, inedible cannibals. Art is not about art, and the best people for artists are their opposites, as His Grace had brightly demonstrated. The Ensor faces indicated that their owners were parasites; not social or economic parasites – though most fell into that category - but people who drew life from others. This accounted for the consumptive intensity of the faces, which were strong – like those in portraits by Soutine – only in richness. They reminded me of the Brussels' sprouts that you leave on the side of a plate. Imagine a plate with no meat, no potatoes, nothing but these discarded sprouts collected from every plate in the land, and you have some idea of that room. It was terribly noisy. Partygoers were trying to "circulate" – to disengage from their interlocutors and so go on to the next joyless union. Passing them at shoulder-level, you saw the agonised, abstracted looks in their eyes as they tried, with partners, to climax, to reproduce - themselves. And then they would gobble up the afterbirth — their passport out of one world and into the universe of the next group of people. Off they would fly – brutally, awkwardly, like queen ants – with nary a backward glance at those with whom, a minute before, they had been so intimate. Why did people put themselves through this? How could they keep on play-acting or pretending that it was pleasurable? Parties (and every other sort of love and friendship?) are like colonic irrigation: well know to be a good thing.

Speaking of colonic irrigation, Gopi Panicker, one of the most prominent of the party, had no-one to talk to. She was pissed. She was holding up her colostomy bag in one hand while she advanced, like the Winged Victory of Samothrace, with a glass of *woyn* in the other. This was meant to attract attention. She was speaking at the top of her horrible Australian voice – a voice which, with its curious, rapid expansion, always sounds like that of a duck being chased across a pond. The colostomy bag as her *"worm"*, she said (her womb); it contained her "trezhah". You could see that she didn't have big tits anymore or a nice face. The great philosopher was about to learn that, once it begins to collapse, a successful woman's body, unlike a successful man's, is never redeemed by its "ghost", its genius. No-one was even slightly interested in her. She walked in circles, alone, bow-legged, bow-backed, as if she wished to urinate. I remember (for some reason) that she was wearing a black smock and black lycra tights that only reached the middle of her calves. Her head, like a spaniel's, was cracked by a vast, wet-looking mouth. Like a spaniel, she seemed to look up all the time. She had big kind eyes and a bad smell. Spindly legs, like a sheep's.

The nimbus around Dew melted the rather tight group through which we were moving, whose extremities were anyway beginning to break off and drift to the tables, where diners were already standing around like people stranded on ice floes. Dinner was being announced in the clammy baritone of a strangely hilarious Bronco. There was a little knot that was not moving, though. They were standing to our right with arms folded, dressed incongruously in dark, beautiful clothes. Their appearance was startlingly different from that of the others, and not just because their exquisite dress and manner – that of a group of discreet, well scrubbed Eurotrash – seemed to come from a distant place, economically and otherwise. "Sand niggers!" said Dew. He seemed to want to deflate in the cruellest possible way the pumped-up public farthingales with which these rig dwellers had sought to conceal their very private foreign parts. "I don't know what *your* liddle ringpiece is gettin' all hot and bothered about," Dew astounded me by saying, "all they are is *Texans*, for Chrissake! Aint one of 'em wouldn't sooner fuck a bison than a four-year-old boy! But look at 'em now - don't they just think they're the dog's bollocks?! . . . Spunk wouldn't melt in their mouth!" I knew enough about Dew's makeup to guess at once he must have become indebted in some way to these people. ". . . They was a-crawlin' about the desert like rats in a Dirt Dunny just th'other day, usin' their own shite for firewood: they make these Boongs look like

Audrey Hepburn and the Agnellis! This mornin' they was a-suckin' on Daddy's cock and a-pickin' Christmas Beetles out of Mommy's whimmy! Tonite they're all dressed up in Donna fuckin' Karan! Well Hah bloody Hah!" "Then why on earth did you invite them?" I replied, annoyed. Dew looked at me obscenely. "You'll see!" . . . Camp, with an audacious air. Then the mysterious mask redescended.

Perhaps Dew was upset because he feared that Nightcliffe and Jingili were unlikely to impress me as much as the "heifer jockeys" had. But funnily enough, his exposure of their identity had utterly dispelled the strangers' mystique. In Proust's novel, the actions and opinions of the Baron de Charlus, which, for much of the book, seem profound and original to the Narrator, become, in retrospect, pitiful and mechanical when their pathological - ie homosexual – origin is exposed. In the same way, the revelation that the seeming citizens of Munich and Juan-les-Pins were in fact Texans completely altered their status and demeanour. Their European elegance no longer appeared organic, the orchid of epoch after epoch of climate and effort. Now it was as deceitful and external as a Nicotine Patch, a shortcut bought with oil money just as easy and unreal. Even worse, their Bohemian weeds, woven from the political and social viscera of Klosters and Milan, stood in ludicrous contrast to the implications of Houstonian life. All that "Miuccia Prada" meant in their case was the buggery of Frat-Boys, trading in Mexican slaves, Tim-Tam in all its peurile, Iron Age horror. . . . One of the party obviously thought herself a thoroughly modern Miss. Peering defiantly out from under a shard of carefully coiffed hair like some *gamine* Milanese, she was clasping one of Gopi Panicker's Feminist classics to her bosom, obviously having just got the Pekinese-faced bore to sign it. "Yeah, great," I thought, "right on, Little Miss Muffet – just wait until they cut your fanny off!"

Suddenly someone was cantering towards us. There was a weirdness in the childish woman. Her legs moved like those of a running cow. Though dressed with the same sombre expensiveness as the others, she looked terribly big. Not fat, big. Awkward, like a labrador in a raincoat. One could sense submission to, and then hopeless defiance of, diets, the loss of other forms of self-control. One glimpsed in her the disasters that always attend those who lack a certain *"je ne sais quoi"*. "What *is* that daft mare saying?" I asked Dew, not realising that she was speaking English. "Probably the same thing as Catherine the Great," said Dew: "*'A horse, a horse, moy kingdom for a horse'* !!!" "Is she a Texan?" I asked. "Her skin is terribly white." "Didga ever see a *non-Texan* that looked like that?" Dew asked. It was true. Arkana's face (that was her name; my guess that Dew knew the Texans was not incorrect) was one unique to women from her part of the world: tender, ugly and intelligent, and vast and oddly naked in its tenderness, like the face of a male gorilla. Seeing such faces, one comprehends the need Texans feel to cover the female face. Such faces are too explicit. They are ugly for the reason that the human genitals, exposed, are. Our own women's faces don't need a covering because they are already veiled, hidden by the ontology – or, if you like, the hypocrisy – of our civilization.

We had reached the gargantuan seated statue, the one with the torrential penis. Before Dew could introduce us, Jingili rushed up from a table to greet me. She had short dark hair and a "sensible" dress with bright chrome buttons. Like a man's business shirt, the dress was ruled with perpendicular stripes in mint-green and pale orange. I could sense Dew watching me for signs of disappointment. Jingili, who held her hands clasped in front of her, had a kind, alert face like a Jack Russell. She had a broad smile and a slightly spatulate nose. A child, naked but for dripping shorts, flitted past the back of her chair. Braith, one of her boys, had just entered the Dining Hall with this brother, Julatten. They had been in the Viceroy's swimming pool. Following, incredulous, the puddles Braith was making on the floor, I noticed the family dog behind Jingili's chair. It was a big black cross between a Persian cat and an Alsatian: it was swallowing a rich pink tongue. The extended Popkiss clan seemed to be treating this exalted occasion as if it were any other old family coroboree: a beach barbie, perhaps, or a picnic. Nightcliffe, for instance, Jingili's husband, was standing with his back to the table, chatting to someone, a "stubbie" (small bottle of beer) cooling in a polystyrene holder in his fist. Jingili tapped him on the shoulder. I feared the worst. Such a long time. He would only vaguely remember. There would be an embarrassing retreat. I would appear effeminate, absurd. "Nightcliffe," purred Jingili, "you remember this *young man*?" He turned: how ugly he looked! I had remembered someone tall and ash blond. Nightcliffe was small, bandyleggèd like his mother, with a long torso. But our eyes grow accustomed to the past, just as they grow accustomed to the dark. I hadn't remembered remembering him; seeing him again, I did, but I was mocked by a very stupid man. Nightcliffe had dirty, badly dyed hair and spoke in a lugubrious drawl, as if he were trying to wake himself up. He had puffy, lidded eyes: he looked like a female dinosaur. He was wearing a short-sleeved tee-shirt with a white collar, the legend *"82 LEAD FARTS"* blazoned across it. I noticed the fine, dark matted hair on Nightcliffe's chest, the metal in his teeth. The rank matureness, as of Gouda, shocked me. I remembered him from my last Australian visit running about with the heroic, mindless virginity of a pullet. His face then (again, like his mother's) had seemed too large for his body, as if given to him, for life, at birth. Now he was finally growing into it. It was hard, synthetic – the archetypal creosote face of Australia – "cooked", translated, not the raw, virginal face of a European. A different sort of human.

Nightcliffe and I shook hands and talked of what had taken place in our families. We sat down at the table. Jingili perched herself on the edge of a chair, hands clasped between her knees – she was offering an excited commentary: the first indication that things might go well. Actually, the first sign was when Nightcliffe ordered one of the Broncos to bring me a drink. (I had made a request for iced coffee). There was something nice about Nightcliffe – I don't know what.

I was inspired to ask Nightcliffe if, like his parents, he was a stalwart of the Australian Labor Party. Apparently, he was not. Instead, he had joined the local Toastmasters' Lodge. One

Toastmaster would move that they should all have a "feed", said Nightcliffe, and then you had to say no, the group here present should *NOT* have a feed. And you would cite the reasons why. "And y' know, Petrick?" Nightcliffe sighed, "it's really hard. You might actually *want* to have a feed!" Nightcliffe described another Toastmaster epic. "Imagine you're a fly, right, and you're in the froth on the head of a schooner. Yer havin' a great old time. *What are your feelings as you go down someone's* throat!?" "You would know all about that, Bon!" said Dewy. Bonnie regarded him with contempt.

Jingili asked me if I watched a lot of "live theatre" in London. "I do try to avoid the other kind," I observed. She introduced me to each of her sons. They were still in swimming costumes – shoulders draped in towels, like Jews, breast and torso muscles heaving like the gills and belly of a fish. Braith, the elder, was drowsy, oily and retarded-looking, slightly cross-eyed; a mouth full of round teeth like fingernails. Julatten had a stupid face, too – the face of a statue. I asked anodyne questions about the dog. Braith said that they owned two such Alsatians – Trent, the one with the candy pink tongue, and Jita, a female. "Trent only poos in the one spot," Jingili observed, "Jita poos all over the place." "There you are, Petrick," Dewy exclaimed, "typical bloody women!" We found Dew enthroned at our table next to Bon, who was also leaning forward on a chair, in her case because thick jars had been placed under its hind legs to ease the strain on her back. "I want a pig and a cow," said Jingili, ingenuously (she meant as as pets). "You've got one," said Bon. "Patrick," Jingili announced, as impervious as her husband to remarks such as this, "this is Lady Bonnie Popkiss, *my mother-in-law*. Patrick, Bonnie has very high blood pressure. Bonnie does Tai Chi. Bonnie gets up at five o'clock every morning." Jingili asked her mother-in-law if she would look after Trent and Jita over Christmas. "Bon'll probably eat the dogfood!" Nightcliffe observed, somewhat shocking me. "What is it," asked Dew, "Kittiecat?" Bonnie again gave us a molten look. I could detect a *frisson* in the air. The whole family discussed someone with allergies. "What about the people who are allergic to the Eighties?" Jingili demanded.

"It's also a matter of how much POYN you can toyk, Jing," Bon observed. "Take Femelle Cooper. She was telling MOY her son had iz kneecaps replaced. Well, it all went wrong and they became *horribly infected*. She said he was *SKROYMING* with the POYN and I thought: '*THAT* I can *BELOYYYYVE*!' . . . He then took ten fuckin' month off work. It would be better if he was fuckin' *dead*, eh? Then he couldn't do fuckin' *shit*!" "God, Bonnie, you're hard," said Dew, looking upset. "Come on, come on," Bon hissed in response, motioning Dew towards her, flowery upturned fingers moving backwards in succession like the blades in a Swiss knife – "NOW yer gettin' there. CHROIST, *YEW* can talk about bein' *CROOOL!!*"

Nightcliffe and Jingili's youngest son, Oak, suddenly crashed in, interrupting this numinous exchange, which was terminated by a pestilential glance from Dew. Oak was more with it, there was a raffish sparkle in his eye. He wore a miniature version of Australia's rugby colours. Sometimes he would grab Braith's seat – but he was always obliged to move out of it. It was obviously a "special occasion".

Braith bashfully asked me if, on entering the house, I had seen the ferns and the other plants that they and their Dad had brought Bon and Dewy from the Rainforest. I said that I had (they were terribly boring-looking things). I found that I could talk to the children with self-confidence, without self-consciousness – the first time this has happened.

When the iced coffee came, I really didn't feel like drinking it; it seemed to be filled with rice – hundreds of little white globules. "It's soya bean milk," Jingili said. "It only *looks* pooky: it's perfectly okeedokee!" Braith and Julatten began to volunteer information about Adelong, one of Nightcliffe's brothers, to whom I had been much closer than to the other siblings at the time of my first Australian visit. It seemed that dreamy academe had suited him even less than Nightcliffe: he was now an ornament of the transport industry; his parents had bought him a fleet of trucks. "Got iz first girlfriend," said Braith, disclosing more than he could ever know. "You would be an expert on that, would you?" sniffed Jing.

Then Julatten revealed what seemed like a highly personal anecdote. Like all Australians, his voice rose a pitch, querulously, at the end of each phrase. His delivery was so slow he sounded like someone who was trying to be sick. "Adelong come in here [*the whole family made bold use of the present indicative*], all dirty from the truck, all oily and that, and, guess what? *—He runs iz hands through iz muthurz hair!*" Julatten referred to his Grandmother – who was sitting right next to us – exactly like that: "his mother". It was wierd . . . There was silence as Bonnie went as red as an aphthous ulcer. Poor Julatten, one sensed, was rather "queer" and in the habit of bringing the conversation to an abrupt terminus. He picked up my map of Sydney, which I had placed on the table, and pointed to an advertisement in one of its panels for a service station in Cronulla. "Lowanna's husband used to own that," he said. Lowanna was the eldest of Dewy's children. She must have been in her mid-teens when last I had visited Australia. I remember having attended one of Nightcliffe's birthdays. I had come upon Lowanna – already wearing the first of many heavy rings – kissing a total stranger in the "carport".

"What was it like?" asked Oak of his father's birthday. "There were lots of saveloys," I said, remembering the lovely sausages on sticks cased in batter and soft with ketchup that Australians call *"Dagwood Dogs"* . . . "It went on all night!" The boys were amazed. "Wasn't one of Lowanna's boyfriends a detective?" I asked. "Policemen, firemen, lawyers!" Julatten recited, proudly. "Oh – she went to the bad," said Nightcliffe, "*heaps* of boyfriends. Crack! All her marriages went *bang*. Mum and Dad built her a house out in Tumutt so she could be near them. *I bet they regret it now!*" Neither Dew nor Bon was prepared to rise to this *soupçon* of sibling rivalry.

"Oko!" Dew suddenly exclaimed. Oak, who had slipped away, was peeing in a beribboned basket of "native flowers" – a gift for Bon – that had been placed behind a statue . . . "Oko, you *dirty little turd*!!"

I pretended to scrutinise my map of Sydney. Every now and then the dog would come up and study me. Its conical head wavered from side to side like the cockpit of a fighter plane; its eyes seemed to be trying to focus. Its mouth was trembling: one of those intense, worried canine simpers. I was reminded of the distorted lower lip of a Spastic I had once seen on the platform of West Hampstead Station: his mad-eyed face had seemed to sheer away, as if I had been something disgusting. The dog, I feared, was about to rip my throat out. I thought: how awful! Imagine ending up having to go into hospital in a place like this! I kept perfectly still and concentrated on the outskirts of Sydney.

All sorts of dishes were being served. Filthy roasts, roast beef for instance, and outside the temperature was still over Eighty! The Bronco who came to serve our dinner looked like a slothful Rubens, but with the slow, sluttish absorption of Rembrandt's *"Bathsheba"*. I asked for some salt and he said: *"It's wrapped up in your napkin!"* It wasn't, but I didn't like to ask again as I already felt like a pest in my long-sleeved shirt . . . the *clientèle* was not that of Maxime's. Everyone was fascinated by the Cricket, which blared in grainy un-verisimilitudinous colour from a set between two of the thighs of the cement sportsmen: the screen was like a painting by Seurat. The sound of the TV, not very far away from us, was turned down, but the Aborigines present watched it hypnotically throughout the ensuing live performance. For the evening's entertainment had arrived in the shape of a tiny girl in a long satinny jumpsuit with ropes of false pearls that plunged to her knees: she looked like the Coptic Pope. She started to massage a Yamaha, belting out the sort of thirty-year-old hits that are the staple of ballrooms in sad Torquay hotels . . . I thought: how dreadful, what a dreadful, awful place. The stupefied Islanders glared morosely like toads as she crashed through several Sixties' favourites. A Kanak, obviously drugged, clapped wildly. She had, most unusually for a Melanesian, straight stringy hair and oily copper features. High cheekbones. " *'Dream Lover'*!", she kept demanding; "*'Dream Lover'*!" Her lover would

167

have *had* to be dreaming, not to say positively wiped out on petrol fumes, which is apparently what these Islanders go in for. I closed my eyes, to see what it was like. It was delightful.

Having just chosen the seafood option, I was also served a Barossa Reisling. The food was actually presented on a stainless steel plate! I tasted the lobster, which was of an overpowering metallic richness: its legs, with their hairy shanks, pronged claws and little, barbed joints, reminded me of an Elephant Beetle. The shellfish was far too warm. The slush sac of the prawns was a transparent yellow-green-black, like an overripe banana. The warmth and richness of the food, especially of the rubberwhite, mineral-flavoured crab, was off-putting. The totalitarian gratuity of the plate imparted a stifling atmosphere . . . Nevertheless, I wanted to enjoy my meal, and so I decided to put my desire to have a pee aside. However, having come so far, and for a once-in-a-lifetime event that could only be enjoyed with a clear, analytical mind, I asked a Bronco if there was a loo. Rather to my surprise, there was. I went off and relieved myself.

"You wouldn't believe we were in Canberra, would you?" said Dew, when I returned to the table. He motioned proudly at the food: "you would think we were in London!" "You can say *that* again," I replied, remembering the wonderful restaurants of Sydney. Later, he said: "I don't think D.H. Lawrence would have been very happy here. I don't think his spirit would have agreed with it!" The brackish green of the disagreeable overpriced plonk had clearly invaded his own spirit. A half-chewed ball of veal on his plate looked like the pithy pink socket you see when someone wrenches the branch off a tree.

Suddenly, Dew grabbed my arm. He said that he wanted me to meet "an international celebrity". Arkana Muckadilla! He was introducing me to the rather odd-looking woman we had seen before. I was astonished to note that she was being guided to the same longish table as my family, and was even being seated on my right: already she was laughing at the fruitbowl. I said "Good Evening", and we shook hands. It was really quite a strange introduction, as Dew, in the course of conducting a conversation with us both, asked for two milkshakes in a row, gingerly popping each of the berries they were crowned with in his mouth. Simultaneously, he would pile his plate with food from a tureen and, ducking and diving, stare, squinting, at the esteemed "black arses" being planted on the neighbouring chairs. "There's a bare bum over there!" he would announce, imprecisely, on espying a particularly tumescent pantyline. The impression was of a possum . . . some greedy, instinctive, bestial thing.

Arkana, at least, took it all in her stride, as behoved a world-famous altruist. For, in addtion to her business interests, she said she was very interested in "native rights". Now that I could study her better, she was a tall, imposing lady with remarkably white skin. She had a nutty, jasmine smell, like truffles. She had made no attempt to conceal her hair, which was most and rich, ecstatically black: the oiled grooves of a record. Wet strands leaked provocatively onto her snow white forehead like the leaves of black grass that you fish out of carafes of red wine in Rome. Like many Texans, her features were large and somewhat angular. With her huge black eyes, high cheekbones and parrot nose, she reminded me of self-portraits by the young Picasso. She wore the sort of "European" clothes that are unique to Texans: curious, old-fashioned things. It was interesting to meet such a famous "face", and we spoke at length. I found her good humoured and gracious, and yet, at first almost unconsciously, one felt a certain unease as one spontaneously smiled at her, especially as I had no idea why Sir Dewy could have introduced us. "I have two two-year old boys," she said brightly, "and a twelve year old girl with Asperger's. She's nearly at one hundred percent – of the kids in her class . . . Did you see that Down's Syndrome couple on TV last night? ... *'Come Dancing'*, wasn't it? It brought a lump to my throat . . . She was a big girl, but she was so light on her feet!"

She always gave you too much information. And "Asperger's Syndrome" she said, not Autism - the dreaded Alzheimer's of the ***Tarka the Otter*** world. What looked like wooden forks for tossing salad protruded from a bun at the top of her head. She asked me if I were on holiday in Australia. When I explained that it was emphatically business and not pleasure, she asked me where I *did* intend to relax that year. I told her I had planned to visit Langres and Hyères, where Raoul Dufy once painted such wonderful landscapes."We are going to Vienna," she informed me, "you know, where Martin Luther came from?" She was obviously trying to "compete" with me. "I never knew Martin Luther came from Vienna," I said, surprised. "Not Martin Luther *the darkie*", she laughed.

Arkana – so opulently turned out - carried not a Gucci *serviette* but a plastic bag with some large, unfolded papers in it that she would check, and then re-check, and check again. She was like one of those perfect houses that you buy with vague, inexplicable misgivings. As acquaintance deepened, her real personality – which had been conducting its existence on some unseen plane in tandem with the well-rounded self she gave the world – showed itself in sharp, frightening vignettes, just as an always secret poltergeist will gradually reveal itself, first faintly, then frequently, as the real spirit of a seemingly lovely "hayume". She would abruptly become upset because she had no emotional "ear". She took everything far too seriously; not intellectually seriously, but emotionally seriously, investing and discerning real feeling in exchanges that should have been mechanical. She was one of those bright, relentless people whose vulnerable and sinister nature is always escaping like juice from a bag of plums. I would speculate that, like many "good" people (and Tim-Tams all think themselves "good" – a condition conferred on them simply by being Tim-Tam), she lacked an external value system. As far as Arkana was concerned, anything that she as a "good person" did and wanted was automatically "good"; anything that opposed her interests naturally constituted "evil". Her charm and kindness were therefore in no way inconsistent with her enigmatic arrogance; in fact, the former depended on the latter.

Despite her turbulent personality – which certainly had depths, even if they weren't the ones she was proud of – I liked Arkana. Though not attractive, she had all the "profligacy" of a beautiful person: the air around her was full of the intoxicating spore that makes us feel we have stumbled on something whose value is not known and is wide open to us . . . Something like the charge Tray Beautous used to say his "man-in-the-street" models gave out, whose star quality only *he* – or so he claimed – was able to detect. In these cases, the magic of the magnetic individual is undoubtedly a feature only of its admirer: but so what? All art – and self-delusion is certainly an art – is necessarily a subjective truth before it can be an objective one. The fact that only the latter – the physical residue – comes to partake of an absolute, attestable reality, but that this reality depends for its birth on an illusion, is what gives life – or should we say art? – its majesty. One does not need to be a homosexual, for instance, to appreciate Michelangelo's *"David"*, but one needed to be one before one could have been deluded enough to create it: we know of the peasant who served as Michelangelo's muse and he looked nothing like the statue that stands outside the Palazzo Vecchio. On the other hand, even the most splendid fuel for a subjective illusion must leave a concrete residue that is sufficiently symbolic, which is to say, universal, before it can enjoy a "David's" career. Before it can live, it must first be minted into a common currency for the simple reason that art that cannot find an audience *does not exist*, and art that *loses* its audience *ceases* to exist – often literally. That was how the historian Niketas Choniates interpreted the melting down of magnificent examples of ancient sculpture by the Crusaders who pillaged Byzantium in 1204:

> *"These barbarians, haters of the beautiful, did not allow the statues standing in the Hippodrome and other marvellous works of art to escape destruction, but all were melted down and minted into coins. Thus great things were exchanged for small ones, and works fashioned at huge expense were converted into worthless pennies."*

Unfortunately, Choniates, a remarkable scholar and antiquarian, was almost unique in the Middle Ages in knowing the true value of classical art . . . Nothing has "intrinsic" value, not even the work of a Phidias, until and unless its price tag can push its way like larva into the sun. By the year 1204, most of the people of Constantinople no longer had the "key" to the masterpieces Niketas mourned: they no longer understood the first thing about them. Far from enjoying them, they feared them, if they felt any emotion for them at all. For the 13th century Byzantine, no less than for the Crusaders, "worthless pennies" constituted an art that had far greater value than the sculpture of Praxiteles, simply because pennies were something that people could still understand.

Because I was drawn to Arkana, and an element of capricious sadism is always present when one is attracted to someone – or perhaps just because I was drunk by this point – I was more forthcoming in conversation with her than I should have been, and expressed priggish, violent ideas that were close to my heart. Not that her own observations were particularly wise or serene. Nor did her arguments have the merit (to me) of consistency. But I would not normally have dignified her pompous Tim-Tammic clichés with anything but polite assent. (Even in those far-off days, you could hear them a hundred times a day in the trite and tabulated form that they seem to have assumed, with the "Kaymart", in some supernatural pre-antiquity). Arkana's delicious, unbecoming hysteria should not, of course, be confused with her political rage, though the same turmoil no doubt informed both. She declared herself full – to me – of all the "official" resentments: about Sunny-Pine, for instance; about the amount of money that the United States gave each year to the Idroolees; about the wealth of the West and the poverty of most of the world's Tim-Tams. (I longed to ask her why the pious oil queens didn't share the billions which Providence – a far bigger patron of the Tim-Tams than the USA is of the Roos - has diverted instead into the local budgets for Chivas Regal, Shepherd's Market hookers and boys).

If only people in the First World knew what it was like in the "Developing World", she said, the Tim-Tammic World! *She* knew, she said accusingly, as if self-knowledge were something remarkable. (In a Tim-Tam, self-knowledge would indeed have been something remarkable, but, alas, it was not one of her attributes). Apart from Texas, the Tim-Tammic world was "so squalid" she fumed, as if it were somehow *my* fault. She loved it though and she kept a terrible picture of it, she said, "in her heart". "It's so polluted!" she wailed, apropos of nothing. I laughed and told her that she didn't need to describe it for me as I was very familiar with more than one Tim-Tammic country and I was perfectly aware of what shit-holes they all were . . . Upturned exhaust pipes like tubas wrapped around overcrowded buses gouting out voluptuous black clouds; puffs as big as from Stevenson's *"Rocket"*. Days as yellow and grey as Townsville crocodile steaks, and with the same slightly fecal taste. Flimsy, out of date modern buildings bulging with far more people than they were made for. Think of the worst, shoddiest modern architecture in the West, and you will be able to picture most of downtown Coonpiss or Gey-Man, where everyone thinks each boring shoebox makes the city look rich and up-to-date, their windows dusty and broken, their walls buckling and stained like wet cardboard dried in the sun. The old, historical buildings wear a look of very modern dilapidation, as if they had just been sacked, which is hardly surprising since their stigmata were mostly inflicted by a recent and meteoric rise in the population. Everywhere hordes of people slither around like rats disturbed in a bin. It is obvious, not only that a complex power and order animates these people – like the occult gravity in a beehive – but that there are far, far too many of them. Human beings, unlike animals, have no humanity, no humanity at all. We do not find female Tim-Tams, for example, as we find female deer, spontaneously inducing mass abortions when their numbers begin to exceed what is locally sustainable: what a high opinion of themselves they must have!

As in a beehive or a fairytale, success in the Developing World, the Tim-Tammic World is never related to genius or effort. A magical dispensation places an arbitrarily-chosen few over the many, as when, during a London transport strike, handfuls of individuals mysteriously manage to find seats on the very few buses. They look impassively out from the top deck on the crowds of tired, distressed and hopeless people on the pavement, much as the Tim-Tammic elect gaze indifferently on what is facetiously called "the Skarab street".

Those faceless unfortunates will get home somehow. And incredibly enough, they do, just as the wretched "masses" in the Third World, the world of Tim-Tam – the word "masses" is suggestive, is it not? – somehow make ends meet, somehow attach themselves to the scams, the accidents that, if only by millimeters, push them and their loved ones forward. In these magical worlds, where reason and fairness have no place, and where nobody – however gifted – is ever wafted to the Abode of Bliss except by a suicide bomb or the Genie – that is perhaps the greatest miracle of all. But "Third World spokesmen" never bother their pretty little heads with things like that. They spit fire in the salons of the North, not because they were ever the losers in their own environments, but because they were among the very few winners. Otherwise, how could the Frantz Fanons and the Tariq Alis have made it to Paris and New York to describe the local misery, and the subsequent rage at the sybaritic West? They talk angrily of the downtrodden, not because they were ever poor or downtrodden in their own downtrodden world, where they stepped merrily on everyone, but because they are not Number One *here*, as they expect to be, as, after all, they were at home. They feel that they are denied their place in the sun here *because* of the "there", *because* of the Third World, for which in fact they feel nothing but shame and contempt. This they translate by the device Freud called "projection" into rage *for* the Third World, and *against* the West to whose bounty and respect they aspire, turning the "base metal" of self-hate into the gold that is hatred of others, and, for the lucky ones, with comparable results. Colonies of them roost like voracious Fruitbats in the orchards of the West: the shrieking flocks literally darken our skies . . . And think not just of the Third World "Revolutionaries" hanging upside down with black and vulpine faces in the Mango trees that are Paris and London. Think of the lowlier bureaucrats from Rabat and Jakarta who are sent to attend international conferences, or posted to organisations like the UN and the World Health Organisation in Vienna or Rome. Which of these Tribunes of the People, their homelands' woe constantly on their lips, comes from any background but that élite whose servants and mansions would be beyond the dreams of most of the Westerners whose guilt they tap? And which of them began their ascent to the International Brothel but unfairly, utilising the crooked ways that have kept most of their compatriots down for centuries? It is therefore no surprise that the ablest hustlers are high-caste Indians, who swamp the international organisations as the Czechs used to dominate the Hapsburg bureaucracy, or Corsicans the Colonial Service of France. The equality and human rights for which these Brahmins call in public and the caste, clan and racial arrogance to which they are committed in private are oddly, even organically related, like the public and private lives of a silk-worm.

I asked Arkana what had originally brought her to Australia. She told me that the United Nations had sent her there years before as "a roving ambassador, exploring diversity". Specifically, she had been commissioned to investigate the Federal Government's treatment of "indigenous minorities". Hence her appearance at our dinner tonight. She then asked me what my own reason for being in Canberra was. When she had learned my frivolous and unaltruistic motives, she accusingly quoted Dr Edward Said at me. Professor Said has written that what she called *"un artiste, un intelligent"* must always be exerting himself in support of the likes of the Aborigines – and the Tim-Tams – because Bohemia should always fight against "power" on the side of the "powerless". "Oh," I said, "so I suppose we should have supported Hitler at the Munich Putsch, and Mussolini during the March on Rome?" I wanted to object that one's support should depend on the extent of a cause or a candidate's morality; it should have nothing to do with how "weak" or "powerful" each might be. But then I remembered how Nietzsche observed that, when people talk about "good" and "evil", what they are *really* talking about *is* power, and that those that find themselves *without* power will always try to make a virtue of the fact, the better to gain - or regain - the whip hand whose blows they claim to resent. Contrary to what Clausewitz once wrote, it is "morality" and not "diplomacy", which is *"the continuation of war by other means"*. I could hardly help but recall that the world's Tim-Tams had raped the world for over a thousand years and that people like Arkana pluck at our heartstrings now (heartstrings no Tim-Tam was ever born with) not because they are oppressed (though they often now are oppressed); it is because they want again to be the oppressor. Their rage comes more from a humiliated hubris than a sense of injustice. Injustice is something they long to re-impose.

"I want to help the helpless . . . I will bring my children up always to protect the weak", Arkana cooed. And what would she have brought them up to be if her civilization had still been powerful, I wondered, rather than retarded and impotent? If what she termed "the glorious Tim-Tammic past" – ie of theft, invasion, genocide (ie precisely what she condemned in others) – was anything to go by, the omens were not propitious. Indeed, even without that power, plenty of Tim-Tammic immigrants behaved in what were, after all, not their own countries, in an amazingly despotic manner.

I decided to ask Arkana about her media empire. How exciting it must be, I said, to own a newspaper! I spoke cruelly and idly because I knew that she had bought her portfolio with what Sir Vidia Naipaul has called *"the unearned wealth of oil"*, and I imagined it was about as "exciting" as owning a bunch of grapes, but her upper lip flared and her teeth didn't move at all; her eyes seemed to sparkle out of a sort of orgiastic coma. When it came to her "work", alas, Arkana's conversation was never limited, as the remarks of someone who knew anything would have been, by time and space; it attained the fantastic open-ended elaboration of true Mongolism. Anyone within earshot of her would find himself waking up to her unstoppable mantra with an encouraging murmur forming on his lips like those noises that dogs make in their sleep and with which he might in fact have been punctuating her monologue for the previous half hour – much as a dog, bewildered by the never-ending vastness of a park, will retreat into its own world and attempt to map or control its environment by issuing a turd. Like many who have never done a stroke of work, Arkana obviously liked to think herself a cynical trooper who constantly had to "pull it off" unrewarded. Rolling up the sleeves of her blouse like someone about to gut a fish, a gold pen in her mouth, her anus as gingerly ajar as the feet on her long, bandy legs were inwardly pointing – she looked, I was told, as if she had forgotten to wipe her bum and the inwardly pointing feet made her resemble a figure by Lowry – "Kana" would thrash around her "office" on one meaningless errand after another, her obscene back and her mincing gait that of some Rugby League player whose feet have been bound after the manner of Chinese gentlewomen. You could identify her from the street below, people said, the dreadful torso bobbing up and down amid the terminals like Charlie Laughton scampering over the parapets of Notre Dame.

And yet Arkana, so unreal in the real world of her audience, appeared utterly plausible within her own. Falseness, like Zionism, can only exist outside its national home, and the deluded person, like the Diaspora, is always true to some reality somewhere. And Arkana just happened to be an utter cunt, one of the least humble psycopaths – in the medical dictionary sense of that term – ever to bestride a newspaper office. No mean achievement, as may be inferred! Yet she never saw herself thus, as she was: spoilt, sick, desperately in need of clinical intervention. She saw herself as the kindly, scatty-savvy career-woman of whom her impersonation had singularly failed to impress her circle. One must add to this, in Arkana's case, the Midas Touch of wealth, which seems – to the wealthy's flattered eyes - to turn every black and bitter heart they touch to gold. It hides them from the truth about everyone: especially themselves . . . But then again, so what? Even "ordinary" people – the sort artists feast on because of their contradictions – exist as one type of individual, and are very much in touch with that life, immersed in it as a fish is by the sea. But they still imagine that they live a completely *different* life, and would be flabbergasted were someone to remove the scales from their eyes – and their backs – and acquaint them with their true environment. In that sense, Arkana was no more a hypocrite than the rest of us. A hypocrite, after all, inhabiting as he does only one *real* persona, *realises* that the other role he inhabits – and exhibits –is false. Arkana, like most of us, moved effortlessly between two worlds which were equally

177

real and true for her precisely because she never considered the one universe – and its veracity – from the perspective of the other.

Her husband Sir Quntee Mush – Australia's most famous sportsman and its first from Texan migrant stock – participated in all her delusions. He, too, was a devout Tim-Tam, and, equally, an infamous pilgrim in infidel cunt. In fact, like the monster in **Alien** and the "seven demons" who once invaded Mary Magdalene he liked to combine his two passions, invariably converting to Tim-Tam the gormless tarts he had implanted more conventionally. Sir Qunt – who had shot to fame as a captain of the ever-victorious Australian cricket team – also laboured under the belief he was a working journalist. He even took the credit - quite unjustifiably – for *"turning Kana's papers around"* – having found them in a state that was decidedly not tumescent. To hear him speak, indeed to read "his" shite-sheets, you would think that he alone had turned them into the playmates the *ne plus ultra* of the Sydney Middle Class they had undoubtedly become, the cattle-prods of a herd as violent as it is skittish; their dildos in fact, no matter how innocent their air of learning, or parlour-like their language. As big and bloody painful as they were unliveable without. The secret working-class lovers - indeed the secret working-class selves – of a race of would-be Lady Chatterleys . . . This was all quite untrue. It was a series of brilliant editors, most of them suggested and – greatly to Quntee's distress – later ennobled by the Labor Government, who had seen to that.

Arkana Muckadilla, meanwhile, was said to have saved her husband's bacon by giving birth to twin boys when his hated brother's wife dropped a shared "escort's" male bastard, thus threatening Quntee's dynastic pre-eminence. "Kana" was said to have been nearly beyond the age of child at the time – in fact she had flushed her uterus down the toilet some time before – but she entered into the spirit of the pregnancy with all the **Camille**-like ardor of a woman risking her life by conceiving *trop tard*, and, in due course, two males of the species were brought forth from behind the permanently closed shutters of the Balinese palace where "her Babyship" had been an unconscionable time a-whelping. ***THEY SAID IT WOULD KILL HER!"*** – was the headline of the *STAR* that day – the letters those clean, sarcastic ones with caps that gave a cold shower of truth to the *STAR'*s bright, *STÜRMER*-like excesses – much as "Zyklon B" had once calmed the naked, raging bodies of the Jews – and, in fact, the two one-year-old brutes that were presented on the front page for the delectation of the fruit-picklers of Moonta would indeed have finished her off had they exited from the orifice whence they were said to have derived. The text that accompanied the photographs said that, prior to the confinement, the Princess of Wales' gyneocologist had examined Lady Muck, and had declared that her "big tent" had been so "spavined" after the birth of her second daughter, "Fanni", that another successful delivery would be "a miracle": a bit of an understatement in the circumstances.

> *"But still she loved and served and served her Beau,*
> *And whoosh! he watched her Fanni grow!"*

– as Penises Freshley, "Woman and Showbiz" Editor, observed in an arch little couplet introducing a four-page feature on: ***"FANNI'S NEW LABOR!"*** – that the Government had suggested the *STAR* run on the occasion of the birth. A fey little piece that counseled "our Chicken Hero" to go easy on Kana's "big tent" for a bit, now that she had (as it were) "pulled out all the stops". Advice which, as Ms Freshley coyly noted, might not in fact be acted upon, such was the insatiable virility of their circumcisèd prince.

It was cogent advice, nonetheless, for, in the years before the advent of AIDS, so many West of Sydney builders, welders and part-time murderers and thieves had negotiated the anus and vagina of the uxorious couple, their internal passages had, at times, resembled the Cahill Expressway at 18.00. Now Sir Quntee, at least, was more circumspect, and kept a troupe of sterilized "Wetbacks" of both sexes in his private apartments at the Sheraton in Dallas, none of them more than twelve years old. (The local clergy had authorised their use as prefiguring the male *"Ghilman"* and female *"Googlies"* that the just – especially those who murder "Tinkerbelles" – will enjoy in Paradise). Three of these children lived permanently in the jacuzzi of his studio, having been trained to gag on his member *à la* the infants that once sported with the Emperor Tiberius in the waters off Capri. For this was the supporter of the *"C'mon Aussie C'mon!"* Labor Government, the modernising "patriot" who had forsaken Australia because he refused to pay even its derisory taxes, the uplifting scourge of Royals, "Tim-Tammophobes," and "pedophiles" [*sic*].

Once a year, the happy couple, the ikon the **STAR** held up to its readers on the blessings of Aussie life, would meet by appointment in Sydney – "Kana" had not been invited to Dallas – and dine in a restaurant considered exclusive by people like themselves - if only those – usually "Pong" in Coogee, where His Highness' "eccentricities" were overlooked. There they would compliment themselves on their Olympian natures and powers as they ate the indifferent Chinese food and surveyed the wall-to-wall Eurotrash with a self-satisfied feeling of having "made it". Under a voluminous tablecloth, two of Sir Quntee's water-babes would administer tongue jobs to the respective genitalia. These tender moments were the only occasions on which Australia's Mrs J. Randolph Hearst *A)* met her husband, *B)* enjoyed "intercourse" with him, and *C)* failed to give the customary 150% of her attention to her food, and then only because the ripening olive in her pudendum reminded her unpleasantly of a pecan that had stuck in her throat when a cake had been shoved down her gob to stop her screaming when she was forcibly circumcised on a date box in Fag-Dad in 1949.

If her husband had sought to elude the dread virus – the Nemesis of the Twentieth Century, the great leveller of the secretly depraved which even wealth and power could not buy off, nor lies conceal the sordid origins of – by confining his non-missionary affairs to children, Arkana had gone further – much further – in her flight. The needs of ladies and gentlemen are different in this respect, and if men require only an empty cup from the banquet of life, the fairer sex (or "the *allegedly* fairer sex", as Knut Fagan used to hail them), are themselves mere empty cups waiting, just waiting, to be filled. In fact, Lady Muck had found that members of the Animal Kingdom were not only free of unmentionable human amoeba, they were as hard and large as their Rooty Hill equivalents – usually even harder and larger – and their owners, while remaining quite as intellectual, were not as given as the denizens of Bankstown and Emu Plains to stupefying pleasantries. One year, visiting Borneo from her château on Bali – the very one, in fact, in which she had "delivered" Trangi and Yarram – she could not help but notice with admiration the masculine profile of the local Simians (not the native Mullahs), and had arranged for one to be imported into her palace. It was only with difficulty that the unhappy creature could be induced to enter the Inner Sanctum, however, and then only from behind and because the somewhat *"tordue"* plesaunce of Lady M, viewed from that angle, bore a passing resemblance to the infibula of one of the female animals he was more familiar with. Nevertheless, the experiment was successful, so much so, in fact, that "Kana" could not help screaming out, in her delight, "*bigger* than a coon, *better* than a coon!", a fit of hysteria that frightened the poor beast, which threw a fit of its own and nearly strangled her to death, messing the connubial bed with its urine and ordure. (The local Kunji had ordered the creature to be stoned to death, basing his judgement on that of the Gulgong himself, who once caused a troop of chimps to be stoned to death for blasphemy). The next day, when it looked like she might not survive, a special edition of the **STAR** was prepared with a pullout that detailed the rise of "the Milk Sheik's" daughter from Fag-Dad, through her marriage to "Aussie Battler Quntee", to her apotheosis as "Queen of the International Jet Set" and "Party-Girl Extraordinaire". A title was sought for this ensemble, and the Night Editor – who had suggested ***"THEY SAID IT WOULD KILL HER"*** - was summarily dismissed.

As if on cue, it was at this point that Arkana, with the meek, devilish air that Tim-Tammic evangelists have made their own, began to recite the "Kaymart" at me. She thought that this would "prove" what she had been saying, as if the Kaymart's "truth" were an external fact everyone conceded rather than the very thing we were in the process of disputing. Its verses sounded to me like the faux-Biblical sayings of the Aunt in *A Portrait of the Artist as a Young Man*, or those gems of wisdom that drunks, fathers and Woodwork teachers force on one, when one is obliged, weakly, to smile. Who, in fact, hearing the Kaymart on the lips of a glib, triumphalist Tim-Tam (is there any other kind?), has not felt disgust at having to take as great trembling pearls such worthless pebbles? No doubt one loses more than the idiom in translation, but then, one could say the same of our own Holy Scripture, and the translated Kaymart quite lacks the Mozartian depth and grace and multivalence of the translated Bible. It is not redolent, as are the Gospels and Torah (or the Upanishads and Avesta) of a civilization at its height. Unsurprisingly, perhaps, given the date of its composition, it has a brittle, Dark Age quality, like a hut in mediaeval Rome made of the badly-integrated spolia of larger, older, intelligent things. There are many echoes of the Bible, but they are peurile and distorted. Arkana informed me that man had created the Bible, and the Lord, the Kaymart, but even God seemed reluctant to claim credit for such platitudes. His hand wasn't exactly easy to spot. Indeed, "Christina", the goddess of Tim-Tam, seemed unrecognisable to anyone raised on the Bible, as spiteful and one-dimensional as the Kaymart's "Moses", "Abraham" and "Jesus", and as given as them to *Bon Mots* which, had one been ignorant of their authorship, one might have attributed to Hitler or Patience Strong.

Though I was, with the usual difficulty, still eating a Mud Crab, Arkana waved a plate of Lamingtons at me – and at the Porno Publisher-type person who appeared as she was kindly indulging my harsh if tentative ideas. I noted how considerately she nudged the conversation in my direction as the Porno Queen expatiated with breezy mock-crestfallen shamelessness on his "success". This individual, who was now in the process of seating himself noisily at our table, was none other than Arkana's husband Sir Quntee Mush: he was wearing a Kenzo leather jacket. (Given the rarefied nature of the event, a Bronco had approached and plucked it from his shoulders). Quntee seemed to talk a lot about gatecrashing. He didn't know whether to crash the **SPECTATOR** party in London in eight weeks, or one at "the Boathouse in Central Park" at approximately the same time. Jingili whispered that he was the "toyboy" of a famous British designer whom he was just then trying to convert. What did that make the dressmaker? A hundred and ten? (. . . His lover turned out to be a surprisingly young woman – *co ûturier*, people had once joked, to the Khmer Rouge: she was famous for having put every socialite in London in wrinkled black pyjamas – though she could as easily have been the nonagerian Pierre Cardin had the publicity been right and Pierre himself not a connoisseur of beauty). I felt sorry for Kana as Prince Charming hardly seemed the ideal husband, but then, as Sir Dewy so sentimentally informed me: "Marriage is like suicide and, like suicide, everyone attempts it at least once".

Sir Quntee was a well-spoken Texan with very white teeth – the sort who, funnily enough, looks rather Jewish – one of that indeterminate group, like a completely new type of human being, whose strange, synthetic representatives seem remarkably alike whether you meet them in Sydney, the Levant or New York. Posh, expensively if repulsively dressed. Not "the real thing". Inherently repulsive to a real person in the world to which they aspire. Like Mercedes-Benz cars, they're too perfect, too frequently encountered: their "polish" off-puttingly "off-the-peg" and ubiquitous. The Texans would resemble the other discreetly despised group even more were they not completely lacking in culture. Absolutely bereft. Absolutely. Helpless – like children – with vaste mansions filled with awful things like the homes of Britain's Indian millionaires. (Quntee's home in Dubai, for instance, was so unrelievedly hideous it would have made the place where we were having dinner look like the Petit Trianon). Sleek, vacuous, pretty – curiously decorative in their pretend Paris clothes – they would remind one of eunuchs or speyed Persian cats were they not as rank and libidinous as dogs.

Sir Quntee's head – meaty, almost spherical – was composed of scores of flat planes. He introduced himself as a "film producer" (it turned out to be something like **A Day in the Life of a Bee**). It was clear that he disliked me intensely. In an effort to make conversation, I would say something: he would deliberately try to speak at the same time. Then he would sarcastically urge me on, quoting my shattered intro as a prompt: *"Yes, and David Hockney ...?"* He was enraged by this because nothing, clearly, pleased him more than the sound of his phoney Bostonian voice. He spoke out of the corner of his mouth, which he would twist it into a moist, uteral triangle. He told a long, unfunny story, presumably for my benefit (he must have thought I was a Nancy, which shows how closely he listened to people), about how Robert Helpmann had once attempted, not without success, to toss him off. He oozed self satisfaction: the slipstreams of butter, mottled with raisins and powdered with sugar, reminded you of his golden skin and juicy, dropsical hair; reminded you of the big unassimilated ideas that clung to him like ticks to a golden labrador. His expression, most unfortunately for a Tim-Tam, suggested the libidinous mirth of a dog. A gap in his front teeth intensified this. There was a yellow film over the whites of his eyes, which made you think – like his pride and stupidity – of a horse. There was a honey-coloured brightness on his black, curly hair. His face was the rich, rich yellow of cold chicken fat, and covered, like the rest of his body, in a drizzly stubble. I took note of his particoloured frame and the play of his black and white opinions. They were always dancing like flames on some dream of power. I remembered the terrifying Australian magpies that plague the lawns outside the Parliament Building in Canberra. They swoop on everything that glitters, gold or not, and they prize blond Barbie-Doll heads no whit less than the bracelets of blow-dried Senators. I am afraid that I devoted to Sir Quntee's horse-like arrogance the intense absorption of the woman scorned, the social inferior, and the intellectual snob. (It is as easy to take refuge in the height of the intellect as in a hot air balloon, a world self-contained and remote from reality). We all find it refreshing, and surprisingly therapeutic, to condemn in others what is just as contemptible in ourselves. My hypocrisy at this point claimed its descent from the virginal nihilism of all young people (I was then one!) Young people look at the world destructively, as a Tim-Tam does, as a child looks at its mother: as if it were omnipotent, a punchbag, not something human and breakable that has been patiently built up by sinners' hands. The young are frequently so successful because, like the Australian "intellectuals" who triumph in more literate countries, they have never been taught how stupid they are. But the world isn't a pagan goddess: every time we violate her, she cannot reclaim her virginity just by bathing in rivers of our piss. "Hell is other people", they say, but what are "other people" but ourselves? When we injure others – secure in the idea that they are invincible, parental, omnipotent – don't we hurt only our own delicate selves? *"If you prick us, do we not bleed? If you tickle us, do we not laugh? If you poison us, do we not die?"* (This was a speech which Sir Quntee, who funded a number of anti-Jewish bioterrorists, had memorised by heart). Dare we dismiss anyone? Isn't everyone equally profound, equally important? Isn't every individual equally sublime?

Artists, after all, are distinguished from non-artists, not by their creativity, but by their *consciousness*, or self-consciousness. The *artistique*, I feel, are aware of their own and other people's creativity, whereas the non-artists, lacking self-consciousness, cannot identify what is significant about themselves: that is the artist's job. As Tray Beautous used to say: *"the painter has to rescue the unique and transient world of others as well as his own: it's a race against time."* He used strongly to agree with Sir Vidia Naipaul, who once complained, in his essay *"Conrad's Darkness"*:

> **"the painter no longer recognizes his interpretive function; he seeks to go beyond it; and his audience diminishes. . . Experimentation, not aimed at the real difficulties, has corrupted response . . . And so the world we inhabit, which is always new, goes by unexamined, made ordinary by the camera, unmeditated on; and there is no one to awaken the sense of true wonder."**

Is not the giddiest bantam, the most empty-headed, Prada-loving queen, as profound, in his constitution, his God-given ingredients, as a Vico or a Kierkegaard? In cretinous little Tim-Tams, say – or in any other non-artist – the profundity is surely present but pathological, whereas in Goya or Shakespeare it has been identified by its human parent, isolated and brought to the surface, like salt that is panned in the sun. In an artist's model, an athlete or a woman, say, *"whose lives and interests,"* (Tray would tritely pontificate), "are worthless in every way," there is yet a residue of power, which is what they *are*, something an artist can isolate, celebrate, but which, because they live it, women and athletes are blind to. I knew that in Sir Quntee Mush, and people like him, profundity rested in something inaccessible, as illness resides in a patient, and that only the unpleasant and irritating symptoms were visible, never the wise and powerful demon within.

He must have had something, after all. Several papers and TV shows – each an Aussie institution – were said to be "under the direction" of Sir Qunt, a fourth generation bison-herd chiefly famous abroad for being married to his wife and for inserting the soubriquet "Prince" under "Occupation" in his Australian passport. (This was not a particular mark of distinction, "Princes" being as common as toilet bowls in the Tim-Tammic world, objects of the same neglect, and more recent). He was supposedly in Canberra to try to buy from Dew the ruins of the demolished statue of Brooklana Fagan on Magnetic Island. This was because Sir Qunt – or so he told us – wished to turn the Piazza San Pietro outside Saint Peter's in Rome into a "sculpture park" or "Garden of Remembrance" dedicated to "Tim-Tammic mar-teers" (Sunny-Pinnian suicide bombers). The idea was to sprinkle Brookee's monstrous beshivered limbs across the plangent veldt like dogs' diarrhoea.

Sir Quntee wished to go one better than the Aga Khan, who had just insisted that the British Government hand him St Thomas's Hospital opposite Big Ben in London so the Ismaili leader could turn it into the world's biggest "Islamic Cen-teer". Sir Quntee had claimed – or so he said – that the Vatican was *morally obliged* to emulate Her Majesty's Government and endorse his plan. As he had sharply reminded Their Serenities, Muslim Arab raiders had once sacked and desecrated Saint Peter's Basilica in the year 846, stealing and melting down the gilded sarcophagus of the Apostle himself. The native Christians had dared to oppose this blessèd act of Muslim piety, and several of the Arabs had been slain and dismembered, their body parts later being used (according to the somewhat *outré* taste of the time) to decorate the city's churches. Brooklana's *"colossal sadomasochistic tidbits"* (to give us Edward Said's name for or them) would, said Sir Qunt, serve as a fitting sepulchre for these *non*-Tim-Tammic (Muslim) mar-teers, as well as for the atomized Sunny-Pinnians. Soon, he said, Rome would be a bigger centre of non-Christian pilgrimage than of Christian, as was only just.

Pope John-Yoko the First had offered to deliver the Piazza into Quntee's hands "with all humility" (according to Mush) when the Organisation of Tim-Tammic States (*OTTAS*) warned that, were he to refuse, the sincerity of his famous apology to the *Muslim* world for the Crusades might (for example) be doubted. The Crusades being an attempt by mediaeval Christians to retrieve the Holy Land from Muslims who had just attacked and stolen it from them, how could the "hurt and distress" inflicted on the Tim-Tammic invaders of 20th century Rome by Christians unwilling to suck dick be any less worthy of reparation? Anyway, according to Quntee, the Pope had managed to convince both Cardinals and Catholic faithful of the "advantages" of surrendering the Piazza with arguments a little more cynical than the Quietist piety that had perhaps inspired him. (Well, that figures!) But once Brooklana's "remains" had been installed, His Holiness declared (in Quntee's version of the tale), the great semi-circular colonnade stretching out like arms to embrace the Piazza from the "torso" that is St Peter's Basilica would resemble the arms of Mother Church holding the broken body of her "daughter", Tim-Tam, a "Christina" crucified by "Pharisees" who had initially begrudged the Texans a mere *"handful of dust"*. It would represent a "variation" on Michelangelo's *"Pietà"* inside the cathedral which shows the Holy Virgin cradling a saviour impaled on the spite of "the Zionist Jews" . . . And that was why Quntee's request had allegedly been approved. (This was *"the verry parfit gentil knight's"* version of the negotiations anyway).

Unfortunately, murdering Christ and an insolent propensity to try to save their own loathesome skins did not exhaust the depravity of the Jewish nation. According to Mush, one of Arkana's business rivals, Sir Mozzy Akimbo, had, out of pure spite, put in an impressive counterbid for the wreckage on Magnetic Island, intending to place it in Jezreel, Israel, in the midst of Silvio Pufulette's "sandpit sculpture", *"Dog Dunny"*, which he had just purchased. Akimbo had announced that the ensemble would form a new memorial to Brooklana Fagan. Jezreel, specifically, had been chosen because it was in Jezreel according to the Bible's **Book of Kings** that the Biblical matriarch Jezebel had, like Brookee, been thrown to her death from a high balcony by two eunuchs. Her broken limbs had then become food for the local mongrel scavengers – hence the intended proximity to *"Dog Dunny"*. To frustrate "the perfidious Jew", and to secure the debris for Tim-Tam – not by outbidding Mozzy, but by bestowing a few little *soupçons* in high places – had required Quntee to make this personal visit. Or so he said. It was not for nothing that he and his wife had been placed at the Premier's table.

Just then I became aware of a movement above my head. I looked up. A pink, transparent gekko – its dark guts quite visible – was darting across the bare, endless ceiling. Short bursts and long pauses, like a spider . . . The noise, the parquet and the humourless brick walls made the salon seem like a Conference Room. It brimmed with the sort of suffocating airiness one finds in stately homes. Blue cigarette smoke filled its limpid zone like a weeping cataract. Here and there a richly polished Chinese vase or censer looked, like the naked statues, painfully alone. Alive both to the emptiness and the paradoxical cacophony, I couldn't relax.

The lady massaging her infernal machine struck up another favourite. "That was *'I saw Mummy Kissing Santa Claus'*," said Dew, sweeping Bon with a meaningful glance. The organist started playing *"The Road to Gundagai"*. I believe it is based on a famous Australian poem: *"Where the Dog sits on the Tuckerbox on the Road to Gundagai"*. "That's a jaunty rendition of the song," I observed. "It goes with the food," said Arkana. "He must have been *here*!" she added, referring, I think, to the dog. She and Sir Quntee had each been served "Game Pie": a hollow pumpkin swimming with what looked like shit. Arkana swore that there was nary an ounce of "game" (Kangaroo or Emu) in it: "It's edible, that's about all you can say." Taking his usual pains with the feelings of his fellow man, Quntee wished aloud that he had booked dinner at the "less expensive" Hilton. "As dear old King Hussein used to tell me," he concluded in his ludicrous Midwestern glissando; "*'Poor show, old girl, poor show!'* "

An old blind man who also had a posh accent, in his case an "Anglo-Australian" one, started fumbling around our table. He tapped our chairs with a white stick, trying to find the toilet and then a place to sit. Nobody seemed to like him. "What am I doing here?" he wailed. His blindness was a bait. He dangled it like a penis, to banish loneliness. He tried, dramatically and with difficulty, to seat himself next to us. *"Sittin' with the boyz agen, Bazel?"* the oafs at the next table jeered. Labor Party activists, they were the insipid oafs of the suburbs. They were not real working-class morons; they just affected to be – a common enough pastime in Australia. "Just like yew to take the piss out of a blind man," the old fatty whined – he was wearing clean white shirtsleeves – but his affected voice meant that he probably was a homosexual. His delicate dead eyes looked like roses. "Have you ever seen me?" he asked. "No," I said. *"Well, thank God for that!"* he replied. He asked me if it were dark outside. I said that it was. "Then why is it bright in here?" He took a torch out of his pocket and turned it on. "Can you see that?" he asked. I replied in the affirmative.

Dew was reaching out to plunder one of the baskets of sweets on the table. "Sugared almonds," he said, crunching one loudly between his molars; " – cinnamon sticks!" He took them out of the basket and laid them carefully on the plate. He described to me watching "beautiful women" undress in the next street from the mezzanine of his Sydney residence. He ordered himself a grotesque sundae and, even though I was talking to him, began rudely to flick through one of those semi-pornographic young professional women's magazines that Jingili had brought to the table. He pointed out one of the pictures in it with excited superior relish, as if the joke were on the model. She was lying stretched out on a beach with her back to the camera, her yellow buttocks covered in sand. The grains looked like ants, as if she were a corpse. Dewy suddenly became agitated: Braith and Julatten were starting to play up again. He seemed afraid of them. "I'll smack yer fuckin' bum," he warned Braith. "Daddy'll smack *you*," Braith replied, in one of the rapid, demented escalations typical of childhood. "I'll kick yer liddle bum, yer liddle turd!" Dew replied. He ate the last of the almonds. "I hope we get some nice chocos with coffee," he noted; " – and give me some of that silver paper." Dew took a sweet out of his mouth, wrapped it in the foil, and put it back in the basket. "Oh, give me some cool air, *ployyyse*!" he suddenly cried. (It wasn't only warm, it was getting very smoky) .

Sir Quntee Mush winked at me. Slumped in his chair on that diaphanous Australian evening, the mighty "Man of Affairs" had the demeanour of a lonely public schoolboy, ambiguous as those plummy, wet-eyed boys always are. His face was puce-red now with the booze. His adamantine geisha bouffant had melted into dripping bangs. He was wearing a mauve blouse open to the waist: his golden paps were black with webbed hair. His "assistant," the Englishman sitting next to him, was a ferrety former soldier. The soldier had a thin, angular face, a large mouth and an enormous forehead; a frog's metallic eyes, a frog's cruel mouth. The soldier had the dark tie of a criminal or an off-duty policeman. The soldier gave us a frenzied account of his military history and was deep in naïvety. He was so naïve, so purely the child, that he wasn't even boasting. A moist, ripe cockney accent – the voice of hairless, muscular bodies, of frogs, of a machismo so purely animal it is reptile. He had won four points out of five in a shooting competition, he said. Soldiers "would flock" to the brothels of Belize. "Well," said Sir Quntee Mush, "they have to keep their spirits up, haven't they?" He sprinkled the soldier's wildly subjective monologue with adroitly neutral asides, as I would have done, but Sir Quntee wasn't nearly as sophisticated as I, which made me curious about him. That being said, he must have been more sophisticated than the average toffee-nosed brute, who, subtle enough to realise that the soldier's tendentious account was boasting, would oafishly have mocked him. But then, what would the average toff have been doing in the company of such a man? And yet, there seemed nothing *unmanly* about the hairy-chested one. He was more like a little boy playing with a dog. The squaddie now started talking about the effect on the Belizian economy of holidaying soldiers. He said that five soldiers would book one double room to crash out and copulate in, but not him, he was too fastidious: "I was born in Canada", he explained . . .

Just then, a door opened between two of the naked statues. A number of Japanese tourists were disgorged, accompanied by a tour guide. Allow me to say I was pretty astonished. The tour guide pointed at our party rudely and began an impassive but analytical monologue, while a hundred flashes exploded over us like snowballs. The clicks and whirrs of the cameras reminded me of sticks breaking in a fire. The Japanese were mostly oldish men. There were a few young women too, who looked like fiendish old homosexuals. They were dressed identically in shorts and floppy white hats. Stony-faced, they pushed their way in crowds into the middle of the room, careful not to discard their listless impersonality. They shot at us and at each other, a quite involuntary act: their faces were like those of urinating dogs. It was somewhat chilling, this sardonic filming amid the alien bustling. A troop of Australian Bull Ants had marched into a nest of termites and had begun sagely to eat the inhabitants. The devoured termites were equally impassive, and were still lost in the contemplation of their own activities. Perhaps they were just stunned. Then the tour guide ushered the trippers out again. "Like fuckin' ants," said Dew, pretending to wipe something off the front of his smock. (Outside, three more Japanese tour buses had drawn up. The denizens had decided not to alight. Instead, the coaches, bristling with every conceivable life-giving image maker, blasted away at the Viceregal Mansion like ships of the line: we could all see flashes of lightning in the chamber's high-set windows).

Sir Quntee suddenly turned towards his soldier assistant. "How's your woman?" he asked. He parleyed with an air of revolting masculinity, and more than a little faux-naïvety, since the woman in question was actually *his* "woman" – his wife Arkana – with whom he had "set the assistant up" a few days' before. Sir Quntee sipped his Foster's nervously, he said to make it last. He was trying to cut down on his drinking, he said, though, "a man must not be very Tim-Tam," he added, smiling. He was going through a semi-portly phase, this Prince of Allambi, and his "real" or Platonic body, nearly as lithe and fit as the soldier's, had swollen milkily. This had always happened when he was in love. Sir Quntee had a broad chest, but his torso was composed, not of muscle, but of that luxurious half-fibrous flab that you see on Rugby-shirted runners in the stockbroker belt. In his Filofax, which had swollen in the same way, and for the same reasons, he had written (according to what Arkana later told me) pages of pathetic possible diets in his tiny, subnormal hand. These had made the cynical Arkana ashamed, she said, when she had rifled the book in order to laugh at him. Next to these diets she had found paragraphs with these headings:

> " *1. Address of Mudludja* [Quntee's divorced mother]
> *2. Address of Kan's boyfriend* [not the ape]
> *3. Fisty and Jurien*"

Sir Quntee would drag their dead daughter Fisty into every conversation ("what are you always digging *her* up for?" Arkana had once insensitively asked), and – said Arkana – he visited the child's cold bed on the eve of every *"Eneaba"* (a Tim-Tammic festival), and on her birthday, too – a favour he rarely bestowed on Arkana. He would look at his hated spouse and find himself unable to imagine his Fisty; he would look at his stomach and be incapable of picturing his willy. The diets were having little effect.

192

Slumped temporarily pot-bellied in the glare of the Nipponese flashbulbs, drenched in the ectoplasmic spume of their ravages, Sir Quntee Mush reminded me of a big, transparent lady spider. Any moment, one felt, his atypically large abdomen would melt like a peach and scores of tiny baby spiders would scuttle out, climbing over each other, scattering everywhere in frightening, teeming sharp bursts like magnetised iron filings. In the meantime, he spun a milky web out of the engorged belly. His enquiry about the assistant's "woman" had produced absolutely no effect, so he repeated it, eliciting nothing more than a distracted: *"She's awright!"* Arkana was looking distinctly uncomfortable.

One could tell that "the Prince" was wondering how to proceed. For all his earthy, matey directness, he was a calculating individual. He was a genuinely simple man, but perversion, which brings self-knowledge to the intelligent, makes stupid people "cunning". Cunning, however, is a way of seeing in the dark which is of no use during daylight hours, and it was a gift which Sir Quntee Mush could certainly not use to penetrate his own darkness. It is no use being a fox if you do not appreciate the taste of pheasant. Sir Quntee's assistant was also unself-aware. He was the product of an ugly, abusive childhood, and (said Arkana) it was apparent to people who knew him well (which did not include Sir Quntee), that he was somewhat disturbed. He displayed all the innocence and spontaneity of the disturbed. Unfortunately, he also displayed all the disturbance of the disturbed, which, from Sir Quntee's point of view, made it extremely difficult to pump him for information. Like a child, he could be sulky, angry, naively sensitive and withdrawn.

When I was a boy (if I may digress for a moment!), I remember that my mother once kept beehives. Watching Sir Quntee trying to interrogate his assistant on a delicate matter – and for the assistant, anything might be – reminded me of how Mum would try gingerly to take sheets of honey out of the hive. Mum absolutely adored the bees, and, I must say, the bees seemed to quite like her! She would stand with a rectangular golden slab in each hand, like the Recording Angel. Quaffing a black beard, sucking a watermelon. The seeds on her lips were insects. But the bees, into whose hard but fleshy oozing one could sometimes drive one's hands harmlessly, as into a bowl of mussels, could turn nasty, even with the belovèd. The oozing beard could become a burning bush. One had to be careful. Keep it all on a cheerful, matey level. Sir Quntee phrased his next question with a charming indirectness. "Have you done the business with her yet?" It would no more have occurred to the ferrety former soldier to conceal anything than it would to reveal it, and he said that he had. One could see that this gave the knight feelings of pleasure. You could tell by his dreamy face that the fact that he didn't yet know all the details of his wife's relationship with the soldier – and would find it hard to get these out of him – endowed their acts with an aching, endless beauty.

Speculation about the operation of nature is swiftly satisfied, by experiment. Tortured by uncertainty as to the existence of God or the devil, we can run away from mental life to the "real" world. God, evil, gravity, don't seem to exist there, which is to say, they don't seem to exist *here*, which is why not only troubled monks, but cowards and evildoers of every sort, find ordinary, everyday life a delicious oasis. But defying the laws both of Physics and Metaphysics, curiosity about concealed human behaviour can never be escaped or resolved. It can lead to an obsessional theorising that is almost physical, and comes to resemble the sexual acts it seeks to pin down, only to find them dissolve, as when we awake from a very real dream. Even now, when he knew that his friend definitely had entertained Arkana, Sir Quntee clearly found it hard to reconcile the glib and childish face of the soldier with the drunken driver of that hard, white, flaky body. It was harder and more exciting still to picture a curved bicep in the trembling palm of his wife's hand, and the horrible concentration on his friend's face, so alien to his obvious stupidity, as he made love. It was quite obvious that Sir Quntee hated his wife for knowing so much more about the beautiful soldier than he did.

Like the Baghdad of *The Arabian Nights*, which was divided into circles within circles, spheres within spheres, a beehive or a simple human being can show a frightening diversity of natures. Sometimes the most frightening comes to the surface first. From time to time, I would fleetingly glimpse the deepest part of Quntee Mush in his face, or hear it in his voice. This was the woundedly sexual part: his heart, "the Commander of the Faithful" (sometimes the Commander of the anything but Faithful). His heart, a big, angry Queen Bee, was something one should never have been allowed to see on the Earth, far from its secret home, just as one should never be allowed to see a meteorite down here on the planet (the form in which Allah is worshipped in the Kaaba in Mekka). It was a part of him that was not particularly happy to have fallen out of its fire, its hell, into the frying pan of the world. I had seen this heart, a big brown Queen Bee, buzzing there angrily like a Cumberland Sausage. That was unpleasant and good.

I now felt very sleepy and a little sick. I rose and made my excuses to my assembled family, to Sir Quntee Mush, to Arkana Muckadilla, even to the stupid assistant. I said that I had to go to bed. Bon announced that the former bedroom of Knut Fagan (surprisingly enough, he and Brooklana had enjoyed separate apartments), unused since his demise, had been made ready for me. An artist favoured by Knut had filled it with frescos, Bon explained, frescos which had not been properly applied. The room, Bon continued, was only ever lit by candles in order to preserve the unstable preparation on its walls. It was kept as a "schroyn" to the statesman; it had not been altered since his death. A Bronco called Zane with a tattoo on his chest showing Cannabis leaves was already by my side. He was holding a candelabra. Like a Christmas Tree, it radiated heat. It dripped like a forest of icicles. "How romantic!" Bon laughed, winking both at me and the Bronco. She told him to take me to my boudoir. "Goodnight ladies!" I cried, as sarcastically as possible.

AN ARSEHOLE AS BIG AS THE RITZ

I followed Zane out of the great oven of the Aula Regia – as bright and noisy as an Operating Theatre – into a warren of pitch black corridors. The air conditioning made them cold: there was a delicious smell of cannabis. The balloon of light that trembled above Zane's hand contained vestigial cloud and bones like a foetus in a fertilized egg. With its palpitating bubbles and burning leaves it reminded me of a jellyfish pulsating through the black deep. Here and there the light scratched what might have been anything from a bookcase to an electric fan. When a diver shines a torch inside a wreck you can never tell what you are looking at. There seemed to be as many receding interiors and exteriors as inside my mother's beehive, a black and yellow lacquer cabinet, a wilderness of slimy rooms. We stopped before the door of one of them. Zane turned to face me, bringing the burning candles towards his chest. I leapt back in fright as a fledgling's horrible beak and its melon eyes jumped up at me in the mottled light. Under the cover of darkness, Zane must have taken the *"Commedia dell'Arte"* mask from his hips and placed it on his face! Not wishing to find out why he had unwrapped his genital, I grabbed the candelabra, rushed into Knut's bedroom and slammed the door behind me.

Some of the candles had gone out, others guttered as the frame swayed in my shaking hand. My face was flat against a suffocating black. A little light puffed around the flames before they could grow strong again. I had sweated: the wetness on my face had become cold. There was an odd smell – the sweet, slightly fecal smell of provincial museums with glass cases of stuffed animals. And, in fact, the walls, washed in the molasses of the steadily growing candles, appeared to be of glass. I seemed to be in one of those aquariums where all the walls are of glass. You feel surrounded by a stormy, silent jungle and there are brief lightning flashes of beautiful white fish. Big yellow things like the undersides of crocodiles were swaying behind the shiny walls. (Or perhaps they weren't moving at all: motion may have been suggested by the distortions of the billowing candlelight). One could make out a faint grid of lines on the yellowy-white ovals, as on the belly of a Sea Turtle. They shook in clear green gelatine against what appeared to be a grainy filigree of sea grass.

My attention was drawn to the middle of the room. An animal sense told me something human was nearby. I became very afraid. The centre of the room was in intense, repulsive darkness. I wanted to run, but I couldn't bear to face the mockery of my family, and especially of the despicable Quntee Mush. Would I even find my way back to the Dining Room through the tangle of corridors I had crossed? What if the eccentric and now exquisitely aroused Zane was awaiting me? The "thing" would have confronted me by now had it been hostile, so I pushed towards where I sensed it . . . I was quickly overtaken by amazement. What suddenly sprang out of the light bubble in front of me – long before I had thought I would reach it – was so pert and foolish I could no longer feel strange. An unreal upturned face like a cake lay on the green pillow of a bed. Its eyes were tightly shut, its mouth obscenely open. It looked exactly like one of those white wooden clowns' heads at the Fair that turn from side to side and into whose gaping mouths you push rubber balls. It was obviously one of the stuffed and lacquered Bronco cadavers but, unlike the others, it no longer rejoiced in one of Bonnie's cast-off Balenciaga frocks. The candlelight, creeping forward like spilt Maple syrup, revealed a perfect naked body. The limbs and torso were more "natural-looking" than the face which – as happens with prepared corpses – had been subject to sugary restoration. The body was quite beautiful. As on the appointed day the ants swarm out of their nests, the queens swarm out, icy with wings, and the ground above the ant colony, so dry and dead, is revealed to have always been immanent, imminent with life, so too the Bronco's body, just before its death, had obviously begun to prickle with an endless neuter masculinity. It would only have taken a few months for the vast chest to resemble, as it did now, a beautiful white fish crawling with ants. I felt like saying – as the Byzantine Emperor Theodore II Laskaris was heard to remark when he first set eyes on the ruins of Pergamum – *"the city of the dead is more beautiful than the city of the living!"* How unusual

197

it looked! The torso was a great wedge of white Stilton. It wept like Stilton, sweated, and the long strands of black chest hair were matted in places like sodden algae. It reminded me of a dead shark I had seen a few days before on Barranjoey Beach in North Sydney: large, lithe, rich and white – gently tapering – bubbling, fluted, muscular as ice cream. Smooth and white, but with a delicious graininess to it like an unstretched canvas or the pitted surface of an egg. Black lashes not feathery but even and granular like thread fawned on its bulges like magnified fingerprints. There were dark patches on the rippling and glittering stomach like the blue veins in a pebbly wet cheese. Bringing the candles close to the body I saw that it was a tattoo, a big wide blue band encircling the navel and comprised of indigo letters. It read: *"This is a SELF PORTRAIT by Tray Beautous"*.

I was instantly charmed by the audacity of a masterpiece of installation art – not usually my favourite type. I remembered the name: that of the painter whose work had impressed me in the National Gallery of Australia. I decided I would very much like to meet this artist and to see his other things – perhaps consider whether it was worth taking his items to London. It might be a shrewd move on my part, as I was certainly not aware of his penetration of that market. No doubt he had a studio in Sydney, like every other Australian artist. I would ask Dew and Bon about it in the morning. Tray Beautous' presence in the Canberra gallery surely indicated a degree of national prominence which might not have escaped even them . . . But I had been so tense. My heart and intestines suddenly unclenched like shoelaces when you pull them open. An unearthly voluptuous weakness overcame me:

> *"I descend my western course . . . my sinews are flaccid,*
> *Perfume and youth course through me, and I am their wake"*

I had to sleep myself, simply had to, I couldn't put it off a moment longer. You know what it's like when you're too tired to even make preparations for bed? I didn't fancy lying on on the mattress with the corpse, but I didn't fancy sleeping on the hard polished floor either, now that my hands had bathed in the cold inviting succulence of the coverlet. It was a double bed so there should have been enough room for me as well but I still couldn't bear the thought of touching "it". Anyway, had I tried to lift it to the floor, it might have broken like a big, foul, perfumed cake. As the Bronco lay slap bang in the middle of the bedspread, I put the candelabra on a bedside table, pinched him gingerly on the right shoulder – the skin felt cold and untouched like an ornament – and tipped him over so that he ended up lying face down on the edge of the bed furthest from myself. Even in the wavering light I could see – at the intersection of two blotchy, blown, staved-in wild birds' eggs – that someone – presumably Knut Fagan – had been using the beautiful corpse-chrysalis for a purpose for which it had not – or perhaps had been – intended . . . I sank down onto the part of the bed that I had exposed. I lay down full length and fully dressed. I now hardly sensed the presence of the corpse lying next to me: it seemed to be as light as thistledown, and no doubt it was, stripped of all its gizzards like a crab. I reached over, blew out the candles, fell back and was immediately asleep. What a series of very odd dreams I had that night!

I honestly believe that to dream is to be born. It is well known that the Australian Aborigines – like the ones I had so recently said goodbye to – believe that this world of ours was dreamed into existence. Is that really as corny, as "touristy" an idea as it appears? After all, it is lost in precisely that ecstatic onward current, like someone falling over Niagra, fleshed by a rainbow, that you remember your origins when you are a very small child. When you are a child, you reach back into your past and what you seem to remember is not starting out, not beginning something, but arriving at a conclusion, ie existing at the end of some fantastic ante-natal drama, some extended epic of wierdness and pleasure. Our first memories – as children – are the memories of dreams that we had when we were very, very small. Or were they perhaps real occurrences? When a child looks back, it is hard to separate the memories with some foundation in the world from those with none, just as historians find it hard, when studying the earliest dynasties of Imperial China – the Shang, for instance – to distinguish the definitely historical episodes from those attributable to myth. At one time the myths – or the dreams, or the facts – moved forward in an enclosed, omnipotent world, free of outsiders, observers, like the monstrous fish that live at the bottom of the sea. Now, like lobsters in the tank in "Décadence Mandchoue" (the international "Art Party's" favourite Chinese restaurant in the suburb of Dee Why, Sydney), their redeemer the historian has plucked them out of their goldfish bowl and cast them, screaming, into the boiling water of Time. Once they were the coral that bloomed on the Barrier Reef: a yellow, Budgerigar-blue or sugary salmon-pink coral. Now, lifted out of the jewel case of the sea, they have become as white and dead as a handful of salt. Once they were alive and conscious of no life but their own and that of the great story – lost to us – that had pushed them further and further out. Now they are dead, or the dream is dead, because the dreamer has survived and surveyed it, as an artist does – the only type of human being to have looked back on Sodom and been turned into a pillar, not of salt, but of society.

My own first memory is definitely of a dream. I had the dream when I was three. The only thing I can retrieve from it is the image of a plane – a fighter plane. (How could I have learned at that age what one looked like? Perhaps from TV: I was born at the start of the Vietnam War). The jet is stationary, alone, only half lit up. It sits, tail down, nose up, in the darkness of a blackened room: a dog sitting on its haunches. The cabin is a bubble of cool, waxy light; it is full of luminous surfaces like the inside of a fridge. The seat is made up of tubes of glaucous, off-viridian white, like the panels of a sweet. The aircraft is covered in a smooth, pine-green metal. The colour of the plane, its deep, deep malachite green, somehow makes it look harmless and sacred . . . This was my first dream – and my first memory. As I can remember nothing before this image (even though, in objective terms, a lot must have happened to me – including being born) – it must be the moment at which I became alive. Because the objective facts of our lives, what other people might see, don't matter. Only what we register or record ourselves constitutes existence. In that sense, everyone is an artist

. . . Anyway, the dreams I had that night in the Viceregal Mansion of Australia were very, very precise – at least as sharp as the primordial dream of the fighter plane. Or what I *remember* of them is precise. I can only recall disconnected fragments of the first, for instance, like the towers of a half-eaten cake.

It was afternoon in the first dream, the holy afternoon of Childhood, when you are just about to get out of school, when you are pining for home, for heaven, as you long for death at the end of life. Especially if it is a FRIDAY, as it was in this dream, when you can be sure, as a child, of enjoying a beautiful, powerful dream before you wake up on Saturday morning. Anticipation which simply adds to the magic of that *Fin-de-Siècle* feeling of freedom, hope and longing. The beautiful decadent sun of a late Summer afternoon came through the sash windows of the classroom, the big Papaya-orange sun of escaping from school, the mellow yet intense Mozart-sun of an asexual childhood, the cider-coloured **Cosi Fan Tutte** Mother-sun of going home. To go home is to cross from the objective to the subjective, from the false to the true: though, for a child, of course, these terms denote the exact opposite of their adult equivalents. To go home from school, as a child, is to cross the abrupt totalitarian border. It is to leave life with its pain and struggle, the external world of the adult, and return to death and love and dream and womb and peace. Doesn't anyone understand that what we miss most about childhood is its peace, or (which is to say the same thing) its freedom? Anything that contradicts freedom destroys peace, and vice versa. That is why old age – however "serene" – is never, ever peaceful. Simply to know the restrictions on freedom – which anyone who has reached maturity can hardly fail to grasp – is to feel anguish, a restless horror. Just as an animal does not know that it will have to die, a child does not know that it will have to live, that it will lose its peace, its freedom. That is what makes childhood – while it lasts – so uniquely radiant.

In this, the first dream that night, I was in a wooden classroom – one of those makeshift classrooms they erect on a temporary basis in the middle of playgrounds. There was a modern feeling in the dream, as there always is in adult dreams that recall childhood, a sexual feeling. The memory of childhood is like an innocent antiquity framed by the serpent; looking back on the Garden from Dante's **_Inferno_** . . . The dream was an Irish-childhood-type narrative, like a Jimmy Cagney movie or a stupid **_Angela's Ashes_**-reacting-against-a-Roman-Catholic-upbringing weepie, and I was part of it. The children were all doing art – the nicest easiest subject and on a Friday afternoon, too, the most beautiful time on the most adored and serene day of the academic week. The walls of our cabin-classroom were made of long, vertical planks which had been painted in a "Cream of Chicken" white. The little pupils were sitting in front of me. Rows of uniforms: blue shirts, grey shorts, grey skirts. Very tanned, like Australian children, and with the wide heads and pin eyes of the very young: they reminded me of cicadas. They made a sort of humming noise, like a cicada when you pick it up . . . "The masturbati!" I heard someone say. It was Sir Quntee Mush, dressed in the white outfit of His Holiness the Pope, right down to the dangerously Jewish white yarmulka. He was sitting in the corner of the room to the left of me, right up at the front, facing the pupils. A huge doll sat on his knee, a doll as big as a man with the gangling spastic lifelessness of ventriloquist's dummy. Sir Quntee was cradling it in the attitude of the Holy Virgin in Michelangelo's _"Pietà"_, except that Sir Quntee, unlike Our Lady, had his hand on his charge's penis. For I saw that what I had taken to be a huge pink toy with jointed plastic limbs was a naked man: none other than the cricketer's soldier assistant, who was looking up at me with the frightened, fatalistic eyes of a dog in a vet's waiting room or a wild bird when one finds it on its nest. Sir Qunt was rhythmically jerking the soldier's penis to the beat of a "Rebel" song he was intoning with false bitterness and in an Irish accent more ludicrous even than his attempt at a New England one:

> **_"The Masturbati_** [he sang],
> **_They drank Frascati,_**
> **_They held a tense and lurid party,_**

At which young Paddy,
The virgin laddy,
Dishonoured Fatherland -
And Daddy!"

In the communal bath of his *"Oyrish Kathoelek Scowl"*, Sir Quntee informed the kids, the soldier had been bathed in "Asses' milk" – in the ambergris of peasants and donkeys. Quntee told the class that he, Qunt, had been Ahab to the soldier's Moby Dick, scrubbing and scrubbing the boy clean of *"the sin of Onan"* – or, as Quntee preferred to call it, *"le vice Anglais"*. "Call me Ishmael!" he announced – most appropriately for a Tim-Tam!

Sir Quntee Mush informed the boys and girls that, upon bathing his assistant, he had discovered an erection. He demanded of the children if they knew that a single drop of spilt Irish milk contained ten hundred thousand murdered Irishmen – spermatzoa that, "cast into the outer darkness", would never fertilize an egg. Oliver Cromwell, he warned the children, was as nothing to the fucking wanker. *"Le vice Anglais,"* he began to chant, like some latter-day Padraig Pearse:

"Le vice Anglais -
Twas in the pay
Of Saxons' turdy treasure,
That Paddy gay,
Denied his fay,
The dower -
Of her pleasure!"

Reposing in the inscrutability, the impertability of the dream, the children hummed away like beehives. They seemed quite indifferent to the errant knight. They were studying me and not him, staring first at their drawing blocks and then at yours truly with the wide abstracted eyes of someone trying to catch an eclipse. "Come boy, out with it!" Sir Qunt admonished the soldier. An erect penis was no more healthy than a swollen finger. Quntee began to finger it attentively, abstractedly, as a child might a hamster that was being passed around a class. Suddenly, white pus flew out, like a frog, spitting. Sir Quntee was left holding the baby, and he bathed it with his own mewling sputum. He lunged at it: a toad lunging at an insect. He gulped the holy milk, like a toad its wife's spawn. "Young Paddy's penis," he mused, again with a false bitterness;

> *"Young Paddy's penis:*
> *The sword of Venus;*
> *His thing of thunder;*
> *His wand of wonder;*
> *His thing of thunder is a joy forever -*
> *So never call young Paddy, 'Trevor'!"*

Then – as often happens in dreams – I suddenly found that I had changed places. I was now a member of the infant audience – a little boy myself, in shorts and cotton shirt – watching a film being projected across the classroom like a laser beam. Members of *"the Bredbo Countrywomen's Association"* – all of them sultana-faced harpies as befitted representatives of "morality" in the modern cinema – were standing up at the front of the classroom. They were showing us a Sex Education film, to the accompaniment of a commentary whose coquettish *pudeur* was meant to illustrate their censorious depravity. Sir Quntee and the mannequin were nowhere to be seen. Instead, the blackboard – which was near where they had been sitting – was hidden behind a bright glaucous square like an electric clock. The beautiful windowfulls of orangeade were gone, hidden by grainy tan blinds. The room was full to the rafters of the brown of clear gravy, but it remained smokily bright from the hot sunshine outside. It was like hiding inside a tent. The Bredbo Countrywomen's Association were none other than the old ladies I had seen in the Australian National Gallery earlier that night. They were dressed in the trademark kneelength white smocks and canvas hats of Australian bowls players: each one looked like a suffragette. (The apparition had no doubt been conjured up by my memory of Les Majesty and his diatribes against the "White Leghorns" who, returning home from bowls, had obstructed his ministerial limousine). Suddenly the bright, muddy screen was full of close ups of caterwauling black sperms with open mouths trembling reedily on thread-like filaments: they were motes in a microscope, faces on waving tails, W.B. Yeats's *"long-legged flies"*, magnified Irishmen:

"We are little Paddies who will never see their Daddies!"

they trilled, in moist and peevish unison, and with the same wretched accent as the "Prince". Then they launched, like him, into an extraordinary, purple "Rebel Song":

> **"Young Paddy's heart**
> **Is often pierced** [- they sang]
> **By many a crool frustration:**
> **The Saxons' lust,**
> **The rebels' dust,**
> **The price of masturbation:**
> **The price of masturbation, Sir,**
> **'Tis horrid to behold;**
> **They farced his arse**
> **With powdered glass,**
> **His Khyber Pass**
> **With gold!"**

which they crowned with the following egregious chorus:

> **"Young Paddies bold!**
> **Saxons so cold!**
> **Hurt him!**
> **And spurt him!**
> **As in days of old!"**

One of the white-smocked harpies began to speak, and I recognised Jaw Majesty under the wide lid of a Panama hat. She at least did not affect an accent, but she spoke with a lapidary firmness quite alien to her usual delivery. "And to think, children," she said, "that a drop of the vaunted British Spunk contains the seeds of only twenty thousand Saxons – that of *yong Pah-dee* contains over a million!" The screen was flashing, pulsating like a police-car light. Upon it, the image of a knife was slicing the ripe belly of a cube of Turkish Delight, a knife encountering resistance, such was the density of the sperm that it was parting, the rich denseness of the Irish sperm, the density of accumulated Irishmen. Then a spoon was shown meekly molding the surface of a saucerful of grey English tea:

"To Saxon suds – the flesh of Spuds!"

the voice of the harpy boastfully intoned, referring to English as opposed to Oyrish Say-Men, and adding that it was specifically to offset this disadvantage that the English had set up "the Altar of Onan" in the land.

The screen went black and then a blazing white. Splotches and hairs started to vibrate across its brightness as the spool finished. Then the film restarted. Suddenly the square was full of rich, fruit-like colour. Pictures from notorious Nineteenth Century English and American magazines like **PUNCH** appeared, magazines purporting to show, with reference to skull size and physiognomy, the "inferiority" of the "Irish race". On one side of the screen were cross-sections of ephebic "Anglo-Saxon" heads with huge brains like ropes of offal, on the other mongol-Paddies in whose vast crania a pickled walnut drifted. This was the "inferiority" of "the Irish race". Then came naked Irish models, as in Edweard Muybridge's "scientific" daguerrotypes. The slides showing their profiles and portraits were constantly and violently alternated, and, like many Nineteenth Century negatives, each looked as if it had subsequently been retouched in nursery green and gold and red. The faces were certainly "Irish" ones, but they unwittingly portrayed the most beautiful persons on earth: withered or moist fool-coloured nipples like a cat's nose or paws; inordinately white skin of a woman or hairy black chest of a man – complex, androgynous faces enclosing the hellishly innocent hen-like eyes. The rich useless complexity and profusion you find in the beauty of the Poles.

An over-rich beauty that finds no animating mental equal and soon goes off, as a beautiful fish does. But the cool turquoise sheen of these wild salmon was so much lovelier, while it lasted, than the domesticated salmon's flyblown red . . . The Pluto-the-Dog Irish faces seemed to be having a ball – notwithstanding their "inferiority". They were like photographs of backpackers carousing in the "Social" section of *THE SYDNEY IRISH NEWS.* The Shamrock Pub or whatever was a flat hinterland like a Pompeian wall painting and these wincing toothy creatures were three-dimensional nymphs and satyrs embedded in it like walnuts in a slab of icing. Each face looked like Magnetic Island seen from a plane: a scored peach stone in the flat glassy blue of the Coral Sea. First of all, the snub-nosed-eyebrows-meeting type of Irish face. Ten different examples, from life. Then the no-lipped snake-like. These ones are. And Dewy Popkiss, who now marched onto the screen, was such a one too: a lipless white Kelt crawling with blackness like the pet snake consumed by ants that had (according to Suetonius) warned its owner, the Emperor Tiberius, that the Roman people would rise up and "devour" him. Dewy Popkiss began to chant a dirge too. His eyes were cold yet tender, like a pigeon's:

> *"Young Oscar Wilde,*
> *Diaalan child* [he sang],
> *By Saxons crude*
> *Deceived, defiled;*
> *From parasites epistulous,*
> *And multiple anal fistulas . . . "*

"Stop, stop, *stop it*" I shouted at the screen, which was instantly submerged, like the classroom, in a stifling, glutinous black. The great physical effort when one tries in the middle of a dream to find and project a voice – a real voice – disturbed me even in my unconsciousness. I realised that I was awake and that I had been crying out in my sleep. The children were still humming but I could tell by the freezing disinfectant breeze that their song came from an air conditioning console nearby. I tried to get up, but I couldn't move. My limbs were as hard to reach as my voice. As I looked up – I was still lying flat on my back – long greyish slicks opened in the Black Sea like clouds when they first appear in the night sky. It was clear that the creamy white oval creatures that I had seen trembling behind two of the walls were also sashaying across the ceiling. Where on earth was I, then? In some greenhouse at the bottom of an artificial lake? Nothing would have surprised me! I knew that the Viceregal Lodge boasted a swimming pool, after all. Though the animals hadn't disturbed me when I had seen them behind the glass of the walls, I didn't like the thought of them moving above my head. I closed my eyes tight so I wouldn't have even to think of them. I was asleep again almost at once, and the second dream I had that night was very distressing.

Its setting, though, was extremely pleasant. In the dream, I found myself walking around Manly with the rest of the International Art party – something I had in reality been doing only a few days' before. Manly is a Sydney resort suburb which is very close to where "the Art Party" was staying on Chinaman's Beach. If one thinks of the South East coast of Australia as a human face looking towards the Pacific Ocean, Sydney Harbour is the slightly open mouth of that face, and Manly its upper mandible. It is a peninsula dropping from the city's northern coastal suburbs towards the opening where the Pacific enters the Harbour. On one side of the peninsula – which is less than a mile wide – you can see the solid Prussian Blue of the Pacific, rimmed by the vulvas of white waves and the rich reddish-gold of Manly Beach. On the other is the Harbour, a vast sheet of clear glass, transparent in the foreground, a fresh piney green further out, black smoke from a ferry staining the pristine cleanness of the burning, ice-clear sky. Surveyed from Manly, the Harbour is ringed by a stupendous amphitheatre of khaki hills, and, further off, on the horizon, you can make out the tiny diamond brooch of the city's skyscrapers. Sydney stands out so clearly from claustrophobic jungles like Paris and New York because of its openness to the sky and the stupendous vastness of its urban panoramas, not to mention the fact that they're fresh and primaeval natural phenomena. Instead of the Trevi Fountain or Trafalgar Square, the Sydneysider has Loch Ness, Ipanema Beach and the Rio Grande.

In the dream's "opening scene" we were facing Manly Beach and the Pacific. It was a hot, hot day at the height of the Sydney summer. In other words, we were enjoying the most beautiful town on Earth when it can be seen at its most characteristic, its most sumptuous and sensual – a porn star at the very height of her powers. The sky was not transparent on this supremely hot Summer's day, it was a dense, raging blue – the appalling synthetic blue of blue ice cream or blue rubber gloves. Native Australian pines – called Norfolk Island Pines – line the Manly beachfront, each formed by a rather spare skeleton of juicy black limbs. They look like very tall Monkey Puzzle Trees, each a tall vertical cartouche of woven Japanese letters. In the dream, we were all standing on the beachfront admiring these trees, towers of wriggling black Japanese calligraphy on the dripping, molten, almost pinkish blue sky. One of the Art Party (in the dream) said that they reminded him of Hokusai's signature. The buildings of Manly – which climb a hill in the middle of the peninsula – are of icing-coloured stucco framed by lines of oxblood brick. The town looked in the dream – as it looks in reality – like a heap of liquorice allsorts. Every vista was a painting – or rather, the print of a *nouveau-riche* favourite by Bonnard of Le Cannet – or Ken Done of Sydney: one of those boringly delicious cards that get stuck up on stuck-up middle-class workplace walls, so you feel suffocated by the sheer wasted niceness and tastefulness and "sophistication" of it all.

In real life – I am not speaking of the dream now – the Art Party and I had enjoyed several visits to Manly Beach a few days' before. Every day we would come across the same couple in the restaurants, closeries and bars: a slightly elderly middle-aged man accompanied by a woman on the verge of middle age – but she was too childishly exuberant to be his wife. Wives, no matter how young, always wear the demeanour of a man's mother: lovers, no matter how old, always look like his petulant bohemian daughters. This was especially true of this woman. There was a wild, insouciant security about her that was revolting, as if she, of all thirty-year-olds, was entitled to play the fool, the girl, the *philosophe*, entitled by the fact that she was "fucking" this man (cue a coltish toss of her mane). And fucking this man was of course an exquisitely tough and incongruous adventure, an experience unique, or fairly unique, in the Earth's history: certainly quite unlike the twenty million other fucks the Earth's animals would administer to each other that evening, and for the same reason – namely, that they were animals like she was . . . This woman – it was part of her blind, introspective zest, her odious girlishness – always carried a tiny black kitten with her everywhere she went. She had a leash for it, but she seldom seemed to use it. The brute scrambled across marble tables like a spider, was allowed to do so by Madam, jumped on the pavement and described wild broken circles like a decapitated hen. I was always worried, as I watched them, lest the cat – which had the fluid range of a child – would rush off into the road and be pulverised before my eyes, but the air seemed to forbid so natural, so inevitable an atrocity. I had been brought up by a loving mother and, ever since those days, adults, even fellow adults, had seemed to leak an impalpable protective nimbus which could override the world and prevent the dangerous from happening. And so, like a pond-skipping insect, the cat was circumscribed – or so I thought – by the treacly water of the lovers' power, no matter how luridly it might stray. Anyway, so much for what had really happened during the Art Party's excursions. What happened in the dream was quite different.

In the dream, we were admiring the Norfolk Island pines when Cloke Wainberg, the Southern Belle from MOMA, New York, drew our attention to what he called "Catwoman" and her friend, who were lounging in a pavement café up the road. After a selfish show of indulgence, the woman let the kitten off its leash and emptied it onto the floor. It zigzagged across the pavement a couple of times and then it made for the other side of the road. A car approached. My stomach contracted slightly but I wasn't really worried. It couldn't happen. The car bore down on the little animal without either slowing down or turning. The drivers of Australia are not vindictive, but neither do they believe in Free Will. The kitten ran across the path of the car's left hand front wheel, and seemed to have cleared the right hand one too as the machine glided away to reveal its corpse lying quite still on the road. Or rather, its head was still, utterly still, but its body whipped frenziedly to and fro, up and down, like a fish that's been landed on the deck of a boat . . . Suddenly, everything became quick that had before been languid sardonic observation, like a film which proceeds normally and is then speeded up. Catwoman shrieked as she crumpled, and cupped her face in her hands. Incredibly, this had all come as a fucking bastard shock to her, an impossible! The lounge lizard her lover sprang up, and – scuttling like a lizard and seemingly as angry – grabbed the kitten by its whipping tadpole tail. He lifted it with ginger loathing and, holding the tail, he whacked the head again and again against the trunk of a Norfolk Island pine. Whacked this thing that they had shown such love, such care for! It flapped wildly in his hands like a decapitated rooster. It really seemed as if he were dusting the pine, not dousing it with feline brains. At length, he tossed the still erotic body over the Sea Wall onto the beach below. And now he lunged at the girl, who sat – elbows on table, face in hands – giving great orgasmic gasps, like somebody under a towel in front of a bowl of menthol. She rushed away, cowering in his extended arm like some escapee from a plane crash or a bomb explosion, as pleased to play a part now, to dramatise, as she had been before . . . It was all too distressing for me and, knowing that it was "only" a dream, I forced myself to wake up. Now that I was awake, I found myself lying in the foetal position, on my side, with my back to the Bronco and facing one of the walls where the white things were. They emerged from the darkness like bushes at the bottom of the garden, slightly less dark than the blackness that was dividing them into separate stooks. They were like individual jars of blizzard, bushells of fragrant, pistachio-coloured wheat, scribbled-on green blackbirds' eggs that you see at the bottom of the nest. For some reason, their intimacy and obscurity, like the flickering life at the bottom of some dim and steamy hedgerow, reminded me of England, of the Northern Hemisphere, of home. I suddenly felt very upset and rather homesick. I remembered something that my old mucker Edward Semper-Adonis had said while we were pottering around Sydney with the rest of the Art Group: "Australia is *far too brightly lit*". I, who rejoiced in the country's blocks of pure acrylic colour, its bleached and fantastically solid surfaces, the impenetrable black cartouche with which the mighty sun enclosed everything – as in some vast mural by Vasarély or Fernand Léger – could never sympathise with, nor even recognise, Edward's point of view. And now I did. I saw that Australia's ferocious light reduced everything to simplicity. It burned away everything but the big and the flat and simple, or it drowned it in a black moat of unspeakable matt shadow. Australians, their eyes and ideas the children of inhuman, autistic light, could have no idea of the furtive, petite frogspawn complexity of normal (ie northern) human landscapes, of normal human associations, of normal human life. Were they to be abruptly confronted with these things, they would find them both more and less than that which they they were used to, like people served sombre vintages and glaucous grey caviar who are more accustomed to red jam and yellow pastry, or great halters of steak like wet doormats, or beer . . . Very soon, I was again asleep.

I am just about to start snoring when there is a blinding light. Livid, grainy white leaves boil up around me like a hailstorm followed, like a hailstorm, by thunder and the most obscene and impenetrable black. Black night. Then there is another crack, a flash of lightning. It is Bonnie, the vision splendid. She is turning on the light. In this: this is Knut Fagan's bedroom. "It's Eight O'Clock," Bonnie announced. Not "Good Morning" or anything like that. Even though I was not properly awake, it struck me that the room must have possessed an electric light – indeed I can see one raging above me like a UFO. The previous evening, Bonnie had assured me there were no such appliances. I suddenly wonder if Dew and Bon have arranged everything that has transpired since Din-Dins as a particularly vile practical joke. I could never have imagined their being so malicious – although as they have committed murder and every other crime under the sun, I accept that this reservation is an irrational one. "The dunny an' all that are down the corridor," says Bon. "You'll find some new togs an' that there too . . . Scrambo and Mushies is at Nine. Church is at Ten. And then it's Sin – Sin with a capital 'Soy'". ['*Cyn*' – *the visit to Cynthia Brownbill. In the 'Hayume'*] . . . I'll come back here in the twennie minutes . . . after youse've had a shower".

I still rejoiced in the previous day's finery, and had brought no change of smalls.

A STATUE OF GOD

Twenty minutes later, I was waiting in a chair in the bedroom – mercifully having bathed: I was as fresh as a rose! Wearing the tee shirt, long baggy shorts and beach sandals that had been laid out for me, which seemed a trifle Bohemian for Holy Communion, even in the "ACT" (Australian Capital Territory). The Bronco cadaver still lay face down on the bed, its knotted torso like the dry shell of a cricket thorax that's been eaten out by ants.

My "aquarium" was just a windowless room. Every inch of each wall, and even the ceiling, was covered by paintings of the Bronco on the bed, endlessly repeated images of the same bubbling white male. Portrayed either from the side or above. He was shown sunbathing in a lush, glittering meadow, the juicy grain of the grass a delicious foil for the flat, matt fibre of the marscapone flesh. Hence the floating pods of floury muscle I had taken for Leviathan, the walls of green water, the oozing threads and noodles of the suppositious weed. The grass formed a continuous "bed" or background for the infinitely repeated Sushi of the sunbather, like the vermicelli-filled fish tanks you see in a pet shop that fill every wall and look like a bank of TVs. The varnish on the walls and ceiling must have been at least a centimetre thick. It was a honey-coloured cataract. It had made me think I was enclosed by glass.

Bon arrived in the same irreverent dress as I and escorted me to breakfast. The passages through which I'd walked with Zane the previous evening resembled those in a Department Store: the furniture and fixtures all seemed to be brand new and to have nothing in common – with either each other or their setting. Bon was complaining to me about one of her daughters-in-law (not Jingili): "But if only she'd *listen*," she said, "instead of babbling away like some incessant . . . *duck*!"

Through one of the windows, I noticed by the swimming pool a big, black square tent, like a kids' climbing frame covered in cloth.

Dewy was waiting for us in the kitchen. Over his dish of mango and papaya, he explained, disconsolately, that the television had blown up. I was surprised to see one in the corner, still in its bobble-shawl mantle. Bonnie went over to the sink to help a Brisbane Bronco who was busy – washing some dishes, I think – naked but for a thong and an oilcloth pinafore. His shiny buttocks wobbled like the shiny green nuts on a coconut palm. Bonnie chatted to him. She had started to prepare the eggs. Whenever Bonnie laughed, wept, shouted, she sounded like a chook: chook chawing and clucking. Always that thin, rasping wafer of sound, never the pure note. In conversational and reflective mood, meanwhile, she sounded like a chook mewing distractedly to itself as it pecked the ground. With her bulky, shapeless torso, she even *looked* like a chook – like the picked carcass of a roasted bird – and her limp made her walk like one, too. I sat down at the table, as startled as ever by Dew's attire. He was wearing a clean white teeshirt, but the words –

CHRISTINA IS A KNUT
–were written across it in large black capitals.

"Well," he said, unnerving me with a relaxed and loquacious manner I was unfamiliar with, "how did you like *His Royal Highness*?!" "I thought he was *ghastly*," I said of Qunt, immediately regretting the British word "ghastly". "Closet queens should be seen and not heard," I announced. "And preferably not seen." To cauterize the "ghastly", I added, as nimbly as possible: "But how long are Sir Quntee and Muckadilla going to stay here?" "Not long, I hope", snorted Dew, "business is business, but I can't stand those liddle Texan Bees [*'bastards'*]. The sooner they fuck off, the better." "I'd rather be on the move, too," I said. "I hate just doing nothing: I don't want to sit around here in Ozzy rotting." Dewy, however, wasn't listening to me. He was still bubbling away over Quntee and "Kana". It struck me again that he must have become indebted to them in some way. "Yeah . . ." he said, "Good riddance to the pair of 'em. They're just like Cane Toads, those fucken Tim-Tams. You let two of 'em inter yer Cunt Tree and, hey presto, there are two million of the fuckers. Nuthin' can kill 'em, nuthin' can eat 'em. They end up eatin' *you*. They destroy a Cunt Tree, just like those foreign Cane Toads destroy the native Aussie mammals. All they do is *shit*. They're not good for a single fucken thing . . . They even *look* like Cane Toads – Cane *Turds*, I should say. *And* they smell like 'em . . . "

But now it was I who wasn't listening: I had become intrigued by a huge, brightly coloured fresco that covered the whole of the kitchen wall. It filled the entire space between the ceiling and the large modern windows. The windows towered over Bonnie, the Bronco, and an Auschwitz-recalling aluminium console of ovens and sinks: they revealed the usual "over-lit" landscape of molten khaki-jade mountains and a violent, plasticene-blue sky.

The fresco was a painting of the giant "Fish Hall" at Darling Harbour, Sydney, where each morning's catch from the Tasman Sea is sold to the private citizens of Sydney and to restaurateurs. It is quite famous and the "Art Party" and I had visited it as part of our sightseeing tour. In the painting, there were slabs heaped with naked men and women from the world's diverse races as well as different types of fish and game. The naked human beings lay on their backs on ice that was as white as salt, jam-red blood trickling from each mouth. The antennae of prawns were plastered to the men's chests like pink pussy hairs – the salt-white ice was strewn with black prawn eyes like the Pau-Pau seeds on Sir Dew's breakfast dish. White signs emerged with atrocious antiseptic blue letters – on metal pins in penis and breast. First *"WHITING"*, *"SNAPPER"*, *"COD"*; then *"IRISH"*, *"ABO"*, *"JEW"*. First art, then life. Or was it the other way around? . . . In the picture, the Fish Hall customers were crouching like the Magi over a burning fountain of perfect flesh that was ever depleted, ever renewed . . . *"The mackerel-crowded seas"*. Genital clusters of gleaming, bowdlerised fowl; strappadoed bunnies . . . I suspected at once that the painting was by Tray Beautous: only he would have had eyes fresh enough to see the potential in the promiscuous riot of the diverse in a big world city. Only he was able, as Sir Vidia Naipaul has put it, *"to awaken the sense of true wonder"* - at what is all around us, *"unexamined"*, *"unmeditated on"* . . . The signs signposted the false analogy between the souls of the various human tribespeople and their bodies. Their bodies were their uniforms ("Irish," "Abo," "Jew"), but their uniform bodies (like the external carapace of "Soldier" or "Nun") also kept the lid on each individual soul – souls that were differentiated and whose unending uniqueness over-egged the mass-produced pudding. Hence the luxury inherent in this pregnant profusion, the sense of an *"embarras de richesses"* . . . Since the Golden Affluence, hair has spread over the Australian chest like the mould on a buttered bagel, but this was not true of the old-fashioned "Soldiers" of the genus *"AUSSIE"* in the picture, from whose navels alone a stream of filth was seen to trickle, like the sediment from the lip of a fountain. The Polish "Nuns'" breasts were like a nest of dead baby mice; the black "Nuns'" breasts were like horses' penises. Everything was perfect and profligate, like Irishmen, like game . . . And to think that all these beauties – like Bonnard courtesans or fruit – were thrashing around us every day of the year – under our very noses – as virile and as dervish-like as ducklings! Unconsidered, unexploited! And unconsidered, unexploited they would have remained had Tray not presented them as they were seen here: as the soft, hot, living bodies of the dead . . . The child is dead, long live the child! Or, as Tray Beautous was apt to put it: "A thing of beauty is a goy forever"!

"Jew like it?" asked Dew. He was following the play of my eyes . . . And then he said: "Can you guess who it's by?" I studied Dew's bloated, lunar head, the wise old eunuch eyes - tiny serrated teeth like the teeth of a dolphin. He was full of surprises today. "Yes," I said, calmly. "I am prepared to bet that it's by an Australian artist called Tray Beautous. They had a painting of his at the Gallery, and I'm sure that all the – things – in Mr Fagan's bedroom are by Beautous, too. I wanted to ask you about him. He clearly does remarkable work and I am convinced that they've never heard of him in Britain or the States. I'd really like to meet him, in fact, if he still lives in Australia – if you or Bon can point me in the right direction." Dew smiled mysteriously. "Oh – you'll meet him alright! He lives up North Queensland way

– in Townsville, in fact, an island off Townsville. *Magnetic* Island, it is – it's just one of the Townsville suburbs now. It's about two thousand kilometres north of here . . . " " *'Townsville?!'* " I said, laughing, " . . . it sounds like the sort of place a serial killer might come from!" "Or go to," said Dew, rudely pulling the pith from a back molar. "But I'm a bit surprised – and, of course, relieved," says I, – "to hear that you know about this chap. I didn't think you would be able to help me . . ." I quickly stopped myself. What was I suggesting? That my Bernard Berenson-like host was some kind of ourang-outang? "Oh, I know about Mister Beautous, alright!" Dew snarled. It struck me that I had never heard him utter so many words in my entire life. "He was a great favourite of my predecessor here – Miss Nancy! [*As in Nancy Reagan: Fagan*] . . . And as for helping you . . . Well – I can help *you* – if you can help *me*." Now I really was taken aback. "How on earth could I help *you*?" "You want to take him to London, don't you?" Dewy said. His tactless penetration shocked me. "Well, I'd be delighted if he went. But if *I* was to suggest it he'd probably fly straight to fucken Bogotá!" I was confused. "But you wouldn't have anything to do with it", I said, "I would be doing it for myself. It would be *in my own interest* to persuade him – and in his, of course. It's obviously no skin off my nose. Quite the opposite . . . I have to tell you that I think Tray Beautous could end up as quite a big noise in dear old Blighty. He could make me a lot of money . . . I mean," – (I corrected myself) – "he could do very well for *himself*. And not only financially. However successful Mr Bee might be in Aussie, Uncle Dew, you don't really exist as an artist unless you exist up there, in that world, in New York, Paris, London!" (*"What a ridiculous thing to say!"* I thought as I said it) . . . "It's like what that famous writer Naipaul says about Australia - I'm sorry, Argentina - in that book of his, **The Return of Eva Peron** (having scanned the painting, my imagination now quite naturally ran to Sir Vid), "– *When the real world is felt to be outside, everyone at home is inadequate and fraudulent*'!" . . . Now it was my turn to be tactless . . . "But what is it, Dewy? Why is it that you want him out from under your feet?" . . . I smiled sardonically. "He isn't due to *sue* you, is he? It isn't a *court case*, or something? . . ." Whenever I thought of Dew and his machinations, I couldn't help fearing the worst.

"No, no," said Dew, as if amused by some private joke, "it's got nothin' to do with *that*. You see, Patrick, I can tell you're a . . . man of the world." Dew looked slowly between me and the fresco in a way that made me slightly uncomfortable. "As I say [*he hadn't said any such thing*], there are two friends of mine – it's a couple they are, very high up, very respected. Very . . . interesting. They've done very well for themselves . . . Contributors, shall we say" – here he winked – "to the Australian Labor movement . . . What I'd like is that you go up to Townsville for me and persuade Tray to *do something* for this pair. If you wanna take him to the UK, you'll have to do this for me first . . . But none of it can come out." (He began to sound childish). "Tray mustn't know that the request came from me . . . It's a commission, see, a commission for a draw-ring – but it's a peculiar one . . . Kinky. That's why you mustn't tell Tray who the sitters are. You see, Pat, my mates want Tray to paint 'em dirty . . . in a certain way . . . In the middle of when they're doin' . . . a certain thing!" "Well," I said coldly, understanding everything, "why involve *me*? You don't need a Tray Beautous to arrange *that*. And why don't they ask him *themselves*?" "After all," I sneered, "a commission of that sort *will* require a certain degree of intimacy! Unless they want to send him a *photograph* of course! Couldn't he paint them 'in a certain way' from *that*? . . . And why *him*? Why Tray Beautous? The world is *full* of mercenary artists. And photographers!" "A photo won't do," Dew insisted . . . "Not even a video!" he chuckled. "Y'see, they'd actually *get off* on *Tray* doin' it. In person, if you see what I mean. And it's got to be him, or they wouldn't get off on it. It can't be nobody else. They've chosen 'im theirselves." "If they're so besotted with him, I presume this Tray Beautous knows them?" "No. Not socially. Not by sight. But they know him alright! By *reputation* . . . They're connoisseurs see. Connoisseurs! That's why it's got to be *him*. No other Australian artist will do". "Are your friends Australian?" Dewy laughed. "They're not Brits, that's fer sure!" "And what makes you think Tray Beautous would agree to such a thing?" I demanded, feeling a little annoyed. The conversation had hardly taken an expected turn. I resented Dew's assumption I would gaily play the Madam. "I haven't a clue if he'd do such a thing, Petrick. That's *your* problem! But I'll tell you one thing, my friend. These mates of mine'll pay *me* to pay *you* good if you win Tray over. They know Tray wouldn't do it if the request came from *them*, or if Tray knew *who they were* – he's incredibly prejudiced against their type. He absolutely hates people from that particular group. Not that he'll get to find out, cos, as far as I'm aware, he doesn't even know this pair: not by sight, anyway . . . This couple approached me cos they think only a Pee Em could sort this kinda thing out. And naturally they're right. They'll get what *they* want, and you'll get to meet your cobber the yartist. Nobody but me is gonna be able to put you in touch with 'im: he's a recluse, see? How many of the Aussie art crowd d'ya think would be able to introduce ya? *'What do they know of artists that only artists know?'* But a Pee Em has access to certain – channels. Not that Tray will realise that it's *me* who sent you his way! I'll make sure he thinks the introduction comes from a Mrs Girly Soukoop, a friend of 'is Gran. I happen to know Girly quite well: Tray doesn't realise that . . . You'll get a bit upfront of course but you'll be paid in full when Tray completes the canvas – he'll be paid, too, it goes without sayin', and big time. You can tell 'im there's a *heap* of shrapnel in it for *him*. Tell 'im that your clients are two rich old English pervs who've somehow found out about 'is work – that they're the ones that put *you* onto it . . . Tell 'im that they'll enjoy every minute of the sittin' – and that so will he! . . . Cos use your loaf, Pat: he wouldn't be against doin' it 'cos it was *kinky*, now, *would he?'* (He looked at me again archly and then, slowly, "significantly" at the fresco) . . . "He's not *perjudiced* in that respect, is 'ee, *perjudiced* like he is with me? . . . I won't go into why. It's not important – it never was, 'cept to Mister Bee ... But – " (and Dew became agitated) " – he would never do it if he knew that *I* was behind it. Or even if he knew who *they* really were." "But Dew," I said, "You *cannot* be serious! Who on earth would waste 'a heap of shrapnel' on a set-up like *that*? I believe what the Spanish call an *'Exhibición'*. Big deal! You could buy yourself twenty whores and have yourself filmed *killing* them for that sort of money." "Who said they've only paid out *'that sort of money'*?" Dew erupted with a laugh which made me realise the seriousness of his proposal. I had forgotten that money is one thing which a thief will never joke about. "They've had to pay me *as well*, remember! It's the singer not the song, Patrick, the singer not the song. It aint just any old *'Exhibición'*, my friend. They obviously want Mister Beautous real, real bad. Why should I care why? Why should you? . . . Maybe his dear ole Gran sucked their Jack Russell's cunt for 'em once when client *'X'* was shootin' 'is bolt up client *'Y'*'s front door? . . . What do I know? . . . That's the whole thing about being rich, Pat, you don't have to *think* about what yer doin'. You finally have the freedom to *just do it* . . . Only the poor think about the *cost* of things . . . Don't you realise that Murdoch and all the other rich cunts deal twenty times a day with so-called 'important' matters that cost a *hundred times* a million dollars – sausage and mash they might just as well flush down the dunny for all it means to them? If you've got as many shekels as our chums here, why not just please yourself? If that's what floats your boat, why not? By the standards of movers and shakers, my friend, I would say our pals are both clever and extremely mean . . . But whether they are or whether they're not, they're gonna spend a packet on tryin' to get Tray anyway. The question is, do *you* want some of it, or do you want 'em to throw it away on some other hustler who ain't my favourite cousin? [*I wasn't Dewy Popkiss' cousin*]. In fact, do you want to meet this amazin' Mister TB at all? Cos I can't see it happenin' unless you cooperate, *can you*? The road to Hell is paved with good intentions, Pat . . . and with the corpses of the cunts who didn't do what I told 'em to! . . . Now are you gonna do this thing for me or aren't chew?"

"A whole heap of shrapnel!" I thought. I was intrigued. A million dollars, a million miles of freedom! For freedom, the final freedom, the final frontier, is what "shrapnel" miraculously bestows. It delivers a life lived on land, with wings, to the one who has been an amphibian all his life like man's first ancestor. But when you are offered something extraordinary, what you could never even have hoped for, it's like getting drunk or high for the very first time. You don't experience the expected orgasm: it is like being taken into a bright, dumb room where you cannot feel anything because it's all new. You do not register the depth of the new environment because it brings with it a new You as well – only the old "you" could have appreciated the intensity, the difference – the old, unhappy You. Only the poor and the unhappy can feel pleasure – because they're the only ones who never *ever* enjoy it.

My intellect, however, did not partake of the general numbness and it acted promptly – on a principle I had long refined for such occasions – should they ever arise! It was a methodology the Baron de Breteuil attributes to one of my heroines – the Empress Catherine the Great – a non-Russian nobody who, against all the odds, won the throne of her adopted land after murdering two of its Tsars, one of them her husband. That advice? *"That one must be firm in one's resolves, that it is better to do badly than to change one's mind, and, most of all, that it is only fools who are indecisive"* . . . "Yes I am going to do it," I told Dew excitedly, "*yes I am!* . . . Or I'm going to *try* to do it, anyway! " . . . "Good lad," said Dew, with an air of patronising if unfamiliar bonhomie, "good lad!"

"Scrambo and Mushee time!" cried the audacious young Bronco, whose lips and eyes – those of Miss Kylie Minogue – were dancing all over the table. He and Bon had come over bearing platters of scrambled eggs, mushrooms and slices of a pomegranate-like pink grapefruit. The cafetière, the toast, porcelain and orange juice had already been set out.

"But Dew," I said, "who *are* these people . . . ?" "I'll tell you later," said Dew, abruptly, "after you get back from Church. Otherwise" (his usual insolence had returned), "you might decide in the middle of *'Cumbaya My Lord, Cumbaya!'* you don't want to do it, eh?" "What the Hell are *you* bullshittin' about?" Bon asked Dew, obviously annoyed. "Just tellin' Pat how beaut you look today, Darl!" "Yeaahh, right . . ." said Bon, contemptuously, as she flung down the butter dish. "Seriously Patrick," Dew continued, when Bon was without earshot, "we can discuss these things over lunch. But even if I tell you *their* names, *you* shouldn't tell Tray *mine*

. . . We'll make all the arrangements for you . . . *Wanko* here will drive you up to Townsville." He indicated a pale, familar-looking young man in black jeans and a crisp blue shirt who was just now tripping into the kitchen. "Sorry oym late, Sir Dee Pee!" cried Wanko. "You can leave in a few days' time," Dewy went on. "We'll have your stuff an' that sent down from Sydney and sort it all out with the 'Dreamin' of Rimmin' bludgers – or whatever the fuck it is they're called . . . Wanko Dykstra is our chauffeur, Pehtrick. So you'll be in *very good hands*. And he used to be a *great friend* of Mistah Beautous . . . dincha Wankee?" Wanko smiled at us maliciously, like a kitten.

I was about to thank Wanko for the services he was about to render me when I became faint with horror. His face had reminded me of someone – I had assumed he must have been one of the Broncos I had met the previous night – but staring into his stupid eyes I realied he was the "thing" I had shared the bed with – or its exact double! The cadaver's eyes had been shut, its face rouged and plastered, which is why I had not made the connection immediately. I again became aware of a freezing film oozing over my neck and arms, and that my face was becoming very hot, which bothered me as I was now as angry as I was shocked and afraid. Whatever its meaning, this was clearly a perverse joke on Dewy and/or Bon's part – as my "commission" perhaps was – and I did not want to give them the satisfaction of gloating over my bright red face. I have to admit that they didn't appear to be paying me much attention, though: in fact, they were in the middle of a heated discussion about the "duck-billed" daughter-in-law.

I tried to get to the bottom of it by engaging Wanko in conversation – discreetly, of course. He had crashed himself down and was tucking into his "scrambo and mushies" with zest. Perhaps, after all, Wanko had once had a twin brother, or something . . . I found it all quite useless – it was like talking to a Rhesus Monkey. Wanko was one of those people who find it impossible to respond spontaneously when confronted with somebody outside their own experience. Instead, like a politician, he met each conversational gambit with a stock of

223

advertisements for himself which had clearly been prepared in advance . . . In Wanko's case, these were related to his profession. He was a policeman, not a sportsman, as I had assumed from his build – which was as powerful as "Sleeping Beauty's". It soon became obvious from his monologue that he inhabited – as do all policemen – an enclosed, enchanted world where Middle-Class salaries settle on muscular young thugs as naturally as Rainbow Lorikeets descend on the shoulders of pirates, a babyish, boy-scoutish world of rules and rivalry where the "difficult job" of the police, their tragic muse, guarantees them the last drowsy paradise in the Civil Service. Here, a career, as in Marx's fantasy of the Millennium, is a supervised ritual like school, punctuated by long breaks and as immune from real work and intelligence as a nudist colony. One might have expected Wanko to be mindful of this and, if not to show gratitude to the civilians over whom he had been set, at least to be indulgent of their little foibles – given his own good fortune – and to regard himself and his cruel duty a little less than seriously. Alas, the Working Class – (as Tray Beautous alone rejoiced!) – are ever unself-aware, and, like the disabled (who are lazy, too), Wanko had come to believe in the fictions Middle Class housewives had attached to his name as avidly as they might cram banknotes into a stripper's jockstrap. According to these narratives, the lives of the police are as *"nasty, brutish and short"* as the Working Class itself. And that was why, towards the public – whose taxes supported his monastic indolence – Wanko remained as hostile and savage as a Praetorian Guardsman, and as unaccountable, as aloof, as manipulative as a Palace eunuch.

"But if only she'd *listen* to me," Bonnie repeated to Dew, "if only she'd listen – instead of babbling away like some incessant . . . *chook*!"

· · ·

An hour or so later, I was sitting with Bonnie in "the Church of the Blue Star," Woden. We were behind a worshipper whose stringy hair was plastered against his head like the hair of a newborn baby. Wanko had driven us over from the Prime Minister's Residence in an elegant old black Mercedes (all the British cars in the Vice-Regal garage had long since been purged). We didn't use the Sacred Chariot (shit cart) as there were only the two of us. The church was a glassy edifice surrounded by heat and bottlebrush; a flat, suburban desolation in what had obviously only been Bush a few years before. There were Australian flags on either side of the altar. I hate to see flags in a church, even the Australian flag – though, with the dazzling white of boiled rice splashing its rich indigo-blue and heartrending red, it is an extremely moving one. I looked out through the glass wall at the mating Australian magpies – they were huge things, like Birds of Paradise – and at the spotty, khaki Budawang Hills. They reminded me painfully of the South Downs. I kept thinking of the first line of *"The Melancholy Hussar of the German Legion"*, a short story by Thomas Hardy, and a great favourite of mine:

> **"Here stretch the downs, high and breezy and green, absolutely unchanged since those eventful days."**

I began to feel terribly homesick, and I wondered how on Earth I was going to be able to endure an extended stay in Australia, even if it *would* result in "a golden shower", which I had begun to doubt. I felt quite bad, quite frightened and ill, still troubled by *"L'Affaire Wanko"*. Fortunately, I was comforted by the hymns. I remember nearly crying over *"Stella Maris"* and *"Ave Maria"*. The emotional climaxes rendered me vulnerable. I don't know why, but there is nothing like religious subject matter for making one's head fill with thoughts of the self . . . I am talking, of course, about the words (considered as literature) of the hymns, because, even for Australia, the singing was incredibly rough. The choir was no better. The sight of an officious old crock waving a ruler at a bevy of ugly, self-important nobodies for some reason annoyed me. "What has this got to do with religion?" I asked myself. There were a series of "sung responses" which the soloists, in their provincial vanity, hilariously muffed.

The layman who read out the "Parish News" was a tall, thin, middle-aged man with a curious, immature face, a greasy moustache, longish hair. He was wearing a white safari suit, a pink shirt and tie, and Levi Jeans. He gave a "religious" homily, too, which took as its theme the foresight of the men who, in the Gospel of St Mark, bring their sick friend to Christ by boring a hole in the mud roof of the house that He is visiting in Capernaum. The Reader compared these individuals to the colleagues of an Australian factory worker he had supposedly known. The worker had seen all his limbs chopped off in turn by a machine, but his "mates" had thrust the "bits" in a bag of ice from the "Offy" (Off-Licence), and the *"so potent art"* of a Microsurgeon had seen them all sewn back on again. Then, in another industrial accident, his head had unfortunately been severed, but, this time, the resulting surgery proved ineffective. "But why?" his friends had asked. "Strewth, mate," the surgeon opined, "he suffocated in the plastic bag!" . . . "The Blood of *Chroist*, who *doyde* for yeugh," said the Altar boy as he thrust the Communion wine towards me. It tasted like Sanatogen, the bread was obviously "Mother's Pride," and the sight of people being "cured" by a laying on of hands in an ante-Chapel, as I left the Altar to return to my seat, played on my somewhat troubled nerves.

The Priest – (it wasn't the one who had advised Dewy and Bon on their conjugal furies) – looked like a giant, gouty baby – like the famous Australian writer Thomas Kenneally, in fact. (Need I say more?) His bald pate was wrinkled and purple, like a passion fruit. He was a really frightful, unhealthy colour; it seemed as if pus would jet from his pursed-up Persian cat-mouth as from an angry wound.

After the service, Bonnie introduced me to Catholic Rotarian-types from the Canberra suburbs. The men looked exactly like the adult males I remember as a boy in suburban London during the 1960s: buck-toothed, fortyish, with brillcreemed 50s' hair. Agreeable enough, if nosey. Wanko was waiting for us on the kerb. Once we had sunk, relieved, into the cold, air-conditioned leather, he introduced me to "another Londoner" who had graced his Juggernaut, a "performer", a polaroid of whose unclad frame – feet and reddish fanny in the air – decorated the windscreen. For my benefit, Wanko then whisked us off on a tour of the "sights" of Canberra: Lake Burley Griffin; the Parliament Building; the Telecom Tower on Black Mountain; the Military Academy at Duntroon . . . Telopea Park. Impossible to describe the sheer horror of the place: imagine Milton Keynes in the Gobi Desert! Bloodcurdling Pentecostalist hymns drifted over the empty, synthetic town: it was the only sound that broke the silence. There wasn't a soul to be seen. It looked like one of those "Potemkin-Facade" cities that they mock up in the Nevada Desert to test atomic weapons on. What I found particularly sinister were the car showroom marquees glittering in the harsh blue light. They were like the skeletons of circus marquees – there was no covering of fabric: just glittering shards of fluorescent plastic crackling and fluttering on the naked ropes. Reflecting rather than absorbing and extinguishing the intensely pure light. The petrol stations and showrooms glittered as you approached them like heaps of broken glass. The vinyl leaves of native Australian plants – of gum trees, for instance – produce the same effect, whereas in England, the light-absorbent leaves of the deciduous trees look like powdery clay bricks on even sunny days.

"*The Lovely Aujourd'hui Veterans' Memorial Nursing Home*" was in Manningreedah, one of Canberra's easternmost suburbs. It was a low, rambling building with a flat roof. Its long rectangular windows were filled with blue-grey louvres: one would have thought from the outside that it was a liquor warehouse or a bowling alley. It was situated – quite appositely, I thought – right next to a boarding kennel for the pets of the local burghers: *"PUSSY NOOK, or, THE BEAUTOUS KENNEL"*. The streets of Manningreedah were full of marigolds, petunias and 1930s English architecture in gingerbread-coloured brick. There was a punishing sun as soon as we got out of the car, and hateful, prehistoric native birds – "Currajongs," I think they are called – hopped around everywhere, one with something silvery and wet in its beak. The dreadful sunlight and the birds rendered this desirable, longed-for English retreat frightful and repugnant.

A cheery bloke was waiting for us at the desk in the foyer of *"The Lovely Aujourd'hui"*, a bearded, brown, tufted, stocky, little chap, like a Yorkshire Terrier. He wore a white dentist's smock which had beautiful gold epaulettes. He was some kind of "carer". "You look familiar!" he said to Bon, in a voice radiant with sarcasm. It made me wonder if Bon had been as attentive to Cynthia as she had said. "Yeah," said Bon, "I'm the undertaker!" Bon signed a book at the desk and motioned to me to follow her down a corridor. "Don't forget to steal somethin' from yer mother-in-law!" trilled the nurse. Bon swung around and marched – hobbled rather – back to the desk. "Just what is your name, Mate?" The nurse, with a stage grimace, pointed with an expiration of breath to the vast badge on his smock: *"Sandi – caring FOR YOU!"* "San-dee," he said with weary, pedantic deliberation. "Fuck off, San-dee!" said Bon. I followed Bon back down the corridor. The place was like a cheap shabby motel and there appeared to be nobody else around. I couldn't see a single nurse. A whiff of ammonia – it rose in a pure, harsh contralto – struggled with a suggestive chorus of fecal – and other – smells. Surely, I thought, the Prime Minister of Australia could have afforded to put Cynthia in a better place than this! When I had visited Australia as a boy decades before, Cyn had been as tender to me as a Grandmother. Part of my reason for coming to Australia was to see her one last time before she died. "You know she's totally gah-gah, dontcha?" Bon asked. "She won't be able to recognise yeugh. Hasn't been able to string a sentence together in three months!" Bon was saying this, I felt, in order to justify the décor. Why waste good money on the care of someone I had once heard her refer to as "the damn chimp"? Now Bonnie told me that vanity had been the cause of Cynthia's decline. Appearances had counted for everything with Cyn, Bon complained. When she had first entered the "Hayume", she would refuse stimulating relationships with unattractive people. "But she's so *ugly*," Cyn would say, "she looks like a *man*!".

228

The first thing I noticed, in the interior of the "hayume", were the empty wheelchairs with the toilet seats in them – nothing underneath the holes in their wooden platforms. Prints of Australian masters on the corridor walls, the noise of an electric saw. We seemed free to wander wherever we pleased. Bonnie opened a door. There were four or five old women in the room; some, who were sitting on beds, propped against a wall, appeared dead. They were utterly motionless. Another, right in front of us, sat, naked from the waist down, in one of the wheelchairs, her knees together, her feet girlishly toe to toe. All, whatever their other dress, were wearing – I suppose as a protective bib – the *"CHRISTINA IS A KNUT"* teeshirts . . . I presumed that such shirts were all the rage in irreverent Oz that Summer. Still, it pained me to see old people wearing – for the sake of the convenience of others – something so young and "with it". It led to humiliation.

Bonnie went into "the House of the Dead" and closed the door. Then she led out Cynthia – carried her, more like, for she could hardly walk. "They don't exercise them at all!" Bon raged. Cynthia's face was deformed by a black moustache. She looked like an unwrapped mummy, with big blotches where her eyes and mouth should have been. She tried piteously to hide her face. I think she said "Hello": I had forgotten the sound of her distinctive voice, but now its timbre came back to me. But then she collapsed and went completely dead – limp. We tried to hold her up, but there was nowhere to put her. As she fell, her blue dress came up above her belly, exposing her pink silk drawers. Even her *"CHRISTINA"* teeshirt threatened to come off. Her tights were about her ankles. She smelled of old haddock. While I staggered under Cynthia's weight – she was surprisingly heavy – Bon ran and grabbed one of the commode wheelchairs from along the hall and I dumped her in it. Cyn slumped forward with a terrible cry – she gasped, appeared to stop breathing. (The sound of her breathing – which was like that of an asthmatic – had been pronounced). Bon became alarmed. She grabbed at Cynthia's hands and took her pulse. Cynthia's hands were smooth, but red, pitted and blotchy, like the surface of an old school desk. Bonnie looked frightened.

"Strewth!" she said, "I'd better go and get that cunt San-dee!" She started hobbling with alacrity down the corridor. I have to confess I didn't feel particularly concerned.

I went to study a print of Russell Drysdale's *"Swan and Clown"* on the corridor wall – a dreadful "happy" work, which, I knew, had been completed after the suicides of the artist's wife and son. "Mistah Beautous – he dead!" I swung around. The corridor was empty but for the mute, annihalated Cyn, whose dribbling head was wobbling on her chest. All I could see was the tangled grey crown of her Lear-like bonce. Unearthly wails and shrieks and the sound of blaring indifferent TVs escaped from the sinister sealed rooms around me, however – the place was a real snakepit. Perhaps the words had originated there.

I went – with some excitement – to look at the next print on the wall, one of Sir Sydney Nolan's immensely well known *"Ned Kelly"* series. My parents had a print of it at home in England and it used to terrify me as a child. The metal bucket protecting the Bushranger's head is a simple black square on a simple black stick. Both are rendered in a flat, unspeakable black, a black utterly flat and yet deep and heinous. By contrast, the face in the rectangular visor inside the mask is not only "moulded" – three-dimensional – but rich and subtle in its colouring. As in Jacques-Émile Blanche's portrait of Marcel Proust, the flesh of the forehead, nose and cheeks is the colour of clotted cream smeared with rose and lemon; the shading around the eyes is a beautiful *crème fraiche* colour mixed with pistachio green and Prussian blue. But the eyes themselves – ovals as big as turkey eggs – are of a flat, bicarbonate white. The pupils are the same fathomless, wretched black as the armour. "Yes! It's our big Chicken!" said a voice behind me. I turned to face her. The eyes of Ned Kelly were looking up at me: black Kalamata olives in bowls of blinding white yoghurt. "Yes," Cyn continued, scrutinising me closely, "it's our big Chicken, for our big state. Barbequed or fried, it sure tastes great! If Queensland makes you feel great, mate – then you'd rather have 'Big Rooster'!" Cynthia had managed to raise her head. She looked miraculously well and composed. Her arms, no longer hanging uselessly by her side, lay folded in her hap. But the voice was no longer Cynthia's voice. It was a voice like the sound of a trumpet: the ripe, gamey bass of Brooklana Fagan. I recognised it from her endless appearances on British TV. I wasn't amazed – that is a weak expression. The shock had carried me so far and fast beyond myself that I no longer even felt strange, just as somebody propelled instantly into the next world by a terrorist bomb does not feel the intense pain endured by a commuter grazed by a mugger's knife . . . I remember once, when I was a little boy, I was very, very sick – with Viral Pneumonia, I think – and I heard things – and saw things. Real things that weren't there. The things were not unreal – or they were not unreal to me. Then, when I was a teenager, I suffered a horrible nervous breakdown, and – the same thing happened. The phenomena would have frightened me terribly had I been well. But in the middle of the "Lost World" of illness – which certainly appears neither irrational nor painful when you are in the middle of it – everything seemed perfectly OK. It was like that now. "Yeah, you're our big chicken!" said Cyn – or Brookee, rather – saliva cascading over the cod roe that was her protruding lip. It had shot out of the "Black Hole" of her mouth like a vulva: it was a lovely coral colour and made me think of a shiny, tumour-like *Foie Gras*. "You're chicken enough not to face up to what you know! You know perfectly well who that 'Labor couple' are, the pair that you're actually prepared – for money, for cash – to try to get Tray to paint! It's our dear old kiddy-fiddler, isn't it, Sir Quntee Mush – and that Arkana bint, his latest squeeze? They're both murdering Tim-Tammic bastards, as you must have worked out, and they both want to *kill* Tray Beautous! You must have guessed that they didn't mean to do him any *good*, anyway, but still you went along with it, didn't you? For a million pieces of Eight, no less! . . . Jude-arse! . . . Well, let me fill you in on the details, *'Pehtrick'*! . . . When Tray paints 'em *'in flagrante'*, Arkana is going to have half a pound of Semtex up her ring-piece, activated by a triggering device. When Quntee shoves it up her – being a Tim-Tam, he can only take the fillies from behind – bang goes Miss Eh [*'A'*], bang goes Sir Qunt, and bang goes Tray Beautous! And bang goes your commission, too! . . . You only get it *after* you get Tray to do the dirty, remember? And who's gonna want to pay you *then*? . . . But don't imagine that *Dewy Popkiss* hasn't already been paid!"

I wondered at this point if I was daydreaming but Brookee's rasping, utterly distinctive voice disabused me. "Think about it, Mister Patrick Amrada Mynts . . . Why do you think you were invited to Australia in the first place? Because Dew and Bon *like* you? Because they *follow your career*? Dew is only using *you* my friend because he knows that Tray would run a mile from anything that *he* proposed! Why else do you think Dew made you agree to all those conditions? He did it cos Tray knows *all about 'im*! He knows *exactly* what Dew did to Knut Fagan and me. And Dew *knows* that Tray knows . . . I mean, Tray was Knut's pet freakshow, after all. And Dewy has also realised – as of course have Qunt and Arkana - that, without your pulling the wool over 'is eyes, Tray would never agree in a million years to be in the same room as two fucking Tim-Tams, least of all 'Sir' and 'Lady' . . . Don't you even *know* what Tray Beautous is famous for? Famous in Australia for, anyway? . . . I mean, even in London you must have heard about the little local difficulty they had over here a while back, the riots between the Tim-Tams and the Anglo-Keltic Aussie boys on Bilgola Beach, Sydney? . . . Well, let me refresh your memory!

What happened was that the Tim-Tammic jimmigrants had been hassling the wee Aussie bints - 'Skippy Hunting' the Texans call it – and the Anzac boys had taught the hairy bastards a lesson, jumped a few of 'em, pulled down their Speedos and humped the bastards – yeah, pork-sworded 'em right up the shitter right down there in the surf like Burt Lancaster in **From Here to Eternity**! The Anzac girlies, the erstwhile Skippys, were standing around cheering. Well, the Tim-Tams just couldn't take it, see, they couldn't take the humiliation, especially the witty reference to their preferred method of backstage entry. And not only that. Sure as night follows day, cue an orgy of *'we are not worthy'* Oz breast-beating and *'reaching out'* to the *'persecuted Texans'*. You must surely have heard of our old mate Rape Foxturd, Hollywood's biggest ever Aussie movie star? Well, to show her soldarity with the 'oppressed' jimmigrants, Rape stages a 'demonstration' for the meeja on Bilgola with two of her chums – Sir Quntee Mush and Gopi Panicker! It's a little play, see, a little *'work in progress'*, in fact, to make amends for Australia's infamy in front of our meeja chums. It's meant to show how Australia should abase itself, beg forgiveness for its 'Tim-Tammophobia'. In honour of which, Rape Foxturd has dressed herself up as Christina Stead, the goddess that them crazy old Tim-Tams worship. Rape's even wearing a special tee-shirt she's had printed, with the word *'DRINK!'* screaming out of it. She's strapped an enormous circumcised dildo around her waist and she's penetrating Gopi, Mother of Feminism. Cos Gopi is wearing one of those kangaroo panto outfits – and Foxy's dildo enters her via a hole under the tail of the panto-kanga shellsuit. Gopi is supposed to represent 'White Australia', see, so while she's being buggered from behind by 'Christina', the great female autonomist is just as willingly noshing on the huge rampant circumcised dick of Sir Quntee Mush, here to symbolise a vengeful, triumphant Texan Tim-Tam. Quntee is wearing a special tee-shirt, too. It reads: *'SUCK MUCKADILLA, AUSTRALIA!'* – much to the delight of the orally passive **SYDNEY MORNING HERALD** and its chums . . . It certainly ain't the first time anybody's 'chewed the fat' on Bilgola, so to speak – as we note by Foxy's injunction to *'Drink!'* – but I bet you anything you like it's the first time they've done it in front of two thousand cheering Tim-Tams and a truckload of hacks from Muckadilla's newspaper! . . . Well, these *'SUCK MUCKADILLA, AUSTRALIA'* tee-shirts become very fashionable, see, among the Tim-Tammic immigrants and the white trash 'liberals' that suck up to them. Suck up to them literally! And so Tray Beautous up there in Queenie gets mighty pissed off with Miss Foxturd and her pals! Nothing upsets him more than cowardly little cunts who advance their careers by towing the Party Line and saying *'I'm brave'*! . . . So 'Let's show the bleeding hearts what *really* being Avant-Garde is all about!' says Tray! 'Why don't we *really* push the boat out? Let's do what *they* should be doing!'. So he creates these 'works of art', my dear! . . . Says that they're just living, walking sculptures! Mobile sculptures!" (She pointed to her *'CHRISTINA IS A KNUT'* surplice and took its fabric between her forefinger and thumb). " . . . No, it's not what you thought, they're not this year's 'must have' in Byron Bay, Patrick! It would be pretty dicey getting away with one in your average 'buffet situation' - even in Australia . . . Knut Fagan liked 'em though. Now *there was an intelligent man*! Bought a whole load of 'em when he was Pee Emm and, when Dewy took over, Bon Popkiss, being the 'Rich Giver' she is, dumped fifty of 'em on *'The Lovely Aujourdh'ui'* . . . Well, as you can imagine, Pat, Tray kicked off a bit of a Nutter-Flutter with these here 'sculptures' of his! Out here in Aussie, at least! What a ding-dong, eh? Quntee and Arkana were jumpin' up and down like two cane toads on a hot tin dunny's corrugated roof! The Tim-Tams were all shook up like a Kitty-Litter . . . And *then* what does Tray do? He's got all these surfies as his nyewd models, see, the sort of limber-hipped gingers that gave the Hairy Hobbits a pasting on Bilgola Beach. And he calls hundreds of the Boys of Summer together while the tide is out and he gets 'em to build a giant sand castle on Bondi, a statue made of hard, wet sand and as big as that idol of yours truly on Magnetic. You should have seen it – hundreds of junior Rugby Leaguers crawlin' over this great, brown, drippin' hundred-foot hive like bees on a honeycomb. A 'temporary installation' is what our artist calls it! Les Boyz are the bees and they sculpt it at Tray's command to make its gob look exactly like Quntee's! They stick in a roast pig's head as the sculpture's circumcised twat, wrestle the top of its turban into a pointy dome like a Mauser bullet, gouge the word *'CHRISTINA'* into Sir Quntee's forehead . . . And what about Miss 'CHRISTINA's' titties, you ask? Why, they're just two ten-foot long rugby balls left over from the promo for the 'Aussie Rules' World Cup . . . Anyway, you should have heard Tray hollering at them Boys of Bummer to get a move on, get it all finished before the tide came in. Because that was the whole point, see, to have it all destroyed, all washed away by the tide. For as soon as the statue is finished – and just in time – the lads winch up an enormous version of one of these tee-shirts here and drop it like a big tent on the bastard's torso. On the front of the megashirt, it says what it says here:

'CHRISTINA IS A KNUT'. That's not surprising, really, cos 'Sir Quntee' has been sculpted to show him stretching out his arm in front of him, the upturned fingers facing the sea as if to force it back. On the back of the tee-shirt, though, the bit the thousands of Bondi sun worshippers can see, Tray has had a giant 'pome' by Black Gin Boree printed:

> ### *MY NAME IS 'AUSSIE', 'MANDY', 'US', QUEEN OF QUEENS: LOOK ON MY QUNT, YE MIGHTY, AND DESPAIR!*

Well, finally the tide comes in. The unending cider snowman collapses like a stob of sorbet in a plate of pipin' soup. Soon there ain't nothin' left but a teeshirt as big as a tennis tarpaulin flapping under the rising surface like a Mantra Ray, the black and white letters shiverin', boilin', billowing' – vomitin' and swallowin' the followin':

> ### *NOTHING BESIDE REMAINS. ROUND THE DECAY OF THAT COLOSSAL WRECK, BOUNDLESS AND BARE, THE LONE AND LEVEL SANDS STRETCH FAR AWAY.*

And that's why Quntee and Arkana want to *kill* Tray, Pat! They want to *kill* the poor bastard, do you hear?! Because he mocked the goddess. Showed that she didn't even have feet of clay. And that's the reason why they want to scatter the bits of Brooklana in St Peter's Square, too: to get back at the Christians for Bondi Beach. But Quntee and 'Kana want to kill themselves, as well, cos their goddess says that, if they do that, in the course of stiffing a Christian, they'll go straight to Pussy Heaven, where Quntee at least will get to fuck fourteen little boys and have as much female arse as the bidet in a brothel . . . But are *you* gonna get to Heaven, Pat? . . . You'll never get to Heaven if you break my heart! Knut – he's broken it already, by suckin' up to Dew! Why else am I telling you this?"

Suddenly Brookee – or, Cynthia, rather – gave a terrible cry. Her eyes flew upwards – then the lids flapped shut, like the "Leica covers" on the bulging eyes of a lizard. Her chin collapsed abruptly into her chest as if the spine – or a thread holding up the head – had just been severed . . . Just at that moment, Bon and Sandi rounded the corner of the far wall and galloped down the corridor towards us. Sandi crouched and took Cynthia's pulse – properly this time. He forced open her mouth and an eye and examined each closely with a cute-looking torch. "Oh, it's nuthin!" he said at length. "She'll live! . . . Better luck, next time, Lady Pee! . . . She's just had a bit of a spell, that's all . . . Must've been all the excitement of seein' her Ladyship since Christ knows when, eh?!" Sandi gripped the handles of Cynthia's wheelchair and opened the door to her room. An acrid smell escaped. Bon grabbed my arm, whispered in my ear: "Time ter go, Patrick! Time to clear *right* fucken out!" I didn't even have time to say goodbye – however laconically – to Cyn, which I greatly regret. We made our way back through the labyrinth of passages, *"the insane in their strong-doored rooms, the sacred idiots"* – as Walt Whitman describes them – caterwauling their *Adieus*.

Bon began again on her subject **du jour**, that of Larrakeyah, her garrulous daughter-in-law. Unlike the selfless Lady Popkiss, Bon explained, Larrakeyah displayed an unbecoming reluctance to devote her waking hours to "those less fortunate than herself" – Cynthia, for example – and her maternal and Maecenas-like faculties also left something to be desired. Bon asked me if "anyone on Earth" could be as self-absorbed as the slut who had married "Wayvil", her Ewe-lamb. Having heard quite enough about Larrakeyah, I assured her that I might certainly fall into that category. "But what about those *less fortunate* than yerself?" Bon demanded. "I don't know anyone less fortunate than myself!" I said. Bon, snubbing me, abruptly decamped, hobbling swiftly ahead out the door of the "Hayume" and down the path to the Merc. With her rolling Quasimodo gait, she looked from behind like a soccer player dribbling a ball past a series of particularly plucky defenders. Wanko was waiting by the car and she told him in no uncertain terms to "step on it" – soon we would be late for lunch at Yarralumla.

My mind floated in a new element. It was full of living pain, like a jellyfish. What had happened seemed so unreal in its intensity that one could be blasé. But underneath a light dusting of leaves, there lurked a hideous, toothache-like fact. Had I really . . . ? The alternative was even worse . . . As I climbed into the Merc, I noticed something on the ground that I initially mistook for chewing gum. It was covered in frenzied ants and surrounded by a circle of rapidly fading damp earth. The poor thing looked so terribly naked in its agony. Slugs and worms and other wet things that crawl on the earth are instantly devoured in Australia. Ants and other predators leave them alone in England. Still, it was good to encounter again, outside the *"Lovely Aujourd'hui"*, the limitless heat and light, the impervious landscapes of Australia. After the foul intimacy of the "hayume", I found them far from sinister, quite bracing in fact. I hoped that the creeping wet inwardness that had opened up in me there would dry out and disappear in the blazing "outwardness", like an ulcer exposed to the sun. I no longer regarded a visit to North Queensland with trepidation . . . But that thing that "Cynthia" had said? Could it perhaps be true?

Wanko started up the engine and we drove towards a solitary Ghost Gum at the top of the hill: it was glittering in the atrocious blue like a tinsel Christmas Tree. *"Oh Christ my Emperor,"* I prayed, trying to remember the famous prayer, *"preserve me from this day!"* "But if she'd only *listen*," Bon couldn't help observing again of Larrakeyah, her wayward daugher-in-law, "instead of babbling away like some incessant . . . *chook*!"

The cicadas began to start up. First a faint hiss, and then a fierce shaking, like a thousand tambourines.

Part Two

THE DEAD PAST

Oh Girly Soukoop, I was so fond of you !

Girly was the old lady I ended up living with in Townsville while I tried to gain the confidence of Tray Beautous. I found out that Tray had left his studio on Magnetic Island so that he could look after his Grandmother in her big old house on the mainland. The mainland part of Townsville was where Girly also lived. Tray's Grandmother had just come out of hospital after an unsuccessful operation on a brain tumour. She was dying, and everybody else in Tray's family had cried off, pleading prior engagements – or *subsequent* engagements, as Oscar Wilde once more accurately described them. Girly and Tray's Gran had always been good friends. Girly had also been close to Dewy Popkiss' parents. I guess the fact that she knew both Beautous and Dew was why Dew had arranged for me to stay with her. But there was this difference between the Popkisses and La Soukoop. Girly, unlike Bon, was the real thing – a real "Aussie aristocrat". She wasn't the only individual the Popkisses knew in Townsville, of course. Girly was a widow – the widow of a famous writer – and she had lived on her own for a long time. So while her lovely villa was being made ready for me, I stayed in another suburb with Freek Bloomers, the Labor MP who represented Townsville in the Federal Parliament. That was an experience!

I am looking now at a photo of the interior of Girly's pretty little Townsville house. The house near the top of the pink sandstone mountain – Mount Kutheringa (also called Castle Hill) – that sat right slap-bang in the city's heart. Its position was marvellous. You looked out through a window of trembling, jellied heat onto the whole of Townsville and its bay. Tin roofs like hundreds of blinding little mirrors; black Mango trees jumping around like toads after the rain. Beyond that, milky-mauve Magnetic Island in the Cancer medicine-blue of the Coral Sea. Given the climate – that of hot, hot places that have buildings just like it – Girly's should not have been an unusual house, but in Townsville, it was. Most Townsville houses are built of wood and sit on high teak poles. They have pointed aluminium roofs.

Painted in so-called "colonial" colours, they often look surprisingly muted: grey; Venetian red; curry powder yellow; combat green. Girly's villa – built, she boasted, by a "Communist hairdresser" in 1930 – was of stucco-faced brick. It sat squarely on the ground. It was completely white – a beautiful white, white, white on that pink mountain! Panelled cubes of white Art Deco inside and out. It had a flat tar roof. In the photograph I am now studying, the white shutters are open on a room full of fish-tank amber light. Spidery, verandah-type rattan furniture. A fat sofa and armchairs in powdery, Pompadour colours. Vertical scrolls with pitch black Chinese letters. The Stilton-coloured walls. Tropical plants with gigantic leaves in radiant sensual brass urns. Coffee-tables and stools in the Oriental-Bohemian style of Cocteau's Singapore. And a forest of wierd, one-off ornaments on every surface. Treacle-brown ashtrays shaped like peach halves. Empty gold candlesticks. Tiny, grotesque Khmer gods. Exquisite little faience horses in Monsoon grey and blue. They create a casual, elegant effect, spontaneous yet precise. Like the quotidian slew – (letters, just-picked mangoes as fresh and doomed as orchids, the newspapers of that very day) – they define Girly's uniqueness, freeze it in time: the vast, vibrant civilization that is just one, randomly chosen human being. Turkish carpets sit in relative isolation on the black stone floor.

It is all gone now: even the floor. All those fantastically particular, peripheral things have flown away like migrating birds. And the same is true, of course, of any other house, any other life. A more typical Townsville interior – even though it would have been furnished like a kindergarten or a beach – would, once photographed, not have seemed less august, less "eternal". And the khaki and silver photographs Girly once showed me of her Edwardian childhood and youth on a "Cattle Station" in the Queensland interior were of a deep, settled world that did not, in reality, prove less fleeting. Girly a blurred young cloche-capped flapper on a sailboat, seen slightly from above, each breast an oyster flimsy with folds, each akimbo arm raised amid rigging like the Winged Victory of Samothrace. "Black Gins" (the wives of Aboriginal stockmen) in frothy bibs like Victorian dolls – with the

240

amazed, contemptuous eyes of dolls. Girly's brothers and sisters on gliding horses. The pet cats you think will never die. Parents and uncles in their Edwardian "Open Sandwich" Sunday Best. Christmas dinner with its chrysalid fowl, its glinting skein of crystal, its crockery a collection of blown wild birds' eggs. The homestead itself on glorious stilts like a Man o' War in full sail – all so seemingly permanent – all gone now – the Christmas crackers, the beermats, the roof beams, the human beings: gone. As if they had never existed.

And this forensic amnesia, this Exterminating Angel which seems such a crime against nature, in fact is one of its laws. For where, for that matter, are the inkwells, the forks and napkins that once graced the Imperial Palace on the Palatine in Ancient Rome? (Let us forget for the moment its absent walls and pillars and frescoes). Just imagine if we were able to scrutinise a photograph of one of its messy, seething rooms, taken at some random, arbitrary hour in Roman history. Ten AM, say, on Sunday, the 8th of August 192 AD? Would we not be amazed at the superfluity and indiscipline – the mess – of details whose existence we could never have imagined? Why, when we picture the ancient past, or even the more recent past, is it always so utilitarian, so workmanlike, so efficient? Why do we always reduce it in our mind's eye to its essentials? Why does it always sit in a sterile moonscape, its buildings whitened skeletons, as if painted by the Belgian surrealist Paul Delvaux? How much more must the Classical Past, say, have resembled the world of the dinosaurs: sunny, pulpy, fabulously decaying and alive, a coral reef of unspeakable, unimaginable detail? Where are they now, those irreducible, endless, adventitious things, which, far more than the essentials, make up the whole picture? They must be somewhere. And who is there to even remember now the instructive lives suggested by these photographs of mine? Lives that were defined by an arbitrary mosaic of perishable dross far more efficiently than by any ghost or statue? How, after all, is Girly any different from any other dead human being, from the billions of others who mean nothing to us? The long, rich civilization of each person to have drawn breath on the earth has been swallowed up like Jonah, as Byzantium was in all its infinity by "the Great Turk", the stupid, peurile conquistador: Death, Islam, *"le Grand Seigneur"*. It is as if, despite its complexity, its size, its huge significance to certain other beings, each lost, loved life never existed at all – as if it were all of fundamental unimportance like a carnation or an icicle or some other complex, unique but prolific item whose passing merits no epitaph. *"And so the world we inhabit, which is always new, goes by unexamined, made ordinary by the camera, unmeditated on; and there is no one to awaken the sense of true wonder."* Who is there to draw attention to these lives – lives that were given their due in their own times, their own circle, but whose orbiting "life-support system" of celebrants and historians has itself now disappeared? Each life was a wilderness of hope and fear and struggle. The ones who participated in each life saw their investment in terms of eternity – but each is as ridiculous and forgotten now as an old bird's nest.

Not perhaps each; but why do we treasure and relate the story of some lives, and not the story of others? Before the unification of those countries, were the many little states comprising Italy and Germany (Hesse, Parma, Baden etc) not as full as France or Russia or Spain of drama, infinity, self-sacrifice? The history of each was ruled by a secret, complex code. It isn't even a question now of lacking the key to the code: the codes themselves have long been consigned to the pit like used-up microchips. It is as if – as we said – they had never even existed. Do the meanings of billions of individual lives, meanings still unravelled at the time of each death, even matter? . . . If only we could be like God and see in all its fullness every life that ever existed on earth. If only we could endow each with the attention, the fascination that each deserves. If only we could retrieve each as we have Pompeii on its last day, develop at full length each accidental polaroid of a messy, once-in-a-lifetime room. Each is just one fleshy frame of the tapeworm, a movie-reel epic wrapped in the ribcage of the whale.

THE ONE HUNDRED AND TWENTY DAYS OF BOWEN

DIARY OF MY VISIT TO TOWNSVILLE

MONDAY 16 NOVEMBER 1987. Woke at 1am this morning, and on several other occasions, worrying about my diary. Slipped into fitful nightmare: I remember finding the glass eye of William the Conqueror – a potent maleficent symbol. I went through mentally what I was going to put in my diary, and I finally wrote it up on waking. I watched a piece on George Harrison on TV. As we breakfasted, I walked around in a dazed pain, bowl in hand. Emporio PM is going to send stuff to "the Come Buckets" as Dewy so delicately calls a Midsummer Night's Dreaming, and they will send it on to Canberra. The buckets must all be back in Sydney by now. Dewy and Bon will send the stuff to wherever I am. And vice versa. Only Dewy and Bon will know where I am, which is food for some delightful thought. I finally plucked up courage and said my goodbyes. Bon came in, quite vexed, with half a toilet roll in case I get caught short. This strange town where I feel so alone already had a glare over it like a swimming pool. I smeared suntan lotion on my arms. It must have been out of date as it was milky, with lumps, like old yoghurt. Walked down the slope of the slight hill where the Yarralumla Gatehouse sits. There were naked Broncos in shorts, mowing. One with a satyr nose and beard looked exactly like Socrates. Wanko picked me up in the Merc. Waved goodbye. I remember a half-naked Dew building a fire with some Broncos in Bonnie's chickenwire chookyard which sits on the grass platform where the Gin Palace is. Homely touch. The infernal imagery of chooks – always such senseless, devilish things. The raucous aluminium orange of the flame looked terribly unfair in this heat. The chooks incredibly frail, as though about to be sucked into the flame like those spiders in Lowell's poem.

We drove past a new sports stadium through fresh suburbs of vinyl orange brick plumped right down in the Bush. The house owners must be like the people who live on the streets of Calcutta. Self-contained, chintzily domestic, utterly oblivious to their environment. Also in the Bush were the big black rectangular tents like room-sized shoeboxes. Just like the one at Yarralumla. The sunlight made their black grey. I asked Wanko what they were. He filled me in on the state of their marriage instead. Her husband spends every weekend at the trotties. The horses never win. Wastes all their "shrapnel". One day, Wanko brought the couple a letter from the Racing Registration Board. Dew was being allowed to call his horse "New Surroundings." "That sounds like a good idea!" she said in Wank's ear. She gestured at their stately pleasure dome and observed: "Livin' on pies in a fucken trailer in Krambach will be like Golden Circle peaches after this!"

A little late drawing out of Canberra and a very violent thump (animal?) put the air conditioning etc. out. "In talking to you there," Wank said, "I've just gone past the exit loop: it can't get much worse . . . I really shouldn't say that at this stage."

Being wise men, we weren't driving to Sydney the way the bus had brought us chillun of the Dreamtime, but "by another route". Due north to Tuena, then due East and a slalom thru the skirts of Holy Sydney before the Pacific Highway at Wyong, just beyond the last burbs. Then the Pacific High would take us up to Townsville: all 2,000 kilometres. The landscape after Tuena was flat, a bright, watery green, with lots of tall, scratchy gums which, from the foothills – we were climbing up into the Great Dividing Range – looked like little creels of Scottish birch. The mountains were as closely forested as Switzerland or Romania, but, strangely, with gums. The eucalypts not the usual sort. They had arthritic cedar-red trunks, shaggy foliage the china blue of damsons. Reminded me of that line by Mandelstam:

> *"You distinguished tree-tops,*
> *The feasts of shaggy trees,*
> *Occupy the place of honour in Ruisdael's pictures -"*

We stopped high up, in Kurrajong – a place called "Old Pansy Junction". I bought four huge opals. They were set in pasteboard earrings, genuine antiques: an absolute pittance. Wanko was there, so I had to send one pair to Bonnie. The shopkeeper said that earrings "were a sore point" with him. To surprise his wife one anniversary, he had bought some on a business trip where Australia's national gem is mined – Atula in the Northern Territory. He had found an expensive modern pair for his wife, the sort that clip on, and, the day before he was due to present them, she got her ears pierced.

Our hotel - the first nice gaff I have had on this continent!

TUESDAY 17 NOVEMBER 1987. I had a nightmare about Cynthia this AM. I dreamt that she was possessed by 5 spirits, hence her hideous staring eyes and misshapen features. One of the spirits, Morphia, "closed the eye of the will." It destroyed one's ability to resist possession. I must have got "Morphia" from *The Faerie Queene.* The spirits were waiting to be born as human beings. If God denied them this, they would refuse to leave the human host.

Descended the eastern slope of the Blue Mountains, which we climbed from the West yesterday. Wanko bolted roughly over a branch in the road. I wound the car window down. It was very early in the morning and the gum forest smelled overpowering in the pure air, like a chapter of Alcoholics Anonymous. The chemical effluvium of the eucaplypts gives the Mountains their name and had spread a wierd "Technicolor" blue like cake dye over the beige-pink sky: it looked like Lana Turner's bathwater in *The Prodigal.* All the way down we heard the beautiful windchime song of the Bellbirds.

Reached the coastal plateau on which Sydney sits and, to the west of the city, stopped for a cup of tea at "Windsor" (these names!) on the Hawkesbury River. Sun already malign. Wandered about in a wet, hot-cheeked daze, worrying. Partly about the nightmare and whether it had anything to do with what took place at Manningreedah, which is madness.

Wanko, after all, has told me that he IS (or was) an indentical twin. I found my way to the river and, looking at the ugly, tacky but suddenly radiant buildings, I thought: "Well, there's no escape. This will be home for the next few weeks. Better make the best of it. And apply, unvarying, the rule I decided upon in Canberra, after the Hayume: FLEE AND FORGET EVERYTHING WITH PAIN ATTACHED TO IT, AT FIRST SIGHT, COMPLETELY AND FOREVER! What better rule could there be for life as a whole?

Purple Jacaranda and that bright crystal olive-green of the Australian scrub and the juicy, churning Latte-brown river and the colonial architecture in yellow stucco and clove-coloured brick. At one of the shops – *"A PORT OF INDULGENCE OFFERING A VARIETY OF DESIRES"* – I saw books. Several things strike you about Australia. "Serious" Australian books, for instance, are huge coffee-table numbers with enormous script – books for the blind. Wanko went to a newsagent to get a paper and a "Golden Rough" (Australian candy). I told him: "Wanko, YOU are a Golden Rough!" I asked him to buy some postcards for me to send to England. He came back with "Colonial Sydney" – a sequence of tarted up eighteenth-century barracks etc. There was a ferociously scrubbed sandstone building with a vibrant, hideously modern sign – an inn of some sort. Ancient, extraordinary, beautiful to an Australian. A British person would, oblivious, have passed it by. Yet it was probably because of their (to him) Olde Worlde splendour that Wanko had thought these particular cards would impress me. I was angry with him because, when you send postcards, you want to convey what is unique about the place in question: in Australia's case, its vulgarity, modernity. Not that modernity and vulgarity are unique to Australia, but they are all it has.

We pierced the placenta of greater Sydney via Castle Hill – White's sainted "Sarsaparilla". Wanko pointed out to me the oldest and most hallowed building on the continent – the headquarters of the first British Governor-General in Paramatta. Then a little isolated town, now deep in Sydney's western suburbs. It dates I would imagine from the 1790s. It was exactly like a little Hampshire pub – but this was the gem, the acme, of Australian antiquity – the Westminster Abbey. It was so tiny, so cosy and undistinguished-looking. There was a park and it was strange to see it against the glaring infinite wilderness over which it had once been set. Its little porthole windows were drowning under luminous gold Buffalo Grass that was at least as high as maize and radiant swatches of Wattle. It was sickening to think of how endless this sea of naked Bush would turn out to be (especially for the Governors), and how holy and homely England is by way of comparison. I really wanted to flee. More terrible by far, however, than the Auschwitz abundance of the Aussie Bush, the outer Sydney suburbs were also visible. Just one of the tasteless brick villas in "Carlingford" or "Tomah" would have dwarfed the one-time centre of imperial power. Set against the menacing Bush on which they had so recently been dumped, they seemed, in their bumptious relish, even more incongruous than what Pasolini once called "the Palace". The holiness and homeliness of Government House spoke of England. I wanted to withdraw there from suburban Australia, just as the earliest Governors had withdrawn there from primaeval Oz.

We then passed some truly ghastly and much poorer suburbs - a whole swathe of Western Sydney is like Staines on Mars. We stopped at a service station in Campsie next to a mosque - nothing looks incongruous in Australia. Interminable sand-dunes, low brownish dying evergreens, refineries, power stations. I remember *"GRACE=DANGER"* painted on the fence of one of them. Most of the people in these suburbs seemed to be recent immigrants. I noticed the parrot-like nose, woolly hair and ubiquitous moustache of the males – outside the Middle East, only now the mark of a sadistic queen. The women – headscarfed like Russian peasants – were sitting complacently under trees.

Our skirting of the inner city, though – before we turned North-East towards the Pacific – really lifted me up! Those suburbs between Central Station and Berala, row upon row of red corrugated iron roofs, pink and yellow and duck-egg blue plasterboard houses, here and there an exquisite, gross Catholic church like a heifer. The houses small, squat, a cross between a Sussex seafront bungalow and a Wild West saloon, valley after valley swarming with vomit-coloured wood and red-painted corrugated iron and, quite apart, a tall, tall palm tree waving on a viscous, silvered white-hot powder blue. The scene reminded me of Delacroix's *"The Fall of Constantinople"*. Or the streets behind Kensington Town Hall in London against a far-off freak of sapphire: hilly, narrow, wooded. But better than England – more of it, better preserved. This Neapolitan Chelsea was made new by the antipodean cleanness and freshness of the white and pistachio green and pink and turquoise-grey houses, by the cubical twin-towers of a Lima-like cathedral in the distance with its stippling grey boa of Ghost Gums. Breezy – I could smell water in the air, I could taste freedom and nostalgia and peace. Then the glittering grey-blue harbour again, ringed with rheumy olive scrub and white and red buildings as fresh-looking as poisonous mushrooms. Then the relentlessly perfect opera house, skyscrapers, bridge – the hairy, delicate yachts like young locusts. It was all stirring, overwhelming. There were a great many schoolkids outside suburban Yagoona station – all oppressively white with rosy panting cheeks and incredibly fussy English uniforms. Disturbingly untroubled, like New Zealand apples.

Suddenly remembering them, I asked again about the wierd box tents. I still got no answer, which was troubling . . . We were now driving through Turra Murra in northern Sydney, "another very tree-oriented area", according to my sagacious coachman. Black boughs. Flickering of black, grey, and green-brown eucalypt leaves like a swarm of stingless native bees. The colours soft and hot and native – Mother-of-Pearl, Lantana-purple, and now a glowing, mutinous sky the bulimic, half-gold grey of Sevruga. In amongst the gums endless Oxblood-brick houses stood like hulking bulls. A shellburst of orange terracotta roofs reminded me of gaudy Takeaway puke on a London pavement. A shocking bang – at first I thought with alarm it was the car – and the world became a waterfall of verdigris and limpid sliver. The gums loured grey and olive and indifferent like the primaeval Australian rain. We cleared Sydney and hit the Pacific Highway at Berowra. We looked out on an endless sodden landscape of low scrub with here and there a tall skeletal gum with a Pom-Pom of foliage and, higher up, a bare finger of branch, like an American cheerleader as depicted by Russell Drysdale.

Australia – intense cultivation of the physical, the sensual (food, sex, nature). The metaphysical's lack of tissue, texture. Underlying spongy sterility like the inside of a tooth – externally hard, white, sensual – airy, sponge-like inside. Just like the Ghost Gum – such an appropriate name! So strange to see living trees – gums – whose trunks and branches are nearly always the white white white of death. After Cooranbong huge wooded valleys of dark olive gumleaf veined with eteliolate white tripe, with corona of cauliflower. Turds strung with tapeworm. Suggestion as in the tooth of a density, of a threshing effulgence that is not, given the feathery folderol of these airy gums. We approached the Myall Lake system: the vision of slate-azure in the milky grey olive-green hills. Reached our motel in the middle of the Booti Booti National Park quite late. It was out on Cape Hawke between Bungwahl and Coomba. There were two little boys sitting there in a huge empty room – a restaurant I imagine. Theirs was the only table – as if the room were still under construction. A plate of French Fries sat between them like a heap of pink carpentry chips. A glass of soft drink belonging to one of them was glowing – a rank orange.

WEDNESDAY 18 NOVEMBER 1987. When I awoke at 8 it was still dark because the rain poured. It poured like a jet roaring in to land just above the roof. It made me feel cosy. I had to turn on the lamp to read the newspaper Wanko had bought at "the port of indulgence". Yellow light on the shingles like the bamboo columns on a cocktail bar made me feel Miss Tiggywinkle-like. I felt like one of the characters in those savage, half-lit paintings by Francis De la Tour or Max Beckmann.

There was a picture in the paper of a Sunny-Pinnian demo – the Idroolees have killed a leading guerilla. One big photograph on the front page – a close-up of a woman in a headscarf shrieking, arms akimbo. Her whole mouth was filled with her tongue, like that of the terracotta Aztec god in the *"Wonder of Tenochtitlan"* exhibition at the Royal Academy a few years' back. Odd prominence in Aztec art given to features ignored in the art of other societies: the tongue, the teeth, the internal organs. Utter Martian otherness of their sensibility. One imagines that, if dogs, say, were to have an art world, that's what they would be interested in. (That and bums of course!) While what is to the fore in the art of all other civilizations – the eyes – were completely neglected by the Aztecs, who always rendered eyes closed tight shut or as skulls with their cheese-like holes. The Headscarf has I find the same horrid effect on the faces of women. The hideous hood and loathesome red-lipped mouth of the lady in the picture, filled by the blade-like pointed tongue made me think of Picasso's picture of the shrieking cockerel. Terrorism seems impossible in Australia.

Driving up through Forster-Tuncurry, not very far north of the Myall Lakes, we got our first glimpse since Sydney of the Pacific Ocean, but very different. Here it seemed a hard-working, human, Atlantic-like sea, not a Lotos-eaten pastiche. Broiling green-blue breakers seen from the hills of which Tuncurry is composed – stupendous crashing iceberg geysers on the edge of beach-fringed cliffs. Deafening bangs of the breaking wave. Brown brown (with sand) boiling springs turning aluminium-olive out to sea. The topography reminded me of St Andrew's in Scotland. Sea seen thru diving hills and the hairy black tarantula fingers of the Norfolk Pine. About twenty tiny tankers standing out to sea in the silvery veil like flies in one of those dense gauze spider nests. The smoky sky mauve and gun grey, silver. The beaches deserted – biscuity blood-orange sand. I couldn't help releasing a cry of delight. I suppose it reminded me of home. "That's why yer uncle wanted me to drive youse up – so you could see the place!" says Wanko. Australia "was the nearest to heaven" that Wanko would ever get – an observation with which I could only agree. "I told Father McAuley," said Wanko, "when oy doy oym taken me sweat band with me! He says: *'You're not wrong there mate!'* "

No need for a sweatband today. The world was copper and olive and pewter and black – we passed endless mangrove-resembling Gum and Casuarina forests, dully glowing bronze lakes. Trees at Nabiac NSW the colour of cooked spinach with the white spines – gum trees the flowery leaves of the cooked spinach, each with a white fistula of spines.

A big river in Taree – a yellowish dog-poo brown, full of hate and primaeval like a crocodile. It went right through the middle of town but the town had wisely turned its back on it. Wondrous lunch at the main "Taree Hotel" – ie pub: a naked brick Art Deco building like a Lido pavilion in 1930s England. Crumbed oysters, a huge steak of river fish with green rice and raisins and the finest pavlova either of us had ever swallowed. A soft, melting meringue with pouring cream, ice cream and a real passionfrut *"jus"*. A coach party also dining – all the food laid out for them *"luxe, calme et volupté"*. The "just-so" preparation of fabulous and lavish and first rate victuals. One expected a Roman figure with a horn of plenty and a bouquet – a cornucopia covered in roses, ears of green wheat and *voile*. Nothing of quality expensive, exigent here, as it would have been in England, yet the salt cellars were just empty coca-cola bottles, the salt mixed with grains of uncooked rice to stop it from congealing in the humid atmosphere. I thought the elderly coach party were foreign tourists at first but their accents betrayed some unassimilated ethnic minority. Mezzogiorno Italians? Sephardic Jews? Old ladies with the grotesque faces of deep sea fish. Small spherical bodies – the soccer ball bodies of snow white hens. Endless harangue of one of the ladies while the spherical gents – fat and tiny, a shiny mottled brown like cowrie shells – looked on. Their concentration was intense. Way "ethnic" Australians say "fully" rather than "really". "That was fully delicious."

We luxuriated too long over our late lunch and darkness (or more darkness) soon sneaked up on us. We passed the Brisbane-bound Greyhound Bus at Port Macquarie. It was picking up passengers outside a supermarket. A fat, bald man in a tee-shirt, a chain smoker, moustachioed, with a strap-bag, was being seen off by his lovers – or daughters. As the bus-driver fussed around him, taking his luggage, the girls would take flash pictures of the scene. Blue flashes. Behind this tableau one saw, by a security light, the dimly-lit largesse of the supermarket, its centrepiece a toy motorbike for 10 cent rides. The bike humanised the sterile town, which, like all Australian country towns was far more desolate than its hinterland. In another "Outpost of Progress", Kempsey (these names!), a little girl – about eight-years old I would imagine – was wandering the empty streets in a woolly lime-green nightgown.

Our hotel was out on Smoky Cape between Arakoon and Clybucca.

THURSDAY 19 NOVEMBER 1987. We left the hotel at nine. Drove through Urunga and Coff's Harbour, stopping briefly.

From the "Shire Museum" in Urunga: "Indigenous peoples of Northern New South Wales": Gumbayngirr Aborigines, aka "the Kumbaingeri", their territory from the Clarence to the Nambucca river, and inland to the Great Dividing Range. When the White Man arrived, very late – in some places as late as the Twentieth Century (for, like much of Northern NSW, this region had simply been by-passed earlier on) – they found only about 1,500 "natives" moving nomadically over that vast expanse. Semi-permanent camps at Bellingen, Karangi, Bostobrik which they would rotate around in endless succession catching the successive local harvests of Grey Mullet, Mutton Birds, Lilli Pilli fruit. (The Court of Louis XVI and Marie Antoinette would move constantly between Fontainebleau, Rambouillet and Versailles to enjoy the discreet *"menus plaisirs"* designated at each). The Aborigines were never at any time numerous. Pre-"Big Mr Bi-Guy", pre-1788 (Australia's "Great Terror", Australia's "French Revolution") there may have been, at most, about 300,000 covering the entire continent.

Coff's Harbour known as "Womboynerahlah" = "Place where Kangaroos camp". The Jita Jita People (a subdivision of the Kumbaigeri) inhabited.

A harbour (ie ANY harbour, a harbour PER SE) was "Gidden Mirreh" = "Big Moon".

The ocean - "Gargil" = "Living Water".

A creek - "Bulungell" = "Drinking Fish" – from the Barramundi that appear to be drinking when they surface to gulp in air.

"Orara" = "Home of the Perch."

"Moonee" = "Small Kangaroo".

"Korora" = "Roar of the Sea".

"Bucca" = "bendy".

Orbost, Central Bucca, Moonbil: the sense of despair one feels when one sees the shopping arcades in these Australian country towns – they offer exotic and elaborate comfits far beyond their equivalents in the UK, but all underwritten by emptiness, illusion. So sad. What comes back to me is what Christina Stead writes about Australia in **A Last Glimpse of the Homestead** – the melancholy, the feeling things are not right, not as they seem; or rather that they *are* right, but out of tune with a correct and definitive version of reality elsewhere. Melancholy baby. Something is amiss. You feel it far more intensely in the country than in Canberra or Sydney. The illusion of a convertible, European reality can be maintained in the city because of the sham human factor's sheer critical mass. Given this density, the city can pass itself off as the analogue of the human element in the real world. But the profound unreality of European Australia cannot be denied in the country towns. There, European-ness slithers just above the top of the indifferent primaeval Bush – which cannot be opened up – as on an intervening layer of thick bleach. It is the sterile syrup which forms the base of the civilisation, not the closed off countryside, to which nobody has the key and which the "civilisation" does not touch. And this despite the brooding Aboriginal names, which only emphasise the failure to connect.

Wank pointed out the Aboriginal Compound just as we were coming into Coff's Harbour. Camp of the original inhabitants. Cut off, like Chekov's *"Ward 6"*. A place not of the conqueror, not of the indigenous people – the Aborigines forced to play a part by the conqueror and his guilt, like Figaro. We saw quite a few Aborigines in Coff's Harbour – the further from Sydney you get – epicentre of 1788's Atomic flash – the more of them you find surviving. If you call it surviving. Which quite a few manage to do as, *pace* the Urunga Museum, there must have been at least 1,500 Aboriginals in Coff's Harbour alone, which indicates an extraordinary level of "resistance", notwithstanding all the whitey snivelling. Wanko however told me that they were "half-breeds" and that lots of even European Australians claim on what might only be a homeopathic tincture of Abo blood in order to gain the special welfare, education and land rights that the Federal Government has set aside for "native people". (So, obviously, the ones handing out the land and money should not be confused with those!) He told me that Australia's registered "indigenous" population was now five times higher than it had been in 1788! So "the Aboriginal Holocaust" has obviously been as fell a phenomenon as the Sunny-Pinnian, which has produced a Sunny-Pinnian community six times larger than it was in the 1940s, when it supposedly received its quietus. (Of course, unlike the Abos, the Sunny-Pinnians were not the first there).

It suddenly struck me that the Aborigines in Coff's Harbour might simply APPEAR numerous because, it being a weekday, everybody else was at work. They drifted around purposelessly, pushing prams, like fat, well-dressed mental patients. There was a huge and spanking Government-funded "Aboriginal and Islander" Support Cen-tah with some farouche pseudo-political porn painted all over it, supposedly "tribal" and evocative of "the struggle". What was it all FOR, I wondered? Given the underlying power structure, the Rousseau-esque raging no less than the seigneurial narcoleptic stupor was all ultimately "permitted". It was the white man who had devised, determined these ways. All this "authenticity", this "authentic" art, these squalidly luxurious mental hospitals and outpatient clinics (because that's what they were). Even these acts of defiance. The *Le Rouge et le Noir* Aboriginal flag for instance cracking above the Cen-tah with the big yellow disk in it like a "Golden Rough" – all quite inconceivable in purely Aboriginal terms. What is "Aboriginal" about a flag, after all? Did the pre-1788 Aboriginals have one?

Surely, even "the violent genocide" alleged by the white Mea Culpists would have been better than this. Hatred, after all, can only ever be bestowed on an equal, or on more than an equal. Like imitation (which surely it resembles), hatred is the sincerest form of flattery. "Respect", the modern West's Cri-de-Coeur, is only ever the expression of a profound contempt. Because whereas previously it had pleased the White Man to destroy, now it pleased him to preserve – like the sentence that Stalin once passed on Mandelstam – *"isolate but preserve"*. After all, as Mandelstam says in that poem of his: *"Permission is always renewed for twinkling, writing, and decay"*! Especially decay. If Nature had been allowed to take its course, the more advanced invaders would simply have annihalated or assimilated the less advanced group. History must have seen it silently happen at least a thousand times. Nobody has ever made a song and dance about it – apart from the White Man, of course. Which is why only the White Man can be criticised for it. It's like Naipaul says: "Only that which criticises itself CAN be criticised."

But how "bad" – which is to say "good" – is the White Man really? What Mother Nature would have done would have been real. "Isolate but preserve" has not led to reality. When the mouse plays with the cat, the cat is still playing with the mouse. It made me feel that all action taken in defiance of the natural order – ie in the absence of the powerful action of the powerful – is a mockery, grotesque. The powerful should and must exercise power at all times. Everything else is sadism – or masochism (which amounts to the same thing).

Lunch at *"FISH, FISH, FISH!"* in Woolgoolga. A real feeling of despair, in contrast to what I had felt at Taree, at the Australian effulgence. A woman under a perfect maquillage, two-toned hair, perfectly combed, like wombat fur, was waiting tables, her effort absurdly incongruous in such a backwater. Her *décolletage* striking – pearls, limbs chic in black like the long-sleeved arms of a chimpanzee. Black slacks. My steaks with "Tassie Scallops" both wonderful and terrible. They put one in mind of the simplicity, *smallness* of the Australian economy: all it can produce is food. A businessman and a crop-haired offenceless Dyke were talking to two Indian businessmen – Indians getting everywhere on the planet, into every nook and cranny, but ruled by their own ancient occult rules wherever on earth they may be, like bees or wasps. Perhaps their presence was less surprising than usual in Woolgoolga, where there is a famous Sikh temple: it looked like the giant cement prawn in nearby Ballina – the same air of impermanence – like a *papier-mâché* animal in a kindergarten. Australian things are not sustained – no animating sustaining spirit in the buildings such as you get in other colonised countries (USA, Mexico). Like zombies – no native spirit, "native title". Artificial – not because the flowers are MADE of paper but because they have never lived on the printed page. Each lacks the spirit of the thing, the spirit of the flower, say: *it is simply the thing in itself.* Land of the living dead. Or of the dead, living. Living, but dead because no ghost. No *"Numen Inest"* – "herein dwells a god": not for the non-Aborigines anyway. Also in the Woolgoolga restaurant a Scots immigrant – he was middle-aged and his Scots accent was incredibly sharp so one wondered at his having given up what must have been a long apprenticeship in the real world for the "prize" that was unreality in an Australian country town. Discussing the rise in the value of his house in the naked Bush with another pretentious "political" bloke. Dreadful sense of immersion in a backwater, of claiming a height in the hierarchy of a backwater, of choices that are not choices because, as Naipaul says: "When the real world is felt to be outside, everyone at home is inadequate and fraudulent." After all the Dyke-friendly businessman's bullshit talk I saw he was wearing a plastic petrol station attendant's badge.

The sun came out after the constant rain and the landscape changed too as we entered what is "Big River Country, Yaegl Shire" – after the Yaegl who once occupied it. A mighty undulating unspoiled emerald-green steppe and the vast violet-blue Clarence River. Not a sign of a human being, of human habitation – which would certainly have intruded in Europe. Such a sense of peace, of freedom – of purity, stupidity, freshness. White egrets in the field next to brown beef cows, a beautiful black swan with a ruby red beak flying through the trees – the wonderful august frond-like gum trees with wattle-flower crests and thread-like foliage.

We stayed the night at the very old fashioned Maclean Hotel in Maclean (capital of Yaegl Shire). Its wooden verandah virtually debouched into the Clarence. After dinner, I went for a walk. Outside, a large and crisply perfect crescent moon and the big star by it, both unspeakably bright, like the kleig light at a night cricket match, and the other stars, all a molten smoky raging white on a limpid, numinous Prussian Blue. Bright light on the waters of the mystic Clarence, as big and wide and lovely as the Dniepr, and twice as innocent – as the Dniepr might have looked about three thousand years ago.

I saw a family in the pitch dark, preparing a barbeque on one of the Barbie platforms of the Riverside Park. Two groups of the *Jeunesse Dorée* of Maclean were squaring up to each other. One group on the "town" side of the road that ran along the river, the other on the other, riverine, bank. The group on the Clarence side was composed mostly of Aboriginals (remnants of the Yaegl?) and had as its citadel a silvery modern people carrier. Out of its side window a little white boy fell.

What is strange is the way everyone in Australian country towns – esp. every male – says hello to you. "Hello Mate!" And this evening I was hailed by a drunk as I walked by the mystic Dniepr. "Hello tiger, how you doin'?!" I mumbled something, which he obviously didn't catch, because the rejoinder was: "Christ! Can't even say hello! What's your problem?!" I doubled back and explained – rather weakly I'm sure – that I HAD saluted him. "O I'm sorry," he said as I scampered off. "I'm sorry for being ignorant". But he said this sardonically.

When I got back, I saw Wanko in the bar. Like Erich Honecker, dictator of East Germany, who is reputedly so fond of African giantesses, he had been watching "Coon-Porn" on the pay per view.

Read Tacitus before my Australian supper sausages, which smell like children and taste so unpleasantly of MEAT (something of which one could never accuse the oleaginous woodchip-filled stockings of Great Britain). The introduction to the *Agricola* , which, for some reason, I find I have brought with me from London. Tacitus is speaking of a long period of tyranny under Tiberius, Caligula etc – though he could be speaking of the Political Correctness of today which, let's face it, is often literally as murderous:

"A few of us, so to speak, survived not only our contemporaries, but ourselves. For so many years have been removed from the middle of our lives, in which the young men among us reached old age - all in silence."

"And so [as Naipaul puts it in *'Conrad's Darkness']* *the world we inhabit, which is always new, goes by unexamined, made ordinary by the camera, unmeditated on; and there is no one to awaken the sense of true wonder."*

FRIDAY 20 NOVEMBER 1987. Bright and hot this morning. We drove along the river to the Ferry crossing near where the Clarence joins the Pacific Ocean at Yamba. The Yamba Ferry transfers to Iluka on the Brisbane side. Beautiful sunrise on the Clarence River. Rising from the far bank a range of mountains dense with steamy gums like a huge pile of jade cabbages. The forests completely untouched by human hand, as when the first "explorers" saw them. A teenage rugby league game or training session was in progress on the parrot green strip by the marvellous cobalt blue river – the river was equally obscene and untouched-looking – the Amazon circa 1502. Everywhere in rural Australia you see rugby or cricket being played. The cold individuality of each member of my Australian circle has blinded me to the profound solidarity, team-mindedness of Australians – sense everyone is the member of one "family" and shares the same attitudes, interests, practices.

Arrogance of the word "Clarence": an Aboriginal reality underlies it, of course. But its European name (narrative) remains valid. After all, only the white man has ever had the decency to put his hand up and say: "Not mine!" If it wasn't for Western self-criticism, Western self-consciousness, there would be no consciousness of the "other" to begin with, and "the Clarence" would appear always to have been that: "the Clarence". In that event, would it ever occur to anybody that there had ever been a world that did not know "the Clarence", that was pre-Clarence? And it could so easily have been that way. Had it not been for Christian guilt, even the memory of aboriginal Australia would have been wiped out as totally as Armenia and Byzantium has been in modern Turkey, or the Latin-speaking Africa of Saint Augustine in modern Tunisia. (In both countries, one is piously assured that Islam and nothing but Islam has ever existed). Had it not been for Christ and His invitation to self-scrutiny, a new past would have been born here, for the founders of new societies are always far more interested in inventing the past than the future, as when an Australian child invests the modern, artificial world he is born into with antiquity and a hoary grace. He opens his eyes on what seems to him a Greece or an Italy, because innocent childhood attaches to everything deep roots and a sense of magic and justice. So is the Australian child's idea of his environment, his analysis, valid? (Not that he analyses). Well, I suppose it is, if he says it is, if he insulates himself, if he keeps out everything but childhood. Which is what ART is, of course. It is staking a claim – asserting the supremacy of one's own subjective eye, one's own "take" on an environment. Imperialism on one level. When you grow up, it is hard to sustain such solipsism – the interpretations that it gives rise to. That is what being an artist is, after all: never growing up! "The child is dead – long live the child!" Warning on the park by the Clarence River: "No loitering or disorderly conduct."
Standing by the Merc waiting for the Yamba-Iluka Ferry in a paddock full of camphor trees, I saw a hand-written notice with the Xeroxed photo of a Stafford Bitch Terrier. It had been

tacked to the frothy milk-caramel bark of a Ghost Gum, a background which horribly intensified its synthetic qualities:

"HAVE YOU SEEN THIS DOG? FEMALE STAFFIE DE-SEXED AND CHIPPED. TAKEN FROM GULMARRAD STREET 16 NOV. VERY ANGRY OWNER! 7 YRS OLD."

I looked around and what should I see but the dog in question! Or a dog very like it. (All dogs, like all children, look the same to me). It didn't look seven years old, though (but perhaps that was "the very angry owner"). A man was waiting to board the Ferry who – we were to learn – was cycling all the way from Adelaide to Brisbane. Attached to the rear of his bicycle was ONE extra wheel, on top of which sat a tray filled by a fluffy bed and a cuddly toy – and the little dog. The dog was secured to the tray by a bridle binding its chest, though it did not seem inclined to stray. It was peering around, alert. An old lady getting off the Iluka boat (which had finally arrived) started a long conversation with the owner. Australians really are that that naked, that forward. I have constantly observed long casually-sparked conferences involving complete strangers which you would think had crowned an eternal friendship. "Where we lived out West," the lady said, "there was a drought. Our little dog – a Blue Hair – never learned to swim. She lived twelve and a half years and there was a drought all that toym."

Wanko, having parked the Merc below, spent the Ferry crossing "chatting up" a young Eurasian girl on the upper deck. I literally could not believe my ears. "I'm a Virgo – oy do a bit of astrology. That's the biggest and the hardest thing. What oy am is a mediator. A self-mediator." "Yair?" said the girl. "It's actually called journalling. I say to clients – write it all down, I'll do it meself. Just note it all down – here are some oydeahs orr might use. Orr do colour therapy too." "Reeeelee?" said the girl. "Warder", said Wanko, "very therapeutic.

Listening to warder. Rain, rain at night. What orr do is energetic hoyling." "Joyyyyyyyy," the girl expired.

Close up, the metallic blue Clarence, shimmering like crushed silk, was black, black, like petroleum jelly. I saw a Sea Turtle floating face up, dead, a grey hanky ballooning out like the tissue from a boiled egg.

From Iluka, we decided to take the inland route to Brisbane via Uki, where we ate lunch. We crossed the border into Queensland just north of Tyalgum . . . Canungra, Beaudesert, Jimboomba – all the Queensland towns on the way to Brisbane (which isn't far from the border) sat not in semi-working farmland like towns in Northern New South Wales but in naked Bush that served as straw for the obscene Hamster-cage furniture of various Theme Parks. We were in the hinterland of the Gold Coast, Australia's playground, which stretches from Brisbane right down to the State line, a sort of hideous, hebephrenic Torremelinos, hundreds of beachfront towers in mustard-yellow and pink nougat cement. "Beaudesert" indeed! We were inland now from the candied coast: olive-umber scrub, tropical houses on stilts (first time I have seen them in Australia), endless honey-coloured creeks and canals meshed with a web of grey mangroves. It was like an Amazonian landscape, like Manaus, and, what I simply couldn't bear, in the middle of it there were freakish sterile video parlours and *"BIG ROOSTER"* outlets under angry blazing cartoon letters. From time to time one would find huge stretches of Bush abruptly and brutally cleared for development. Giant hoardings full of aseptic colour – so strange amid the sluice of grey and brown and brassy olive – anticipated the delights of "KOALA CITY" opposite "DREAMWORLD". There was a "FARMWORLD" and then (of all things) a "BOOKWORLD". (I wonder what that was like!) Unnatural desolation upon the natural variety: it spoke of my alienation, loneliness, fear. Reminded me of what I had come to Queensland FOR – consideration of which I could no longer put off. Images like these gnawed away as we approached Brisbane, the illuminated "Expo" Pavilions rising like pointy Arabian Nights tents on the other side of the mighty Brisbane River, the darkened town disclosed by pink and red signs that drifted off the top of huge unseen skyscrapers . . . We stayed the night at the Metropolitan Motor Inn, a tall metal cylinder with strange triangular bedrooms like wedges of birthday cake.

SATURDAY 21 NOVEMBER 1987. It was a big shock coming out of the air-conditioned cold of the hotel this morning – it was delicious inside – the cold perfume of roast coffee beans. Our first day in the Tropics. The wet heat was like a facecloth in a Chinese Restaurant. For the first time that unmistakable smell of the Tropics – that smell of petrol and Frangipani and the sight of glutinous waxy Frangipani flowers crushed on the pavement like grasshoppers. I was amazed to see a little yellow budgerigar sitting in the grassy verge by the hotel entrance. Here was a wild little Australian bird ("Budgerigar" means "good food" in Aboriginal) right in the heart of a great city of over a million people. It looked lurid and false – something that could have had its feet in a cake.

The city of Brisbane was hard to look at as I had lost my shades. The light must have been three or four times brighter than that in Sydney – itself about five times cleaner and more intense than London on a limpid day in early June. The feeling you always get in the Tropics that you won't be able to do – to get at – ANYTHING, that the wet heat and the light are too big for you, that they hide in their intensity everything that they magnify. It's like being dwarfed, hemmed in, marginalised by something that should be a partner, a friend – part of the furniture. You feel like a Wren turning around in its nest to find that its brother is a Cuckoo.

We set off from the hotel on Wickham Terrace – which sits on a cliff overlooking the "CBD" (Central Business District) – very early. Like Sydney, Brisbane was founded as a penal colony and the conical shape of the Metropolitan Motor Inn was in honour of the oldest and most important building in the city, which lay right next door, a wretched little lime-washed stone windmill erected by the early convicts. (Well, we had already seen the most important buildng in Sydney!) When one studied the profoundly human scale and dreadful workmanship, one got the same feeling as when surveying the ill-made, dwarf convict churches that cower like Chihuahuas at the feet of the Victorian behemoths and hypertowers of Sydney. It was impossible to associate them with the Assyrian scale and repulsive tofu finish of the more recent buildings below, impossible to imagine that the word "Brisbane" could have denoted both this partridge covey of hovels and ALSO the Elephants' Graveyard that one saw down there, or that the former could in any way have given rise to the latter. We were making for the Inner City Bypass and Luttwyche Road. This would become the Bruce Highway, the name, in Queensland, of the Pacific Highway and our *entrée* to Townsville, a mere eight hundred kilometres or so north up the coast. "The Deep North", as they call it here. We passed the Conrad Hotel and the Casino on George Street and crossed the mighty Brisbane River via the Victoria Bridge, admiring the Performing Arts Centre that swam into view on our left (Richard Meale's opera **Voss** was playing). We lurched right into Grey Street, our route to Roma Street and the Bypass.

I noticed an "adult" store on Hope Street: "PLEASURE ON HOPE".

In Grey Street, I watched as a group of schoolchildren in uniforms no less stuffily Edwardian than those in Sydney emerged from "the Queensland Art Gallery and Museum". Their white faces seemed to wince in the blinding light, like shallots. Too fresh. The air of something that isn't meant to be seen – or not in the sun – something moist and delicate and from under a stone that would be burnt up in this unwonted clime. Poor featherless squabs with the glassy grey agate flesh of chicken fillets, and yet shrieking, leaping, as gregarious as goslings. Completely untainted, nonetheless, by the ecstacy of "ethnicity", the sordid charisma of "the Street". They were what Britain's schoolchildren must have looked like in the Nineteenth Century, before the immigration. Before the genocide. The idea that a white society could be as vibrant, as homogeneous as this was incredible. I had grown up in Britain with the idea that the **Wind in the Willows** certainties of an all-white life were a thing of the past for white children, that homogeneity and electricity were open only to immigrants and the poor. Provincialism (?) had preserved in Brisbane what had been eradicated everywhere else by a wandering of peoples unprecedented since the fall of the Roman Empire, a hurricane of invasions which had rendered bizarre and rare the parochial white childhood I myself had enjoyed, a childhood which, before the fall, had been bored by itself, contemptuous of itself, of its "eternal" nature, of the "eternal" vistas of its superfluous and yet organic rites. I could well imagine the pathetic tasks which the Grey Street children had been set, like the idiotic tasks I myself had been given by the teachers at my Thames Ditton Prep in the National Gallery in Trafalgar Square. How beautiful, integral, those rituals seemed now, now that the world which had devised them was gone! The clipboard list of things to see and do; the meaningless favour of the teacher; her meaningless *dis*-favour; the coveted place in the classroom's class system, the glut of gold and silver stars like a Byzantine mosaic. Cos now I saw them, not as I had immediately after their demise, when they had seemed merely to be resting, but as they were in reality, gone for good. In just such a way must the Greeks and Romans of the Sixth Century AD have watched the passing of philosophy and mimetic art, complacently, as something that would come back, not realising that the Golden Age was packing its bags for good. The decline of the Ancient World, so mysterious, so magical and swift when studied from the present day must, at the time, have appeared to Late Antiquity much as the West's decline appears to white and Western people today: as an elaboration rather than an abdication of the past. The people of Late Antiquity, like the white West, must have thought that the past was moving forward among them like a statue in a Catholic procession, a statue of the past. A past that would bestow upon them the same universe they had always known. But it is the future, not the past, which is "another country". The past, like the poor, is always with us and we cannot imagine what it will be like to live in a world utterly separate from it. It was left to Petrarch and to Michael Akominatos, the mediaeval bishop of Athens, in the nuclear winter that followed the end of Antiquity, to mourn, to realise, to apostrophise the value of what had vanished, just as I was now doing in Brisbane.

Because somehow, that magical Western world of health and safety had survived here in the **Pollyanna** set that was Southern Queensland. Like the gold stars, the Golden Age had returned, foretold, like Virgil's, by the birth of a child, by the Catholic Christ. For it was obviously Irish individuals who had arranged it. These Grey Street children – one could tell it by their faces – were of Irish descent. Ireland – like Eastern Europe – was Australia's hairy hope – supplying it with as endless a supply of Christian natives as Armenia had once poured soldiers into Byzantium. Ireland was a bottomless stewpond of overripe, too-handsome men and women who tumbled into the rest of the Australian population like fresh water into a dirty bath: *"The mackerel-crowded seas"* ! What the children said to me was that there was a tang of the end of the world about Brisbane, as with Sydney and every other port city. A moral grandeur clung to it and also to its inhabitants – it reminded me a bit of Liverpool, also intensely "parochial" and Irish. The Brisbaneites' epic liveliness and rawness as if a skin, a psyche lighter was that of joyful mating dogs. As if like "the Horses of Patrokles" in Cavafy they were eternal and their world, Brisbane, which had once fitted them, could no longer support an epic, spastic life. Because the city was clearly now as dead as its people were alive, as grandiloquent to be sure, the great mercantile offices by the water as large and pompous as anything in Glasgow or Bordeaux, but silent, functionless now, as the vast temples and arena of Rome must have been in the era of Alaric and his Goths. Not ruined as yet, not even moribund (which is when the human vultures come to pluck at flesh *sans* soul, *sans* associations). For the original function of Brisbane's distilleries and shipping offices was still remembered, as that of the Temple of Venus was in the Rome of St Jerome's time, when (the Saint exults), the vast cult statues – like those of Cook and Kitchener in Brisbane – had only *"spiders and bats"* for company. (In Brisbane's case, it was fruit bats!) All life had fled Brisbane – albeit recently – all life but the life of its people, which clung to the ruins of the city as the plague is said to have hovered over Baghdad after the Mongols sacked it in 1258, when their army is said to have massacred over five hundred thousand people – the number of Brisbaneites supposed to have debouched to the satellite towns since 1975. I found inner-city Brisbane heavy and rain-rinsed under a hot, condensed-milk sky, of grey stone like certain parts of Edinburgh, evidence of a provincial merchant class which could no longer, one imagined, support the big, porticoed dwellings or the artificially independent identities of posh neighbourhoods that amounted (as in Edinburgh) to no more than a few blocks (not inner-city suburbs in the Sydney or London sense) a mere dual carriageway away from the City Cen-tah. That sense one got in so many towns in the North of England of the natural gradation of imposing central to smaller peripheral buildings having been destroyed in the Sixties, when a desire not to be left out of the world's modernisation had caused the City Fathers to see every old building as a recherché embarrassment, and every new one as a miraculous passport to glamour and power that could put the town in the same category as New York and LA. If only all the old buildings could be got rid of! The result, now that the old buildings were seen (rightly) as the bestowers of originality, was the isolation, the murder of both old and new, each of which had been rendered unsupported and insupportable by the intrusion of the other. It was then that Brisbane must have lost its organic wholeness, its life. The old buildings stood apart, exquisitely scrubbed, removed from the economically creative purposes for which they had been built – museum pieces – while opposite their sheared-off backsides and a *Cordon Sanitaire* of unearthly grass rose the new "working" buildings in tropically blackened concrete: nests of the new gentility, the new bureaucracy, the new Telecom, the new tourism. (Tourists in Brisbane! A concept that could only have arisen with the city's death!) No wealth was ever produced in these buildings, nothing was ever made, but inside, and through the stained glass of the wine bars and bistros that infested the old monumental headquarters of long dead shipping and mining concerns, was a luxury, an ersatz unearned comfort, besides which the sumptuousness of the past, the product of reality, creativity, paled into insignificance.

What made Brisbane particularly bizarre was the fact that the unreachable Mother Nature of tropic Queensland was even more contemptuous of European Australia's Lilliputian pretentions than the unreachable Mother Nature of New South Wales. I felt particularly the INNOCENCE – the VIRGINITY – of the trains and buses. They looked like toys compared with those in London. Great blazing lava walls of flower trees – Frangipani, Bougainvillea, Ponsietta – crashed down the sweating uptight marble streets, vast slicks of a smoky, milky white and mauve, cerise and orange. Stands of Giant Bamboo and Coconut Palm shot up everywhere in the most unlikely places, like wierd lupins on ruins. The seaside sewerage smell of mangroves, like the voluptuous diarrheoa smell of fallen mangoes, was everywhere. And amid the glinting unnatural skyscrapers tinkling flocks of budgerigars a silly pink floated like clouds of powdered chilli. Then rasping dirty black fruit bats settled in starling blizzards on the Moreton Bay Figs, their flying machine wings slow and painful like the wings of vultures. Its setting made the whole town look absurdly pretentious and out of place, like a jungle necropolis . . . Wonderful names as we cruised through the last, most northern Brisbane suburbs – "Beachmere", "Mango Hill", "Chermside". On the car radio, for the first time, the *"BIG ROOSTER"* song:

> *"I'd rather have a sunny day,*
> *And I'd rather have Big Rooster,*
> *I'd rather live the Queensland way,*
> *And I'd rather have Big Rooster;*
> *Yes it's our big chicken, for our big state,*
> *Barbequed or fried, it sure tastes great,*
> *If Queensland makes you feel great, mate,*
> *Then you'd rather have Big Rooster!"*

A minister in the first post-Petersen Queensland Government was described on the radio news as "no more than a raw prawn".

"Geebung", "Nundah", "Toombul" – as we drew past these last dregs, I noticed a little girl standing in a graveyard, looking at a grave. She made it seem so deserted: it wouldn't have looked that way had she not been there. The statues of angels and the gravestones covered in a black tropical mould. A schoolgirl in one of those tension-inducing innocent Australian uniforms. We passed a big, duck-blue plank shed: "THE PACIFIC GYMNASIUM". There were large crude paintings of gymnasts on the walls. A curious style, like the sort of do-it-yourself political graffiti they go in for in Vietnam and Nicaragua. Black – they looked as if they had been painted with a wide, house-painter's brush. We began to climb Mount Mee. A white horse cantered up to a low "Queenslander" ("Queenslander" = house on stilts – in Australia, they are unique to Queensland). The horse looked like the owner, about to enter the house. We passed a low wire shed filled with thousands of chickens. You could reach out and touch the grass, the tall, sharp, lime-green grass I remember from my first childhood visit Down Under in the 1960s. Proustian: the memory only came back to me with the smell – a honey-like smell, intoxicating.

Being mostly of wood, everything human in rural Queensland looked even more crude and recent and unreal than its New South Wales equivalent. Not to Wanko. Such and such was the new "million dollar" Toogoolawah Court House, the "beautiful" Roman Catholic Church in Quinalow. That house – a bad plank impression of a Swiss Chalet – would sell for "two hundred thousand dollars" (what one might expend in London on a chemical toilet!) The Swiss Chalet was set right in the middle of the Bush – termite hills, interminable gums. Ghastly heat. Ghastly heat up here in the fabled cool of the Goombungee mountains. Wanko pointed out a garden in Yarraman. Its owner had clipped a box hedge (hedges are quite rare in Australia) in the shape of a gigantic engorged Zeppelin. The Zeppelin had cabins – or testicles. "Queer shapes," he non-commitally observed. A man in a wheelchair, strikingly out of keeping, it must be admitted, in the prevailing sterility, issued from one of the clapboard houses in Nanango. He was brown, bare-chested, like a shrub growing from his silver wheels. "Poor man in a wheelchair. Very sad, oy always think," said Wanko serenely.

Near the mountain tops the trees gave out – their slopes became raw and vast and a fresh, bright green like rotten meat. Reminded me of Scotland – the bald hills near the border just north of Carlisle – or like pictures I have seen of Zimbabwe: the same air of fertile, open menace. Historyless – for the white man. "It's so RICH" said Wanko of the pleated rust-red earth, which escaped here in great wet roils like the guts of a harpooned whale. The crust of the watermelon mountain was formed by the sharp blades of the murderous lemon-green grass. Not the sort of grass you would want to picnic on – though that's what the deceptively plangent scenery seemed to invite. Too few trees though. Too empty. A land too open, too recently violated. A land prised from its original associations incredibly swiftly and still without new ones. All this had been Aboriginal land, hardwood rainforest – teak, mahogany – until a mere 70 years ago, every stand of it felled now to build the ubiquitous "Queenslanders". "This red dust would go all over my nappies," noted Wanko (a parent), completely without explanation. We dined at Lake Barambah in an empty sixties-style café with canned music. A tough, boneless reef fish, like chicken. Not disagreeable . . . A cruise on the lake – a volcanic crater in the mountains – a boat made of recycled aluminium cans. The captain threw meat to the hawks and eels, corn to the guinea fowl scratching at the water's edge. They – and the English coots – were all there was to see. Amazing how you find sparrows – also "introduced" – absolutely everywhere in Australia. Somewhat macabre to see them in the Tropics. On the boat, I noticed an elderly Australian in front of us – the spitting image of my dead maternal grandmother. Her companion was an Englishwoman with the quavering voice of a homosexual comic. "I love Bundaberg," said the Australian.

269

"I've got quite a soft spot for that." "Alison's in Perth," said the Englishwoman. "She was so in love with Chip," the Australian responded, " . . . he must have had a terrible life".

I visited the Orchid House at the "Lacustrine Cen-tah" – orchids I imagine one of the rare blessings of tropical life. The usual Australian non-event. There really isn't ANYTHING here worth seeing. Show them a cyclone-proof Civic Hall and they think they're looking at the Pitti Palace. They think a foreigner is looking at it too. The stems of the orchids were held up by thread from the roof, which made them look even more iniquitous than usual. The Cattelyas were ravishing – straight out of Proust's *"Un Amour de Swann"*.

We drove down the mountain, the clouds drifting over the road like fog. The view to our right was more awesome than anything in Switzerland. "Aweful" – in its original sense. I have never been so high up, or seen mountains and valleys and forests of that violence and magnitude. Queensland landscapes like those hellish quilts of preserved Sicilian fruit in Palermo shop windows. No gradation, no nuance. Violent transition between mosaic cubes of soft-drink splinter, as in a kaleidoscope. Down on the coastal plain (we had to go to Noosa to see one of Dew's rellies), we stopped briefly at Imbil and Tewantin. The heat was appalling. The day on the flat land by the sea hideously bright and clear like a cough sweet. Tropical Queensland only has two gears, hot and hotter, bright and brighter. Nothing in-between. No nuance. There was a great mirror rippling in the sugar cane like some grim lake in Central Africa where an undiscovered dinosaur lives. The beaches of Noosa cliffs of white salt like runnelled Lemon Sorbet, the sea a rich purple like freshly picked blackberries. I remember a lady in a white dress and a golden turban – the outfit totally absurd in this clime and anyway rendered peurile by a light that might have been reflected off Mount Palomar, such was its intensity. It turned her "DOLCE E GABBANA" into the tinsel and bedsheets of a Nativity Play. Beverley Brownbill, Dew's relly – a widow. The incredibly mangie old Kelpie (ie Dingo cross) at her side trembling and expectant. I feared its intense worried canine simpers. Something in Beverley's manner reminded me of the dog. Her ravaged plastic face looked like a Chocolate Sundae. She wore a shock of titanium hair over one eye and a necklace of huge wooden blocks. Her daughter, Kay, who was getting ready to leave for a friend's, was just as radically chic. "Kay-ee, you won't go running ovah the road, now, will yoh?"

After the preposterous scenery, Beverley's home, "Capricornia" – Wanko had "sold" it as spectacular, "Citizen Kane"-like – looked subdued. Crushed, like everything else, by the light. Peeling and temporary-looking like a painted cement animal in a school playground. Its design failed to move me – the Guggenheim Museum in NYC turned upside down – each of "Capricornia's" cylindrical upper storeys being smaller than the one underneath. We crossed the moat surrounding it on a spindly, rusting iron bridge. The moat had been a swimming pool as you could see by the tiles at the bottom. Now it was full of blue native lilies and algae like *"The Bridge at Giverny"* in the painting by Claude Monet. Within, like the Guggenheim and all circular buildings, "Capricornia" felt unusually cramped (for Australia). It was all shiny vinyl maroon wood like the furniture in a yacht, the lush stuffs the jarring tone of a housewife's acrylic sponge. The air conditioning, after the heat, was delightful though, cosy. You feel how "shut in" tropical Queensland is and has to be, like Russia. The semi-transparent black ears of Kay's mice in a tank on an overcrowded table were oddly beautiful. Reminded me of violets. Of England. Of home.

We met Bosun, Beverley's new young "neighbour", and Rad, his brother. Young Australian men all have bushy goatee beards – often goatees without moustaches. "Ever met Wanko?" Bev asked Rad, who was the younger and prettier. (A sensible family, Rad was clearly being groomed as the next Ganymede). "Once, five thousand years ago." The entire household had the same grandiose hustler manner. Iced beers all round – "Four X" up here, tiny squat brown bottles, called "stubbies", like Pompeian lamps. Radley, sullenly, and, I thought, with an air of understatement and self-sufficient maturity, made himself a plate of sandwiches. "Oh Rad," cried Bev, flicking the fronds from a caramel brow, "oym SO sorry – oy gayve the starff the day ORFF!" She must be joking, I thought. She wasn't. Rad looked insular and tragic. Silently, he went outside. Framed by the window, I saw "Benjy" poke his head through a hole in the front gate, barking. Beverley is angry because the "Pakis" on the next property (another vile gimcrack *Mon Repos*) feed the dog cakes and ice cream. She handed me a letter she had received via Dew from Tia, my London housekeeper. Tia said my postcards had subjected her to "emotional liability", which upset me, since I try to censor and qualify them as much as possible:

> *"What sort of food are you eating? Healthy, I hope. Do you have enough cool clothing? Let me know. A horrible smell of tomcat in the conservatory this morning. Possibly that odious 'Tabby Tyger' spraying around. Heaven help him if I encounter him there . . . YOU must decide what is best for you, and how long you want to stay. It is your life, dear . . . Traumatic here yesterday afternoon, as the bloke from Katz Castle came for the little feral family (fat, spitting, black balls of fury). He got mother cat in the trap easily with one kitten, as she loves pilchards, then the three others were alone in the conservatory, but one escaped, but came back in last night poor little soul, and is now in the kitchen hiding behind the pot plant, and crying piteously. All too much for me -"*

I began to feel terribly homesick. How I miss England! I remember it as small and voluptuous and delicate like a beating heart. Its nature and built environment a filament of veins – like lines in a Beardsley drawing – organs INSIDE the body. In Australia human beings, nature, buildings look obscene – organs OUTSIDE the body – the incredible lungs and bowels of a whale heaped up on the deck. You get the sense that they SHOULDN'T be seen. Intimate things of Britain like "modern" (ie mediaeval) mouseholes of Pergamum when Theodore Lascaris visited it in the 13th Century: Australia the sterile superhuman ruins of antiquity. And how I miss London! The brown streets of London like first World War trenches, everything seen as in a fish tank of oaky yellow urine. Pale fleshy faces floating in the impure element like matzoh balls in a clear soup. The eternal clouds like preserved

a novel

ginger in its crystals. Cloudy panal of the honeycomb. No milky rose-corn nor fawn nor bran nor sweet translucent pewter in tropic Queensland! Everything harsh and unnatural (ie natural). Planchette-fed queen, I need the unclean. I need the unclean spirit. I find I do not lust after the concrete young. I need what Santayana called *"the salad of illusions"* in its sluice. Slushy Sushi in its juice. Delicate watery pink. Silk-worm veins of silk that frame a spiny green buttermilk. Green English leaves in the tender underwater night. A May night: rosé wine, then a pale green light. The pigeon grey of sweet green May. Sweet spermy air. Tender watery pink of port wine jelly. The clement English weather that brings the delicate, the human, right up close: in Queensland everything is reduced to gigantic atomic blocks like a Rothko painting. Everything human – including man himself – hiding from the Hiroshima of the sun. Big things glimpsed quickly.

Bev and Wanko (a parent himself) discussed the "Sex Ed" programme at Kay's school. They are showing films of animals giving birth. "Bitches are good for children," Bev observed. Rad came in and said, as we were about to leave: "Your tyre's flat." We had run over a branch on the way down the mountain. Bosun offered to replace the wheel. Wanko demurred. He pointed out that he (ie Sir Dewy Popkiss) paid the local equivalent of the RAC "so much money". Let THEM replace it. I was frantic with depression and anxiety. I want to get on to Townsville – get everything over and done with. We really did dally in NSW, taking much longer than was necessary, but, as I've told Wanko, I have no intention of wasting time in Queensland. In the end, the "RAC" didn't come until dusk, so we had to spend the night at "Capricornia". Bosun kindly prepared an Australian classic for dinner – Kangaroo Tail soup, with a *ragoût* of the tail in rice like a Lamb Shank. Wanko was on Cloud Nine because somebody in a shop in Imbil or Tewantin had given him a free can of deodorant. He never buys "Essence de France" himself because he has "so much" of it at home. (I hadn't noticed). We watched Kay (who had returned with friends) go through a disco routine with a gaggle of other red-rumped infants. Being forced to watch these kids in leotards and hear all this talk about stupid school committees was a sharp insult. Kay brought the depilated mice to the table as we were having dinner. "You've never got this far," Bev reminded Wanko, "you've never had a toy [tea] from moy."

Another night in a horrible wedge-shaped room. I visited the Dunny on the top tier, the top catfood tin of the ziggurat, and it was wierd. Can you imagine what a small circular room is like? You are always turning around and someone is always behind you – in this case some "hideous kinky" portraits. Who did them, I wonder? They looked oddly familiar. Very claustrophobic: a circular wall. A continuous frieze – fresco – of naked people. Something very nasty going on like "the Circle of Manias" in Sade's **The One Hundred and Twenty Days of Sodom**. It was like Buchenwald – a Jewish woman being raped by a Muslim dog, and giving birth to puppies. "The Circle of Excrement": Goldilocks forced to eat the three turds of the bears in three white porcelain bowls – just like Prince Minski's guest in the divine Marquis's **Juliette**: "Who's been sleeping in MY bed?"

The brushwork on the fresco reminded me of Lucien Freud. Each head recalled the "slug prison" that Tia has installed in my Surrey garden – a bucket of beer into which shoals of slugs are lured. Each face consisted of woven worms of yellow paint in a consommé of shit *à la Freud*. They put one in mind of the face of the narrator's grandmother in Proust's novel, who was dying of kidney failure, and to whose temples a fashionable doctor has attached a web of writhing white leeches. I felt that, like Proust's grandmother, Bev had perhaps chosen a famous rather than an inspired practitioner. The painter had gone to great trouble to render everything with tortured exactness. Great knots of paint popped out of tense features like veins from a weightlifter's neck. What he had perhaps not done was LOOKED at what he was painting, even though he had clearly been staring anatomically at it for a very long time. The silkworm had gorged itself industriously – too industriously – on mulberry leaves, just as an artist digests ordinary lads in order to excrete the divine, but had, instead of silk, produced a dull, mass-produced-looking shag. The woolly cocoon was there, like the fluff on a gramophone needle, but the moth (which the Greeks saw as a symbol of the soul) had gone. There was no flame, no warmth, to attract it. It seemed to me that the facile dexterity of the artist was meaningless, and had been sidetracked into the sort of loving realism that is pointless, because rootless. It was sad to see such ascetically exacting draughtsmanship wasted on its own cause – just like the starving of the Irish Famine who, in return for Government slop (Bev's largesse) were forced to break rocks and build roads that led nowhere. To me, this sort of Freudian "realism" is no more an end in itself than is its opposite, abstraction, and no less devoid than abstraction of what distinguishes PAINTING from ART, which must surely be the existence of an IDEA that is *unique to the artist himself.* An idea which, being personal, unites him with his subject as the Priest is united with the believer at the Eucharist, ie THROUGH A SHARED BELIEF. A pre-existent *esprit de corps* which does not depend on or derive from its means of expression (as, of course, a mechanical scholasticism like "Realism" or "Abstraction" inevitably must) . . . "Who the FUCK!" I cry, nearly dying of shock as something red and mottled like a prickly pear shoots out of the floor. It was "Big Ann", one of Beverley's friends from "Tazzie", a stupid kindly parasite who had been given a holiday in Noosa at Bev's expense. "Big Anne" had not meant to introduce herself. Obviously not *"entre nous"* enough for presentation, "Big Ann" had been having a late "toy" in her room. This lay below, and was reached by the spiral staircase that shot up, like her head, from a manhole in the Dunny floor. She had not wished to make my acquaintance, but the sound of my voice had tormented her. Like any freeloader, she was terrified by the exclusive juxtaposition of her patron to another human being, being quite unable to imagine her friend having any relationship than one which involved a degree of exploitation. This idea, which is common to all jealous women – which is to say, women – assumes, of course, that Lady Bountiful KNOWS she is being exploited, an idea as naive as it is cynical. Beverley no longer had any of the realistic instincts about others that would have surrounded a poorer person, the greatest wealth, like the hardest drugs, having the effect of reducing the hallucogenic horror of existence to a nice bourgeois dream. It is only those who are not rich, like those undergoing an operation without anaesthetics (on the British National Health Service, for example), who are forced to confront human nature in all of its frequently Strindbergian candour.

SUNDAY 22 NOVEMBER 1987. I had a dream this morning – an "Irish" dream like the one sung by the reedy Semen. It was about Gaybum Fortnightly, the architect of "Capricornia". Beverley was digressing about him last night. This was what the tadpoles were singing, and at 3 AM:

> *"Gaybum Fortnightly,*
> *The Saxons excite me,*
> *They sing of young Paddy - Ye gods!*
> *Limp wrist of the Saxon,*
> *Hot piss from his dachshund,*
> *The kiss*
> *Of the crool*
> *Senapods . . . "*

At breakfast, Mrs Brownbill handed me a book of her poems: ***Enchanted Tongue***. She watched me read them with the attentive look of a Yorkshire Terrier – a little withered bat face staring out of elaborately coiffed shards of hair. Ingenuousness of her verse that spoke of the self-indulgence of this rich Roo-ish woman who thinks her far from amazing sensitivity to her own banal existence worthy of record. Hilarious results - poems about "the Stolen Children" of the Aborigines interspersed with, in the same text and context, going to the cunt waxer or to have her hair permed, each expedition presented as a molten sacrament. Artless revelation, as in the indiscretion of a queen, of some very simple reigning passions. The "compliment" I paid Bev was obviously transparent because she stared at me like an enraged hyena. After another absurd scene with Bev we took the road north. I told Wanko to put his foot on it – I don't want to bugger around any more.

The scenery just beyond Noosa was impressive – the last really wonderful things we saw. Lush, histrionic green felt mountains: half were in shadow, half in light. Polished lakes with pink lilies, low African scrub, solitary gums in the foreground a spidery lime-gold, picked out in the sun like thread against the dark wooded hills beyond. Then endless forests of a different sort of gum tree began, dryer, greyer than the trees in NSW . . . I loved Maryborough though.

Stopped to eat at a Transport Caff in Bundaberg. It was draped in the human entrails of a Greyhound Bus. Beautiful tropical smorgasbord of cold roast chicken, pork, freshly picked penguin-sized local pineapples, glaucous orange mango bites like the mouths of nestlings, cold noodles, hibiscus flowers, blood-red watermelon. I had a shot of the famous Bundaberg cane rum with coke and I lunched on dripping Dolmades. The Greek lady from whom I got them was obviously flattered – everyone else was asking for Chicko Rolls. As we partook, an Aborigine came and sat next to me, which I thought ominous. Her daughter stood and wept in a high mewling voice a few paces away. These "aubergines" – as the Greek termed them – are always sitting about with elaborately dressed children. Nothing to do. A video of an idiotic police comedy was playing, which the Australians present followed with lascivious relish, the TV dangling. There were a few beefy Poms with a cassette recorder. I remember one song in particular: *"Didn't We Almost Have it All?"* Felt suddenly upset: thought of all the things I might have done had I not come out here to Oz.

The day was dark green and orange on the outskirts of Bundaberg, on the flat, tropical Savannah. My attention was drawn to the house of her most famous son, the early aviator Bert Hinken, transplanted brick by brick from his birthplace in England. It looked so odd, this emissary of another world, so tiny and alien, like a porcelain soup dish lying in a meadow. Curious pangs . . . I slept most of the way to Gladstone – ditto the journey from

Gladstone to Rockhampton. An utterly unvarying scene of endless identical gums for hundreds of miles, these ones so dry and skeletal they looked dead, like burnt matches. Darkness had fallen by the time we dined in Rockhampton on a gorgeous steak sandwich (*"Rockie - Cattle City!"*). Awoke near Mackay. We were in "the Deep North" – Blue Singlet country. Some gentlemen sitting on the steps of a pub whistled at me as I alighted in a pale green Simpson's jacket. They were all wearing Akubra hats and the eponymous undergarment, pig dogs growling at their feet. So humid – walking to the hotel was like pushing through a jacuzzi – could hardly breathe. The crickets were coo-cooing.

MONDAY 23 NOVEMBER 1987. In the morning, Mackay was low, sterile, pink, geometrical. Our car was parked next to a macabre pet shop. We took the road north quite early, the Tropics surprisingly chill at dawn. Endless fields of sugar cane. Turreted black sugar refineries like the factories in a Lowry painting. Windmill-pumps with propellers like Lowry's coal-mines – the beautiful horseshit and liquorice smell of molasses. The grey sands and waters of Port Bucasia hove into view on the plain below, the black bulk of the sugar mill vertical against the golden horizon. Its "industrial estuary" feel reminded me of Rouen. "Bowen Shire – Home of the Mango". Then a huge concrete (20 foot high) statue of a mango, half vermillion, half lime green, so pure, so shocking. Lewdly swollen. "GUNS AND AMMO" written on a shop in Bowen itself. I fell into fits of sleep. I remember Guthalungra, Home Hill, crossing the mighty Burdekin on a bridge like the rail bridge over the Firth of Forth. The creek at Barratta, Giru.

At Wathana, there was a beer advert on a hoarding at the side of the road:

> *"TOOHEY'S NEW:*
> *WHAT MATES DO!"*

then, ominously, at Bobawaba, another:

> *"DO IT FOR A MATE!"*

Biscuity red-brown colour of the surrounding mountains, or milky cinnamon splashed with a goose-shit green like mould-speckled loaves.

A sign – *"TOWNSVILLE: CITY OF YOUTH"* – and beyond it, in the distance, you could see tin roofs glittering like glass around a bald pink mountain. The mountain was puce from where we were because the sun, beyond it, was shining right in our faces. An aerosol blue horizon – the Pacific.

Wanko informed me that Townsville was the second biggest city in Queensland with "42 suburbs and 110,000 inhabitants". Perfect colonial houses in wood, and public buildings in fondant-coloured stucco: all intense yellow, bluish-green and crab-pink under a torrid milk and crystal sky. When we saw the great sandstone mountain from the other side, lit by the sun, you realised that it was lightly forested, the gums a feathery gold. I didn't know what to think as we glided through the louvred slat bungalows of a suburb called "Railway Estate". Peeling grey, dark green and milk-blue board cottages sitting on thick wooden poles, with corrugated iron roofs, and crinkly brown glass in the windows. A painted tin hood sheltering every door and window. Everything to filter out the murderous light.

We passed one of the plank cottages trembling on the back of a juggernaut. Wanko said it was being taken to a new set of stilts. Often people "moved house" in Townsville by swapping one nest of stilts for those of a "mate". The mate's "humpy" would then migrate to the original podium . . . I became alarmed. We were behind another trailer, and this one had a black cube frame tent swaying on the back of it, like the tents I had seen in Canberra. I pointed it out, shocked, to Wanko – he waved his marriage band at me. He was annoyed, said he would tell me all about it later. We were just about to turn into "Cummins Street". We drew up at the place I'm staying at, a "Queenslander" like the others. On stilts. It was painted a curious milky orange, its windows and door-frames picked out in greyish chocolate: both are very popular colours up here. We mounted the ladder-like steps to the front door.

Freek Bloomers was friendly enough. Tall and skeletal. A mate of Fagan, the former Oz premier. Freek is a "polly", Labor MP for Townsville in the Federal – ie national – parliament. (A separate individual sits in the Queensland Assembly in Brisbane). Face a wrinkly gelatinous brown with saucer eyes like a kipper. The whites of Freek's eyes seem to partake of his skin's brown, as in the brownish draylon eyes of a kipper. I was shocked because we seemed to have caught Freek in his underwear. I soon found that most people in Townsville, male, female, of whatever age or *éclat*, don this uniform: skimpy shorts; skimpy teeshirt or singlet; flip-flops. Sometimes women will wear open sandals and men ankle-length boots with very short black socks poking just above them. Individuals of both sexes wear wide straw hats or floppy baseball caps.

It was hard to believe that two of the most gorgeous eyes in La Fagan's peacock train had once belonged to homely Freek, a former "art model" (hence I suppose his suitability as host) who now writes books on "Hoons" (juvenile delinquents – his circle is admittedly extensive), social trends – fashion even, though he dresses like a Crack Fiend – weary, fabulous books. There really is no contradiction as his analytical gift springs from a sexual feeling that seems utterly remote. Proust says that: *"no exile at the South Pole or at the summit of Mont Blanc separates us more from others than a prolonged holiday in a hidden vice"*. He might have added that such a "holiday" separates us far more from ourselves than it does from other people. The moment he picked up this pen, *"the Queen of the Night"* – as Freek signed himself – became as unaware of the Sun Bum of Cummins Street as Dr Jeckyll was of Mr Hyde ... Anyway, he has certainly come up in the world. "Between the back-stabbing and the arse-licking, there was never a dull moment!" as Dewy used to say of "Miss Nancy"'s" chums. ("Nancy Reagan" = "Fagan"). Anyway, Freek is very well known up here as he identifies social groups as they emerge, names them, is much in demand as a television sociologist, a commentator, and as a titterer among rich cunts in the marbled coffee-table magazines of *"le Tout Queensland"*: **COW'S HOOF, HARPIES AND QUEENS, CONSTANT**

SCREAMER. In his articles on society he affects a cynically left-wing masculine sobriety, but is in reality a piffling bantam, lending hysterical weight to the small and his own paucity to the large . . . Oh, and he's also a pillar of the Returned Servicemen's League (RSL).

Inside, a Queenslander is like a tree-house, surprisingly small beyond the verandah that surrounds its cabin. (Sometimes, except for the railings, the verandahs are completely open, sometimes they're screened with wooden slats or trellises). It was humid and dark in the cubby-hole beyond the verandah. Everything felt flimsy, cluttered, second-rate. There were vases of plastic flowers, messy dressing tables, broken ornaments. Like a White Wedding, they seemed to be a concession to an outmoded principle – the feminine principle, the principle of beauty. How often have I seen such sad, broken things in the house of a widower! A huge fan hung face down from the ceiling like a Spitfire propeller: no air-conditioning in these old Queenslanders.

I still couldn't sort myself out. I was living on so many different levels and the most superficial, pain, cancelled the more profound levels out. My first thought was: how could I ever live in Townsville – even for a few weeks? The heat and light were indescribable – it was worse than Noosa. From Freek's verandah one saw a molten blue sky, milk-white heat of cloud, livid scarlet Ponsietta. Wanko, who had obviously read the alarm on my face, declared: *"Don't be such a Barbie, Patrick!"* It wasn't an inappropriate observation as the whole house was filled with Barbies – the sort of dolls with wide, knitted skirts they cover toilet rolls with. Perhaps Freek collects them. Out the back there was half an acre of the short, wide-leaved grass that you see in tropical parks. It is of a scandalous green like plastic. Rich-smelling Paupau and Banana trees. Wire around a chook run and a little chook house with a delicious dirty, savoury smell, *"Petit Hameau"* – like in its daft cosiness. The chooks, Marie-Antoinettes all, walked as gingerly as ballet dancers in their enormous white bustles, as if treading hot coals. They pretended to appear self-absorbed. A lady next door was calling: "Froy-ak, Froy-ak!" (Freek, Freek).

We had lunch – the lady saying "Freek" prepared it. Battered steak and *Oeufs Maire-Antoinette* from the hen run. I've never seen steak crumbed or battered before but it's so cheap in North Queensland they can do it any old way, like monkfish. Freek showed us the "Thank-You" cards he has had printed to send to people who have offered condolences on the passing of his wife. (Melanoma, which is horrible). All printed by a young man – a "close friend" of his who suffered a frightful accident. He had been lying under a car when the jacks slipped. The car fell on top of his head, crushing his chin into his chest, so he couldn't cry for help. His mother went looking for him when he didn't come home for lunch. His spine was broken, and he became subject to ghastly fits. Spasms would hurl him across the room into the stereo. The Doctor told his father that the boy should undergo spinal shots to paralyse him completely, but he gave the father the final say. The gentleman, a former "Digger" (soldier – Freek is the President of the local RSL) came up to ask Freek what to do, as he wasn't on speaking terms with his wife. Ultimately, the shots were administered. The RSL has set the boy up with a printing press and now he prints these cards. I asked Freek where the RSL was – he said Mundingburra, a nearby suburb. There had been a controversy in the Clubhouse about condom vending machines: the younger members wanted them in the Gents'. Freek had argued that the machines should be put in the Ladies' instead. (The *habituées*, he intimated, were "rough as a badger's arse"). Freek couldn't work out why the condoms were orange flavoured – I guess he's never used one!

After a dessert of fresh Paupau, Wanko got in the Merc and away he drove. I couldn't believe he could face so abruptly the long drive south again. Before going to Canberra he is stopping for a holiday somewhere near Brisbane – his estranged wife and kids. It's curious, but I'll miss him.

I remembered I had forgotten to ask Wanko about the tents. Freek said that I should ask Tray Beautous about THAT – Freek has arranged our first meeting for tomorrow. Freek said the tents are the result of a commission Prime Minister Fagan (the one before Dew) gave Tray to commemorate Australia's "Aboriginal Genosoyde". Tray had made up several hundred of these rectangular black tents in imitation of the Holocaust Memorial in Berlin, which is composed of a forest of huge black marble bricks on a giant open-air marble podium. Tray's tents weren't meant to be seen together, though, like the "bricks" in Berlin. There was meant to be just one tent each for every town and city in Australia. It was quite ingenious. They were cheap, weatherproof, and suitable for permanent or temporary installation. Given what was likely to be a volatile local context, politically, they were easy and cheap to set up or take down, to keep in storage – to dispense with completely. "Was that it?" I asked, "just a black tent? What's so intriguing about that?" "You should have seen what was INSOYDE 'em!" says Freek. Apparently the black canvas was meant to make people think of a birdcage with a black cover on it. "In mourning". If you looked through the holes cut in the sides – which let in sunshine that illuminated the interior – you saw a dead gum tree full of black cockatoos – meant to represent the souls of the massacred "aubergines". Imprisoned in the birdcage "prison" of "White Australia": *"La Cage aux Folles"*. "Black parrots?" I said. "You said the idea was supposed to be cost effective! Filling tents with galahs hardly seems very efficient to me! Just think of all the mess. Anyway, isn't it cruel?"

"They wasn't LIVE cockies, ya dill!" cried Freek, "they woz STUFFED. Dead – like the Boongs!" I said I'd seen smoke coming from one of the tents I'd seen, others peppered like a colander. "Yairs. Well, those was the peepee-holes, see. And the smoke, that was the poison gas escapin' from the peepee-holes. Cos Knut, he wants to make out that the Boong Cull was like when the Krauts locked the Four-be-Twos in the jacuzzi with the Agent Orange". "The Zyklon B?" I ventured. "Well, whaddever. You know what I mean. When the Huns was crop sprayin' the Kosher Nostra with the Yeed killer. That's what the smoke was meant to represent. Weed killer. Puffs of the paraquat fart. It was meant for ter bring a tear to yer eye. Smoke gets in yer eyes, see? And so you croyde and croyde and croyde for the big Boong darkie genosoyde. Just like when the Nasties had a perv at the dyin' Yeeds through the peepee hole at Clausewitz". "I doubt if many tears were shed then!" "I doubt if many tears was shed for the Egg-and-Spoons, either, mate!" "Then where did the smoke come from?" I asked. "From a burnin' termite nest, me old China! Flambéed like a pyklet and put in each tent. They're just like Chrissie puds, see, those white ant nests, all made of leaf mulch and chewed up Bo Trees and farmers' verandahs. They burn ferocious, like a cowpat. Lotsa smoke. And Tray Beautous, he sees 'em as symbolic. His 'ervra' is full of 'em. *You've seen that fer yerself, I berloyve!"* "Indeed", I replied, shocked that Freek had been informed.

I thanked him for his florid explanation.

After taking a nap, I walked to a nearby bank. Bright heat on the Charters Towers Road – I remember the ladies with black umbrellas. I popped into a chemist where I bought sunglasses, a supermarket, another chemist. It was a sickening experience, visiting these places, worked up but idle. I wrote a few postcards, my sweaty arm sopping the glass-topped table, posted them. Returned to Cummins Street.

I wandered around outside the house. It looked like a dog kennel perched on a birdfeed pole, as do all these nestbox houses. On the telephone lines the corpses of electrocuted fruitbats hung like dwarf umbrellas. They reminded me of the carcases of crows that farmers in England hang up *"pour encourager les autres"*. The thought of English crows suddenly made Townsville seem so strange, so primitive. "This isn't my element!" I cried. Under the house, in the area framed by the stilts, I was introduced to "Mort", one of the Blue Singlet brigade, another "friend". A "Fishie" – fisherman, that is. Not for the first time I wondered: how do these uneducated, almost autistic people manage – jobs, money, relationships? And in so odd a backwater? Living at the centre of the world I hardly find them manageable.

Felt very worried about my meeting with Tray. Decided to go to church, as I missed it yesterday and when I miss a service I always have bad luck all the following week. It had to be a Catholic service of course, it being a weekday. There were details of the Townsville churches in the local paper. A taxi dropped me at the Strand, an interminable street that runs along the beach in front of Mount Kutheringa. A lovely Canteloup-orange beach that faces Cape Palleranda and Magnetic Island. In the thin strip of park between the Strand and the beach huge black cockatoos of all things, waddling through the grass like seals. Some shuddered through the Sugar Palms with an equal erratic inelegance, diving and jolting like crazy biplanes. The shrieking was frightful. I crossed the road and asked some pimply convent girls lolling on the grass where "St Joseph's" was. They directed me up a side street. The church, in simple white stucco with simple square stained glass windows that one could open, like the windows of a Queenslander, was most agreeable, the service impressive. There were painted clay reliefs of Christ's ministry along the walls in the pale colours of hard candy. It was the best Mass I have attended, and I was impressed, considering where we were, by the priest's orthodoxy (so rare in English clerics) and intellectual scope (even more rare). He compared what he called "the New Religion" to those of "the pagan Mediterranean" (wierd when an acid blue "pagan Mediterranean" and purple Magnetic Island were just beyond the door). Christianity has never been *anti*-intellectual, the priest said, but it has always insisted on the utter gratuitousness of Christ's saving grace. There was a refreshingly mad scramble for the Eucharist, quite unlike the orderly queue for Communion in a simpering Protestant temple. It was all so casual and radiant that I was surprised to find we were partaking of a Funeral Mass for one "Chuck Angry", an erstwhile grocer. Chuck was described: "One hundred per cent Townsvillean".

Back in my dreadful box room in Cummins Street, it was hard to write as Freek always has the TV blaring – keeps the sound at about a thousand decibels. I fell asleep with my wet forehead on the desk in the middle of a letter to Tia, the fan soughing.

TUESDAY 24 NOVEMBER 1987. Another day of unspeakable light and heat: the sky was so blue it looked like painted concrete. Breakfast – fresh eggs, steak, juice squeezed from the yellow oranges on the tree in the yard. Then Freek drove me in his little red Lancia to "Hambeluna", the house where Tray Beautous is staying. It overlooks the sea on one of the lower spurs of the big pink mountain – you can see it from everywhere in the city – Mount Kutheringa. Also known as "Castle Hill". A shabby, mauve-grey Queenslander on a simply vast scale, Hambeluna shoots straight off the side of the hill at a right angle – a big flat square biscuit tin on stilts. It's pretty old, dating, I would say, from the 1890s, supported on one side (where the front door is) by the slope and on the other, overlooking the sea, by a forest of high stilts. The whole shebang, house and stilts, is sheathed in a wall of wooden louvres, apart from those sides of the living area facing the sea, open but for a balustrade. Despite its size, you can hardly catch even a glimpse of the house from the rest of Townsville. Everything beyond its white paling fence – which encloses a whole city block – is hidden under a dome of African Tulip Trees, huge dark Tamarinds, smoky lipstick-pink Bougainvillea, a fleshy volcano that looks, smells and – with the fruitbats and lorikeets – sounds – cacophonous. Tray's grandma – whose name is Marilyn – had been a very keen gardener, but everything has run riot since her cancer.

I opened a gate in the fence and followed a jungle path down the slope to the front door. It was like going down a mine, the walls veined by recent and ancient deposits, but when you think only of your own safety, of escape. The door was ajar. Wooden windchimes hung burbling from the lintel like wisteria. A footstopper – I was shocked by what looked like a small artillery shell – held open the door. I went in and I called Tray's name. There was an incredible smell of camphor mothballs. A wide verandah sealed off by the glowing louvres enclosed an inner chalet. The verandah was scattered with elegant rattan furniture, fantastic tropical plants in jardinières, polished tables with clay and leather knick-knacks like fetishes. Even inside Hambeluna you could hear the buzz-saw drone of the cicadas and the sudden rapist shriek of particularly loud birds. Also a pitter patter in the ceiling and a deafening stampede as of feral children: possums. Every few minutes there was an eerie series of delicate double hoots. Recalling as it did the cooing of a wood pigeon, it emphasised more even than the avowedly tropical sounds the othernesss of Townsville, for it was no dove. On my right stood the plank wall of the inner bungalow, plated with windows and French doors. Their lead tracing, in flower shapes, held panes of dark stained glass in red, mint green, burnt orange. To the left, on the other side of the verandah, a line of wooden railings beyond which is a sheer drop to the plunging slope of the hill. The slope isn't open on this side but enclosed in a glass atrium or greenhouse made of musty yellow panes, a tank of yeasty light that fills the whole house like a lamp. Pots full of orchids suspended on twine were dangling from the roof of the atrium. They reminded me of the Christmas Puddings they hang from the beams of the Spread Eagle Coaching Inn in Midhurst, West Sussex. Down below, one could see that the mud "floor" of the atrium was littered with hideous Cane Toads hissing like fresh cowpats. There were ceramic beer jars, too, like Winnie-the-Pooh honey pots, frothing with fern and wild chives. I later learned that this atrium was called "the Bush House". Tray supposedly used it as a studio.

As I entered the verandah, Tray's Grandmother Marilyn hobbled out of a glass door in a dirty old shift, barefoot, her face and hair white. Her face, and her speech, were distorted. She looked like General de Gaulle. Offered me a shuddering tray with two cold drinks and some water biscuits wet with curling anchovies. Shocked and embarassed, I felt awful. Why was I intruding? Freek, who hadn't seen her since her illness, had warned me of a "Diana Vreeland Dragon" with "chick" (*"chic"*). "Gorgeous dyed red hair". How were the mighty fallen! After an exchange of the usual rubbish, Marilyn asked if Freek had brought me. Then, why he had omitted to accompany me in. She said that, after she got "crook", she told a lot of her friends "Out West" not to come and visit her —to remember her as she had been. But she wouldn't have minded if Freek had come. A bead of brown amber collected; a brownish tear ran down. I was taken aback. Obviously, I didn't know this individual: it was a bit intense. Returning things to normal, I asked about the door stopper. She said it was an unexploded Japanese bomb – one of the hundreds dropped on Townsville during the Second World War! Which was good to know. She asked me not to tell Tray that the bomb was "alive". Apparently, he's a "worrier". *"So am I!"*, I said.

A crackle behind me. I was taken aback. Disappointed and also surprised as Tray Beautous emerged. Just a very ordinary Australian, like some short, brown professional cricketer from Wollongong with a hairy chest, a primitive, snub-nosed face, and one of those provincially fashionable haircuts with a feathery ball like a Grebe's perching on his head. He reminded me of a tropical fruit, where an outlandish blandness meets precocity. He certainly looked nothing like his statuesque "self-portrait" on the bed at Yarralumla. I noticed however that his eyes – the effeminate, idealistic eyes of an ox – were completey at odds with this face and body – as was the texture of his repartee. He spoke with the slow quizzical Queensland accent but his hirsute mongol voice delivered words of a mocking shrewdness. I told him this was my very first visit to "The City of Youth". "Don't worry," he said, "you haven't missed anything!"

I gave Tray the spiel I had agreed with Dewy. I told him I had come all the way to Townsville to see Girly Soukoop, the widow of a local novelist. That I was a gallery owner in London but had a particular interest in the art of "Alastair" (1887-1969), the pseudonym of Baron Hans Henning von Voigt, a German imitator of Beardsley known for his erotica. I said that the vendor of an "Alastair" drawing I had purchased in Holland had told me that a writer called Shoom Soukoop, who lived in *"Townsville"* – the name had intrigued me – owned the biggest known "Alastair" collection in the world. I told Tray I had been informed that Shoom had inherited the art from his Dutch family, who were linked with this German, "Alastair", in some way. I could find no clues to the Townsville contact details of Shoom in London or the Continent, I opined. In desperation, I said, I had looked up the Deputy who sat for Townsville in the Australian Federal Parliament. Freek, who was so famously "artistic" himself, had then kindly written saying he could put me in touch with Shoom's widow. So here I was. "So you've been living out the plot of ***The Aspern Papers***?" said Tray. "Yes," I replied, though the analogy didn't strike me. "*'What will survive of us is love'*," I sighed, referring to Girly and Shoom. "Not true!" Tray pouted. "What will survive of us . . . *is me*!" ("Typical pretentious illiterate", I thought to myself. I was obviously in for a cute time of it.) "What trace does *love* ever leave?" he demanded. "And what trace does anything else leave? Most people – even the most successful – devote their entire lives to things that never get them noticed. They waste their entire lives. Only painters are alive. Only *we* are engaged in work whose residue will last!"

He seemed full of himself, or rather full of something quite different from himself. He had the ironic, exasperated manner of a spoilt teenager who has discovered a big idea – Communism, say, or religion. He was like a terrorist in that his personality was something he had absorbed from somewhere else and identified with. He struck me as both inflexible and brittle, like a coral reef that takes on the contours of the sunken ship it colonises. Or the sacred Banyan Tree, that basket of tendril suckers that has swallowed and hence mimics the pineapple appearance of the Neak Pean temple at Angkor Wat. What amazed me is that life lets us exist like that. Not only that these "off the peg" illusions survive their collision with reality, but that *we* survive this collision too. That despite the false consciousness that propels them into so many disasters, whenever we meet them after a gap of years, we invariably find artists, like schizophrenics, fanatics and upended cockroaches, somehow clinging on, not only to life, but to their strange "inner" life, about which they will invariably have "learned nothing and forgotten nothing". Human beings really are as tough as the devil.

"I completely agree with you!" I told Tray, knowing very well how to deal with artists. As President Nixon once noted, three types of human are susceptible to flattery: men, women and children. And artists, of course. "I'm just as interested in living painters as I am in dead ones," I told Tray. "I'd be interested to find into which category I can put *you*! As soon as I arrived here Freek kept telling me about a wonderful artist that Townsville itself had produced – never mind Alastair – that I simply *had* to meet you. Who knows? I might even like your work enough to represent you in London!" "And what exactly has Bloomers told you?" Tray asked, not sounding particularly gratified. "Well", I said, "he told me about those black tents of yours. I've even seen a few of them. Only from the outside, of course". I said how intrigued I was by the idea of black cockatoos sitting on jerky white gums: like angels sitting on wiry stratus clouds. But black. "If you peeked in", I said, "caged birds really are so immobile the viewer probably would think the cockies were alive". Tray laughed. "I thought they were your protest against genocide?" I shot back. Tray laughed again. "For a hypocritical race, the English are remarkably credulous. What do *I* have against genocide? As Whitman said: *'What have I in common with it? Or what with the destruction of it?'* I can't imagine there's anything wrong with the idea *in principle*. Of course, Hitler gave genocide a bad name." "You *could* say that!" I observed. "Well, it's all so ridiculous!" Tray hissed. He hates being interrupted. "I mean, if, instead of the Five-to-Twos, you'd popped the *Texans* into a microwave, who the hell would have complained? What contribution have *they* ever made? If every Tim-Tam, say, were to drop dead tomorrow, what would the effects on the world be but positive ones?" "But you don't believe in *killing* them?" I gasped. "Not very practical, I'm afraid," said Tray. "Abu Faraj, the historian of the Arab conquest of Egypt tells us that, when the Muslims found the great library of Alexandria, repository of all the learning of the ancient world, they destroyed its contents in their entirety. The Caliph of the day had said that: *'if what is written in these books of the Greeks agrees with Muhammad, it is not required; if it contradicts him, it must be destroyed.'* The volumes, Faraj writes, were distributed among the four thousand baths of the city and their furnaces, we are told, took no less than six months to devour every one of them . . . But it would take even the Gay Bath Houses of New York considerably longer than six months to incinerate every damn Tim-Tam, I imagine." "Well, Tray", I laughed, "I did hear you were rather *Tim-Tammophobic!*" "Not like you eh?" he replied. "A few days back what should I see but a piccie of you in **THE AUSTRALIAN** with Arkana Muckadilla and that husband of hers, the nonce cricketer. It was at that 'feed' you were at in Canberra". "Oh God", I thought to myself, "*'Never crap a crapper'* ! Those pervy Japs and their Nikon cameras!" I clutched at straws. "Well, er, yes. We really didn't speak though. I had to fly to Canberra first, you see, to meet Freek. Freek was kind enough to get me invited to that event. Because his party leader hosted it, you see?" I could have kicked myself. What did I have to go and mention Dewy for? "Anyway" I said, changing the subject, "what *do* your tents signify? . . . I mean, if they're not about *geno-soyde*? What is inside them? What causes that smoke?"

"You wouldn't want to know", he sniffed. "Probably that's why Freek tried to mislead you – it's not nice . . . Certain things I do actually regret. In any case, it's ancient history. I did that art *years* ago". "Well," I asked, "what are you working on now?" He beckoned me towards a room off the corridor, in the inner chalet. Marilyn, who had been sitting on a cane pouffe, sipping Freek's drink, said something about having a "spell". She stumbled into the Bush House. Was there a nurse, I wondered? Tray seemed anything but solicitous.

"The Gun Room", Tray called it. Cold musty smell inside. Frosted French Windows that faced the verandah piercing two of its walls, their panels full of light – grey light glowing. Tray opened the doors of the cupboards that hugged the walls to show me the collection of rifles and pistols his grandfather had assembled, also the toy locomotives that he said his Dad had played with. Tray showed me the old 1930s train sets, the boxes of green-gold bullets. He opened the doors and he showed me. There was a sort of erotic intensity in the cold luscious bullets – I grasped them like wriggling maggots in a Fishie's bucket – the black Mausers, Lugers like dead beetles, their metal cold and priapic to the touch. There was something sensual, too, in the rich bottle-green or glassy Black Cherry colour of the long tube-like snouts of the toy locomotives: each was as big as a wild duck. Rich colours are so uplifting. The doors of the carriages had tiny gold handles on them like wild rose thorns, the chambers within each an erotic, anal cubbyhole. I adored the yellow consommé glass of their windows and inside the exquisite banqettes and cornflake-box toy tables. It made you wish you were one inch tall and could climb inside. Then Tray pointed to the bare plank floor. In the middle of the square room a series of circles within circles – curving toy railway track – concentric circles of it like a dartboard. Along the tracks the trains rushed endlessly like chooks, each coming to an orgasm like a sewing machine. (Outside, on the verandah, I had taken the metronomic choking for the coughing of kookaburras). My eyes crept to the centre of the spider's web, to the target of the dartboard. Suddenly, I heard myself scream. This, alas, set Tray shrieking with mirth like the batshit pansy in **Silence of the Lambs**. For sitting in the Bull's Eye like a monstrous Redback Spider was the mottled face of "Big Ann" poking through the hole again. But it was actually a cake, a cake just lying there on the floor. It was shaped like a human face, like a death mask looking up at the ceiling, a ripple of bumps in the flat grey sea: it was "Magnetic Island". Like Magnetic it was very colourful, the eyes, skin, hair delineated with cochineal and other dyes in blazing synthetic blue, saffron, pink – exactly the synthetic colour washes that you see on Warhol's famous *"Marilyn"*. For this, too, was a Marilyn: the cake was an exact life-sized replica of Marilyn's face. Tray said he had taken a mould from his granny's gob with industrial gelatine, turned it into a tin baking mould and Marilyn herself had poured cake mix into it. Tray said that it was a sponge and that his grandmother had baked and iced it at his direction. "I mean, Andy [Warhol] used to get *his* people to make *all* his art for him. It's actually a very 'Duchamp' situation. I mean, in the end, who actually *is* the artist?" ("Oh God", I thought, "not the 'Duchamp' speech. I've only heard that about sixteen thousand times before.") I asked him what this "work of art" was called and, pointing to the face with its pulsating Hornby haloes he said *"Medusa"*. Trains running endlessly around a face on the floor. Cake like a death mask. She'd cooked her own goose. He said he was going to make her *eat* her own goose, too. Eat her own death. "Like this".

He picked up a gun – an American Smith and Wesson, the sort with a revolving cannister for the shells, and he put the barrel in his mouth and bit it. He pulled the trigger. Nothing. No bullets in the gun. Then, he said that, because I'd gazed on "Medusa", I had to die, too – what a wanker, I thought – and he pointed it at my head and "click". No bullets. Probably not even a real gun. Tray suddenly seemed different: wild-eyed, wiry and fair like the hero in a Herzog movie. He asked me some very obvious question: I remember the unreason I could sense behind its stupidity. I told him to put the revolver away: he was waving it around as a monkey might. He was wearing a white djellaba like a ball gown, the everyday dress of an Arab male, said he often wears one in Townsville "for the heat". He reminded me of a voodoo priestess in Haïti with her long white shift and toque twirling a black chook above her head: the gun had all the dignity of a headless rooster. I felt like laughing but there was a horrid bang like a balloon and dust and a thudding screaming of the unseen possums above. I looked up and saw a pink hole new torn in the plank ceiling, blood like ink – possum blood I hope – skittering out, red spots pittering on Marilyn's icing face. Tray shoved the handle of the gun at me with the smug pride of one showing off a tattoo. Holding it by the barrel, he opened the canister: two bullets snug in the chamber like lovely silk grubs in a honeycomb. "Here. Another piece of my art. *'Romulus and Remus'* is what I call it". . . Wanker! Upset and not knowing what to say, I asked Tray what he would do when his Grandmother died. He gave me some meretriciously urbane flapdoodle about things *"sorting themselves out"*. Amazing how rational self-indulgent lunatics can be when it comes to their own self-interest. Tray put down the gun and asked me if Freek had taken me to see Girly yet. "No" I said, "but Mrs Soukoup knows I'll be coming to stay. She knows what I'll be looking for." Tray asked if I would like him to introduce us. He told me that Shoom's widow lives not far from Hambeluna and is a good friend of his Gran, that he knows Girly well. "Yes, oh yes!" I said. Anything to get us out of that room.

We found Marilyn lying quite still on a chaise by the louvres like a stuffed dog. After being introduced to Marilyn's old tabby cat "Jim" (another brown bead rolled down), Tray walked me along a back road to Girly Soukoop's house. I shall be moving there in a few day's time. I couldn't get over the unearthly intensity of the tropical colours – the tropical light: the smoky silver of the zinc roofs – the deep polar blue of the sky above Marilyn's garden - the fluttering shadows on the hot milky flanks of purple Magnetic out in the bay, its texture so pure and raw, like a passionfruit. The bay was the colour of a chemical toilet, a bright viscous green so unnatural-looking you'd think it was polluted.

Girly's house – "Araluen" – sits high up on Mount Kutheringa, directly under the summit. There are staggering views over the Coral Sea and Magnetic Island. Not a Queenslander but a square white stucco villa in an attractive Art Deco style like a villa in Tangier. Too sardonic for Townsville. Because of the gradient, Araluen is built on the top of a series of stone terraces – like Inca terraces. They project at right angles from the face of the hill. On the crown of each terrace is a luscious well-trimmed lawn, the grass like the moss at the bottom of a spring. On the third terrace down, where the villa is, are striped awnings and parasols, spindly white iron chairs and loungers like in *The Great Gatsby*, a little ivy arbour with a swing sofa. Pots of manicured dwarf orange trees with tiny scented Bergamot oranges like peppers.

We climbed up the stone steps, knocked, and a thin lady like a skinny sexless old man answered the door: the cleaner. She looked us up and down with a capricious air. Brightening when she learned who we were, she led us by the storm drain that ran up the side of the house to the back garden, which was throbbing with banks of curry-coloured marigolds. Their bitumen smell reminded me of childhood. Shaded by massive Bo Trees, the back garden, like the front, ascended the hill in a series of terraces. We climbed up a staircase made of orange rocks to find Girly Soukoop watering the plants on a vertiginous Inca lawn. She was sitting on on a shooting stick under a huge picture hat, a little transistor strapped around her wrist. She had a long kind face like a foal and, like Marilyn, a soft, quavering semi-English voice that made her sound like a Sydney waiter with gay cancer. She was very pale; the older, upper-class Australians, unlike the posh rough young ones, taking enormous pains to keep out of the sun. She apologised and asked us to wait as she listened to the *dénouément* of the cricket. Then she apologised for her work clothes, explaining one is only allowed to water in Townsville for a few set hours each day. I was struck by the ironic elegance of her *déshabillée*: slacks, a man's pyjama shirt, a Liberty's silk scarf. It looked quite astonishing in Townsville.

She introduced us to her gardener, Kade – he is also her chauffeur. Kade wore nothing but blue shorts and a wide straw Chinese peasant-woman's hat. He was about 20 and resembled a subnormal Elvis. Girly and Tray – who seemed to employ Kade as a "model" – were swift to ply me with confidences. Kade suffered from "a lack of focus", which wasn't earth-shattering news. It was because his parents had both gone out to work. It had taken a long time for "treatment" to bear fruit. ("I bet!" I smiled, thinking of his vocation). You had to take him back to earliest childhood and then guide him back to adulthood along the right path. (It sounded like what I was doing in Australia). Kade, used to the "centrality" of his affliction, didn't mind this discussion. Only the outsider, who didn't share his egocentric world, felt a strange apprehension. By the same token, I was unprepared for the interest they took in me: as a Londoner, I suppose. I expected them to see Townsville as central because it was central at the time to me. I made no allowances for the city's real place in the world, its peripherality, isolation, which Girly and Tray must have felt quite keenly.

We went inside. The villa was cool and dark, like the interior of a hacienda, the shutters were flung open on the bay. Exquisite furniture and artefacts. A windchime – brass this time – gurgled over Magnetic in a blazing square sapphire window that lit up the table. Somewhat

295

to my irritation, Tray noisily deployed his molars to crunch the ice in the drinks that Girly brought. Shortly afterwards he decamped for Hambeluna. Girly said that Marilyn had told her that, on one occasion, she, Marilyn, had seen something white in the garden, late at night, and had played the torch on Hambeluna's front lawn. It was Tray, sitting naked, cross-legged, staring at the moon! "*Meditation*, that's it," said Girly. "I wonder if he's one of these *Moonies*, you know, these South Africans that are terribly affected by the moon? It's a country I would have *loved* to visit. I've known several South Africans and they were all a bit queer." Well, that was the 24th of November. I still find it hard to write my diary in the evenings at Freek's place. The noise crushes and stamps on the flimsy Queenslander as if it were one of those local Green Ants' nests made of Tea Tree leaves. Casting about in my aviary for some way of getting to sleep, I decided to fixate on Tray's philosophy and analyse it, like counting sheep. Is it really true that "all that survives of us is art"? I suppose it is. After all, does anyone today remember the fact that Caravaggio murdered his rent-boy models, and even slit the throat of his patron, his "Patrick Mynts"? All that we remember, I guess, are the eternal victims of his stiletto Muse. Then, of course, there was Pier Paulo Pasolini – a sort of Caravaggio in reverse. Killed, like Sebastian in **Suddenly Last Summer**, by a pack of the male whores he was wont to patronise. One could hardly imagine a more horrible or shameful end. At the time of his lapidation on an Ostia beach in November 1975, the journalists of Roma were sneering. They placed in their copy a variation on the famous ditty piped by the Paris rabble when the self-indulgent Louis XV kicked the bucket in 1774:

> *"Louis a rempli sa carrière*
> *Et fini ses tristes destins,*
> *Tremblez, voleurs, fuyez, putains,*
> *Vous avez perdu votre père!"*

("Louis has fulfilled his career
And come to the end of his unhappy road,
Tremble, thieves; flee, whores,

You have lost your Daddy!")

But who remembers the Ostia incident now? Or the newspapers in which it was recorded, which were Panini wrappers long before Pier Paulo's body was even cold? All that people recall, and will recall, is Pasolini's radiant cinema and verse, peopled by the boys who kicked him to death. Boys transformed from base metal into gold, from trash into the eternal algrebra of art. Hasn't Pasolini made his murderers into the creators of his life, the creators of his *real* life? Perhaps that was why he called them, in that poem:

> **"sons turned into fond fathers"**

because -

> **"Little by little**
> **they have become stone monuments**
> **thronging my solitude in their thousands."**

And haven't they come to throng our more public piazzas, too: our bookshops, our cinemas, our lecture halls? And didn't the *"tristes destins"* – of the likes of Louis XV – point the way? After all, when Louis XV, "fond father" of "thieves and whores" snuffed it, exactly two hundred years before Pier Paulo, didn't the Paris mob place a placard around the neck of the equestrian likeness that was raised in his honour? *"Statue Statuae"*, it read: "the statue of a statue". But what higher compliment could there be? Didn't it unwittingly reveal how the patron of Rameau, Boucher and Fragonard would come to be assessed, the man who invented Sèvres china and Louis Quinze chairs? The man who gave the world the Petit Trianon and the Place de la Concorde? And wasn't it an epithet that disclosed, too, why the "Big Daddy" of "thieves and whores" would melt away like ice? After all, how many of us even get to be *statues*? So how many even of the pin-stuck "voodoo dolls" among us will live to become the *statues* of a statue? I hope I will!

In the living room, where Freek was sitting bare-chested with a stubby, I heard something on the infernal TV about "soldiers of the old queen". *"For Captain Gunn, there has only been one quoyn. In his cupboard, a piece of her wedding cake, in his garden a Troy grown from her bouquet."*

WEDNESDAY 25 NOVEMBER 1987. Freek dropped me at the restaurant at the Casino out on the Breakwater, which has been built between Magnetic and Townsville's industrial port. Opened only a few years ago, it was like a "modern" hotel in Cairo – scruffy, blackened marble with cracks, a "post-modern", Thatcherite red carpet – red to show the dirt. Lots of gold. Girly was waiting in the foyer in a coffee-coloured silk dress rippling with shocking black spots. She had invited me to lunch. She sported white elbow-length gloves and a rakish wide-brimmed hat – big blue "Jackie O" shades. Yet again, she had stepped off another planet. We had a sumptuous if hardly delectable meal, though, as I was sick with anxiety, even the choicest viandes would have been as ashes.

We discussed the Australian artists Donald Friend and Russell "Tassie" Drysdale. Drysdale, apparently, had been a friend of her family and, in her infancy, a neighbour. (A big fan of Drysdale, I was intrigued). She told me how she and Marilyn were given revolvers and horses as five year olds and would gallop over the Bush shooting snakes on the adjoining "Stations" (ranches) where they grew up, close friends, near Baratta – it's about twenty miles away, between Townsville and Home Hill. This was before the First World War. They would post the snake skins "Down South" to a shoe and hat maker in Sydney to pay for the toys they wanted. Or, at the request of the Chinese cook, they would blast away with their Lugers at the poor little Galahs to provide him with the *mis-en-scène* for his favourite, "Pallet Pie". (I couldn't help thinking of the Black Cockatoos and the Shoah of the Aubergines). In those days, Girly airily insisted, every little upper class girl was a "brute": every single one had an automatic weapon. Girly's mother, too, always carried a revolver to shoot dead the Station cats when they got too numerous. *("Would that there were a similar Nemesis that stalked the Tim-Tams!"* Tray later mused). Marilyn and Girly had a pet kangaroo called "Ginny" – from "Black Gin", demotic for a female Abo. Ginny lived under the stilts at "Ivanhoe", Girly's family home. She would graze there on the piles of old newspapers. One day, alas, Ginny's attention strayed to a precious volume narrating the family's distinguished history back "home" in "the old country". Intrigued, Ginny partook, leaving nothing but a heap of confetti. Girly's mother, alas, blew Ginny's head off with a Browning pistol. I snapped the femur of a "Sandie" (sand crab) here, finding this a bit cruel. I dipped the femur in a boat of *Sauce Marie-Rose* . . .

Girly told me that the "Black Hands" on the station would take the little girls out hunting, *à la façon des Aubergines*. "I've tasted goanna *of course*. Which is delightful – imagine a terrine of crab and pheasant. Possum is more like grouse. A beautiful flesh, as sweet as roast baby kid – but *strong*. It can taste horribly of turpentine – because of all the gum leaves they eat, you see?" She told me that the Aboriginal Stockmen would tell them about the spirits – the "Lightning Spirit", Namarkon, and the spirits of the sacred trees and plants and animals. How to answer when such and such a spirit might speak to them as they were crossing a certain Billabong. What Girly called "spirits" are no doubt what Freud calls "totems" – in the long piece about the Australian "Aubergines" with which he opens **Totem and Taboo** in about the same year – 1912 – as the infant Girly was riding down the possums with the "Boongs":

> **"The totem is the common ancestor of the clan; at the same time it is their guardian spirit and helper, which sends them oracles and, if dangerous to others, it recognises and spares its own children."**

Sometimes, said Girly, the stockmen would warn them not to go out at all: "Bad tribe about today!" . . . So, even in 1912, there were still unconquered tribes! Strange to think that within Girly's lifetime a whole world stretching back a hundred thousand years had been destroyed and another with its vast penumbra of suburbs and bidets created – conjured out of nothing like the mythical city of Kitezh in Rimsky-Korsakov's **The Maiden Fevroniya** :

"Behold, I tell you a mystery -
We shall not all sleep,
But we shall all be changed,
In a moment, in the twinkling of an eye - "

We caught a taxi back to "Hambeluna", hoping to meet Eurong, "a wee buck nigger" (Girly's expression, not mine) who had grown up with Marilyn on "Dululu", her family "Station", and had accompanied her to her married residence as a handyman. He is too old to work now – very reclusive. Apparently, he lives in a hut in the wilderness under the "Hambeluna" stilts. Eurong is supposedly the son of a chief of the Warrigal, a local tribe. He has tasted human flesh, a privelege reserved in Abo as in Aztec society to the *"Noblesse d'Épée"*. Girly to tease me told me that he is a *"Maban"*, a sorcerer in the tribal way, wielding the power of life and death. She told me that Tray had only been able to make the "Black Tents" in such large numbers with Eurong's assistance. (Laughed dismissively when I gave her Freek's account of their nature and origin, but she was rather tipsy by then). Tray, she said, had given some of the tents he created the title *"Black Box Recorder"*, some *"I am a Camera"*, because each was meant to be "a statue of God . . . or maybe of the you know who." So that everyone who bought one could have their own "monotheistic idol", their own "Ark of the Covenant", like the Hebrews in the Wilderness, which is what Tray said the European Aussies really were. Others he apparently dubbed *"Angkar Leou"* because, like the "Higher Organisation" in Khmer Rouge Cambodia, each with its many perforations boasted the all-seeing "eyes of a pineapple". Others still, said Girl, he had styled *"Plato's Cave"*. But every tent was identical and each, she assured me, performed the same function. They were meant to work like an old Black Box Camera, she said, such as you can make at school by boring a tiny hole in a shoebox: the pin of light prints an image of the outside world on the primed greasepaper within. Thanks to a fetish supplied by Eurong and placed within each tent, she said, the billowing walls inside each had been "primed" by the occult, and, when you peered

300

through one of the holes, the "light" of your spirit, heavy with the spore of your everyday deeds, would stream in and illuminate your future in the next world. You would see yourself writhing in the three dimensions of Heaven or Hell and, if the latter, the tent would fizz with Hell-Fire smoke, such as I myself had seen pouring out of more than one of them. "He came up with all that?" I asked, amused. "God, what a medicine show! Tray is one Hell of a hustler!" "Maybe he should have called his black tents *that*," Girly observed, " *'One Hell of a Hustler'* !" "What about 'Death of a Salesman'?" I laughed.

Unfortunately, when we arrived, we discovered "Hambeluna" in chaos: Eurong was forgotten. (He is very shy anyway and apparently goes "Walkabout" with some frequency). Marilyn, we found, had fallen in the bathroom and had been immobile for hours as her lunch burned away in the oven. She hauled herself towards us like a goanna, naked under a cheap dress like a dishrag. She had been trying to contact Tray all day long, she said. (Why not Eurong?) Tray was out kicking up his heels on Magnetic Island. We laid Marilyn on a *Chaise* on the breezy verandah and awaited *Cher Maître* Beautous' return. When he came in, boiling, Tray spat in an aside that M. had fallen "deliberately" to make him feel guilty.

On my return to Cummins Street, I was upset because, as usual, I couldn't write my diary. My room was like an oven, and the cool section, with the Spitfire propeller, was full of a thousand radiant decibels.

THURSDAY 26 NOVEMBER 1987. Today, after lunch, I walked all the way up to Hambeluna to see Tray. I need to get him to agree to "the Plan". On the way, I was threatened by some drunken Abos staggering home from the pub to their camp in the mangrove swamp. At first I thought they were in one of those races where the runners tie their legs together. They all had arms over each others' shoulders.

To escape them I had to bolt off the road into the swamp itself. Keeping to threads of dry land, I plunged through the bushes: each was buzzing, literally trembling with cicadas. I kept on running: I thought I was being chased. There was what the poet Ezra Pound calls *"hot wind from the marshes"*, that rotten egg smell of sulphur-rich mud unique to the tropical zone. The little mangrove trees thinned out and a stagnant pond shuddered by on my right, a leafless, dead white Ghost Gum rising out of the black water like a hand. I didn't have time to investigate but, extraordinarily, the fresh corpses of beautiful naked Abo women were actually swinging upside down from the arms of the gum like catkins, their bodies striated and voluptuous like bees. They were twirling from their bound heels like fruitbats, as nubile as ears of roast maize. At the time, the adrenaline dissolved my shock – and afterwards I could only doubt what I had seen. I kept on running, though this time through hissing blocks of fragrant mauve Lantana. I finally emerged from the swamp at the "Lou Litster Park" and doubled back through what is called "Penny Lane" towards town. I admired the wooden pubs with the verandahs lining West Flinders Street, especially the one with the painted statue of a Foster's Lager Can perching on its roof like a funnel on the Queen Mary. Townsville certainly has more character than Canberra, perhaps more character than Sydney. I walked to the middle of a bridge in the town centre that crosses the Ross Creek. The water was a flat polished jade, the single line railway bridge in the distance unfenced, frail-looking, like the Sydney Monorail, the red and white brick Victorian Gothic station on the other bank – the zenith, to Townsville, of olde-world "Tchick" – small and crude and, to my eyes, modern.

I walked back to Flinders Street past one of the ubiquitous Aboriginal "cen-tahs", complete with Aboriginal flag and "Aboriginal" murals. This idea that the dispossessed are blessed is a European idea, not an Aboriginal one, and the abstract painted animals on the walls were fake and depressing. Aboriginals serving up, in art as in life, a European idea of their victimhood. An idea utterly alien to the pre-existent culture they claim, thereby, to uphold. After all, have the non-Western peoples of the world ever been troubled by dispossessing one another? The Aboriginals did it themselves, with the Tasmanian Aborigines, a completely different race which once covered the entire continent and whom they exterminated to a man – leaving the Europeans to finish off the remnant that had survived on the island of Tasmania. Racism, colonialism – call it what you will – is a neutral and universal human process. Every human group has been responsible for it, and every human group has been its victim. Only its most recent practitioner, the White Man, turns it into something immoral.

These Aborigines, when they claim to be rejecting European culture by appealing to the consciences of their dispossessors – since, in the whole history of mankind, it is only the Caucasian who has ever *had* a conscience – are simply borrowing their usurper's trite ideas. (Which they are claiming thereby to reject!) A continent as vast, as defenceless as Aboriginal Australia would certainly have been conquered at some time or other, by someone. The idea that underlies the Aboriginal *schtick*, that it would, and could, have remained inviolate forever, is absurd. The Abos should just thank their lucky stars they were never conquered by another *"oppressed"* community! There would have been no guilt or handouts then! Genocide and oblivion would have been their lot. Look at what the Indonesians, those anti-colonial paragons, are doing to the peoples of East Timor and West Irian. Had the UN not insisted that the Portuguese and Dutch be ousted from those places, the Timorese and West Irians would be free and independent by now. Instead, the Indonesians – who are racially distinct from both communities – were allowed to "liberate" them. To be oppressed by the White Man for a strictly limited period is evidently bad; to be exterminated or enslaved for all of time by a fellow person of colour is a beautiful form of "liberation". Isn't nature wonderful?

Anyway, once a country is colonised, whether by white or brown, the link between culture and race among the pre-existing natives quickly unravels. From now on, they will be distinguished from their conquerors by their race, not by their ideas. Even the Abos who live today in the Bush, as their ancestors did, and who access traditional Aboriginal culture,

303

do so in a permitted, parasitic way, because it has always been in the power of the conquerors to destroy them. And these Abos' own understanding of their environment, even where it remains unchanged, is violated by profoundly European concepts, by the mere knowledge of the new power in the land and their own marginality. Who can doubt that we have completely lost the Aboriginal Australia from which today's "natives" claim to speak, an Aboriginal world seen from within and without the retrospective gloss that Western scholars have given it? The Australia that didn't know Europe and wasn't known by it was dead by about 1810. The Dead Past. We have lost that ancient Eden and that ancient Sodom: Sodom because its law, like that of every tribal society, was the law of the stronger, the law of the killer and the paedophile and the thief, Cain's law. What we have today are not "Aboriginals", not the murderers and abusers of old who exulted in imperialism and genocide, but Europeans who, by virtue of their Aboriginal blood, recite purely European clichés hostile to invasion and killing and by so doing imagine that they are rejecting Whitey. An Aboriginal of today has no more in common with a "real" (pre-1810) Abo than a lobster in "Décadence Mandchoue", cooked with bean curd and black chilli sauce, has with one gambolling on the Great Barrier Reef, and the same ontological barrier, of course, divides an artist like Tray from his fellow humans.

As I arrived at Hambeluna, I met a "Blue Nurse" climbing up the jungle path. Thinking I was a family member, she told me that Marilyn was in no fit state to live in the seedy old mansion with the possums and the gekkos and the dirt. As she was speaking, I couldn't help noticing a dead cane toad on the path. It was lying dried out and as flat as a pancake, like a stick of dried ginger. The front door was still held ajar by the dark green Japanese bomb. Marilyn was lying on a filthy nylon bed in the Dining Room, the first room off the verandah, talking out of the side of her mouth. She seemed to think Girly, whose birthday it apparently is today, was coming at 3 PM for tea. Tray, whom she summoned with repeated blows to the old Dinner Bell, which was like a ship's bell, appeared with a tray of sandwiches from

COLE'S. Out of earshot, I told him that the nurse had said that she was going to ring around and see if Marilyn couldn't be put in a "home". Marilyn, I reported, had allegedly agreed with the nurse about this, but only in the distant future: a future she would never see. Tray disputed its necessity. Defying reality to the last, he said that Marilyn had always "fallen beautifully". The Greys, for instance – a group of maiden ladies from a Townsville oligarch family next door – were in the habit of "falling badly". I wasn't able to get him to discuss even a fragment of what I hope might become our "arrangement". Tray reserves the right to decide the date of his "negotiations" in advance, since everything he does is a "performance", and he is distinctly strange out of character. (Though not as odd as he is "in" character).

I walked down the hill to Flinders Mall, Townsville's Champs Elysées, and bought a nice caddy of tea for Girly's birthday in *DAVID JONES*. When I returned to the house Marilyn was still lying in bed. Then Girly arrived. A sort of diffident, dreamlike stoicism prevailed. Here we were in the elegant midden of an obviously dying woman. Ching vases were sitting next to common earthenware pots of mummified ginger on the bookshelf: they were fifty years' old, pungent and unopened. There were Drysdale originals on the plank walls with Nineteenth Century watercolours of native Australian birds. Girly, Tray and Marilyn were discussing butterflies. Tray brought in the butterfly net from his childhood home. Suicides were discussed, descents into madness, "bludgers" – the suicide of "Tassie" Drysdale's "sponger" son, Tim, who had been bought a Maserati. There was a wierd abstraction about it all, an acknowledgement of emotional intensity, yet a refusal to succumb to its attractions. Tray showed Girly a glass panel of crumbling rare butterflies he had brought Marilyn for Christmas about ten years before. Girly, Tray and I were sitting around the Dining Room table, the dishonourable sandwiches bristling with flies. The "Bush House", which we could see through the doors beyond the verandah, lighted the darkened protagonists like a Vermeer. Girly's indigo white-spotted dress and her wide straw hat were framed by the slanting panel of the coffee-coloured afternoon. The repartee evoked a vivid and unwitting picture of degeneracy. To think the pioneers' dynamic stock has come to this, the likes of Girly and Marilyn and Drysdale junior, shut-in, stay-at-home, parasitic failures. *"Who breaks a butterfly on a wheel?"* Who indeed? I think the climate has influenced these families – this land was never meant for the White Man. In that sense, the Aborigines are right.

All the talk about butterflies reminded me of the "lubras" hanging juicily like chrysalids and I cautiously broached the subject of the "Swamp Thing" in the hope I'd be told I had *actually* seen something quite different. I was disturbed when they looked at each other warily. "You shouldn't really have gone there," said Tray. "That's their cemetery – the lubras' graveyard anyway. Everyone knows they wind-dry their dead like the Incas, turn them into crispy bacon – it's the process they use in Biltong, that dried meat. And they always 'bury' their dead by hanging them up in the branches of a tree. Haven't you ever seen **Walkabout**, that movie by Nicholas Roeg? Jenny Agutter was in it. Remember the scene where the Abos hang up the mummified corpse like it's a Christmas bauble?" Somewhat abashed, I caught a taxi back to Cummins Street. I was so upset that I mentioned the incident to Freek. I had only found myself near the "sacred grove", I insisted, by accident. "So Tray Beautous told yew *that*, did 'ee?" Freek laughed. "Well, hoy *would* say that, wouldn't 'ee?" Freek said that, as elected representative for the area, he could assure me that what I'd seen were just *papier-mâché* shells! They are created on the living model from a mould composed of newspaper steeped in glue. Then the Abos wait for them to dry and varnish each cocoon. They turn them into what look like brown bottles by brushing each with Tea Tree resin. The "balloons" were hanging upside down like that to represent Fruit Bats. Freek said that the tribe that had made the "dolls" had only arrived recently in Townsville. They had left their ancestral land up in the Bush at Deeragun to live as pariah dogs on the White Man's vomit. But though they had exchanged their hunting spears and boomerangs for the turps bottle and the welfare token, they had not abandoned the ancient cult. This particular tribe regarded the Fruit Bat as their "totem" or "spirit ancestor". In that sense every single tribesman was a fourteenth generation Fruit Bat. The chief of the tribe had recently died and he would be cremated in the open, said Freek, like a Roman Emperor. It was cremation, according to Freek, and not tree inhumation, that formed the usual Abo obsequy. The paper Fruit Bat lubras, representing the chief's many wives, would be burned at the ceremony to provide him with a seraglio in the spirit world. I informed Freek that this was the same thing that happened when important men in pre-Mao China had kicked the bucket: paper-lantern-like models of their servants, lovers, favourite fruits, etc, were incinerated at the same time as the corpse. Freek said that it also explained why the breasts of the "women" I had seen looked so young and pert, and had not hung fat and flat like a Basset Hound's ear – as is the case with the usual Abo titty.

Freek made a great point of saying that he had carefully hosed the plastic chairs underneath the house (which is, of course, on stilts). I was huffily invited to write my diary *there*, but sitting as I was right beneath the television, I was just as cruelly deafened.

FRIDAY 27 NOVEMBER 1987. Amazing the persistence of chook imagery in North Queensland. The Townsville fast-food emporium is *"BIG CHOOK"*, I lunched today on a "Chicken Hero", and there is, of course, the advertisement on TV (which I can hardly escape) that goes: *"I'd rather live the Queensland way, and I'd rather have Big Rooster."* Freek's chooks are a sorry looking crew – attributable, no doubt, to the recent death of his wife – their bottoms, the bits above their tails, bare. Pink and shiny and bloated. It must be terribly distressing for them.

I am interested to note, re-reading this diary, that I used the word "Morphia" when I was describing a dream. Last night, Freek told me that Dr Toots Rasy, his predecessor as Townsville MP, had started life as a pharmacist and had written out a prescription for

"Morphia" (not "morphine") on the night that Marilyn's husband died. (He also died of cancer). Isn't that peculiar?

I spent the morning under the house, composing my diary and a letter to Bonnie and Dew. In the afternoon, Dingee, Freek's daughter, called. I thought it must be one of the "subjects" for his book: this beautiful woman in a green car. She had obviously put on an effort for me. Though what an "effort" means in Townsville deserves to be noted as it demonstrates Girly's heroism: yellow, striped pantaloons; wide-shouldered cotton blouse; Egyptian earrings – big, gold and white enamel panels with hieroglyphs. I was so intrigued that I had Freek take my and Dingee's picture. After tea, fleeing the usual cacophony, I sat under the orange tree and penned my diary. It's all so painful now but later, I will look back on this and wonder why I didn't enjoy myself more. In a way, it really is beautiful here.

SATURDAY 28 NOVEMBER 1987. On the phone this morning to Dewy's office in Canberra, explaining what might be a delay. Then moved with my stuff to Girly's place in a taxi. My room here in "Araluen" is lovely, like a room in Somerset Maugham's *Eastern Tales* – panacotta-coloured stucco with Art Deco moulding; simple, exquisite furniture; a stupendous view of the whole bay and Magnetic Island. It was Nirvana after *"Le Freek, c'est Chic"* (sic) and my gratitude was profuse. Freek has to go back to Canberra for a few days, anyway.

Girly and I went by appointment to Marilyn's place for afternoon tea. A childhood friend of hers, Nanya Veldten, had flown in from Mount Isa in Western Queensland. I suppose to see M. for one last time. She arrived in an old chauffeured Pontiac with her brother Elgar, just as Kade was parking Girly's beautiful maroon 1966 Humber Super Snipe, all polished walnut and silver inside with plump grey leather seats. Elgar – who owns a big Cattle Station between Calen and Mumu – was so called because his family thought he might prove "musical". He had a white moustache like a quivering rabbit's tail, a tiny corn-cob of teeth like an angry poodle. Nanya reminded me of an Albino Billy-Goat. Elgar had been in Britain's Royal Flying Corps during World War One. He stared with horror at the possum shit dripping down the walls: we ate at a table on the verandah overlooking the yellow atrium. The conversation was characterised by a banality that wasn't even stoical. Stoicism would have been too much effort. These people, Australians of the old school, just seem to accept their fate. How different they are from Dewy and Bon! You understand, too, what they mean by "whingeing Poms". Nanya had lost both her grown-up children in tragic accidents, but they talked mostly about food. "I used to take Rum and milk," said Elgar, a millionaire, "but it got too expensive – twenty cents a shot!" He meant it.

Marilyn tried to to fill her glass with water from a pitcher but it spread all over the table. The sandwiches and water and biscuits she attempted tumbled from her twisted mouth. When she spoke – her speech and co-ordination have definitely deteriorated – she sounded like an abnormal child. Once the height of sophistication, but sitting there in her bare, dry, swollen feet, she wasn't without dignity, even now. Tray had to translate what she said for Nanya, who was deaf. Sometimes what Tray had to shout was embarassing. Wasn't one of Nanya's grandsons a truck driver? "Why *of course not* Marilyn! Maybe he drives the truck around the *Station* sometimes!" There was a plague of flies, which added to the delirious atmosphere. Marilyn mentioned that, in the years before World War One – when she, Nanya and Girly had boarded at Frensham together – the last word in luxury was an "oyster cocktail": nobody *then* would have dreamt of putting "raw prawns" in a vase of *"Sauce Marie-Rose"*! (Frensham is a famous Australian girl's school – we passed it on the drive from Sydney to Canberra. The three girls would travel there by ship, Marilyn said, even though each of their estates had its own railway station on the Townsville-Sydney line). Elgar said that he could "never bear" an oyster. He had visited Sydney in a party in 1913, and, for breakfast, they had served him a single raw oyster on a plate. "That was enough for me. Ugh! I've never touched an oyster from that day to this!" Tray's contribution was typically bizarre. He leant over the table and shouted at Nanya: "There was a list of five things the United Nations said you should always do, and the first was: always have a proper breakfast. Also, they've done a survey of rude drivers and they found that most of them never eat a proper breakfast. It produces irritability." He shook his hands repulsively in emphasis. Through the arch made by his body, I could see flies crawling over the sandwiches. Pieces of savoury biscuit, like flakes of old paper, were visible in Marilyn's mouth. "Did you make these biscuits yourself?" Nanya asked facetiously. "They're Arnott's Cheds", said Tray, in cold and bitter earnest.

Later, when Nanya and Elgar had gone, Tray told me they were related to the Lascelles, who are related to the Royal Family. The interest he takes in these things is frankly pathetic. It seemed amazing that an artist, of all people, doesn't realise that precedence, such as he seems to believe his own family possesses (!) has to be earned – even in this epic backwater – not only by those who make the name, but by each succeeding generation. If you sit on your laurels, nobody is going to notice them. Living, as he and Marilyn do, in and off the past, they are oblivious to the squalor all around them. The once glorious house – rotten pulp of a dying seed – overrun by cats, lizards and leering possums.

Tray and Marilyn said how nice it would be if I could stay here "up North" for Christmas.

Girly told me, as Kade was driving us away, that Nanya, the lady who had called, had been a very innocent young thing. "Donald and I are going down to the boat," Russell Drysdale would tell her, "down to the water to pick up a few whores". "Oh, look Tassie" she would say, "don't do that, *don't* do that!"

In the evening, at Araluen, I added to my diary and chatted to Girly about her travels in Europe before the Second World War. Also about the Soukoops, her late husband's people. Another rather sad, blasted line – sons, but they all died in their prime. A maiden lady called Betsan, who still lives in the Hague, is the last surviving family member. "Sometimes," Betsan wrote in her last letter, "I feel so lonely".

a novel

SUNDAY 29 NOVEMBER 1987. This morning as I pondered my predicament in church I became upset. Australia has been surprisingly traumatic – without considering other matters. Some people say: keep your dreams of the place you once saw. Don't go back, don't puncture them by comparing them with reality. But I say, no; go back, deflate your dreams. Dreams can keep you awake.

Not really having explained to Girly the nature of my mission here (though Dew may well have told her), I nevertheless hinted at my hope of aborting it and going home. "I think it's mad, this business of going back to England," said Girly, "I don't see why you can't stay here, until Christmas at least".

"But I hate not having a job to do", I said, "something to occupy me. I'd rather be on the move, on the way to somewhere. Not just sitting here – *rotting like a mango*". The air here is thick with the scent of mangos and the ground with their slushy corpses. "And what about making Marilyn happy?" Girly demanded, "isn't *that* a job? She'd be *so* happy if you could stay". I suddenly realised how lonely Marilyn must be. How little Tray must be a comfort to her, how interesting I must appear! Thinking only of myself, I suddenly saw the force of Girly's view. It will be Marilyn's last Christmas. Of *course* she would like me to stay.

In the evening, I finally got through to Dew. The television news was on. Girly came out of the kitchen and said: "Is that you, Pat? . . . *'Goodness'*, I thought, *'doesn't President Reagan sound like Patrick?!'*" I talked to Girly about her visits to Malaya and Singapore in the 1920s. "I don't wonder that some of those people went a bit mad after the war and wanted the British out", she observed. She and a Baratta friend, Eucla Bloodworth, had stayed with a bachelor planter up in the jungle who had "tried it on". Eucla had stayed there before and, afterwards, the bachelor posted her a pair of knickers that had mysteriously disappeared at his "hacienda". " 'And gosh', we said, 'you ought to see the way he eats *MANGOES*!' . . . As for those people who suck the *STONE*!" Girly tossed her head back and fiercely rubbed her eyes.

311

Asking me about Dew, she told me that his parents used to buy their son "great novels" to read. I laughed, and loudly doubted it. "Everything's a novel, I suppose," said Girly, "as long as it's interesting."

MONDAY 30 NOVEMBER 1987. I walked down the hill to lunch at the Seaview Hotel on the Strand, an Art Deco building in margarine-coloured stucco dating I suppose from the 1930s. I've always wanted to sample it, but it was packed. One had to eat in a garden and order one's meal at a counter. My long range vision seems to be failing and I couldn't read the blackboard menu that lay in darkness on the other side of the counter. I went across the road to a *"BIG CHOOK"* instead.

I walked along the beach until I found a bench in the shade of a Banyan Fig. No sooner had I attacked my prawn cocktail and Hawaiian Chicken than a couple drew up in a Mazda and started to tuck into their own takeaway. Then another car drew up and the vixens inside hailed a group of passing boys, who sauntered over warily. Then a truck arrived. It was like a sketch on one of those bad Saturday night comedies. I washed my hands in the sea and proceeded to the Ozone Café, a Townsville landmark. Partook of a vanilla milkshake – and a pumpkin scone, as iconic a Queensland delicacy as *paté de foie gras* in the Auvergne. As I was walking up East Flinders Street to the Library two youths hailed me with a wolf whistle and a *"Hey you, in the orange!"* (I was wearing a subdued cheesecloth *chemise*). Kept on walking. Wrote and posted Christmas cards to friends in London. Everything shut.

Walked up the hill to Hambeluna to see Tray and try to sort something out. Rather shocked to find the door wide open and the invalid alone, incapable, on the bed. I asked where Tray was. Marilyn said he had decamped "for a snack" at 2.15: it was now half past four. I waited with her, talked, noticing a child's plastic lunch-box on the floor. It seems she's using it as a chamberpot. Marilyn was upset because Tray doesn't seem to be working anymore. He isn't painting much, she thinks – even though he has the whole "Bush House" as his studio. I didn't tell her that Tray says that, at her beck and call, he can't concentrate enough to paint. So was amused to hear her insist that, were he more focused on his art, he would be around more to look after *her*! Rummaged through the tomes on the bookshelves of the Dining Room, where, for convenience, Marilyn's dirtly little nylon-covered camp bed has been installed. Found a pile of Kipling volumes rotting in a sandy grime like birdshit, Balzac's **Cousin Bette**. "They're Shoom's", she said. "Girly's husband?" "Yeah. Girly didn't want anything to remind her of him". "Why on earth not?" I asked. "You'll find out soon enough. Just look through the photos at Girly's place. You'll find more of *my* husband than hers". (Girly told me that Driss, Marilyn's husband, used to own the sugar refinery here). "How did Girly and Shoom meet?" I asked Marilyn. "At the surf" (ie bathing inside the stockade that protects swimmers from fatal jellyfish on the Strand beach; Girly told me, though, that they had met at the amateur races here). "Kipling very popular now," Marilyn observed (I'm used to her distorted wail). "He wasn't before". A literary *aperçu* that surprised me. Marilyn said she was glad I was staying for Christmas. *I* was glad to learn that a nurse is coming in to bathe her.

At about 5.30, Marilyn tried to get up onto her frame to walk to the kitchen. She fell on the threshold. The frame went flying. She lay curled in the doorway like a prehistoric corpse – a mere scrap of a thing, a hatchling dropped from its nest, but I found her heavy to lift. I felt, what with her frailty and heaviness, that I was going to tear off the spindly arms she offered as if they had been the wings of a roast chook. Miraculously, just then, Tray Beautous entered. No longer "in character", Tray presented a most unusual spectacle – like a ferret, two dark furious eyes set in the chunky irregular blond head like raisins in a scone. No longer "beauteous", just odd. With his pale beard and longish pudding bowl hair he looked like a New Malden pacifist. I noticed a bald patch. "Very bright out, isn't it?" he snapped. I noticed from his dropped bag that he had bought a book, a paperback of **My Art, My Life**, the famous autobiography of the Mexican mural painter Rivera – another to add to the

313

hundreds in his filthy meaningless library, which I had been rifling through elsewhere in the house. On Magnetic Island, without distractions like bookshops such as even a dump like Townsville offers, he apparently worked furiously, constantly. No doubt why he had chosen to locate his studio there. Just as, in **Cousin Bette,** the sculptor Steinbock is a genius only as long as he is slave-driven by his gaoler, the eponymous Bette. Clasped instead to the intoxicating bosom of the Montparnasse of the North, Tray seems as idle in Townsville as Steinbock becomes in the arms of Hortense, the indulgent lover to whom he escapes. Diego Rivera; the squalid accident; books; unearned food; the refusal to face reality; the decreative urge to consume, the failure to act, to analyse – how it depressed me. How it reminded me of myself. It's just like Balzac says in **Cousin Bette** (I'd plunged a nail file in the page):

> *"There are men of talent in Paris who spend their lives in talk, and who are satisfied with a sort of drawing-room celebrity. Steinbock, in imitation of these attractive eunuchs, contracted an ever-growing disinclination for work . . . Happiness, in the person of Hortense, had reduced the poet to indolence. A normal state for all artists, for to them idleness is itself an occupation. In it they enjoy the pleasures of the pasha in his seraglio; they toy with ideas, they get drunk at the springs of the intellect."*

They do nothing . . . As he rushed me out the door, all talk of business forsaken, Tray said in that curious staccato way, edges of his mouth tightly sealed, speaking through pursed lips: "Something like this happens once a week". Once a day, more like. "She's still OK, though", he said. "Maybe going downhill a little". I asked him when next we would meet: "We have things to discuss, Tray". "For Christ's sake," he shouted, nodding at Marilyn, "can't you see what my life *is*?! . . . Please don't hassle *me*, I'll hassle *you*!" Feeling rather embittered, I walked back to Girly's place. Took a picture of the city below – the flat gold and olive plains, the far mountains a lovely steamy blue. A small cane toad as swollen as a mango lay at my feet, seething with ants. Girly was shooing a Rock Wallaby out of the kitchen as I came in. "He leaves his pills and piddles all over the floor," she complained. Eyes set like single black olives in its head – no white or pupil – the smooth coarse fur like a labrador's. There is also a mother dingo, apparently, which lives up on Castle Hill. It brings its pups down to the villa's old laundry room. We sat looking out over purple Magnetic, tumblers of Black Label a jar of honey in each fist. A long talk about the Beautous family. How Driss, the worm in the bud, was the cause of it all: the gradual decline of the house, and of the dynasty. Once both were the envy, the acme of North Queensland – if one can imagine such a thing! Now look at them. "Don't fuss". That was Driss's motto, and it became Marilyn's motto too. They were too alike, said Girly, they should never have married, just as Dewy and Bon were too alike and shouldn't have wed. I couldn't see the resemblance. "Oh, you will," Girly replied. According to Girly, Driss and Marilyn were each diffident, phobic, withdrawn. Driss, spoiled by his mother and sisters, was charming but peculiar, an unpleasantly childish man. Imagined himself a great wit but only managed to say things that upset people by their stilted maladroitness. Like Tray, a great reader, but, again like Tray, a black hole, book-wise – he couldn't talk about what he had read, relate what he read to life. "They say Mussolini lapped up every great book you can think of," said Girl. "It might as well have been a plate of spaghetti for all the good it did him. Whereas dear old Uncle Joe [*Stalin*] read Machiavelli and Pareto and didn't *he* put it to good use!" She laughed convulsively. When Girly's brother Hart left school – a boarding school housed at that time in the British Governor's Residence that we saw in Paramatta – he stayed for a while with Marilyn and Driss at Hambeluna. One day Driss went out into the garden and whacked the heads off all Marilyn's Gerberas with a golf club. It was for a "laugh", he said. They were her pride and joy. When they went out in the car – a big old Daimler-Benz – Driss would drive wildly and pretend that he intended to crash. Marilyn was deeply in love with him all her life, but his foibles made her cynical. Why should she bother, married to someone like that? "Don't fuss" indeed! Girly said that she saw an awful lot of Driss in Tray, except that Tray incubated a real talent while Driss was simply an attractive eunuch. "Just like one

315

chook'll lay fertile eggs, and its sister won't. Just look at Dickens' kids – or Shakespeare's even!" "One of them came out here," I said, referring to Dickens' wastrel émigré son. "Don't end up like him," Girly warned me, suddenly in earnest. "What's the point of being a tasty sandwich if you're thrown away to feed the ducks?" I didn't quite comprehend this *Bon Mot* ! I share what I suspect was Driss's hidden power, but also his illness, his painful, paralysing fear of pain. And soon I'll share his affluence. What a curse. "Oh!" said Girly suddenly. "Look, it's a full moon!" A glorious green tropical moon: I couldn't help thinking of Tray!

Magnetic Island swam like a whale in a mystic broth, a net of glittering green fish following in its moonlit swell. Girly offered me some Camembert. "Isn't it rather strong?" I demurred, sniffing the rancid air. "It's *not* strong. It's terribly delicate!" "He's singing away and nobody's listening to him," she said, guillotining an old queen who was serenading us from the TV. The crickets were whirring.

I rang Tray, and Dewy's daughter Kommode Thalanga, she of the Australia Council. She of "the Art Party".

TUESDAY 1 DECEMBER 1987. We were discussing the Tropics and Girly told me how the Chinese Gardener at "Ivanhoe", the "station" on which she grew up, could grow everything under the sun. Peanuts, grenadillas, sausagefruit. She and Marilyn would have a pineapple each as big as a coffee pot, cut off the top and eat the flesh with a long spoon. The homestead was on a lagoon and the Chinaman would dip kerosene cans in the water. He would carry the perforated cans around the property on a yoke, watering the crops like an animal. She and Marilyn would wait for the refinery train early every morning, climb up on the fig trees drooping over the railway line, steal pieces of sugar cane from the wagons. As very small girls their hands got all calloused from riding all day and constantly firing revolvers. When Girly went to dinner at the Drysdale mansion at Giru, and the Japanese servants would offer her the hotplate, the slightly hysterical daughters of the host would shriek *"Oh don't burn her hands, her lovely little hands!"* And she would look at her hands and think they looked like Toadfish.

I lunched on the rissoles that Girly had kindly prepared for me – and I spent the first half of the afternoon in idle misery, trying to relax. I tried to compose letters to distract myself from a soggy, stomachy anxiety but the deafening cicadas and the appalling heat and light as I inscribed hoary Yuletide greetings only added to my feeling of unease. I thought back to the black snowy London of December exactly ten years ago. I had bought a Christmas card for Leah Groundling in Bentall's of Kingston because, rather unexpectedly, she had brought one in for me. Those lovely girls who gave me Christmas cards that year – their merciful features, their striking clothes and voices – charming and middle-class girls. Where are they now? That was the dawn of the "New Wave" era, the last youth renaissance. One could suckle on its placenta. People of our age then, and in an age like that, think that friendship and youth are a permanent feature of life. That friendship and youth will go on forever. That's why they forget to "seize the day". Those casual, gratuitous friendships – *"To Dear Patrick, from Netty"* – they were real, but of the moment: no-one knew how long the moment would last, or even that the moment was finite. What were they going to do, those girls? They were all going to do "art", I think. That's what I should have done!

I vividly remember the card I bought Leah – you could get such strange, out of the way things at Bentall's then. It was a tiny card. A Moghul miniature of a little girl standing in profile against a star-pitted pine-green sky. Carrying what? A ewer? A pot? The dominant colours were cherry red, green and marine blue. I remember the lovely lighted Christmas Card section of the store – I had decided to post and not to hand it to her. I waited for ages for a bus home – it was the last day before I had to fly to Sicily on holiday – a Thursday. There was a thick fog, and snow. The bus fare home was 21 New Pence. I think we waited for two and a half hours. The lady behind me told a little boy in the queue she was going to write to London Transport. I remember how dark it was. It had been a wonderful Autumn: I was getting to grips with people for the first time in a relaxed and syncopated manner. That night, though, as I was lying in bed, I heard a tapping noise on the wallpaper above my head. In that split second I could have decided to do the reasonable thing – to turn over and ignore it – probably air in the paper or a bird trapped in the chimney. Instead, "to be on the safe side", I surrendered to the terror that had crept over me. I fled the room, refusing to sleep there ever again. I made my first surrender to "reasonable" unreason, like Proust with the goodnight kiss. I was beginning to live by internal rather than external standards. Autumn had promised things, but the long night had descended.

I came down to dine. Girly was reading from Tray's book on home-made ice-cream. "Breakfast in a glass," she said dreamily, "healthy drinks, healthy drinks!"

WEDNESDAY 2 DECEMBER 1987. At breakfast, Girly told me that she remembered very vividly the outbreak of the First World War. Her family were holidaying in New Zealand at the time, in Rotorua. Her father stayed behind while "Mother" took them on a tour of the mountains, Girly and several friends and siblings – Marilyn too – shoe-horned into a huge old Packard car: "We were like vixens in a sack!" "Mother" saved on petrol by only using the engine during the ascent of each summit. When she reached the top she would just turn off the ignition and down they would swoop shrieking into the fathomless valley below. They stayed long enough to see the first wounded Maoris come back from the front. She remembered their eerie, blissful songs. They would stick out their tongues in the acclaimed way and tell the children secret places in the lakes and inlets where they were sure to find trout.

I took my cup of China tea out to admire the bay from under the parasol in the front garden. I found Kade already sitting there, at the F.Scott Fitzgerald white iron table. He had been mowing, his torso like a dripping orange iced lolly: he was sipping a bottle of Bundaberg

Root Beer. I asked him about the sort of "modelling" he had done for Tray. He told me that his last assignment had been in one of the "black tents", of all things! *("Ah,"* thinks I, *"now I'll get to the bottom of this!")*

Kade said that Tray told him that the cubical black tent was meant to represent the temple of Apollo in Delphi in ancient Greece. Apparently, Tray had shown Kade a picture of the ruins of this temple from **NEWSWEEK**. (I myself have visited it). Like the rest of ruined Delphi, the temple sits under a cliff on a ledge of rock high up in the mountains near the modern city of Lamia. Delphi's setting at the foot of a curtain of raw pink sandstone looks, in fact, identical to the area under the summit of Castle Hill here in Townsville where – according to Kade – Tray installed his own black "temple". In ancient times, of course, the Delphi ruin was the site of the most famous oracle in the Greco-Roman world. Here the god Apollo would answer questions about the future that were put by pilgrims who flocked to Delphi from every corner of the pagan Mediterranean. He spoke through his prophet, a priestess who would scream riddle-like answers while sitting in a copper basin set up on a tripod in the Holy of Holies. In classical art, Apollo is usually represented as a figure of light, all white and gold with a halo and wings like the Archangel Michael. The myths of Greece tell us that, before building the Delphi temple, Apollo killed a giant python that lived in a cave on the site, dramatising the victory of reason over the intuitive forces of nature and absorbing its satanic power into his own. Hence his name in ancient Greece, "Pythian Apollo". Hence the name of his temple prophet, "the Pythoness".

To prepare him for his part in this "installation", Tray had made Kade dress up as Apollo, but a good ole' Aussie Apollo. It would appear Tray had forced Kade, in fact, to dress like a giant Fruit Bat in a specially made black panto outfit. (Australian Fruit Bats are also known as "Flying Foxes" because they have tiny vulpine faces like ferrets. They have serrated ant-egg teeth and are covered all over in black, cat-like fur. They have shiny black eyes like elderberries, black ears like a hamster's ears and leather wings like the black, webbed feet of

319

a swan. They are disgustingly dirty creatures – if extremely sociable. They shriek like pigs and smell appalling).

Up on the hill, said Kade, Tray would guard the tent in a sentry-box or "booth", taking the money off the good burghers of Queensland who wanted "Apollo" (or *"Othello"* as Tray called *"the Bat Kade"*) to tell their future. This "payment booth" was comprised of Tray standing outside the tent dressed in a full-length burka with a black Ned-Kelly-can helmet on his head. The punters would each push two envelopes through the eye visor of the helmet, as if through the mouth of a postbox. One contained cash, the other the question pertaining to the future. In return, Tray would hand each of the *"paying pervs"* an opera glass – which is like a little telescope – and they would go up to the black cube and stick the "monocular" through one of the holes in its wall . . . What a treat would greet their eyes! Inside, "Apollo" would be masturbating with one furry hand – his catsuit (or "bat suit") strategically ajar – the great PVC wings flapping and clattering on his back. And with the other hand he would be turning a live baby crocodile tied to a spigot over a basin of steaming charcoal on an indoor tripod barbeque. This sort of cheap Aussie barbie – where a spit and a roasting tray perch on a bowl of burning coal – rests on three iron legs like a tripod or easel. The envelopes containing the questions for the "Pythoness" – the little female croc – would be burned in the bowl and the "priestess" would, said Kade, scream out her replies, her mouth foaming whitely in agony like his own ecstatic cock. On the floor inside the black tent a tape recorder would sit immortalising the animal's cries. Then the tape was played backwards. The idiotic pervs would always say that they could discern intelligible words that answered their questions. After all, they would hardly have parted with their cash in the first place had they not been the sort of moron who can always find meaning in a pikey's crystal ball or see the face of Christ in a scone. The opera glasses had to be handed out, said Kade, so that the "pilgrims" could see through the smoke, which would pour out of the holes "like them holes in a burnin' paper hornet's nest."

Kade said that, because of the tape deck, Tray *had indeed* called this "work of art" *"Black Box Recorder"*, but he also sometimes referred to his "installation" as *"An Angel at My Table"* (because of the Black Angel Apollo and the roast croc, an exquisite Queensland delicacy). In the beginning, though, thanks to the smoke from the tripod barbeque, Tray had provisionally entitled his "multi-media experience" *"Ghost in the Machine"*.

All the above info was related in Kade's limited vocabulary and in his usual fantastically slow, subnormal Queensland accent, an accent so laconic you sometimes wonder whether a heavy irony is not intended. But if Kade was pulling my leg, how could a redneck cretin like him have invented the scenario?

This afternoon, I took a long nap. I've decided that, in this heat, it's not worth forcing oneself to do *anything*. Over dinner, Girly and I talked about the care Marilyn was – or was not – receiving at Hambeluna. This led us on to Freek's late wife, Yenda Bloomers-Vane, one of Queensland's first female oncologists. I asked whether she had borne Freek children other than Ding. Then – with unbelievable effrontery, given that Girly herself appears childless – *why* she might not have. "Did she have an abnormality?" I asked. "Well," Girly replied laconically, ". . . she *was* a woman!"

THURSDAY 3 DECEMBER 1987. I do so hate writing this diary. The heat makes it difficult to compose myself, and to compose sentences. I suppose tension is working on me too. Progress on my Tray Beautous project hardly appears remarkable. Least of all to Dew. I dreamed this morning that *my* family had visited New Zealand. And then, suddenly, we were climbing a tropical wooded mountain in a train. We were on our way to some resort, but it was a Soviet resort. A sort of grotesque, Soviet Funfair. Lots of metal, and emblematic plaques – a generally 50s atmosphere. We alighted in a room at the top of a mountain. There were Soviet women and children standing around with long glasses in their hands, bulges at the tops of the glasses. There were sets of *"The World's Greatest Books"* for sale. Crudely printed Soviet editions. Each volume was about six inches thick and a yard square. Each page bore the legend *"AIRMAIL PAPER"*. Nightcliffe Popkiss introduced himself as general factotum to my brother, Candide Mynts, and Frances, Candide's ex-wife, was there as well. Candide bought Francesca one of the sets of "classic books". "I'd far rather have Daddy well and working again", said Francesca (her father actually committed suicide two years ago). "But Fran," I asked her, "do you really *like* these books?" The volumes included a few Ian Flemings and an autobiography of Rupert Murdoch. I woke at 7 AM.

I was turning yesterday's development over when Freek – who has just flown back in from Canberra and was taking me to lunch – drew up in the Lancia. He had a coppery ephebe called Dirk in tow about whom he is writing a new book. Dirk used to be in a cult where you had to sleep with your mother. (He looked as if he would have preferred sleeping with his father). When I got to the door Dirk was familiarly hosing the lower garden and Girly was mounting the steps – she thought I might be asleep. I was struck by the pathos of her Shooting Stick lying on the ground: it spoke of the violence, the vulgarity of the pollie's invasion. Freek drove us to some Chinese place and we ate a takeaway meal in Cummins Street.

Freek and Dirk were all aflutter about a meeting they apparently had with Dew in Canberra. They want me to get Tray to do a painting of Dirk *"making the beast with two backs"* with his dear old Mum. Dirk's Pa, Kenny, who in real life is something fantastically respectable, the Head of Revlon Australia or something, is behind this request. Kenny is the "prophet" of Dirk's old "religion", you see, and he'll be having a good old perv if ever I get to arrange the production of this masterpiece, which Dirk described without irony as a "tribute to Sir James Frazer's book *Adonis, Attis, Osiris*"! Kenny, apparently, has had a "revelation" from an angel called "Whyalla" (sigh) and it seems that the kid that Tray would paint being conceived is "the Anti-Piste", from *"la Piste"*, which in French means "the Track". When it's born, Whyalla says the cult are going to have to call the kid "Off Piste". ("What are you going to call the child you conceive with Freek?" I asked Dirk). Their religion has to have the "Isis and Horus" painting to control "the Anti-Piste", you see: it is all so very sensible. Once he's been born into the world, the Piste (with two backs) can be controlled by this picture because it will apparently imprison the Piste's "primal essence". It's an icon they'll be able to manipulate and ask favours of, like Aladdin's Lamp or that ring in Tolkien's stupid novel. Dirk said that his Ma and Pa are shortly to arrive in North Queensland by sea: I told him I couldn't wait. Dirk and Freek asked me what they should call the "icon", should it ever be painted, and I suggested, after that classic by William Frederick Yeames, *"When Did You Last See Your Father?"*

After lunch, we all went for a slow stroll to the chemist's shop which the old Townsville MP, Doctor "Toots" Rasy, still runs in the Charters Towers Road. I also met Treacle Witts, Doctor Feelgood's "silent partner", who originally put up the money for his political campaigns and his string of shops. I was taken aback when I realised that these rough old plebeian-mannered old men might be pansies too. The former MP regarded me intensely from the cubby hole where they make up the prescriptions. "The silent partner" looked like one of the caricature self-portraits Edward Lear used to draw – spindly legs, a spherical torso. His eyes were as obsequious as a Merino Ram's; deep they lay in bushy cavities. He was bald. Tall white hairs sprouted from his chest, wide and coarse like Winter grass.

We returned to the house and Freek and Dirk settled down in front of the deafening TV. I had hoped to make my escape after the end of a stupid American comedy but **Anne of Green Gables** came on and I decided to stay till the end of it, since they were obviously engrossed, and, even had I just risen and called a cab, I would have disturbed them. O, the wickedness, the brutality of the inane! It went on for two fucking hours! I got back to Girly's to find that "Emporio PM" had phoned in my absence. I was furious.

FRIDAY 4 DECEMBER 1987. I woke up at about 3 AM with a terrible pain in my stomach – that stupid bloody Chinese dinner! I hoped and prayed I wouldn't want to heave, which is usually the next stage. Fortunately, I became more and more tired. I put out the light and turned on my side. The pain diminished and I fell asleep. Woke again at 5, then at 6.30, and then, after another little dream, at 8 AM.

I decided to call on Tray. I really need to force the issue now. I must: time is running out. I bought three prawn cocktails from *"BIG CHOOK "*and two meat pies, one for me and one for Tray. I entered "Hambeluna" via the back gate. It was all rather sinister. The cicadas were hissing, cats and lizards darted across my path. I struggled through the Bougainvillea and Cactus Fern. Nobody answered the door. Suddenly there was a crash and I saw what I thought was an "Aubergine" in yellow – a meths bottle glinting in his hand – flutter through a screen of Wattle. I shouted "Hey!" and ran after him – probably some tribesman from the park sleeping off a turps and *"ROOSTER"* orgy. But he ran through a hole in the trellis into the massive black cave beneath the house and I didn't want to follow him *there*. Back at "Araluen", Girly, glued to the cricket, eagerly accepted my offer of Tray's pie.

SATURDAY 5 DECEMBER 1987. Moist, broiling day. The day was dusty with moisture – sparkling dust. Townsville was grey and olive green, the sky an implacable Oxford blue between the watercolour grey of storm clouds all blotted and scalloped and veined. I watched a storm over Magnetic Island from my room – the green and pink lightning like tentacles from a jellyfish on a black sky.

When it stopped raining I tried to drop mangoes at Hambeluna for Marilyn. There was the smell of some dead animal by the door. I knocked. There was no reply, so I hid them beneath the short flight of wooden steps. Just then, just like yesterday, there was a tinkling flurry in the bushes and I ran towards it. Someone – or some *thing* – was definitely there. Off the path leading from the gate to the front door is another track that I've never taken. It leads into the densest part of the Hambeluna jungle, its entrance a cave in a green cliff, and there was movement beyond the black arch, a crockery-like crash of branches and leaves. I followed it, the darkness suddenly a cosy mineshaft with beams and vines. The track was strangely soft, thickly carpeted with tiny leaves like used tea. There was that smell of overripe tamarinds that is the smell of every jungle in the world, a smell like furniture polish. The path zig-zagged so that all I could see in front of me was a waterfall of leaves constantly jerked to one side like a bullfighter's cape. I couldn't be sure if the sound of crashing steps was not my own. Finally, sweating and shivery, I came out in a clearing. The birds and cicadas kept up a Phil Spector-like "wall of sound". Light poured down like dry ice.

In the middle of the clearing was a circular pond, its rim a ring of concrete, with a circular island in the middle of it. The island was also a concrete cake-tin, one that emerged from the pond and was filled to the top with earth. The water was a milky green like Pernod, and what looked like an upended dugout canoe formed a bridge between the bank and the island, which was covered in the same brown mash as the path and clearing. Rising from the island in a column of gold air from the forest ceiling was one of Tray Beautous's infamous black cube tents. It was as big as a caravan and, in the strong light and up close, it was almost a light pistachio-grey in colour. Holes flecked its haunches like the feathery stubs in the flesh of a plucked chook, and it was only these which appeared truly black. They reminded me of the holes peppering the face of the dirty classical ruins in modern Rome – the holes where the mediaeval pillagers dug out the iron wall clamps. "Good!" I thought, forgetting my fear, "now I'll finally find out what this is all about!" I skipped across the dugout, which seemed to undulate underfoot like a caterpillar, and crept up to the tent's wall. It was made of hessian like black Levi jeans. When I adjusted my right eye to a hole in the canvas wall, I found my left eye staring through a hole as well, as if the fabric were a mask.

At first the interior looked like one of those photos taken from space of the continent of Europe at night, with powdery pulsing ribbons and beads of light where the cities or, in this case, the holes on the far side of the tent were. But our eyes grow accustomed to the dark, just as they grow accustomed to the past. The beads of light in the tent started to weave waxy nests like candles. Faces formed around the bristling lights, bodies bubbled up like glittering fountains, and it became apparent that the three of the internal walls of the tent I could see were covered in the same sort of continuous nude group portrait as had graced Beverley Brownbill's dunny at "Capricornia". The paint was implied in the same sinewy impasto, so it was probably the same artist as well. As at "Capricornia", an inter-racial orgy scene was described, but in this one Aboriginal women with rows of tits like black teeth were fucking and sucking white men. Many of the retching penises, mouths and vulvas were blanked out with the kind of strategically placed white disk you see in prurient newspaper photos of knickerless starlets climbing out of limousines. On each white disk was printed a black letter and, taken together, these black capitals spelled out the legend: "*RAPE OF THE SABINE WOMEN*". Didn't Peter Paul Rubens do a painting with that title? (The scene from Roman history that Rubens – early in the Seventeenth Century – was depicting was the episode in which the ancient Romans invade the land of the Sabines to rape and steal the women, because there are none in their own country). As the features of the painted rapists became clear, I was shocked to recognise the faces of the Broncos whose stuffed and lacquered corpses I had seen at the Viceregal Mansion in Canberra, and, in their midst, the face and body of the creature that had shared my bed there, the crispy brute who looked like Wanko! The black women, meanwhile, were the ones whose faces I had seen hanging upside down from the Ghost Gum in the mangrove swamp. I now realised that the holes in the walls through which the sun was streaming, lighting up all within, had been cut where the orgiasts' eyes should have been. Inside the tent, in the middle of the bare earth floor, sat a dark conical stone (?) like a giant onion-shaped dog turd.

Suddenly the "eyes" of the "Wanko" figure twinkled and went out. Instead of two stars there were two furtive jittering bees in the sockets like polished berries. Somebody on the other side of the tent was staring at me through "Wanko's" eyes! I screamed like a pig and fled, jumping onto the stony, peat-like surface of the dugout. It reared wildly like a stallion, sent me hurtling through the air. Luckily the mulch with which the clearing was carpeted broke my fall, but when I picked myself up I saw a giant crocodile – whose back I had taken for a canoe – lunge at me from the pond, hissing like a cat. It was as big as a motorbike, its mouth splayed open like a pelican's, and like a pelican's the mouth was a revolting egg-yolk orange, the teeth all of different shapes and embedded higgledy-piggledy like the broken glass that they stick on walls. I screamed and screamed and all in vain as the birds and cicadas were making a noise that would have made the soundtrack of *The Texas Chainsaw Massacre* seem like a Bach *motet*. I turned tail and ran for my life. Down the jungle track I ran and up the path to the gate.

SUNDAY 6 DECEMBER 1987. Communion this morning at St James's, the Episcopalian (ie Anglican) Cathedral. All the fans were going in the crematorium-like brick nave. The thunder thudded away. One of the Readers, referring to the suicide-bomb massacre of Idroolee mothers and infants that the assassination of the Sunny Pine guerilla has occasioned, prayed for "neither condemnation nor condoning." She was a small, striking, hideous woman – a head like a cauliflower in cheese sauce. She gave God thanks for the new Cathedral photocopier and then, in the same breath and context, she gave Him thanks for Jesus Christ. I prayed with assiduity about the disturbing events of the last 24 hours.

When I returned to Hambeluna to give Marilyn the mangoes I'd hidden by the front doorstep (I steered well clear of the jungle), I found her unable to move in or off the bed. I tried to pull her up on her pillows and again, I rather feared I might tear her apart. Tray finally appeared and, as it was impossible to get him to discuss *anything*, I just asked if I might borrow a few books. I chose *The Ancien Régime in Europe* and a biography of Prokofiev, among others. Back at Araluen, I lunched on exquisite lamb cutlets. "Have you ever tasted Snow Peas?", Girly asked, "I eat them all before I can cook them! They're so sweet! Sweeter than sugar! I had to wait ages before I had a nice pea." Girly poured me some tea. "It looks horribly weak," she said. "I'm sure it's delicious," I replied. Girly has such wonderful taste. There were black olives in the base of a white scallop shell, white and blue Japanese porcelain bowls, one heaped with green grapes, the other with purple cherries. I returned to my room and did a little more writing. I noticed the encomium on a jar of mosquito-repelling unguent above my bed: *"Fragrant, non-greasy protection"*.

MONDAY 7 DECEMBER 1987. Girly was complaining this morning about a neighbour who evades the Townsville restrictions on watering one's garden. This you may only do at certain times early every morning and evening. He contributes to follies dear to the hearts of the local politicians – "FOOTIE WORLD", for instance – and so is sure of escaping justice. "Old greybeard!" she growled, of the philanthropist, then: "I talk about everyone being old – I forget, half the time, I'm older than they are!" I told her how much I'd love to visit Karumba, on the Gulf of Carpentaria – it looks so remote on the map, so concrete. This led to a discussion of her gardener, Kade – he of the glistening coca-cola bottle torso who is never to be seen without a pair of 1970s dark glasses. Apparently he has a band and he and his band have played Karumba. He lives in a "humpy" up on Castle Hill and grows cumquats. Then Girly got herself into a lather about the remarkable number of tourists in the Gulf who have recently been eaten by crocodiles. Reading from the paper, she described the demise of one, a Danish girl who went swimming in a Karumba tide pool after a party. "And the old croc was waiting there and he said: *'Here's my dinner – a nice big fat one!'* " She laughed uproariously.

Suddenly, there was a rap on the shutters. "It's Tray Beautous here!"

Tray was panting. He had obviously jogged all the way. He said that Marilyn was immobile, unintelligible. He could no longer cope. He thought Marilyn should go into hospital. When he isn't "on", Tray's conversation is repetitive and trivial. He talked in a famished, obsessive way about the weather, glad to have got the ordeal over, to have done his duty. His reaction to the event was that of a child. Misfortune hurts: at the same time, the drama – the glamour – carries you above the pain. What happens to the other person makes you, the child, a victim: it makes you the one they will have to tend to. Adults (and Tray is an adult) should realise that they are going to have to face the world alone. For a child, tragedy is like tragedy on the stage, a personal catharsis but unreal – your own precious suicide performed by others.

Tray went over and over the fiasco of her breakfast and *toilette*, reliving the drama, the glamour. Girly went and rang a Doctor Redslob and asked him to get Marilyn into the "*Mater Misericordiae*" Hospital – one of Townsville's very few towerblocks, built in the Fifties between Araluen and the Strand: it's right next to Saint Joseph's Convent, quite near the Canteloup-orange beach. Why hadn't Tray done all this, I wonder? Why had he run all the way over to Girly's and laid the problem at *her* feet? Why, when he finally made his way back to Hambeluna, did he walk all the way down to the North Ward Taxi Rank (almost as far as it is to Marilyn's place) and get a *cab* home, instead of walking there? As we approached Hambeluna thirty minutes later (we too had rung for a cab – Kade being away), we saw Tray's chimp-like form crawl from the waiting car and amble across the carriageway. His broad chest was round-shouldered with fear, his arms were straight at his sides, fingers curled tensely upward towards the wrist, eyes not so much scanning the road as timidly downcast.

Inside the house, Tray tried to explain what he called his "project for Marilyn". When Tray talks, repetitively, he makes these terse, angular gestures with his hands, first to the left, then to the right. As he makes his point his downcast eyes flash open and upwards revealing a green yolk of pupil isolated in white lunacy, like the eye of a doll. He gives a nervous little laugh and his downturned mouth discloses its camel-like teeth. His head jiggers from side to side like a car toy. Marilyn became agitated on her rancid sheets and started to wail. Girly slapped her thigh. In her dreamy, distracted voice she said: *"Eowoo! Something's biting meah!"* Dr Redslob, who looked like Fidel Castro, came and told us that Marilyn was "very poorly" and hadn't long to live. He wrote a letter for the hospital and asked Tray to phone a private ambulance. Then Redslob left. Incredibly, Tray couldn't find the number, which he must frequently have had recourse to. He rang the emergency line instead! When the ambulance man arrived he sat on the bed with Marilyn and put her arm across his shoulder. "Isn't anyone going to help me?" he snarled. He looked at us parasites with contempt. I rushed forward, as Tray seemed to have no intention of assisting, and placed her other arm around my neck. We carried her out of Hambeluna for the very last time. (She has lived there for 65 years). Outside, we laid her on the trolley stretcher and pushed her up the jungle path. Tray climbed into the ambulance, too, which shuddered and roared off trailing the cawl of a ludicrous wise-after-the-event siren.

Back at Araluen, Girly prepared herself a stiff whisky. It had all been pretty shocking.

TUESDAY 8 DECEMBER 1987. Late in the morning, I arranged to go with Tray to the hospital. I feel I will now be able to draw him close. Now that I'll have him to myself, I shall get what I want. Marilyn looked very pale, but so much more peaceful than of late. She recognised Tray and tried to speak. She said one intelligible thing – I wish I could remember what it was – and drifted off to sleep. Tray asked a nurse – one of the Australian variety, who look like wheedling hookers – how long his grandmother might live. "I DON'T KNOW. I'll have to get someone to tell me who DOES, WON'T I?" she said. After a long time, a Polish doctor appeared, a small, fat squishy woman who told Tray no-one could predict Marilyn's death – it could be tomorrow, it could be next month. She had intense, self-important eyes, like Lotte Lenya in *From Russia With Love*. Long fat lips of the self-styled "professional" type. I wanted to stay – if only to talk to Tray on his own – but he said he would appreciate some "quality time" with Marilyn, which I found a little arch as he hasn't exactly gone out of his way to keep her company before.

I walked over Melton Hill into town. The heat in Townsville in the middle of the afternoon – the worst time of the day – is of an immobile, atrocious type one associates with Classical Antiquity or the paintings of Claude Lorrain. I bought stamps, a hat (an antidote to skin cancer) and a "cooked chook" at *BIG ROOSTER*. Back at Araluen, Girly was kind enough to prepare me some gravy and vegetables. I wanted to tell her about a wonderful meal of wild duck and honey I had once enjoyed at "The Spread Eagle" in Midhurst, West Sussex; I began to describe Petworth, a lovely Sussex town nearby and she said: "Oh, I've been there!" It made me so homesick as she described the places she and her husband Shoom Soukoop drove through when they visited England late in the 1940s – Midhurst, Horsham – Surbiton even (whence they caught the train to Epsom for the Derby)! A friend of Girly's from Bambaroo, North Queensland, was living at the time in Surbiton. (The famous Australian novelist Christina Stead also once set up home there). Shoom and Girly would stay with Russell Drysdale's spinster aunt in Maidstone, Kent. Miss Drysdale had lived in Russia before the Revolution and she rented out her London flat to an Englishwoman who had also lived in pre-Bolshevik Moscow. The flat was beautifully furnished with Russian quilts and icons. This lady owned a clothes shop in Duke Street, St James's, and would have woollens embroidered, *à la Russe*, with the sort of coloured beads beloved of Dewy and Bon. She described her workers as "maggots". "*Put the maggots over there*", she would cry. Queen Mary once visited the shop and the *soi-disante* Muscovite's fortune was made.

WEDNESDAY 9 DECEMBER 1987. Got a taxi to a Chinese shop on Akuna Street in Mundingburra, a suburb in the west of Townsville, and purchased some provisions. There was a group of middle-aged to elderly people blocking the pavement in front of me, dumpy, in formless clothes. They were holding hands. I thought at first they must be a party of retards. Each woman reminded me of *"The Drover's Wife"*, that painting by Russell Drysdale. They were just an ordinary Australian family, their faces vacant but powerful.

Back at Araluen, I found Girly fearful lest I had succumbed under the blows of "the darkies". I told her about Marilyn, whom I visited with Tray this morning, that she had seemed awake, but that she didn't recognise us. Her one good eye, the eye once full of anxiety, of command, had seemed utterly vacant. Girly thought she might in fact have been lucid, and attempting to convey something. "I used to think it was awful when they put people in, oh, mental homes I suppose there were at the time, asylums, and they weren't *sillih* at all. And all they wanted to say was: 'Now, look, I'm not as *sillih* as you think I am!' "

THURSDAY 10 DECEMBER 1987. I had a series of unpleasant dreams this morning. I dreamt that my Hindu London friend Sheila (Thapar) invited me to India. Her brother-in-law was in the Indian Army. "Pippy" was his name. She had bought the lower half of a door "wholesale" from some terribly cheap local tradesman. Sheila would show off the door to her friends but Pippy had somehow botched the business of installing it. I woke at about One AM. Then I dreamt I was trapped in Canberra with Dewy and Bon. I dreamt I was Russell Drysdale's grandson. I dreamt that Marilyn was his second wife. When Marilyn died, a collection was taken up for me at St Martin's School of Art in the Charing Cross Road. I was trapped in Canberra and I badly needed to escape. I remember, though, looking at the gold coins in the hat – which only came to the equivalent of some four Australian dollars – and thinking: "Why, *I* don't need that: thanks to Dewy, I will soon have, if I play my cards right, a quite enormous heap of 'shrapnel'!"

I really must get Tray to submit to Dew's plan. I must.

FRIDAY 11 DECEMBER 1987. This morning a singular breakfast: cheesecake and lychee nuts. One peels a lychee like a boiled egg. The spermy flesh resembles the boiled blue-white of one of those gulls' eggs at Fortnum's, and the brittle brown rind its shell – the perfume of freesias when you burst the flesh in your teeth! I had to put the frozen bought cheesecake out in the sun to thaw it out. It sat on top of the wall overlooking the bay. Framed by the shutters and the acrylic blue sea, the slice of incongruous yellow cake looked like one of those surreal studies of simple household objects that René Magritte used to paint. Girly was reading from *THE TOWNSVILLE BULLETIN:*

> *"The English language is being murdered on the streets of Paris and nobody is saying a word."*

According to *"the Bully"*, a horse-drawn Townsville bus from the early 1900s has been discovered. Girly said she remembers catching horse-drawn buses and cabs to the railway station here in the years before the First World War. At that time, enormous crocodiles would bask under the eaves of the railway bridge or on the banks of the Ross Creek, right in the middle of town.

Spent the morning on the phone to Dew relating the extent of my success, or lack thereof, and lunched on a *BIG CHOOK* prawn cocktail, a pepper sandwich, and the last of the cheesecake. To justify this formidable repast, I observed: "That's why I do so much walking." "Why?" Girly demanded, "so you can eat so much?" Girly was nuzzling a misty glass of Johnny Walker even though it had only just struck noon. "When you feel like things, it's gorgeous to have them," she averred, spooning the bloody, brain-like prawns down with a two-pronged silver fork. Marilyn, Girly affirmed, hadn't looked very well that morning: she and Kade had just returned from the hospital in the Humber Super Snipe. "But, oh! Those lovely pale, pale, pale blue sheets!" And Tray, she said, had been waiting by Girly's car, a book and ridiculous iced lolly trembling in his hand, expecting a lift home. Something he never usually wanted. He had seemed frightened. " . . . I hear that you've been in his

Black Books as well," Girly said archly. What was *that* supposed to mean? Are "the Black Books" yet another name for his stupid tents?

We discussed death and funerals. Her own husband, Shoom, hadn't wanted his ashes buried under an Ilex Tree: *" 'Think of the fucking cyclones!' "* They put him under a crawling patch of wild cucumber instead.

Wasn't it "shocking", Girly cried, reading aloud from the *"Bully"*, about the tourists who had been forced to jump off the catamaran that had caught fire yesterday on its way to the reef? "Think of the old girls like me with their handbags and everything! I don't know what I'd have done. I'm terrible at things like that. I used to dream of the *Titanic* as a girl. That big black thing like a Black Swan's behind sticking up in the air. They would have had to push me, I suppose".

She related how she had nearly drowned in the Condimine River as a teenager. A friend called "Kaiser" Barnes had saved her life. She had plunged in and lunged and flailed about until she reached the middle: then she had sunk like a stone. "Well, you don't like to admit that you can't swim, do you?" She saw a white arm – a fish? – thrashing about in front of her, and grabbed it. "Kaiser Barnes was always a very strong swimmer!"

SATURDAY 12 DECEMBER 1987. Infinite confused debate between Girly and Tray at Araluen over funeral arrangements. Again: why? What has it got to do with Girl? I couldn't get Tray to myself. I wrote Christmas cards to friends in London all morning, and posted them, with a note I had written Tia, on my walk to the Mater Misericordiae to meet up again with Tray. Marilyn was rather less well than yesterday; very pale, and impossible to understand. But, the pity is, she was lucid, and was trying to ask for things. She kept pointing at a pillow. A nurse came in and asked what her favourite drink was. Marilyn is eating, but in danger of dehydration, because they cannot get her to drink. Tray wasn't able to enlighten the girl, and Marilyn, though she tried to inform us, could only sigh. Tray asked the nurse if she were uncomfortable. The nurse said they were no longer administering morphine, as she isn't in pain. (But how would they know?) Marilyn managed to wave good-bye as we left. On the way back, having been rebuffed again by Tray, I purchased a takeaway prawn cocktail for Girly at *BIG CHOOK*. A note awaited me at Araluen.

" *PATRICK*

> *Would you ring -*
> > *Mr Bloomers?*
>
> *Cynthia Brownbill has died in*
> *Canberra "*

I rang Freek. Apparently, poor Cynthia passed away early this morning. Dew had wanted *Freek* to tell me. His conscience is troubling him, I suppose. Freek said he would drop by with my mail at 1.45 PM, which rather spoiled my enjoyment of lunch – a delicious exigent steak. Freek and I talked for a while, sitting under the pergola by the dwarf orange trees. He said that Dewy thinks there's no point in my going to Cyn's funeral as I have "more important things" to do. I rang Tray. He seemed upset about Cynthia, much more than he is over Marilyn. He actually refused to receive me at Hambeluna! He even seemed to cry. Rather shocked me by telling me to "fuck off"!

I tried to work on my diary but the heat confused and paralysed me. Girly returned from the hospital to report a marked decline in poor old M. Girly was full of the fact that one of the nurses was an Allingham – one the "families" up here. "You know, Joss Allingham? He drank. He used to say there's nothing for it in Summer but to lie down in the creek and let the water run right through you. What did he say? Flat like a goanna. And Bunty. You must have heard of Bunty Allingham? No, perhaps not. And Moya, his sister? She married Mick.

Mad Mick, mad as a Coon Dog. Her mother was an uppy person, Moya's, a *Melbourne* sort of person!"

Worked some more on my diary. Girly called me down for tea, Gruyère cheese from "*DAVID JONES*", water biscuits, prawn cocktails, and an ice cream Girly had kindly bought for me at Short's. She scrutinised with curiosity the steering wheel cover Bon has sent her up for Christmas (Freek brought it). "This would go twice around my steering wheel – I think it's for a tractor or something!" She talked about Freek's late wife: she had been amazed to find her so attractive (I was equally surprised). She had expected her to be "built like a brick shit-house: most of these lady doctors are".

"You know when Cynthia Brownbill went mad?" Girly asked of the other *infanta defunta*. "When she travelled back home to England". A family friend had promised Cynthia £1,000 in his will. (Australia had pounds, shillings and farthings until 1965). "Well," Cynthia had said, "I don't think *that's* very fair. I'd rather have my money *now*!" She used it to go back "home" and to visit France and Tangier in 1937. She met, and courted, Drysdale, who was studying then in Paris, but he remained faithful to "that Stevens woman". Cynthia, said Girl, returned to her grazier uncle's estate at Yelarbon with a charlatan she had picked up on the boat. He began charging his gambling debts to her family. It was then that she married Piers Brownbill, from the nearby "Mutton Hole" place. One shouldn't be too hard on Piers (also now dead) Girly insisted – Cynthia had always been a handful. "Full as a goog!" She would seize the keys and throw them out of the car when Piers was driving. Crashed innumerable cars herself.

We talked about Drysdale, by whom I am naturally fascinated. Girly used to visit his London studio in Chelsea in the 1950s when he was painting the Outback "Abo" series from memory. "I'm sorry, Tassie, I just don't understand that one", she would tell him. "But what about the *colours*?" he would say. He would sit with his feet up on the empty canvas looking at it for hours before he would paint anything. Girly could have picked up his work dirt cheap – she always had an invitation to his Sydney and London shows, even the *Vernissage* in New York, but Shoom, her husband, wasn't keen on it. "I don't think my other paintngs would like them!" he would say. "What other paintings?" I asked, not having seen any. She changed the subject.

Drysdale came up to Townsville quite a lot – he and Donald Friend used to paint in the North – and he did quite a few drawings of "Araluen", but his wife, "the Stevens woman", tore them all up. She would destroy everything she didn't think "worthy" of him before he could sign it. "Was jealous of, more like!"

I went to bed full of sadness. How I would have *loved* to be a painter!

SUNDAY 13 DECEMBER 1987. Advent service in the Cathedral. Tray rang to apologise for his behaviour. We have agreed to meet tomorrow morning.

MONDAY 14 DECEMBER 1987. Wrote a few Christmas cards. On the way to the hospital, Tray and I breakfasted by arrangement under a Yum-Yum Tree in the Botanic Gardens – a meat pie and a bottle of Bundaberg Sarsaparilla – but I couldn't draw him out at all. When he's "off", boy, is he "off"! He said he was thinking of his grandmother, which I very much doubt. Marilyn had obviously been given morphine. She recognised Tray, and even said "Patrick!" When I asked her how she was, she amused me by sarcastically replying: "Better!" She fell asleep, breathing heavily. There was a bubbling as of mucus.

Having again been snubbed by Tray, I returned to Araluen and worked on my diary. Kade drove me to the Uanda Laundry in the Super Snipe. Left a dark suit and a few cotton shirts to be dry-cleaned for the funeral and walked across the road to the Great Northern Hotel, one of Townsville's wooden, verandahed "Wild West" pubs. Lunched on ghastly watery Oysters Kilpatrick and a Steak Diane glassy with gristle. Shan't go there again. Purchased a few more Christmas cards at *DAVID JONES*.

"Gosh" the ingenuous androgyne at the counter observed, "you buy cards *every day*!" "There are a lot of people on my list," I said. "I have to write to all of them". "How many?" he demanded. "Ooh, a lot" I stammered, rather taken aback. "It's . . . quite expensive" "I reckon!" the pansy averred. It must be strange to be an androgyne in Townsville. I mean, even the fairies are stupid.

I bought a few stamps and sent a few more cards. God, I'm sick of doing nothing. In the insane yellow heat the Post Office clerks were wearing furry Santa caps. They looked like disgraced members of the middle class after a particularly nasty revolution.

Back at "Araluen", Girly and I had a long talk about the Drysdales. Miss Drysdale, the maiden Maidstone aunt, owned a Soutine. She had bought it for £150 and the Director of the Tate (where it now hangs) offered her £700 for it. "No" said "Tassie", (this was during Girly's visit to Europe in 1938), "tell her not to sell! It's worth at least a grand!" Drysdale himself was "mad on Soutine" (one of my own favourites). From Girly's description, I should guess the picture was one of the landscapes at Auxerre with tall, bending trees that Soutine completed in 1936. "I was *sillih* about this painting," Girly sighed, "it used to hang in Miss Dee-Dee's Sitting Room". The Drysdales had originally come from Kilree House in Scotland. "They were always very kind to us and I remember we always used to write to to Kilree House, Kirkaldy, Fife!" The first Drysdale to come to Oz – John – had been an engineer and surveyor in Burma and the Far East. Russell's father, Lee, was in the Black Watch, but had to leave the regiment in India when he took off with the bandmaster's daughter. Isabel, Russell's mother, led him many a dance. She had a boyfriend, Bertie Beeston, whose cousin, Miss Kininmoth, was a teacher at Frensham when Marilyn and Girly went to school there. Isabel had a horse, *"Blue Wheat"*, and she and Bertie (Girly imitated her pronunciation of the loved one's name) would ride everywhere on *"Blue Wheat"*, even to the outdoor "pictures". There were other boyfriends: it was the talk of Giru. Girly remembered visiting old Lee Drysdale in Melbourne during Regatta Week when Russell was at Geelong Grammar and finding the agèd cuckold distraught. He took her aside and and told her: "They are all purely platonic you know, these boyfriends!"

TUESDAY 15 DECEMBER 1987. Read from a few of the books by Shoom Soukoop that I borrowed from the Dining Room in Hambeluna. There are none of his things at Araluen, which I frankly find quite odd. Girly says that to have anything that would remind her of her late husband would "upset" her. Shoom's novels are all set in Australia but I find them incredibly pure and bloodless. The action they depict may as well take place in Denmark because they seemed to me – always so amazed by the Australian reality – to be untouched by any awareness of the local environment. Perhaps he was too much of his environment to notice it (which means, of course, to criticise it). The books seemed to proceed, as it were, from first principles. The stories read like abstractions which did not depend on the external world and had always existed in the writer's mind. Or they had existed in his mind from that period – always difficult to define – at which our parents form and pervert our psychology. One novel was called *The One Hundred and Twenty Days of Bowen*. It must have been based on Sade's *The One Hundred and Twenty Days of Sodom*, which, according to Tray, Shoom had never read, as interpreted by Pier Paulo Pasolini in his film *Salò*, which – or so Tray alleged – Shoom had seen well over one hundred and twenty times. According to Tray, Shoom relished the scenes wherein Pasolini's naked teenagers are tortured, forced to eat excrement etc by a group of bourgeois grandees (priests, businessmen etc) in the puppet state of Salò. (Hitler set Salò up for the deposed Mussolini in Alpine Italy in the closing days of World War Two. Sade's *Cent Vingt Journées de Sodome* are supposed to occur in a castle in the Ardennes in the time of the degenerate Louis XIV: Pasolini transfers the action to a villa in wartime Lombardy).

Apparently, Shoom had not been very fond of children . . . Or perhaps he had! Tray said that Shoom and Girly were being troubled at the time of the book's composition by children who would knock on their door and then run off. One had even lit a fire at its base. In his novella, which is set in Bowen, in the prim Australian boondocks, an outwardly respectable couple lie in wait for the brutish youths and *"thick-lipped shikses"* (local girls) who are given to tormenting them in this way. They capture one of each and expose them to all sorts of sexual malfeasance for one hundred and twenty days before, finally, they anally impale them on two tall sharpened poles of wild North Queensland sugar cane. These they set up in a field of peanut plants on the outskirts of Bowen with all the other scarecrows, *"pour encourager les autres"*. That was the story. Not much of a story, when you think about it, although its brittle genius might have inspired a whole canvas by Tray Beautous or some other priggish conroversialist, to say nothing of a religious ruling by the Tim-Tams in one of their more *"'Christina' means 'Peace'!"* – like tantrums.

WEDNESDAY 16 DECEMBER 1987. Tray rang. This was itself unusual. I wonder if he's been avoiding me because he saw me in the garden that day? Peeking at his "object" – or *in* it, rather? He might find it odd to face me, knowing what I now know. I asked Tray if he was lonely and gingerly broached the subject of Marilyn's demise. How would he cope? He parried my questions and kept everything on a bright and paltry level. He was used to her being "in hospital", he said, making it sound like she was going to come out again. We agreed to meet.

Chatted to Girly. She talked about her visit to London in 1938. One of her Frensham friends gave her a letter of introduction to a Miss Alicia Stubbings. Alicia was an orphan. JP Morgan, Junior, the millionaire American banker, was her guardian. Alicia's mother, his lover, had made him promise to look after the girl. Alicia lived in a magnificent studio flat in Wilton Place, Knightsbridge. Edward VII had entertained his girlfriends there. One approached it through a warren of Mews houses where they kept thoroughbred horses. Girly, armed with the *entrée*, passed someone in the courtyard carrying an armful of puppies. (For some reason,

I pictured Chihuahuas, a mantle of bronze, onion-like Chihuahuas). "Are you Girly Akers?" the onion lady asked. "Yes!" "Then why didn't you speak to me? *I* am Alicia Stubbings!" "Well," said Girly, "I didn't know who you were. I don't like going up to English people and talking to them, you never know how they'll react. I have an Australian accent, as you see!" Alicia would take Girly riding in Hyde Park with Princess Marina and Queen Farida, the wife of Farouk of Egypt. (I remembered the famous song attributed to the Desert Rats: *"You can't fuck Farida if you don't pay Farouk"*. Or was it the other way around?) Princess Marina was being taught to ride so she could cope in *Terra Australis*, where her husband the Duke of Gloucester was to be made the Governor-General. A little boy would come up to Girly and say: "That *beast* has given my pony to Princess Marina. She's hurting him terribly!" Alicia invited Girly to visit Switzerland with her, but Girl decided to go there with another friend instead because Alicia was planning a detour to Morgan's French château and Girly didn't think she had the right clothes.

Girly began to rummage through the things on her desk. No, she said, she wasn't going to send a card to Dewy's daughter Kommode (the one who heads up the Australia Council). Kommode hasn't sent *her* a Christmas card in years. When Dewy and Kommode visited Townsville a year ago – they both had "business" up here, Girl mysteriously added – they arrived at "Araluen" in Freek Bloomers' red Lancia. On their way back to the South, (Dew explained to Girl over tea), he and Kommode were planning to stop at Noosa. Girly promptly gave Dew an old gold watch and chain to give to Kay, Beverley's daughter, who had taken her stepfather's death rather badly. The pocket watch had belonged to Shoom, Girly's husband. "You know what Beverley will do with that watch-chain, don't you?" hissed Kommode. "She'll hang it around her neck!" Which is apparently the fashion here. "I thought: 'You jealous little monk-ee, you're *just* like your mother!' " As they were leaving, Kommode looked at Freek's Lancia Beta and hissed: "I do so *hate* red cars!". Girly's Humber is, of course, a deep carmine red.

THURSDAY 17 DECEMBER 1987. Remembering my conversation with M. in the Dining Room at "Hambeluna", I asked Girly if I could see the photographs she says she has of Marilyn's Sydney wedding. I was curious to see whom Driss resembled. The album was full of other photographs taken before and just after the First World War depicting life on the "stations" where Girly and Marilyn grew up. Each was composed like a Vuillard – diffident gestures, beautiful faces and clothes. Tea things, native flowers and animals. Raffish diagonals of light. Elegant, vertiginous "Japanese" designs. I cannot get over what incredible languid beauties Marilyn and Girly were in those wide flapper hats, dangling pearls and light, voluminous, almost Arabian clothes. After much prevarication, I asked Girly if I could keep the photographs and she surprised me by consenting. I suppose she wants them to go where they will be disseminated and externalised.

Girly and Kade went in the Humber and brought Tray back to Araluen from the "Mater" (in more ways than one). He'd bought *another* book – on home-made ice-cream! He never makes a thing! He is a compulsive shopper, heedless of the hoard of needless trash "Hambeluna" already groans under. I asked him how Marilyn was and he shocked me by saying, brightly, that she looked "extremely well"! When I tried to get on to my "commission" Tray interrupted me. He said that, on the way to the hospital this morning, an old Taxi Driver had told him about the bunker in Garbutt whence General Macarthur had apparently directed American operations in the Pacific during World War 2. (Garbutt is in Townsville's northern suburbs: it's an aboriginal name). This Taxi Driver's brother had apparently done all the bunker's wiring. "What would you do without tea?" asked Girly, dreamily sipping a cuppa. "What would you do to get it?" Following rather disturbing reports, I wrote a somewhat minatory letter to my London colleagues at the gallery. Dew rang me at about 6.

a novel

FRIDAY 18 DECEMBER 1987. I called on Hambeluna without warning. I am really now getting desperate. Not wishing to broach my own business first, I asked Tray if he was going to have a funeral service for Marilyn in a church or whether it would simply be a graveside ceremony. He was spooning ice-cream from a family-sized tub and I couldn't get any sense out of him at all. He agreed with every course of action I mooted, whether with regard to funerals or Dew's commission – and with each of the various alternatives. Finally, I suggested he move the Drysdales and the centuries old Chinese porcelain from the Dining Room. The interior of the house, with its epic, open verandahs (even if they are some way off the ground) is enchantingly accessible. If anyone wandered in – and Tray is out for such long periods – they could just pop the priceless bibelots into a *sacoche*. Tray wasn't having any of it. He would definitely consider moving the pieces if they ever had a "big party" at the house. Not before. I was astounded. As if there would ever be any more "parties" at Hambeluna!

SATURDAY 19 DECEMBER 1987. This morning, I asked Girly about the pictures of slaughtered foals in her album. One is of a boy like Charon standing over a paddockful of equine corpses – soft, lolling testicular buttocks – with a hammer in his hand. "Did you ever eat horsemeat, Girly?" She recoiled in horror. "But you *have* eaten crocodile, haven't you?" "Yes," she said, "it tastes just like rabbit!" She and Marilyn, she said, used to ride out with the "Boongs" when they went "tailing" the cattle. By night the stockmen would hunt crocodile and koala: both animals sleep during the day and it would have been unsporting to ensnare them then. "And have you ever *dined* on koala?" "Oh yes, but *strong*! It tastes like, oh, Tea Tree flowers. Native food, I suppose. I don't know how they eat it though, it's so awful." We discussed the Aborigines for a while. "And the Islanders," I said, "they're different, aren't they?" "Oh!" said Girly, shaking her head, "they're awful, disgusting! They

343

let themselves go. *And* they smell. They all have something wrong with them – Diabetes, I think. The children are lovely."

Somehow we got on again to her holiday in the mountains of New Zealand in 1914. The children fought "like dogs" and her mother would pay them so much a day to shut up. "We were never frightened of getting stranded up there because there were so many lovely streams – lovely crystal streams and watercress everywhere. We had it on our sandwiches. Baby lambs' tongues. It was like England. Even when you listen to that chap" – she mentioned a Kiwi cricketer – "you can tell he isn't an Australian". "But that's what I like about Australia – that it isn't like England. It's harsh," I said, "unique!" "Yes," she replied, "it's certainly harsh, but it's not quite *unique* any more. They're copying the Yanks." It was England that used to be the model. Why, she wondered, had the Australians become so anti-English? "They've always been like that," I laughed. "They've always had a chip on their shoulder and it's the size of the Aral Sea. An inferiority complex". Girly shocked me by agreeing. "And what I can't stand about them," she went on, ". . . *'them'*, I say, I mean *'us'!* . . . Why do they have these people who have to make out that everybody is the same?" "Like Paul Hogan?" I ventured. "Yes," she said, "that everyone has to be alike." "And *Dewy Popkiss*?" "Dewy too!" she cried. "That nobody can be *different* from anybody else. It's all so bloody cretinous. That's what I loved about England. You could walk down Half Moon Street naked I suppose, and no-one would bat an eyelid . . . And being Catholics has a lot to do with it." (Her sectarian provinciality amused me). "They all stick together like bison". "Well, you certainly couldn't include *my* family among the conformists!" I said, trying gently to draw attention to her arrogance, for which, however, she showed a predictable aristocratic partiality.

I was wrestling with my diary when she came to my room before driving off to see Marilyn at the hospital. Dressed up, as usual – a wide hat, silk dress, pearls, elbow-length gloves. "I leave the world to darkness," she said, "– and to you!"

SUNDAY 20 DECEMBER 1987. Early church at St James's. They're starting to take an interest in me. Must remember to avoid the place. A man with teeth like peanuts and an oily face like Count Ciano's directed the "visitor" to a choice seat between two of the Deacons. The singing was particularly hideous today. The choir no better. The Bishop invited it to *"Burst into Joy"*. The theme of the Bishop's sermon was "small beginnings". He told us about a doctor who visited a sick child and saw a map of the world on the boy's wall. There were white pins in the map – where missionaries were at work. The white pins preyed on the doctor's mind. He became a missionary himself. He married and had nine children and all of his children became missionaries. And all of his children married and all of his children's children became missionaries. ("They must have been Tim-Tams!" I said to a neighbour). The way it turned out, in just one three month period, the doctor's extended family was able to put in a thousand years of missionary work. And all because of those little white pins. Rather paralysed by this *tour-de-force*, I couldn't face trying to beguile Tray any more, so I walked down to Torakina Street and bought milk and pies. Most annoyed to be intercepted on the way back to Girly's by a woman who had seen me carrying "our" parish magazine. She was wearing a vast hat like a lifeboat. "I wasn't wearing this in church", she explained. Girly prepared a delicious luncheon of lamb chops, fried Choco Fruit, and mash with wild chives and pepper.

MONDAY 21 DECEMBER 1987. This morning, over breakfast, Girly told me about Marilyn's wedding, which took place in Sydney in the 1920s. Girly was staying in Nangus, New South Wales at the time with the family of a friend her brother had made at the King's School, then located in the Governor's House, Paramatta (the place I saw). Then she moved next door to stay with the friend's uncle, a Mr "Ripper" Armitage, at Coolamon. Mr Armitage would take her into Sydney to watch the Polo at Neranda. He would even pay Girly's bills at the Hotel Australia. "Hotel life," sighed Girly, "that's the life for me!" She would take a little suite all by herself close to the lovely shops of Pitt Street, poke her head out the window into Rose Street to see what the weather was doing, breakfast at Farmer's. A languid arrangement: one sat in one's armchair sipping a cup of Oolong tea, luxuriating over the obituaries in *THE SYDNEY MORNING HERALD*. Then the news came like thunder: Marilyn was to be married! Girly had to join her family in the ultra-fashionable Astor Flats in Macquarie Street. "That's when we got stuck into prawns!" They had no servants with them so, instead of preparing meals, they would send down to Romano's for "fresh shrimp" – the repulsive debris was voided by shute.

We talked about London for a while: she swooned remembering the shops in Knightsbridge in the 1930s. I felt quite homesick and played Vaughan Williams' *On Wenlock Edge* on my tape recorder. Visited Marilyn with Tray. I worry about how hard it increasingly is to get through to him.

Maybe he'll lighten up after his Grandmother's death (horrible to appear to wish it forward). Though I doubt if Tray has *ever* been susceptible to the other person's point of view. *"To judge is to equal"*, as Raphael says, and for someone like an artist – whose life is built on a life-denying pose – accepting the validity (ie the equality) of a stranger's interpretation would be suicide. Tray is just like a Tim-Tam in that respect. So how on Earth do you get him to do the things you wish of him? By getting him to think it's what *he* wants, I guess.

Marilyn looked rather better, better colour, more comfortable. She was breathing more easily and the nurse said she had spent a peaceful night. We were relieved to discover that Redslob visits her every day and that she is never in pain: morphine is administered on an eight-hourly basis. Tray called her name and her eyes opened but they fell shut again. I sat and prayed by her bed and Tray kissed her goodbye. I could forsee the drama prolonging itself: the nurse said that Marilyn might even lapse into a coma and live for months. Tried to accompany Tray back to Hambeluna but he brushed me off: got the impression he resents my even coming to the hospital. Hope I haven't committed some dreadful *faux-pas* – not that I care one way or the other but it might make executing "Plan Me" *un peu difficile*. Purchased jiffy bags, bubble paper and stamps to send Girly's photo albums back to England. I don't fancy lugging them onto the plane. Lunched in a very disagreeable Greek caff on *"Baby Barra 'n' Veggies"*. There was a group of tropical youth at the next table and a wild-haired girl came and waved a pink slip at them and repeated some frenzied delighted set-piece over and over again. I thought it must have been her exam results but she read it out to another girl and it turned out to be a Mash Note from some boy. I picked up my suit from the Uanda Laundry and walked over to the railway station to get a taxi back to Araluen. Then I dipped into one of Girly's biographies – of Lilly Langtry it was – very homesick-making.

I spent the entire afternoon in my room writing a very long letter to one of my colleagues at *"EMPORIO PATRICK MYNTS"*. I am inserting it in the parcel I am sending to London. I came down for a glass of ginger wine. Dewy rang and we discussed Marilyn – among other things. Said he wouldn't ring again until Wednesday as there didn't seem to be imminent developments on any of the various "fronts". "You look rather worried", said Girly, when I'd put down the phone. "I'm extremely tired", I demurred. I lay on the sofa re-reading the letter to my colleague. I felt painfully stubbly and oily about the face. I walked up to the bathroom to shave. I had just applied the Phisohex and shaving foam when the telephone rang downstairs. I knew exactly what it would be about, so I swept the blade briskly about my chops. "Patrick", Girly called from downstairs, "that was Tray. The hospital has just phoned: Marilyn died! He asked me if I wanted to go down but I don't think so. Do you think I really ought to?" "No," I said, distracted. "They asked Tray if he wanted a priest sent up and he said no, she wasn't a Catholic, but there *are* Anglican priests, aren't there?" "Yes there are". "My husband Shoom said that in England they would never get away with what they get away with here. Some of them are very 'high', aren't they?" "They certainly are," I said, remembering that Cloke Wainberg had told me that his father, an Episcopalian – ie Anglican – priest was "higher than Mary [*Cardinal of the Americas*] Spellman". I went downstairs. I remember the sound of the leathery beating wings of the Flying Foxes in the Mango tree outside. I flopped down in a cane chair. Girly suggested we eat the fresh prawns she had bought at Short's. Tray, she said, had bought some too, to share with Marilyn's cats. Mention of her cats suddenly made me upset. "I've put them in tomato sauce. It's such a pity I couldn't get any cream." I really didn't feel like them but I spooned the bloody gobbets of lychee-locust into my mouth. Full and fat and white. And crunchy. Slivers of bone, like the undercarriage of a moth, dangled from the empty shells. They reminded me of the abandoned hood of a hibernating cicada.

TUESDAY 22 DECEMBER 1987. I awoke this morning at 3 AM exactly and then, marvelling at the accuracy of my internal clock, on the dot of 5. Girly stumbled past in the doorway. My back was wet with sweat and when one rubbed it one's fingers slid away on rolls of dead paste. I came downstairs tearful and fresh. I must admit it: I am worried about the future. The right thing to do is to stay on, the brave thing, the thing I'll regret *not* doing if I *don't* do it. Unfortunately, I don't *want* to do it. I've been counting the days till my release like a prisoner on remand. One half of me wants to abolish all thought of Dewy and his "commission", which has absolutely ruined and corrupted whatever "leisure" I have enjoyed here. The other half wants to make a holiday of the rest of my stay, visit Melbourne, Darwin – Karumba!

I asked Girly for a ruler and scissors so I can send some of the amusingly naïve articles in **THE TOWNSVILLE BULLETIN** to my colleagues in London. She gave me a ruler she bought when the Australian Chancellor brought in a new fringe benefits tax: "Isn't he a bastard, that Paul Keating, bringing in something like that?" One of the pieces I cut out was a fascimile printed in today's *"Bully"* of part of its edition of exactly one hundred years ago. The page from 22 December 1887 has an editorial in the form of a poem:

> *"Great changes have occurred.*
> *New kingdoms have been founded.*
> *Mighty empires have been swept away.*
> *New cities have been formed.*
> *But the greatest event that has ever occurred has happened in*
> *our own days, viz:*
> *The rise and progress of the Great Empire of Britain,*
> *With its immense dependencies,*
> *Its vast colonies,*
> *Its huge centres of commerce:*
> *Among which can be numbered*
> *Those great Emporiums of Trade, viz:*
> *London on the Thames -*
> *And -*
> *Townsville on the Ross. "*

Tray arrived, then the undertaker. Tray picked up the newspaper and astonished me by nervously reading it throughout the ensuing discussion. Dew rang but I warned him that Tray was in the room. The Funeral will take place in an Episcopalian church in a suburb called Oonoonba. There will only be the four of us. Marilyn didn't want any of her old friends to be informed. Girly asked if there would be hymns. She was relieved to discover that, as most organists are unpaid, and have to work during weekdays, there would not. She was suddenly fascinated: "And what do they DO?" she demanded. If not their "organs", what did they play? During the week?

I walked down to the hospital to collect Marilyn's effects – Tray said he couldn't bear to. I nearly cried myself, don't ask me why, when they gave me her handbag – the one she had frantically sought when they took her away. There was the useless lipstick and powder puff – amazing how I could understand her garbled delivery when she was asking for it. It was listed on a card itemizing her possessions with *"MARILYN BLANADET BEAUTOUS"* at the top. At a clothes shop near Short's I bought the blackest tie I could find. A blackish satin tie with cream spots. From a few feet, you would think it really was black. I had to turn the list card over in my hat so that the prying lady in the shop wouldn't realise whose funeral I was attending.

I was bitten by a DINGO of all things on the way home! Aborigines in the Bush of course keep them as hunting dogs – it was the Abos who brought Dingoes into Australia over the land bridge that then existed with Godwanaland tens of thousands of years ago. It is very rare though for an urban Australian to keep one, even though the Dingo cross-breeds like Pig, Dogs and Kelpies abound. They are vicious horrid things like blond wolves: Hitler would have loved them! Imagine an Alsatian with the fur of a Golden Labrador. Even in the Bush they are always attacking campers and carrying suburban babies off to picnic on in their eyries as per *L'Affaire Lindy Chamberlain.*

Anyway, here is how it happened. I was climbing up a street of low, shabby Queenslanders and passed a tumbledown one with a windmill pump and a boat on a trailer. It was in a pit of green shadow, almost completely hidden by trees, like one of those old collapsed nests you see in England in Autumn hedgerows. Suddenly the brute shot out from under the house like a fish from the reef, its bark a horrid staccato cracking. I watched it resignedly, reconciling myself to a stay in the hospital from which I had just emerged. Miraculously, just then, its owner roared up behind me on an extraordinary silver-coloured motorbike with two sidecars. He was an old black man, one of **"*L'École de Boree*"** (Blue Singlet Brigade), and he ordered the brute to desist. He beat it repeatedly with a branch that was lying by the road – a sound like an egg hitting the pavement. I proceeded up Castle Hill in shock and was relieved to discover that, despite the arc of saliva on my trousers, there wasn't even a mark on my skin. I lunched on roast Roo tail and partook of a wonderful nap.

Girly woke me at 4PM to help her arrange the wreaths. She told me she was going to buy "strong sweet biscuits" for Mr Barscrub, Marilyn's solicitor: "the others are very delicate!" Dewy rang, to monitor my progress, and, for some reason, I told him about the Dingo. Girly prepared me some lovely salmon sandwiches on a rectangular plate and they just filled it. They were delicious – onions, butter and sweet malt vinegar had been added. They were decorated with green lettuce and calimari olives – always the big LITTLE touch with my dear friend Girly, the little *je ne sais quoi* that means so much!

I was afraid lest Dewy become worried about my being bitten – though Girly found the idea hilarious. I wanted to ring again and tell him I had *not* been hurt. "You *are* a worrying sort of person, aren't you?" Girly demurred. "Yes I am," I replied.

WEDNESDAY 23 DECEMBER 1987. I woke at 4AM this morning, quite agitated. I wanted to ring Dew and tell him the Dingo bite wasn't serious – and certain other things. I didn't wish him to worry. (*Dewy*, can you imagine? That's how deranged I was). I didn't want the worry of his worrying hanging over me at the funeral today, though the very idea was insane. Even without my current difficulties, I usually find it impossible to enjoy my environment because, in the background, there is always some general, long-term anxiety. This morning, in the merciful dark before the tropical dawn, I realised what an elegant, comfortable room I was in. Why wasn't I enjoying it? The local, immediate worry about the Dingo bite, like the bite itself, had banished the bigger, broader, thematic concern.

I waited until about 6, when I heard Girly moving about, and asked her if I could use the phone. I told Dewy about the Dingo. He laughed dementedly. Having given in to compulsion I returned to bed with that weak bladdery feeling you get when you know you are powerless in the hands of a neurosis. The cicadas began to surge. Strange to hear them beginning, as if they were half-aware of their awful mission. The sound of a tap running. I wanted badly to fall asleep. I didn't think I *was* asleep, but realised the truth when I found myself in a rococo barley-sugar Townsville waiting for Marilyn's funeral. A sort of Saint Petersburg. For one blessèd moment I thought it was London – but there was the pink hulk of Castle Hill against the endless, stoned blue sky. Tray was chiding a funeral director – "Yes, you can go for a *bend* [crap], but I think you're being very selfish!" I rose at 8.

There were a few calls – people asking about Marilyn. Girly was furious – blames the Florist. Marilyn had wanted the funeral strictly *entre-nous*. The chauffeurs from the funeral parlour arrived in a black 1970s Japanese limousine and hearse. Small Japanese cars are so functional but this large one (and one so seldom sees large, luxurious Japanese cars) had an expressive quality – its lines were baroque. I felt curiously vacant during the service. There was only Girly, Tray, myself, Freek (in a tropical shirt – well, at least he *wore* a shirt!), and Mr Barscrub of "Barscrub-Keem", who looked a bit like a puppy with his big dark eyes, his big black smudgy mouth. I glanced at Tray. He looked as if he were holding his breath, as if his emotions had been heightened and tightened so much of late that they remained in knots somewhere unspeakable. He couldn't untie the knot, loosen the knot, let the waters flow. I was struck by the illustrations behind the altar when I went up to receive Communion: the church was very modern. They were flat figures cut from brightly painted synthetic boards. On the left of the Cross were a soldier, a schoolboy and a miner. On the right a university professor, a schoolgirl and a bare-chested navvy in shorts. In the middle was a beardless Christ in a white jellaba rather like Tray's (not that Tray was wearing one today). Christ wore a red dressing gown and a tall tinsel crown like a schoolboy dressed as one of the Magi. More even than the crude draughtsmanship, the superfluous salacity suggested a local artist, almost certainly a woman. I've said it before and I'll say it again: I don't know why but there is nothing like religious subject matter for making one's head fill with thoughts of the self. I revolved my own problems over and over again. Hence God's injunction against imagery. To approach God you have to repress your awareness of the *self*. Religious art, especially in churches, always strikes me as insolent, self-absorbed. An overdressed altar girl sitting on a box next to a fan added to the makeshift pantomime quality, but the Sistine Chapel is just as bad.

I talked to Mr Barscrub about a contract I want him to draw up. Mr Barscrub talked about his wife, who "hasn't been the same" since an operation to remove a growth in her pituitary gland. Like Bon, he was the nice cheerful type. The church, whose glass walls were open down each side, was very noisy – there were gums all around full of cicadas screaming like a pressure cooker. Very few people in Europe can imagine how noisy cicadas are – how much their noise oppresses the public space in Australia. There were many uneasy moments when we were told to sit and stand and we couldn't hear the vicar's instructions. "Stand, I said – *stand*!" It was breezy, but there were a lot of mosquitoes. "Look," said Mr Barscrub, "there's a mozzie on your shirt!" (My yellowish cheesecloth *chemise*). "I won't crush it or you'll be covered in blood!" My heart sank resignedly, as when I was bitten by the dingo. There is no Malaria here but Dengue Fever is endemic.

The service ended unexpectedly and Freek, *Maître* Barscrub, Tray and I shuffled out to take our positions as pall bearers in the porch. Marilyn's magnificent cedar coffin, which had lain on a trolley next to us in the aisle, was wheeled out and the four of us each took a silver handle. We were driven right around the city, right around Castle Hill, to Belgian Gardens Cemetery. Our limo was behind the hearse. We were driving very slowly. The orange pyramid of rock was everywhere, shivering with red and black, like tinned salmon, the vast blue sky grey with heat. The bleaching sun, the tumbledown Queenslanders in their straggling gardens, the emptiness – a few children, stupefied, watching us – the roar of the cicadas, the unearthly austere panorama rolling by – it wasn't without meaning.

Finally we reached the cemetery. Mile after mile of densely packed white graves in an endless Wadi of grey sand, like chickenbones in ashes after a fire. I could see where a grave had been opened. A funeral pansy went ahead and stuck two black umbrellas in the earth, then he came back and led Girly to the spot and unfurled one over her head. We carried the coffin from the hearse and followed the vicar in his fluttering white robes as he began to intone the "Office of the Dead" under the vast blue sky, the innumerable pebbly white bones in the ashes, the roar of the cicadas. There was a breeze. The grey sand sank beneath our feet. It felt strange – like walking on a beach with shoes on. We mounted a platform covered in green baize and shaky underfoot. The blue metal rods supporting the coffin were removed and we lowered it into the earth on green straps. I couldn't hear what the vicar was saying. We went and stood by Girly, a picture under the black umbrella held by the catafalque fairy, head resting to one side in a cupped palm like a Giotto Madonna. Afterwards, the vicar asked me how long I was staying in Australia. I didn't answer, but moved forward and took the silver trowel of earth the funeral queen was offering and threw it on the coffin. It was a strangely satisfying gesture.

Tray's wreath of roses had been lowered into the the coffin, my wreath and Girly's are to be put on the top of the grave, as are the flowers from the other members of Marilyn's family, who couldn't be bothered to come and didn't even visit the hospital. Tray pointed to the desolate cemetery and said how different I must find it from the lush English variety. In England, he said, they even have picnics in the cemeteries. "Marilyn wouldn't have wanted it any other way", I said. "No," said Tray. "This is *her land*!" I nearly broke down for the first time: God knows why, she wasn't *my* grandmother. "But yes," I thought, surveying the desert, so alien to me, "this *is* her land". I realised how totally Australia, which once seemed so attractive, had died in me. Walking back to the car, I got a scoop of sand in my shoe. "Yes" I thought, tears pricking my eyes, "this *is* her land". I shook it out . . . *Right* out. We drove back to Girly's place past the hospital and Mr Barscrub joined us for drinks. He was a delight: he talked about his wife. He is taking her to Brisbane on January 12th for six weeks of radiation treatment. "Eat, drink!" he said, pointing to the whisky tumbler Girly had provided for the beer, ". . . for tomorrow!" Tray rudely and nervously buried himself in the papers and refused to be drawn on any subject at all, grunting contemptuously when

I suggested, privately, I come to stay with him at Hambeluna: "Isn't it wierd for you to be there all alone?" I asked him if he were returning to Magnetic Island – whether I could see his studio there – what would happen to Hambeluna etc. Another grunt.

Freek Bloomers talked about Magnetic Island in the old days. There was no ferry then – you had to get a fishing smack across. No reticulated water. Cans of cow dung hung burning in the badly partitioned hotel rooms to kill the mosquitoes.

Freek left, and then returned to ring a service station because his car wouldn't start. Tray left by taxi and then returned for some reason with some vanilla ice-cream and his father's Christmas card for Marilyn, which had perversely just arrived at Hambeluna. Girly laced the ice cream with Boronia Sherry, an Australian liqueur fortified with the cordial of the Boronia Tree flower. It was delicious! Tray seemed much more cheerful now and talked about Marilyn's estate (maybe that was why he was so cheerful). We lunched on tongue sandwiches and talked for a long time, but about nothing "important". Tray would open the singing Christmas Card from Bonnie and Dew and let it play *"Jingle Bells"* for minutes on end. He would obsessively turn Girly's pocket radio on and off, pretending to listen to the Children's Programme: *"'Cuddlepie had a dream. In this dream, Buff called out:* 'Cuddlepie, Cuddlepie!'"

Girly told us how she got to know the Hollywood movie star Peter Finch, then a little boy, in Sydney just before World War Two. He was illegitimate and had been taken in by a relation who was a friend of one of Girly's cousins in Neutral Bay. Finch would steal from this benefactor. Girly would meet him on the steps leading down to the Neutral Bay Ferry and he would tell her of how much he loathed Greta Garbo. Later, he shared a flat with the artist Donald Friend and became his *mignon* or *"protégé"*.

I was more interested to hear from Girly about what Sydney looked like before the *First World War* but she couldn't remember, as she didn't stay in Sydney for long periods then. The only pre-14 visit she could really recall was when her mother took them to the city so she could give birth to Girly's younger sister, Weeta. The children were sent to a Presbyterian school in the central business district, "which was harsh, all built of ugly, hot brown stone like demerara sugar". When her mother moved to the Blue Mountains to convalesce, they were sent to a Roman Catholic establishment in Katoomba. Girly's class would be given ribbons of different hues. They would have to shake them in unison and chant: *"Rainbow, Rainbow, All Hail to Thee!"* in the Virgin's honour. Girly's efforts were hopelessly lacking in coordination and the nuns warned her she would be kept behind until she could enact the observance perfectly. "I thought: how awful to be kept behind when everyone else has gone home, so I ran away!" But the nuns ran after her and Girly got tangled up in some barbed wire.

We discussed the book in my lap – a beautiful old 19th Century guide to Rome that Shoom must have bought. Girly bemoaned the loss of a guidebook to the West Indies: she and her husband had gone island-hopping there from New Orleans in 1952: "The natives with the lovely expressions on their faces – it was too gorgeous for words!" I was feeling tired and I excused myself.

An hour or so later I was awoken by a tapping noise. At first I thought with horror that it was the tapping in the wall that had terrified me in London in 1977; then I realised it was coming from the corridor outside the bedroom. I poked my head around the door and saw what looked like a grey baby in the window at the end of this corridor, a mummified, naked two foot-high version of Marilyn clawing at the pane, trying to get in. I was about to shriek when I realised it was a possum attempting with its frog-toe-like fingers to open the window. (Possums adore invading Australia's abodes where they set up home in the attic or in the spaces between the walls. They make a frightful noise – not considering other matters – and very few householders emulate the evident delight that Tray takes in their company). I moved towards the window to scare the brute away but the possum – which looked like

Yoda from **Star Wars** and was clinging with its other mit to the mango tree that climbs up the side of the house – was nothing if not brazen.

There is a diagonal line of windows that pierces the mango-ward wall of Araluen. It follows the sweep of the staircase as it snakes down to the front door, and, as I chased it, the possum simply swung down through the mango like a gibbon to the next highest window and then the next, and the next, trying at each to force the glass leaves open. I had nearly descended to the ground floor before it took fright and scrambled off into the treetops. I was about to return upstairs but, where I now was, the indistinct voices that had been rumbling away in the Living Room assumed a shape definite and astonishing that forced me to pause.

Peering around the wall that hid the stairwell, I could see the back of Freek and Girly's head at the end of the open-plan interior. They were sitting side by side on the "Pompadour" sofa downing a jug of the local firewater with alacrity, Tray and Mr Barscrub obviously having decamped. (Prior to the Wake, I had watched Girly carefully hiding the Scotch). From what Girly and Freek were saying, I would guess that they were talking about Marilyn's will. I was utterly taken aback by Girly's intonation which had a bitter, contemptuous quality I was quite unfamiliar with – at least outside the world of art! "I mean, *I'm* not getting anything out of it!" Girly hissed. "What did *I* ever gain from our friendship? Nothing!" "Isn't *'nothing'* exactly what yer want?" Freek retorts. "Soon enough *yer won't be getting Tray*! Isn't *that* what yew want?" "What I *'want'* is for Tray to just sign the damn thing off, take what he's offered. Mother of God, it's not as if he hasn't spent his whole life trying to get it! Why doesn't he just take it?" "Sometimes", Freek enigmatically replied, "it's more sensible to make it look like yer *don't* want it!" "Well I agree," says Girl, "that if you have to fight someone for something, sometimes it's better to affect disinterest. But he's being offered it all on a plate!" *"But don't yew see,"* gasped the "polly", "it's pre-*soycely* because it's there for the toy king that he doesn't have to toyk it *now*? Don't yew re-*a-loyze* he's got *bigger* fish to froy? That he won't even get the bird in 'iz *hand* unless he covers the bush *first*? . . . I mean, the same waffle yew want from Cole's today'll still be there termorrah. *And* the next day. *And* the day arf-ter! It's not as if there won't still be pungkin [*pumpkin*] scones at the Ozone Caff if yer don't get one *terday*! But yerv got to pay for the fucker *first! And it's not Cole's that Tray's gotta pay, Girl!* That sheila at Cole's may very well want to let Tray have 'iz cream horns for free, hand 'em to 'im on a fucken plate. *But the lady at Cole's ain't the one makin' the decisions, luv!* Unless Tray compensates the Coons first, them Boongs'll never let the feral ['*Federal*'] Government get what we want. *Our guy* ['Ergo'], the ferals [ie the regime] will never let *Tray* get what you think he just has to pick up off the floor like a pyklet! Understand? Until Tray bakes a cake for the Boongs, it's no deal!"

I presumed, upon hearing this, that the Abos have made some claim on Marilyn's property under the "native title" laws and that Tray won't get his inheritance until he submits to the usual shakedown. I had been mesmerised by the revelation of Girly's sinister misanthropy but it suddenly struck me that I was eavesdropping on a private conversation about a stranger's money, than which there is no greater crime for a "burgher queen" (ie a member of the middle classes). I scampered up to bed ashamed.

After another nap, I came down to find Girly alone and agreeably tipsy. "I don't want to hear any more about those Greenies!" she shouted, turning off the TV. "I thought a country girl like you would love them," I said, surveying the misty quotidian tumbler empty at her side. "I hate them!" she said. "They all have hairy arms! They're lesbians!" She wanted to talk about the old Hotel Boolba, an extraordinary minareted Anglo-Moghul fantasy on the Strand, now an Aboriginal Cen-tah, once the resort of "*le tout Queensland*", if one can imagine such a thing. What the Plaza in New York City was to the East Coast Wasps, and the Shelbourne in Dublin to the Anglo-Irish aristocracy, the Boolba had apparently been to the *Faubourg Saint-Germain* of Ant Hill Plains. Girly remembered staying there as a child in 1909. They had a "Bush House" where they would grow fresh palms for the lounge. She remembered the grossly fat wife of the manager, who had great social pretentions, falling through a rotten verandah during a Flappers' Ball, and how she had to train her forbidden pet Pig Dog, Suzie, to hide under the bed at a given signal when the maids were sniffing around.

Girly asked me what I wanted for dinner. "Vanilla ice cream and Boronia Sherry!" I cried. I complimented her on her unerring gratuitous good taste when she brought it to me beautifully laced in a bowl shaped like an apple. "Patrick, you're a funny boy", she said.

Kommode Thalanga rang, Dewy's daughter. I spoke to her for a while and then I put Girly on. Kommode told her about the "bond" I had supposedly forged with Marilyn. Girly thought she was talking about the *bomb* that Marilyn used to keep behind the front door. Kommode had warned me that if I don't get Tray's consent to Dewy's plan by the New Year, the whole thing is off and Dewy doesn't want to see or hear from me ever again. I was intrigued by the way he always deputes the delivery of these glad tidings to an underling. (And, as Shakespeare said: *"it is not in our stars, but in ourselves, that we are underlings"*). It isn't cowardice on Dewy's part, but the mark of a shrewd dictator. You're always left wondering whether the tyrant's *actual* words were kinder or could give grounds for hope. Wasn't that why ordinary people always used to think so highly of Stalin, Hitler, Mao Tse Tung? "Oh, if only Uncle Joe *knew* what his *mignons* were doing!"

THURSDAY 24 DECEMBER 1987. This morning, I dreamt that there was a group of young people lying naked face downwards on a beach. The naked lover of a young woman was murdered by ruffians – stabbed in the back, I think. The transvestite singer who had been serenading the group began to wail in grief. He stripped off his leathery purple outfit and wig as if removing scalp and skin to reveal what were discoloured brown bones, purple joints, and sticky brown-grey muscles. He was pulled along on his back screaming in the wake of the funeral procession. All this happened in Cairns. A "punk" with a naked abdomen appeared – an "outrageous" Australian. I thought at this point I was in the middle of an Australian movie and that, as usual, the director wanted to show us how "sophisticated" Australia was. The punk girl was out and about looking at "normal" people, as if at a spectacle. "Gee", she said, "they even have totally naked dogs!" Her own belly was covered in gelatinous grey bumps like lychee nuts and boasted a row of teats like a pregnant cur. I dreamed of Australian midgets – local council workers in yellow shirts – breakdancing on upturned rubbish bin lids. I was shocked to see they didn't have any arms, just little sea anemone hands waving at their shoulders like Thalidomide brats. The stumps would move fleshily in the breeze like tinned pears in a womb of syrup.

I rose at 6.20 – asked Girly for something for my stomach and received a dose of Eno's Salts. Read from the Prokofiev biography and did some writing. Tried to ring Tray to confirm a meeting. There was no reply so I called a cab and visited Hambeluna in person. Tray had unplugged the phone. He showed me a copy of Marilyn's Will and then a box of books from Shoom's library. I was amused to find the biography of the painter Kumi Sugai that Michiko Naruse was working on when I visited her in Granchester outside Cambridge about six years ago. I tried to talk to Tray about art, about viewing some more of his artwork and representing him in London, about Dew's "clients" and what they wish Tray to do (without, of course, alluding to either Dew or "clients" by name), but I got nowhere. He simply agreed with everything I proposed in a peurile automatic way that made it clear he would probably forbear to do a thing.

Tray showed me a recording of the opera *La Mère Coupable* by Darius Milhaud and, attempting a new tack, I questioned him about classical music. He said he "got into it" by listening to the "meditation" records he would buy, and he showed me these. Each was actually a recording of a very famous ballet – *Les Biches* by Francis Poulenc, for instance; Debussy's *L'Après-Midi d'un Faune* – but the LPs were entitled *ENVIRONMENTS*. They had covers suggestive of mental illness. Each sleeve featured the backside of a naked girl with a film projected onto it. A bum full of lightning on one sleeve; in the second, the movie projected onto the naked female rump portrayed another girl frolicking quite nude in the surf. I asked him where he had come upon such things and he said he had first listened to them in Edgecliff, Sydney, where he had once attended a workshop for people with "nerves". (Girly had already described for me Marilyn's account of this "programme". Marilyn apparently used to visit Tray in Sydney in the period when he was an unknown young painter in Woolloomooloo. You would enter a sitting room and the "nervous", Marilyn said, were all lying in armchairs, heads back, eyes staring vacantly at the ceiling . . . It sounded fantastic!)

A tense silence ensued. Perhaps Tray felt ashamed of these "nerves". To break the ice, I picked up the Marquis de Sade's *Juliette*, one of the novels that had been conveyed from Shoom's library. Knowing it to be quite amusing, I started reading aloud from it, beginning at the point where the eponymous heroine arrives in Naples. She is touring Italy late in the Eighteenth Century and surprising all sorts of famously pure real-life contemporaries in somewhat embarrassing situations – the saintly Pope Pius VI Braschi, for instance, whom she finds conducting a Black Mass in the Vatican. In Naples her hosts are the then actually reigning monarchs, the deeply pious Ferdinand IV, King of the Two Sicilies, and his icily virtuous queen Maria Carolina, aka "Charlotte", the daughter of the Hapsburg Emperor of Austria and the sister of Marie-Antoinette. "Juliette" and her lesbian friend "Clairwil" are ushered into the presence of the royal couple at Portici, a palace where the Roman and Greek sculpture newly excavated from nearby Pompei is being displayed. ***"Among other masterpieces***", I declaimed, reciting the first-person narrative of the insolent "Juliette":

> *"I quickly distinguished a superb effort representing a satyr coupling with a goat, an astonishing work of art, beautiful in its conception, striking in its precision of detail.*
>
> *'That fantasy is quite as agreeable as it is alleged to be extraordinary,'* *Ferdinand commented. 'It is,' he went on to say, 'much in usage*

hereabouts; as a Neapolitan, I was eager to experience it, and I do not hide from you that it gave me the greatest pleasure.'

'I can believe it,' said Clairwil. 'Many and many a time in my life I have thought of the idea, and I have never desired to be a man except to enact it.'

'But you know, a woman can perfectly well surrender herself to a large dog,' the King reminded us.

'Certainly,' I rejoined, in such a way as to suggest I was not totally unacquainted with that practice.

'Charlotte,' pursued Ferdinand, 'was of a mind to try it. It suited her to perfection.'

'Sire,' said I, speaking so as to be heard by Ferdinand only, but with my accustomed frankness, 'if all the princes of the House of Austria had but confined themselves to goats, and if all the women of that House had conversed with bulldogs alone, the earth today would not be plagued with this accursed race, whereof its populations shall never otherwise be rid save through a general revolution.' "

Tray winked at me. "Sir Quntee Mush please note!" he said, alluding to the pubic scalps Mush is given to nailing as trophies to his 'missionary' positions. "Yes," I replied, "but I doubt if anyone would need to *ask* Quntee Mush to fuck goats".

As Tray and I were waiting outside Hambeluna for our cab, Girly drew up enthroned in the back of the Humber, but Tray just waved her on. I noticed that hard falsetto Tray uses when he's upset as he gave the taxi driver our instructions. At Araluen, Girly and I opened the Christmas presents Tray had brought. I had received a lovely silver hip flask. "That cost fifty-four dollars", Tray explained. He buys affection with what costs him nothing: money. I do feel sorry for him, for he is an affectionate, moral person. Girly played with the cheap Spanish doll that came with her expensively wrapped atomizer and soap. There was a harsh shriek as Tray sprayed the air with her radio. He described the joys of sailing in the moonlight – a launch company offers moonlit party cruises nowadays on the Barrier Reef. Girly and I glanced at each other. To Girly's protests, he earnestly described how "Sappho Dereby" had died of drink and her husband was found dead one day on the floor in the kitchen. "No," he said, as if reciting the height of Everest, "Marilyn said that *all* her friends had died of drink!" Afterwards Girly said: "He does make me laugh. All this talk about death. He says it so casually. *'He was found dead in the kitchen!'* . . . As if they were bandicoots!"

FRIDAY 25 DECEMBER 1987. The strangest Christmas Day I can remember. I woke up, feeling distressed and distinctly un-festive, just before 7 AM. I decided to lie back and luxuriate and think pleasant thoughts but Bonnie rang. I had to fetch Girly, who was watering the garden. She only has two hours in the early morning and resented the interruption. I completed a rather elaborate *toilette* and arrived downstairs at about 8.15. There was a brief moment of peace and semi-happiness as Girly and I exchanged presents. Weather overcast for the first time in days – as if it were deferring to auspicious Yule. I started to worry about the call Dew promised to make on Christmas Day. The trouble is, when I know I have to say something, especially within a short, fraught space of time and in a final, comprehensive form – so that I don't feel compelled to ring later to qualify or add –I dread it. The time until the moment to speak comes is ruined. I resented the idea of ruining Christmas Day – especially the expensive lunch Girly has booked at the Hotel Bedourie. I wondered whether I should decide *not* to relate my news to Dew so I wouldn't have to worry about his call. An obsessional debate arose which quite spoiled the service I attended at the Cathedral. As I was walking down the road to Communion, the stillness and the unfamiliar cloud finally made it feel Christmassy. A car drew up. A lady and a young man alighted and said Ho, Ho, Ho. An Australian voice from within the house they were making for said: "Heyo, Heyo, Heyo" back. I arrived at 9.04, shortly after the service had begun. The gentleman in front of me had a tattoo of Australia on his arm. He and his wife went up to the font and took part in a Christening. His wife took flashlight photographs of the event in a vexatious, obtrusive way. I remember a blue flash as the Bishop was dilating on "the light of the world". As they returned to their pew, the gentleman made the sign of a gun with his fingers, pointed it at the head of the baby, and fired . . . "Boosh!"

There was an Islander behind me who intoned the hymns like a racist comic impersonating Idi Amin. Something about him seemed familiar.

After church, I called in at "Hambeluna". Tray shouted that he was "working": he wouldn't open the door. I wandered around the garden, wishing I was "hayume". Finally, he let me in and I wished him a "*Joyeux Noël*". He brought the carton of Shoom's books in for my further delectation and I drank a glass of gin and "it". Invited Tray to join us for lunch. (I didn't want to broach the subject of Dew's "commission" on Christmas Day). Tray complained again that Marilyn had "staged" the fall in the bathroom on the day I had lunched with Girl at the Casino. He said she hated to think others were enjoying themselves when she was unable to. "What a thing to say!" I thought, but I assured him that on that particular day I had anything but enjoyed myself. Tray said he has been taking the phone off the hook because an estate agent rang up the day after Marilyn's funeral telling him she had a buyer for Hambeluna.

I went to the kitchen for a drink of water: it was not as dirty as I'd feared. I noticed the notes Marilyn had scrawled on the plank walls summarising the deaths of her beloved cats: "*Tildy, five past eleven PM, 12th of February 1984*" . . . Sad. I left, alone, with Freya Stark's **The Valleys of the Assassins**. Returned to Araluen and read nervously from Roderick Cameron's book **My Travel's History**. Girly said she was at Frensham with his aunt. I changed, Tray arrived, and the taxi ("Bob Kade-shit" naturally has the day off) took us to the Hotel Bedourie, a hideous conical skyscraper in the middle of town known as "the sugar-shaker". The meal was frightful: Townsville really doesn't have any good restaurants at all.

Back on the ground floor, Girly asked for the Free Taxi token the restaurant had advertised. The receptionist said she knew nothing about it. Girly marched over to where we were waiting and related all this at the top of her voice. The girl called her back. Someone from the restaurant would come down with it. One of the incompetent young waiters arrived. He walked in long, mincing strides, on tiptoes; his upturned mouth, fair upswept hair and baby face reminded me of Velasquez's portrait of the Infanta. The taxi driver we got said he had chosen us (another party disputed our possession of the cab) because "*we can't disappoint the regulars*, can we?" This contemptuous remark was directed at Tray. "Three Victoria Street isn't it?" he enquired (Hambeluna). "No," I said, slightly puzzled, " *'Araluen'*. 340 Stanley." He began to sing – always a bad sign. He was the direct but nervous type and obviously expected a tip. It was, after all, Christmas Day! Tray and Girly, following the Australian custom, *never* tip. We arrived and the driver wouldn't accept the Taxi Token. "I want *paid*!" he roared. There was an ugly edge to his voice; you could sense all the contempt he felt for eccentric abnormal parasites.

Home at last, Girly had a nip of the Black Label I had bought her for Christmas. There was a savage grey storm: it made me feel drowsy and I fell asleep on the couch. Tray made his excuses and I went upstairs and lay on the bed. The fan was on me. I thrashed about, dipping into Graham Greene's thin, trashy novel, but it depressed me. I came downstairs unrested, conscious of having wasted a great deal of time – I couldn't even face my diary. "How on earth could they give that man a knighthood?" Girly asked of Barry Humphries' character "Sir Les Patterson", who was regaling us red-nosed and gorgonzola-fanged from the TV, a gorgette of spittle and filth flickering on his lapel. "He slobbers so!" She was under the impression "Sir Les" really was an Australian politician, and who can blame her?

Dewy rang.

SATURDAY 26 DECEMBER 1987. This morning, I dreamt of Kokoschka's last paintings, including his nude self-portrait, *"Time Gentlemen, Please!"* My own interpretation of these paintings, of course.

Woke at 5, rose at 6, finding sleep impossible, and came down and looked in the paper for Marilyn's funeral notice. I thought of visiting Tray, to press him re the Dew proposal but, remembering how, yesterday, he refused to answer the door, I quite lost heart.

I found letters awaiting me in the sitting room and Girly engrossed in the cricket. (I have been amazed to find a television blaring with it on in every shop in Townsville). I was intrigued by the appearance of the Australian cricketers – tall and stocky, but also soft and brown and voluptuous, like rock stars. Overripe. The sheep and wheat and fruit of Australia are bigger, lusher than their originals in Europe but blander somehow, and the same is true of the people.

"They're so nice, those New Zealanders", Girly observed, not for the first time. "They're not rough and crude like the Australians. They used to have a microphone down there behind the wicket and the *profanities* that went on! You've no idea of the language of these people!" (*Her* people, of course).

Girly is totally engrossed in the current "Test". She told me how she had obtained the autographs of the infamous English "Bodyline" cricket team that toured Australia in the 1930s. She happened to be on the "Manunda", the ship from Townsville to Sydney they were travelling on. She collected their signatures on a menu card as they played quoits, sunbathed etc. She found Jardine, the notorious captain, in a deck-chair upstairs. He wouldn't even look at her as he scrawled his signature. He was a "gentleman amateur". The rest of the team were professionals and he scorned their company.

I hinted at the difficulties I was having with Tray. Girly wasn't surprised and dilated on his peculiarities. He refuses to honour appointments - by waiting until they're over. Then he pops up and says sorry. Girly remembers Knut and Brooklana Fagan inviting him for a "feed" - (Bush locutions are surprisingly common among "*Le Tout Ant-hill*") – at the Prime Minister's residence in Sydney. He didn't seem keen but agreed to go. Well, he jumped off the Manly ferry and ran straight into "Jonah Tatsine", a Lebanese Croesus who invited him for drinks at his penthouse in Cabarita. Tray seems to have grabbed at the chance to waste time, and arrived chez Fagan-Hag hours late to find the *déjeuner intime* cleared away. His hosts were *"disgusted"*. "Even though I know him quite well, I'd never get on the wrong side of Tray", Girly mysteriously observed.

I poured a cup of tea and worked on my diary. Then I spent the rest of the morning on a letter to some London colleagues. Two telegrams from Dew arrived after lunch with an *"I warn you"* implication. I chatted briefly to Girly's gardener Kade. Girly was chewing something noisily, which was most unlike her. "Arabs eat cucumbers all the time," she announced. "They do?" "That's why they carry them about with them. *This* one happens to be a nice one." She studied the Florist's bill for the funeral. "Just hark at what they call the nest they put the flowers in: '*A Wet Oasis*'!" . . . "A wet o-a-sis, a wet o-a-sis," she sang. I went upstairs and wrote another letter.

Kade called up and asked if I wanted a run into town as the mechanic had arrived with Girly's Humber. (It broke down this morning on Cape Palleranda). Kade and I were driven back to his garage in sainted South Townsville. Then Kade drove me in the Humber to a liquor store, where we picked up some grog. The inside of a tiny, flimsy Queenslander was visible a few yards away. The windows were open, it was a glaring hot day, and the crucifix and tinsel on the plank wall of what might have been a dog kennel made me want to scream and flee right home to London straight away. Never have I felt so oppressed by Australia's isolation, artificiality, nothingness.

Kade drove back to Araluen and I walked from South Townsville to the City Cen-tah and enquired at the "North Australian Travel Agency" about visits to Karumba. It can hardly be Rome-like, but being so small, so dwarfed by nature, the human element there might not to the same extent be the occasion of ironic pain. I bought Girly some little boxes of Russian tea in *DAVID JONES* and finished composing my telex to Dew in the Government Bookshop. I sent it at the Post Office next door. In the bookshop, I pretended to be reading a brochure on the Australian flag so I could use a table: a government publication that showed one how the Australian flag was to be held and hung in pageants, multinational gatherings etc. A superfluous book that gave me a desolate feeling.

Walking back to Araluen, I picked up a stick near the cutting so I could beat off the Dingo – should it appear. But the stick had become so hot lying in the sun that I had to cast it away. In the Tropics everything you touch burns, having absorbed so much sun – leaves, plates, car doors especially. I saw a taxi draw into Araluen. It was Girly! Kade had left the mended Humber's engine on when he had popped into the Bookie's while she was shopping and all the water had run out of the radiator! A "horrid" man, apparently, had pushed Girly in the taxi queue. Treeda Quamborne, from one of the "old families", had approached and asked her about Marilyn. She was with her son: they too were waiting for a cab. They usually shop at "Nathan Plaza" in the suburb of Thuringowa on the burning plain in the interior behind the mountain. The son is in his forties. "He's you know – what is he? – not quite normal". The image of dependency juxtaposed with "Nathan Plaza" and its trifles in the pitiless glaring Bush was singularly horrific.

More mail arrived from London and I started yet another letter. I lay on the bed but I couldn't rest. I went into the back garden and took a few photos of the wallaby. I met him in the front garden as well. Girly was sitting on her shooting stick, watering. I walked down to Short's to pick up a few more copies of the *TOWNSVILLE BULLETIN.* The funeral notice has also appeared in the Brisbane *COURIER-MAIL,* so I bought a few of those as well. We dined on cold schnitzel with salami and olives. Girly raved tipsily about a tub of ice cream I had bought. "I thought you said you didn't *like* ice cream?" There were veins of brownish syrup in its flesh and she said: "I don't, but it's the chocolate, the divine, the lovely chocolate!" Girly showed me photographs she had taken of holidays at Palm Beach, NSW, in the years just after the First World War. They were entertained there by the parents – mostly doctors – of her Frensham chums. She showed me the picture of a classmate – Gretel – the media mogul Kerry Packer's mother. Strange seeing the Lion Islands, Pittwater – places I know which are now deep in Sydney and poxed with acrylic suburb – just virgin sepia Bush like New Guinea. (The Soap Opera *Home and Away*, supposedly set in the Outback, is actually now filmed at Palm Beach). Girly showed me a photo of a man named Horton – the brother-in-law of one of the Anakoua-Durbets she stayed with at Nangus. He poured a pot of boiling water over her head after she'd bet him he wouldn't. (A lot of Girly's anecdotes seem to involve boiling water). "They were picking blisters out of my hair for weeks", sighed Girly. She was speaking as if with a blocked nose and in a rich, quavering pansy accent.

SUNDAY 27 DECEMBER 1987. Today I felt very worried. Anxieties about my long-term future – or any future at all – are behind it all. And yesterday Bonnie's Christmas present for me arrived in a plastic ice-cream box. I was sick with rage. It was a vulgar, two dollar mug (these people never drink out of delicate cups) and it weighs a fucking ton, but I shall have to drag it all the way back down South, to prove with what rapture I received it. It also places me under the obligation to buy *her* something.

I woke up this morning in a terrible state and for some reason the service at Saint Matthew's, Oonoonba (I thought the funeral church might be a jolly alternative to Saint James's), did little to dispel my mood. The service started at 9 and I only got up at 8.30. I called a taxi and dropped my post off in the Eyre Street box on the way but still arrived in plenty of time. There was a skinny malformed Islander in front of me with an incongruous pot-belly: he looked like a little tree toad. I was intrigued by his tropical saffron shirt: somehow it seemed familiar. He was at a loss – couldn't find the hymns etc – he kept on glancing back and scrutinising me. The rest of the congregation was oppressively white. I admired him. There were no fans hanging from the ceiling, only a few household appliances whirring away on tall stalks like perching cicadas. The Islander was sitting right in front of me. His crinkled brown skin reminded me of old cold cooked sausages. The hymns were agreeable. On the way back to Araluen, I bought pies and a Lemon and Bitters for our lunch. I rang Tray again – again without success but at least he's reconnected the phone. Afterwards, I lay on the bed and tried to think pleasant things but sleep was like being chained to a torturer – frightful inescapable anxiety and debate throughout the ensuing dream. Oh God I feel so homesick, so worried and depressed. I wish I could just fly home tomorrow. Read from **The Comedians** by Graham Greene. Amazing how unconvincing his characters always are. Turned over on the bed the better to peruse my letters – the thunder was snapping away like a distant howitzer. A preposterous deafening storm ensued. There was a Christmas card from Edward Semper-Adonis, now back in England, and, in Tia's letter, a card from Sir Pedro Veech, one of my gallery's best customers. Apparently he'll be in Darwin in March. Edward (to whom I had sent a Queensland postcard) wrote how much he envied me the *"drunkenly green"* mountains of Yarraman! Suddenly I felt so much better. I have been alone in a nightmare, but when you see it through the eyes of the living, of the waking, the time involved seems shorter, the Australian scenery human and sublime, "exotic". I fell asleep – the cool, cool sleep of the storm – and awoke, amazed, to see purple Magnetic all lit up a blazing autumn gold. A band of black cloud filled the top of a transparent gold sky. It was raining. I wanted to get up and take a picture but I fell asleep again. The phone awoke me. It was Tray! . . . *Tray!* I arranged to go and visit him at Hambeluna on Thursday.

I went back to bed incredibly relieved. Now, though it was sunny, the sky was a solid mass of black and grey set off, here and there, by little wisps of pink cloud that seemed to drift just outside and in front of it. Just above the sunlit mountain-tops of the island, the cloud was white. There was a rainbow in the middle of this white cloud, like the red, green and

a novel

yellow tracks you find in an ice-cream after you have removed the glacé fruits . . . Could it be an omen?

Went down and dined on a burnt pie.

MONDAY 28 DECEMBER 1987. This morning I woke up when it was dark and very still: I was startled and I wondered why. Then remembered I was in the Tropics where the night with its possums and fruitbats is a banshee even less scrupulous than the day. I fell asleep again and dreamt I was staying at "Hambeluna" with Tray and I heard someone walking along the path outside the louvred verandah wall. The police were called. It was a deranged soldier who liked to stand and look at the front door. I will never forget the swish of the palm he was carrying on the concrete path as he walked, invisible, past those louvres. Tray was interviewed about it on television. He told the presenter he had earned more money through doing interviews than he had from his art . . . Then I heard Girly up. I rose and washed.

Donned my hat and dark glasses and walked down Stanley Street into town. I posted a card for Dewy, and, after a bit of a wait at the Greyhound place, collected my bus tickets for Bowen. I *have* wanted to go on an excursion and Karumba is a bit too far away. Also, having read ***The One Hundred and Twenty Days of Bowen***, I want to "trace the Nile to its source". I want to try to absorb, as Shoom must once have absorbed, the *physical* Bowen he was too familiar with to describe in his book. And yet without whose suggestive physical presence the bloodless book could no more have arisen than alcohol can exist without grain.

Visited the "REEFWORLD" aquarium in East Flinders Street – somewhat unwillingly, but knowing I would regret afterwards not having done so. There was the usual tautological film sponsored by the ferry companies that are destroying the Reef and the delights of whose effluent-disgorging floating hotels etc featured prominently. Then the screen

371

electronically withdrew and we we were looking into a vast sunny tank of coral and tropical fish. I was amazed by the variety of their synthetic colours and shapes. Did each of these incredible species have a name? What would they look like, lifted out of the water, gutted and cooked? What would they taste like? A gigantic fish hung like a balloon right next to the glass, eyeing us sideways. A milky mother-of-pearl white, with brown stripes like chocolate. Incredible to think something so colourful and beautiful could be tangible, physical, real. I also visited the Townsville Museum in Denham Street and learned that Townsville was founded in the 1860s by the agents of a landowner, one Robert Towns (so its name is *not* a tautology). Towns wanted a port north of the Burdekin as an outlet for the produce of his estates on that river. The Wulguru were the local tribe.

I'd bought some recherché ice-cream at *COLE'S* and lunched with Girly at Araluen. She read out a letter she'd received from Dew. He felt *"so sad"* about *"poor old Marilyn"* but *"death is part of life and the way we all go in the end"*. "Well," I said, "you can't argue with that!" Dew wrote that he *"can't help looking back"* to the old recondite Australia of ranches and oligarchs *"but that's no good – got to keep looking forward – such as when is* 'New Beginnings' *going to win a bloody race?"* Girly seemed a bit tired and cranky: I suspect I may be exhausting my welcome. "I'm eating fresh vegetables and you're eating ice cream!" she said. "Well," I replied, "you can see which one of us . . . " I was going to say, "will go to heaven" when Girly broke in: "is the stupidest. Is stupid, *stupid*!" She started talking about the dawn chorus. "In England, everything seemed so alive. Miss Drysdale would wait for the first nightingale". "Not like the awful cicadas here," I observed, with deliberate rudeness. "Quite," she said tersely. Was she annoyed? "How do they make that sound anyway?" she asked of the cicadas. "I believe they rotate their anuses," I replied. "Just think," she said, "if human beings did that. Can you imagine the noise that certain people would make?"

TUESDAY 29 DECEMBER 1987. This morning I dreamt I was living in Tray's studio in the "Bush House". I was sitting on the front lawn outside "Hambeluna" with Bonnie Popkiss. She was shaking her head with sultry gravitas. All eyes were upon me, she warned. People were jealous of me because of the beautiful tumbler she had sent me. Nightcliffe and a few of the other brutes appeared. I had to think on my feet. How could I convince them that I was in fact *unfortunate*? I awoke: it was 5.45. I rose and peed but I couldn't get back to sleep. I was worried about the "anti-national" remark I had made to Girly about the cicadas. I decided I would apologise, but once I decide to do something that involves nervous energy, I have to get it over with right away. Otherwise I worry about its hanging over me. This is what kept me awake. I got up at 6.50, washed, went downstairs, and explained myself. "Oh, that's alright," said Girly. "It didn't even register. Different people are sensitive to different things. I remember in Singapore I used to hear all night the clack clack clack of the Chinamen's clogs on the cobblestones. I used to think: 'I really don't like this. This is going to keep me awake'. But in the end, I came to love it." I drank a little tea and threw the rest out. I didn't want to have a full bladder on the bus.

Walking into town, I was approaching the Cutting, avoiding the dead toads, when I realised I would be passing the site of "Ivanhoe" on the coach. I rang Girly from a call box in Sturt Street. She said I wouldn't see the site of the homestead from the road, but when I crossed the Baratta Creek, I would know I was on the property. She was listed in the phone book in the telephone box under her address and "Miss K. D. Akers" – her maiden name! I asked her why. I wanted to avoid having the compulsion to ask hanging over me during the trip to Bowen, which would spoil my enjoyment. Instead of telling me why she forebore to use her marital *surname*, she said that her real *Christian* name was "Karalee" (hence "Girly"), an Aboriginal word such as were popular with Australian oligarchs then (viz. "Treeda", "Eucla", "Weeta" etc) . *"Work that one out if you can!"*

At the Greyhound Terminal, I knew something was amiss when we were each given a plastic box with an apricot tart and melon balls in it. It was described as a "compo payment". I added to my diary in the Waiting Room. When the call came to board we found ourselves on a mangy old 60s charabanc utterly bereft of air-conditioning or light-sensitive glass. The usual luxurious coach was unavailable due to what was delicately described as *"a customer under the bus"*. The trip down was an ordeal due to the heat, the scratchy chorus of headphones, the glare from the undarkened windows. And the ghastly scenery. There was nothing between Home Hill and Bowen but flat ashy grey soil, dead black trees and here and there a mountain like a heap of orange cinders. The gentleman next to me fell asleep, his head flopping onto my shoulder like a brick. My spirits rose briefly when we arrived. There was a wide main street of low, sunbleached, wildly coloured stucco falling to a turquoise sea. I have never seen a blue like the blue of the Bowen sea: radiant, metallic, veined like Fortuny silk. I walked down the street to the waterfront: there was no beach – a strip of grey earth simply collapsed abruptly into the water. The stone orange arms of a breakwater were enclosing the bay. On one side lay an industrial port with its chimneys and antennae, on the other a Marina for pleasure craft. Pale sulphur-blue mountains were visible in the pure sky beyond the breakwater. After the last pub, I passed an unearthly Bingo Hall. A few fat, rosy young matrons – white people look so incongruous in the Tropics – were standing next to a tricycle on the pavement. A man's voice, calling out the Bingo numbers, drifted out of a low white shed in a wasteland next to the railway line. "Three and Seven, Thirty-Seven!" A horse stood among the cinders next to the track with the acid sea beyond. Its ribs protruded and I was shocked to see there was a chain around its neck. There was nowhere for it to retreat to in the pitiless sun. I sat on a bench under some Leichardt Trees in the ashy seafront park and ate my Apricot tart with the fresh cream. (We had been forbidden to eat it on the bus). Sandy white lumps swam about in pools of whey. The motion of my jaws made me aware of my hat and interfered with sensations of pleasure, so

I removed it. A group of introverted seagulls stood around looking not particularly hopeful of a bite to eat. Amazing how they spring into raucous, committed life when you throw them something; they usually look so diffident.

Having seen the sea, I walked around some of the back streets of Bowen. They were laid out geometrically like the streets of every other Australian town. I was struck by the very wide desert margin between each pavement and the road proper. The old "Queensland" houses were smaller and less ebullient than those in Townsville, their gardens drier. They looked even more shut up and deserted. It was like a ghost town, peopled solely by mad drivers. I was amazed by the vast, glossy mango trees. Bowen is famous for its mangoes. A local postcard showed a girl lovingly fingering their great green testicles: *"BOWEN MANGOES, ONE OF THE MOST SOUGHT-AFTER TREATS OF THE TROPICAL TABLE-LAND!"* How sick Bowenites must get of them – their only claim to fame! I wondered how the huge threshing mango trees get enough water – you could see how the malachite colossi would dwarf very small dry gardens. I walked past one which completely overhung the pavement. There were mushy disembowelled mangoes everywhere, and, right in front of the gate, a great heap of half-bruised corpses. The sweet stench - like that of roast game – was appalling.

I passed a newsagent – *"Louis L'Amour Western Novels in Store!"* - and glimpsed a nicely dressed lady sitting upright in a dress shop, *"Peaches of Bowen"*, primly eating her lunch. The ridiculous effort implied by the fulsome name and her dress and manner in this meaningless desert at the end of the world quite shook me. The more so in that her lewd gluttony violated and so accentuated her prim manner. The penile finger she licked was like the one the little boy put in the damn. And here she was withdrawing it, licking it, positively *luxuriating* in the salty blue tsunami beyond! She regarded me slyly and with horror. I lunched myself in "the Bowen Tuckerbox". The usual lunatic came and sat next to me. This one was wearing a green boilersuit whose trousers ended half-way up his legs. He talked to himself incessantly about "Chrissie-massie Boongs".

 Then, leafing through *__THE BOWEN BUGLE__* or whatever it was, a local paper lying on the table, I nearly choked on my prawn cutlets. There was a huge two-page feature on a century-old local priest, "Father Tudor Crean". *"THE COD FATHER"* (for thus the piece was titled) had spent Sunday (Dec 27th), his one hundredth birthday, baptising his five hundredth Bowenite, *"Miss Araby Buraneer"*, daughter of *"Gordo and Belkina"* at *"St Agnes-Lips-of-the-Jewfish Roman Catholic Church, Magazine Creek"* – a region of Bowen. The left hand page of the spread was devoted to the not very interesting life of the hoary androgyne, the right to a huge photo of him holding Araby at a font as of she were a dustbin, *"Gordo"* and *"Belkina"* flanking him on either side. Below the picture, the legend *"1987"* blossomed in big shivering numerals. Around this oval image, like rhinestones ringing the opal in a brooch, were little rosettes containing much smaller photographs of the priest baptising kids on the same seventh year of other decades (1927, 1937, '47 etc), starting with his very first Bowen Christening in 1917. The names of the children baptised on *those* occasions were not, however, printed. There was a Dorian Gray-like feeling about the sequence, the jugged-hare resembling cleric advancing in perfumed decay, preserved in what was clearly alchohol, while the mothers, fathers and babies, like the victims of some vampire, beamed up forever young, forever pure and retarded. *"The One Hundred and Twenty Days of Bowen"*, indeed!

It was the image from *"1957"* which astonished me. By that date, Father Crean already looked like the skinned rabbit that Catherine Deneuve has forgotten to put back in the fridge in Polanski's *__Repulsion__* on its eighth day of putrefaction. But standing on his right was a man who looked exactly like Wanko does now (and of course exactly like the "shark" who shared my bed at "Yarralumla"). On the priest's left, meanwhile, perched a woman who was the spitting image of a (much younger) Girly! Even the features of the boy (or girl) cradled in the gin-soaked pansy's arms recalled Wanko's! Could it really be a family resemblance? On the drive up, I got the impression, from the way he was praising it, that Wanko came from the region of Mount Glorious, deep in the south of the state, while Girly, as far as I am aware, has never had any kids at all and in 1957 would have been about twice the age of the girl in the picture . . . . Wierd.

I paid a brief visit to the Bowen library and wrote photo cards to friends in England to give them some idea of the Australian Nirvana. I had them franked in the fondant-coloured Art Deco Post Office, which was charming. Took an afternoon tea of a *"Dagwood Dog"* and a chocolate milkshake in a pleasant café - *"A TASTE OF NUDGEE"* - and wandered down to the sea. All I could think of was England . . . I thought: "Wait a minute! When you're back you'll wish you hadn't recriminated so much! You'll wish you had kept your eyes open and absorbed Australia!" I took off my dark glasses and looked at the cindery soil of the Rotary Club Park. How strangely real it looked! This whole trip has been such a nightmare you half expect things *not* to be real. I carefully deposited my paper cup and made my way back to the bus stop.

Waiting for the bus, a toothy young Aboriginal was engaging a fat old German lady in conversation. She shook him by the hand and they talked about Collinsville. I can't get over the Europeans – English people, Irish, Scots, Germans – who have actually *emigrated* here! And to a place called "Collinsville"! (Better than "Townsville", I suppose!) How *can* they do it? I so admire them. To stay here for the next few weeks seems an evil enough eternity – but to commit yourself for *life*! To an eternity without history! As the bus passed Giru, I noticed the large monument to John Drysdale, Russell Drysdale's forefather, who features in so many of the stories Girly tells me.

Back in Townsville, I was overwhelmed by the heat of the evil afternoon. I bought two pies in the North Town Arcade and walked back to Araluen. "There was a shocking show at the Sheraton," Girly announced as I entered. A headline in the *"Bully"* about a floor show there - " 'STUNNINGLY DIFFERENT' *by Mike Boys*" – winked at me from the table. She waxed lyrical about Frensham before the First World War. Then how she had learned from "the Black Gins" at "Ivanhoe" never to feed wallabies cows' milk. It gives them diarrhoea. "Let them eat cake!" she tittered. And drink tea. Not what she had obviously been drinking. The wallaby had been in that afternoon and she had served him a plate of Rose Poochong, remembering the "Lubras" of 80 years before.

Sitting under the lamp, I was eaten alive by mosquitoes. I dined on a pie, and Girly on half a pie. "They say curries are cooling", she said. "That's why the darkies always eat them".

WEDNESDAY 30 DECEMBER 1987. This morning I dreamed I was watching the opening images of some television programme about the sun setting on the British Empire. Ships, seen from above, were sailing in a line, one after another, over a blue, mildly dented ocean. The ships were leaving a British colony. Schools of minnows seemed to be darting under the boats. Torpedoes. At the end of the line one saw a ship lying on its side just beneath the water gently rocked by wave after wave of torpedoes. The tall funnels were moving slightly under the water, like the tentacles of a sea anemone.

I came downstairs at about 8.30 and read, nervously, from Shoom's book on Leipzig. I knew I had a lot of an onerous nature to do: I am very near my deadline. Girly came in and began spooning juice out of an orange over the sink. She said it was most important to avoid the pith. The juice was a cure for arthritis. "When you're an old man yourself you'll remember what old Girly told you about arthritis!" Then, in a mood of *tempus fugit*: "The other day I was going to pay my cheque at the Main Roads place and these two great youths ran up from behind and said: *'Out of the way, Grandma!'* I thought: 'You cheeky brutes!' . . . Larrikins, I suppose."

Rang Bonnie and asked her about my mail. She greeted the news of the funeral with grievous sighs, a knowing expiration of breath.

Chatted to Girly about London and Paris in the 1930s. She told me how you could buy *coûture* dresses then for next to nothing, had they already once been worn by the Paris models. She went over to Europe, apparently, on a Vestey's meat boat. They'd sit gambling (which wasn't allowed), and a lady from Gol Gol, New South Wales would come and sit at their table with her daughter and show them photographs of the Tilapia Cod her husband had caught in the Murray River. "The Chief Engineer – he was a breakup!" She arrived in Paris on Bastille Day, 1939. (How fascinating that would have been, I thought, the last Bastille Day of the old, *authentic* Paris! Paris has been a parody of itself ever since). "Oh, it was divine. The Spahis with their Arab grey horses!" She was travelling with a girl named Alison Edols. Girly and Marilyn used to stay with the family at their property at Cudal, New South Wales. Alison Edols' sister was married to the brother of the British *coûturier* Teddy Tinling. Teddy designed clothes and his brother designed planes. Teddy had made his name with the "Gorgeous Gussy Pants" he had created for America's female tennis players. A member of "the Queens' Club" (I bet he was), he was able to get Girly tickets for Wimbledon. Girly would visit his fashion house in Hanover Square while Alison was being fitted for gowns. "I remember the beautiful, oh, beige – or were they off-white? – curtains with *'TINLING'* written in a line down to the ground. You know, like stripes. He was really quite an awful-looking person. He's quite bald now." (Girly has a disconcerting habit of referring to the deceased in the present tense).

After Paris, Girly and Alison went to Switzerland and the taxi taking them to their *Pensione* in Muzot (where Rainer Maria Rilke died) stalled half way up a mountain and the chauffeur couldn't find water for the radiator. When he opened it, they were all drenched by a scalding geyser. They rolled around shrieking. "Oh, it was so *funn-ih*, like having a hot hotel breakfast thrown over one!" The *Pensione* was even lovelier than a hotel – the grub-like eiderdown, the cosy porcelain stove. They enjoyed every minute. They had to return, though – war was about to break out. "When we sailed back into Sydney Harbour, everyone said: *'Australia,*

379

Australia! Isn't it *wonderful* to be home?!' And I thought: *'Oh God!'*. . . It suddenly seemed like the ends of the earth. After Europe, well, Sydney seemed so . . . so *harsh*, so *geometrical*." I felt the words she was looking for were "sterile", "artificial", "association-less". When her delicate friend Princess Marina came out, Girly said, the British papers wrote that she was being sent to *"the Siberia of the British Empire"*. The description amused me.

. . . I am almost hysterical with homesickness as I write this note. This hiatus in Townsville – I can't leave until I lay my hands on Dew's money – makes everything unreal. The idea of all I have to do has crazed me. I keep thinking: "I shall close my eyes and, when I open them, I shall be back in England!" It seems impossible that it can be so far away. I keep on thinking how apposite the "Siberia of the British Empire" line is. Australia is Siberian in its harshness, true, in its climate and in the fact that, during the Nineteenth Century, bad people were sent here as to a sort of Hell. (Heavenly America, founded by idealists, was naturally the reward of the just). But Australia is Siberian most of all in its tedium. And – ugh! – as if in reproof, a Blue-Tongued Lizard has just crawled across my bed! . . . That doesn't mean I want to *reject* Australia. What would be the point? It would be like trying to "reject" your parents. We're stuck with each other.

I spent the whole day writing and, when not writing, in nervous anticipation of writing. I really felt awful today. Recrimination prevents me from returning home immediately, as I would like, and recrimination for what I am missing out on in England prevents me enjoying myself here. Girly, meanwhile, bemoaned the fact that they show one of her favourite imported British TV dramas, about a vet, at dinnertime. "Just as you're having your seafood cocktail, they're diving into a cow's whimmy or something!"

THURSDAY 31 DECEMBER 1987. Woke at 2 or 3 AM feeling oily and uncomfortable, still fully dressed. With some effort I rose, showered, got into bed. I dreamt that I sailed back to England with Edward Semper-Adonis. There was a woman on the ship who became mentally ill. Her servant said his mistress had been invaded one day by a spirit just as she was about to sit down to dine. In the dream, you saw her about to seat herself at a table. Suddenly she was jumping up like a chimp and shrieking: "Oh Suzy!" Suzy was the name of the spirit. (It was also the name of Girly Soukoop's Pig Dog, of course). I descended the stairs at around 8 and chatted to a naked and profoundly laconic Kade, who was even at that unearthly hour pruning the mango tree.

Breakfasted on doughnuts, a pie, camembert and rich black olives. This got Girly onto "gorgeous, gorgeous canapés" (not to be confused with Teddy Tinling and his "Gorgeous Gussy Pants"). The Malayan planters had used to serve her "gorgeous, gorgeous canapés" in the 1920s. She was reading from a book Tray had lent me on the Malayan Raj. "Ah yes," she sighed, "*the British adviser opens a new bridge'* ". Back in the 20s in Penang, one planter would lend her his car and "syce" (chauffeur) by morning, another would give her his limousine in the afternoon. She would omit to tell either benefactor about the munificence of the other.

I set out for the Eyre Street Post Box at 9.45, and then I climbed the hill to "Hambeluna". This is my "big day". Tray was wearing a professional pool player's short-sleeved red satin shirt, which made him look even more sinister than usual. I sat on the old green chair on the verandah and found myself having to perfect my daily prayer. It was very hard, as I tried to pray, to resist reverie. It was hard to concentrate. I was badly bitten by Anopheles mosquitoes.

Tray and I walked down the hill into town. It was hot, blustery and grey. On our way to a shop to pay Tray's radio rental people, I saw an Aboriginal girl, one of the several who adorn the Mall, half-lying on a concrete ledge. She had a long, elegant neck, sleepy, elfin eyes. She reminded me of a dead lizard. She seemed the personification of the Aboriginal tragedy. Her childish dress (she must have been in her twenties) was bunched up around her thighs, and I remembered how Kipling, in **Something of Myself** (one of the books I have borrowed from Tray), said that his Ayah had told him in childhood that *"Hubshees"* ("curly hairs") always sleep that way and it makes it very easy for "black spirits" to enter their bodies. On our way back to the taxi rank, Tray stopped and fumbled in his breastpocket, drawing out a great wad of ten and twenty dollar bills, like a green ants' nest. His voice became soft, his eyes narrowed and seemed far away. He said he didn't have enough money and would have to return to the bank for more. So *this* was what *I* looked like in a state of compulsion and neurosis! The behaviour and excuses of the subject are superficially reasonable, but the softness, the terror in his manner fill the air with a withering oddness.

We stopped at the Uanda Laundry where I picked up my washing and we lunched at the Yongalla Lodge – a Greek restaurant off the Strand opposite the church where I saw Chuck Angry's funeral. It was a two story colonial building with verandahs. Tray told me several times (he has a habit of neurotically repeating himself) that it was one of the very few multi-storey "Queenslanders" built as such. (Most two-storey colonial buildings were originally raised as traditional plank bungalows on stilts, and sometimes the stilts would simply be enclosed to make a "ground floor"). We must have looked an unusual pair – Tray in his red silk shirt like a jockey, black stains under his arms like a darts' champion. I was wearing a bright lime cheesecloth chemise and a straw hat and carrying a bundle of washing in an old duvet bag.

We took a table on the verandah upstairs. There was a sombre atmosphere, and suddenly crashes of thunder like someone dropping a piano in another street. On one side of the rail stood a towering Tamarind tree, and St Joseph's Convent, whose school, Tray told me, he had attended as a little boy. On the other side of the verandah a door opened into a room which was meant to be representative of Nineteenth Century Townsville. Period furniture, life-sized waxworks in period clothes – one woman in a white Victorian shawl by the bed was grotesquely life-like and I got an appalling shock every time I turned my head. The restaurant is called the "Yongalla" after a ship of that name that sank early this century during a hurricane off Rockhampton. Tray's great Grandmother had booked a passage to Melbourne on the *Yongalla* – Marilyn and Girly were to accompany her (travelling by rail to Melbourne then would have taken much longer than by sea) – but she backed out when she heard that the captain was in the habit of entertaining his tarts on the bridge when he was meant to be steering. Everyone on board the ship drowned. One of the victims owned the house that became the eponymous restaurant. Hence the sinister Victorian "shroyn" to its passengers.

Now it was hot and still and grey. I still didn't say much – I had too much on my mind. Behind us a group of shop managers – the only other diners – were carrying on a "with it" conversation. One of them was a Chinese lady who spoke in a rich and animated way. "Carnations – I like all kinds of carnations but somehow never the red ones. They remind me of death". She mentioned "Barcelona", pronouncing it, for effect, with a Spanish intonation. "Do you bath-a-lone-ah?" one of her male colleagues demanded.

Taking advantage of my silence, Tray began to talk about auto-hypnosis: he was beginning to remind me of Wanko! When Barbara the cat was ill, he said, Marilyn took her to the "doctor". Near the "doctor" was a shop that sold psychic paraphernalia. He, Tray, wished to heal Barbara and one could listen to these hypnotist's tapes from the shop with their subliminal messages and visualise red and white circles, beautiful scenery. Then they would appear to you when you were about to fall asleep. Then, with application, the neophyte began to see them with his eyes open. Tray is trying to look at his cats and visualise a white circle around them. This will protect them. He also thinks of a long, glowing blue bottle of medicine and sets it against an image of his favourite cats and possums. It is the beautiful colour – not necessarily the chemical properties – that will cure them, he thinks. He has already cured a possum's eyes in this way. His own eyes become sore and he becomes "irritable" when he practices this meditation after watching TV, so he has refrained from watching it. These things he is trying to summon up with open eyes appear real – they aren't

383

mental images. He goes over all the objects in the Gun Room at Hambeluna, and, when they appear before him in the kitchen, it is as if they are actually there, on the table. "Then why be an artist?" I asked him, rather bored with this conversation. "Isn't it about recording things that *are* really there? Doesn't it depend on the real thing?" As soon as I broke in Tray was obviously rattled and started mouthing things, talking to himself as I kicked off aloud. He certainly doesn't like to be interrupted and his remarks always have the air of a "set piece". But I find him more interesting when he is forced not to be mystical and narcissistic, when he thinks on his feet. It was also the case, perhaps, that, like a cow in a field, whose mind (I suppose) is generally on the cow god, or the local bull – or anything, in fact, but the procedure whereby it produces milk – Tray, like most artists I have known, is seldom moved to talk about painting. "I mean, what about when you're drawing from the model?" I asked. "Well, what's the difference?" he shot back. "They may as well not be there. It would save me a lot of time if they weren't. Because you're right – all the artist wants is the *form*. We're not trying to capture their 'inner soul'. But just try and tell *them* that. They all think you want to fuck them or something." He said this sarcastically, I think in a dig at me and my "pretentiousness" in raising the subject. "People like you," he sneered, "are always telling us you have to go through the mask, the external, to get at the reality. Any artist will tell you that you have to go through the deep end *first* to get at the *external*! People are like bananas whose peel is on the inside; you have to go through 'the hidden truth' to get at the wallpaper. Calm the boyfriends and the girlfriends . . . I've had to sit through a good few knickerbocker glories in my time, I can tell you! . . . And why? All to draw a pickled walnut! Nobody realises that strangers are nothing to each other. Models don't realise that they have have nothing to lose because they *are* nothing." "What do you mean?" I asked. He had come alive, like a carnivorous flower.

"Well," he went on, straining for words (he clearly preferred spinning his hokum about cats), "say you ask someone to sit for you. You can put the magnitude of that request, of the relationship it suggests, in a few superficial words: a piece of bread floating on the water. Your mind swims, a fish, to the surface. To the light, where that little crust is floating. You deal with things in an automatic, contingent way. You are surrounded by the darkness, the depth of that request. That indeed is your element, but you are looking up at that little crumb in the light, that piece of pie in the sky. That is all you see. And there's something thrilling in that – the thought of controlling another being, the unspoken emotional size, made flesh in a wafer. The bread of heaven – like in a communion wafer. That's what I *love* – insignificance, but abundance if you want it. *'Cast your bread on the waters, and it will be returned a thousand fold!'* . . . The model is wholly your fantasy: the explosive, the nervous, contained in the local, the neutral. The tiniest scratch could bring out the big – a boil is so easily burst. It can so quickly get out of hand, like when a nestling falls in a boiling Billy Can, or an Alka Seltzer in a tumbler of champagne". Tray started to gesture with this hands. "Now, for the first time in my life, I feel *surrounded* by that vastness, Pat, that social or sexual bigness, raw to it, sensitive to it, and I don't know what to do. I'm trying to extract the sands of the Seltzer from the Goldfish bowl, trying to put the genie back in the bottle . . ." Tray laughed. He has a lovely laugh.

"How do you became an artist?" I said, stupidly. "An artist's relationship with the world is that of a *knife*", Tray observed, "the non-artist's is that of a *fork*. So the way to become an artist," he said, "the first emotional line that you cross is: you detach yourself. Not from others, from yourself. Those who do that are *de facto* artists. It's precisely because models haven't learned this distinction – between the self that they know and the completely different individual known to others – that they always take the painter's approach the wrong way. People are born blind, you see, like mice." "Or is it," I said, putting on airs, "that the painter, like Oedipus, is blinding *himself*? It seems to me that you're deliberately maiming yourself, Tray, by refusing to have 'friendships'. You're like those people in India who want to become beggars: you've deliberately crippled yourself. It keeps you in a state of wanting, needing, that is propitious for you." "And what is 'friendship' to an artist?" he laughed. "I don't have any time for my *enemies*, let alone my friends!" "So what you paint is your enemy?" "Not really. I'm just . . . I'm not putting it right. It's like when I'm painting. When I get something down I sense the subtlety of, but find difficult to explain, I make a few rough strokes and later, looking at them, I realise what it was I wished to say. I elaborate; but by then the complexity comes naturally - like Peroxide fizzing in a wound." He laughed again. "Here I am again, now, effervescing – I'm just an Alka Seltzer sizzling in the great big sea!" "Out of the frying pan into the fire, eh?" I replied. "Tray, I'd love it if you *were* a silly little Alka Seltzer! You could cure a very big headache of mine! It seems all I ever get is your *placebos*, though, your dead little sugar pills!" I was referring to his usual "set piece" mode, of which our discussion was not an example. "But of course!" he laughed. "Everybody's got to wait for the 'Cum Shot', haven't they? Everybody wants the Cumshot, and nobody wants it to end. Least of all dealers, people like you! But it's like when you open a bottle of champers. How are you going to pour yourself a stem unless it's stopped effervescing? The foaming at the mouth, the poetic *petit-mal*, the descent of the Muse, it all has to come to an end. Otherwise how can the work actually begin? After all, you'd hardly want me to give you the first febrile crayon to sell, would you? You'd want me to give you the finished paintng?" This penetrating sally took me aback. As did: "I might as well tell you, Pat, I can read your mind!"

Fortunately for me, he couldn't. He started to talk about Jung and Jung's theory of the collective subconscious. It was something he had learned from a book he had bought at the psychic paraphernalia shop, how to read the minds, the innermost thoughts, of his circle. I said that I didn't think it would be a very profitable occupation – not in Townsville anyway! "No", he earnestly agreed, the curtain coming down again, "some people are very sad and it might not be very good". Hoping he would agree to my plan, I said that what one took for other people's thoughts were usually one's own. That analysing other people only ever led you further into yourself. Tray seemed appalled. Like me, he often tries to neurotically distance himself from what he says. This was a case in point. He also laughs, ironically, at what he says, his long, sensitive teeth lost in the bloated lunatic head. I felt sorry for him, for I realised he was savouring, perhaps for the first time, the pleasures of conversation.

He had progressed so far down the road of reading people's minds, he said, that he could make people materialise just by thinking of them. He found it hard to sleep, sometimes: "My grandfather did, too". Often, he said, he would stay up all night, take a short nap, and start painting at midday. He enjoys staying up: "Sometimes I feel the most tremendous vitality!" But when he's had too little sleep he finds it "hard to smile". That is when he wants to avoid meeting Mr Barscrub. "I like Mr Barscrub but sometimes you don't feel like smiling at people". He would find himself avoiding thinking of Marilyn's solicitor or he would end up meeting him. He started calling Castle Hill "Mount Kutheringa" once – the Aboriginal name for it – and he immediately started meeting Aboriginals. One night at Hambeluna, (for example), he couldn't sleep and he went out to check the mail box (a euphemism, I thought, for one of his "Owl and Pussycat" adventures). What should he see but a group of three "Boongs" marching up the starlit boulevard? Then there was the very attractive brunette who used to work in "Pat Molloy Jewellers" (he intoned it as if invoking the shade of "Asprey's" or "Cartier"). He would deliberately think of her. He ended up meeting her day after day, sometimes coming up behind her or surprising her in embarrassing situations. She got annoyed and he stopped doing it.

"And look at the way you bought that cocoa!" he said, of a fancy tin I'd found Girly at *DAVID JONES*. "I was getting very into cocoa at the time!" It was a Jungian coincidence. One couldn't approach the subject, he warned, in a "carefree" manner. If you got out on the wrong side of the bed one morning and thought of someone whose mind you wished to read, you might do them real harm. "But you're just about the most benign person I know", I said, revolting myself, hoping to draw him out. "Yes," he said, he was now, but it wasn't always thus. "Certain things" had happened in the recent past that had made him "very angry". He gave me a captious "knowing" look. I became afraid.

Suddenly, "I think I'll sign that contract now," he said of the legal document I had asked Mr Barscrub to draw up: I had mentioned it to Tray once before. He began to fumble around for a pen. What an absurd obstacle, I thought, just think how many times a momentous opportunity has been lost because someone couldn't find a pen! He started to write. There was a clatter of thunder; the cicadas began hissing again. It struck me how operatic it all was. I became tenser. "*Nineteen-*" he said. "Do you spell it with one or two 'tees'?"

I thanked him profusely and suggested a toast. "The character is rich, luscious, sweet!" said Tray, reading from the label, the crystal in his hand a gamey, menstrual red. "Relieved" is a word I would not use of my feelings then.

I caught a cab home to find that Girly had strained her shoulder leap-frogging a low wall. This happened as she was helping Kade to cut the bougainvillea and clear a drain. Now she found it difficult to lift her arm. She had been forced to ask a gentleman to pluck a can for her from the topmost ledge at a supermarket. "He looked like an old wharfie but he was so very nice. He looked like one. A real old roughie but they're terribly sweet".

I mentioned the protest the Aboriginals are planning tomorrow to mark their Bicentennial "year of morning". (A Freudian – perhaps a Jungian – slip. I meant to write "mourning"!) They say they're going to wear white, as a deliberate inversion of the whites' association of the colour black with sorrow. "Aren't they *funn-ih*?" Girly said. "Poor things . . . Appalling really." Eagerly I agreed with her, pointing out that, had the white man lived by the purely Aboriginal values which today's Abos claim to extol, the genocide would have been total, and unaccompanied by reflection.

Girly slipped into her book. "Shanghai's a place I would have loved to see," she sighed. "I'd love to have puffed on an opium flute. And Mahjong – I never ever played it. But it was a great game in the Malay states because it didn't take a lot of energy. The way they play games now everything's got to have a lot of energy. Too much, I think."

I asked her about Kade's band. I said I found it hard to visualise him singing. "Oh," she said, "I don't think they have to *sing* – they only have to look as if they're in agony. I don't know if *he* looks like that!"

I wondered how *I* looked, as I certainly was in agony. The significance of what I had done had begun to dawn on me.

FRIDAY 1 JANUARY 1988. Another hard day, at least initially. I awoke at 2, aware that the New Year was upon us, and I was still languishing in irresolution and pain, but in a sort of oasis now that I have Tray's consent, looking forward to the hours of sleep before the guilty debates began on waking. All I look forward to now is sleep. That's the only time I feel happy. (Except, of course, when night is hot with nightmare). Well, I can blame no-one but myself. Surrounded in England by a great rich dung cake of association, I capriciously chose the glamour of nullity. I simply cannot understand why - when I could have been happy at home – I reached out, as if to a hornet's nest, and willingly swallowed this awful pain. And I've suddenly realised what has been wrong with me. I have been lonely. Just the feeling – not to be borne when it comes on you unawares – that you are alone with your problems far from home.

I woke at 5.30, and couldn't get back to sleep, debating whether or not I should ask Dewy – presuming he rang – whether I must stay to supervise the portrait and how the identity of the sitters, when he lays eyes upon them, can be concealed from the artist, who may very well know all about them. (I haven't actually apprised Dew of this detail, not wishing to lose my cash). And I can't work out – (if I put these questions to Dew) – the precise form in which the enquiry should be couched. These interstate phone calls, with Dew hollering down the other line, are like operations for a tumour. Every detail must be cleared up at once, without a single fragment remaining that might torment one into further expensive surgery. An atmosphere of breath-held terror prevails, the more dreadful for its promise of release. But the time leading up to the call is much, much worse, which makes you want not to make it at all, and, if so, to "get it over with" as swiftly as possible.

I went downstairs and compulsively ate cheese biscuits, turning the problem over and over in my head. I noticed the phone bill on a coffee table and perused it. Girly has paid a price for my neurosis. It added to the tension. I apologised to Girly, without directly alluding to the bill, which I didn't want her to know I'd read. "That's alright", she said quietly. This disturbed me: it was ingenuous proof of her annoyance. When people *really* don't mind, they make a great play of saying they don't mind, not because they really don't, but because, with the temporary abandon of a saint, they write it off in a higher cause. I went back up to my room and tried to read – some local tangential pleasure in which the past and the future could lose themselves – a licking of "Continual Dew" off the leaves. And, as so often when I've had time before Dewy's call, the pleasure, without giving me pleasure, went deeper, spread, so that the hours whizzed by and I still hadn't decided the precise nature or wording of my exposition . . . And so I started to panic, like one who hasn't done any revision before an exam. Girly called me down for lunch. I was genuinely confused. I decided, without going into specifics, to ask for Girly's advice. A woman born for stupor and delicacy and yet strong enough, intellectually, for my purposes. It was strange to see her respond, quite spontaneously, to such strangeness, such seriousness, like watching yourself in a dream get what you imagine you'll never enjoy. Often, in an impasse, I will ask for advice like this, seeing no way out, and yet hopeful of some miracle. It's as if I exist on two planes. "Your trouble" she said, "is that you keep on changing your mind. I would get into a *frightful* mess if I decided upon *one* thing and then did *another*!" I chewed my lovely steak and broccoli without delight. "Yes", I thought, "I'll stay with my original plan. I'll sweat it out. Do what needs to be done!"

Eventually, unable to bear the suspense any longer, I decided to pre-empt Dew's call and ring him up, but from Hambeluna's phone, not Girly's. It was one of those "split second" decisions. I rang Tray and warned him of my arrival. I grabbed my hat and said goodbye to Girl, whose arm was in a sling. She was reading greedily from the book about the Malayan Raj. As I walked down Stanley Street I thought what a pity it was I couldn't enjoy the delicate yellow afternoon – that, in different circumstances, I would be happy. I bade Tray a glorious New Year and asked if I could use the phone to ring my London colleagues about the contract which he and I had agreed upon. Consenting with flair he withdrew to the kitchen and I rang Dew's private number. I noticed the pathetic notes on Marilyn's desk: instructions for exercising the fingers etc the Blue Nurse had dictated. The phone bleeped and bleeped. I rang Dew's public number and asked whether the private number were in abeyance for the holidays. No, a husky Bronco replied, it was probably just in demand. I rang again. The phone purred over and over again and I was already vaguely reconciled to the frightful likelihood of having to stifle my assault. Resisting neurosis when you have already made a decision, however abstract and token, to give in, is much more difficult than refusing, in advance, and however unsuccessfully, to accept the possibility of defeat. Strange that the decision to give in – as neutral and cerebral as the belated countermanded desire to resist – should unleash such occult convulsive furies. I was stunned to hear a new Bronco at the other end: "Yeah mate, whadya wand?" . . . Dew sounded sleepy. Without addressing him then or later by name I offered up my "Happy New Year" with a passion that came of wanting to get things over with as swiftly as possible so I could proceed with the matter in hand. "Happy New Year," said Dew, "I have a *baby* in bed with me!" Which wouldn't have surprised me in the least but it turned out to be his grandchild. After giving Dew the "good news", I was careful to spell out my problem in metaphorical terms that Tray, should he overhear, would not be able to comprehend. I also tried to make sure that no misunderstanding could arise between Dewy and I that I would later feel compelled to

391

clarify. "There," thought I, "it's over and done with, and no addition to the presentation has so far occurred to me! Should any suggest itself later, I shall not have to worry about a call in which I may need to bring it up!" *"Now, listen Pehtrick"*, said Dew, after we'd discussed the issue, *"I hope that's an end to your stupid worrying!"*

I went and thanked Tray in the kitchen and we returned to the verandah. He sat opposite me, in profile, on the other side of the table that still lay as Marilyn had set it for her last "celebration", the tea for Nanya Veldten. "What day are you thinking of leaving?" he asked. He had obviously overheard me say I would be leaving Townsville around the *"_th "* of the month. "You can stay here in Hambeluna for a few months if you like". I was silent. This after avoiding me, after giving me the runaround for ages! My neurosis would once have made me embrace the issue, dreading a "future imperfect" when my interlocutor might pull me up on some supposed mutual pact. Now, however, I was serene and I said nothing at all. After all, the end was in sight. We talked about the contract and I thanked him again, as repulsively as I could, for agreeing to sign it. I remember thinking what a good Australian film the scene would make – Tray with the downcast eyes and the sharp, sad edges on his mouth – something realistic, pensive, autochthonous, strange. Something so unlike the neutral international settings and soap opera "psychology" adored by Peter Weir *et al.* I went to the other side of the verandah, not quite able to believe that this torture might finally be over. I prayed to God: "O God, may nothing more occur to worry me; may this truly be the end!" . . . I was so optimistic that the fact that I may now be embracing the Great Beast didn't trouble me in the least! I wondered, though, if I would ever be happy enough, relaxed enough to daydream again, to fantasise.

We took a taxi down to East Flinders Street and walked through the Reef World Mall. A winey tropical dusk, Fruit Bats hopping around and screeching like toads. The houses of South Townsville like nesting boxes on the other side of the creek, pale blue mountains. I saw an "ethnic Australian" café advertising crocodile steaks *("Behold The Tourists' Revenge!")*.

We were the only diners – not an unfamiliar phenomenon, according to the owners, a couple who told us they were just about to sell up. It struck me that "*LARRIKINS*" with its crystal and linen juxtaposed with barbie favourites and "Bush Tucker" – making an in-joke, an expensive irony of what most locals would have associated with Abos and the poor – must have gone right over Townsville's head. The failure couple, who were middle-aged, too old to start over, divided between themselves the honours of the kitchen and the *Table d'Hôte*. They went into the back. We heard them arguing and there was a nasty edge to it. They came out again and now they were dressed in the restaurant's soon to be discarded uniforms: shorts and teeshirts with *"LARRIKINS"* written jauntily on the breast pocket. We ordered roast Emu. Each tiny portion arrived sculpted into a ridiculous dog-turd: it wasn't hard to see why the enterprise had failed. The husband, who looked like Goebbels, pounced on my accent and said that he had been "brought" to Australia as a child. "Oh!" I said. "You are a *'stolen choyld'*!" He had been born in Angmering – a ghastly piece of 30s ribbon development on the bleak West Sussex coast. Had never been "able to afford" to revisit "the old country". Then, forgetting that diners seldom enjoy talking to waiters, even – indeed especially – in an empty restaurant, he demanded all sorts of personal details. And then if my visit – I suddenly realised that Townsville must seldom receive tourists – was "business or pleasure"? "Pleasure!" I intoned, as sarcastically as possible. "Well," he blurted, "it must be nice for *some* people, swanning around the world the whole bloody time!" Tray smiled drily. Not for the first time I was left utterly speechless by the Australian audacity. It wasn't rudeness really. Rudeness requires a degree of sophistication, differentiation, that doesn't really exist in Australia – a consciousness of breaking the rules. In Australia there *are* no rules. Nobody wears a mask in the first place: everybody says the first thing that comes into their heads, as in an asylum or a kindergarten. Nothing is driven by malice, because, like kindness, it is a form of subterfuge.

I must have been wrong about the tourists as Madame Goebbels came up and offered a selection of Townsville tourist brochures from what I saw was a smorgasbord, a cornucopia, behind the bar. All soon to be swept from the overstuffed aborted restaurant like the crystal and the chilling uniforms. It seemed to speak of the pointlessness of all of Australia's largesse. Perhaps I would turn out to be Townsville's last tourist as well as its first.

Tray and I walked up Flinders Mall to the taxi rank. At Hambeluna, the possums awaited us. Tray fed the first of the filthy things – it perched on a rail of the verandah – introduced it as the "mother". He said that he could recognise each of them, that the Aborigines had regarded them as the choicest form of food. I borrowed books about Constantine Porphyrogenitus, Jack Kerouac and the Ispahan of Shah Abbas the Great and caught a taxi back to Araluen. Girly was watching a nationwide telecast which was in celebration of the Bicentennial, which began today. Australia's famous expatriate know-it-all Clive James (an "intellectual" as in "Germaine Greer, intellectual") tried pitiably to advertise his mastery of Russian, Japanese, Mandarin etc. A local celebrity, his fellow compère, humourlessly extemporised, clearly resenting the smartarse competition. Vintage colonial performances all round.

SATURDAY 2 JANUARY 1988. The ***BULLETIN*** announced today that they're taking the toys off Flinders Mall. When first Flinders Street, Townsville's Champs Elysées, its Nevsky Prospekt, was "pedestrianised", gaudy plastic tables and seats, like play furniture for infants, were strewn where the traffic had roared, surreal palms and other tropic plants were set in tubs, giant plastic toys scattered for adults and children. A pavement, for instance, striped like a chessboard, was painted pink and white for chessmen the size of dwarves. A tiny train took people on paid rides through the White Trash tupperware horror – which formed Townsville's only "attraction". In postcards that are still being sold of the "new" Mall in its heyday, it looks like it has been decorated for Christmas or a parade, that "normal service" will soon resume, that playtime will soon be over. But playtime was never meant to end and, as a result, real life in the Mall has been choked off as well. For the stupor and the play and the absence of movement and life drove away the shoppers and the shops, most of which are now thrift venues. As part of the vicious circle, the drunken Abos decended on the arctic infant furniture from their camp in the Mangrove Swamp, and, even before dark, the place of peurility and the immobile became sinister. (The *"Bully"* was rejoicing in the headline *"HOONS IN THE MALL!"* a few days ago). Even *DAVID JONES* is to move soon, to the out-of-town incubus known as "Nathan Plaza". In an attempt to win back the crowds, a "Farmers' Market" is now held in what was once Townsville's Downtown every Sunday – the pineapples and sweet potatos sitting in mounds in front of the boarded-up shops as in some cannibalised colonial town in Zaire after independence. Nobody seems to have seen how fragile it would turn out to be, the real, the civic life. The City Fathers must have thought it was all so strong it could be abused, that the only problem was that real life had to be reined in somehow. And now real life is revealed as a delicate growth like a truffle plant that depended on the careful preservation of a precise concatenation of circumstances. It is all so reminiscent of the careless way Australians today treat the racial-political infrastructure they have inherited from the Brits.

In any case, it now means that Townsville has joined the ranks of every other Australian city. For the cities of Australia – even Sydney – are vestigial. They are interminable suburb with these little "dead hearts" at their core. ("The Dead Heart" is the name of the desert beyond the Blue Mountains – the desert of which Australia is mostly composed – the inhabited coasts are the merest mould of green rind). In other countries, the middle of a city is its pump, its brain, its first freshwater well. Life is pumped from there to the suburbs. In Australia the city cen-tah is more like an appendix. This is true of Sydney but even more of the provincial towns, which are not cities in any real sense at all. And what is wrong with that, you may ask? What *dérangement* could one possibly find in the Manningreedahs and the

Mundingburras, in the interminable, luxuriant pulp? Isn't one obliged to compare Australia and its sterile luxury – its peace – with the situation in its immediate neighbours? Isn't one obliged to compare Tarcoola and Streaky Bay with Ho Chi Minh City, Chungking, Rangoon? Would it not be more fair to compare the way Australians live with the way *other* Asians live? Why compare Townsville or Canberra with London or Paris? Behold the clean shops on every kerb in Oonoonba, with an array of refigerated delicacies that would put Fortnum's to shame and you realise what a survivor of the Khmer Rouge might see in it. Initially, I was surprised when I saw so many Kampucheans, Greeks, Koreans etc inhabiting Sydney. How could these ancestral peoples bear the lack of associations, the pastlessness, the empty, interminable future that I, a mere British visitor, sensed with such horror? But tupperware is better than pain.

This morning, I worried about the return of the leitmotif, the guilt obsession. I made an attempt to finish my letters early, so I could devote the afternoon to pleasure, to reverie, which I have missed. You can only enjoy daydreams if you can create a *cordon sanitaire*. I lunched, *without* pleasure, on greenish prawn fritters. I finished writing my diary shortly afterwards and looked forward to luxuriating over my books. I tried not to read the Kerouac as I want to save it for the journey back to London. Tomorrow I'll have to start worrying about that but today is officially an hiatus of pleasure. But I couldn't enjoy myself – that hornet's nest in the stomach feeling again. I threw myself into the books – even the ones I had been "saving" – as a mere aspirin, a local analgesic. I was denied the right to savour them in tranquility, like a vase of sherry. I remember turning away from **Shah Abbas' Isfahan** in disgust.

Unable to settle, I climbed up through the back garden to Mount Kutheringa. The whole hill is naked, solid rock of an incredible baked pinkness, like a saddle of *"Trout Belin"*. There is a light covering of earth – after the rains, it is suddenly very verdant – a forest of fragile gums. It is difficult to know how they survive - they seem to grow straight out of the paltry earth. When it rains, the hill is veined with hundreds of little streams: they look quite white, sometimes silver, like guano. The leafage of the lovely gums was lit up a transparent lime-gold against a great cliff which was dark, completely in shadow. It seemed too new, too synthetic in its purple pinkness to support associations and – given the infinite repetition of these features in every direction (the pink mountains with their mist of gums that look blue at a distance) – too featureless. It was difficult to locate here the particularity that would support spirit life, nostalgia, because the elements of specificity that did exist were infinitely repeated in every direction, and the sheer weight of the infinity appeared to crush them. The unique is only interesting when there is a finite number of unique objects: this is the attraction of a cosy little landscape like England's. When there is an infinite number of unique objects, the landscape seems to close up, defy analysis. I find it hard to understand the Aborigines' affection for this land; they are certainly welcome to it as far as I am concerned! There was something hostile up there on the hill. The land definitely has its own genius. I defined it in a note as a homesickness other than my own, but I wasn't thinking of the Aborigines. The Australian landscape seems alive. The English countryside is like a house, it breathes with the breath of mankind, it exhales the purely human note, the human side of world history. It has been possessed - fabricated. But the Aborigines haven't created the Australian landscape in the way the English have created "England". Australia is alive and it was alive a long time before they were. Australia is a bad thing, like a Killer Whale.

Just as I was about to return to the house I heard a sound like a cat behind a row of huge boulders. I went to look but couldn't see anything. I was turning back when the sharp mewing began again, seemingly right in front of me. I scanned the bare pink rock: again I could see absolutely nothing. Then, a fissure cracking the surface a few meters further up the hill vibrated again with a flat cat-like cry. When I climbed up, I saw that what had seemed, from below, like a horizontal line slicing the cliff was the lip of a crevice which was divided from its further wall by a deep pit. I looked down into the hole: it reminded me of

Marilyn's freshly opened grave. At its base, surrounded by a dandelion-spore spray of Aboriginal white-dot paintings, I couldn't believe what I saw: a horrible Dingo suckling two human babies! It was truly appalling, the naked gurning babes chewing on the monster like two bald Osprey chicks tearing at the guts of a big hare in a shit-spattered nest, each trying to push the other aside and screaming like bug-eyed owlets. The Dingo bitch looked up at me complacently like a woman being fucked. I picked myself up and stumbled down the hill, thumping along as fast as I could. At Araluen, I screamed for help but nobody was home. Nobody. Kade had driven Girly out to the "Villa Vincent" Retirement Hamlet to see the Misses Grey, Marilyn's erstwhile neighbours. (The sylph-like grimalkins have just been moved there). I had to rush back up Mount Kutheringa all alone. Completely alone. The great baking rocks like knuckles of bacon all looked the same. So did the crevasses that veined them. In none did I find any trace of the Dingoes' nest or Aboriginal painting. Or infants! The hill was silent now, malign. I felt afraid. And I felt light-headed, diffident, as on the night of the tapping ten years ago, which also followed an episode of extreme tension. Should I duplicate my error then, go with the flow of what could only be an hallucination? How could a Dingo possibly be suckling two little white babies? Isn't it all a bit too much like the trauma induced by the Dingo bite? Anyway, anyone listening to me would think I was insane. And what could anyone do about it were I not? What would the ensuing procession of events *entail*? The last thing I need is a further complication *now*. I'm not even going to mention it.

SUNDAY 3 JANUARY 1988. The city was immobile this morning under a glass of catatonic heat, the sea a hot grey-turquoise colour. "We can use sprinklers, which is gorgeous," said Girly, "I can turn mine on today!"
I studied my return air ticket to London with Continental. It's still valid – the one I got from the Australian Govt. Happily, I am now in a position to buy my own. But should I perhaps

keep to my original schedule? . . . Still, what a schedule! The thought of the 17 hour wait at Honolulu, of dragging one's baggage around Newark Airport in the middle of a mugger-infested Winter night, trying to catch a tiny crowded minibus through the slums of New Jersey to the next airport, rather spoiled my enjoyment of Communion. Whenever I return to my pew in the Cathedral, I see a black cat in one of the chapels. It seems to be wrong somehow. It strolls insolently, indifferently through the nave, throwing the proceedings into vivid relief. It strips away the context we had invented, making us see it all as it is, as an atheist might see it.

The sermon was impressive. The Yorkshire Bishop bade us an insincere farewell at the door. He was wearing a home-made (?) robe stitched with yellow and green felt shapes. Once more, I felt a shiver of horror as I imagined myself in *his* shoes. Who would be a career diplomat, for instance? After only a few months in Australia, the romance of foreign travel appals me. Foreign travel is for people who never really leave home. It is part of an epicentre, metropolis mentality, this feeling that the faraway is desirable. How exotic Townsville must have seemed from Yorkshire, for instance! And it *is* exotic – but only in the metropolis. So when you are actually in Townsville, what you miss most of all – even about Townsville – *is* the metropolis. Like the chapel whose superficiality and pretentiousness the black cat had brought to view, the Bishop's robes suggested a society that had had to make an effort at pain, a society to which reality had never come naturally. After church, I walked up Melton Hill from the Cathedral to look at a lovely old Queenslander like a cat basket. Then I climbed the spur of the hill and gazed out over the delirious blue to Magnetic Island. Yes, so nice, to see this scene from London, to think of it from there. So painful to contemplate it from here.

As the guilt-over-Tray-Beautous obsession took a hold, I continued to toy with the "official" idea of trying to forget the debate, only to jump willingly into some further arcane point, like a man diving underwater, coming up for air only so he can plunge back down again.

This is what obsession is – and anger too. All one needs to terminate either is a decision to pause, to stand outside oneself. The artificial treadmill, in which there is an element of wilfullness, of play, will come to a halt. But it is so much easier to stay inside oneself – even in a futile cause – to stay with the seemless narrative, which has its own momentum, than to breathe the coïtal and destructive air of reality. And soon enough it is, instead, the passion, the obsession that is real. It is the same with writing – with writing this diary, say. It seems so difficult to begin. At the beginning, one's mind seems superficial, superficially involved. But with application comes concentration, a concentration which one always feels one has had enough of, which one is always trying to escape, but a concentration which does not come from within. This is when – perhaps for the painter no less than the writer – the *pièce de-résistance* arrives. First you are scared by the prospect of nothing – and then there is too much. You feel you can never get it all down – you try to escape it. Just as I was deciding light-headedly to try to forget the guilt debate, I must have crossed this point, for I just as light-headedly decided to succumb and tell Tray about the "clients" on the morrow, to pull the whole thing down. But this of course would become a big thing and ruin the day until I decided to tell him. I toyed with the idea of going down to the GPO to check Dew's Sydney number (he is in Sydney at the moment), just to satisfy myself I had it. With one ridiculous part of my brain I convinced myself I wouldn't use it, wouldn't tell Dew that I'm backing out.

By the time I arrived at Hambeluna I didn't know whether I was worried or not. Whether the guilt debate was a legitimate area of concern, or (as I hoped) something superficial and "neurotic". There was a deep underlying anxiety, a light dusting of leaves. I was quite absorbed in all this mental activity when Tray greeted me and I was aware of my rootless responses to his. I fastened on the little relaxations his books and conversation afforded. If I let them grow, they might show the pain I felt to be unreal. I had only expected a brief interview. I wanted to return to Girly's, compose myself, and work out where I stood vis-à-vis my obsession. I was therefore surprised and depressed when Tray suggested that we lunch together. Still, I girded up my loins. I know how foolish all this worry will appear in retrospect, in a few months' time. I will no doubt think then that I wasted a whole *"saison"* not *"en enfer"* but in *"en paradis"*. And so, in the midst of what seem to be overwhelming, important problems, I always try to write. From the future, I know it will strike me as the only worthwhile thing I did. I am reminded of those *papier-mâché* heads we used to make at kindergarten. We covered a pert balloon with paper and glue; by the time it had dried the balloon had shrivelled. This balloon, this awful, ontological Townsville life will one day shrivel, and what I will be left with is an interesting hardened epic. Even though the act of writing now seems distracting, somewhat painful, it is a weary act of will which I know, by instinct, to be correct. In this spirit, I called Tray grimly for pen and paper and made a note of this morning's sermon.

The Yorkshire Bishop actually said that the concept of the soul and its immortality is falsely attributed to Christ because it is alien to the Jewish tradition and is nowhere mentioned in the Gospels! He wanted to tell us about the debt we owe, as Christians, to Plato's Greece. He told us about a philosopher who walked out of the ancient city of Ephesus one day and plunged his hand into a stream. He had taken out his hand and said that the stream was now different from what it had been only a second before, that life, like the stream, is constantly unique, and that each succeeding moment is eternal only in its difference. The only *permanent* uniqueness in a life of anarchy is, the philosopher had said, *"Logos"*, "the Word". (In other words, "Logos" is like my diary!) Its permanence is not the permanence of what will never be again, but the permanence of what will *always* be. What will always be *the same*.

It was Philo, said the Bishop, a Jewish leader who lived in ancient Alexandria, who had first reconciled the Greek with the Semitic tradition, who linked the Greek concept of "the Word" – the unchangeable uniqueness in a chaotic universe – with the Jewish idea of God, the changer who makes an ordered world out of chaos. And it was St John, the Bishop reminded us, who called Christ *"the Word made flesh"*. The Bishop told us that Christ, by giving man eternal life, a soul, has given an ever-changing universe its unity and eternity, just as God the Father brought the universe itself out of madness. So salvation involves finding that particular "world" which tallies with "the Word", and vice versa . . . As an afterthought, I decided I would make *no attempt* to contact Dewy before pulling everything down, before leaving for Sydney.

As I had never seen them, Tray showed me the maze of internal rooms beyond the verandah at Hambeluna, each a foot and more deep in books and papers. The squalor a lapse, an easily correctable slip that had latterly become despotic. I feasted on a giant map of the world, trying to make my date of departure nearer by staring at it. I picked a biography of the Australian "polly" Bob Hawke up off the floor. It blew him up as a "phenomenon" like the other, the real countries have. I sat in the green armchair on the verandah, reading books about Vietnam and the Australian artist William Dobell, squashing mosquitoes. The air of the books was of desert fruits, dry on the outside and moist within, the whiff of an incredible waste, just-bought books, a hopeless excess of them that had already gone to seed. They gave off a mothballed smell as you opened them, the cool, damp unread smell of their new yet past-it pages.

Midday when the restaurants open struck and we rang for a cab to East Flinders Street. Really fiercely hot and bright. Dined on "Croc-burgers" again (a great favourite up here), the flesh a pungent yellow-grey web like the swallows' nests in Bird's Nest Soup in China. Then Tray said he wanted to go for a walk along the Strand. He would show me the famous public urinal he designed, the one that was meant to recall the *Ara Pacis Augustae* in Rome. He pointed out the Hotel Boolba on the corner of Ching Street, informed me how he had seen so and so there (all colonial nonentities) with his parents when a little boy. We passed the Tobruk Baths by the seashore, a delightful Art Deco building in pink and blue stucco like icing sugar. Strange to see the great beaches empty, for fear of the jellyfish, the great parks empty, all those naked people crowded into a little wire pen around an artificial pool. Somehow it reminded me of Auschwitz. *"Water, water everywhere, and not a drop to drink!"* The hot, monstrous red face of Castle Hill swung into view. Tray talked about his family, his grandmother, how and whom they had entertained. Mention of these supposedly effulgent families – of dying Marilyn and her once "great" name, important only in a backwater then and meaningless now (even here) – it pained me. How strange Tray looked on the beach with his kinky satin shirt and limp and baggy trousers, his arms held rigidly at his side, hands curved upwards, inwards – his falling-down trousers and squint! To the glaucoma-like glare of the beach he had forgotten to bring dark glasses, making him appear not only over-dressed but almost nude. It was hard to pull my shoes out of the flour-like sand. I noticed he was talking to himself.

Suddenly he stopped dead and said he had decided that I oughtn't to see his Stately Pleasure Dunny after all. After all that. That the "atmosphere" *"wasn't right"*. I wondered if it was because I might recognise some of the Broncos "sculpted" there from the *"Ghosts"* he might know I had studied in *"the Machine"*.

We stopped for a "spell" (a rest) when we got back to East Flinders Street, the trees glittering in the sun amid the colonial masterpieces of South Townsville on the other side of the creek. As we drew breath, Tray warned me against jogging, said that several Sydney joggers had fallen down dead, and, on examination, their brains were found to have boiled in the shell like turtle eggs.

The lady taxi-driver who picked us up at *DAVID JONES* made an effort at polite conversation: I had to repeat her light pleasantries for Tray's earnest attention. Walking down the jungle path that leads from the gate of Hambeluna to the door I noticed some plants I remembered from my childhood visit to Australia in the 60s, though I had never thought of them since. Wierd that they should spark my recognition now. (*"Quel Marcel!"*)

Each was a few inches tall, a cone of leaf rising straight from the soil. Each cone contained a pool of dark red pungent water. When Marilyn first fell ill, Tray said, he would water them assiduously but the red pools disappeared and the plants appeared to die. Marilyn told him one day to pour the water straight into the cones, and they revived. The continuity of the cones over decades, their sudden sickness, the childish relationship – the sick mother-figure who was no longer there – it all made an unbearable impression on me.

Now that Tray was there to protect me, I asked to see under the house, where Eurong lives, the vast dark space sheltered by the pillars. We climbed down into the Bush House, the "Secret Garden". Tray said that they used to leave food for the poor homeless feral cats right at the top of these stairs, where the cane toads couldn't get at it, but that the toads would leap right up the steps and appear right there on the threshold of the living area. The image of the turd-like toads besieging them, lapping up the turd-like food, disturbed me. In the end Tray and Marilyn had to give the ferals up or face living with the turds *en famille*. I noticed that the door that leads into the Bush House from the garden wasn't locked, couldn't be locked – I expressed alarm. Tray sent up a screen of the usual flannel. He really doesn't care about anything.

There were a number of rooms under the house and it was very dark - like the night I went to the room with Zane at the Viceregal Mansion. I wanted to see Eurong's room. Eurong was the Aboriginal gardener. Tray said that his grandparents had inherited him from a relative, that he was a "wild Myall" [*sic*] caught straight from the Bush. Eurong would sit outside the gate on his days off in a white sailor's cap and one of Tray's grandfather's tuxedos, his bottom half quite naked. One day, said Tray, an ambulance took him away – I was reminded of Marilyn. "Eurong was a tribal leader" said Tray, "a king – he had tasted human flesh. I remember seeing cult objects in Eurong's room in the 1960s – a shiny green emu's egg; its shell was a centimetre thick. There was a real magic boomerang. Marilyn made us a present of it. We had a neighbour, unfortunately, called Summer Casey, a hateful

adopted orphan – he broke it by hurling it against the drive".   Tray remembered being
sickened – the hot, stony grey bitumen, the broken flesh-coloured "sacred" wood. It made
Tray think, he said, of the nestlings Summer had said he "had" to kill – how could he put
them back in the nest above the Ginger Tree again? Yellow jelly on the concrete beneath
the Caseys' house in Buna Avenue; the flailing abodomen of the locust Tray said that
Summer had boiled alive in a Billy Can in the Chillagoe Gardens. He was aware, Tray told
me, of the magic boomerang's delicacy, antiquity, and how it had been violated. Yet Tray
also told me of his unease, incomprehension, at Marilyn's fiery anger. Adults were supposed
to understand. Her indignation, he said, had made the delicacy, antiquity, mysterious and
sickening. Her slightness, standing there in the street, was, he said, sickening to him against
the hardness of that hot grey bitumen afternoon. Her little brown silk dress, the long white
gloves and the wide hat that she – like Girly – always wore were as sickening as the broken
flesh-like wood.

The Emu Egg was gone, but, in Eurong's room – (an ancient wooden wireless like a mummy
case stood in the corner) – Tray showed me boxes of wild birds' eggs that Marilyn and Girly
had collected eighty years' before on the Billabong at "Dululu". Nothing looks as forlorn as
an abandoned egg collection. A collection is the essence of something, the elixir of a life,
and to see these selections, these concatenations tossed away, discarded like this, was to
confront all the wasted effort, the rotting intensity of the house. In the next room, which in
the 1930s had belonged to the Japanese Butler, there was a collection of old chequebooks.
It produced the same effect on me. They were made out in the name of Tray's great
grandfather. He was his own bank – the chequebooks were records of the payments he
would make to his Dululu staff. The Lascar cook and some of the native stockmen had
signed their stubs with thumbprints. What impressed me was the abundance of the
chequebooks and the other historical documents, the carelessness with which they had been
abandoned to this rotting, termite-ridden midden. There were great dry ulcers in the books

where the termites had been at them, hundreds of little woody eggs in the wounds. I plucked a few away to show Girly – Tray insisted I should keep them. My hands were black with dirt.

There were little bones all over the floor in the Butler's room, chickenbones I presume, as if someone had recently enjoyed a *BIG CHOOK* pigfest there. I was surprised however to see what looked like a human tibia amid the debris. I suppose it was actually a drumstick.

As we were about to go back upstairs, I went to retrieve my hat. I had stuck it on the point of a draped object sitting on a table *Chez Eurong*. "What's this?" I asked, intrigued. "A statue," Tray nervously replied. "One of yours?!" I demanded. I insolently whipped away the drape. I was amazed to see up close the vile turd I had glimpsed on the floor inside the black tent in the middle of the pond here, an irregular, up-ended flowerpot thing that rose to a tip like a tarboush. It seemed to be made of rough cement; its surface was as sandy as a sugar cube. It was dark in Eurong's room but for a glittering lattice panel at the top of the plank wall. Nonetheless, I could now see that someone had used a primitive home-made pigment to paint the wizard's hat a purplish black with red spots, the spots multiplying towards the top so that the crown itself was completely red, except for the very point of the tip, which appeared to have been burned like charcoal. "What's this?" I asked. "I thought you told me it was a statue?" "It *is* a statue," Tray replied, "it's an Abo statue, a statue of Magnetic Island. The name they give it is *'Yunbenen'*. That's what the Boongs *call* Magnetic Island". It transpired that the "tarboush" was some sort of potent fetish that had belonged to Eurong. It was actually a little termite nest, such as I'd seen hundreds of in the Bush, its surface daubed with native alum to make it resemble the island in the Bay. Tray said that for thousands of years the island had been sacred to the local Aborigines, central to their cult. The local tribes had apparently called the island *"Yunbenen"* because this was their word for the crocodile – which breeds there - their "father-creator", their "ancestor spirit" or "totem". That meant that it was taboo – at least for the Abos here! - to incestuously eat the flesh of the crocodile or to take its eggs. Nonetheless, observed Tray, any group of children must naturally emulate their ancestor. And, just as the tribes for whom the koala was the totem were obliged ritually to eat eucalyptus leaves and the "children" of the echidna had to sup on ants, the Abos in the environs of Townsville were religiously compelled to partake like the croc of human flesh, becoming virtually the only cannibal tribes in Australia. Of course, they did not view themselves as such, for they would devour members of the neighbouring clans in their *crocodile* rather than their *human* capacity. (Which didn't necessarily improve their reputation: these were the "bad tribes" of whom the native stockmen down in Giru had warned Girly in Edwardian times).

According to Tray, the local "nations" known as the Wulguru and the Warrigal didn't eat human beings at all times, only on special ritual occasions. Like the Aztecs, they would mount razzias against other Abos with the sole purpose of seizing groups of sacrificial victims. The women they would skin, leaving the scraped pink cadavers out by the Ross Creek for the "totem-father" to crunch like Girly's bloody white *BIG CHOOK* tiger prawns. Then they would treat the women's flayed shells with resin and inflate them by leaving inside the hide before sealing a little dead kangaroo-rat whose decomposing body would produce gas. (Hence the sort of puffy brown pupae I had seen hanging from the Gum Tree in the Mangrove Swamp, perhaps?) Afterwards, they would tie bunches of these buoyant lifelike pillows together with koala gut and make rafts. Taking their male captives with them, alive, and bound with the same twine, the Wulguru and the Warrigal would sail out to "Yunbenen" once a year on fleets of female human inflatables. There, on the top of Mount Cook, the highest point of the island, where Brooklana's vast statue would one day stand, they would sacrifice the bound men to the crocodile totem and devour them. They would hang the men upside down from gum trees and smoke them alive over a forest of the termite nest fetishes which they would light at the top like candles.

These pyramid-like woodchip fetishes, Tray told me, represented three things. First of all, each was intended to recall a bloody breaking crocodile egg with the red baby, which was struggling out of the top. Secondly, and analogically, they were meant to represent the regularly erupting volcano which, according to Aboriginal legend, Magnetic Island, and in particular its Mount Cook, had once been. Thirdly, each egg and its volcanic ejaculation simultaneously stood for womb, penis, menstrual blood and sperm (the sperm being the smoke given off by the burning wood-mulch of the termite nest). It was a symbol for Aborigines of the cyclical, circular interaction of these elements, with penis, baby and sperm endlessly breaking the perfect egg-like womb, just as the lava and pyroclastic flow breaks and makes its prison, Mother Earth, during a volcanic eruption. "For the Abos, the *primeval* universal creation myth reflected the personal," Tray informed me. Indeed, Tray insisted, it could well have been a volcanic eruption that originally brought fire and hence life to Northern Queensland. "It's well known" he said, getting into his familiar "preachy" stride, "that, though some tribes developed flints and fire-sticks before the Europeans, many Aborigines had no idea even of the simplest way to create sparks. Let's take the Tasmanians. They carried little fires around with them all the time in bark trowels that they were obliged continually to feed with grass. Fires which their forefathers had found at the site of lightning strikes or volcanoes. If the sacred flame died, so did the tribe. That's why the Europeans found it so easy to wipe them out". "But Magnetic Island never *was* a volcano!" I protested. "How do we know that?" Tray shot back. He pointed out that the Aborigines have been in Australia for over ninety thousand years. Modern science, he said, keeps on proving the accuracy of the historical lore handed down within the tribes and formerly dismissed by the White Man as fable. He led me back up the "Turd of Toad Hall" stairs to the kitchen and showed me a copy of **THE AUSTRALIAN** from a week back. In it was an article about the "Birpai" people of what is now Port Macquarie, who have been amusing tourists in the acrylic slum for years with tales -

"that there was a time when the coastline was a different shape, and that there were active volcanoes in the area. These memories, going back for 10,000 years or more, have now been confirmed by scientists".

I have to admit I was impressed. Who knows? Perhaps I have been unduly harsh on the poor old "Aubergines"?!

I had returned a good few books to Tray's library (Tray pedantically checked each one back in), but I decided to take back to Girly's a few more – *China: The Dragon Awakes* by Christopher Hibbert (interesting that the symbol of China, the dragon, is probably derived from the Yangtse crocodile) and Carl Schmitt's *The Concept of the Political*. I packed the chequebooks in with them. "Decadence" I said, as I looked back down at the smoky blue Cactus Pines as I closed the gate.

I walked over the mountain to Araluen. Girly told me about the lady who had encouraged them to collect the eggs out on the lagoon all those years before. The phone started to ring while she was out watering the garden. It was Dew. He asked what had been arranged and when I intended to return. He then asked Girly if I was driving Freek's car. He asked too about the maps belonging to Tray's great grandfather, a famous explorer who apparently opened up the Gulf of Carpentaria. They are of immense historical value and are lost in some midden in Hambeluna's guts. He complained that his own father had left a valuable rifle at Hambeluna when he stayed with Marilyn and Driss in the 1940s and, when he asked for it back, the stock had been completely devoured by "white ants".

MONDAY 4 JANUARY 1988. What I remember this morning is Kade parking the Humber on the corner of Armati Street near the centre of town. He was congratulating himself on finding himself such a "possie", congratulating himself in childish, archaic terms. I went to the Foreign Transactions Desk of the Commonwealth Bank to make sure I could indeed escape with the loot – take as much cash as that out of the country. I remember the suspicious intrigued eyes of a neighbour in the queue and my own rising above it. I have lived so long in pain that I smile grimly, suspend myself. Reassured, I was re-directed to a teller. I remember the straw hat bulging embarrassingly in the carrier bag between my legs. Blessed with so much, I didn't want to wear it – didn't want to appear an eccentric sponger, a sordid Sardanapalus, a remittance queen. I remember waiting behind some outlandish almost naked couple (it is quite common to see the air-conditioned cold of banks and official buildings here thronged with the bare-bummed and -chested). When the queue was dissolved and I joined another, a kindly factotum picked me out and asked a young lady, who was going off duty, to see me anyway. I warned her I had a large sum to dispense, to transfer abroad. Noticing that the creditor held an account with the same bank, the teller went to see if the money could be paid in at once. This would obviate the creditor's ability to recall it later. (Hooray!) As the girl conferred with a Simone de Beauvoir lookalike, I studied the clerks. I tried to picture my own statusless security in a milieu like this, in the desolation of the sun-dead calm of Townsville. Simone de Beauvoir regarded me with frantic romantic contempt and advised me to consider a different account – a more remunerative rate of interest. As I emerged, I was rather tempted to enter the yawning silver chasm of the Quantas Office next door. But why, I thought? I won't change my mind about a new ticket Sydney-London whatever the Qantas people say. I would defend neurotically a once-made decision.

Leaving the Mall, I was shocked to see Tray standing by the pavilion selling tropical fruit, belly stretching a formal but untidy shirt like a convict. He was laboriously spooning in a tiny tub of Pau Pau chunks: with his big upturned fingers he resembled a gorilla. As our eyes met, I thought I had better speak to him, but he seemed not at all keen, as if he were waiting for someone. No: he just wanted to receive *himself*. He divides his life like this. Into compartments. This was not the time for "entertaining".

I didn't fancy anything hot and sticky like a pie in the miasmic heat – decided to lunch on seafood instead. Seafood is so cool and clean, its flesh transparent and salad-like. I remembered a dish I once saw offered by the Iron Knob Hotel: Moreton Bay "Bugs" in Prawn and Chilli Sauce. The dining room was crowded but the doors were locked; a reception mmust have been in progress. I made my way to the Hotel Nullagine instead, which overlooks the emerald, Abo-strewn park where I could see about twenty of the Chillun of the Dreamtime jerking the unseen turps bottles to their lips like trombones. It was painful to make a detour in the bright heat, my bag weighed down with melting ice cream and an oily reproachful sack of doughnuts. (I had been prevailed upon in COLE'S to purchase six doughnuts for one dollar instead of three for 90 cents, and had already scoffed a few, which added to my sense of joyless glut). The mixture of heat (in frozen England, the mother of life) and emptiness was another disagreeable paradox: the emptiness but for the Abos of a glaring glassy park where, in England on such a day, a hundred Bug-fleshed beauties would be sunning themselves. In Australia one always has the sense, not of looking into a goldfish bowl, but of being in one, something completely sealed off from and refusing to acknowledge the moonscape beyond. And you realise that this cloying artifical world is as desolate as the wilderness outside.

After lunch, I crossed over the George Roberts Bridge to the southern side of the Ross Creek and walked westbound through Townsville's *soi-disant* "Central Park", keeping to the water's edge. The town and Castle Hill sailed by on the other bank, the hill a milkshake-pink wave with the city a crumbly stain climbing its back or lolling like stagnant slicks of litter in its wake. I walked far beyond the city cen-tah, almost as far as Railway Estate, and climbed up into a Yellow Acacia tree – which completely hid me, especially from the sun – to rest in its branches. The water of the creek below was a beautiful tawny amber like Tokay wine. The bank was made of huge orange rocks with the crisp sides of cut watermelon: they glittered with silver filament. Overhanging the creek, bushes of mauve and yellow flowers filled the hot air with the aching incense smell of Lantana. A kookaburra skittered by like a moth with a fish of gold in its mouth. I looked up into the gum trees above me, which stood as white as bone against the blue: a whole flock of kookaburras had begun to chatter and bark in them like monkeys. I wondered what could be disturbing them. Though buildings were still visible in the distance, the other side of the Ross was now deserted. There was nothing but a paddock of tall white Elephant Grass dotted with dark Mango trees. Under the trees, Brahmin bulls with their Viking horns could be seen in silhouette, flicking their ears against the flies. (Indian cattle are the only sort that can survive in tropical Queensland because of the ticks and snakes). I noticed that a discarded washing-line pole sticking up out of the creek had begun to rotate: I looked at it more carefully and almost crashed out of the tree . . . It was a periscope! Then I became aware of the rasping sound of a lawnmower in the white grass across the creek. A silver motorbike with two sidecars ridden by an old yellow-shirted Abo roared up to the bank overlooking the part of the current sliced by the pole. The periscope promptly rocketed out of the water followed by one of the little yellow fibre-glass submarines they take tourists out in when they show them the Reef: it bobbed up and swayed in the water like a giant plastic duck. They're quite common up here and are hardly submarines at all, really, being capable of plumbing only very modest depths: they have transparent floors and noses, enabling the punters to study the coral and the brilliant humming-bird fish beneath. I was surprised to see one this far up-river though. The "Yellow Submarines" usually dock a long way downstream in East Flinders Street near where the Ross Creek meets the Pacific, at the wharf where you board the ferry for Magnetic Island. That's where the submariner-tourists embark too for the Reef excursions.

Just then, the tower of the submarine peeled open like a banana. Two naked people pulled themselves out, one a man, one a woman – they looked like roast chickens. Each was wearing a mask with a big curling down Toucan nose. The man's skin was brownish-pink, like a black rat. As they clambered over the orange boulders to the bike, they reminded me of baboons with toadstool fannies scurrying over the Rock of Gibraltar. Bright stone is such an unhappy setting for the nude! Each struggled into a sidecar – the vinyl must have been very hotty on their botties! - and the Abo put his foot down and roared off through the Mango trees, the black heads of his passengers like a joey in the pouch on each side. A little later I saw the unmistakeable motorbike rising like a star up the back of the pink mountain. It came to a rest at exactly the street and – I am reasonably sure – at the house from which the Dingo had dashed out and bitten me.

I stopped at *BIG CHOOK* on the way home. The young man at the counter, a Philippino by the look of it, was covered in oily lumps. There were some rather threatening types nearby. When I ordered, I thought they would notice my accent and become indignant. The tannoy was playing a number from the 1970s. As so often in Australia, I found myself floating on the anxiety, hoisted high above events by a helium balloon of pain. It's my element - my oxygen tent. I just tell myself: exist, float on, it will pass. Don't let it get you down – whatever happens you will still be alive at the end of the day. You'll still be in a position to make sense of it. That is why living with Freek enraged me so. The heat and noise and the brutal vulgarity and the drives and meetings I was obliged to attend prevented me from writing. They prevented me from doing what divided me from the despair in which I lived. Once you describe chaos and waste, it is chaos no longer.

TUESDAY 5 JANUARY 1988. A morning walk down Stanley Street – the honey yellow of the early tropical light, the verandahed houses, the big black mango trees, the pinkish-blue of the sea at the end of the road, a colonial house with four tall coconut palms at each edge, all of it sitting on the musty yellow grass of the bare mountain like the scenery in a Ray Crooke painting.

I made for the Cutting and asked at the Commonwealth Bank about the discrepancy in my statement after I got the first of Santa's payments. "New South Wales taxes" said the girl. Queensland doesn't have them. She looked frightened. You could see her tremble and detach herself, mentally.

I passed a stereo shop in Flinders Mall. A modern rendition of *"Pretty Flamingo"* with its echoes of the Fulham Road in 1966 blasted out. How poignant. I entered an arcade. Was amused to see, in one of the tacky newsagent-cum-gift shops, bowls of synthetic "Aboriginal" flags as well as those of European Australia. I felt touched, gratified, by how far this lunacy has gone. The unself-conscious pretentiousness of ordinary people. Ordinaries, otherwise reactionnaries, embracing "anti-racism" in a mute, self-serving way. Rather like America's totalitarian capitalists self-consciously co-opting blacks in those Quisling Cosby Shows. As in America, there's probably quite a market for this sort of derangement. When you see these sloth-like creatures, their fantastic idleness, the incongruity of their clothes, the incredible slowness of their movements, when you think of how many of them there are in the Mall area, awash with dole, you realise what ripe fruit, what rich pickings they represent. Finally exploitable now that they are state prisoners. (I meant to write "state pensioners" but it amounts to the same thing!)

I noticed a Cricket magazine in the shop and bought one for Girly. There was an article in it anticipating the Bicentennial match between England and Australia. Why was it so important? Well, the writer said, few people of Irish descent *"had anything good to say about those on the other side of Saint George's Channel"*. (You can say that again!) And then there was *"the relationship between coloniser and colonised"* (the Irish-Australians usurping here the prerogatives of the Aborigines). The Sage went on to write of his own exciting English *entrée* under the purple hills of Lancashire, of love as well as hate in the *Ola Porrida*: it all made me terribly homesick. Purchased some roses in a tube from a Florist's ice-box.

After a *"Déjeuner Araluen"* (steak, sherry and ice-cream), I wrote *"to dear Marilyn, with love, Patrick"* on the whimsical Florist's card I had bought. I popped it in the tube, like one of the butterflies Tray used to catch. Kade offered to run me to the cemetery but, as he was working in the garden, I called a cab instead. There were several necessities dangling in my bag. A sticky grey silence on the empty mountain. To see the cab appearing, secretly summoned out of all that emptiness, was a little sinister. We cruised through North Ward - I saw directions to the airport. How I wished I was on the way to it now! Then the two ramps, the gate, the endless empty graveyard, the cinder-grey sand, tombs the white of very old dog turds like in a Carlo Carrà painting. I recognised the Celtic Cross headstone of Tray's grandfather and bade the driver stop. Driss and Marilyn's grave was nothing but a long mound of ashes and the wreaths had withered to brown seaweed. I placed the flowers, so fresh and artificial, on the sand, stood back and tried to evacuate my mind. I tried to feel something, to resist the compulsion to imagine the unholy. I resumed my place in the car and resumed, too, my necessarily silent, exotic personality.

I bade the taxi on to the Barber's way down on Punari Street. I remember the fantastic checquerboard mansions against the raw red back of the hill. Everywhere empty, silent. At Townsville's Mister Teezy-Weezy, two half-Aboriginal girls. I learned that "Lindelle" was pregnant and the sensation of her full, hard stomach against my head was suddenly disagreeable. The other girl was talking to a dark suburban wrinkly who adored inverts. "Gay goys are *so patient*!" (Gay nymph boy hairdressers, she meant). I found it difficult to connect with the serene sensitive I saw in the mirror as I am such a mass of nerves, and yet, for the Friseuse, I played the part of the sage cosmopolite, asking Lindelle why she didn't come to work in London. "Love my shrapnel too much, I guess!"

It was incredibly torrid outside – I felt the heat clinging to my skin like napalm. The morning had been overcast and now, as in a painting by El Greco, there was a moist, silvery edge to the intermittent light. I wanted to ring for a new cab. I had to wait an age before what looked like a pair of one-parent families and their indiscretions vacated the phonebooth on Yoolante Street. It was standing full in the sun, the children a vulnerable pink like baby mice: European pinkness, as of fresh raspberries, so horribly out of place in this ungracious atomic light. As I was waiting, I watched several shambling Islanders enter a flimsy plywood apartment building. There are so many in this area - a family visit, I suppose. I wondered at their social life - the dole-paid homes, the useless, pretentious clothes. The father was grotesquely fat and superfluous. A Michael Jackson motif on his tee shirt completed an appalling picture.

The cab driver was one Tray and I have had before. Wierd and terribly subnormal. Said he kept falling asleep at the wheel, which showed one how keenly he habitually honed his marketing skills. If it was a long journey, say, from the City Cen-tah to Palleranda, he found himself anaesthetised by the air conditioning. A gold and thundery sky. Picked Tray up at Hambeluna to take him for a "thank-you" dinner in Townsville's "most exclusive" eaterie, *"Chez Wandelle"* in the basement of the Hotel Moondene, the Strand's only skyscraper. Tray's behaviour most unusual throughout the journey: talking to himself, etc. Took me on a tour of various of the Moondene's "opulent" salons when we arrived. Sterile ice-cream marble and fake Sheraton gold in this wasteland and the provincials who live here think it inestimably chic etc, not realising that it is a "house style" you find everywhere in the world - admittedly a surprise in the spinifex and sandstone wilderness of North Queensland, but repulsively so. *"Pleasure on Hope"*, as that Brisbane porno shop called it. Pleasure on despair, more like!

"You wouldn't think we were in Townsville, would you?" said Tray, reminding me of Dew. "Wandelle's", Townsville's *"Tour d'Argent"*, was freezing in our flimsy clothes, its air-conditioning as brutal as its shiny black marble walls. Its décor reminded me of that of sumptuous lavatories. Tray said he's just bought a collection of short stories about people who have "popped the cherry". He talked at the top of his voice, childishly, hinting, as a child might, at urbanity outside his experience. I dined on rather a dull yabbie salad and a wattle-flower sorbet – lovely pistachio colours, though. I noticed how badly Tray was limping as he took me out onto the windy lawn in front of the Moondene, which faces the Strand. The hotel swimming pool was lit from underneath, like a volcano, and one could almost smell the immense mauve sky and the frightening bulk of Magnetic Island beyond the Breakwater. Mysterious red and yellow lights fluttered on the top of Mount Cook, Magnetic's Island's highest eminence. As far as I am aware, there aren't any houses there. More eccentricity in the taxi ride back to Hambeluna, which was dark and sinister. We had a cup of local Tea Tree tea, which isn't tea at all, but the leaves of a eucalypt that taste similar – it's what the white "pioneers" used to boil in their Billy Cans. To lull Tray into a sense of security, I discussed the arrangements for his arrival in London. (He presumed this would take place after and not before the forthcoming "portrait session"). There was a full moon. I got a bit concerned: his manner had become frantic. He absented himself for an ominously long time on the verandah facing the Island. He put on the outside light and, when my taxi arrived, we climbed back up the path together to the front gate. The crickets were purring.

WEDNESDAY 6 JANUARY 1988. Compulsions and obsessions always begin like this. Not even as ideas, but as a fear of ideas. A fear of intellectual engagement – paper-thin, acknowledged to be absurd – that comes to dominate the mind without engaging, let alone defeating the intellect. I was determined to resist this compulsion – which arises from my guilt - but also somewhat regretted not submitting to it earlier. This must be what the British intellectuals felt like during that Falklands war in 1982. This minute degree of British self-assertion after such a long dearth of that sort of thing and you would have thought, from the shrieking of the TV whores, that we were back in the heyday of Victorian imperialism. It was like watching the desert bloom. All it took – as in my neurosis – was the frailest, briefest shower and suddenly the tramp-dyke women were beating their unbra'd tits and the men were running fingers through hair that hadn't seen a comb since Suez.

It was a brilliant silvery day. I marched down to the Qantas office. The act of physically moving myself seemed sufficient to force me to my decision to buy a new ticket home, to deflate the fled thing. The Creek was beautiful, like transparent mint jelly. The pink and lemon stucco of East Flinders Street made me think of "Edinburgh Rock", a chalk-like

Scottish candy. I tried to ring Dew and Bon from the leisure complex on the Creek where the "Maggie Island" boats depart but they were out, which deranged me, as I wanted Dew's consent before I booked my flights. I tried to secure seats on a few of the planes I'd identified, but all were fully booked. I am incapable of making split-second decisions, and, when I was rebuffed, I lunged for the next best flights in a sort of naked limbo – I would have preferred to return to Girly's and ruminate. Dewy was still unavailable when I phoned him a second time from the public phone next to the Port abbatoir. I went back and unthinkingly plumped for tomorrow's twelve o'clock out of Townsville – on that plane, a seat was available. It was a way of "physically" making up my mind.

I was nearly run over at the crossing near the Wedding Cake technical school on my way back to Araluen. How awful, I thought, to be run over here just as I've finally got it all, just as I'm about to flee. I could just picture myself as others must see me, my full complement of dangling Mother's Boy bags and unrolled-up sleeves swaying across the road in pathetic haste. I remember a transparent silver heat that seemed to push up the sky.

Girly was quite amazed when I told her I had booked my escape flights home. She said that I should ring Tray, which I proceeded to do. Always the wary enthusiast, the giggling, empty, agreeing voyeur, he treats every important piece of news as a platitude to be nodded at. That is what most distresses me about Townsville, about Tray's company: the banality hiding the decay, the superficial, ritual *"everything is alright"* when everything is all *wrong.* He said "Oh gee, oh yeah, you're going" as he might have said "yes" to some remark about the cornflakes. He said he would come and see me at Girly's tomorrow, just before I leave. Yet I know how bitterly he regrets my leaving. It clouded over and there was a fierce thunderstorm, which matched my turmoil, and a rainbow which I hoped portended better things to come. I rang Freek Bloomers and various "significant others" telling them I was off - it was a real ordeal. Freek kindly said he would pick me up and drive me to the airport. After the immediate relief of getting that over with, the background horror, the guilt, redescended. I realised I had locked myself into a course of action from which there is no turning back. Not for the first time I thought "I really can't go on", and then I thought: "You *will* go on - physically. After all, how can people fail or forbear to go on? Whatever happens and whatever they may feel or do the night will follow the day and they'll be in it."

THURSDAY 7 JANUARY 1988. Girly came in as I was packing with the shirts I had washed. She had a piece of pressed batik for my housekeeper. A young man called to see about the leaking roof in Araluen's piano room. He left in mysterious circumstances, without having been paid. Girly told me that he lived in "Roseneath", some very distant outlying suburb, practically in the next town. When it rained in Roseneath, she said, it didn't rain in the city cen-tah, and vice versa. "Roseneath". The very word made me shiver. The dignified English name seemed to want to make one part of the Bush "local", special, to separate it from the infinite sameness of the rest of it. The horror of these suburbs is the impenetrable Ghost Gum sameness that begins just outside them, a sameness which can begin but which can never ever end. The suburban anti-demonism of the world "Roseneath" – as if holding the Bush at bay, but not so. The Australians give suburbs and towns these unctuous Olde English names out of their limited-to-Australia experience. Paradoxically, this is blind to the Bush and to what the Bush entails. It is therefore blind to the incongruity of setting settlements down in it and of giving them these names whose foreign luxury would suggest that one part of the Bush is more hallowed than any other part. But what made me unhappiest when I thought of the Roseneath boy was the realisation that "Roseneath" (or "Heatley" or "Cranbrook", two other outlying Townsville suburbs) was for him what "Petworth" and "Chiddingfold" are for me. He will never know the pang I feel when I see the incongruity of the one - (a satellite in remote space brought into bizarre, moonscaped relief by the obscene settledness of the Home Counties name) – set against the organic wholeness of the other.

419

I took a few pictures of what (I hope) I will never see again: the villa's sculpted "Cubist" white front door with its Art Nouveau border of purple convolvulus, the **Tender Is the Night** front garden with its 1930s furniture.

I looked at the mad blue sky one last time; it suddenly reminded me of something Conrad once wrote about the Congo: *"There was no joy in the brilliance of sunshine"*! A momentary sense of relief carried me out of the Tropics on a great wave of pleasure. Then Tray arrived with some books and we all sat around the table reading. I was anxious lest my neurotic compulsion to reveal and reverse the whole thing return. I sat with a feverish "high" feeling in the top of my stomach like someone recently recovered, "real" again, who has to keep on his convalescent toes lest his assumption of reality and health ignite the illness from which he has escaped. To that end I read, and Tray and Girly read, the latter two with that stay-at-home failure's absorption, that pretence that the trivial is important, that must characterise the blind bland ferocity of house-builders in the Bush. Luxurious comforting platitudes were exchanged, giving no relief. I studied Tray: always that tiny, overlapping untidiness – the extra, overbought book brought – that makes you think that, if only that little detail could be taken care of, all might be well. It would be a start but, neglected, the inferno begins. The Babel of bought books rises and rises and rises, reality retreats. As for Girly, it wasn't that she believed in these valium clichés, but that she couldn't be bothered to go deeper and engage with the virile and complex decay. Who does not prefer the aspirin lilypond cliché, which after all will fend off reality for an hour or two? And there are ever so many clichés, ever so many books, and here we all were sitting around the table reading them furiously, furiously, Girly with a sort of calm.

I was very struck by the theatrical gestures Tray so often makes, his nodding of the head, the confirming rabbit smile, the saucer eyes, the pushing away of problems, realities. Well, he'll soon face reality alright!

The book he had brought with him (the one on ice-cream was still littering Girly's desk, the first spore, if uncleared away – and it would be so easy to clear away – of a frightful forest), the book Tray had brought was on Nineteenth Century Australian cooking. Something I would have been very interested in had I been in England and Australia a romantic nebula ten thousand miles away, awaiting only specifics. But here, looking at the book's illustrations – at the superfluity of the yellow varnished haunches of meat like portmanteaus – it was unbearable. And Victorian England was also provincially mimicked in these colour plates, the luxury and class stuffiness as ever in Australia despised and yet desired, as one could see by the polyester pretence of the badly dressed models. Had I flicked through the book in England, I would have pined for this kangaroo haunch, this "elegant" old Aussie banquet on a Bush station, oranges piled scientifically like cannon balls. They would have appeared strange, sought-after gems. These specifics, enviable from England, are something I've now had too much of. Not so much *"Après moi, la déluge"*, as *"Après la déluge, moi"*! Now these details oppressed me. They were the first isolated drops of a downpour, the start of an interminable desert of just desserts. They offered no compensation for the provincial void depicted in the plates which, from Europe, would have appeared an exotic, specific – and hence finite – existence. It struck me with painful force that the Victorian Australian ladies evoked in the illustrations – many of them, of course, born in England – would never have been able to turn these pages. Their existence was not the pinned-down butterfly it appeared to a European reader, but an infinite orgy, unhallowed by the relief (which dignifies it) of life in Europe. Those crocodile steaks would have been unexotic to such women, and now they were unexotic to me. Like the mangoes of Bowen, they have to be faced every single day.

I worried about what might crop up in the next few days, refusing to believe I might have a trouble-free future, and yet believing in it, too, and so there was a heady, shiny, cardboard quality to the day. I checked the briefcase several times for my checquebook, bank statements etc. I brought down the big bag. As I dragged it past the Piano Room, where the young man had been, I saw, of all things, a silver opera glass sitting shining like a crystal tumbler on the grand piano. At first, I thought it was my hip flask. I have never seen an opera glass in the house before – though I've seen plenty of hip flasks! Where could it have come from? For a reason I will never understand, I stole the opera glass – I put it in my pocket.

Girly said I was lucky that Freek was driving me. Kade has the day off until lunchtime and she read out a report in the Townsville *"Bully"* about a young divorcee who has been supporting her children by taxi-driving. She had driven a young man to one of the outlying suburbs, the "Olde Worlde" ones, and he had dragged the mother into the Bush and cut her throat. It seemed a strange crime for Townsville, which is nothing if not wholesome, and the image of some young European with his shiny draylon hair cutting her pink offenceless throat in Olde Worlde "Cluden" against a background of relentless grey leaves was oddly sickening. The taxi drivers have staged a strike in protest and I probably wouldn't have got a cab. I was moved by the thought of this woman trying to make mortgage repayments in such an "outpost of progress" where one's reward for the investment is so awful, so unreal. It had never occurred to me that the facts of economic life could apply even in such a forum as Townsville. Why make sacrifices for *this?* Why not make them, if you have to make them, in London or Paris or New York?

There was a toot and I looked down and saw Freek's red car in the drive. He was with Dirk, the coppery androgyne. I ran down and greeted them. I returned to get my cases which I dragged on to the grass. I put on my hat and bade my farewell to Tray and Girly on the front lawn. I guessed it could be the last time I might see them, whatever the content of my and Tray's agreement. This idea must have occurred to everyone. I think this is why Tray said I could come back and stay with him "anytime": he shook my hand with a repulsive vigour. Girly, whom I kissed, was more restrained, but I think that she, too, knew the extent of what was happening and was eager to get it over with. I thanked them both profusely. In the sudden coolness of the car, Dirk wanted to know if Tray wished to come to the airport with us. All the odious little hustler wants to do is stare at the poor devil for Tray does look a tad eccentric. I don't know why Dirk said this. He'll soon have plenty of time for looking at Tray! Freek asked me what I had been doing with myself. Obviously not paying him court, and hence the reproach. I looked up as we drew off and there were Girly and Tray – the last time I would ever see them? – arms raised like two triumphant statues on a Roman arch. I thought of Tray, a light lunch, the last superficially comforting moments with Girly and then – she glad to get rid of him – a wasteful chauffeured Humber ride home to that vast empty eerie rotting house. And then what? His "future perfect" of "anytime". No wonder he wished me to stay. But I have been thinking only of myself. I mentioned the taxi strike as we approached the Cutting. No response from Freek or the lustrous ephebe. It was overcast. We drew up at Townsville Airport. I remember a couple of almost naked girls in its pompous halls: I shall never get used to the Tropics! Surprised myself by the theatrical confidence I achieved when offering my thanks to Freek and Dirk but I suppose I was just so glad to be rid of them. Dirk helped me out with my bags. I bade the wretched Pickle Smokers another goodbye and made my way to the terminal. I knew it was only a matter of time before my continuous mental life, the painful background to my existence, reasserted itself, but for the moment I felt neutral, placeless and serene. I was amazed as I sipped a "Flat Latt" in the top floor Airport Café to look down at the carpark and see the elegant old Mercedes Wanko had driven me up in amid the ranks of serried Holdens and Datsuns. Why on November 23rd did Wank tell me he was driving back down south when he must obviously have *flown* home that day? Surprised – I don't know why – to find our plane propeller driven. The clouds cleared as we walked onto the runway, the air hot and icily transparent. The last shiny malachite-green mango trees slid by as we banked to the right and I pictured Araluen and Hambeluna far below. Even the vast pink carcass of Castle Hill looked green after the rain – a mottled pistachio-pink like a cassata ice-cream. From our really extremely modest height the white streets of Townsville seemed utterly deserted and one realised (apropos Marilyn's door stop) how emotionally easy it would have been for airmen to bomb the foreigner's city during World War Two. Though I suppose for the Japanese, *anything* is emotionally easy: they're pretty wierd! I scrutinised the buildings, aware it would be the last time I would ever see them. (I shall fly directly from Magnetic Island to Sydney, whence a plane to London. Tray thinks that I am flying to Sydney today). I wasn't so much interested in Townsville as in my reactions to it, and whether these were appropriately literary, symmetrical and intense. They were. The ocean beneath us was a purple-grey, prinked with tiny waves like dandruff, and suddenly there was a densely wooded wedge in the middle of it like a tray of steamed broccoli. First there was nothing but sky and then there was nothing but black and olive as we bumped down on the funky little Horseshoe Bay airstrip on Magnetic Island. I caught a taxi to the motel I'd booked at the nearby and appropriately named Nelly Bay (obviously solidarity with the slit-throat had not infected the cab drivers of Magnetic). The taxi lumbered over a darkened river as I contemplated the anguish I'd escaped.

I showered, changed, and went for a walk along the Esplanade. I have primarily come to have a "sticky beak" at Tray's studio while he's away, but I've always wanted, too, to study the ruins of Tray's statue of Brooklana Fagan on Mount Cook, Magnetic's highest eminence. From Magnetic, Castle Hill was a cupful cone of orange, the merest mound of spices sitting on a ribbon of Biro blue. Felt happier than I have for a long, long time. It is more explicitly "tropical" here: for all its oily humidity, the orange stoniness of Townsville imparts a dry, Moroccan quality. After I passed the Nelly Bay pier, where the yellow submarine and ferry had docked, the scenery became quite spectacular. In the foreground, a golden meadow, lit by the sun, and then a curtain of tall, irregular, deciduous-looking trees – the first such trees

I have seen in Australia – and beyond that, in shadow, vast, closely wooded mountains. The seafront, of grey mud that smelt of sulphur - obviously recent mangrove scrub - was unimpressive, but generally the little resort has as pleasant an aspect as Townsville. There was a bandstand and an impromptu pop concert. The theme of the songs was "Expo" in Brisbane and the Bicentennial. The sort of elaborate, optimistic lyrics that probably look good on paper but which struck me as too intellectual, ideological, for the audience – the stunned, naked, thong brigade, and the ubiquitous fat, dead-looking Aborigines. An amusing audience for a celebration of the "Bi".

When I got back to my room, I set myself the task of working on my diary for a full three hours. This completed, I went across the road to an old Queensland café to dine on Barrimundi (tropical fish) and a chocolate milkshake. I was in quite high spirits – an "eye of the storm" type of feeling. I knew the pain would redescend, so I was sorry I hadn't brought a book. I love to luxuriate over a book, eating.

FRIDAY 8 JANUARY 1988. I dreamed this morning that my old cat had a "pipe" in his eye, a black vein, making him squint. Or maybe it was Marilyn's cat, Barbara. Overcast and thundery again – we're getting into the Cyclone season now.

In the Breakfast Room of Motel Nelly I asked the waitress how to find Tray's studio and the ruins of Brooklana Fagan. I had assumed Tray was well-known here but not as well-known as turned out. "You're a bit old for 'im arntcha?" Typhoid Mary brightly piped up. Like many Australian women, she had a sort of dead ripeness about her like flowering rhubarb.

Apparently, you can't get to the Brooklana ruin: the Aborigines have claimed it as a "sacred site". One of the most important Aubergine "Ancestor Myths" of "the Deep North" (even I have heard of it) involves the two Wawilak sisters, fertility gods who once polluted a sacred waterhole with their menstrual blood, thus causing the resident "ancestor", a giant python, to devour them whole and vomit them up again in little bleeding gobbets. Almost all the northern "Aubergines" attribute the division of Abos into separate tribes to this primeval and piecemeal regurgitation. A local "activist group", no doubt getting wind of what Sir Quntee Mush is prepared to lay out to secure the Brookee fragments, has claimed that the scattered colossus is in fact the broken anatomy of one of the Wawilak gins! This claim might appear insane, not least because the remains of Tray Beautous' "*Statue Statuae*" are man-made, Western, and only a few years' old, but elementary considerations such as this have done nothing to stop a slew of other Aboriginal claims, including the current demand for the "return" of the gleaming (and highly valuable) skyscrapers and shopping malls of central Brisbane.

Fortunately, Tray's studio – known locally as "Thunder Egg Farm" – is a less problematic proposition. In fact it nestles in the grid of streets behind the hotel and Esplanade here in Nelly Bay. Winking at me, the waitress drew me a map showing its location on the back of a postcard.

I felt sick with excitement as I mounted the muddy pavement and passed an oleander where I saw a boy high up in the branches collecting golden chrysalises that glittered in the leaves. Hundreds of black butterflies with milk white spots on the wings were fluttering around him like pigeons. I loved the wide streets, the vulnerable, open weatherboard houses perching on stilts with crenellated tin roofs painted a gamey red or dark green, their stained glass, wide grass pavements, wire fences, louvre walls, ferocious dogs, each in a different style, each an individual masterpiece. Some far gone in a decay that made them even nicer, like sprawling rotted pheasants. As I entered the first street a loud speaker perched on the roof of a shop started blaring *"The First Nowell"* of all things. The street was empty but for a man in shorts and his dog.

In Bottigery Lane, where Tray was supposed to live, there was another man in shorts on a truck, hosing. And his ugly wife. Her face, like that of a long dead fish, shocked me. I told them I was English. "What, with that accent, mate?" They redirected me to "Mandalay Avenue", which runs straight uphill from the seafront to the foot-hills of Mount Cook. I knocked on a door. Below me a piece of some animal was crawling with ants. What sounded like a dog scraped at the door but nobody answered. There was a smell of rancid motor oil and stagnant seawater. "Thunder Egg Farm", like Hambeluna and Araluen, was built on the side of a hill. It stood on a shelf of polished cement that projected from the slope: I had reached it by a flight of concrete steps. I found the house at the very end of the resort's farthest street, where Nelly Bay meets the Bush, and it stood a long, long way from any other Queenslander. Unlike them, it was made of asbestos plates like greyish kitchen towels. (Asbestos was very popular up here for a while because the wooden buildings were always burning down and asbestos is one of the few things that termites won't eat). Thunder Egg's windows were louvred with fuzzy glass, which struck me as odd for a studio, where the premium must surely be on light. I couldn't see what was inside but some animal was clearly gliding around the darkness like a carp. The building had two storeys and, at the front, the upper storey projected over the lower. On the ground floor, only the stilts at the back had been plated in asbestos – those at the front, supporting the top floor, formed the pillars of a "porch". Under this balcony, I found that the front door, painted powder blue and clearly filched from some other building, was extremely wide: it seemed to have come from a garage. The pyramid-like roof of Thunder Egg Farm was of raw corrugated iron, so rusty that its surfaces looked like those triangular toasted sandwiches with ribbed burn marks that they sell at *COLE'S*. I walked around – the sharp elephant grass was waist high – I couldn't find a soul. In the back garden, which climbed up Mount Cook, there was an upended tube of corrugated iron sitting on a wooden platform like a giant lidless soup can. It must have been six feet wide. It was brightly painted. You find these tanks, which are erected to catch soft rain water, behind almost every Queenslander – they often have little taps at the bottom like cartons of supermarket wine. Until the 1960s, these tanks – and the local artesian wells, if you were lucky enough to have one - were the Deep North's only source of potable water. You couldn't drink the piped water from the rivers, which was full of parasites. Even today, few in Townsville would drink water from a tap. Standing next to the tank in the long grass was a wooden outdoor dunny like a furniture crate. It reminded me of one of Tray's tent "statues".

I watched as the back garden crawled up the slope. The grass gave out and the forested face of Mount Cook raised itself like a densely sculpted Hindu temple. A flight of cement stairs, like those that led to the podium of the house, wound up through the trees: I felt compelled to follow it. The forest – which looks purple from Townsville – is actually made of Travellers' Palm, Milky Pine, strange little gum trees with thin black trunks. It was terribly hot, intermittently sunny, and the trees were now a dark grey-green, now a rich bright solid olive like tinned asparagus. The thunder began. Everywhere the trees had to struggle out of a thicket of black boulders: with their brownish velvet surface they made me think of giant puff balls.

After I'd been climbing for about an hour, a big hoarding dwarfed the steps, a sign painted in the colours of the Aboriginal flag. The top half was black, the bottom red, and the triangle of a yellow Magnetic Island with its highest peak rose from the line of the "red sea" in the middle. In white, in the black sky above the yellow island, was written:

"NYUNTU ANANGU MARUKU NGURANGKA NGARANYI!
YOU ARE NOW ON ABORIGINAL LAND!"

"Good!" I thought. "If I keep on going I'll reach the Brookee statue!" After climbing for about another ten minutes I had to pause for breath. The thunder got louder; the air was milky and glowing. I grasped my knees and raised my sweating face from the ground. As I did so, a boulder on the right caught my attention. Sitting on a natural ledge, half hidden by wattle, it seemed to be trembling, jittering like a newborn moth. It was one of Tray's black tents, the fabric bubbling and flapping in the pre-storm breeze! I was very excited. I jumped off the steps and clambered up to the tent through the Bush, keeping my eyes peeled for thorns and snakes. (And, of course, for crocodiles!) I peeked in through two of the "eye holes" in the side and saw something that made me jump back: in fact, I nearly toppled backwards. Luckily the thunder was now booming, the trees clattering and thrashing. Nobody inside would have heard me, especially as they were rather emphatically "otherwise engaged"!

Inside the tent I had seen Tray Beautous painting from the life a naked Sir Quntee Mush and his wife Arkana Muckadilla, each of whom was having sex with a frantic, whimpering drunco! I recognised their naked bodies: they were the bodies that had climbed out of the yellow sub on the Ross Creek. Quntee was on all fours doggy fashion, with the drunco underneath him on its back, his hair brushing his big forehead. He was gulping Quntee's dick like a dog gulping horsemeat from its bowl, fiercely closing its eyes as a dog does when it's chewing sideways. Quntee, in turn, his back arched, was slobbering like a drag queen on the drunco's little penis. The drunco's willy was pumping away like a tongue: it looked like a human heart in the middle of a transplant operation, about to explode. And it wasn't alone! For Arkana was on all fours behind Quntee, another drunco wrapping itself around her back and thighs like a mating fox, its face a picture of idiocy as it penetrated her vagina from behind. At the same time Arkana with her one free hand was frantically pushing the green Hambeluna doorstop into Quntee's upraised anus. She really was going for it hammer and tongs! (Those who may discount the feasibility of such an exercise should study Andy Warhol's *"Landscape"* series, a collection of male nudes featuring bodybuilders "fisting" each other, ie ramming their buxom arms up to the shoulder into what is delicately termed "the bull pussy" . . . So you see, the sight that greeted me was hardly unusual. After all, didn't everybody say of Sir Quntee that *"his circle is surprisingly wide"*?)

And then there was Tray. I presume it was Tray: all I could glimpse was his beeswax-coloured carcas from behind and a sweaty backside. His buttocks and the top of his back were grotesquely hairy. He was utterly absorbed in rendering the lovely scene with his brush on the far wall of the tent, the one directly opposite the wall whose apertures I was peering through. One of the conical termite nests stood on the floor by a table that held his paints. Quntee, Arkana and the druncos were scuffling and gasping in the space in between us.

As I considered the scene I realised that the green shell might detonate at any moment. Hadn't Marilyn warned me that the bomb was active, and that Tray wasn't aware of that fact? Wasn't the scene I had witnessed just the sort of scenario that Brookee-Cynthia had warned me about in the "hayume" in Manningreedah?

Now I was more determined than ever to reach the Brooklana ruins: I wanted to salvage what I could from the nightmare (or the *day*-mare rather). I stumbled back through the Bush to the cement staircase and ran up towards the summit as fast as my legs would carry me. Sure enough, about a quarter of an hour later there was an almighty roar behind and below me. The ground shook and the milky air covering the hill flashed blue. I couldn't be sure whether it wasn't just thunder and lightning, though, until I looked behind me. Then I saw smoke whipping away from the grove where the tent had been. A golden Castle Hill was shining in the brown sea like a poached pear.

A few flights further and I realised I wasn't far from the summit: above me I could see the end of the staircase framed by trees. The sun finally broke through these trees: a molten white star pulsing with purple stains. Then, suddenly, the sun was swooping down on me like a UFO, bumping bigger and bigger as it bounced and spun down the stairs from the summit, bearing right down on me, bounding down the steps I was mounting! As it came closer I suddenly realised it was an old-fashioned pram that was crashing down the steps! It was rising and diving, blazing, its rocking cabin full of a raging flame – the old-fashioned sort of pram that sits high like a landau on four big bike wheels. As it neared me – I was too stupefied to move – a siren rose above its rasping wheels, the unmistakeable siren sound of babies wailing. As the pram flew by I recognised the heads of the "Romulus and Remus" children from Castle Hill, the kids I saw being suckled by the dingo. Their waving arms were burning, as were the bedclothes, the screaming heads were washed in bluish flame. One head, like a flaming Christmas pud, was poking out of the front face to face with its brother (or sister) who was lying shrieking in the back. After standing there like an idiot for a second, I rushed down the steps to try to catch the pram and save the two kids. Suddenly, there was an almighty roar of thunder. All at once the rain poured down as hot as piss, but instead of extinguishing the fire in the pram it seemed to make it flare up, as when you pour water onto a paraffin lamp. The screaming of those poor children was frightful.

I found it hard to keep my footing on the slippery cement, or even to keep track of my quarry in the streaming grey-green mirror that had opened up beyond me. The burning chariot was gaining speed the further downhill it bumped: it looked just like that pram that tumbles down the Odessa steps in *The Battleship Potemkin*. Suddenly, leaping down the stairs without looking, I slipped and went sailing through the air like a dolphin. I crashed head first, luckily not into cement but a giant termite "Twin Towers" by the side of the path. A real White Ant nest, not one of the portable, painted fetish variety.

I woke with a cracking headache – as night had fallen, I presume some hours later. The storm had passed, the air was exquisitely fresh. I was soaked and covered in ropes of larvae that looked like White Mulberries – and in the ruins of the termite Gotham, which I had completely destroyed. There was a powerful insect odour like the smell of castor oil beans. A dark red tropical moon was shaking above my head. But it wasn't a moon. It turned out to be a face flickering craggily above a flaming torch! A moment later and I recognised the old Black Man in the yellow shirt that I keep meeting in church! "Hoy, moy name is Eurong!" he said in a deep and childish voice, and with the somewhat *faux-naïf* intonation

431

of an Aborigine. "Pee-pul tell moy yew wanna soy moy!" In his right hand, Eurong clung to a bottle of methylated spirits, the neck corked with a burning rag like a Molotov Cocktail. "Well, now yew soy moy," said Eurong, plucking the rag out with his left hand and using the right to snatch a swig . . . "And now yew don't!" And he threw the rag away. It dribbled though the air and, before reaching the ground, out it went. Everything was black again: I couldn't see a thing.

I lay still for a long, long time and perhaps I fell asleep. I remember searching in the sky for the Southern Cross, which gradually became visible. It was good to hear the soothing whistling and burring of the crickets. But I became aware by the regular bass notes and an insistent far-off scraping and stamping that it must in fact be human activity I was listening to. Shocked, I got up and brushed myself down. I peered up at the top of Mount Cook, from where the chanting seemed to come. A stupendous orange glow rose from the crown of the hill, turning the trees that fringed it into tiny black icicles. It reminded me of the glow that fills the night sky when you look for the site of London from the South Downs. I mounted the steps again and I climbed towards the summit.

When I reached the top I found that the peak of Mount Cook was in fact an enormous flat plateau, an undulating sea of tussocky grass. There were only a very few trees. What I first took to be boulders – like the ones that carpeted the slopes – were in fact the giant severed limbs of Brooklana Fagan, here a tit, there a ten-foot high fist, over there a head. It was very hard to make out the details of these colossal fragments as the light covering the meadow was intermittent and it was far from strong. It came from the extraordinary centrepiece of the plateau, a fifty-foot high pyramid bristling with lights that sat right in the middle of the plain. It was here, I presume, that Brooklana Fagan's memorial had once stood. I thought at first it must be a building, a copy of "Capricornia", Beverley Brownbill's villa in Noosa Heads, for four circular white storeys like giant coins, each at least ten feet high, stood on top of one other, each one much smaller in diameter than the "coin" underneath it – the effect was of a slightly conical multistorey wedding cake. Along the external wall of each storey, near the top, a horizontal line of buttons or lozenges was affixed. I realised a second later that they were face-cakes like the one Tray had shown me at our first meeting in Hambeluna. (I was studying all this through the opera glass I had "teefed" at Araluen). The effect that they produced was horrible, though not as horrible as the "candles" that stood in thickets on the flat roof of each "storey" - nothing more or less than the sort of stuffed and lacquered corpses that I had seen thronging the Viceregal Mansion! The naked effigies were both male and female and almost all of them were burning, the flames peeling off them like billowing silk: they were human torches. On the top storey, the most narrow, standing like the little model of "Man and Wife" on the top of a wedding cake, were the naked gilded cadavers of Quntee and Arkana! They were holding hands! These particular mummies had not been set alight. Neither had two cadavers standing in the middle of the storey just beneath them, the second most lofty eminence. One of these was the varnished corpse I had slept beside in Canberra – I recognised it not only from its features, which were identical to Wanko's, but from the blue circle around its navel. Standing right next to this terrible object was another unburnt stiff that resembled it in every respect, ie that resembled Wanko in every respect. I noticed that there was no blue lettering around the navel of this one.

The flambéed statues sent out great waves of wavering orange like sweeping searchlight beams and, on the tussocky plateau, hundreds of aborigines, naked but for their white body paint, were dancing in the light of these beams, chanting. They were in "tribal" mode, jogging around the conical ziggurat in a great wide column, rhythmically shaking spears and beating sticks together, singing in their famous nasal buzzing drone like cicadas. (It was only when I saw the spears that I realised the danger I might be in). I dashed behind a six-foot high Brookee thigh fragment where I couldn't be seen. It took me all my power to repress a shriek however when one of the two unburnt figures on the penultimate storey started

433

moving! It was the one without the blue writing on its stomach. It bent down, picked up a megaphone, and started to address the dancing "Aubergines"!

"Moongs, Murkies, Countrymen! -"

the announcement began. It was Wanko! It was Wanko's voice exactly! I would have recognised that voice anywhere! Immediately every Abo stopped dancing and fell silent. They all turned to look up and listen to the figure with the megaphone. *"Wanna say a few words before you eat this cake here!"* Wanko observed, indicating the ziggurat. *"It's a hash cake - the fucken leaves was marinaded in meths and molasses, eh?!* [Loud cheers welled up]. *The oyssing's real. Real oyssing. It's a thank-yew cake from the Proy Minister, Sir Dewy Popkiss. A Billy Doo for youse Aboriginal people. Tray Byoodus made it for yew at Sir Dewy's request. It's a work of aaart so youse bedder enjoy it eh?* [More loud cheers] . . . *And who am oy you're askin'?"* the statue demanded. *"Well, friends, moy name is Wanko Dykstra and oym wunna Dewy's best mates. Oy've been livin' here on the oyland for the last few months, down at Tray Byoodus' place. And Sir Dewy wannett me to say a few words to yew. He wannett me to let yew know how generous our Proy Minister can boy. How if yew know howta tickle old Dew's Niagra Falls he'll scratch yours good and proper, eh? . . . Now take Tray! Yew all know Tray Byoodus, dontcha? . . .* [Derisive jeers]. *Well look at what Dewy's done for Tray. Oy come up here from Canberra a few months back with a goy from Pommieland called Paddy Mynts and Tray wants ter be a big shot in the Lun-dun art world, eh? And Dew tells 'im he can fix it for 'im with this pommy pooftah Minty if Tray Byoodus does Dewy a liddle fayva. Cos this Minty, he's a fucken Bigshot gallery owner over in Pommie Poof Central, eh?"*

Wanko went on to say that he and Tray had spent the last few weeks on Magnetic arranging for the baking of the giant ziggurat cake, even when Tray had been obliged to dash back and forth because of his obligations to yours truly. The cake, Wank said, was to thank the Abos and particularly their tribal leader Eurong for the potent and massively effective magic fetishes they had been producing. Wonderful advantages had descended on Dew because of these fetishes, Wanko said. Then he described how the secret power of the fetish had been revealed.

Wanko first of all informed the "Boongs" that he, Wank, was the son and heir of Thallon Dykstra, *"the world-famous Bowen Rugby League player"* (!), and of Almaden Soukoop, only daughter of Girly and Shoom Soukoop. Shoom, he intimated, was equally well-known, an aside which raised another long and derisive jeer.

Wanko said that a few decades ago, not long after he was born and when his Dad was about the same age that he, Wanko, was now, Tray Beautous had started to produce a series of artworks based on the famous *"dago dauber"* Goya's last "dark" paintings. These were the notorious images the Spanish depressive created of witches' covens, massacres, cannibals, victims of the Inquisition. (Wanko hardly needed to go into all this: it must have gone right over the Aubergines' heads. I reflected on how typical it was of his "a little learning is a dangerous thing" pretentiousness). Goya, Wanko correctly observed (Tray must have been his informant), had painted his nightmares on the internal walls of a specially rented house known (because he was *"A.I.F"*) as *"la Quinta del Sordo"* – "the House of the Deaf Man". Tray, inspired by the master's example, had started to produce "sculptures" each of which he used to call *"the House of the Blind Man"*. These were none other than the black tents! Tray used to promise any patron who'd buy a tent to create on the internal walls of each a scene of satisfying retribution; he promised each potential buyer, Wank said, that he would paint a continuous tableau of the patron's least favourite racial, social or religious group dying in agony in a Gas Chamber! That was what each black canvas cube was meant to be: a Gas Chamber! To make it more authentic, Tray offered to ignite in each tent one of the termite nests he had found in Eurong's room at his Grandparents' house. This would produce a simulacrum of the Chamber's poisonous miasma. Tray would cut holes in the eyes of the agonised "portraits" he would paint, Wank laughed, to let the "gas" escape. He would present the lucky patron with an opera glass so that he – or she – could scutinise the scene

435

in gloating comfort. (*"Smoke Gets In Your Eyes"*, as Nat King Cole once sang, but not if you have an opera glass). Hence the ironical title, *"House of the Blind Man"*.

Shoom, Wanko informed the "Boongs", had been Tray Beatous' first customer, and he had asked Tray to produce a tent with an internal fresco showing naked Abo girls and white "ockers" dying in a state of oral intimacy. Shoom insisted, said Wank, that he "detested" these groups [*methinks the lady did protest too much!*] and that Tray should call the piece *"Le Rouge et le Noir"* after Stendhal's epic novel; "rouge" for the "rednecks", "noir" for the "Boongs". But Tray suggested *"Rape of the Sabine Women"* instead because of the scenario's *"colonial dialectic"*. Shoom Soukoop deferred to him, but specified that the male "models" for the painting should be the current "Townsville Tree Frog" Rugby League Football team, then captained by his son-in-law Thallon, in whom he took a more than paternal interest. The "lubras" were brought on board as models, Wanko ironically added, after Tray had procured the services of their ladyfolk from the Mangrove Swamp tribesmen with a case of industrial grade turps. [*More derisive jeers*]. The black tent was set up, the painting completed. But after the smoke from Eurong's fuming termite nest had passed through the eyes of the painted sitters, the models all perished. One morning their partners and lovers woke up screaming to find nothing but these glittering mummies in each conjugal bed: Wank indicated the icy effigies to his right and left. Then, *"Meet me Dad!"* Wanko cried, pointing to the chrysalis with the blue tum tattoo at his side. Wanko's Ma, Almaden, had *"naturally"* been very upset, Wanko bathetically added, and Dewy got to hear of the appalling development through *Almaden's* Ma, Girly, who was a friend of Sir Dewy Popkiss' family. Poor old Girly was obviously distraught. Dewy, however, did not enjoy ministerial power at that time, and Tray later sold the *"zombies"* to his most important current patron the then Prime Minister Knut Fagan, who went on to decorate his Canberra residence with them.

"Now," Wanko tells the "Boongs", *"fast forward a coupla years!"* Dewy has taken over from Knut and, with the fall of his mentor, *"Tray is up shit creek in a chickenwire canoe; the groyvy troyn is well and trewly turned* OFF!"

Then, one day, says Wank, Tray happens to read in the "Bully" that the world-famous cricketer Sir Quntee Mush and his Media Mogul wife Arkana Muckadilla are shortly to visit Dingo Beach, North Queensland. [Dingo Beach is an "exclusive" resort just south of Bowen between Mookarra and Earlando]. As behoves the two best-known Aussie members of their faith, Quntee and Arkana, Tray reads, are to be the honoured guests of *"TWATT"*, "the Townsville Association of Tim-Tams". *TWATT* is to organise the Dingo Beach beach-party as a Tim-Tammic circumcision ceremony for Quntee and Arkana's twin boys Trangi and Yarram. It has been decided to make it a beachside celebration to mark the couple's *"we will fight them on the beaches"* victory over the infidel at Bilgola. All at once, says Wanko, a plan suggests itself to Tray, a plan that will enable Tray both to give his old enemy Quntee a kick and to get himself into the new Prime Minister's good books. And, what is more important, his order books!

Tray, says Wanko, knows enough from his previous connections to realise that Dewy Popkiss utterly loathes Quntee and Arkana and longs to be rid of both of them. Now that he's PM, they're calling in all the favours they've done him, making demands. Arkana is reminding Dew of all that media puffery, Quntee of the money that he (or rather his wife) has lent the old shitbag. At the very least, Quntee wants to lay his hands on the shards of Brookee colossus that he has, after all, paid for so that he can carry out his plan for the Vatican in Rome. This he is desperate to do now that "Christina" has been "insulted" on Bondi Beach. Quntee wants revenge on the whole of Christendom, and Dewy, as a good Catholic boy, is not very anxious to hand it to him. Also, (Wank hypocritically lies), *"the Proy Minister loves the Aboriginal pee-pul"* and doesn't want *"the Texan sand niggers"* to steal the shattered fragments of their *"Sacred Soight"*! On the other hand, Dew knows that it wouldn't do to piss off two media players as powerful as Quntee and Arkana, not with all the shit *they've* got on his ass. " '*Oh Chroyst* ' ", he thinks, " '*if only I could just make the pair of 'em* disappoyar!' " And it's at this point, says Wank, that Tray Beautous steps in.

There have been a lot of dingo attacks on kids of late on Fraser Island, which is not that far south of Earlando. So nobody is surprised when the *TWATT's* circumcision ceremony is attacked on Dingo Beach by a huge pack of the eponymous beasts: *"The Devil Rides Out"* Texan bison-fuckers are completely overwhelmed. Little Trangi and Yarram are sitting on special little thrones, dressed in the red capes and Christmas-cracker crowns that Tim-Tammic circumcisees wear on these occasions. Two massive dingoes bowl them over, seize each boy by the cape, and, with one of the babes dangling from each jaw, haul them off screaming into the silvery Bush. *"It's just what happened, remember, when the fucken dings siezed Lindy Chamberlain's baby Azaria at Ayer's Rock, eh?!"* says Wank. A few days' later the dingoes appear in Townsville and present the kidnapped infants to the Abo *"Maban"* or sorcerer Eurong, who holds the brutes in his supernatural power and who has been acting as both Prospero and Caliban to his old friend *"beautous Tray"* for years.

Tray contacts Dew with the story: Dew isn't inclined to believe him. But last year Dew and his daughter Kommode – she who holds the Australia Council purse strings which Tray is so anxious to unloose – pay a visit to Townsville and, after calling on Girly, climb up Castle Hill and verify that Eurong's dingoes have indeed seized the Texans' "wolf cubs". At that point, Dewy and Tray cut a deal, says Wank. In return for the "Pee Em's" patronage, Tray will help Dew rid himself of Quntee and Arkana.

"And this is how ee duz it!" Wank declaims.

Dewy flies back down south and tells *"Q and A"* that, thanks to contacts available only to the Prime Minister of Australia, he can assure them that their old sparring partner Tray Beautous can lead them to Trangi and Yarram. But that, being a kinky, vindictive, and yet essentially harmless *"Optic Nerve"* ["perv"], Tray will only assist if the two agree to pose for him in the revolting fashion I have just seen the pair of them attempt. Tray also asks the power couple for a *"management fee"* to scrape together a *"sweetener"* – allegedly for yours truly! Kommode is inviting me to Oz for the "Dreaming of Coming" Festival, Dew informs the Tim-Tams, and Dew needs the cash so I can be *"persuaded"* to accept Tray onto my London roster – which he presents to them as one of Tray's demands! (*Needless to say, I have only seen a tiny fraction of the figure which Wank gives as my* "Billy Doo". *I am quite certain that Dewy must have "teefed" the rest of it*).

Quntee and Arkana, says Wank, assent to all the conditions, and elaborate precautions are made so that they can arrive in Townsville by tourist sub and in mufti, keeping the matter - for obvious reasons - well away from the "sticky beaks" or the Fuzz. Not to mention Arkana's rivals in the *"meeja"*, of course! Wank says that Eurong has been hosting the Texans at his Townsville home (the very "home" from which the Pig Dog rushed out to bite me). Before they actually agree to "sit" for Tray, Eurong has shown them that their twins are alive and well. But the children are out of reach, guarded by dingoes on nearby Castle Hill. And now, Wanko announces to the assembled Aubergines, the deed has been done! Quntee and Arkana have actually completed Tray's outlandish pose. Eurong's magic incense burner, too, has done its stuff in the black tent down on the bouldered slope below. *"And so good ole Dewy and the Black Fellers have two less Sand Niggers to worry about, eh?"* And with that Wanko points mockingly at the "wedding couple" corpses at the very peak of the cake. And *"good ole Eurong"* has already enjoyed *his* reward, too, Wank assures the crowd. With Mum and Dad out of the way he has "pigged out" on little Trangi and Yarram! *"It's an old Abo recipe!"* Wanko "jokes". *"A* soupçon *of meths on the trussed squabs and you push 'em down a hill in a burnin' pram! When they hit the bottom they're* 'done', *eh?! . . . And now it's your turn to enjoy a good ole feed!"* With this, Wanko hurls an "esky" of meths bottles into the dusky throng and gesticulates wildly towards the cake.

The "Boongs" appeared spellbound by the above peroration so I take the opportunity to make tracks while Wanko is still quacking away through the megaphone. The distortion is terrible, like when you haven't tuned a transistor to a radio frequency properly, and, of course, there are quite a few observations lacking in refinement that I have sensibly omitted. I haven't really tried to give a flavour of his bonhomie. But I have to say I never doubted the truth of Wank's incredible homily – it explained so much! Girly's puzzling coldness towards the memory of her husband, for one! It wouldn't take a genius to guess why she would cooperate with Dewy's plan – even to the extent of putting up yours truly at her villa. Where, of course, she could spy on me for both Dewy and Tray, revealing to each how desperate I was to get Tray signed, thus enabling Tray to play "hard to get" while he finished the all-important "compo cake" for the "Boongs"! Of course, it has to be remembered that Tray and Dew were each working to mutually exclusive timetables and had very different agendas, and so I presume that Dewy was constantly pressing me to get Tray signed – which he knew would happen anyway - only as a way of hassling the painter, of forcing him to make haste.

In any case, how bitterly Girly must have resented the artist, how badly she must have wanted him out of Townsville altogether! Especially now that Tray seems to have his beady eye on *Kade*! How delighted she must have been at the contract I got Tray to sign, obliging him, not only to paint Quntee and Arkana *in flagrante*, but to follow me back to London! (Not that I thought he would ever be in a position to do *that* !)

But how can I find an explanation for all those other black tents I saw? The one on the back of the truck, for instance, the wigwams I glimpsed in Canberra? . . . Who knows? Perhaps Dew – or even some other bigshot – had other enemies he wanted Tray to "take care of".

So there you are . . . I have been Tray and Dewy's fool all along, and the only reason Dew pretended to me that Tray held him in contempt was so I would never guess they were working as a team!

I slipped away from the plateau, with great difficulty finding my way down the steps by the light of the stars and a bright crescent moon, and I made my way to the motel.

L'APRÈS-MIDI D'UN PRAWN

EMPORIO PATRICK MYNTS, LONDON, MONDAY, 5 JULY 1993:
TO EDWARD SEMPER-ADONIS, TATE GALLERY

Dear Edward,

I have been asked to comment on the following unsent letter. It was typed but there
is no date or signature. Given what they call my "special knowledge of the subject",
the police want to know if I think it was composed by Tray and, if so, what clues it
might give as to what later, you know . . . *happened*. They found the document in
Tray's studio in Petworth, West Sussex. (As you know, he lived there because it was
where one of his idols, Turner, lived). What do you think I should say?

In some anxiety (as usual),

PAT

Yaffle Studios, Rosemary Lane, Petworth, England

Dear Kurwen -

*I found myself back in London today, in the half-rural fringe of London I stayed in with Patrick when first
I came to this country. I was standing between an avenue of trees: gorgeous, deciduous English trees, dense
and ripe and grainy, like fruitcakes - so different from the sterile, pre-pubertal eucalypts of Australia.*

*On the other side of the street, a cliff falls away and then sweeps down to the river. The woods that crumb
the endless hills of South-West London float above the hazy Thames like bluish clouds. It was oddly
wonderful to see that low grey sky again, and that rich, flickering bright green - that grey sky and that dense
green that make every landscape in London look timeless because you seem to see them in an eternal room.
Nothing brightly lit, everything dull and intense, like a fish tank.*

442

a novel

From the edge of the cliff, I gaze down onto the slope that rolls to the very flat land by the river. The scene is tense with a profound, historical atmosphere - with squat or grandiose chocolate brick pubs, always standing epic and alone, always iced with creamy white plaster borders and big, black Victorian letters. Then flat industrial land, speaking of ancient Empire, now cleared, and green and saffron with weeds; so ordinary, so ravaged and recent-looking, yet made unfathomable by history, as an Australian building site would not be. Then the inscrutable grey flats by the Thames, which, like the black banks of the Nile are eternally drained, eternally drowned by history - and the silver light purling off the flats, a rheumy silver like spring water; everything heart-stopping, precise, uncelebrated, unexplored: the tumuli of Troy before the excavations of Schliemann. I felt like Cyriac of Ancona in the Greece of the 1440s. I felt like I was the only one aware of the histories of these overgrown Spartas and Delphis, their contemporary residents - the direct descendants of those who had built them - completely ignorant of and indifferent to the undisturbed tombs. Everything in the scene was fixed by brooding history to this smoky, silvery room before me, as collections of insects are to the glass.

The view from the cliff was extraordinary - or extraordinary to me, who had grown up with the truly extraordinary in Australia. Shit-coloured railway tracks meandered off into the plain below. Trees tumbled down. I could have been in the middle of Cornwall but for the grey towers and the glimpses, here and there, of the ossified brown of the backs of houses. Right in front of me - on the horizon at the end of the tracks - rose a closely wooded hill. I watched it, its leaves turning, mewing and mottling under a windy grey sky, a pyramid of cubed sugar burning with green tea - the trees rich, clear and human; human in their dignity, human in their pregnant reticence. A powerful spirit lived there - you could feel it, it was quite strong. Australian trees are never human.

I left the street that circled the plateau, gingerly lowered myself over the cliff at its edge, and crawled, crab-like, down the slope into the trees. I have done this repeatedly for what I call "the same pleasure." I can tell by the rich bright green of the leaves and the grey flowers that I am moving through a damp, early Summer. It was dry now, but the wind blew, and the union of the grey cloud with the green of the hill, and the constant windy, whitening hiss of the leaves, pricked here and there by the shouts of kids and the bark of a dog, was

443

oddly gripping, moving, mysterious; oddly expressive of what is quintessential and timeless about London. You always feel so free in London, so exquisitely alone.

I entered a copse that bordered a Golf Course. Through the last silhouetted leaves and branches I could see oblongs of green sky and blue sky, separated on the horizon by a line of brown brick cottages, an old white pub and a new white church, and a red brick mansion with barred black windows picked out in white. In front of the pub and the church and the house a burning pond was glowing. Uneven swatches of blue and green and purple Oak and Beech crowned the buildings, tall black Poplars shot up behind. The Copper Beech and the Poplars were reflected with painterly aplomb in the purple-copper water. Blue and grey blotches swam on the hot sky like watercolours on a white enamel lid.

It was hot, for London, but windy and changeable. I became separate from myself and I was able to watch myself, a figure moving further and further into the green golf course, overtaken by waves of shadow as the clouds glided overhead.

Suddenly there was a commotion in a nearby spinney, like the sound of Jackdaws raiding a nest. As on those occasions - when all the other songbirds rally around the raided mother, seeing who can squawk the loudest - there seemed to be competition as well as desperation in a group of hectic male voices. An impersonal physical crisis will always assert its supremacy over a metaphysical drama touching only the self, and, drawn by the urgent cries, I veered back over the Golf Course to find out what was wrong.

A spinney, like a magpie's nest, is domed as well as walled: a teepee of stunted trees and bushes. I pushed my way into the empty heart of the dome and found myself facing the backs of four or five golfers. There was a little red-haired boy, too: presumably their caddy. They were all shouting at each other and pointing at something on the ground.

I am, to put it mildly, surprised to find a huge pig, shiny and mottled like an uncooked sausage, lying under a stunted Rowan tree. I am even more surprised to see two very, very young (human) babies, like purple knotted turds, lying on the ground swaddled in oversized tee-shirts, each one sucking on one of the monster's teats . . . The whole production reminds me of a "Jew's Sow" - one of those sculptures - very few of which now remain - which used to grace nearly every cathedral in Europe and which usually depict a scrum of hideous, fully clothed Jewish dottards nuzzling like puppies on the udders of a monstrous female pig.

"What the Hell is going on?" I hear myself demand.

The red-haired boy - who is quite as stupid as I - replies that they are trying to find their golf ball, which they saw drop out of the sky into this copse.

"I'm not talking about that, *you idiot," I say in a tone of command. "I'm talking about* that, *that damn White Spot porker! And what the fuck are those Bubyoolums doing hanging on its nipples? Who the hell wrapped them in those toerags?"*

I notice - though the lettering on banked-up fabric is hard to read - that one of the teeshirts bears the word "ROMULUS" *(yellow letters on green), and the other* "REMUS" *(yellow letters on red).*

"Don't you swear at us, Mr Soft Whip!" one of the golfers retorts, "why should we know more about it than you? We only just saw it ourselves. We were looking for our ball."

"How dare you!" I cry.

The golfer responds with a defiant expression of Lèse-Majesté, *and a series of far from fastidious insinuations.*

"I know how it happened," the little red-head suddenly interjects. Everybody stares at him, as at the village idiot. A shiver of pleasure runs through his body: he is like a cat which is about to be stroked. The red-haired boy points in the direction of the railway line. Beyond that line of trees screening the railway embankment, he says, is a "City Farm" owned by his uncle. ("City Farms" are suburban zoos where the children of Britain's inner-city underclass are taken to see farm animals, which they otherwise might gaze upon as often as a book or their natural fathers).

"Ginger" says that a few days ago, the "Gilded Youth" of the "Yassir Arafat Council Estate" in Plumstead, South London, paid the farm a visit, accompanied by their parents - or whatever ancestral detritus laid claim to that title. One of the children was a foreigner and her "Mum and Dad" had made a particularly strong impression on the boy. The heavily pregnant mother was "very scary", he says, "all wrapped up in a black rubbish bag like a Dalek". Even her face had been hidden by a hanky - "like a

445

bank robber". The father, meanwhile, was just as fat and "waddled around the farm in a dress with a big beehive beard." He had looked like "a dirty squirrel".

According to the boy, before the arrival of the children, Plumstead Council had contacted his uncle and ordered him, at the insistence of the Balle Masquée, *to hide the pigs in the Milking Shed, as it offends the lofty sensibilities of the circumcised to find themselves face to face even briefly with* "the Swinish Multitude". *(The feeling is no doubt mutual!) When "Nunky-Poo" objected that hiding the pigs would deny the majority in the party who were* non-masqués *the pleasure of their company (ie the pigs' company), he was threatened with the police and warned that Plumstead was a Council that "values diversity".*

Thus it was that, on the day of the "visitation" - as our Ginger informant called it - Nunky-Poo was compelled to herd his pigs into the Milking Shed (the cows were grazing in the Water Meadow at the time). The Dalek couple had only brought one of their children on the farm visit, a six-year-old girl whom they had - for reasons best known to themselves - smothered in a foulard.

Dalek Woman was larger than the average expectant Mum, according to Ginge, because, true to the precepts of her faith, she had - though obviously prodigiously fecund - deliberately undergone fertility treatment - funded by "perfidious Albion", *of course! (Plumstead Council had been Ginger's informant). Yea, for the sake of the belovèd goddess she would become a faster breeder than Three Mile Island! Having pupped four brats already, she was now - thanks to Dr Feelgood - carrying another seven. According to the red-head, she was vast and moved though the farm with some awkwardness - "like a rolling tugboat" - and she, her husband and child eventually became separated from the rest of the Plumstead visitors.*

This was no great loss, according to Ginge, as they regarded the local infidels as "unclean" . (Not that their own fraîcheur *was "anything to write home about", according to "Simply Red", who said that "even the goats" had run from their odour of sanctity).*

The three foreigners were approaching the point where the Milking Shed intersected with the high wooden fence enclosing the farmstead when, said Ginge, there was a stupendous bang. It was like a missile detonating a Zeppelin: Dalek Woman had exploded!

Everyone and everything - with the animals leading the vanguard - ran flapping and screaming in each direction like a colony of disturbed Fruit Bats. Unlike the "Grande Mademoiselle," *however, cousin of Louis XIV, whose corpse - bloated with fetid gas - erupted with the force of a Vacuum Bomb when she was lying in state in the* Sainte Chapelle *in 1693, suffocating not a few of Louis's court, blinding others with a Tsunami of liquid ammonia, and perforating the eardrums of several,* Madama Dalek *had not been the cause of numerous casualties. The force of the explosion had only decapitated her daughter and spouse, fortunately, the child's head hurtling through the ether with its train of unfurled headscarf like a toilet roll, Squirrel Nutkin's "burning bush" drifting serenely over the Duck Pond like a comet.*

The blast had also flattened that section of the wooden fence that was nearest to the Milking Shed, which it had partly atomised, freeing those pigs it had not reduced to shreds of Chorizo and pastrami. The pigs came thundering out, screaming with the voices of cockatoos. They trampled the bones and entrails of "Three Mile Island" into the stinking mud when not - like a dog which has found another's poo - sharply braking and - suddenly tender and absorbed - sniffing and eating. And that wasn't all they ate! The remains of the babies which had exploded in the Dalek Mother's womb were lying all over the farmyard, and "Ginger" said that he had seen a little white sow munching on a foetus's head "like a sucking pig at a wedding with an apple in its mouth."

Incredibly, two of the babies were found alive in the soft ruins of a haystack, whither they had been flung wholly intact. His aunt had wrapped each of their struggling, taut, raspberry-soft bodies in the "ROMULUS" *and* "REMUS" *teeshirts, which she had bought for her own twins because (according to Ginger) these twins were profoundly attached to the family's wolf-like Alsatian, "Sieglinde". His Aunt had been carrying a straw-filled wicker basket at the time (she had been going to show the visitors how she collected eggs from the Hen Runs), and she had tenderly lain the infants in the straw at its base. (The Dalek had been about eight months' pregnant at the time and the children were fully formed). His Aunt had then set this basket on the ground and run off to calm a lumpen Inner City "chyle" who was screaming hysterically, having found a baby's severed black penis like a leech in her bloodied hair.*

The pigs - being more intelligent than the other animals (which were all content to careen around their prison like Goldfish) - made a run for it. They stampeded through the demolished fence to the Golf Course and freedom. One pig, however - a shiny pink sow "like a big fat wrestler" - made a detour towards the egg basket. The plaited wicker handle it seized in its jaws. Off it galloped through the gap in the fence like the Pied Piper, Aunty and the other adults in high voice and hot pursuit. Unfortunately, they soon lost "Rusalka" (for that was the female porker's name) in the scrub beyond the trees.

All this, said the red-haired boy, had taken place just a few days' before. Nothing more had been heard of "Rusalka" or "the Babes in the Wood" . . . Until now, that is. I turn to the other adults to discuss these incredible events, but there is a horrible sound like a fart.

"Hey Beaut, it's me!"

I turn again sharply - the pig under the Rowan tree is talking to me! It is talking to me in the voice of Arkana Muckadilla: the pig's lidded octopus eyes with their heavy lashes are Lady Muckadilla's exactly! "You never did get to eat my children - sorry, meet my children - did you, Beaut?" says the pig, motioning briskly with its head towards the babies nuzzling its dugs . (How horribly its dirty elephant ears flap!) "This one's Trangi, the one over there is Yarram". I am speechless, but the golfers and the red-haired caddy - who are talking animatedly among themselves - seem not to see or hear a thing. "My daughter's built a big mausoleum for us. It's called the 'Taj Maiale' . . . 'Maiale' *is Italian for 'pig'," she hastens to add .. . The* 'mausoleo' *is way over there, beyond the pub, on the other side of that pond. Isn't it an amazing shape? It was Martin McGuiness's idea. Just think: a mausoleum 'Wasp' built in my honour! And in the form of a giant She-Boar, all yoghurt pink, completely hollow! Instead of the traditional dome, a 'Belly of Pork'! Eighty feet high with a big slit so the worshippers can get in and out: it's like a giant piggy bank! But the slit is under the tail, not on the back, Tray. There's a ladder up to it. Yep, a ladder! There has to be: the* 'Taj Maiale's' *legs are twenty foot high at least! And the 'doorway' around the slit has been 'circumscribed', of course".*

"Of course!", say I. "But where did you say this mausoleum of yours was?" "Just over there, beyond the trees" says the pig. And off towards it I run.

I finally reach a felled and scooped-out tree trunk lying sideways at the very edge of the Golf Course. It looks like a cylinder and it serves as a sofa - it faces the pond. The sky seems threatening. The wind grows stronger. The luminous clouds are disgustingly raw and fast and near and vast. Some are pregnant spider sacs of black drifting across the shocking blue with a fringe of web, like motes in a microscope. Every few minutes the sun becomes free of the clouds, and the leaves and brick of the red mansion are lit up like opera props against an inky puce sky. Fearing it's about to rain, I go to sit in the nearby pub, which is called "The Alma" - I presume after the battle in the Crimean War. I ask for a bottle of Coca-Cola, a glass of ice, and a packet of cheese and onion chips ("crisps" as they are called in England).

"A coke and a bag ah cheese and onion crisps?!" cries Dewy Popkiss, who just happens to be the publican. I have to tell you that our old friend was wearing a jaunty pink and green Hawaiian shirt. I notice things about his body that I never used to when it emerged from his familiar attire. His arms are hairy now and his left forearm bears a single tattoo: an Irish Cross. He simulates the upwardly mobile masculinity beloved of publicans. His chest is a dry, and now depilitated brown, his nipple - he pushes open the shirt quite widely to scratch it – is pale and flaccid. His face is the only one I have ever seen which offers no possibility of an even sadistic warmth and, as he chats to me, he ends even apparently neutral sentences with "understand?" *It wasn't normal, this intimacy. Dew's hostility, as you know, is always there, but it never usually becomes human. Why had Dew withdrawn his impersonality? He was exaggerating his Australian accent now, and the slightly angular way he moves his arms and head. It was as if, like me, he were looking at himself and sending himself up. He turns on the pub jukebox without paying for it, glances over at me again and again and again, accompanies the old Rock and Roll song that emerges on an imaginary piano. When the song climaxes, his hands are still spread out, and he jerks his head towards me as if heading a ball. He cries* "POUM"! . . . *I felt as I had done bathing once at Yeppoon when a fish - an ordinary fish - swam up to the shallows by the beach and bit me. His behaviour was that odd.*

I suddenly realise that this performance is in honour of his wife, Bonnie, who is sitting in a baby's high chair behind the bar wearing the slatternly weeds of a London publican's wife (no change there, then!) In honour, too, of Beverley Brownbill: Bev is perched on a stool facing the bar and is decked incongruously in the garb of a teenage English slut (no change there, either). Bev's eyes are hidden by a teepee of fizzy, metallic, blond hair. Her cheekbones are oily and wildly rouged. Her breasts are hardly larger than her stomach and they perch on it, not protruding far, as she drops, cross-legged, on the stool. Her bum and legs - a bursting sheath, bedenimmed - balloon from fluorescent, acid-white stilettos: sausages from a machine. Bev is carrying a shoulder bag which is also an acidulous white. A much older girl, plain, with dull pink corduroy slacks and a ponytail of greyish blond hair - I notice with a start that it is Klima Mastny - is standing nearby, showing Bev photographs of newly-born puppies. Bev looks at Klima piercingly, indulgently: "Which are the ones with no plums?"

Bev is nursing, not a petite tumbler of the sort of Australian lager I am used to, which is as clear and yellow as Strega, but a huge British pint glass filled with English ale. It is brown and milky, and full of indistinct half transparent clouds, like a pint jar of Blue Gum honey with a comb inside.

I settle myself in a corner of the pub near the window: it overlooks the pond. I open a volume of Proust that I have brought along and I drink a little Coca-Cola to quench my thirst and clear the decks. It was I, "a (praying) Aussie Mantius, rough as a badger's arse" who had to introduce my supposedly *soigné English dealer Patrick Mynts to Proust! And to Byzantium and the Golden Age of Islam. His education began, as you know, in the library at Hambeluna. I have had to be* his *Svengali, not he mine!*

I intend to savour the Proust as a sacrament of self-experience, which is why I have forborne alcohol, which would dull my powers of analysis. I detect the piney scent of coke as I pour the bottle into the schooner. I fondle the jagged edges of the crisps through the skin of their tight anaesthetic bladder. I break its wind (the bag splits). I raise a pungent plate of dandruff to my lips and I suck on it a while and, once the cheesy onion-ness has aroused another thirst, I douse it with a gout of lemonny coke: I am careful to suck the crisp resinous sting of the coke through the corpse of its now castrated wafer. I luxuriate over a chapter of **Sodome et Gomorrhe***, straining the last motes of magic from its pages as if they were cheese and onion crisps.*

Suddenly, there is a growling noise and I look up. I peer through the window across a picket fence to the pond. A silver car with a buxom lady in it flickers in the white palings: it shudders to a halt. A little girl with a face the colour of salted butter is sitting in the back. I feel a sick thrill in the roof of my stomach. I pick up my drink and put my **Sodome et Gomorrhe** *in a bag, which I am surprised to find contains a drawing block and a handful of pens. I leave the dark wooden interior for the Beer Garden, where I study the beautiful silver car - a Seventies Jaguar - from which the driver has now alighted. "Frou-Frou, son of Argie", the publican's Jack Russell - his arse an oyster, his tail a chipolata - is bounding around the car in endless circles, barking hypnotically, like an Iranian. Dewy is telling him by name to "leave it out!"*

Arf, arf, arf! Wot a larf! Frou-Frou runs in clumsy leaps, front and back legs thrust outwards together, as horses were thought to do before the invention of photography. His cone of head emerges - like that of the bronze she-wolf which suckles Romulus and Remus in the Capitoline Museum - from widening ripples of fat. I am struck by his face - the furious, spotty, adolescent face of a Tasmanian Devil . . . I suddenly realise that I am looking at the famous Afghan cricketer Boondil Dakabin: that Frou-Frou is uncannily "'Sledger' Dakabin", albeit "Bin" with the limbs, ears and torso of a Jack Russell! (In fact, I wouldn't have been surprised if the real *Dakabin, naked, hadn't been endowed with something like Frou-Frou's wasp-like body! The Thirteenth Century Byzantine historian George Pachymeres describes the Turks as "dog-faced", but it is the famous Musa Qalaian priapist whose face would look more normal, in my view, on the shoulders of a Doberman).*

Suddenly Frou-Frou stops, and pisses against a hubcap. He seems to be preparing his inner poo for space, and the final frontier. He lifts his leg again: a line of champagne dangles in the sun.

He waddles a little to the middle of the dirt track. He halts. He crouches. Frou-Frou is approaching climax. Those exquisite doors are being rammed by the boulders of bliss. His eyes roll skywards and become neutral and serene. He pushes his lower lip inside out. His chin is advancing in ecstasy past his wet black nose. Out it comes: the wing-plastered brown abdomen of a locust . . . "Dakabin" doesn't even look at what he has done. He bounds back towards the car, his face relaxed, with a flaccid open mouth and bored eyes. Dogs, like children, believe that the world is kept going by others. I ponder the spectacle. People who breed dogs, like people who breed children, are basically anti-social.

I am in two minds as to whether to go and pick up the glistening chrysalis poo, but I suddenly remember that I have nothing to put it in . . . In the early part of my career, as you know, I loved to collect such prodigies and paint their perfection, incongruous, haggis-like, on a rich white Doulton plate. I like to think that my special gift as an artist lies in bringing to the attention of the world ordinary and yet untapped - perhaps even unacknowledged - items of beauty. "A thing of beauty is a Goy forever" is, as you know, my Cri de Coeur.

"Frou-Frou, FROU-FROU!" Bonnie, the publican's wife, is calling her doggy. I can see through the window of the pub that Bon is eating a home-made cheeseburger molten with onion rings and tomato sauce. She is addressing another dog in babytalk, a Rottweiler. It is sitting on a footstool next to her highchair. She is shaking her head in its face. Incredibly, it is the face of the famous London socialite Peewee Kish, another of my dearest friends! Is it not the "Vag Hag's" vast snout that juts out like a jet Jackdaw's beak from the "Black and Tan" velour of the Rottie's slithering muscles? Bon is asking the canine to kiss her and "Heavy Petty" Peewee is licking off the fluid that has collected around her lips. Bonnie has an unfortunate, associative sense of humour and when her husband reminds her of etiquette, she complains that he, Dewy, hardly ever kisses her - nor does he often indulge in foreplay. (The word she uses - making an even greater mental leap - is "horseplay").

Frou-Frou is still barking at the lovely car, one shaped and scented like a cigar. Around and around the Jag Frou dances, yapping to the beat of his four feet as they fling him off the ground. The strange car has been parked across the mouth of the dirt track, denying Dewy's lunchtime patrons access and parking. The little girl is now the only occupant of the Jaguar. She resembles a malicious tomcat. In her face, a preserved fig, I am surprised to find the features of my esteemed "marchand" *Patrick Amrada Mynts! And yet Patrick is indubitably a little girl. The old anchorite is undoubtedly a girlchild. Dewy takes advantage of her* faiblesse *to luxuriate in his* soupçon *of Irish blood: "What the fuck do you think this is, Free Derry?" "Mah - um," the little girl intones. She explains that her "Mah-um", "a middle-class per-sun", has gone into the nearby church "to confess her sins". Dewy, contradicting her, contends that "Mammoy" can be "nothin' but a damn crack whore". He insists that Mammoy has stolen the Jag "in Cobham" and alleges that, cruising through those hanging (and birching) gardens of Babylon that provide us with our first glimpse of the capital, "Mammoy" has seen directions for the Jumble Sale in a nearby Church Hall. Swerving to the left, she has parked the Jag "any ole way", and, oblivious to the daughter and car keys left behind, dashed off "to teef Jogging-Jew strides". Without another word, Dewy jumps into the driving seat and roughly reverses and realigns the car. The boot hits a tree with the sound of a slammed desk . . . It is crushed, an exquisite cigar stubbed in its silver foil. "Ooh dear," the publican simpers, "I seem to have scratched your car!" Dewy and his passenger have alighted and are gazing complacently at the wreckage.*

"Yes," Chylde Patrick remarks, pointing to something on the ground under the rear, right-hand door, " - you have also squashed your dog!"

Blubbery testicular flesh mangled with pigeon-grey redness. The publican past me in badness madness. When the impossible happens, everything can happen. The air has broken like an egg, like the viscous water of the white of an egg. Frou-Frou has exploded like a cigarette, like a match in the room of pregnant waters, in the room of gasses. And now he lies smouldering in the greyness-pinkness like a naked rent boy by Frances Bacon. He looks, literally, like something the cat has dragged in. His innards - including, pathetically, a little withheld poo - have spurted out in blue and reddish whorls through his erect hind legs from where a tyre has completely crushed his ribs. Its trajectory has inflicted an exquisite freize on his silver coat. I am suddenly struck - apropos of nothing - by the similarity between a dog's anus and the vagina of women: the lipped black slit in wet and yellow beeswax like the cut flesh on an unbaked pie. He put in a thumb, and pulled out a plum, and said what a good boy am I! . . . A gelatinous string of plums has shrieked indeed from poor Frou-Frou's anus. It reminds me of a live birth, or rather of a live death - a miscarriage. A miscarriage of justice.

The little girl, obscenely dispassionate, runs off to her "Mammoy," who is emerging from the big white Church with a priest. They are both in masks. I can't remember exactly what clothes they are wearing except the priest is strangled by a dog collar and both wear the funny bug-eyed masks with the long long curling noses - like Mr Punch in the "Commedia dell'Arte". By the pond, sections of cut up tree trunks are lying around. Other trees, hollow and dead, remain standing, bereft of branches and crowns, nothing inside them, the trunks abruptly pruned about eight feet off the ground, black liquid running down the grey and pistachio bark. There are holes in the sides of the hollow trees like windows in Hansel and Gretel houses. Three of the hollow trees stand together and, as well as window holes, each has a rather larger fissure, opening at the root, that looks like a door. A vandal has spray-painted in red the word "ROMA" on one of the trio, "YERUSHALIM" on the second tree, and "BYZANTIUM" on the third. The priest goes into the hollow tree marked "YERUSHALIM", "Mammoy" into "ROMA", and the little girl into the trunk with the legend "Byzance" painted on it. I soon hear a humming and a moaning from the trees and I move closer. The woman is giving the priest her "confession". The hollow trees are confession boxes. The priest is telling the woman, who is "confessing", that she is a "bad mother". Patrick is confessing that he is "a bad child". (And so he is!)

Dewy, meanwhile, gazes at the wreckage of the dogchild he can never father and he becomes that dog, that child himself. There are moments in his life when he touches base like this, moments when, he feels, the odds against him become so self-evidently great that no reasonable observer could possibly expect him to refer the situation to his masculinity, to his sixty odd years. (And they have been odd: oh God, they have certainly been odd!) It is at moments like this that he flings the gauntlet at God's feet with wondering defiant expectation of parental contrition and reward . . . Unfortunately, Dewy has no experience of God. It is not that he has abjured belief, just that he has never reached those levels - to which the backward soon fall and the over-educated rise - where belief, or its rejection, becomes necessary, where the idea of God, of Christ, impinges.

Like most people with no mental life, the Publican believes in "Justice" - but not in the way that the French Revolutionaries (also Godless) believed in "Reason". Rather, he has a passionate religious sense of the absence of Justice in his life. "The sleep of Reason," said Goya, "brings forth monsters" - and so does the sleep of Justice. Dewy is one of them. The injustice of his own invadvertent murder of the only being he has ever loved goes so far beyond what he has ever been able to bear that it robs him of himself, of his need to respond. He rushes raging to the Mammoy-God to fling the event wondering at her feet . . . There, what are you going to do about it?

A Rottweiler is fellating her chops. A vision like that of Picasso's "Minotaur" ravaging an ox-eyed nubile: a caterpillar clings to her eyelashed pudendum. "Frou-Frou is dead," cries Dew, blasphemously; "

'Dakabin' *is dead!" He sweeps Beverley Brownbill's big brown pint of English Bitter tinkling to the floor. I saunter back into the delicious interior to enjoy the floorshow. Dewy and Bon (who has descended from her highchair) are weeping and screaming at each other, unburdening themselves of all the appalling and necessary things they have foolishly with-held in the world beyond. "Peewee the Rottweiller" also descends, clambering down from the stool with heavy gangling awkwardness, like an ape. She also starts barking, baring hideous, cocoon-like teeth. The waters have broken, and life comes streaming in. Everything is observation, and then, suddenly, everything is life. First art, then life. I am whipped right into the scene like vanilla essence. Terror has unfolded in the way all terror unfolds before an observer, immediately enveloping me in its atmosphere, in reality, whereas before, in a time of peace, of unpain, one can look at the world and feel completely separate from it. When an accident happens it is as if the air is conspiring against us, becoming suddenly alive with the pain of life. That is when the air, that pane of glass separating us from life, becomes water surrounding both ourselves and the victim, and we all find ourselves struggling and drowning, and yet each remains impotently apart.*

Suddenly, I really am alone again. I can no longer hear the hideous afternoon. I am in one of those silver bubbles of air in which pond-skipping insects live, immune to my surroundings.

I slip back to the table where my "crisps" lie. Yellow light is making transparent the wax at the top of a brown candle: my ice-filled glass of coke. I sit down, sip, and retrieve the volume of Proust from my purse. Do you remember **The Tin Drum**, *that novel by Günter Grass? Do you remember that scene in it in which they fish for eels in the canal with a horse's head as bait? If you want to attract attention in an English pub, just sit in the corner dandling a great "horse's head" of a book - Proust, say, or* **The Faery Queene**. *Somebody interesting will certainly approach you! Well, sure enough, "Tray Beautous!" someone hails me. My revery melts like a house in a forest of summer hail. The cola dregs, a lucent spine of wine threading the boulders that jump, with the shock, to my nose, collect quickly at the back of my throat and have to be gulped. The usual lugubrious offices cannot be performed. I am furious. I recognise the distinctive carping voice of Gopi Panicker, who always used to sound like a Merino Ram.*

The voice emerges from the gross form of "Mammoy" - still wearing her Mister Punch-like mask. She lowers herself onto a chair by my side.

I ask her why she is wearing a mask.

"I am married to a Tim-Tam, remember!"

Her hair, however, is perfectly visible: she is still wearing it in a hive. Her arms remain disturbingly long in relation to what are now pendulous breasts: huge, harmless, hollow-looking breasts that lie plastered over her torso like two cold hot water bottles. They are the monstrous breasts of a much older woman who, though fit and fertile, has never suckled children. The dugs of a blown old colly who will never find her nose near those exquisite drifts of pebbly sheepshit again. Gopi had never used to wear those body-hugging black prophylactic sheaths that the more pious of Tim-Tam women go in for. By concealing her highly animated face, she has somehow made herself ugly. For the first time in her life she lacks that insect-like energy that turns so many female cockroaches into great and attractive lovers. She has regressed to the drowsy imago stage, a pupating beetle stuffed with lard for a journey she is never going to make, a ripe and unripe queen! She is a House of Lords few male members will ever enter, its bowels full of an explosive which can neither be cleared nor ignited. It seems unlikely that "the right Guy" (Fawkes) will ever light the fuse.

I am so displeased at the prospect of having to make conversation and, perhaps, love with this individual who has given me no warning - so shocked by the sudden fall of my "Empire of the Senses" - that I do not reflect upon how strange it is to meet her.

"You will think me a very untender old bender, I'm sure," I explain; "however, I do not wish to go to bed with you!"

"Beautous!" she cries, "Is that all you can say after all these years?"

According to my guest, we had last met when she and I had graced a ballet performance together a couple of years ago: this was shortly after I arrived in the Northern Hemisphere. Needless to say, a charity performance, the money from the tickets going (or so the mask says) towards finding a cure for "MAITTS", a mysterious illness that has just arisen and which is being widely blamed - as was "AIDS" of course - on

the CIA. "MAITTS", you see, only afflicts Tim-Tams. "So what exactly is 'MAITTS' ?" I ask her.
['Mothers-and-Infants-of-Tim-Tam,-triggered,-are-torn-to-tiny-Shreds']

The symptoms are terrifying, according to Mrs Punch. Gopi tells me that Tim-Tammic women are forming foetuses full of an explosive protein. Before the child reaches full term it blows itself up in the womb, taking "Mammoy", and - not infrequently - the rest of "the Holy Family" with it. Just as baby sharks, apparently, try to eat each other while still in Mummy's tummy, "the Exterminating Angel" is no longer awaiting birth, let alone "Jeunesse dorée", before unfurling itself like a butterfly in a wall of flame. Even by the time of our interview, quite a few of the spontaneous combustions have occurred in "Walmart" or "Toys'R'Us"; ie in detestable Christian countries. This ensures that a good few infidels have been obliterated as well. But "MAITTS" strikes Tim-Tammic women everywhere, even in the heart of the so-called "Bummah", even in Texas and the rest of the Tim-Tammic "Via Sacra". The whole Tim-Tammic schtick of breeding everyone else to death like aphids hangs in the balance.

His Holiness Pope John-Yoko the First, who has always prided himself on his titles - "Pontifex Maximus", "Vicar of Christ", "Slapped-up Bitch of Tim-Tam Number One" *- is aghast, she says. So he dedicates "Christina" -* "the Old Sow that eats her own Farrow" *(as James Joyce described Ireland) - to the Sacred Heart of Jesus and he sets up this "Benefit" at which Panicker and I were to dance the Fandango like Pavlova and Nijinsky.*

We apparently thought it rather insensitive of the Roman Catholic Church - which had organised the evening - to put **L'Après-Midi d'un Prawn** *on the programme - a ballet by an Aussie composer, Okelle de Bahn. Don't they know that bivalves are as abhorrent to Tim-Tams as the lips of a clitoris? In other ways, however, the "Cattle-ticks" - as they are hailed in Oz - have displayed an exquisite "sensitivity". We present the ballet before a hand-picked audience of Tim-Tammic heffalumps in the Pantheon in Rome: the marble floor is cold and slippy under our satin pumps. His Nibs John-Yoke has staged tonight's "divertissement" to celebrate the fact that he is giving Rome's Tim-Tammic immigrants the domed, "Wasp"-like building in which we perform. The Roman Emperor Hadrian had erected it as a pagan temple in 129 AD, and the Byzantine Emperor Phokas made it over to Pope Boniface IV in the year 608 to use as a church.*

Reconsecrating it to "Christina" - a goddess whose appetite for blood exceeds that of the Mayan, let alone the Roman "pantheon" - is described by His Holiness as the last stage in the building's "sacred journey". . . "For lo!" His Holiness intones, "the prophecy in **The Book of Revelations** *has come to pass!* 'Mystery, the Mother of Abomination' *now sits on the Seven Hills of Rome as on the Seven Heads of* 'the Great Beast'*!" And so, having already conquered Jerusalem, Alexandria, Antioch, Byzantium - Christendom's four other great Patriarchal seats -* **"what rough beast"** *(as John-Yoke now demands),* "slouches towards Bethlehem" *but Rome itself, the first and greatest?*

I have, at His Holiness' specific request, painted a continuous, Rubens-like Bacchanal of naked Roos writhing in their terminal agonies on the inside wall of the drum of the new "Wasp": an internal wall which forms as perfect a circle as the dome it supports. The poisonous aroma in "the Gas Chamber" *(as we call it) is designated by a dancing mesh of mosquitos - or swastikas - the ethnicity of the victims is indicated by a pentangle picked out in blue on each arm. The death camp known as* "Clausewitz" *ought to be evoked to* "show respect" *for* "the beliefs and sensitivities" *of the Roodophobic Tim-Tams, the Servant of the Servant of God confides, rather like the* "Minbar" *he has had installed - or* "the Minibar" *as Gopi not inaccurately calls the black, fridge-like object.*

Anyway, the second piece we offered the Tim-Tams that night was apparently entirely conventional: **Tamara** *(or* **Tim-Tamara** *as we hailed it), the famous* Jeu d'esprit *by the composer Balakirev, as choreographed by Fokine for Diaghilev's* Ballets Russes.

Unfortunately, the mask informs me that, at the end of our performance, as Gopi and I are sinking Bellinis in the Via Sallustiana and the slaves of Christina are prostrating themselves on the opus sectile *for the very first time, bums akimbo, fifteen members of the youth wing of the MSI, Rome's divine* Fascisti, *clamber all over the Pantheon, locking its Second Century bronze doors and dropping walnut-sized rocks of Zyklon B through the aperture in the crown of its dome. Then the Blackshirts seal the dome with one of the circular Iron Age shields from the Etruscan Museum in the Villa Giulia: it fits the glary blue porthole exactly. Etruscan shields always bore images to terrify Etruria's enemies, and this one, staring down on the Tim-Tams* "as God comes a loving bedfellow" *(as a poet once put it) is a vast frogspawn eye like the eye of God on an American dollar. (The Etruscans had probably wished to delineate the face of a Cyclops). The adherents of Christina expire jumping writhing jumping like chooks in a burning henhouse, their attitudes increasingly redolent of Agesander's "Laocoön" in the Vatican, a marvellously erotic* finale *which - in my manifestation as "Tray el Pintor" - I greatly regret having missed! The Eye of Christina, however, catches everything, just as the Kommandant of Clausewitz once used to spy on the naked, raging Roos through a specially bored peephole.*

Gopi is still sitting there in front of me. She is reminding me of all these details, relating the whole context of our alliance. We are still in the pub - "The Alma". The past is lounging seductively on the table dividing us: it is playing gooseberry.

"What are you wearing a mask for?" I ask Gopi again, stupidly.

"It is because I must not let the Poobah see my pabulum."

"But they can *see your pabulum," I say, pointing to the great orange baboon cunt she is sitting on. It is as big as a potty. It pokes out of a hole specially cut in her violet slacks - a dribbling wrinkled cylinder of French goat's cheese and intensely pungent.*

"Why do you show that, *when you won't even show your* face?"

"Because we pious ladies must prove to the world that we are circumscribed. *Just as our coverings are supposed to hide us, but in fact draw people's violent attention to us, we show that we are chaste circumcised* Tamteema *- that our menfolk have rendered us incapable of pleasure - by pushing our big fat smelly cunts in people's faces."*

It was a familiar Tim-Tammic strategy!

"But," I said, pointing, "you quite clearly haven't *been circumscribed!"*

"But that's the whole point!" she says. "We show, by flaunting, the importance of modesty. We invite circumscription by showing we are not being circumscribed!"

I am about to ask Gopi to clarify when I notice that faces are peering in at us through the pub windows. First I think they are women wearing "Tooraks": a metal mask that covers what is not hidden by the hood of the "Gingin" or "Binbag". Fierce red eyes peek out from under towering foreheads; noses are squat metal

459

triangles like the hoods over the holes on a cheesegrater. The noses are placed high up, right on the line of Neanderthal brows. From the nose to the mouth (a mere slit set very low) is a long, bulging oval - like one of those earthenware casserole lids that are shaped like nesting birds. The "wing" on each side is ruled with horizontal lines. One of the slits yawns into a bowl of porridge swimming with blood and I realise that this isn't a mask but a face, the face of a baboon! I am looking into the eyes of a troop of baboons! The troop is peering in at us. It is as if they have been spying on us making love! I am enraged - I rush to the windows. Using both front and back legs, they leap over the picket fence like Cane Toads.. They scatter across the Golf Course, jerking and tumbling awkwardly this way and that like toads, like pissing fireworks! They shriek: they have the rasping voices of gulls. They are wearing full length Jiljabs, which make them look odd, like pantomime horses. The great genitals poke out of specially cut holes like an orange fungus.

"What have you done, what have you done?!" Gopi cries, rushing up to the window. "Don't you know that when the monkeys leave this place, Tim-Tammic rule over Britain will end?"

"Aren't you talking about Gibraltar?" I object.

"Don't you talk about Gibraltar to ME!" she flashes back.

"I didn't mean to refer to that," say I. "I mean that the legend surely is that when the baboons leave the Rock of Gibraltar, British rule over Gibraltar will end. You know, the colony with the - the big hill sticking out of the sea? It's just like your cunt! It looks just like Townsville, remember? Just like Castle Hill in Townsville, like a tin of red salmon rising up out of the Coral Sea. It was named after Tarik Abu Zara, the man who conquered Spain. Remember? 'Gebel Tarik': 'Gibraltar'!"

Gopi surprises me by bursting into tears. She delves into an unusually large maroon-coloured handbag and plucks out a hanky. I notice when she blows her nose that it is covered in blood.

"The apes have gorn," she wheezes through snuffling gasps, "the apes have gorn! The clock strikes twelve: 'Oh Cinders it's you!' they say. The Tim-Tams are gonna turn back into niggaz! I mean piggas! The Tim-Tams are gonna turn back into pigs!"

"Well," I point out, "why should that bother you? Aren't you supposed to be rather Roo-ish?"

"I was Roo-ish," she says, "but I converted. I got cream-bunned by Quntee."

"By Quntee?!" I nearly cry out. "Sir Quntee Mush? . . . That's ridiculous!"

"Yeah," Gopi laughed bitterly, "just about as 'ridiculous' as getting a Boong-sized Bratwurst up your shitter, eh?"

"So you were bumfucked then," I whisper, finally believing her.

"Mmm," she said. "It's sort of like a Bar Mitzvah. Since I got bummed, I've been trying to convert as many people as possible."

"What, you bumfucked them?" I ask. "How did you do that?"

"I've been cutting off the cocks of the men I've been to bed with."

The words tremble in the jellied air.

"I beg your pardon?"

"I am Circe and I circumcribe. Or Circe-cum-scribe, if you prefer," Gopi explains. "I am like Circe, anyway. Circe turned men into pigs. I've been turning men into pigs, too. I've been circumscribing them - cutting their cocks off."

"Would you mind if we went outside, darling?" I whisper, "this pub isn't exactly 'Rive Gauche', you know!"

I look around nervously to make sure that none of the strapping regulars have overheard us. I retrieve my satchell and my volume of Proust, etc. We leave the pub and walk towards Marney's Pond. Gopi opens her handbag and extracts a long tube of Smarties.

"Are you addicted to those?" I ask.

"Yes I am. We were born into slavery."

"Well, speak for yourself," I retort, "we're not all fucking Tim-Tams, you know!"

Gopi throws some Smarties one by one to a pair of large, mongrel ducks in Marney's Pond. The lurid colours float for a surprisingly long time in the tea-coloured water. The ducks rifle them with their bills, but clearly do not enjoy them, for they swim up, mount the bank with jaunty infant legs, and, heads down, run, cackling, to chase the two adipose virgins away.

We clamber over to the Sycamore trunk, the tree that lies like a cylinder and serves as a sofa, the Sycamore seat that looks out over the pond and the pub and the church and the dark feathery Copper Beech and the Poplar. The surfaces of the buildings are still lit up. The light makes them look solid, like solid gold. Black clouds pour into the swimming-pool blue of the sky just as smoke does from a burning tyre. Gopi relates to me the story of her existence - or the story of her existence since we last embraced in the Hotel Lux in Via Sallustiana.

She had been in love, she says. He had "made" love to her. He could "make" love, she could only be "in" it. Or rather, "it" could only be in "her": there was no way that she could ever change or penetrate him. *Having been* "a good Tamteema", *intercourse had changed her quite appallingly both in body and mind, leaving her lover unchanged and intact. And so it would go on, his always virgin desire deconstructing woman after woman. Unless he, too, could be mutilated; or, better still, unless a single stricken woman could play the role each man plays among women. Luring lover after lover in and then - unchangeable herself - cutting them off in their prime like sausages from a string! Out of the frying pan into the fire! . . . Such a heroine would restore balance to a disordered world. By ensuring that coïtus deflowered men as well as women she would be protecting those Tim-Tams as yet undevoured, and giving those who had been a new, true parity with their lovers. The native-ity and nativity of a gonad-gored girlhood would come in future only with the sexual death of a member-less manhood. They would share a common desuetude: they would be "virgins of the unvagine". In two or three years, Gopi insists, she has trimmed a whole hedgerow of* Homo Erectus. *She has modelled herself, quite consciously, on King Shahrayah, Scheherezade's husband in* **The Arabian Nights**, *the prince who, until he meets his lovely bride,* "marries" *hundreds of virgins one by one for one night only, slaughtering each the next morning* "in order to save himself from the cunning and treachery of women".

It seems like a very tall story to me! After all, why haven't we ever heard of these unfortunate eunuchs? What has become of them? . . . Perhaps, drugged and docked while still abed, their peckers popped into the freezer like shalotts, they would have been too mortified to expose her. By so doing, they would only have exposed themselves. (That admittedly would have been difficult).

I could hardly verify whether there had ever been an outcry over these malheureux *. . . And yet, there they were in the mouth of her moist red leather handbag (which she had opened again to retrieve another tube of Smarties); there they were: wrenched, cut, writhing, smitten; frozen in agony like Winter dog turd; harder in cold and death than ever they could have been* "hotcheeked and blushing". *Like soldiers' corpses in* rigor mortis *they lay on top of each other in fantastic attitudes of repose. Their red and white and blue had become much more clear in the dribbled pathways of their melting patina . . . It had been an awfully long time . . . Which one of them was mine?*

Finally, I recognised it. Just then, a huge dingo with the face of Arkana Muckadilla romped up and started growling at us viciously. It must have been about five years old at least (born in '88), conceived when the Dingo impregnated the "Meeja" Vicereine in the "Black Box" on Magnetic Island. To my utter horror, Gopi hurled my severed penis at its head. It jumped up and caught the object in mid-air and started pawing and chewing on it like a bone. "Hey!" I cried. Seeing I wanted to snatch its prize away, the dingo bared its hateful teeth and off it ran, the frozen penis still welded to its jaw . . .

END